NOTRE-DAME OF PARIS

VICTOR HUGO (1802–85) was the most forceful, prolific and versatile of French nineteenth-century writers. He wrote Romantic costume dramas, many volumes of lyrical and satirical verse, political and other journalism, criticism and several novels, the best known of which are *Les Misérables* (1862) and the youthful *Notre-Dame de Paris* (1831). A royalist and conservative as a young man, Hugo later became a committed social democrat and during the Second Empire of Napoleon III was exiled from France, living in the Channel Islands. He returned to Paris in 1870 and remained a great public figure until his death: his body lay in state under the Arc de Triomphe before being buried in the Panthéon.

JOHN STURROCK is a writer, critic and translator who, since 1993, has been the Consulting Editor of the *London Review of Books*. He has written a number of books on French and Latin American literature, on Structuralism and on the theory of Autobiography. He was one of the translators of the new Penguin edition of Marcel Proust's *In Search of Lost Time*, published in 2002.

VICTOR HUGO

Notre-Dame of Paris

Translated and edited by JOHN STURROCK

PENGUIN BOOKS

To the Memory of
Cyril Jones

PENGUIN BOOKS

Published by the Penguin Group
Penguin Books Ltd, 80 Strand, London WC2R ORL, England
Penguin Putnam Inc., 375 Hudson Street, New York, New York 10014, USA
Penguin Books Australia Ltd, 250 Camberwell Road, Camberwell, Victoria 3124, Australia
Penguin Books Canada Ltd, 10 Alcorn Avenue, Toronto, Ontario, Canada M4V 3B2
Penguin Books India (P) Ltd, 11 Community Centre, Panchsheel Park, New Delhi – 110 017, India
Penguin Books (NZ) Ltd, Cnr Rosedale and Airborne Roads, Albany, Auckland, New Zealand
Penguin Books (South Africa) (Pty) Ltd, 24 Sturdee Avenue, Rosebank 2196, South Africa

Penguin Books Ltd, Registered Offices: 80 Strand, London WC2R ORL, England

www.penguin.com

This translation first published 1978
Reprinted with new Further Reading and Chronology 2004

030

Printed in England by Clays Ltd, St Ives plc
Set in Monotype Fournier

ISBN-13: 978-0-140-44353-0

CONTENTS

INTRODUCTION

'HE bought himself a bottle of ink and a huge grey knitted shawl, which swathed him from head to foot, locked his formal clothes away so that he would not be tempted to to go out and entered his novel as if it were a prison. He was very sad.' This engagingly domestic report on Victor Hugo sitting down in the autumn of 1830 to write *Notre-Dame of Paris* is by his wife, Adèle, who in the 1860s published a quaintly titled memoir (dictated, some have hinted, by its subject himself): *Victor Hugo Recounted by a Witness of His Life*. The remark about her husband's sadness is a shade enigmatic, for it was not necessarily the prospect of composition which had depressed him; Hugo was also having to compete at this time with the writer and critic Sainte-Beuve for the affections of his wife and in November of that year he even seems to have offered, very generously, to let Adèle choose between them. But the marriage somehow survived this crisis as it later survived his own spectacular infidelities.

Whatever its origin, Hugo's sadness soon passed; once the book was under way, his optimism returned and Adèle deduced that he was feeling better when she found him working with the window wide open, defended no doubt against the autumnal cold by his voluminous wrapper.

Her image of the novelist being incarcerated in his novel is a picturesque one and is justified by two details in Hugo's biography, one literary, the other financial. In the first place it follows neatly on from his previous work of fiction, *The Last Day of a Condemned Prisoner*, which had been published the year before. This is the supposed testament of a man in the condemned cell, waiting to be guillotined on the self-same Paris square where La Esmeralda is executed in *Notre-Dame of Paris*. The form of the book is a monologue and its aim polemical, since it was Hugo's object to make prisons less brutal and to outlaw the ultimate enormity of capital punishment.

Here, then, the prisoner is a writer, giving an increasingly desperate account of his final six weeks of life; he is anxious to live yet fascinated by his inescapable extinction. But the weakness of the book is the shifts Hugo is forced into by a first-person narration, which means in the end that his hero has to scribble down his dying thoughts on the scaffold itself and so keep the executioner waiting. When it comes to the composition of *Notre-Dame* the terms of this curious equation are reversed: now it is the writer who is a prisoner, condemned not to death but to a period of unnatural seclusion in order *not* to keep his publisher waiting.

For the second justification of Mme Hugo's image involved money: the manuscript of *Notre-Dame* was long overdue. Hugo had started making notes for a historical novel of this kind two years back, in 1828, when he had read industriously in the archives and the old historians of Paris – the fruits of his research are freely and sometimes awkwardly incorporated in the text of the finished novel, making it at once more convincing as history and less plausible as fiction. In November 1828 Hugo sold the first year's rights in the unwritten novel to a publisher, Charles Gosselin, for a sum roughly equivalent to £900 (of 1978 money); the manuscript was to be handed in 'around 15 April 1829'.

But it was never in fact begun; Hugo was at once sidetracked by his own unusual versatility as a writer. Even by this time, when he was still only twenty-six, he was the author of a substantial and varied *œuvre*: lyric poetry, literary journalism, two plays – the preface to the first of which, *Cromwell*, is the most resonant manifesto of an outright Romanticism in French literature – and two exotic works of fiction, *Bug-Jargal* and *Han of Iceland*. The first of these was originally written in a fortnight for a bet, when Hugo was eighteen, and is a steamy tale of the Negro uprising in San Domingo in 1791; *Han of Iceland*, published when he was twenty-one, is rather more characteristic of the later Hugo, dwelling as it does on the ferocious and grotesque. But the fact that these two callow romances should be set one in the lush Caribbean and the other in the chill of Norway is a convincing sign that even at this stage Hugo wanted his writing to embrace the world's antinomies.

When he should have been starting *Notre-Dame* Hugo turned back instead to the theatre, and wrote two more plays, *Marion de Lorme* and *Hernani*, both costume dramas that embody uncompromising conceptions of honour, love and loyalty. *Marion de Lorme* was suppressed by the censorship, which was afraid that the historical King of France portrayed in it, Louis XIII, might be taken by alert audiences to be a slander on the unloved Charles X. So Hugo wrote *Hernani*, a melancholy play in which a romantic passion is stifled by the bigotry of age and authority. *Hernani* is celebrated now less for its merits on the stage than for having been the occasion of the most tumultuous of all public confrontations between the Classics and Romantics of Paris. The so-called 'battle of Hernani' was unarguably a crucial incident in the aesthetic history of the nineteenth century. It was joined in the theatre itself at the first performance of the play and perpetuated afterwards in newspapers, journals and reviews. It was a kind of literary Dreyfus Affair, when the literary world could let it be known whether it sided with Classicism, which stood for restraint, formal rigour and an adherence to the prevailing conventions of art, or with Romanticism, which stood for the overthrow of these stale ideals and a fresh approximation of art to life itself. *Hernani* takes what now seem quite polite liberties with the prevailing conventions of the French drama, yet, aggressively promoted, they were scandalous enough to polarize opinion and enlist the rowdy backing of the young. Hugo, already the accredited theorist of a Romantic ideology, after the preface to *Cromwell*, was now acclaimed for bringing practice into line with precept.

Understandably, these turbulent events kept him away from his projected novel. Gosselin, however, had money invested in it and became pressing. In June 1830 he got Hugo to sign a fresh contract; the text was now to be delivered by 1 December of that year and Hugo would pay a fine of 1,000 francs (a quarter of the total advance) for each week it was late. He was not rich, he had four children and a very pregnant wife; the incentive to begin was finally there.

He started writing on 25 July, which was a comically unlucky choice of date. On the 27th there was a revolution in the streets of Paris, and on the 28th his wife gave birth to their fifth child, a daughter, also called Adèle. Both as a parent and as a political thinker in rapid evolution from an ultra-conservative monarchism to an egalitarian social democracy, Hugo was distracted by these events. After three days of popular insurgency, the 'three glorious days' as they are often known, Charles X was driven out and Louis-Philippe, a more constitutional king, brought to the throne.

In the words of Chateaubriand, worth quoting here for their aptness, Paris had just seen 'yet another government flinging itself from the towers of Notre-Dame'.

The birth of a child would not have been enough on its own for Hugo to convince Gosselin that he must extend his deadline, but a revolution, however succinct, was a more ponderable excuse. The interruption had been real and the Hugo household was near enough to the action for bullets to pass over the garden. Hugo renegotiated with Gosselin; he explained that he had lost crucial notes while transferring his papers to greater safety and claimed, opportunistically, that the times were bad for fulfilling literary contracts: 'it may of course be in your own interest', he told his publisher, 'that the manuscript should not be delivered so close in time to the revolution as 1 December.' Whether or not Gosselin challenged this ambiguous postponement – it is hard to see why the mere delivery of a manuscript should be thought untimely – he allowed Hugo a further two months.

Hugo began to write in earnest on 1 September; the novel was finished, incredibly, on 14 or 15 January the following year: a book of almost 200,000 words written in four and a half months. Even allowing that Hugo's notes were made and the novel itself planned in outline, this was a formidably single-minded achievement. Adèle, who has, admittedly, a weakness for imposing coincidences on the otherwise dull chronology of her married life, claims that Hugo finished novel and ink simultaneously, and that the huge manuscript was the product of a single bottle of fluid. Victor, she says, toyed with the idea of calling the book 'What There Is in an Ink-bottle'.

Notre-Dame went on sale in March 1831. The reviews were not good, and one or two of Hugo's more fastidious fellow writers were quick to condemn the book. 'I should be in despair', said Prosper Mérimée, whose own historical writings were altogether more cautious than Hugo's, 'if that were the sort of thing this century wants,' while the venerable Goethe complained to Eckermann that the novel was too schematic and its characters marionettes. But the book was a success with the public, who found it easy, as they always will, to swallow the vulgarities so distasteful to the likes of Mérimée or Goethe. In the first eighteen months after its publication, 3,100 copies were sold, which was good, and by 1833

Notre-Dame was well enough established to be invoked by the great historian Michelet, who, like Hugo, was very willing to see words as a counterweight to masonry, and wrote, in his *History of France*, that Hugo had built 'alongside the old cathedral, a cathedral as solid as the foundations of the other, as tall as its towers'.

Notre-Dame was the book by which Hugo became famous in England; between 1833 and 1839 no less than four different translations of it appeared, evidence certainly of the novel's popularity if also of the disorganization of the local publishing business. Even before it was translated for the first time, British readers had been advised of its success in France and in 1831, in the *Foreign Quarterly Review*, Henry Southern declared that when reading it one was not 'as in the writings of our Horace Smith [whose novels are a bad imitation of Scott's], overwhelmed with masses of crude and undigested lore', and concluded, in one of the perennial and incredible clichés of the literary publicist, that the book 'would appeal to an appetite which is shared by the peer with the peasant'.

The first English version to appear was made by William Hazlitt the Younger and was published in August 1833. Hazlitt, an active and unyielding Liberal, also wrote an introduction which made much of the anti-royalism of the novel, as revealed in the unflattering portrayal of the devious King Louis XI, and tried to enrol Hugo as a foreign subscriber to his own political faction. In October a second translation came out, this time under the compelling but unsuitable title of *The Hunchback of Notre-Dame*, by which it has usually been known in English ever since. The switch of attention from the cathedral to its weird inhabitant was understandable but unfortunate, since it also meant a switch of attention from the book's strengths to its weaknesses, from its ideas to its plot. To start with, and for a long time afterwards, *Notre-Dame* was commonly enjoyed as an accomplished weepie: 'The concluding passages', wrote a lachrymose English reviewer in 1835, 'offer some of the most pathetic pages we ever remember to have bedewed with (irresistibly flowing) tears.' Mercifully, we can now read the book with harder hearts and see (I shall try to show how in a moment) how much more intelligent and topical a work it is than one would suppose from reading these early accounts of it.

In the late 1830s and following decades, Hugo went into something of a decline in England, as his social and political beliefs moved towards an outspoken socialism, and even though he spent a large part of his years of exile from Paris, during the Second Empire of Louis Napoleon, in the Channel Islands. The romancer of *Notre-Dame* had emerged as a worryingly subversive radical. In this early novel, Hugo's philosophy is tentative or incomplete; by the time of his longest, best and most majestic novel, *Les Misérables* (1862), it has achieved some sort of parity with the narrative elements, so that the story of the regeneration, against many obstacles, of the former convict Jean Valjean is at once an individual, a social and even a cosmic event, illustrating Hugo's indomitable hopes for the future of the human race.

By the end of the nineteenth century, Hugo's popularity, restored perhaps by his death in 1885, was again surprising. According to the diligent K. W. Hooker, in his *The Fortunes of Victor Hugo in England* (New York, 1938), no less than thirty-six separate editions of *Notre-Dame* appeared in England in the thirty years between 1885 and 1915. Hugo had found some imposing champions among English writers; Swinburne wrote flatteringly of his novels and so did Robert Louis Stevenson, while Kipling, writing long afterwards in his *Souvenirs of France* of his first visit to Paris as a child in 1878, recalls: 'I discovered on my own account Quasimodo's Notre Dame. (I believed profoundly in the phantasmagoria of *Notre Dame*, including Esmeralda and her Djali (translated).)'

All through these years, it was reasonable that Hugo, whose novels were both congenial and accessible, should have been seen abroad as *the* French novelist of the nineteenth century. It is in the twentieth century, with its demands for a greater intellectual seriousness and power of innovation, that he has fallen back into the second rank of French novelists, though still admired, if often grudgingly, as the greatest of French lyric poets. Nowadays, it is Stendhal, Balzac and Flaubert who are taken, rightly, to be the novelists who matter most, while Hugo, like Dickens in some quarters, suffers from having so obviously written down to a popular audience. Yet without that writing down there could be no 'phantasmagoria', to use Kipling's apt term, and the 'phantasmagoria' of *Notre-Dame* is effective still today.

Notre-Dame of Paris is, it goes without saying, a historical novel;

the action takes place in the year 1482, the year before Louis XI of France died. But what *kind* of historical novel is it? In many ways, an astonishingly modern kind, in that the history which it contains is more easily assimilated to contemporary historiography than to the historiography of Hugo's own day. Unlike the great majority of historical novels, including most modern ones, *Notre-Dame* has little to do with the noisier events of recorded history, with battles, treaties or the squabbles of dynasties. Indeed, Hugo is quick to tell us, in only the second sentence of the novel, that the day in the past to which we have been removed – and he dates it, 6 January 1482 – 'is not a day of which history has kept any record'.

As a novelist, then, Hugo does not mean to compete with historians in the interpretation of great events or the possible motivation of historical figures; he is preoccupied with what in recent years in France has come to be known as the 'history of mentalities', or the state of mind of a population at a given historical period. The sub-title of the novel is simply '1482' and Hugo's wish is to give us a convincing sense of what daily life might have been like for various classes of Parisian in that year. Thus the history in *Notre-Dame* is diffuse, it is to be found in representative attitudes and tendencies: the superstition of the populace, the hierarchy of the lawless truants, the movement towards a centralized administration, the capriciousness of justice, and so on; and to be found, too, in the very elaborately reconstructed décor of life, its buildings, institutions and ceremonies. The sole intervention of a more orthodox history is the presence in Paris of Flemish ambassadors, sent to agree marriage terms between the Dauphin of France and Margaret of Flanders, daughter of the imperial house of Austria. This marriage was arranged but finally abandoned several years later, and even here Hugo exploits rather than merely registers the few sure facts, such as the names of two of the ambassadors, Guillaume Rym and Jacques Coppenole, which are given in the best-known of primary sources for this period, the *Memoirs* of Philippe de Commynes; Hugo turns the hosier Coppenole into a precocious symbol of social democracy and of the eventual elimination of the monarchic principle from France.

The peculiarities of *Notre-Dame* become clear when one compares it, as one should, with a slightly earlier historical novel also set in France in the reign of Louis XI, Sir Walter Scott's *Quentin*

Durward. Scott's impact in Europe as a novelist was, we know, immense; he was esteemed, above all, as the first historical novelist to have documented himself intelligently on the periods he was writing about and the first to have made the past seem something more alien than a mere prototype of the present. *Quentin Durward* is the story of an untried Scottish youth who arrives in France to join the king's renowned corps of Scottish archers. He eventually wins glory and an aristocratic bride in the service of the crown. Durward's career is closely bound up with the incessant warring and scheming of Louis XI, and with the principal territorial conflict of his reign, against the Duke of Burgundy; Scott's history is of a more public and eventful kind than Hugo's.

Now Hugo knew Scott's novel well, having reviewed it at some length when a French translation appeared in 1823 (made, curiously enough, by the wife of Gosselin, the eventual publisher of *Notre-Dame*, who later said she found Hugo's novel inferior to Scott's). Much of the admiration that Hugo gives to Scott's work is of a conventional kind; he is impressed by Scott's ability to deal as competently with the lower as with the upper classes, with 'the rags of the mendicant and the robes of the king', and by the 'minute accuracy of his chronicle', a fulsome phrase which he then goes on to disprove by listing some of the Scottish writer's more glaring historical blunders. Perversely, one might think, he also complains of the choice of Louis XI as a fit king for a romance, which he attributes to the dimness or the malice of 'the English Muse'.

But the most significant passage of the review – a very mature and assured piece for a critic only twenty-one years old – comes when Hugo criticizes Scott for his lack of colour and ambition, and for missing altogether the lyricism of the past. He himself has a different and higher idea of the possibilities of historical fiction: 'After the picturesque, but prosaic romance of Walter Scott, a different romance remains to be created, yet more beautiful and complete in our view. This is the romance, at once both drama and epic, picturesque but poetic, real but ideal, true but great, which will enchase Walter Scott in Homer.'

This breathtaking prospectus is all of a piece with the propaganda that Hugo was later to make for Romanticism, and it is both just and sensible to apply its terms in the judgement of *Notre-Dame* itself. Young as he was in 1823, Hugo knew that he wanted to do not the same as Scott but *more*, he wanted to include in a historical romance elements that Scott had omitted, either from reticence or ignorance. In the same way, the essence of Hugo's Romanticism, as it has been the essence of so many aesthetic reform movements, was the transcending of artistic conventions which were too exclusive. Romanticism is critical of Classicism because it finds Classicism stiff and inadequate in its representation of the world; Romanticism demands and tries to provide a wider, looser realism.

In view of the indiscipline of some Romantic writing, and such feverishly operatic plots as that of *Notre-Dame*, it may seem eccentric to argue that Romantic conventions are more realistic than the ones they replaced. But one should remember that realism is not reality, it is simply the level of lifelikeness that readers find acceptable in a given literature at a given time. Comparisons with what actually happens in life are beside the point; the only comparisons worth making are with previous conventions and with the expectations of contemporary audiences.

For Hugo, therefore, Romanticism entails the expansion of literature in terms of what it may and may not treat, as well as its deliverance from obsolete formal or linguistic constraints. There are few topics, genres or styles that he himself felt unable to pursue. He wrote a vast amount and was fond of the largest subjects: God, Satan, Napoleon, Shakespeare, nature, humanity, the city, war, revolution, the sea. The plot of a novel like *Notre-Dame* is contrived in part to display his own great range of interests and skills; he engages with every social class: royalty, gentry, burgesses, students, clerics, the lower orders; he describes the insides and outsides of buildings, and buildings of different scales and functions; and as if to deny the restrictions of an urban scene, he at one point expels the demented archdeacon Frollo from Paris into the countryside to show that he is as well equipped to write about nature as about townscapes. Much has been made of Hugo's love of antithesis – rich against poor, light against dark, good against evil – but the antitheses themselves are a way of achieving comprehensiveness, since between their extremes, we must suppose, lies the whole of humankind.

This quest for size and completeness is the Homeric aspect of Hugo, and it is supported by his technique of enumeration, his taste for encyclopedic digressions. Hugo spares us little of his own specially accumulated knowledge of the world and its contents; the will to enlighten is strong. Once he touches on a subject – as he touches on architecture in *Notre-Dame* – he likes to write of it in the most extensive way imaginable; in this case a potted, dialectical history of the architecture of past and present, East and West. In other novels, these pedagogic interludes are even more massive, involving a god's-eye view of the battle of Waterloo in *Les Misérables* or a natural history lesson on the octopus in *The Toilers of the Sea*.

Yet the proportions of epic are not to be achieved by simple accretion and one must look elsewhere to specify what it is that gives *Notre-Dame* a dimension absent from a novel like *Quentin Durward*. It is, without question, the ideas that Hugo deploys in the novel or, to use a more prestigious term, his ideology. Hugo was not, and has never been mistaken for, an intellectual, because he lacked all the detachment and finesse that we now associate with that title. But he was a man of many ideas and convictions, and eager to impose them on as many people as possible. It is worth, therefore, uncovering in *Notre-Dame* what is not always obvious, and that is the cluster of social and literary principles which are at work in it.

The first readers of the novel seem to have missed them, mesmerized as they must have been by the sentimental fantasies of the plot. Hugo was nettled by their blindness: in the introduction which he wrote for the so-called 'definitive' edition of 1832 – a splendidly pragmatic document which appears on pp. 26–9 of this translation – he expresses a rather wistful gratitude to those discerning readers of the novel who had troubled to look for something deeper than the story and who had consequently grasped that *Notre-Dame* was intended to be more than an entertainment. Some of Hugo's ideas are easily located in the text, and are formulated openly and at length; others are more obscure or even tacit.

Given the title of the novel, a brief account of his ideas should start, logically, with architecture. *Notre-Dame* is a book written in praise of, and to some extent in imitation of, the Gothic style of architecture. This was a style that had long been under a cloud in France, from which it took Romanticism to save it. Hugo was not the first French writer o campaign in favour of the Gothic; Charles Nodier and Madame de Staël were already its champions. Nevertheless, even by late adolescence, he was aware of the injustice and partiality of current architectural preferences, which could accept the Romanesque style that had preceded the Gothic and extol the inert Classicism that finally succeeded it, while having only contempt for what it saw as the disorder and uncouthness of the Gothic itself.

Notre-Dame is thus meant in part as a redemption of an architecture in eclipse. Hugo redeems it not simply with his applause and the attention he pays to its visible merits, but also by associating it with the Romantic spirit of the age, with the congenial movement of the contemporary mind towards a greater flexibility of thought. The Gothic style, for Hugo, is one of populism, aspiration and caprice. He compares it, whenever practicable, with the style that came before it in north-western Europe, the Romanesque. The Romanesque, whose defining characteristic is the rounded arch, he judges to have been a hierarchical and dogmatic style, the imposition of a superior caste on an immobile society. The Gothic, in which the rounded arch has been replaced by the pointed arch or ogee, is, on the contrary, a freer style, encouraging licence and dissent from authority.

It is also an architecture of the vertical rather than the horizontal axis. Hugo, in the words of Nodier, was early seized by 'the demon ogee' and all through *Notre-Dame* he lays stress on the pointed, upward aspects of Gothic architecture – its spires, steeples, staircases and lancets – as well as on the altitude of the cathedral itself. This pervasive feature of the Gothic consorts perfectly with Hugo's humanist philosophy, because he saw humanity as engaged on a long but inevitably triumphant ascent from ignorance and crime to a harmonious state of grace on earth. Hugo cherishes the sky-scraping side of Gothic because it represents the opening of men's minds to hopes denied them by the autocracy he reads into the Romanesque, and the cathedral of Notre-Dame, begun in a Romanesque age and finished in a Gothic one, is presented, very reasonably, as a monument of the transition from one style to the other and thus, more important, of the transition from one outlook to the other. It is an impoverishment of the novel to suppose that

Hugo's interest in architecture was merely that of a connoisseur or antiquarian; one should bear in mind that he interprets architecture as a sign of a much larger ideological shift.

There is something else besides in the Gothic which he esteems and on which he capitalizes, and that is the part it allows to the grotesque, as in the gargoyles on the cathedral of Notre-Dame. Hugo felt much solidarity with an art form which had realized a part of his own Romantic programme by acknowledging that reality was compounded of both the beautiful and the ugly and had given the ugly at least a token part to play in a harmonious whole. This was to enlarge the art and at the same time to popularize it, for Hugo is clearly right to maintain that the inclusion of such motifs is a blow against the élitism of classical styles.

It is here that we come to the most meaningful of *Notre-Dame*'s parallels between the inanimate and the animate, for it is obvious that the architectural juxtaposition of beauty and the beast, the rose-window, let us say, with the grinning water-spout, is repeated in the commerce in the novel between the beautiful gypsy, La Esmeralda, and the hideous bell-ringer, Quasimodo. Hugo works hard to identify Quasimodo with the building into which he has been received as a foundling and establishes him as its presiding genius. Quasimodo has his place there not in spite of his bodily deformity but because of it, and his professional function of ringing the bells makes of him the agent of its harmony.

Quasimodo, like all of Hugo's central characters, like the bandit Hernani, or the ex-convict Valjean, or the lovelorn sailor Gilliatt in *The Toilers of the Sea*, is a social reject, the most typical of Romantic heroes. But Quasimodo is a reject because he is so repulsive to look at; he is an aesthetic reject, not a political or psychological one. Without wishing to dematerialize him into a symbol, one can say that he is a plea for a more enlightened aesthetic, one which can first find room for deformity and subsequently thrive on it. Quasimodo has aspirations, towards the conventional beauty of La Esmeralda and towards the cathedral he lives in, which he is able to scale with an abnormal agility – a skill, this, shared with Jean Valjean in *Les Misérables*, who is also able to climb upwards (never downwards) with inhuman ease; he is a benighted soul granted instincts by Hugo that are a promise of some ultimate social reconciliation. There is no such reconciliation in *Notre-Dame* because when he wrote it Hugo's own social ideas had not developed fully; in *Les Misérables* the reconciliation between Valjean and society is total, even euphoric.

But before coming to the political and social attitudes that Hugo introduces into *Notre-Dame*, there is a final point to be made about the architectural concerns of the novel, for as the introduction of 1832 makes quite clear it is an episode in Hugo's long-standing campaign against the vandalism of his contemporaries. I have said that before the Romantics championed it, the Gothic style was under a cloud, which would have been harmless enough if that were the full story; but often it was under the worse threat of decay, demolition or a philistine restoration. The Gothic spirit needed protection not only in the abstract but also in its substance, and some of Hugo's most venomous polemic was directed against its enemies – generally, like today, municipal authorities. In his early travels about France, he came across grievous examples of threatened buildings of the Gothic or earlier periods and he eventually summarized his deep resentment at France's neglect of its old architecture in a pamphlet which he called, fierily, *War on the Demolishers!*. It was published not long after *Notre-Dame* though most of it had been written several years before. It is one of Hugo's most rollicking performances as he sets about the town councillors of Laon, in north-east France, who were talking of knocking down a famous old tower in their ancient city. Hugo's prose style on these occasions has a bite and animus well worth quoting: 'It took the nineteenth century, the marvels of progress! A goose quill, drawn more or less at random across a sheet of paper by a few infinitely insignificant men! The miserable quill of a fifth-rate town council! A quill that haltingly draws up the idiotic dictates of a peasant divan![1] The imperceptible quill of the Lilliputian senate! A quill that makes mistakes in French! ...' And so on, for page after vituperative page.

The tower, admittedly, came down, but Hugo's verve was not altogether wasted, he had helped measurably to alert intelligent people to the neglect or destruction of much precious architecture. In 1830 the incoming Prime Minister, Guizot, formed a Historical Committee for Monuments and the Arts, and Hugo served on it between 1838 and 48. Later, Baudelaire wrote that 'it was his powerful instigation which, by the hand of erudite and enthusiastic

1. In the sense of a Turkish court of justice.

architects, is repairing our cathedrals and consolidating our old memories of stone'. This last phrase will have gratified Hugo above all, concurring as it does with his own remarkable defence of architecture in *Notre-Dame* as a form of script suitable to the ages that preceded the invention of printing, and as the most majestic and permanent repository of the national memory.

The social and political ideas involved in *Notre-Dame* were quite new to Hugo at the time when he wrote the novel. In the early 1820s he had been an extreme monarchist and orthodox Catholic, and the first literary review that he founded, with his brothers, was called *Le Conservateur littéraire*. But in September 1830, after the overthrow of Charles X and just at the moment when he was starting to write *Notre-Dame*, he recorded in his Journal the shift in his political opinions: 'In the last ten years my former royalist and Catholic conviction of 1820 has crumbled piece by piece before age and experience.' He was on the way to becoming as radical in politics as he had been for several years in art, in what still today seems a progressive awareness that styles of art may reflect social and political options and that the revolutionary artist is called on to be a revolutionary *tout court*.

Hugo's democratic beliefs can be observed gathering strength in *Notre-Dame*, supported *passim* by his espousal of an architecture itself valued for its populism. They are attached, mainly, to the figure of the Flemish hosier, Coppenole, a menacing and incongruous stranger to the feudal society which Hugo depicts. Coppenole is aggressively plebeian and much appreciated for his egalitarianism by the cowed plebs that witness it. Coppenole, predictably, is the master of ceremonies of the great popular cultural manifestation in the novel; the contest in face-pulling, which is so very much more successful a spectacle than the classical morality play of Pierre Gringoire. The face-pulling is subversive both artistically, in that it is a Romantic insult to a dead tradition, and socially, since it brings about the aggrieved withdrawal of the royal representative at the morality, the Cardinal of Bourbon. So it is no great surprise when, much later in the book, the outspoken Coppenole warns the King of France himself that the time will come when the people will rule the country, a warning delivered, with conspicuous irony, in the Bastille, whose storming in 1789 has always been taken for the true symbol of the French Revolution.

Hugo has allowed himself this prophecy for the good reason that he believed in the *inevitability* of democracy, sure that once this benevolent ideal was lodged in enough people's minds nothing could prevent its final realization. For him the French Revolution was the pivot of human history, a telluric event that might be deplored in detail but could only be accepted as a whole because it was unavoidable. 'The Revolution', he wrote in *1793*, his last novel, 'is a form of that immanent phenomenon that crowds in on us from every side and which we call Necessity.' In *Notre-Dame*, though there are still three hundred years to go before the Revolution, Louis XI is also shown to be conniving in that distant event. His efforts to break the power of the feudal aristocrats and to centralize the government of France in his own hands are presented by Hugo as the first stage of a process that would continue with Richelieu in the seventeenth century and end with Mirabeau in the late eighteenth. Hugo was always a man for the long, evolutionary view of human affairs and the historical components of *Notre-Dame* have been shaped accordingly.

What is necessarily missing from the novel is the prime agent of social improvement: enlightenment. Rather than political change, Hugo believed that the world would be saved by a social regeneration, and that regeneration could only be brought about by educating the masses. His trust in education was quite utopian. In his Journal for 1830 – entitled *Journal of a Revolutionary of 1830* – he looks radiantly ahead to the day '... when the shadows have at last finally and everywhere disappeared, when every head is in the light, when everyone governs everyone else'. If there is a political choice underlying this golden vision, it could only be anarchism, and Hugo often seems to have shared the puzzling faith of anarchists that an end of ignorance means the end of social conflict.

In *Notre-Dame* the struggle between darkness and light remains very much a pictorial element, a taste for chiaroscuro which Hugo indulges in such scenes as the nocturnal attack on the cathedral, with its interplay of inky blackness, the truants' torches and Quasimodo's lofty bonfire. In this respect, *Notre-Dame is* an early work, to be corrected in *Les Misérables*, where Valjean exchanges night for day after an encounter with an heroically altruistic bishop. Valjean, an ex-convict, steals the bishop's one valuable possession, his candlesticks, but is saved from a further savage sentence in the hulks when the bishop untruthfully attests that the candlesticks were a gift from him to Valjean. The symbolism is easily penetrated: what has been transmitted from one to the other is the precious gift of light. This symbolism is foreshadowed in *Notre-Dame* in the lyrical account that the archdeacon Claude Frollo gives of his experiments with the hermetic philosophy. But just as Frollo is doomed irrespective of his intellectual attainments, so the creatures of darkness, the sordid hierarchies of the Court of Miracles, are brutalized far beyond the point of no return. Even so, they are only ignorant, not evil; for Hugo the creatures of darkness are criminals, that is to say anti-social, so that their eventual reconciliation with society can be achieved easily enough by removing those inequalities and injustices which create fresh contingents of social outcasts in each generation.

And though Frollo, unlike Valjean, is not saved, he still testifies to the supreme equation of power with knowledge. Above all, he is the guardian of the recorded word, a reader of manuscripts and a prophet of the coming age of printing. The doctrine he puts forward in his speech to Jacques Coictier and the 'Compère Tourangeau' in the chapter called 'This Will Kill That', of books replacing buildings as the permanent record of human thought, is, delivered in 1482, an exotic prophecy; written in 1830, it is Hugo's retrospective account of the Gutenberg revolution and a strong statement of his own belief in the power of the word.

The whole novel, he says in the preface, was derived from a single inscription on a wall in Notre-Dame. That inscription was, to him, a challenge to resuscitate the past and reinvent the circumstances of its first appearance. Hugo's novels are full of such inscriptions, whether in Frollo's alchemist's cell or in the death cell of *The Last Day of a Condemned Prisoner*. They are the poignant and the potent relics of a particular human life, a proof that we can leave messages for posterity and that words survive deeds. Hugo had a robust faith in words of the kind traditionally associated with French writers: 'The inkpot will smash the cannon' was a typically ebullient slogan, justified in his scheme of things by the undeniable fact that the inkpot has time on its side as against the immediacy of the cannon.

It is proper that a writer should hold such beliefs in the power of writing, however deluded they may look to us today. In Hugo's case they were in any case guaranteed by his vatic assumption that he was the spokesman of providence. His determinism, unusually, was a thoroughly optimistic philosophy, whereby in the long term the moral and social betterment of the human race was assured.

Notre-Dame ends pathetically and badly, and over it presides the forbidding Greek word 'ANÁΓKH, or Fatality. But the plot of the novel hardly lives up to this sombre legend and its disasters can be traced to a single flaw, which is the celibacy of the priest, Claude Frollo. Had Frollo been in a position to act instinctively and satisfy his lust on the gypsy, all would have been well; there is nothing pessimistic ultimately about what transpires in the novel, since the trouble is brought on by observance of the rules of a specific society, and is not endemic in the structure of the universe. For Hugo the force of nature is benign and overwhelming; it is exemplified in *Notre-Dame*, as elsewhere in his work, by the unbreakable bond between mother and child. Hugo, like Rousseau before him, sees an unsatisfactory society as the source of human misery and the preferably peaceful renegotiation of the social contract as the means of its evolution into something better.

I hope that even so cursory a synopsis of the ideology of *Notre-Dame* will stop any one reading the novel as if it were merely picturesque. It undoubtedly *is* picturesque, because Hugo's powers of visualization are remarkable. But there is more to *Notre-Dame* than the prolonged, often lyrical descriptions of Paris, its cathedral and its inhabitants, and much more to it than the melodramatic sufferings of the principal characters; it is, in short, something richer and less lowbrow than the mixture of 'grandeur and absurdity' described by Tennyson.

Notre-Dame has been regularly retranslated since that first outbreak of English versions in the 1830s. I have not consulted all these translations but those which I have seen have all seemed to me to betray Hugo to some degree by making him read like a historical novelist of a much stiffer, more archaic kind that he actually was. The striking thing about the French of *Notre-Dame*, as about Hugo's style generally, is its formidable directness and resourcefulness, directness in syntax and resourcefulness in vocabulary. Stylistically, it was Hugo's democratic intention to bring written French closer to spoken French, from which it had drifted apart during the long years of Classical hegemony. There is no strong sense, reading *Notre-Dame* today, of a story written in the French of 1830, and no disloyalty at all, consequently, in translating it into plain, colloquial English.

This translation has been made from what was at the time of writing, before the appearance of the Bibliothèque de la Pléiade edition of *Notre-Dame*, the best established French text, that edited by M.-F. Guyard in the Classiques Garnier; I have also drawn on M. Guyard's very useful notes on a number of occasions. There is one specific difficulty in translating this novel, which is Hugo's tireless introduction of archaisms, including, to make things worse, the archaic jargon of the 15th century underworld. Hugo believed – and the belief was certainly rarer then than now – that by reproducing the idiom of a given social group one could reproduce its mental outlook in a specific and informative way, and he loves the lexicology of secret languages. I do not see much point in the translator of Hugo striving to recreate these languages from the more arcane resources of his own language, and the vast majority of the ancient, very occasionally wholly obscure, French words in *Notre-Dame* have therefore found their way on this occasion into contemporary English. One exception seemed worth making: the enumeration of truants in Book Two, Chapter Two, rough equivalents for which I have taken from Thomas Harman's lively *Caveat for Cursetors*, a traveller's guide to comparable English rogues of the sixteenth century.

John Sturrock

NOTRE-DAME OF PARIS

A FEW years ago, when the author of this book was visiting, or rather exploring, Notre-Dame, he found, carved by hand on the wall in a dark recess of one of the towers, the word:' ΑΝΑΓΚΗ.[1] The Greek capitals, black with age and cut quite deep into the stone, the forms and attitudes of their calligraphy, which had something peculiarly Gothic about it, as if to show that the hand which had inscribed them there was a medieval one, and above all their grim and fatal import, made a keen impression on the author.

He wondered, and tried to guess who the tormented soul might have been who had not wanted to depart this world without leaving behind, on the brow of the old church, this stigma of crime or misfortune.

Since then, the wall has either been distempered or scraped (I forget which) and the inscription has gone. For such is the treatment accorded to the marvellous churches of the Middle Ages for close on two hundred years. Mutilation has come on them from all sides, from both within and without. The priest distempers them, the architect scrapes them, then along comes the populace which demolishes them.

Thus, apart from the fragile memento here dedicated to it by the author of this book, there is today nothing left of that mysterious word engraved in the gloom of the tower of Notre-Dame, nothing left of the unknown destiny of which it was so cheerless a summary. The man who wrote that word on that wall was erased from the midst of the generations several centuries ago, the word in its turn has been erased from the wall of the church, and soon perhaps the church itself will be erased from the earth.

This book was written about that word.

1 March 1831

1. 'Fatality.'

Note added to the Definitive Edition of 1832

THIS edition was wrongly advertised as augmented by several *new* chapters.[1] That should have been *unpublished* chapters. If by new we mean *newly written*, then the chapters added to this edition are not *new*. They were written at the same time as the rest of the work, they date from the same period and share the same intention; they have always formed part of the manuscript of *Notre-Dame of Paris*. Their author, moreover, fails to understand how brand-new developments could be added to a work of this kind at a later date. One cannot do that at will. In his view, a romance is born in a more or less necessary way, with all its chapters; a stage play is born with all its scenes. You must not think that there is something arbitrary about the number of parts that make up the whole: that mysterious microcosm which you call a play or romance. Grafts or welds take badly on works of this kind, which should issue forth in a single draft and then be left alone. Once the thing is made, do not change your mind, do not tamper with it. Once the book is published, once the sex of the work, whether virile or not, has been recognized and proclaimed, once the baby has uttered its first cry, it is born, it is there, it is the way it is, and neither mother nor father can do anything more about it, it belongs to the air and the sunlight, you must let it live or die as it stands. Your book is a failure? Too bad. Don't add a chapter to an unsuccessful book. It is incomplete? You should have completed it when giving birth to it. Your tree is stunted? You won't straighten it. Your romance is consumptive? Your romance won't survive? You won't give it back the breath it lacks. Your drama was born lame? Don't, believe me, fit it with a wooden leg.

The author is thus particularly anxious for the public to know that the chapters added here were not expressly written for this reprinting. There is a very simple reason why they were not published in the earlier editions of the book. At the time when *Notre-Dame of Paris* was first being printed, the folder containing these three chapters went astray. This meant either rewriting them or

1. Book Four, Chapter Six; Book Five, Chapters One and Two.

doing without them. The author reckoned that the only two of these chapters long enough to have some importance were chapters on art and history which in no way affected the underlying drama or story, that the public would not notice they had gone and that he alone, the author, would possess the secret of this lacuna in the text. He chose to go ahead. Also, if we are to make a full confession, his laziness recoiled from the task of rewriting three lost chapters. He would have found it quicker to write a new romance.

Now, the chapters have been found again and he has taken the earliest opportunity of restoring them to their place. His work is thus now whole once again, such as he conceived it and such as he wrote it; be it good or bad, long-lived or short, it is the way he wants it.

These rediscovered chapters will no doubt be judged of small worth by those otherwise very discerning people who have sought only the drama, the story, in *Notre-Dame of Paris*. But there may be other readers who have found some profit in studying the philosophical and aesthetic ideas concealed in the book, and have been willing, when reading *Notre-Dame of Paris*, to enjoy teasing out, from beneath the story, something which is not the story, and to pursue – if I may be permitted these somewhat ambitious expressions – the system of the historian and the intention of the artist through the creation as such of the poet.

It is for them, above all, that the chapters added to this edition will complete *Notre-Dame of Paris*, always supposing that *Notre-Dame of Paris* deserves completion.

In one of these chapters, the author expresses and enlarges upon the current decadence of architecture and the now, in his view, almost inevitable demise of this king of the arts, a view, unhappily, deeply rooted in him and deeply pondered. But he feels the need to say here that he very much wants the future one day to prove him wrong. He knows that art, in all its forms, has everything to hope for from the new generations, whose as yet embryonic genius can be heard germinating in our studios. The seed is in the furrow, and the crop assuredly will be a good one. He is only afraid, and you will be able to see why in Book Five of this edition, that the sap may have withdrawn from the old soil of architecture, which for so many centuries was art's most fruitful terrain.

Yet there is today so much life, so much potential, so much what one might call predestination in our young artists that, at this moment, particularly in our schools of architecture, the professors, who are execrable, are creating pupils who are excellent not only without knowing they are doing so but altogether in spite of themselves; the exact reverse of the potter in Horace, who conceived amphoras but produced cooking pots. *Currit rota, urceus exit.*[1]

But in any case, whatever the future of architecture and however our young architects may one day settle the question of their art, while we wait for new monuments we must conserve the old. We must, if it be possible, inspire the nation with a love of its national architecture. That, its author here declares, is one of the chief aims of this book; it is one of the chief aims of his life.

Notre-Dame of Paris may have opened up a few true perspectives on the art of the Middle Ages, that marvellous art hitherto unknown to some and, what is worse, misunderstood by others. But the author is very far from considering the task he has voluntarily set himself as over. He has already pleaded the cause of our old architecture on more than one occasion, he has already spoken out loudly against many profanations, demolitions and impieties. He will not tire of doing so. He has pledged himself to return frequently to this subject, and he will return to it. He will be as indefatigable in defending our historic buildings as the iconoclasts of our schools and academies are zealous in attacking them. For it is distressing to see the hands into which the architecture of the Middle Ages has fallen and the way in which our present plaster-smearers are treating the ruins of this great art. We who are intelligent men should feel ashamed when we see them at work and are content merely to jeer at them. Nor am I talking here only of what is happening in the provinces, but of what is going on in Paris, on our own doorsteps, beneath our own windows, in this great town, this town of letters, the city of newspapers, talk and ideas. To end this note, we cannot forbear indicating some of the acts of vandalism projected, debated, begun, continued and quietly brought to a conclusion every day under our very eyes, under the eyes of the artistic public of Paris and in the face of critics bewildered by such audacity. The archbishop's palace has just been demolished, a building in poor taste so the harm is not great; but along with the archbishop's palace they have also demolished the

1. 'The wheel turns, a jug emerges' (*Ars poetica*).

bishop's palace, a rare relic of the fourteenth century that the demolishing architect was unable to tell apart from the rest. He has pulled up the wheat with the tare. Who cares? They are talking of razing the admirable chapel of Vincennes, so as to use the stones for some fortification or other, for which, by the way, Daumesnil felt no need.[1] They repair and restore an ungainly pile like the Palais Bourbon at great expense, and let the wonderful stained-glass of the Sainte-Chapelle be blown in by the equinoctial gales. For the past few days, there has been scaffolding on the tower of Saint-Jacques-de-la-Boucherie, and one of these mornings the pick-axes will get to work on it. Some mason has even been prepared to build a small white house between the venerable towers of the Palais de Justice. They have found another to castrate Saint-Germain-des-Prés, the feudal abbey with three bell-towers. Be in no doubt, they will find another to lay low Saint-Germain-l'Auxerrois. All these masons claim to be architects, they are paid by the town authorities or by the royal purse and wear the green coats of the Academy. All the harm that false taste can do to true taste, they are doing. At the moment of writing, one of them – and what a lamentable sight it is! – has hold of the Tuileries, he is making a scar right across the middle of Philibert Delorme's face; it is by no means one of the lesser scandals of our time to see this gentleman's leaden architecture splayed so insolently right across one of the Renaissance's most delicate façades!

Paris, 20 October 1832

1. Daumesnil was a nineteenth-century governor of the Château de Vincennes who three times defended it successfully against attack.

BOOK ONE

ONE
The Great Hall

THREE hundred and forty-eight years, six months and nineteen days ago today, the people of Paris awoke to hear all the church-bells in the triple enclosure of the City, the University and the Town in full voice.

Not that 6 January 1482 is a day of which history has kept any record. There was nothing noteworthy about the event that had set the burgesses and bells of Paris in motion from early morning. It was not an assault by Picards or Burgundians, it was not a reliquary being carried in procession, it was not a student revolt in the vineyard of Laas,[1] it was not an entry by 'our most redoubtable Lord *Monsieur* the King', it was not even a fine hanging of male and female thieves on the gallows of Paris. Nor was it the arrival, so frequent in the fifteenth century, of an embassy, in all its plumes and finery. It was barely two days since the last cavalcade of this kind, that of the Flemish ambassadors charged with concluding the marriage between the dauphin and Marguerite of Flanders, had made its entry into Paris, much to the annoyance of Monsieur the Cardinal of Bourbon, who, to please the king, had had to put on a smile for this uncouth mob of Flemish burgomasters, and entertain them, in his Hôtel de Bourbon, with a 'very fine morality, satire and farce', as driving rain drenched the magnificent tapestries in his doorway.

What had 'excited all the commonalty of Paris', as Jean de Troyes puts it, on this January the sixth, was the twin ceremony of Twelfth Night and the Feast of Fools, which had fallen on the same day since time immemorial.

Today, there was to be a bonfire on the Grève, a maypole at Braque's Chapel and a mystery play at the Palais de Justice. These had been trumpeted at the crossroads the previous evening by the provost's men, in their handsome actons of mauve camlet, with large white crosses on the breast.

And so, first thing, the crowd of townsmen and women had shut

1. The scene of student disorders in 1548.

up their shops and houses and made their way from every side towards one of the three appointed sites. Everyone had made his choice, some for the bonfire, others for the maypole, others for the mystery. We must pay tribute to the ancient good sense of the sightseers of Paris and tell you that the greater part of this crowd was making either for the bonfire, which was highly seasonable, or for the mystery, which was to be given in comfort and under cover in the great hall of the palace, and that by common consent they left the poorly arrayed maypole to shiver all alone under the January sky in the graveyard of Braque's Chapel.

The people were mostly flocking the approaches to the Palais de Justice, for it was known that the Flemish ambassadors, who had arrived two days before, were intending to be present at the performance of the mystery, as well as at the election of the fools' pope, likewise due to take place in the great hall.

It was no easy matter to get inside the great hall that day, although it had the reputation at the time of being the largest covered enclosure in the world. (True, Sauval had yet to measure the great hall of the Château of Montargis.) To the onlookers at their windows, the palace square, which was packed with people, resembled a sea into which, like so many river-mouths, five or six streets were constantly disgorging fresh torrents of heads. As they continued to swell, the waves of people collided with the corners of the houses which, here and there, jutted out into the irregular basin of the square like so many promontories. In the centre of the palace's tall Gothic[1] façade, twin streams flowed up and down the great staircase without interruption and then, after breaking halfway, below the entrance steps, spread down the two ramps at the sides in broad waves, so that the great staircase emptied ceaselessly into the square like a waterfall into a lake. The shouting and the laughter and the tramp of thousands of feet made a great noise and clamour. At times this noise and clamour were intensified, and the current that was sweeping all these people towards the great staircase faltered and turned back on itself, forming eddies. An archer had

1. In the sense in which it is generally used, the word *Gothic* is altogether improper but altogether hallowed by age. We accept it, therefore, and adopt it, like everyone else, to characterize the architecture of the second half of the Middle Ages, whose principle is the pointed arch and which succeeded the architecture of the earlier period, engendered by the semi-circular arch (V.H.).

just lashed out or a provost serjeant's horse reared up to restore order: an admirable tradition which the provosts bequeathed to the constables, the constables to the marshals, and the marshals to our own Paris gendarmerie.

Doorways, windows, dormers and roofs were alive with the calm, law-abiding faces of thousands of good burgesses, who asked for nothing better than to stare at the palace and the mob; for many people in Paris are content merely to gaze at the gazers, and for us a high wall behind which something is going on is in itself an object of keen curiosity.

Were we, men of 1830, to be granted the power of mingling, in spirit, with these Parisians of the fifteenth century, and accompanying them as they shoved, elbowed and stumbled their way into the vast hall of the palace, so constricted on that 6 January 1482, the spectacle would lack neither interest nor charm and everything around us would be so old as to seem, to us, quite new.

If the reader agrees, we shall try to recapture, in the mind's eye, the impression he, like us, would have got as he crossed the threshold of the great hall in the midst of this throng in surcoats, actons and cote-hardies.

And right away, our ears are dinned and our eyes dazzled. Above our heads, a double Gothic vault, with carved wood panelling painted sky-blue with gold fleur-de-lys; beneath our feet, a pavement of alternate black and white marble. A few yards away, an enormous pillar, then another and another; in all, seven pillars along the length of the hall, supporting the springings of the double vault at its mid-point. Around the first four pillars, the stalls of tradesmen, sparkling with glass and tinsel; around the last three, oak benches, worn away and polished by the hose of litigants and the robes of attorneys. All round the hall, along the high wall, between doors, casements and pillars, the endless row of statues of all the kings of France since Pharamond: the indolent kings, their arms dangling and their eyes lowered; and the valiant warrior kings, with head and hands raised boldly to heaven. Then, in the tall, pointed windows, stained-glass of every colour; at the wide exits from the hall, rich, delicately carved doorways; and the whole thing, vaulting, pillars, walls, door-frames, panelling, doors and statues, splendidly illuminated from top to bottom in blue and gold; this illumination was already somewhat tarnished by this time and had almost completely vanished beneath the dust and spiders' webs by the year of grace 1549, when Du Breul could still admire it out of tradition.

If you now picture this vast rectangular hall to yourselves, lit by the pallid January daylight and invaded by a noisy, motley crowd drifting along the walls and swirling round the seven pillars, then you will already have a confused idea of the general picture, of which we shall now try and fill in some of the curious details.

Certain it is that if Ravaillac had not assassinated Henri IV. the documents for Ravaillac's trial would not have been deposited in the record office of the Palais de Justice; there would have been no accomplices to profit from the disappearance of the aforesaid documents; hence, no incendiaries obliged, for want of a better method, to burn down the record office in order to burn the documents, and to burn down the Palais de Justice in order to burn down the record office; and so, finally, no fire of 1618. The old palace would still be standing together with its great hall, and I could say to the reader: Go and see it; and so we would both be spared, I from writing and he from reading a make-shift description of it. Which goes to prove this brand-new truth: that great events have incalculable consequences.

True, it is very possible in the first place that Ravaillac had no accomplices, and then, if by any chance he did have some, that they had no hand in the fire of 1618. There exist two other highly plausible explanations for this. First, the great flaming star. a foot across and a cubit high, which, as everyone knows, fell from the sky on to the palace after midnight on March the seventh. Secondly, Théophile's quatrain:

> A sad sport indeed it was
> When in Paris Dame Justice
> Ate too many sweeteners
> And caused a palate-ial fire.[1]

Whatever your views on this threefold explanation – political, physical or poetical – of the burning-down of the Palais de Justice in 1618, the unfortunately certain fact is the fire. Thanks to this catastrophe, and thanks above all to the various restorations which

1. The joke works better in French where the slang word for 'bribe' is *épice*, or, literally, 'spice', thus justifying the palate-ial fire.

successively finished off what it had spared, very little remains today of this first residence of the kings of France, a palace senior to the Louvre and already so old in the days of Philip the Fair that they searched for traces there of the magnificent buildings put up by King Robert and described by Helgaldus. Almost everything has gone. What has become of the chamber in the chancellery where Saint Louis 'consummated his marriage'? Or the garden where he meted out justice, 'dressed in a camlet tunic, a surcoat of wincey without sleeves, and a cloak over-all of black sendal, lying on rugs, together with Joinville'? Where is the Emperor Sigismund's chamber? Or Charles IV's? Or John Lackland's? Where the staircase from which Charles VI issued his Edict of Grace? The flagstone where, in the presence of the dauphin, Marcel cut the throats of Robert de Clermont and the Marshal of Champagne? The wicket-gate where the bulls of the anti-pope Benedict were defaced, and whence those who had brought them departed again, mockingly clad in copes and mitres, to make honourable amends all over Paris? And the great hall, with its gilding, its sky-blue, its pointed arches, its statues, its pillars, its huge vault all jagged with carvings? And the gilded chamber? And the stone lion that stood at the door, head down and tail between its legs, like the lions of Solomon's throne, in the attitude of humiliation proper to might before justice? And the beautiful doors? And the beautiful stained-glass? And the carved ironwork which so disheartened Biscornette? And the delicate joinery of Du Hancy? What has time done, what have men done to these wonders? And what have we been given instead of all that Gallic history and all that Gothic art? For art, the heavy, depressed arches of M. de Brosse, the clumsy architect of the Saint-Gervais portal, while for history we have the garrulous memoirs of the big pillar, still echoing to the backbiting of our Patrus.[1]

Which is not much. But we must return to the real great hall of the real old palace.

The two extremities of this giant parallelogram were occupied, one by the famous slab of marble, so long, so wide and so thick that, as the old inventories put it, in a style to whet the appetite of Gargantua, there never was seen 'such a slice of marble anywhere in the world'; the other by the chapel, in which Louis XI had had

1. Olivier Patru (1604–81) was a well-known lawyer.

himself sculpted kneeling before the Virgin and to which he had had moved, not caring that it left two empty niches in the line of royal statues, the statues of Charlemagne and Saint Louis, two saints whom he imagined to be very influential in heaven because they had been kings of France. This chapel was still brand-new, having been built barely six years before, and was throughout in that charming style of delicate architecture and marvellous carving, with fine, deep incisions, which marks, with us, the end of the Gothic era and is perpetuated up until around the middle of the sixteenth century in the entrancing fantasies of the Renaissance. In particular the little open-work rose-window above the doorway was a masterpiece of slenderness and grace, like a lacework star.

In the centre of the hall, facing the main door, and with its back to the wall, was a platform of gold brocade, on to which a private entrance had been made by way of a window in the corridor of the gilded chamber; it had been erected for the Flemish envoys and other important persons invited to the performance of the mystery.

The play was to be performed, as was customary, on the marble slab. This had been got ready early that morning; its rich expanse of marble, scratched all over by the heels of the lawyers' clerks, supported quite a tall woodwork cage, whose upper surface, visible from everywhere in the hall, would serve as a stage, while the inside, hidden by tapestries, would serve as a dressing-room for the characters in the play. Communication between stage and dressing-room had been ensured by a ladder, set artlessly up on the outside, whose steep rungs would do for both entrances and exits. No matter how unforeseen the character or how dramatic the turn of events, they would be obliged to climb up by this ladder. The art and its machinery were then in their innocent and venerable infancy!

Four of the palace bailiff's serjeants, the necessary guardians of all the people's pleasures, on feast days as on execution days, stood at the four corners of the marble slab.

The play was to begin only at the twelfth stroke of noon from the great palace clock. This was no doubt very late for a theatrical performance, but they had had to take their time from the ambassadors.

But this great multitude had been waiting since morning. A fair number of these worthy sightseers had been shivering since break of day in front of the great steps of the palace; a few even declared they had spent the night athwart the great door so as to be sure of being the first ones in. The crowd was getting denser by the minute and, like water exceeding its own level, had begun to rise up the walls, to swell around the pillars, to overflow on to entablatures, cornices, and window-ledges, and wherever the architecture projected or the sculpture was in relief. And so, long before the hour when the ambassadors were due to arrive, the discomfort, impatience, boredom and licence of a day of cynicism and excess, the quarrels that broke out at the least provocation over a knobbly elbow or a hob-nailed shoe, the fatigue of a long wait, all added a sour and bitter note to the clamour of a crowd compressed, pent, crushed, crammed and suffocated. All that was to be heard were complaints and imprecations against the Flemings, the merchants' provost, the Cardinal of Bourbon, the Bailiff of the Palace, Madame Marguerite of Austria, the tipstaffs, the cold, the heat, the bad weather, the Bishop of Paris, the fools' pope, the pillars, the statues, this closed door, that open window; all to the great amusement of the bands of students and menservants distributed among the crowd who added to its discontent with their teasing and their pranks as, so to speak, they stuck pins into the general ill-temper.

One group in particular of these merry young demons had broken in the glass of a window and sat boldly down on the entablature, whence their stares and raillery plunged alternately down inside and out, into the crowd in the hall and the crowd in the square. It was easy to tell from their mimicry, their hoots of laughter and the derisive repartee they exchanged with their fellows from one end of the hall to the other, that these young scholars did not share in the boredom and weariness of the rest of the audience but knew very well how to turn what they could see into a spectacle for their own private enjoyment and one which gave them the patience to await the other spectacle.

'Upon my soul, it's you, Joannes Frollo de Molendino!' shouted one of them to a sort of small, fair-haired devil with a pretty, malicious face, who was clinging to the acanthus leaves of a capital. 'Jehan of the Windmill is the right name for you, your two arms and two legs look like four sails going round in the wind. How long have you been here?'

'By the Devil's mercy, more than four hours,' replied Joannes Frollo, 'and I certainly hope they will be credited to me against my time in Purgatory. I heard the King of Sicily's eight cantors intone the first verse of seven o'clock high mass in the Sainte-Chapelle.'

'Fine cantors,' rejoined the other. 'their voices are even more pointed that their hats! Before he founded a mass for Monsieur Saint John, the king should certainly have found out whether Monsieur Saint John likes Latin chanted in a Provençal accent.'

'He did it to give employment to the King of Sicily's confounded cantors!' screeched an old woman in the crowd at the foot of the window. 'I ask you! A thousand *livres parisis* for a mass! And out of the taxes from the Paris fish market, what's more!'

'Quiet, old woman!' answered a fat, serious personage standing next to the fishwife and holding his nose. 'He had to found a mass. You didn't want the king to fall ill again?'

'Bravely spoken, Sir Gilles Lecornu, Master-furrier of the King's Wardrobe!' shouted the small student clinging to the capital.

A burst of laughter from all the students greeted the unfortunate name[1] of the poor Master-furrier of the King's Wardrobe.

'Lecornu! Gilles Lecornu!' said some of them.

'*Cornutus et hirsutus*,'[2] put in another.

'No doubt,' went on the young imp on the capital. 'Why the laughter? An honourable man Gilles Lecornu, the brother of Maître Jehan Lecornu, Provost of the King's Household, and the son of Maître Mahiet Lecornu, First Gatekeeper of the Forest of Vincennes, all burgesses of Paris, all married from father to son!'

The merriment was renewed. The fat master-furrier made no reply but struggled to escape the stares levelled at him from all sides. But he puffed and sweated in vain; his efforts merely caused his broad, apoplectic face, purple with resentment and ire, to become more solidly embedded among the shoulders of his neighbours, like a wedge sinking into a piece of wood.

One of these neighbours, as short, fat and venerable as himself, finally came to his aid.

'Disgraceful, students addressing a burgess in that tone! In my day, we'd have taken a birch-twig to them and burned them with it afterwards.'

The whole band exploded.

1. Unfortunate because *Lecornu* would mean 'the one with horns', i.e. cuckold.

2. 'Horned and hairy.'

'Yoohoo! Who's that singing scales? Who's the owl of ill-omen?'

'Hold on, I know who it is,' said one, 'it's Maître Andry Musnier.'

'Because he's one of the four sworn-booksellers of the university!' said another.

'Everything in that place comes in fours,' cried a third. 'Four nations,[1] four faculties, four feast-days, four proctors, four electors, four booksellers.'

'Well then, we ought to give them what *for*,' put in Jean Frollo.

'We shall burn your books, Musnier.'

'We shall thrash your servants, Musnier.'

'Musnier, we shall dishonour your wife.'

'Nice, fat Mademoiselle Oudarde.'

'Who's so fresh and jolly you'd think she was a widow.'

'Go to the devil,' muttered Maître Andry Musnier.

'Shut up, Maître Andry,' Jehan went on, still hanging from his capital, 'or I shall drop on your head!'

Maître Andry looked up, seemed for a moment to be calculating the height of the pillar and the young scamp's weight, and multiplying the weight by the square of the velocity in his head, and then shut up.

Jehan, the battlefield his, went on triumphantly: 'I'd do it too, even if I am the brother of an archdeacon!'

'A fine lot, our university people, not even having our privileges respected on a day like today! After all, there's a maypole and a bonfire in the Town, a mystery play, the fools' pope and Flemish ambassadors in the City; and at the University, nothing!'

'Yet the Place Maubert is big enough!' put in one of the scholars posted on the entablature of the window.

'Down with the rector, the electors and the proctors!' shouted Joannes.

'Tonight we must make a bonfire in the Champ-Gaillard,' went on the other, 'with Maître Andry's books.'

'And the scribes' desks!' said his neighbour.

'And the beadles' staffs!'

'And the deans' spittoons!'

1. The students at the University of Paris were then divided into four 'nations': France, Picardy, Normandy and Germany.

'And the proctors' sideboards!'

'And the electors' breadbins!'

'And the rector's stools!'

'Down,' chimed in little Jehan, 'down with Maître Andry, the beadles and the scribes; the theologians, doctors and decretists; the proctors, electors and the rector!'

'So it's the end of the world!' murmured Maître Andry, stopping his ears.

'And talking of the rector, he's just going past in the square!' shouted one of those at the window.

They all tried to be first to turn and face the square.

'Is it really our venerable rector, Maître Thibaut?' asked Jehan Frollo of the Windmill, who was clinging to an interior pillar and so could not see what was going on outside.

'Yes, yes,' answered all the others, 'it's him, it's him in person, Maître Thibaut the rector.'

It was indeed the rector and all the dignitaries of the University, going in procession to meet the embassy and just then crossing the palace square. The students crowded in the window greeted them as they went by with sarcasms and ironic applause. The rector, walking at the head of his company, bore the brunt of the opening salvo, which was a fierce one.

'Hello, Rector! Yoohoo! Good morning!'

'How's he managed to get here, the old gambler? Has he left his dice then?'

'Look at him trotting on his mule! Its ears aren't as long as his.'

'Yoohoo! Good morning, Rector Thibaut! *Tybalde aleator!*[1] Old idiot! Old gambler!'

'God preserve you! How many double sixes did you throw last night?'

'Look at that grey, jaded, haggard face and the bags under his eyes, that's what dice and gambling do to you!'

'Where are you off to, *Tybalde ad dados*,[2] turning your back on the University and trotting towards the Town?'

'I bet he's going to look for lodgings in the Rue Thibautodé,'[3] cried Jehan of the Windmill.

1. 'O Tybald, dicer.'
2. Kitchen Latin, 'O Tybald of the dice.'
3. i.e. Thybaut-aux-dés, or Tybald of the dice.

The whole band took up the pun in a thunderous voice, clapping their hands furiously.

'You're going to look for lodgings in the Rue Thibautodé, aren't you, Rector, your game's the devil's game.'

Then it was the turn of the other dignitaries.

'Down with the beadles! Down with the macers!'

'I say, Robin Poussepain, who's that one there?'

'That's Gilbert de Suilly, *Gilbertus de Soliaco*, the Chancellor of the College of Autun.'

'Here, here's my shoe, you're better placed than I am, throw it in his face.'

'*Saturnalitias mittimus ecce nuces.*'[1]

'Down with the six theologians in their white surplices!'

'Are those the theologians? I thought they were the six white geese Sainte-Geneviève gave the town for the fief of Roogny!'

'Down with the doctors!'

'Down with cardinal disputations and quodlibetarians!'

'Here's my cap for you, Chancellor of Sainte-Geneviève! You did the dirty on me. It's a fact, he gave my place in the Normandy nation to young Ascanio Falzaspada, who comes from the province of Bourges, because he's Italian.'

'That's unfair,' said all the students. 'Down with the Chancellor of Sainte-Geneviève!'

'Hi there, Maître Joachim de Ladehors! Hi there, Louis Dahuille! Hi there, Lambert Hoctement!'

'I hope the devil chokes the proctor of the German nation!'

'And the chaplains of the Sainte-Chapelle, with their grey amices. *Cum tunicis grisis!*'

'*Seu de pellibus grisis fourratis!*'[2]

'Yoohoo, masters of arts! All the beautiful black copes and all the beautiful red copes!'

'They make a fine tail for the rector.'

'It's like the Doge of Venice going to his nuptials with the sea.'

'I say, Jehan, the canons of Sainte-Geneviève!'

'To hell with the canonry!'

'Abbé Claude Choart! Doctor Claude Choart! Are you looking for Marie la Giffarde?'

1. From Martial, *Epigrams*: 'We send you, herewith, Saturnalian nuts.'
2. 'Or trimmed with grey fur.'

'She's in the Rue de Glatigny.'

'Making the king of the ribalds' bed.'

'He pays her four *deniers*, *quattuor denarios*.'

'*Aut unum bombum*.'[1]

'Do you want her to pay you face to face?'

'Friends, Maître Simon Sanguin, the Elector of Picardy, with his wife riding pillion.'

'*Post equitem sedet atra cura*.'[2]

'Bravo, Maître Simon!'

'Good morning, Elector, sir!'

'Good night, Madame Elector!'

'How lucky they are to be able to see it all,' sighed Joannes de Molendino, still perched in the foliage of his capital.

Meanwhile, the sworn-bookseller of the University, Maître Andry Musnier, lent towards the ear of the Master-furrier of the King's Wardrobe, Maître Gilles Lecornu.

'I tell you, monsieur, it's the end of the world. Never have we known such behaviour from the students. It's all those accursed new inventions that are ruining everything. Artillery, serpentines, bombards, and especially printing, that other plague from Germany. No more manuscripts, no more books! Printing is killing the bookshop. The end of the world's at hand.'

'As I can tell from the way velvet is coming in,' said the master-furrier.

Just then, it struck twelve.

'Ah!' said the whole crowd as one. The students fell silent. There was a great shifting about, a great movement of heads and feet, a great detonation everywhere of coughs and nose-blowing. Each one settled himself, took up his position, drew himself upright, got into a group; then there was a great silence; every neck stayed craned, every mouth agape, every eye trained on the marble slab. No one appeared on it. The bailiff's four serjeants still stood there, stiff and motionless, like four painted statues. All eyes turned towards the platform reserved for the Flemish envoys. The door stayed closed and the platform empty. The crowd had been waiting since early morning for three things, twelve o'clock, the Flemish

1. 'Or a fart.'

2. 'Behind the horseman sits black care' (Horace, *Odes*).

embassy and the mystery play. Only twelve o'clock had arrived on time.

It was too much to bear.

They waited one, two, three, five minutes, a quarter of an hour; no one came. The platform remained deserted, the stage mute. But impatience had given way to anger. Irritation was being voiced, if only in an undertone as yet. 'The mystery, the mystery,' was the subdued murmur. Heads were in a ferment. A storm, still no more than a growling, floated on the surface of the crowd. It was Jehan of the Windmill who drew the first spark from it.

'The mystery, and to hell with the Flemings!' he shouted at the top of his voice, writhing like a serpent around his capital.

The crowd clapped its hands.

'The mystery,' it took up, 'and Flanders can go to the devil!'

'It's the mystery right away,' the student continued, 'or my idea is we hang the palace bailiff and have that as a comedy and a morality.'

'Well said,' cried the populace, 'and let's launch the execution with his serjeants.'

Loud cheers followed. The four poor wretches looked at one another and started to turn pale. The crowd began to move towards them and they could see the fragile wooden balustrade that divided them already giving and bulging inwards under the pressure.

It was a tense moment.

'String them up,' came the shout from every side.

At that instant, the tapestry over the dressing-room which we have described above was raised, to allow through a person the mere sight of whom suddenly halted the crowd and, as if by magic, transformed its anger into curiosity.

'Silence, silence!'

This person, extremely ill-at-ease and trembling in every limb, came forward to the edge of the marble slab with a great many bows which, as he got nearer, looked more and more like genuflexions.

Meanwhile calm had slowly been restored. All that remained was that faint buzz which the silence of a crowd always gives off.

'Messieurs and mesdemoiselles,' he said, 'we are to have the honour of declaiming and performing before His Eminence Monsieur the Cardinal a very fine morality play, entitled *The Right Judgement of the Virgin Mary*. I shall play Jupiter. At this moment

His Eminence is accompanying the most honourable embassy of Monsieur the Duke of Austria, which has been delayed at the present time at the Porte Baudets listening to the address from the Rector of the University. As soon as the most eminent cardinal arrives we shall begin.'

It is certain that, short of the intervention of Jupiter, nothing could have saved the palace bailiff's four luckless serjeants. If we had been fortunate enough to have invented this very true story and so to be held responsible for it by Our Lady Criticism, it is not against us that the classical precept of *Nec deus intercessit*[1] could be invoked at this moment. The Lord Jupiter's costume was in any case a very fine one and had helped not a little to pacify the crowd by attracting its undivided attention. Jupiter was clad in a brigantine covered in black velvet, with gilt studs, and a bycoket decorated with buttons of silver gilt; and but for the rouge and the huge beard which each covered one half of his face, but for the roll of gilt pasteboard, much bespangled and bristling all over with strips of tinsel, which he carried in his hand and which knowledgeable eyes easily recognized to be his thunderbolt, but for his flesh-coloured feet, tied with ribbons like a Greek's, he might well have borne comparison, for the austerity of his costume, with one of the Duke of Berry's Breton archers.

TWO
Pierre Gringoire

As he addressed them, however, the satisfaction and admiration universally aroused by his costume were dispelled by his words; and when he came to his ill-found conclusion: 'As soon as the most eminent cardinal arrives, we shall begin,' his voice was drowned in a storm of catcalls.

'Begin right away! The mystery! The mystery right away!' the people shouted. And Joannes de Molendino's voice could be heard above all the others, cutting through the din like a fife in an orchestra of pots and pans:

'Begin right away!' shrilled the student.

'Down with Jupiter and the Cardinal of Bourbon!' bawled Robin Poussepain and the other scholars perched in the casement.

1. 'Let not a god intervene,' a precept from Horace's *Ars poetica*.

'The morality right away!' the crowd took up. 'This instant, right away! To the gallows with the actors and the cardinal!'

Poor Jupiter, haggard, terrified and ashen beneath his rouge, dropped his thunderbolt and took his bycoket in his hand; then he bowed, shook and stammered out: 'His Eminence ... the ambassadors ... Madame Marguerite of Flanders ...' He did not know what to say. Basically, he was afraid of being hanged.

Hanged by the populace for waiting, hanged by the cardinal for not waiting; either way he could see only the abyss, that is a gallows.

Fortunately someone came to extricate him from his dilemma and assume responsibility. A person standing on the near side of the balustrade, in the space left unoccupied round the marble slab, whom no one had so far noticed, his tall, thin figure having been completely sheltered from every line of sight by the diameter of the pillar against which he was leaning; this person, as I say, tall, lean, pasty-faced, fair-haired, still young although already lined on forehead and cheeks, with shining eyes and a smiling mouth, dressed in black serge that was threadbare and shiny with wear, approached the marble slab and signalled to the poor victim. But the other was so put out he did not see him.

The newcomer moved a step closer. 'Jupiter,' he said, 'my dear Jupiter!'

The other did not hear.

Finally the tall, fair-haired man grew impatient and practically shouted in his face: 'Michel Giborne!'

'Who's that calling?' said Jupiter, as if starting awake.

'Me,' answered the person dressed in black.

'Ah!' said Jupiter.

'Begin right away,' the other went on. 'Give the people what they want. I'll undertake to pacify the bailiff and he'll pacify the cardinal.'

Jupiter breathed again.

'My lords the burgesses,' he cried at the top of his voice to the crowd, which continued to hoot at him, 'we are going to begin right away.'

'*Evoe, Jupiter! Plaudite, cives!*'[1]

'Nowel! Nowel!' shouted the populace.

1. 'Evoe, Jupiter, applaud, citizens!'

There was deafening applause and the hall was still vibrating to the cheers after Jupiter had gone back in under the tapestry.

Meanwhile the unknown figure who had so magically turned 'the storm into a lull', as our dear old Corneille puts it, had modestly returned to the penumbra of his pillar and would no doubt have remained there, unseen, unmoving and unspeaking as before, had he not been drawn out by two young women who, being in the front row of the spectators, had observed his conversation with Michel Giborne-Jupiter.

'Maître,' said one of them, beckoning him over.

'Hush, Liénarde, my dear,' said her neighbour, fresh, pretty and very spruce in her best clothes. 'He's not a cleric, he's a layman; you musn't call him *maître* but *messire*.'

'Messire,' said Liénarde.

The stranger came up to the balustrade.

'What can I do for you, mesdemoiselles?' he asked eagerly.

'Oh, nothing!' said Liénarde covered in confusion, 'it's my neighbour Gisquette la Gencienne who wants to speak to you.'

'No it isn't,' Gisquette put in, blushing, 'it's Liénarde who said *maître* to you and I said you should say *messire*.'

The two girls lowered their eyes. The other, who was only too ready to engage in conversation, looked at them with a smile:

'So you've nothing to say to me, mesdemoiselles?'

'Oh, nothing at all!' answered Gisquette.

'Nothing,' said Liénarde.

The tall, fair-haired young man made as if to withdraw. But the two inquisitive girls did not want to lose him.

'Messire,' Gisquette said quickly, with the impetuosity of a flood-gate opening or a woman making up her mind, 'so you know the soldier who's going to play the part of the Virgin Mary in the mystery play?'

'Do you mean the part of Jupiter?' the unnamed man resumed.

'Ha, yes,' said Liénarde, 'isn't she silly? So you know Jupiter?'

'Michel Giborne?' replied the unnamed man. 'Yes, madame.'

'He's got a gorgeous beard!' said Liénarde.

'Will what they're going to say up there be beautiful?' asked Gisquette shyly.

'Very beautiful, mademoiselle,' replied the unnamed man without the slightest hesitation.

'What will it be?' said Liénarde.

'*The Right Judgement of the Virgin*, a morality, if it please you, mademoiselle.'

'Ah, that's different,' Liénarde went on.

A brief silence followed, broken by the stranger:

'It's a brand-new morality, that hasn't been used yet.'

'So it's not the same one as they gave two years ago, on the day of Monsieur the Legate's entry,' said Gisquette, 'when there were three beautiful girls playing characters . . .'

'As sirens,' said Liénarde.

'And stark naked,' added the young man.

Liénarde chastely lowered her eyes. Gisquette looked at her and did likewise. He went on, smiling:

'And a very pleasant sight it was. Today it's a morality written expressly for the Princess of Flanders.'

'Will they sing pastorals?'

'Really!' said the stranger. 'In a morality play? We mustn't get the genres muddled up. If it had been a satire, all well and good.'

'That's a pity,' Gisquette went on. 'That day at the Ponceau fountain there were wild men and women having fights and putting on different faces as they sang little motets and pastorals.'

'What's right for a legate', said the stranger somewhat drily, 'is not right for a princess.'

'And near by several bass instruments were having a contest to see who could play the loudest tune,' Liénarde added.

'And to refresh the passers-by', Gisquette continued, 'the fountain was spouting wine, milk and hippocras out of three mouths, which anyone who wanted could drink.'

'And just below the Ponceau,' Liénarde persevered, 'at the Trinité, there was a tableau of the Passion but without speaking.'

'I remember!' exclaimed Gisquette. 'God on the cross and the two thieves to right and left!'

At this point the young gossips, warming to the memory of the legate's entry, both began to talk at once.

'And further on, at the Porte-aux-Peintres, there were other people very richly dressed.'

'And at the Saint-Innocent fountain, that hunter pursuing a hind, with a great noise of dogs and hunting-horns.'

'And at the Paris shambles, those scaffolds representing the fortress at Dieppe.'

'And when the legate passed, Gisquette, you know, they sounded the assault and the English all had their throats cut.'

'And there was a lovely tableau against the gate of the Châtelet.'

'And on the Pont-au-Change, which was draped all over.'

'And when the legate passed, they released more than two hundred dozen birds of every sort above the bridge; it was very beautiful, Liénarde.'

'It'll be more beautiful today,' finally put in their interlocutor, who seemed to be listening to them impatiently.

'Do you promise us the mystery will be beautiful?' said Gisquette.

'Certainly,' he replied; then he added with some emphasis: 'Mesdemoiselles, I am its author.'

'Really?' said the girls, flabbergasted.

'Really!' answered the poet, puffing out his chest a little. 'That is to say, there are two of us: Jehan Marchand, who sawed up the planks and erected the framework of the stage and all the woodwork, and I who wrote the play. My name is Pierre Gringoire.'[1]

The author of *Le Cid* could not have announced more proudly: 'Pierre Corneille.'

Our readers may have noticed that a certain length of time must have elapsed between the moment Jupiter went back under the tapestry and the moment when the author of the brand-new morality suddenly revealed himself to the simple-minded admiration of Gisquette and Liénarde. Remarkably enough, this great crowd, so turbulent a few minutes earlier, was now waiting submissively, after the actor's promise; which goes to prove the eternal truth, still tested every day in our theatres, that the best way to make an audience wait patiently is to declare that you are about to start right away.

The student Joannes, however, had not dropped off to sleep.

'Yoohoo!' he suddenly shouted in the middle of the expectant hush that had followed the upheaval. 'Jupiter, Madame Virgin, devil's tumblers! Are you having us on? The play, the play! You start, or we shall start again.'

1. Pierre Gringoire was a historical dramatist, born in 1475; Hugo has aged him considerably.

They needed no further prompting.

Bass and treble instruments were heard to play from inside the scaffolding, the tapestry was raised and four motley characters emerged, wearing make-up, mounted the steep ladder to the stage and, once they had reached the upper platform, formed up into a line in front of the audience, to whom they gave a deep bow; the symphony fell silent. The mystery was starting.

The four characters accepted ample repayment for their bows in applause and then, in the midst of a religious silence, launched into a prologue which we shall gladly spare the reader. In any case, as still happens in our own day, the audience was even more taken up with the costumes they were wearing than with the parts they were reciting; and this indeed was only right. They were all four of them wearing half-yellow, half-white robes, only distinguishable from each other by the material they were made from; the first was gold and silver brocade, the second silk, the third wool and the fourth sacking. The first character carried a sword in his right hand, the second two gold keys, the third a pair of scales and the fourth a spade. And to assist such lazy intellects as might be unable to see through these transparent attributes, there could be read, embroidered in huge black letters: at the foot of the brocade robe, MY NAME IS NOBILITY; at the foot of the silk robe, MY NAME IS CLERGY; at the foot of the woollen robe, MY NAME IS COMMERCE; at the foot of the sacking robe, MY NAME IS TILLAGE. The gender of the two masculine allegories was clearly displayed for any discerning spectator by their shorter robes and the tasselled caps they wore, while the two female ones were less abbreviated and wore hoods.

It would have needed much ill-will also not to gather, from the poetry of the prologue, that Tillage was married to Commerce and Clergy to Nobility, and that the two happy couples were joint owners of a magnificent gold dolphin, which they intended to award only to the greatest beauty. They thus went through the world in search and quest of this beauty, and after having successively turned down the Queen of Golconda, the Princess of Trebizond, the daughter of the Great Khan of Tartary, and so on and so forth, Tillage and Clergy, Nobility and Commerce had come to rest themselves on the marble slab of the Palais de Justice and spout at the worthy audience all the sentences and maxims which could then be expended in the Faculty of Arts on the examinations, sophisms, determinations, figures and acts at which masters of arts acquired their degree-caps.

It was all, indeed, very beautiful.

Meanwhile, as the four allegories competed in swamping it with metaphors, there was no ear more attentive, no heart more athrob, no eye more haggard, no neck more craned anywhere in that crowd, than the eye, ear, neck and heart of the author, of the poet, good Pierre Gringoire, who, a moment before, had been unable to resist the delights of telling two pretty girls his name. He had returned behind his pillar a few feet away, and there he listened, watched and savoured. The good-natured applause that had greeted the opening of his prologue still reverberated deep inside him, and he was utterly engrossed in that sort of ecstatic contemplation with which an author sees his ideas falling one by one from the mouth of an actor into the silence of a vast auditorium. Worthy Pierre Gringoire!

It pains us to say so, but this first ecstasy was very soon disturbed. Hardly had Gringoire carried this intoxicating cup of joy and triumph to his lips before a drop of gall was added to it.

A ragged beggar whose takings had suffered, lost as he was in the midst of the crowd, and who had no doubt failed to find adequate compensation in his neighbours' pockets, had had the idea of perching himself in some prominent position so as to attract both eyes and alms. During the opening lines of the prologue, therefore, and with the help of the pillars of the reserved platform, he had hoisted himself up on to the cornice along the bottom of the balustrade and there sat down, to solicit the attention and compassion of the multitude with his rags and with a hideous sore that covered his right arm. For the rest, he uttered not a word.

His silence allowed the prologue to proceed without hindrance, and no noticeable disturbance would have ensued had ill-luck not decreed that the student Joannes should become aware of the beggar and his ridiculous pantomime from on top of his pillar. A wild laugh took hold of the young rogue and, unconcerned about interrupting the performance and breaking the general concentration, he gave a hearty shout: 'I say, that counterfeit crank asking for alms!'

Anyone who has tossed a stone into a pond full of frogs, or fired a gun into a flock of birds, will have some idea of the effect these incongruous words had in the midst of the general attentiveness.

Gringoire shuddered as if from an electric shock. The prologue stopped dead and all heads turned in uproar towards the beggar who, far from being put off, saw the incident as a good opportunity for gain and began to say plaintively, half closing his eyes: 'Alms, please give me your alms!'

'Well, damn it all,' Joannes went on, 'it's Clopin Trouillefou. 'Hey there, friend, was your sore such a nuisance on your leg that you've put it on your arm?'

So saying, nimble as a monkey, he threw a *petit-blanc* into the greasy felt hat the beggar was holding out in his bad arm. The beggar accepted the alms and the sarcasm without turning a hair and went on in a piteous tone: 'Alms, please give me your alms!'

The audience had been much distracted by this episode and a fair number of spectators, with Robin Poussepain and all the scholars in the van, were merrily applauding this weird duet that had just been improvised, in the middle of the prologue, between the shrill-voiced student and the beggar, with his imperturbable psalmody.

Gringoire was highly displeased. Having recovered from his initial stupefaction, he endeavoured to shout to the four characters on the stage: 'Go on, confound it, go on!' without even deigning to bestow a contemptuous glance on the two interruptors.

At that moment he felt himself being tugged by the hem of his surcoat; he turned round, rather bad-temperedly, and had some difficulty smiling. He had to nonetheless. It was the pretty arm of Gisquette la Gencienne that had reached through the balustrade and was attracting his attention in this way.

'Monsieur,' said the girl, 'are they going to go on?'

'Of course,' answered Gringoire, somewhat taken aback by the question.

'In that case, messire,' she continued, 'would you be courteous enough to explain to me...'

'What they are going to say?' Gringoire broke in. 'Well, listen!'

'No,' said Gisquette, 'what they have said so far.'

Gringoire jumped, like a man touched on an open sore.

'Pestilential, silly, brainless girl!' he said between his teeth.

And from then on, Gisquette no longer interested him.

Meanwhile, the actors had obeyed his injunction and the public, seeing they had begun to speak again, began to listen once more, though the kind of soldering operation performed on the two abruptly sundered portions of the play had deprived them of a great many beauties. Gringoire reflected on these bitterly in an undertone. But calm had gradually been re-established, the student had fallen silent and the beggar was counting the small change in his hat; the play had the upper hand once again.

It was in truth a very fine piece of work, of which, with one or two adjustments, something might still be made today. The exposition was somewhat long and vacuous, i.e. within the rules, but simple, and Gringoire, in the candid sanctuary of his heart of hearts, admired its clarity. As might be imagined, the four allegorical characters were a little weary after voyaging over three-quarters of the world without managing to unburden themselves fittingly of their golden dolphin. Whereupon, a eulogy of this marvellous fish, together with many subtle allusions to Marguerite of Flanders's young fiancé, at that moment an unhappy recluse in Amboise who little suspected that Tillage and Clergy, Nobility and Commerce had just circumnavigated the world on his behalf. The aforesaid dolphin, or dauphin, then, was young, strong and handsome and above all (magnificent source of all kingly virtues!) he was the son of the lion of France. I hereby declare that this rash metaphor is an admirable one and that the natural history of the stage, on a day of allegory and royal epithalamium, is in no way affronted by a dolphin who is the son of a lion. It is just such rare and Pindaric mixtures that prove enthusiasm. Nevertheless, to allow criticism too its say, the poet might have developed this noble idea in less than two hundred lines. Still, the mystery was to last from noon until four o'clock, in accordance with Monsieur the Provost's ordinance, and they had to say something. Moreover, it was being heard in patience.

Suddenly, right in the middle of a tiff between Mademoiselle Commerce and Madame Nobility, and just as Maître Tillage was uttering the miraculous line

Ne'er dwelt in forest a more triumphant beast

the door on to the reserved platform, which had so far remained so inopportunely closed, opened more inopportunely still; and the booming voice of the usher brusquely announced: 'His Eminence my Lord Cardinal of Bourbon.'

THREE
Monsieur the Cardinal

POOR Gringoire! At this solemn and dramatic moment, the crash of all the great double petards going off on Midsummer's Day, the discharge of twenty arquebuses, the detonation of the famous serpentine on Sunday 29 September 1465 at the Tour de Billy during the siege of Paris, which killed seven Burgundians in one go, or the explosion of all the gunpowder stored at the Porte du Temple, all would have been less brutally ear-splitting than those words, dropping from the mouth of an usher: 'His Eminence my Lord Cardinal of Bourbon.'

It was not that Pierre Gringoire was afraid of Monsieur the Cardinal or that he looked down on him, he was neither that craven nor that overweening. Gringoire was what today we would call a true eclectic, one of those elevated, steady, moderate, calm spirits who manage always to steer a middle course (*stare in dimidio rerum*) and are full of reason and liberal philosophy, while yet making due allowance for cardinals. A precious and unbroken line of philosophers to whom wisdom, like a second Ariadne, seems to have given a ball of thread, which they have been paying out through the labyrinth of human affairs since time began. They are to be found, quite unchanging, in every age, that is, ever in conformity with the times. Quite apart from our Pierre Gringoire, who could represent them in the fifteenth century if we managed to restore to him the celebrity he deserves, it was their spirit for a certainty that inspired Father du Breul when, in the sixteenth century, he wrote these sublimely innocent words, worthy of any century: 'I am a Parisian by nation and a parrhesian by speech, for *parrhesia* in Greek signifies boldness of speech: the which I have employed even towards my lords the cardinals, the uncle and brother of the Prince of Conti: at all times respecting their greatness and without offending any person of their retinue, who are many.'

So there was no dislike of the cardinal nor scorn for his presence, in the disagreeable impression this made on Pierre Gringoire. Quite the reverse: our poet was too sensible and his tunic too shabby for him not to be especially anxious that many of the allusions in his prologue, and in particular the glorification of the dolphin who was the son of the lion of France, should be caught by such a very eminent ear. But the noble nature of poets is not ruled by self-interest. Suppose the entity of the poet to be represented by the number ten: then it is certain that if a chemist analysed or pharmacopolized it, as Rabelais would say, he would find it composed of one part self-interest to nine parts conceit. But at the moment when the door had opened for the cardinal, Gringoire's nine parts conceit, swollen and tumefied by the breath of popular admiration, were in a state of prodigious increase, beneath which the imperceptible molecule of self-interest we have just isolated in the make-up of poets had disappeared as if suffocated; it is, for all that, a precious ingredient, a ballast of reality and humanity without which their feet would not touch the ground. Gringoire revelled in feeling, in seeing, in so to speak fingering an entire assembly – admittedly of nobodies, but what did that matter – which had been stunned, petrified and as if asphyxiated by the inordinate speeches forever pouring forth from each participant in his epithalamium. I can state that he himself shared in the general beatitude and that, unlike La Fontaine, who, at the performance of his comedy *Le Florentin*,[1] asked, 'What bumpkin wrote this rhapsody?' Gringoire would happily have asked his next-door neighbour 'Whose is this masterpiece?' So you may now judge the effect that the abrupt and untimely arrival of the cardinal had had on him.

What he may have been fearing was only too well borne out. The entry of His Eminence threw the audience into a turmoil. All heads turned towards the platform. You could no longer hear yourself speak. 'The cardinal, the cardinal,' every mouth took up. The unfortunate prologue stopped dead for a second time.

The cardinal paused for a moment in the doorway to the platform. As his gaze strayed somewhat indifferently over the auditorium, the uproar was renewed. Everyone wanted a better look at him. They competed to set their own heads on their next-door neighbours' shoulders.

He was an exalted personage indeed, a sight of whom was every bit as good as a stage play. Charles, Cardinal of Bourbon, Archbishop and Count of Lyon, Primate of the Gauls, was related both to Louis XI, through his brother, the Lord of Beaujeu, who had married the king's elder daughter, and to Charles the Bold, through

1. The actual author of this play was Champmerlé.

his mother, Agnes of Burgundy. Now the dominant trait, the distinctive and characteristic trait in the character of the Primate of the Gauls, was his courtierism and his devotion to those in power. One can imagine, then, the countless difficulties that this double connection entailed, and all the temporal shoals between which his spiritual barque had had to tack so as not to be dashed to pieces either on Louis or on Charles, the Scylla and Charibdis who had engulfed the Duke of Nemours and the Constable of Saint-Pol.[1] Heaven be praised, he had survived the crossing pretty well and reached Rome without mishap. But although he was now in harbour, and precisely because he was now in harbour, he could never look back without anxiety on the various hazards of his political life, for long so full of alarms and hardships. Thus he had a habit of saying that 1476 had been a 'black and white' year for him, meaning that in that one year he had lost both his mother, the Duchess of Bourbonnais, and his cousin, the Duke of Burgundy, and that one bereavement had consoled him for the other.

For the rest, he was a good fellow. He led the gay life of a cardinal, liked to get merry on the royal vintage of Chaillot, was far from averse to Richarde la Garmoise and Thomasse la Saillarde, and bestowed alms on pretty girls rather than old women; for all of which reasons he was very popular with the 'commons' of Paris. He always went about in the midst of a small court of bishops and abbots of good family, who were bawdy, lecherous and great carousers should need arise; more than once the good worshippers at Saint-Germain d'Auxerre had been shocked, when passing of an evening beneath the lighted windows of the Bourbon mansion, to hear the same voices they had heard chanting vespers during the day intoning, to the clink of glasses, the bacchic proverb of Benedict XII, the pope who added a third wreath to the papal tiara: *Bibamus papaliter*.[2]

It was no doubt his justly acquired popularity which saved him, as he entered, from any rude greeting from the crowd which, a moment earlier, had been so disgruntled and was little disposed, on a day when it would be electing a pope, to show respect to a cardinal. But Parisians nurse few grudges and having, in any case,

1. Both of whom were beheaded as third parties caught up in the perpetual power struggle between Louis XI and Charles of Burgundy.

2. 'Let us drink papally.'

had their own way over starting the performance, the good burgesses had scored off the cardinal and that was triumph enough. Monsieur the Cardinal of Bourbon, moreover, was a good-looking man and wore a very fine red robe, which looked very well on him; which is to say that the better half of the audience, the women, was on his side. It would certainly be both unfair and in poor taste to jeer at a cardinal for keeping you waiting in the theatre when he is a good-looking man and wears his red robe well.

He made his entry then, greeted the spectators with a grandee's hereditary smile for the common people and walked slowly towards his scarlet velvet armchair, his thoughts seemingly on something quite else. His cortège, or what we would nowadays call his staff, of bishops and abbots burst on to the platform in his wake and the turmoil and curiosity in the pit was redoubled. They all tried to point them out to one another, to put a name to them, to know at least one of them personally; with some it was the Bishop of Marseilles, Alaudet if I remember aright; with others the first canon of Saint-Denis; with others still, Robert de Lespinasse, Abbot of Saint-Germain-des-Prés, and the libertine brother of one of Louis XI's mistresses; it was all as cacophonous as it was inaccurate. The students meanwhile were cursing. This was their day, their feast of fools, their saturnalia, the annual orgy of the schools and the legal fraternity. On that day, depravity of every kind was a right and something sacred. In the crowd, what was more, were such wild wantons as Simone Quatrelivres, Agnès la Gadine and Robine Piédebou. On such a beautiful day, and in the excellent company of churchmen and whores, surely one could expect to relax and to swear and blaspheme against God a little? So they did not stint themselves, and in the midst of the hubbub, all these tongues, the tongues of students and clerks held in check all the rest of the year by the fear of Saint Louis's red-hot irons, were released in a terrifying cat's chorus of blasphemies and enormities. Poor Saint-Louis, how they insulted him in his own law courts! Each of them engaged one of the newcomers to the platform, either a black, a grey, a white or a purple cassock. As for Joannes Frollo de Molendino, he, as the brother of an archdeacon, had boldly taken on the red one and was singing at the top of his voice, his insolent eyes fixed on the cardinal: '*Cappa repleta mero!*'[1]

1. 'A cope filled with wine.'

All these details, which we have laid bare here for the edification of the reader, were so drowned by the general uproar as to be erased before reaching the reserved platform. The cardinal would in any case have been little put out by them, so habitual had the licence of that day become. What is more, he had something else to worry about, which, as his preoccupied expression showed, had been pursuing him closely and had come on to the platform at almost the same time as himself: the Flemish embassy.

He was no great politician nor did he feel responsible for the possible consequences of the marriage between his cousin Madame Marguerite of Burgundy and his other cousin Monsieur Charles, Dauphin of Vienna; it little troubled him how long the agreement patched up between the Duke of Austria and the King of France might last, or how the King of England might take this spurning of his daughter,[1] and each evening he did honour to the wine of the royal vintage of Chaillot, little suspecting that a few flagons of this same wine (slightly revised and amended, it is true, by Doctor Coictier) would be cordially presented by Louis XI to Edward IV and would one fine morning rid Louis XI of Edward IV.[2] 'The most honoured embassy of Monsieur the Duke of Austria' brought the cardinal no such worries, but he found it bothersome for other reasons. As we have already hinted on the second page of this book, it was somewhat hard on him, Charles of Bourbon, to be obliged to welcome and entertain these mere burgesses; he, a cardinal, they, civic dignitaries; he, a Frenchman, fond of the table, they beer-swilling Flemings; and in public moreover. It was, truly, one of the most irksome smiles he had ever had to force in order to please the king.

So, when the usher announced in ringing tones: 'Messieurs the envoys of the Duke of Austria,' he turned towards the door with the best grace in the world (so practised was he at it). Needless to say, the whole hall did likewise.

There then arrived, in twos, with a solemnity that contrasted with the spirited ecclesiastical cortège of Charles of Bourbon, the forty-eight ambassadors of Maximilian of Austria, with at their head the Reverend Father in God, Jehan, Abbot of Saint-Bertin, Chancellor of the Golden Fleece, and Jacques de Goy, Sieur

1. Previously engaged to the dauphin.
2. Edward IV was not, in fact, poisoned by Louis XI.

Dauby, High Bailiff of Ghent. A profound silence fell on the gathering, accompanied by laughter, muffled so that they could listen to all the outrageous names and civic titles which each of these notables communicated imperturbably to the usher, who then hurled names and titles in any order and much mutilated among the crowd. There was Maître Loys Roelof, Syndic of the Town of Louvain; Messire Clays d'Etuelde, Syndic of Brussels; Messire Paul de Baeust, Sieur de Voirmizelle, President of Flanders; Maître Jehan Coleghens, Burgomaster of the Town of Antwerp; Maître George de la Moere, First Syndic of the *Kuere*[1] of the Town of Ghent; Maître Gheldorf van der Hage, First Syndic of the *Parchons* of the aforesaid town; the Sieur de Bierbecque, and Jehan Pinnock, and Jehan Dymaerzelle, and so on and so forth; bailiffs, syndics, burgomasters; burgomasters, syndics, bailiffs; all of them stiff, starched and formal in their best velvet and damask and carmagnole hoods of black velvet with huge tassels of gold thread from Cyprus; good Flemish heads, all of them, with stern and dignified faces, of the same breed as those which stand out so grave and powerful against the black background of Rembrandt's *Night Watch*; personages each of whose brows declared that Maximilian of Austria had been right 'fully to trust', as his manifesto put it, 'in their sense, valiance, experience, loyalty and probity'.

With one exception. This was a sharp, intelligent, crafty face, a bit like a monkey's or a diplomat's, towards which the cardinal took three steps and gave a deep bow, yet whose name was simply 'Guillaume Rym, Counsellor and Pensionary of the Town of Ghent'.

Few people then knew what Guillaume Rym was: a rare talent who, in a time of revolution, would have shone brilliantly on the surface of events but who, in the fifteenth century, was reduced to subterranean intrigue and to 'living in the saps', as the Duke of Saint-Simon puts it. But he was esteemed by the leading 'sapper' of Europe: he schemed on familiar terms with Louis XI and frequently took a hand in the king's undercover activities. Of all of which things the crowd was completely unaware as it marvelled at the cardinal's courtesies to this puny-looking Flemish bailiff.

1. The body of magistrates.

FOUR
Maître Jacques Coppenole

WHILE the Pensionary of Ghent and His Eminence were exchanging low bows and a few words in even lower voices, a man tall in build, with a broad face and powerful shoulders, stepped forward so as to enter abreast of Guillaume Rym; he was like a mastiff alongside a fox. His felt bycoket and leather jacket were a blemish on the velvet and silk all around him. Assuming it to be some groom who had lost his way, the usher stopped him.

'Ho, there, my friend, you can't go in!'

The man in the leather jacket shouldered him away.

'What's this scoundrel on about?' he said in a raised voice which drew the attention of the entire hall to this strange conversation. 'Can't you see I'm one of them?'

'Name?' asked the usher.

'Jacques Coppenole.'

'Titles?'

'Hosier, at the sign of the Three Small Chains, in Ghent.'

The usher recoiled. Announce syndics and burgomasters, yes, but a hosier was too much to bear. The cardinal was in torments. The whole populace watched and listened. For the past two days His Eminence had been striving to lick these Flemish bears into shape and to make them a bit more presentable in public, and this outburst was a bit hard. Meanwhile Guillaume Rym went up to the usher with his artful smile:

'Announce Maître Jacques Coppenole, Clerk to the Syndics of the Town of Ghent,' he breathed to him very softly.

'Usher,' put in the cardinal loudly, 'announce Maître Jacques Coppenole, Clerk to the Syndics of the illustrious Town of Ghent.'

This was a mistake. Left to himself, Guillaume Rym could have avoided any difficulty, but Coppenole had heard the cardinal.

'No, by the Holy Cross!' he exclaimed in a voice of thunder, 'Jacques Coppenole, hosier. Have you got that, usher? No more and no less. By the Holy Cross, there's nothing wrong with a hosier from Ghent. Even *ghent*-lemen like the archduke wear my hose.'

There was a burst of laughter and applause. They are quick to see a pun in Paris, so it is always applauded.

We should add that Coppenole was of the people, just as the crowd around him was of the people. Thus the contact between him and it had been prompt, electric and, as it were, on level terms. The Flemish hosier's haughty quip had humiliated the courtiers and aroused, in all these plebeian souls, some sense of dignity as yet, in the fifteenth century, dim and uncertain. This hosier who had just answered the cardinal back was an equal: a sweet thought indeed for poor devils used to showing respect and obedience to the servants of the serjeants of the bailiff of the Abbot of Sainte-Geneviève, the cardinal's train-bearer.

Coppenole bowed proudly to His Eminence, who returned the bow of this all-powerful burgess, of whom Louis XI stood in fear. Then, while Guillaume Rym, 'a wise and malicious man' as Philippe de Commynes puts it, followed the pair of them with a mocking and superior smile, they each went to their places, the cardinal very much put out and preoccupied, Coppenole calm and haughty, no doubt reflecting that after all his title of hosier was as good as the next man's and that Marie of Burgundy, the mother of the Marguerite whom Coppenole was today marrying off, would have feared him less as a cardinal than as a hosier; for no cardinal could have stirred up the people of Ghent against the favourites of Charles the Bold's daughter; no cardinal could have fortified the crowd with a word, against the tears and entreaties of the Princess of Flanders, when she came and pleaded with her people for their lives at the very foot of the scaffold; whereas the hosier had merely had to raise his leather elbow for your two most illustrious and noble heads to roll, my lords Guy D'Humbercourt and Chancellor Guillaume Hugonet![1]

But the poor cardinal's troubles were not yet over; the chalice of finding himself in such low company must be drained to the dregs.

The reader will not perhaps have forgotten the beggar who had come and clung shamelessly to the fringes of the cardinal's platform as soon as the prologue began. The arrival of the illustrious guests had by no means caused him to let go, and while prelates and ambassadors, like true Flemish herrings, packed themselves into the stalls on the rostrum, he had made himself comfortable, boldly crossing his legs on the architrave. No one noticed such uncommon impudence immediately, their attention having

1. The two were executed in Ghent in 1477.

been turned elsewhere, while he, for his part, noticed nothing in the hall; he swayed his head as blithely as any Neapolitan, repeating from time to time amidst the din, as if from an automatic habit: 'Alms, please give me your alms!' Indeed he was probably the only one in the entire audience who had not troubled to turn his head at the altercation between Coppenole and the usher. But as chance would have it, the master hosier of Ghent, with whom the people had already sympathized so keenly and on whom all eyes were fixed, came and sat in the front row of the platform exactly above the beggar; and they were surprised not a little to see the Flemish ambassador, after scrutinizing the rascal immediately below him, bestow a friendly pat on his tattered shoulder. The beggar turned round; there was surprise, recognition and then the two faces broke into smiles, etc.; then, quite oblivious of the onlookers, the hosier and the counterfeit crank began to converse in undertones, their hands clasped, while Clopin Trouillefou's tatters, displayed against the gold cloth of the platform, looked like a caterpillar on an orange.

The novelty of this remarkable scene evoked such wildness and merriment in the hall that it was not long before the cardinal became aware of the noise; he half leaned over but from where he was placed he had only a very imperfect view of Trouillefou's sordid cloak and thought quite naturally that the beggar was demanding alms. Outraged by such audacity, he exclaimed: 'Palace bailiff, throw this scoundrel into the river.'

'By the Holy Cross, my Lord Cardinal,' said Coppenole, without letting go of Clopin's hand, 'this is a friend of mine.'

'Nowel, nowel!' shouted the mob. And from that moment on, Maître Coppenole had 'great credit with the people' in Paris as in Ghent, 'for there are plenty of such men', says Philippe de Commynes, 'when the people are thus unruly'.

The cardinal bit his lip. He leant towards his next-door neighbour, the Abbot of Sainte-Geneviève, and said to him quietly:

'What charming ambassadors the archduke has sent to publish Madame Marguerite's banns to us!'

'Your Eminence is wasting his courtesies on these hog-faced Flemings,' replied the abbot. '*Margaritas ante porcos.*'[1]

'Or rather *Porcos ante Margaritam*,' answered the cardinal with a smile.

1. 'Margarites (pearls) before swine.'

The little becassocked court all went into ecstasies over the pun. The cardinal felt somewhat consoled, he had now got his own back on Coppenole, he too had had his jibe applauded.

And now those of our readers who have, as the modern style puts it, the power to generalize an image or an idea must allow us to ask them whether they have formed a clear picture of the spectacle offered by the vast parallelogram of the great hall of the palace at the moment when we have arrested their attention. In the middle of the hall, with its back to the west wall, a large and magnificent platform of gold brocade, on to which, through a small, pointed door, solemn personages are entering in procession, announced one by one by the strident voice of an usher. On the front benches many venerable figures already, their heads swathed in ermine, velvet and scarlet. All around the platform, which remains silent and dignified, below it, everywhere, a great crowd and a great hum. The populace is staring in its hundreds at each face on the platform, and whispering over each name. A curious spectacle, indeed, well worth the attention of the spectators. But right down at the far end, what is that sort of trestle with four multi-coloured puppets on top of it and four more down below? And who is that man beside the trestle in a black smock and with a pale face? Alas, dear reader, it is Pierre Gringoire and his prologue.

We had all completely forgotten him.

Which is exactly what he had been afraid of.

From the moment the cardinal entered, Gringoire had not ceased to fret for the safety of his prologue. At first he had enjoined the actors, who had been left in suspense, to continue and to raise their voices; then, seeing that no one was listening, he had stopped them, and during the quarter of an hour or so that the interruption had lasted, he had been like a cat on hot bricks, ceaselessly tapping his foot, calling out to Gisquette and Liénarde, and urging his neighbours to press on with the prologue; but all in vain. No one would budge from the cardinal, the embassy and the platform, which was the one centre of this great circle of lines of sight. You must also believe, and it pains us to say this, that when His Eminence arrived to create such a terrible distraction the prologue was beginning to annoy the audience just a little. After all, the spectacle on the platform was the same as that on the marble slab: the conflict between Tillage and Clergy, Nobility and Commerce. And many people preferred seeing them quite simply living, breathing, doing, rubbing shoulders, in flesh and blood, in the Flemish embassy and the episcopal court, beneath the cardinal's robe and Coppenole's jacket, rather than made up and dressed up, talking in verse and, as it were, stuffed beneath the yellow and white tunics in which Gringoire had dolled them up.

However, when our poet saw that calm had been partially restored, he conceived a stratagem that might save the day.

'Monsieur,' he said, turning towards one of his neighbours, a fat, patient-looking man, 'supposing we began again?'

'What?' said the neighbour.

'Eh? The mystery!' said Gringoire.

'If you like,' rejoined his neighbour.

This half approval was enough for Gringoire, and he did his own spadework; merging as far as possible with the crowd, he began to shout: 'Start the mystery again! Start again!'

'Hell!' said Joannes de Molendino. 'What are they chanting down at the end there?' (For Gringoire was making enough noise for four men.) 'I say, fellows, isn't the mystery finished? They're trying to restart it. That's not right.'

'No, no!' shouted all the students. 'Down with the mystery! Down!'

But Gringoire was in half-a-dozen places at once and shouting all the louder: 'Start again! Start again!'

The shouting attracted the attention of the cardinal.

'Palace bailiff,' he said to a tall, dark man positioned a few yards away, 'those rascals are making an infernal din, what's got into them?'

The palace bailiff was a kind of amphibious magistrate, a sort of bat of the judicial order, a cross between a rat and a bird, a judge and a soldier.

He approached His Eminence and, highly fearful of his displeasure, stammered out an explanation of the people's impropriety: that midday had arrived before His Eminence and that the actors had been forced to start without waiting for His Eminence.

The cardinal burst out laughing.

'Well I never, monsieur the Rector of the University ought to have done the same. What say you, Maître Guillaume Rym?'

'My lord,' answered Guillaume Rym, 'let us content ourselves with having been spared half the play. That at least is something.'

'Can these scoundrels go on with their farce?' asked the bailiff.

'Go on, go on,' said the cardinal, 'I don't mind. I shall be reading my breviary meanwhile.'

The bailiff went forward to the edge of the platform, held up his hand for silence, and cried:

'Burgesses, villeins, inhabitants, in order to satisfy those who want it to begin again and those who want it to end, His Eminence orders it to continue.'

The two camps could but resign themselves. However, both author and public long felt bitter towards the cardinal.

The characters on the stage therefore resumed their commentary, and Gringoire hoped that the remainder of his work at least would be heard. It was not long before this hope was disappointed like his other illusions; silence had in fact been restored among the audience, after a fashion, but Gringoire had not noticed that at the time when the cardinal gave the order to continue the platform was far from being full and that behind the Flemish envoys new figures had appeared, also part of the cortège, whose names and titles wreaked considerable havoc on his dialogue as they were intermittently hurled into its midst by the shout of the usher. Imagine, in fact, an usher barking out in the middle of a play, between two rhymes and often between two hemistiches, such asides as:

'Maître Jacques Charmolue, King's Procurator in the Ecclesiastical Court!'

'Jehan de Harlay, Squire, Keeper of the Office of Chevalier of the Night Watch in the Town of Paris!'

'Messire Galiot de Genoilhac, Chevalier, Lord of Brussac, Master of the King's Artillery!'

'Maître Dreux-Raguier, Inspector of Waters and Forests of our Master the King, in the regions of Champagne and Brie in France.'

'Messire Louis de Graville, Chevalier, Councillor and King's Chamberlain, Admiral of France, Warden of the Forest of Vincennes!'

'Maître Denis le Mercier, Warden of the House of the Blind in Paris,' and so on and so forth.

It was becoming intolerable.

Gringoire was the more indignant at this strange accompaniment, which was making his play hard to follow, because he could not hide from himself the fact that the latter was growing in interest all the time and that all his work needed was to be heard. Indeed, it would be hard to imagine a more ingenious and dramatic construction. The four characters of the prologue were bemoaning their mortal quandary, when Venus in person, *vera incessu patuit dea*,[1] appeared to them in a beautiful cote-hardie emblazoned with the ship of the town of Paris. She had come in person to claim the dolphin promised to the greatest beauty. Jupiter, whose thunderbolt could be heard rumbling in the dressing-room, had seconded her, and the goddess was about to succeed – that is, in plain terms, to marry the dauphin – when a young girl, clad in white damask and carrying a marguerite in her hand (a transparent personification of the Princess of Flanders) came to do battle with her. This was the turning-point of the drama. After an argument, Venus, Marguerite and those players in the wings agreed to leave things to the good judgement of the Holy Virgin. One excellent role still remained, that of Dom Pedro, the King of Mesopotamia. But it was hard to make out, through all the interruptions, what his function was. All of them had climbed up by the ladder.

But the play was doomed. None of these beauties had been either heard or understood. It was as if, when the cardinal entered, a magic and invisible thread had suddenly drawn all eyes from the marble slab to the platform, from the south end of the hall to the west side. Nothing could disenchant the audience. Every eye remained fixed there and the new arrivals, their accursed names, their faces, and their costumes formed a continual distraction. It was heartbreaking. Except for Gisquette and Liénarde, who turned away now and again whenever Gringoire tugged at their sleeves, and except for his fat and patient next-door neighbour, nobody was listening, nobody stood facing the poor abandoned morality. All Gringoire could see were profiles.

How bitter he felt as he saw his whole scaffolding of fame and poetry crumble piece by piece. And to think that this crowd had been on the point of rising up against the bailiff, so impatient were

1. 'Her very walk revealed the goddess' (Virgil).

they to hear his work! Now that they had it, they paid it no heed. This same performance, that had begun to such unanimous acclaim! The everlasting ebb and flow of popular favour! To think how close they had been to hanging the bailiff's serjeants! What would he not have given to be back at that moment of sweetness!

However, the usher's brutal monologue ceased. Everyone had arrived and Gringoire breathed again. The actors went bravely on. And now if Maître Coppenole, the hosier, did not suddenly stand up, with every eye upon him, and Gringoire heard him deliver this abominable harangue:

'Burgesses and squireens of Paris, by the Holy Cross, I don't know what we're doing here. I can certainly see on that trestle over there in the corner some people who look as though they want to fight each other. I don't know if that's what you call a *mystery*, but it's not much fun. They're quarrelling with their tongues, that's all. I've been waiting for the first blow for the past quarter of an hour. Nothing's happened. They're cowards, they just scratch each other with insults. They should have brought some wrestlers from London or Rotterdam, that's the stuff, then you'd have had fisticuffs they could have heard from the square! These ones are pathetic. They should at least have given us a Moorish dance, or some other mummery! This isn't what they told me. I was promised a feast of fools, with the election of the pope. We have our own fools' pope in Ghent, and there's nothing you can teach us about that, by the Holy Cross! But here's how we go about it. We gather a crowd, like here. Then everyone in turn goes and sticks his head through a hole and pulls a face at the others. The one who pulls the ugliest face and gets the most applause is elected pope. There. Highly diverting. Would you like us to make your pope the way we do it in my country? At least it'll be less tedious than listening to these chatterboxes. If they want to come and pull a face at the window, they can compete. What do you say, burgesses of Paris? There's a grotesque enough selection of both sexes here for us to have a good Flemish laugh, and we've got enough ugly faces to hope for a really good winner.'

Gringoire would have liked to reply, but stupefaction, rage and indignation deprived him of the power of speech. Moreover, the popular hosier's motion was greeted so enthusiastically by these burgesses, flattered at being addressed as *squireens*, that all resistance was pointless. He could only let himself be swept along by the torrent. Gringoire hid his face in his hands, not being lucky enough to have a cloak with which to cover his head like Timanthes's Agamemnon.

FIVE
Quasimodo

IN a twinkling, Coppenole's idea was all ready to be put into effect. Burgesses, students and lawyers' clerks had set to work. The face-pulling contest would be staged in the small chapel opposite the marble slab. It was agreed that the contestants should stick their heads through a round hole in the stonework of the pretty rose-window above the door, where the glass had been broken. To reach this, they merely had to clamber up on two barrels, fetched from somewhere or other and roughly balanced one on top of the other. The rules were that each entrant, man or woman (for they could choose a female pope), should cover his face and stay out of sight in the chapel until it was time to go on, so that the face he pulled might have its full and virgin effect. In no time at all, the chapel was full of competitors and the door closed behind them.

From where he sat, Coppenole was in complete command, organizing and arranging everything. The cardinal felt just as affronted as had Gringoire, and, under cover of the upheaval, he withdrew, along with his retinue, on the pretext of business matters and vespers to attend to; the crowd, among whom his arrival had caused such a stir, was not in the least concerned by his departure. Guillaume Rym was the only one to observe His Eminence's discomfiture. The attention of the populace continued to revolve like the sun; it had started at one end of the hall, had halted for a time in the middle and had now reached the other end. The marble slab and brocade platform were things of the past and it was the turn of the Louis XI chapel. The way was henceforth open for all kinds of excess. Only the Flemings and the rabble were left.

The face-pulling began. The first face to appear at the window, eyelids turned up to show the red, mouth agape like an animal's, and forehead creased like a pair of Empire riding-boots, brought an explosion of such irrepressible laughter that Homer would have taken all these villeins to be gods. But the great hall was very far from being an Olympus, as Gringoire's poor Jupiter knew better than anyone. A second and a third face were pulled, then another and another; and the laughter and joyful stamping of feet were renewed. There was something about this spectacle which made the head spin, it had some peculiar power to bewitch and intoxicate hard to convey to a reader of our own day and from our own *salons*. Picture to yourself a succession of faces displaying all the known geometrical shapes one after the other, from triangle to trapezium, from cone to polyhedron; every known human expression, from anger to lust; every age of man, from the wrinkles of the newly born to the wrinkles of the dying crone; a whole religious phantasmagoria, from Faunus to Beelzebub; every kind of animal profile, from jaws to beaks and from muzzles to snouts. It was as if all those mascarons on the Pont-Neuf, nightmares turned to stone by the hand of Germain Pilon, had taken on life and breath and had come, one by one, with their burning eyes, to stare you in the face; as if all the masks at a Venetian carnival had followed one another under your lorgnette; in a word, a human kaleidoscope.

The rout was becoming more and more Flemish. Teniers would give only a very inadequate idea of it. Imagine Salvatore Rosa's battle-scene, only as a bacchanal. There were no longer students, or ambassadors, or burgesses, or men, or women; no longer any Clopin Trouillefou, Gilles Lecornu, Marie Quatrelivres or Robin Poussepain. All had been obliterated in the common licence. The great hall was nothing more than a huge, fiery furnace of shamelessness and joviality, where every mouth was a shout, every eye a flash of lighting, every face a grimace, every individual a posture. And all shouting and yelling. The strange faces which came one by one to gnash their teeth at the rose-window were like so many brands being hurled into the brazier. And, like the steam from a furnace, this whole seething multitude gave off a sharp, shrill, piercing sound like the whir of a gnat's wings.

'Hey! Damnation!'

'Just look at that face!'

'It's no good.'

'Next one!'

'Guillemette Maugerepuis, look at that bull's snout, it only needs some horns. Isn't that your husband?'

'Next one!'

'Pope's belly! What sort of face is that?'

'Hey, that's cheating. You're only to show your face.'

'Damn that Perrette Callebotte! She would do that!'

'Nowel, nowel!'

'I'm choking!'

'There's one whose ears won't go through!'

And so on.

We must meanwhile give our friend Jehan his due. He was still to be seen on top of his pillar, in the midst of this witches' sabbath, like a cabin boy in the topsail. He was hurling himself about in an unbelievable frenzy. His mouth was open wide and a shout was coming from it which couldn't be heard; not because it had been drowned by the general uproar, intense though this was, but because it had no doubt attained the upper limit of perceptible sound, Sauveur's twelve thousand vibrations or Biot's eight thousand![1]

As for Gringoire, he had recovered his equanimity, after that first moment of dejection. He had steeled himself against adversity. 'Go on!' he had said for the third time to his talking machines on the stage. Then, as he strode up and down in front of the marble slab, it crossed his mind to go and appear himself at the chapel window, if only to have the pleasure of pulling a face at these ungrateful people. 'But no, that wouldn't be worthy of us; no vengeance! We must fight to the end,' he repeated to himself. 'The power of poetry over the people is great; I shall bring them back. We shall see which wins, face-pulling or literature.'

Alas, he was the only spectator left at his play!

It was much worse than before. He could see only backs.

I am wrong. The fat, patient man, whom he had already consulted at a critical moment, was still facing the stage. As for Gisquette and Liénarde, they had deserted long ago.

Gringoire was deeply touched by the loyalty of his solitary spectator. He went up and addressed him, shaking him gently by the arm; for the good man was leaning on the balustrade and was somewhat asleep.

'Monsieur,' said Gringoire, 'I thank you.'

'Monsieur,' answered the fat man with a yawn, 'what for?'

1. Joseph Sauveur (1653–1716), a French physicist and pioneer of musical acoustics; Jean-Baptiste Biot (1774–1862), also a French physicist.

'I can tell what's annoying you,' the poet went on, 'all this noise is stopping you hearing properly. But don't worry, your name will go down to posterity. What is your name, please?'

'Renault Château, Keeper of the Seal of the Châtelet of Paris, at your service.'

'Monsieur, you are the one representative of the muses here,' said Gringoire.

'You're too kind, monsieur,' replied the Keeper of the Seal from the Châtelet.

'You are the only one who has seen fit to listen to the play,' Gringoire went on. 'What do you think of it?'

'Eh!' answered the fat magistrate, half awake. 'Pretty lively in fact.'

Gringoire had to be satisfied with this praise, for their conversation was cut short by a thunder of applause, mingled with deafening cheers. The fools' pope had been elected.

'Nowel! Nowel! Nowel!' people were shouting on all sides.

And the grimace just then lighting up the hole in the rose-window was wonderful indeed. After all the pentagonal, hexagonal and unclassifiable faces that had succeeded each other at the window without realizing the ideal of grotesqueness formed by imaginations over-excited by the rout, it took all of this sublime grimace, that had just dazzled the throng, to decide the voting. Maître Coppenole himself applauded; and Clopin Trouillefou, who had been a contestant and whose face was capable of achieving an amazing degree of ugliness, acknowledged himself beaten. We shall do likewise. We shall not try to give the reader any idea of that tetrahedral nose, of that horseshoe mouth, of the tiny left eye, obstructed by a bushy red eyebrow, while the right eye had vanished entirely beneath an enormous wen, of those irregular teeth, notched here and there like castle battlements, of that horny lip on which a tooth encroached like an elephant's tusk, of that cleft chin, and above all of the facial expression itself, with its crowning mixture of malice, astonishment and sadness. In all, a sight for you to imagine, if you can.

The acclaim was unanimous. They dashed towards the chapel. The lucky fools' pope was brought out in triumph. But it was now that the surprise and admiration reached a crescendo. The grimace was his real face.

Or rather his whole person was a grimace. A huge head sprouting red hair; between the two shoulders an enormous hump, the repercussions of which were evident at the front; a system of thighs and legs so strangely warped that they met only at the knees and looked, from the front, like two scythe-blades joined at the handle; broad feet and monstrous hands; and somehow, along with such deformity, an appearance of formidable energy, agility and courage; a strange exception to the eternal rule which says that strength, like beauty, results from harmony. Such was the pope whom the fools had just given themselves.

He was like a giant broken in pieces and badly reassembled.

When this sort of Cyclops appeared in the doorway of the chapel, motionless, squat and almost as broad as he was tall, 'square at the bottom' as a great man put it,[1] the populace recognized him instantly by his half-red, half-mauve surcoat, dotted with silver campaniles, and above all by his perfect ugliness. They shouted as one:

'It's Quasimodo the bell-ringer! It's Quasimodo, the hunchback of Notre-Dame! One-eyed Quasimodo! Crook-kneed Quasimodo! Nowel! Nowel!'

As you can see, the poor wretch had nicknames and to spare.

'Pregnant women watch out!' shouted the students.

'Or those who want to be,' put in Joannes.

And in fact the women were hiding their faces.

'Horrible ape,' said one of them.

'And as vicious as he's ugly,' put in a second.

'He's the devil,' added a third.

'I live near Notre-Dame, worse luck. I hear him all night long prowling on the tiles.'

'With the cats.'

'He's always on our rooftops.'

'He casts spells on us down the chimney.'

'He came and pulled a face at me at my dormer the other night. I thought it was a man. Gave me a proper turn!'

'I'm sure he goes to the witches' sabbath. One time, he left a broomstick on our leads.'

'Nasty-looking old hunchback!'

'He's got an evil soul!'

'Ugh!'

1. Napoleon.

The men on the other hand were overjoyed and applauded.

Quasimodo, the object of this uproar, was still standing at the door of the chapel, sombre and serious, letting himself be admired.

A student, I think it was Robin Poussepain, went up and laughed in his face, but he came too close. Quasimodo merely picked him up round the waist and hurled him ten yards amongst the crowd. All without uttering a word.

Maître Coppenole approached him in wonder.

'By the Holy Cross, I've never seen anything so beautifully ugly in all my life! You deserve to be pope in Rome as well as Paris.'

So saying, he laid his hand cheerfully on his shoulder. Quasimodo did not move. Coppenole went on.

'I can't wait to split a bottle or two with a rogue like you, even if it does cost me a brand-new silver shilling. What do you say?'

Quasimodo did not answer.

'By the Holy Cross,' said the hosier, 'are you deaf?'

He was in fact deaf.

However, he was beginning to grow impatient of Coppenole's goings-on and suddenly turned to him with such a formidable gnashing of teeth that the Flemish giant recoiled, like a bulldog from a cat.

A circle of terror and respect then formed around this strange personage at least fifteen geometrical paces in radius. An old woman explained to Maître Coppenole that Quasimodo was deaf.

'Deaf!' said the hosier with his rough Flemish laugh. 'By the Holy Cross, he's the perfect pope!'

'Ha, I know who he is,' cried Jehan, who had finally come down from his capital to take a closer look at Quasimodo, 'it's my brother the archdeacon's bell-ringer. Hello, Quasimodo!'

'Infernal man!' said Robin Poussepain, still concussed from his fall. 'He appears and he's a hunchback. He walks, and he's crook-kneed. He looks at you and he's one-eyed. You talk to him and he's deaf. I don't know, what does this Polyphemus do with his tongue?'

'He talks when he feels like it,' said the old woman. 'He went deaf ringing the bells. He's not dumb.'

'It's the one thing he isn't,' remarked Jehan.

'He's got one eye too many,' added Robin Poussepain.

'No he hasn't,' said Jehan shrewdly. 'A one-eyed man is much more incomplete than a blind man. He knows what he lacks.'

Meanwhile all the beggars, manservants and cutpurses had joined with the students and gone in procession to the lawyers' wardrobe to fetch the fools' pope's cardboard crown and mock chimer. Quasimodo allowed himself to be dressed up without moving a muscle and with a sort of proud submissiveness. Then they seated him on a multicoloured litter. Twelve officers from the brotherhood of fools lifted him on to their shoulders, and a sort of bitter, disdainful joy spread across the face of this cyclops as he saw all those handsome, straight, well-made men's heads beneath his misshapen feet. Then the yelling, ragged procession got under way to make, as was customary, its circuit of the internal galleries of the palace before parading the streets and crossroads.

SIX
La Esmeralda

WE are delighted to have to inform our readers that throughout this scene Gringoire and his play had stood firm. His actors, spurred on by him, had not left off reciting his drama, nor had he left off listening to it. He had resigned himself to the din and was determined to see it through to the end, not despairing that the audience's attention might return. This glimmer of hope was revived when he saw Quasimodo, Coppenole and the deafening cortège of the fools' pope noisily leaving the hall. The crowd rushed eagerly after them. 'Good,' he said to himself, 'the trouble-makers have all gone.' Unfortunately, the trouble-makers were the whole audience. In a twinkling, the great hall was empty.

In actual fact, there were still a few spectators left, a few individuals, the rest collected around pillars – women, old men or children who had had enough of the din and the disturbance. A few students were still astride the entablatures of the windows looking down into the square.

'Oh well,' thought Gringoire, 'there are still as many as we need to hear the end of my mystery. There aren't many of them, but it's an élite audience, a literate audience.'

A moment later and a symphony which was to have produced a great effect at the arrival of the Holy Virgin failed to sound. Gringoire realized that his orchestra had been led off by the pope's procession. 'Keep going,' he said stoically.

He approached a group of burgesses who seemed to be discussing his play. The snatch of conversation he caught went as follows:

'Do you know the Hôtel de Navarre, Maître Cheneteau, which used to belong to M. de Nemours?'

'Yes, opposite Braque's Chapel.'

'Well, the treasury has just leased it to Guillaume Alixandre, the historifier, for six pounds eight *sous* a year *parisis*.'

'Rents *are* getting dear!'

'Come on!' Gringoire said to himself with a sigh, 'the others are listening.'

'Comrades,' one of the young rogues at the casements suddenly shouted, 'La Esmeralda, La Esmeralda in the square!'

This word had an effect like magic. All those still in the hall rushed to the windows, clambering up the walls so as to see, and repeating: 'La Esmeralda, La Esmeralda!'

At the same time loud applause could be heard from outside.

'*La Esmeralda*, what does that mean?' said Gringoire, wringing his hands in distress. 'Oh, dear! it seems to be the windows' turn now.'

He turned to the marble slab and saw that the performance had been interrupted. This was the precise moment when Jupiter should have appeared with his thunderbolt. But Jupiter was standing motionless at the foot of the stage.

'Michel Giborne!' cried the poet in vexation, 'what are you doing there. Is that your role? Go up!'

'Alas,' said Jupiter, 'a student's just taken the ladder.'

Gringoire looked. It was only too true. All communication between his plot and its resolution had been severed.

'The scoundrel!' he murmured. 'Why's he taken the ladder?'

'To go and see La Esmeralda,' answered Jupiter piteously. 'He said: "I say, there's a ladder not being used," and took it.'

This was the last straw. Gringoire accepted it with resignation.

'Go to the devil!' he said to the actors. 'If I get paid you will be.'

He then made his retreat, head bowed but the last to leave, like a general who has put up a good fight.

And as he was going down the winding stairs from the palace: 'A fine herd of clods and donkeys these Parisians,' he grumbled under his breath. 'They come to hear a mystery and don't listen to a word! They show interest in everyone, Clopin Trouillefou, the cardinal, Coppenole, Quasimodo, the devil, but not in the Virgin Mary. I'd have given you Virgin Marys, you gawpers, if I'd known. I came to see faces and I only saw backs! I'm a poet and I had as much success as an apothecary! True, Homerus begged round the Greek villages and Naso[1] died in exile among the Muscovites. But the devil skin me if I understand what they mean with their Esmeralda! What *is* the word, first of all? It's Egyptiac!'

1. i.e. Ovid (P. Ovidius Naso).

BOOK TWO

ONE
Out of Charybdis on to Scylla

NIGHT comes early in January. The streets were already in darkness when Gringoire left the palace. He was pleased that night had fallen, he was in a hurry to meet with some unlit and deserted alleyway where he could think things over at his ease and where the philosopher could apply the first dressing to the poet's wound. Philosophy, as it happened, was his only refuge, for he had nowhere to spend the night. His theatrical venture having come so resoundingly to nought, he did not dare return to the lodgings he had been occupying in the Rue Grenier-sur-l'Eau, opposite the Port-au-Foin, for he had been relying on what the provost was to give him for his epithalamium to pay Maître Guillaume Doulx-Sire, farmer in Paris for the cloven-hoof tax,[1] the six months' rent he owed him, to wit twelve sous *parisis*, twelve times the value of everything he possessed in the world, including his hose, shirt and bycoket. He took shelter temporarily beneath the small wicket-gate of the Treasurer of the Sainte-Chapelle's prison and, having thought for a moment about where to lay his head for the night, being free to choose any of the paving-stones of Paris, he remembered having noticed, the previous week, in the Rue de la Savaterie, by the door of a parliamentary councillor, a stepping-stone for mounting mules, and having told himself that should the occasion arise this stone would make a mighty good pillow for a beggar or a poet. He thanked providence for having sent him this good idea; but as he was preparing to cross the palace square to reach the tortuous labyrinth of the city with all those sinuous old sisters, the Rue de la Barillerie, the Rue de la Vieille Draperie, the Rue de la Savaterie, the Rue de la Juiverie, and the rest, still standing today with their nine-storey houses, he saw the pope's procession also emerging from the palace and charging across the courtyard with loud shouts, a great glare of torches and his, Gringoire's, musicians. The sight reopened the wounds to his vanity; he fled. In his bitterness at his theatrical misadventure, anything which brought

1. A tax payable on all cloven-hoofed animals entering the town.

back the day's festivities soured him and drew blood from his wounds.

He wanted to cross by the Pont Saint-Michel; there were children running up and down with slow-matches and rockets. 'A plague on all fireworks!' said Gringoire, and fell back on the Pont-au-Change. Three flags had been attached to the houses at the head of the bridge, depicting the king, the dauphin and Marguerite of Flanders, together with six smaller flags on which were 'portrayed' the Duke of Austria, the Cardinal of Bourbon, M. de Beaujeu, Madame Jeanne de France, M. the Bastard of Bourbon, and Heaven knows who else; all lit by torches. The crowd was admiring them.

'Lucky Jehan Fourbault the painter!' said Gringoire with a deep sigh, and turned his back on the flags, large and small. There was a street in front of him; it looked so dark and abandoned that he hoped there he might escape all the repercussions and radiations of the festivities. He plunged down it. After a moment or two, his foot met an obstruction; he stumbled and fell. It was the bundle of beech twigs which the lawyers' clerks had laid that morning outside the door of a president of the Parliament, to mark the day's solemnity. Gringoire bore this new encounter heroically. He got to his feet and reached the edge of the water. After leaving the Tournelle Civile and the Tour Criminelle behind him, and walking along the unpaved strand past the high wall of the king's gardens, where the mud was ankle-deep, he came to the western tip of the Cité and stood in contemplation for a while of the cow ferryman's little island, which has since vanished beneath the bronze horse and the Pont-Neuf. In the gloom, the island appeared as a black mass on the far side of the narrow, whitish channel dividing him from it. In the beam from a small light he could just pick out the sort of beehive-shaped hut where the ferryman took shelter at night.

'Lucky ferryman!' thought Gringoire. 'You don't dream of fame and you don't write epithalamiums. What do kings getting married or duchesses of Burgundy matter to you! The only marguerites you know about are the ones the April meadows give to your cows to graze on. Whereas I, a poet, have been barracked, and I'm shivering and I owe twelve *sous* and my soles are so transparent you could use them in your lantern as glass. Thank you, ferryman, your hut is a sight for sore eyes, it makes me forget Paris!'

He was aroused from his almost lyrical ecstasy by a great double petard, suddenly going off in the idyllic hut. It was the ferryman sharing in the day's celebrations and loosing off a firework.

The petard made Gringoire's skin crawl.

'Damnable holiday!' he cried. 'Are you going to follow me everywhere? Dear God, even at the ferryman's!'

Then he looked at the Seine at his feet and an awful temptation took hold of him:

'Oh,' he said, 'I'd be only too happy to drown myself if the water wasn't so cold!'

Then he came to a desperate decision. Which was, since he could not escape from the fools' pope, Jehan Fourbault's little flags, the bundles of beech twigs, the slow-matches and the petards, to penetrate boldly to the very heart of the celebrations and go to the Place de Grève.

'At least there I might perhaps get a brand from the bonfire to warm myself,' he thought, 'and sup off the crumbs from the three great coats of arms in the king's sugar they must have erected on the public buffet.'

TWO
The Place de Grève

TODAY only one all but imperceptible trace is left of the Place de Grève as it was then. This is the charming turret which occupies the northern corner of the square, which has already been buried beneath the shameful paint clogging the sharp edges of its sculptures, and will soon perhaps have gone, submerged by the spate of new houses so rapidly engulfing all the old façades of Paris.

Those people who, like ourself, never cross the Place de Grève without bestowing a glance of sympathy and compassion on this poor turret, throttled between two Louis Quinze ruins, can easily reconstruct in their mind's eye the group of buildings to which it belonged and so recover the old fifteenth-century Gothic square in its entirety.

It was, as today, an irregular trapezium, bordered on one side by the quay and on the other three by a series of tall, narrow, gloomy houses. By day, one could admire the diversity of its buildings, all carved in stone or wood and offering complete specimens of the various medieval styles in domestic architecture, ranging from the fifteenth century back to the eleventh, from the casement window, which was beginning to oust the pointed window, back to the semi-circular romanesque arch, which had been supplanted by the pointed arch but still occupied, underneath it, the first storey of the ancient house of the Tour-Roland on the corner of the square overlooking the Seine, next to the Rue de la Tannerie. By night, all that could be made out of this mass of buildings was the black saw-edge of the roofs, unfurling their chain of acute angles around the square. For one of the radical differences between towns then and towns now is that nowadays it is the fronts of houses that overlook the streets whereas then it was the gable-ends. In the past two centuries, houses have turned about.

In the centre, on the eastern side of the square, stood a heavy, hybrid construction formed from three adjoining mansions. It was known by three different names, which explained its history, its purpose and its architecture: the Maison-au-Dauphin, because Charles V had lived in it as dauphin; the Marchandise, because it had served as a town hall; the Maison-aux-Piliers (*domus ad piloria*), because of the row of fat pillars supporting its three storeys. Here the town could find everything a fine town like Paris needs: a chapel, for praying to God; a court-room, for holding court and putting the king's men in their place, if need be; and, in the attics, an arsenal full of artillery. For the burgesses of Paris know that situations can arise when it is not enough to pray or to plead for the city's freedoms and they always keep a good rusty arquebus or two in reserve in an attic of the town hall.

The Grève already wore that sinister aspect still preserved today by the hateful image it evokes and by Dominique Boccador's gloomy Hôtel de Ville, which has replaced the Maison-aux-Piliers. It must be said that a gibbet and pillory, a 'justice' and a 'ladder' as they were then called, stood permanently side by side in the middle of the paving and helped not a little to avert people's gaze from that fateful square, where so many human beings full of life and vigour had met their death, and where, fifty years later, 'Saint-Vallier's fever' would be born, that sickness of the terror of the scaffold and the most monstrous of all sicknesses because it comes not from God but from men.

It is a consoling thought, be it said in passing, to reflect that capital punishment, whose iron wheels, stone gibbets and whole panoply of tortures were set permanently into the ground three hundred years ago and obstructed the Grève, Les Halles, the Place Dauphine, the Croix-du-Trahoir, the Marché-aux-Pourceaux, the ghastly Montfaucon, the Barrière des Sergents, the Place-aux-Chats, the Porte Saint-Denis, Champeaux, the Porte Baudets and the Porte Saint-Jacques, not to mention the innumerable 'ladders' of the provost, and the bishops, chapters, abbots and priors with legal authority, nor the judicial drownings in the river Seine; it is comforting, as I say, that today, having lost all the pieces of her armour one by one, her superfluity of torments, her inventive and fantastic punishments, the torture for which, every five years, she remade a leather bed in the Grand-Châtelet, this old suzeraine of feudal society has been almost eliminated from our laws and our towns, has been hunted down from code to code and driven out town-square by town-square, until now, in all the vastness of Paris, she has only one dishonoured corner of the Grève and one miserable guillotine, furtive, anxious and ashamed, which always vanishes very swiftly after it has done its work, as if it were afraid of being caught in the act!

THREE
Besos Para Golpes[1]

BY the time Pierre Gringoire reached the Place de Grève he was frozen stiff. He had crossed by the Pont-aux-Meuniers so as to avoid the mob by the Pont-au-Change and Jehan Fourbault's little flags, but he had been splashed by the wheels of all the bishop's water-mills as he went by and his smock was soaking. He fancied moreover that the collapse of his play had made him even more sensitive to the cold. So he hurried to be near the bonfire, blazing splendidly in the middle of the square. But it was ringed by a considerable crowd.

'Damned Parisians!' he said to himself, for Gringoire, being a true dramatic poet, was given to monologues, 'now they're getting in the way of my fire! But I certainly need a chimney-corner. My shoes are taking in water and all those confounded mills that wept over me! Blast the Bishop of Paris with his mills! What on earth can a bishop want with a mill! Does he think they're the mills of God?

1. 'Kisses for blows' (correct Spanish would have *por*).

If all he needs for that is my curse then I give it to him, and to his cathedral and to his mills! Let's just see if these loafers will move themselves! What are they doing there, I'd like to know! Warming themselves, how enjoyable! Watching hundreds of faggots burn, how interesting!'

On closer inspection, he realized that the circle was much bigger than it needed to be to warm itself at the king's fireside, and that this press of spectators had not been attracted there solely by the beauty of the hundred burning faggots.

In a huge space left free between the crowd and the fire, a young girl was dancing.

Gringoire, sceptical philosopher and ironical poet that he was, was so fascinated by this dazzling vision that he could not immediately make up his mind whether the girl was human being, fairy or angel.

She was not tall, but so boldly erect was her slim figure that she looked it. She was dark, but you could tell that in the daylight her skin must have had that lovely golden sheen of Roman or Andalusian women. Her tiny foot too was Andalusian, for it looked both constricted and comfortable in its graceful shoe. She danced, she spun, she whirled on an old Persian carpet thrown carelessly down beneath her feet, and each time she spun and her radiant face passed in front of you, her great black eyes flashed lightning.

Around her, all eyes were fixed and all mouths agape; and as she danced, to the drumming of the tambourine she held above her head in her two pure, round arms, slender, frail, quick as a wasp, with her golden, unpleated bodice, her billowing, brightly-coloured dress, her bare shoulders, her slender legs, uncovered now and again by her skirt, her black hair, her fiery eyes, she was indeed a supernatural creature.

'Truly,' thought Gringoire, 'it's a salamander, a nymph, a goddess, a bacchante from Mount Menalaus!'

At that moment, one of the 'salamander's' plaits of hair came down and a yellow copper coin that had been fixed to it rolled to the ground.

'Ha, no it's not,' he said, 'it's a gypsy girl!'

All illusion had vanished.

She began dancing again. She picked up two swords from the ground, balanced the points on her forehead and made them rotate in one direction as she rotated in the other. It was in fact, quite simply, a gypsy girl. But though Gringoire may have felt disillusioned, the scene as a whole had something marvellous and magical about it; it was lit by the harsh red light of the bonfire, which flickered brightly on the encircling faces of the crowd and on the dark forehead of the girl, while at the far end of the square it cast a pale glimmer, mingled with the swaying of the shadows, on the black and wrinkled old façade of the Maison-aux-Piliers on one side and the stone arms of the gallows on the other.

Among the innumerable faces tinged scarlet by the glow, there was one which seemed even more rapt in its contemplation of the dancer than any of the others. This was the face of a man, austere, calm and saturnine. This man, whose dress was concealed by the crowd around him, did not look more than thirty-five; yet he was bald, having no more than a few tufts of thin and already grey hair at his temples; his high, broad forehead was beginning to be lined but his deep-set eyes shone with an extraordinary youthfulness, a burning vitality and a profound passion. He kept them constantly fixed on the gypsy, and as the sixteen-year-old girl danced and flitted wildly about to the general delight his own meditations seemed to become more and more sombre. Now and then a smile and a sigh would meet on his lips, but the smile was more sorrowful than the sigh.

The girl became out of breath and finally stopped, and the people applauded her affectionately.

'Djali,' said the gypsy.

Gringoire then saw a pretty little white goat come up, quick, alert and glossy, with gilded horns, gilded feet and a gilded collar; he had not noticed it before, for up until now it had remained sitting on a corner of the carpet watching its mistress dance.

'Djali,' said the dancer, 'it's your turn.'

She sat down and held her tambourine prettily out to the goat.

'Djali,' she continued, 'what month of the year are we in?'

The goat raised its front hoof and struck the tambourine once. They were indeed in the first month. The crowd applauded.

'Djali,' the girl went on, turning her tambourine round another way, 'what day of the month is it?'

Djali raised his little gilded hoof and struck the tambourine six times.

'Djali,' continued the gypsy with yet another adjustment of the tambourine, 'what hour of the day is it?'

Djali gave seven taps. At that very moment, the clock on the Maison-aux-Piliers struck seven.

The people were full of wonder.

'There's witchcraft at work there,' said a sinister voice in the crowd. It was that of the bald man who had not taken his eyes off the gypsy.

She shuddered and turned away, but the applause broke out and drowned this surly exclamation.

So completely was it erased from her mind in fact that she continued to question her goat.

'Djali, what does Maître Guichard Grand-Remy, the captain of pistoleers,[1] look like in the Candlemas procession?'

Djali stood up on his hind legs and started to bleat, walking with such charming solemnity that the circle of spectators all burst out laughing at this parody of the captain of pistoleers' self-interested piety.

'Djali,' the girl went on, emboldened by her growing success, 'what is Maître Jacques Charmolue, the King's Procurator in the Ecclesiastical Court, like when he preaches?'

The goat sat down on its backside and began to bleat, waving its front legs in such a peculiar way that, except for his bad French and bad Latin, it was Jacques Charmolue to a T, both his gestures, his accent and his attitude.

The crowd's applause grew.

'Sacrilege, profanation!' the voice of the bald man resumed.

The gypsy turned round again.

'Oh,' she said, 'it's that horrid man!' Then she stuck her bottom lip out beyond the top one, gave a little pout that seemed to be habitual with her, pirouetted on her heel and began to collect the crowd's donations in her tambourine.

It rained *grands-blancs*, *petits-blancs*, *targes* and *liards*.[2] Suddenly she passed in front of Gringoire. Gringoire put his hand to his pocket so unthinkingly that she stopped. 'Blast!' said the poet, finding reality, i.e. emptiness, at the bottom of his pocket. Meanwhile the pretty girl stood there, staring at him out of her big eyes,

1. Cavalrymen armed with pistols.
2. Small coins of the time.

holding out her tambourine and waiting. The sweat was running down Gringoire.

If he had had Peru in his pocket he would assuredly have given it to the dancer; but Gringoire did not have Peru and, what is more, America had not yet been discovered.

Luckily, an unforeseen incident came to his aid.

'Will you go away, you locust from Egypt?'[1] cried a shrill voice, coming from the darkest corner of the square.

The girl turned round in fright. It was not the voice of the bald man any more, it was a woman's voice, a pious and spiteful voice.

But the cry, which frightened the gypsy, delighted a band of children prowling nearby.

'It's the recluse in the Tour-Roland,' they shouted, laughing uproariously, 'it's the *sachette*[2] grumbling! Hasn't she had her supper? Let's take her some scraps from the buffet!'

They all rushed towards the Maison-aux-Piliers.

Meanwhile Gringoire had taken advantage of the dancer's agitation to remove himself. The children's yelling reminded him that he too had not dined. So he ran to the buffet. But the young rogues had the legs of him; when he arrived, they had stripped it bare. There was not even a dry cake left at five *sous* a pound. All that remained were the slender fleurs-de-lys on the wall, interwoven with rose bushes, painted in 1434 by Mathieu Biterne. They made a meagre supper.

To go to bed without any supper is unwelcome; to have neither supper nor any idea where to sleep is even less attractive. This was Gringoire's case. Neither crust nor resting-place; he found necessity crowding in on him from all sides and thought necessity mighty churlish. He had long ago discovered this truth, that Jupiter created man in a fit of misanthropy and that, throughout his life, the sage's destiny lays siege to his philosophy. Personally, he had never experienced such a total blockade; he could hear his stomach sounding the chamade and thought it quite uncalled-for that an ill fate should starve his philosophy into submission.

He was sinking further and further into these melancholy reflections when a song, strange yet full of sweetness, suddenly wrenched him from them. It was the young gypsy singing.

1. i.e. gypsy, gypsies supposedly having originated in Egypt.
2. A name given to female penitents because of the sackcloth (*sac*) they wore.

As with her dancing and her beauty, so with her voice. It was both enchanting and indefinable: something pure, resonant, aerial and winged, so to speak. It dilated continually, into melodies and unexpected cadences, into simple phrases scattered with sharp, sibilant notes, and leaps up the scale that would have defeated a nightingale but where the harmony was never lost, and then into gently undulating octaves that rose and fell like the young singer's own breast. Her beautiful face followed each caprice of her song with a peculiar mobility, from the most dishevelled inspiration to the chastest dignity. At one moment she seemed a madwoman, at the next a queen.

The words she sang were in a language unknown to Gringoire and seemingly unknown to her also, for the feeling she put into the song bore little relation to the meaning of the words. Thus, in her mouth, these four lines took on a wild gaiety:

Un cofre de gran riqueza
Hallaron dentro un pilar
Dentro del, nuevas banderas
Con figuras de espantar.[1]

While a moment later Gringoire could feel tears come to his eyes at the way she sang this verse:

Alarabes de cavallo
Sin poderse menear
Con espadas, y los cuellos
Ballestas de buen echar.[2]

Yet her song breathed joy above all and she seemed to sing like a bird, out of serenity and a light heart.

The gypsy's song had disturbed Gringoire's daydream but only as a swan disturbs the water. He heard it in a sort of rapture,

1. 'A chest of great value
They found inside a pillar,
Inside it, new banners
With terrifying faces.'

2. 'Arab horsemen
Unable to move
With swords, and round their necks
Crossbows that shot well.'

oblivious of all else. It was the first time in several hours that he had not felt he was suffering.

But not for long.

The same woman's voice that had interrupted the gypsy's dance now interrupted her song.

'Will you shut up, you cicada from hell?' she cried, still from the same dark corner of the square.

The poor cicada stopped dead. Gringoire blocked his ears.

'Curse you, you toothless old saw,' he exclaimed, 'you've broken the lyre.'

The other spectators meanwhile were grumbling, like him: 'Devil take the sachette!' more than one of them said. And the unseen old killjoy might have had cause to regret her aggression towards the gypsy, if they had not at that very moment been distracted by the procession of the fools' pope, which, having paraded a great many streets and crossroads, was now emerging into the Place de Grève, with all its din and its torches.

This procession, which our readers saw leaving the palace, had been organizing itself as it went and had recruited all that Paris had to offer by way of rogues, idle thieves and available vagabonds; it looked quite impressive by the time it reached the Grève.

In front marched Egypt. The Duke of Egypt at their head, on horseback, with his counts on foot, holding his bridle and stirrups; behind them the Egyptians, men and women, in any order, with their young children yelling on their shoulders; all of them, duke, counts, common people, in rags and tinsel. Then came the kingdom of the argot, that is to say, every thief in France, graded in order of rank, the lowest going in front. Thus there filed past in column of four, in the various insignia of their grades in this strange academy, the majority crippled, some of them lame, others with only one arm, the upright men, the counterfeit cranks, the rufflers, the kinchin-coves, the Abraham-men, the fraters, the dommerars, the trulls, the whipjacks, the prygges, the drawlatches, the robardesmen, the clapper-dogens; an enumeration to weary Homer. In the centre of the conclave of palliards and demanders for glymmar, the King of the Argotiers, the 'Great Coëzra', was just visible, squatting in a small cart pulled by two large dogs. After the kingdom of the Argotiers came the empire of Galilee. Guillaume Rousseau, Emperor of the Empire of Galilee, walked majestically in his purple wine-stained robe, preceded by clowns beating each other and dancing pyrrhics, and surrounded by his macers, myrmidons and the clerks from the counting-house. Lastly came the legal fraternity, with their maypoles crowned with flowers, their black robes, their band which would have done for a witches' sabbath and their huge yellow tapers. In the centre of the crowd, the high-ranking officers of the brotherhood of fools were carrying a litter on their shoulders more weighed down with candles than Sainte-Geneviève's reliquary in time of pestilence. And on this litter, resplendent in crozier, cope and mitre, was the new pope of fools, the bell-ringer of Notre-Dame, the hunchback Quasimodo.

Each section of this grotesque procession had its own band. The Egyptians were playing tunelessly on their balafos[1] and African tambourines. The argotiers, a somewhat unmusical breed, had not got beyond the viol, the buccina and the twelfth-century Gothic rebec. The empire of Galilee was scarcely more modern; its one instrument seemed to be some wretched rebec from the very infancy of the art, still imprisoned in the *doh-re-me*. But it was around the fools' pope that the full musical resources of the age were deployed, in a splendid cacophony. Here it was all treble rebecs, alto rebecs and tenor rebecs, not to mention the flutes and the brass. Our readers will recall, alas, that this orchestra was Gringoire's.

During the journey from the palace to the Grève, Quasimodo's hideous and unhappy face had opened out to a degree hard to convey and now looked both proud and self-satisfied. This was the first taste he had ever had of the delights of vanity. Hitherto, he had known only humiliation, contempt for his condition and disgust for his person. And so, stone deaf though he was, he relished the acclamation of the crowd like a real pope, that crowd which he had detested because he felt it detested him. What did it matter that his people was a pack of fools, cripples, thieves and beggars, it was still a people and he its sovereign. And he took all the ironic applause and mock respect seriously, although it should be said that mixed in with it, among the crowd, went an element of very real fear. For the hunchback was strong; his crooked legs were nimble; his deafness made him vicious: three qualities that tempered the ridicule.

For the rest, we cannot really believe that the new fools' pope

1. A sort of xylophone from E. Africa.

had acknowledged to himself the feelings he was experiencing or the feelings he was inspiring. There was necessarily something deaf and incomplete about the mind that dwelt in that misbegotten body. And so to him what he was feeling at that moment was altogether dim, blurred and confused. Joy alone had broken through, pride was dominant. There was a radiance about that sombre and unhappy face.

Thus it was with some surprise and alarm that suddenly, just as Quasimodo, in this half-intoxicated state, was passing in triumph before the Maison-aux-Piliers, they saw a man dash out from the crowd and, with an angry gesture, snatch from his hands his gilded wooden crozier, the badge of his foolish papacy.

This reckless man was the figure with the bald forehead who, the moment before, had been mingling with the group round the gypsy and had made the poor girl's blood run cold with his words of menace and hatred. He wore ecclesiastical garb. The moment he issued from the crowd, Gringoire, who had not noticed him until then, recognized him: 'Good Lord,' he said, with a cry of astonishment, 'it's my hermetic master, Dom Claude Frollo, the archdeacon! What the devil does he want with horrid old one-eye? He'll be eaten alive.'

And a cry of terror had indeed gone up. The formidable Quasimodo had leapt down from the litter and the women were turning away their heads so as not to see him tear the archdeacon to pieces.

He bounded up to the priest, looked at him and fell to his knees.

The priest snatched off his tiara, snapped his crozier in two, and ripped his tinsel cope.

Quasimodo remained kneeling, his head bowed and his hands joined together.

There then began between them a strange dialogue of signs and gestures, for neither of them spoke. The priest upright, irate, threatening and imperious, Quasimodo prostrate, humble and supplicant. Yet it was a fact that Quasimodo could have crushed the priest under his thumb.

The archdeacon finally gave Quasimodo's powerful shoulder a rough shake and signalled to him to get up and follow him.

Quasimodo got up.

Whereupon the brotherhood of fools, having recovered from their initial amazement, tried to defend their abruptly dethroned pope. The Egyptians, the argotiers and all the lawyers' clerks surrounded the priest yapping.

Quasimodo took up position in front of the priest, flexed the muscles in his athletic fists and stared at his assailants with bared teeth, like an enraged tiger.

The priest resumed his serious, gloomy look, signalled to Quasimodo and walked silently off.

Quasimodo walked in front of him, scattering the crowd as he went.

Once they had traversed both the populace and the square, the flock of onlookers and loafers sought to follow them. Quasimodo thereupon took up the rear and walked backwards behind the archdeacon, squat, scowling, monstrous, shaggy, bunching his limbs, licking his boar's tusks, grunting like a wild animal and inducing great oscillations in the crowd by a look or a gesture.

The pair of them were permitted to enter a dark, narrow street, where nobody dared venture after them. The chimera of Quasimodo gnashing his teeth was more than enough to bar entry to it.

'All very wonderful,' said Gringoire, 'but where on earth am I going to find some supper?'

FOUR

The Drawbacks of following a Pretty Woman through the Streets at Night

GRINGOIRE had begun, quite at random, to follow the gypsy. He had seen her take, with her goat, the Rue de la Coutellerie; he had taken the Rue de la Coutellerie.

'Why not?' he said to himself.

Gringoire, that practical philosopher of the Paris streets, had noticed that nothing is more conducive to meditation than to follow a pretty woman without knowing where she is going. Such voluntary abdication of one's free will, such a subjection of one's own fancy to that of some unsuspecting other person, has about it a mixture of whimsical independence and blind obedience, a sort of compromise between servitude and freedom which appealed to Gringoire, whose mind was essentially a mixed one, both complex and indecisive, holding gingerly on to all extremes, constantly suspended between all human propensities, and playing one off against the other. He readily likened himself to the tomb of Mahomet, attracted in opposite directions by twin lodestones, and eternally hovering between the up and the down, the ceiling and the pavement, the ascent and the descent, the zenith and the nadir.

Had Gringoire lived in our own day, how beautifully he would have bisected the Classics and Romantics!

But he was not primitive enough to have lived for three hundred years, which is a pity. His absence is a gap of which we are only too keenly aware today.

Anyway, there is no better frame of mind in which to follow passers-by (especially female ones) through the streets, as Gringoire was happily doing, than not knowing where you will sleep.

So he walked pensively after the girl, who quickened her step and made her pretty goat trot as she saw the burgesses making their way home and the taverns closing, they being the only shops that had been open that day.

'After all,' he thought, approximately, 'she must live somewhere and gypsies have kind hearts. Who knows . . .?'

And who knows what graceful thoughts were contained in those points of suspension with which, mentally, he followed his reticence.

From time to time, however, as he passed the last groups of burgesses shutting their doors, he caught some snatch of conversation which broke the train of pleasing hypotheses.

On one occasion it was two old men accosting each other.

'It's cold, Maître Thibaut Fernicle, d'you know that?'

(Gringoire had known it since the start of winter.)

'It is that, Maître Boniface Disome! Are we going to have another winter like three years ago, in '80, when wood cost eight *sous* a bundle?'

'Bah, that was nothing, Maître Thibaut, compared to the winter of 1407, when it froze from Saint-Martin's Day to Candlemas, and so fiercely that the Clerk to the Parliament's pen froze every three words in the big chamber, which stopped them recording the cases.'

Further on, it was two women at adjoining windows, holding candles that spluttered in the fog.

'Did your husband tell you about the accident, Mademoiselle la Boudraque?'

'No, what was it, Mademoiselle Turquant?'

'M. Gilles Godin, the notary at the Châtelet, his horse took fright at the Flemings and their procession and knocked down Maître Philippot Avrillot, a Celestine oblate.'

'Really?'

'Just like that.'

'A civilian horse, that's rather hard. All well and good if it had been a cavalry horse!'

And the windows closed again. But Gringoire had lost the thread of his ideas all the same.

Happily, he soon recovered it and retied it without difficulty, thanks to the gypsy and thanks to Djali, who were still walking in front of him: two slender, delicate and charming creatures. He admired their tiny feet, their pretty contours, their graceful movements, and they almost merged as he watched them; their intelligence and friendliness made him think they were both young girls; their lightness, agility and nimble gait made them seem like two she-goats.

Meanwhile, the streets were getting darker and emptier by the minute. The curfew had long since sounded, and only rarely now was a passer-by to be met with along the pavement, or a light in the windows. In following the gypsy, Gringoire had entered that inextricable labyrinth of alleyways, intersections and cul-de-sacs which surrounds the ancient burial-ground of the Saints-Innocents and resembles a skein of thread ravelled by a cat. 'Not much logic about these streets!' said Gringoire, lost amidst the countless twists and constant turns, through which the girl was following a route she seemed well acquainted with, without hesitating and at an ever brisker pace. He, on the other hand, would have been quite ignorant of his whereabouts, had he not, at a bend in the street, caught sight of the octagonal mass of the pillory of Les Halles, whose openwork superstructure stood out stark and black against a still lighted window in the Rue Verdelet.

In the past few moments, the girl's attention had been drawn to him; she had looked anxiously round at him several times, and had even stopped in her tracks once and taken advantage of a shaft of light coming from the half-open door of a bakery to look him hard up and down. After this look, Gringoire saw her give the little pout he had noticed earlier and continue on her way.

The little pout set Gringoire to thinking. There was certainly both contempt and mockery in that pretty grimace. And so he had just begun to look down and count the paving-stones, and to follow the girl at a rather greater distance when, just as a bend in the street hid her from view, he heard her give a piercing cry.

He hurried forward.

The street was full of darkness. But a wick soaked in oil, burning in an iron cage at the feet of the Holy Virgin at the corner of the street, enabled Gringoire to make out the gypsy struggling in the arms of two men who were trying to muffle her cries. The poor little goat was terrified, it had put its horns down and was bleating.

'Help, messieurs of the watch,' cried Gringoire, and advanced bravely. One of the men holding the girl turned towards him. It was the formidable figure of Quasimodo.

Gringoire did not turn tail, but he advanced not a step further.

Quasimodo came up to him, hurled him four yards away on the paving-stones with the back of his hand and plunged rapidly into the shadows, carrying the girl folded over his arm like a silk scarf. His companion went after him and the poor goat took up the rear, bleating plaintively.

'Murder, murder!' cried the unfortunate gypsy.

'Stop where you are, wretches, and let that ribald go!' suddenly thundered the voice of a horseman abruptly issuing from the nearby crossroads.

It was a captain of archers of the king's ordonnance, armed from head to foot and with a broadsword in his hand.

He snatched the gypsy from the amazed Quasimodo's arms, laid her across his saddle, and just as the redoubtable hunchback had got over his surprise and was dashing forward to recover his prey, fifteen or sixteen archers, who had been close behind their captain, appeared, clutching their large swords. It was a squadron of the king's bodyguard acting as counter-watch, on the orders of Messire Robert d'Estouteville, Warden of the Provostry of Paris.

Quasimodo was smothered, seized, pinioned. He roared, he raged and he bit and if it had been broad daylight there can be no doubt that his face alone, made even more hideous by anger, would have put the whole squadron to flight. But at night he was deprived of his most fearsome weapon: his ugliness.

His companion had vanished during the struggle.

The gypsy sat up gracefully on the officer's saddle, rested her two hands on the young man's two shoulders, eyed him fixedly for a few seconds, as if overjoyed at his fine bearing and the fine succour he had just brought her. She it was who broke the silence by saying to him, softening her already soft voice:

'What is your name, *monsieur le gendarme*?'

'Captain Phoebus de Châteaupers, at your service, my beauty!' answered the officer, drawing himself up.

'Thank you,' she said.

And as Captain Phoebus turned up the ends of his Burgundian moustache, she slid down from his horse like an arrow falling to earth and ran off.

A flash of lightning could not have vanished more swiftly.

'By the pope's navel!' said the captain, tightening the straps on Quasimodo, 'I'd rather have kept the ribald.'

'What do you expect, Captain?' said a man-at-arms, 'the song-bird has flown and we're left with the bat.'

FIVE

The Drawbacks (*continued*)

STUNNED by his fall, Gringoire still lay on the paving in front of the good Virgin at the street-corner. His wits slowly returned; first he drifted for a minute or two in a sort of half somnolent daydream, which was far from unpleasant and in which the ethereal figures of the gipsy and the goat were allied to the weight of Quasimodo's fist. This state was short-lived. A fairly keen sensation of cold, from that part of his anatomy that was in contact with the paving, suddenly aroused him and brought his mind back up to the surface. 'Whence the cold?' he asked himself abruptly. He then noticed he was more or less in the middle of the gutter.

'Blasted hump-backed cyclops!' he grumbled between his teeth, and sought to stand up. But he was too dazed and too bruised. He would have to stay where he was. His hand at least was more or less free; he held his nostrils and resigned himself.

'Paris mud,' he reflected (for he thought he was sure the gutter would definitely be his lodging for the night), 'And what can we do in a lodging except dream?'[1] 'Paris mud smells particularly un-

1. A quotation from La Fontaine.

pleasant. It must contain a lot of nitrous salvolatile. That's the view of Maître Nicolas Flamel and the hermeticists, anyway...'[1]

The word 'hermeticists' suddenly made him think of the archdeacon Claude Frollo. He recalled the violent scene he had just glimpsed, that the gypsy had been struggling with two men and that Quasimodo had had a companion; and the haughty, morose face of the archdeacon passed vaguely through his memory. 'That would be strange!' he thought; with which datum and on which foundation he began to erect a fantastic edifice of hypotheses, that card-castle of the philosophers. Then, coming suddenly back to earth once more: 'Ah, damn it, I'm frozen!' he exclaimed.

His position had in fact become less and less tenable. Each molecule of the water in the gutter had removed one molecule of the calorific radiating from the small of Gringoire's back and a painful equilibrium between the temperature of his body and the temperature of the gutter had begun to be established.

But all of a sudden he was beset by trouble of a quite different kind.

A band of children, of those barefoot young savages who have always roamed the streets of Paris under the eternal name of *gamins* and who threw stones at us too, as children, when we came out of school in the evenings, because we did not have torn trousers, a swarm of these young scamps was running towards the crossroads where Gringoire lay, shouting and laughing in apparent disregard for anyone sleeping near by. They were dragging behind them some kind of shapeless sack or other, and the mere noise of their clogs would have awoken a corpse. Gringoire, who was not yet quite that, half got up.

'Hey, Hennequin Dandèche! Hey, Jehan Pincebourde!' they shouted at the tops of their voices. 'Old Eustache Moubon, the blacksmith on the corner, 's just died. We've got his palliasse, we're going to make a bonfire with it. It's the Flemings today!'

Whereupon they threw the mattress down exactly on top of Gringoire. having arrived next to him without seeing him. At the same time one of them picked up a handful of straw and went and lit it from the good Virgin's wick.

'Christ's death!' muttered Gringoire, 'am I going to be too hot now?'

1. Flamel (1330–1418) was a notorious alchemist and dabbler in the occult.

It was a critical moment. He was about to be trapped between fire and water; he made a superhuman effort, like a forger trying to escape being boiled alive.[1] He got to his feet, threw the mattress over the urchins and fled.

'Holy Virgin!' cried the children. 'The blacksmith's haunting us!'

And they fled in the opposite direction.

The battlefield belonged to the mattress. Belleforêt, Father le Juge and Corrozet[2] assure us that the following day it was gathered up with much pomp by the local clergy and taken to the treasury of Saint-Opportune's, where up until 1789 the sacristan earned quite a fair income out of the great miracle of the statue of the Virgin at the corner of the Rue Mauconseil, who had, merely by her presence, on the memorable night of 6–7 January 1482, exorcised the deceased Eustache Moubon, he having played a prank on the devil when he died by slyly hiding his soul in his mattress.

SIX

The Broken Pitcher

AFTER running for a time at top speed in any direction at all, knocking his head against many a street-corner, vaulting many a gutter and traversing many an alleyway, cul-de-sac and cross-roads, as he searched for a way through and out of all those old, meandering pavements of Les Halles, and explored in his panic what the beautiful Latin of the charters calls *tota via, cheminum et viaria*,[3] our poet suddenly halted, first of all for want of breath and then because he had, as it were, been taken by the scruff of the neck by a dilemma that had just arisen in his mind. 'It seems to me, Maître Pierre Gringoire,' he told himself, putting a finger to his forehead, 'that you're a blockhead running away like this. Those young scamps were just as frightened by you as you were by them. It seems to me, as I say, that you heard the sound of their clogs escaping southwards, as you escaped northwards. Now there are two alternatives: either they have taken to their heels, in which case the straw mattress they must have left behind in their terror is the very

1. The contemporary punishment for forgery.
2. All sixteenth-century annalists of Paris.
3. 'All the paths, roads and passages.'

bed whose hospitality you have been seeking ever since this morning and which the Virgin has now sent to you by a miracle to reward you for writing a morality in her honour together with triumphs and mummeries; or else the children have not taken to their heels, and in that case they will have put a torch to the straw, and there in fact is the excellent fire you need to cheer you up, dry you and warm you. Either way, good fire or good bed, the mattress is a gift from heaven. Perhaps the blessed Virgin Mary at the corner of the Rue Mauconseil made Eustache Moubon die just for this; you're foolish to be running away like this with your tail between your legs, like a Picard from a Frenchman, leaving behind you what you're looking for ahead of you; you're a fool!'

He then retraced his steps, searching for his bearings with nose to the wind and ears cocked as he struggled to locate the blessed mattress. But in vain. It was nothing but intersecting houses, cul-de-sacs and converging streets, in the midst of which he was constantly hesitating and wondering, more securely hobbled and ensnared in this tangle of dark alleyways than he would have been in the actual maze of the Hôtel des Tournelles. He finally lost patience and exclaimed solemnly: 'A curse on all crossroads! The devil created them in the image of his fork.'

This exclamation relieved him somewhat, and a kind of reddish reflection which he spotted at the same moment down the end of a long, narrow alleyway completed the restoration of his morale. 'God be praised!' he said, 'it's down there! There's my mattress burning.' Then he added piously, likening himself to the mariner foundering in the darkness: '*Salve, salve, maris stella!*'[1]

Was this snatch of litany addressed to the Virgin Mary or the mattress? Of that we have absolutely no knowledge.

He had only taken a few steps down the long, sloping alleyway, which was unpaved and became increasingly steep and muddy, when he noticed something rather peculiar. It was not empty. Here and there, dim and shapeless figures of some kind were crawling down it, all making for the light which flickered at the end of the street, like those ponderous insects which haul themselves at night from one blade of grass to another towards the shepherd's campfire.

Nothing makes one adventurous like a hollow feeling beneath

1. 'Welcome, welcome, star of the sea.'

the waistband. Gringoire continued forward and had soon come up with the laziest of these larvae, as it dragged itself along behind the others. As he came nearer, he found it was merely a wretched legless cripple hopping along on his hands, like an injured harvest-spider with only two legs left. As he passed close beside this sort of spider with a human face, it raised a piteous voice to him: '*La buona mancia, signor! La buona mancia!*'[1]

'Devil take you, and me with you,' said Gringoire, 'if I know what you mean!'

And he pressed on.

He caught up another of these travelling shapes and examined it. It was a cripple, both halt and one-armed, so halt and one-armed that the complicated system of crutches and wooden legs supporting him made him look like a walking builder's scaffold. Gringoire, whose comparisons were noble and classical, compared him mentally to the living tripod of Vulcan.

This living tripod saluted him as he passed, but stopped his hat level with Gringoire's chin, like a shaving bowl, shouting into his ear: '*Señor caballero, para comprar un pedaso de pan!*'[2]

'This one seems to talk too,' said Gringoire, 'but an uncouth language and anyone who understands it is a luckier man than I.'

Then a sudden association of ideas made him strike his brow: 'Come to think of it, what on earth did they mean this morning with their *Esmeralda*?'

He tried to walk faster, but for the third time something barred his path. This something, or rather someone, was a blind man, a short, bearded blind man with a Jewish face, who was rowing about him in the air with his stick as he was pulled along behind a huge dog; and said through his nose, with a Hungarian accent: '*Facitote caritatem!*'[3]

'We're in luck!' said Pierre Gringoire, 'someone who speaks a Christian tongue at last. I must look very charitable for them to ask me for alms with a purse as undernourished as mine. My friend (and he turned to the blind man), I sold my last shirt last week; or, since you understand only the language of Cicero: *Vendidi hebdomade nuper transita meam ultimam chemisam.*'

1. 'A donation, sir, a donation!'
2. 'Sir knight, to buy a slice of bread!'
3. 'Be charitable!'

Having said which, he turned his back on the blind man and continued on his way; but the blind man began to lengthen his own stride at the same time, and now the cripple and the legless man came hurrying up from different directions, their begging bowls and crutches sounding loudly on the stones. Then all three began jostling at poor Gringoire's heels, and chanting their refrains:

'*Caritatem!*' sang the blind man.

'*La buona mancia!*' sang the legless man.

And the lame man provided the counterpoint, repeating '*Un pedaso de pan!*'

Gringoire blocked his ears. 'What a tower of Babel!' he exclaimed.

He began to run. The blind man ran. The lame man ran. The man with no legs ran.

And then, as he penetrated further down the street, the legless, the blind and the halt came swarming around him, together with the one-armed, the one-eyed and the lepers with their sores; some emerged from the houses, others from the small streets near by, yet others from the air-vents of cellars, yelling, bellowing, yelping, all of them hobbling and limping as they hurried towards the light and wallowed in the slime like slugs after rain.

The dismayed Gringoire, still followed by his three persecutors, and with little idea of what might be about to happen, walked through the midst of the others, skirting the lame ones and stepping over the legless, his feet caught up in this ant-heap of the maimed, like the English sea-captain who was sucked down by an army of crabs.

It occurred to him to try and return the way he had come. But it was too late. The whole legion had closed up behind him and his three beggars were holding on to him. So he went on, urged forward by fear, by this irresistible tide and by a confusion of mind that had turned the whole thing into some awful nightmare.

At last, he reached the end of the street. It opened out into an immense square, where hundreds of scattered lights flickered in the hazy night mist. Gringoire leapt forward, hoping that the speed of his legs would save him from the three infirm spectres who had battened on to him.

'*Onde vas, hombre?*'[1] cried the cripple, throwing away his

1. 'Where are you going, man?'

crutches and running after him on the soundest two legs that ever measured out a regulation yard on the pavements of Paris.

The legless man, meanwhile, was on his feet, and had put his heavy iron bowl on Gringoire's head, while the blind man was staring him in the face with blazing eyes.

'Where am I?' said the terrified poet.

'In the Court of Miracles,' replied a fourth spectre, who had accosted them.

'Upon my soul,' Gringoire went on, 'I can see blind men staring and lame ones running, but where's the Saviour?'

The answer was a peal of sinister laughter.

The poor poet took a look around him. He was indeed in the redoubtable Court of Miracles, where no law-abiding man had ever penetrated at such an hour: a magic circle where those officers from the Châtelet or provost serjeants who ventured into it vanished in small pieces; a city of thieves, a hideous wen on the face of Paris; a sewer from which that stream of vice, mendicancy and vagabondage that is in constant spate in the streets of capital cities flowed each morning, and to which it returned to stagnate each night; a monstrous hive to which all the hornets of the social order returned in the evenings with their booty; a bogus hospital where gypsies, unfrocked priests, ruined students and wastrels from every nation, Spaniards, Italians, Germans, and of every religion, Jews, Christians, Mohammedans, idolators, were beggars covered in artificial sores by day and transformed themselves by night into brigands; in short, a vast dressing-room, in which the entire cast of the everlasting comedy performed in the streets of Paris by theft, prostitution and murder, donned and removed their costumes.

The square was vast, irregular and ill-paved, as were all Paris squares at that time. Here and there gleamed fires, with strange-looking groups milling around them. All was bustle and shouting. There was the sound of shrill laughter, squalling babies, women's voices. The hands and heads of the crowd stood out black against the background of light, gesturing weirdly. Now and then a dog that looked like a man or a man that looked like a dog would go past along the ground, where the flickering light from the fires merged with the great indeterminate shadows. In this city, the boundaries between races and species seemed to have been abolished, as in a pandemonium. Amongst this population, men, women, animals, age, sex, health, sickness, all seemed communal; everything fitted together, was merged, mingled and superimposed; everyone was part of everything.

The feeble and uncertain radiance of the fires enabled Gringoire to make out, for all his agitation and right around the huge square, a hideous frame of old houses, whose stunted, decrepit and wizened façades, each broken by one or two lighted windows, looked in the shadows like the enormous heads of monstrous, crabbed old women, arranged in a circle, and staring at a witches' sabbath through blinking eyes.

It was like some new world, unknown, unprecedented, shapeless, reptilian, teeming, fantastic.

Gringoire, more and more alarmed, held in a pincer-like grip by his three beggars and deafened by the crowd of other faces that surrounded him, foaming and baying, the hapless Gringoire tried to gather his wits and remember whether it was a Saturday. But his efforts were unavailing, the thread of his memory and his ideas had been snapped. Doubting everything, drifting from what he could see to what he could smell, he asked himself this unanswerable question: 'If I am, is this? If this is, am I?'

At that moment, a distinct shout went up from the vociferous mob pressed around him: 'Take him to the king! Take him to the king!'

'Holy Virgin!' muttered Gringoire, 'the king of this place must be a billy-goat.'

'To the king, to the king!' every voice took up.

He was dragged off. They vied to get their claws on him. But the three beggars had not loosed their hold and snatched him away from the others, screaming, 'He's ours!'

In the struggle, the poet's already ailing doublet gave up the ghost.

As he crossed the ghastly square, his brain cleared. After a few steps, his sense of reality returned. He was starting to get used to the atmosphere of the place. At the outset, smoke, a vapour as it were, had risen from the poet's head or perhaps, quite simply and prosaically, from his empty stomach, and had drifted between him and objects, so that he had glimpsed them only through the incoherent mists of nightmare, through that darkness of dreams which makes every outline waver, every shape grimace, and which makes objects conglomerate in disproportionate groups, whereby things are dilated into chimeras and men into phantoms. To this hallucination there gradually succeeded a less distraught, less magnifying vision. Reality dawned around him, it struck both his eyes and his feet and demolished, piece by piece, the terrible poetry by which he had earlier thought himself surrounded. He was made to realize that he was walking not through the Styx but through mud, that he was being jostled not by devils but by thieves, that it was not his soul that was at stake but quite simply his life (since he lacked that valuable peacemaker which is so effective an intermediary between bandit and honest citizen, a purse). In short, when he took a closer and less feverish look at the rout, he descended from the witches' sabbath to the tavern.

The Court of Miracles was in fact no more than a tavern, but a tavern of brigands, as red with blood as with wine.

The sight that confronted him once his tatterdemalion escort had set him down at the terminus of its journey was not such as to return him to poetry, not even to the poetry of hell. Here, more than ever, was the brutal and prosaic reality of the tavern. If we were not in the fifteenth century, we could say that Gringoire had descended from Michelangelo to Callot.[1]

Around a large fire, burning on a big, circular flagstone, whose flames were licking at the red-hot legs of a temporarily unoccupied trivet, a few rickety tables had been set up, dotted about haphazardly, such that the lowest minion, however geometrically-minded, would not have deigned to set them in parallel lines or looked to see that at least they did not intersect at too improbable an angle. On the tables gleamed a number of jugs, dripping wine and barley-beer, around which was gathered many a bacchic face, purple from the wine and the firelight. There was a man with a big belly and a jovial face, noisily embracing a fleshy, thickset whore. There was a sort of fake soldier, a ruffler in the language of the argot, whistling as he unwound the bandages from his fake wound and restored the circulation to a sound, vigorous knee, swathed since morning in innumerable bindings. In total contrast, a counterfeit crank was getting his 'God's leg' ready for the next day with celandine and ox-blood.[2] A couple of tables away, a cockler, in full

1. Jacques Callot (1592–1635), an engraver of sordid, realistic scenes.
2. With which he caused a healthy leg to look pitifully diseased.

pilgrim's outfit, was spelling out 'Sainte-Reine's lament', with all the right nasal intonations. Elsewhere, a young hubin was taking lessons in epilepsy from an old froth-blower, who was teaching him the art of foaming at the mouth by chewing a bit of soap. Next to them, a dropsy sufferer was deflating himself and had caused four or five female thieves, squabbling at the same table over a baby they had stolen that evening, to hold their noses. All of which circumstances, two centuries later, says Sauval, 'seemed so ridiculous to the court that they served as a pastime for the king and as a curtain-raiser for La Nuit's royal ballet, divided into four parts and danced on the stage of the Petit-Bourbon'. 'Never', adds an eye-witness of 1653, 'have the abrupt metamorphoses of the Court of Miracles been more happily portrayed. Benserade got us in the mood for them with somewhat amorous verses.'

From everywhere came bursts of loud laughter and obscene singing. Everyone wanted the stage to himself, swearing and discoursing with no ear for his neighbour. Mugs touched, quarrels flared at the impact, and chipped mugs tore holes in rags.

A huge dog sat on its tail staring at the fire. A few children formed part of the orgy. The kidnapped baby, who was crying and yelling. A second one, a fat boy of four, sat dangling his legs on a bench that was too high for him, with the table under his chin, not saying a word. A third one was solemnly smearing the molten tallow running from a candle over the table with his finger. A small one finally, squatting in the mud, had almost vanished inside a cauldron, which he was scraping with a tile and extracting sounds that would have sent Stradivarius into a faint.

Next to the fire was a barrel and on the barrel was a beggar. This was the king on his throne.

The three men holding Gringoire led him before the barrel, and the entire bacchanal fell silent for a moment, except for the cauldron occupied by the child.

Gringoire dared neither breathe nor raise his eyes.

'*Hombre, quita tu sombrero*,'[1] said one of the three rascals to whom he belonged, but before he had understood what this meant the other took his hat off for him. A miserable bycoket it was, true, but still good for a sunny or a rainy day. Gringoire sighed.

Meanwhile, the king addressed him from the top of his cask.

1. 'Man, take off your hat.'

'Who's this scum?'

Gringoire shuddered. The voice, for all its menacing tones, reminded him of another voice which only that morning had dealt his mystery play its first blow by snuffling out in the middle of the auditorium: 'Alms, please give me your alms.' He looked up. It was indeed Clopin Trouillefou.

Clopin Trouillefou was clad in his royal insignia, but no less ragged for that. The sore on his arm had now gone. In his hand he carried one of those whips with white leather thongs called *boullayes*, which tipstaffs then used to compress crowds. On his head he wore a sort of ringed head-dress closed at the top; but so alike are the two things that it was hard to tell whether it was a baby's burlet or a king's crown.

Gringoire, meanwhile, though he did not know why, had felt some hope when he recognized the king of the Court of Miracles as his accursed beggar from the great hall.

'Maître,' he stammered, 'My lord ... Sire ... How should I address you?' he said finally, having reached the topmost note of his crescendo and no longer able either to go up or come down again.

'My lord, Your Majesty, comrade, call me what you like. But get a move on. What have you got to say in your defence?'

'In your defence?' thought Gringoire, 'I don't like that!' He resumed with a stutter: 'I'm the man who this morning...'

'By the devil's fingernails!' Clopin broke in. 'Your name, scum, and that's all. Listen. You stand before three powerful sovereigns: I, Clopin Trouillefou, King of Thunes, successor to the Great Coëzra, supreme suzerain of the kingdom of the argot; Mathias Hungadi Spicali, Duke of Egypt and Bohemia, that yellow old man you see there with a duster round his head; Guillaume Rousseau, Emperor of Galilee, that fat man who isn't listening to us but is fondling a ribald. We are your judges. You have entered the kingdom of the argot without being an argotier, you have violated the privileges of our town. You must be punished, unless you're a canter, a palliard or a hooker or, in the jargon of the law-abiding, a thief, a beggar or a vagabond. Are you anything of that sort? Explain yourself. State your occupations.'

'Alas,' said Gringoire, 'I haven't that honour! I am the author...'

'That's enough!' Trouillefou put in, without letting him finish. 'You will be hanged. It's quite simple, messieurs the burgesses of

Paris! As you use our kind among you, so we use your kind among us. The law you apply to the truants, the truants apply to you. If it's a vicious one, that's your fault. We need now and again to see a respectable face above a hempen collar; it makes the whole thing honourable. Come, my friend, share your rags gaily out among these young ladies. I shall have you hanged for the amusement of the truants, and you shall give them your purse to buy a drink. If there's some mummery you need to do, there's a very nice God-the-Father in stone in the pulpit over there which we stole from Saint-Pierre-aux-Bœufs. You've got four minutes to throw your soul at his head.'

It was a formidable speech.

'Well spoken, so help me! Clopin Trouillefou preaches like the Holy Father the Pope,' exclaimed the Emperor of Galilee, breaking his mug in order to prop up his table.

'My lords, emperors and kings,' said Gringoire coolly (for he had somehow or other recovered his firmness and he spoke with resolve), 'you can't mean it. My name is Pierre Gringoire, I am the poet whose morality was performed this morning in the great hall of the palace.'

'Ah, it's you, maître!' said Clopin. 'I was there, God's head. Well, comrade, is the fact you bored us this morning any reason why you shouldn't be hanged this evening?'

'It's going to be hard to save myself,' thought Gringoire. However, he made one more effort. 'I don't see why poets shouldn't be counted among the truants,' he said. 'Aesopus was a vagabond, Homerus a mendicant and Mercurius a thief...'

Clopin interrupted him. 'I think you're trying to confuse us with your gibberish. Damn it, let them hang you and stop all the fussing!'

'Forgive me, my Lord King of Thunes,' replied Gringoire, contesting every inch of ground. 'It's worth it... one moment!... Listen to me... You shan't condemn me without a hearing...'

But, in fact, his unhappy voice had been drowned by the din going on all around him. The little boy was scraping his cauldron more energetically than ever; and to cap everything, an old woman had just put a frying-pan full of fat on the red-hot trivet, and it was yelping in the flames with a noise like the shouts of a band of children following a masquerade.

In the meantime, Clopin Trouillefou seemed to confer for a moment with the Duke of Egypt and the Emperor of Galilee, who was completely drunk. Then he cried shrilly: 'Silence there!' but since the cauldron and the frying-pan did not hear him but continued their duet, he leapt down from his barrel, gave one kick to the cauldron, which sent it and the boy rolling ten yards away, and another to the frying-pan, which overturned all the fat into the fire, then climbed solemnly back on his throne, indifferent to the muffled tears of the child and the grumblings of the old woman, whose supper had gone up in a lovely white flame.

Trouillefou made a signal, and the duke, the emperor, his henchmen and his lieutenants came and stood round him in a horseshoe, with Gringoire, still tightly held round the body, at its centre. It was a semicircle of rags, tatters and tinsel, of pitchforks and hatchets, of wine-stained legs and great bare arms, of sordid, vacant, lifeless faces. At the centre of this round table of beggarhood, Clopin Trouillefou, the doge of this senate, the king of this peerage, the pope of this conclave, dominating it first by the full height of his barrel and then somehow by his expression, fierce, haughty and formidable, which made his eyes sparkle and attenuated, in his savage profile, the bestial type of the race of truants. His was a boar's head amidst the snouts of pigs.

'Listen,' he said to Gringoire, stroking his misshapen chin with a horny hand, 'I don't see why you shouldn't be hanged. It's true you seem to find it repugnant, but it's quite simple, you burgesses aren't used to it. You make too much of it. After all, we wish you no harm. But here's one way you can get out of it for now. Will you be one of us?'

You may judge the effect that this offer had on Gringoire, who had seen life slipping away from him and had begun to release his grip on it. Now he clutched it tightly to him once again.

'I will indeed, I certainly will,' he said.

'Do you agree,' Clopin went on, 'to enrol with the cutpurses?'

'The cutpurses. Exactly,' answered Gringoire.

'Do you admit you are a member of the parasites?' the King of Thunes continued.

'Of the parasites.'

'A subject of the kingdom of the argot?'

'Of the kingdom of the argot.'

'A truant?'

'A truant.'

'In your soul?'

'In my soul.'

'I would point out to you', the king went on, 'that you'll be hanged just the same.'

'Dear God,' said the poet.

'Only,' Clopin continued imperturbably, 'you will be hanged later on, with greater ceremony, at the expense of the good town of Paris, from a fine stone gibbet, and by law-abiding men. That's a consolation.'

'As you say,' replied Gringoire.

'There are other advantages. As a parasite, you won't have to pay for street cleaning, the poor or lighting, to which the burgesses of Paris are liable.'

'Amen,' said the poet. 'I agree. I'm a truant, an argotier, a parasite, a cutpurse, whatever you like. And I was all that in advance, Monsieur the King of the Thunes, for I'm a philosopher: *et omnia in philosophia, omnes in philosopho continentur*,[1] as you know.'

The King of Thunes frowned.

'Who do you take me for, my friend? What kind of Hungarian Jew's talk is that? I don't know Hebrew. I may be a bandit but I'm not a Jew. I don't even steal any more, I'm above that, I kill. Cutthroat, yes: cutpurse, no.'

Gringoire tried to insert some apology between these brief words, which anger was making more and more staccato. 'Please forgive me, my lord. It's not Hebrew, it's Latin.'

'I tell you,' Clopin went on, heatedly, 'I'm not a Jew and I'll have you hung, synagogue's belly! like that little swindler from Judaea next to you there who I hope one day to see nailed on a counter like the counterfeit coin he is!'

So saying, he pointed at the little bearded Hungarian Jew who had accosted Gringoire with his *facitote caritatem*, and who, understanding no other language, watched in surprise as the King of Thunes's bad temper spilled over on to him.

My lord Clopin finally calmed down.

'So, scum,' he said to our poet, 'you want to be a truant?'

'Surely,' replied the poet.

1. 'And all things are contained in philosophy, all men in the philosopher.'

'Wanting to isn't everything,' said the surly Clopin. 'Goodwill never put another onion in the soup, it's only good for going to paradise; but paradise and the argot aren't the same thing. To be received into the argot you've got to prove you're some use, and to do that you must search the dummy.'

'I'll search anything you like,' said Gringoire.

Clopin gave a signal. A few argotiers left the circle, to return a moment later. They were carrying two posts finished at the bottom in two timber spatulas, which gave them a firm foothold on the ground. To the top end of the two posts they fitted a crossbeam, so that the whole thing formed a very pretty portable gallows, which Gringoire had the satisfaction of seeing erected in front of him in the twinkling of an eye. Nothing was lacking, not even the rope swinging gracefully underneath the crosspiece.

'What's their game?' Gringoire asked himself in some anxiety. At the same moment the sound of little bells put an end to his anxiety. It was a dummy which the truants had hung from the rope by its neck, a sort of scarecrow, dressed in red, and so laden down with sheep-bells and tinklers you could have harnessed thirty Castilian mules with them. These hundreds of bells shivered for a time with the swinging of the rope; then gradually grew faint and were finally silent, the dummy having been brought back to rest by the law of the pendulum, which has ousted the hour-glass and the sand-glass.

Then Clopin, showing Gringoire a rickety old stool set underneath the dummy: 'Up on there.'

'God's death!' objected Gringoire, 'I shall break my neck. Your stool limps like a couplet from Martial; one foot's a hexameter and the other a pentameter.'

'Up,' resumed Clopin.

Gringoire climbed on the stool and managed to recover his centre of gravity, though not without some swaying of the head and arms.

'Now,' the King of Thunes went on, 'twist your right foot round your left leg and stand on tiptoe.'

'Are you absolutely set on my breaking a limb, then, my lord?' said Gringoire.

Clopin shook his head.

'Listen, my friend, you talk too much. Here, briefly, is what you do. You will stand on tiptoe as I say; that way you will be able to reach the dummy's pocket; you will search it; you will pull out a purse from it; and if you do all that without us hearing any bells, fine; you will be a truant. And we shall only have to beat you black and blue for a week.'

'God's belly! I'll take good care not to,' said Gringoire. 'And if I make the bells play?'

'Then you'll be hanged. Understand?'

'I don't understand at all,' answered Gringoire.

'Listen once again. You will search the dummy and take its purse; if a single bell moves while you're doing it you'll be hanged. Understand now?'

'Right,' said Gringoire. 'I understand. And afterwards?'

'If you manage to remove the purse without the sound of bells, you're a truant, and we shall beat you black and blue for eight consecutive days. No doubt you understand now?'

'No, my lord, I do not understand. What do I gain? Hanged in one case and beaten in the other...'

'And a truant?' Clopin put in, 'and a truant, is that not something? It's in your own interest that we should beat you, so as to toughen you up for beatings.'

'Many thanks,' replied the poet.

'Come on, get a move on,' said the king, stamping on the barrel, which boomed like a bass drum. 'Search the dummy, and let's get it over with. I warn you for the last time that if I hear a single bell you will take the dummy's place.'

The band of argotiers applauded Clopin's words and formed a circle round the gallows, laughing so heartlessly that Gringoire could tell he was amusing them too much not to have everything to fear from them. There was nothing left to hope for then, unless it were his outside chance of success in the fearsome operation prescribed for him. He made up his mind to chance it, but not before he had addressed a fervent prayer to the dummy he was about to rifle and which would have been more easily moved to pity than the truants. The myriad small bells with their little brass tongues looked to him like the open jaws of so many asps, ready to hiss and to bite.

'Oh,' he said, under his breath, 'is it possible that my life should depend on the least vibration of the least of those bells! Oh,' he added, hands clasped, 'don't bell, bells! Tinklers, don't tinkle!'

He made one more approach to Trouillefou.

'And supposing a puff of wind comes?' he asked him.

'You'll be hanged,' answered the other unhesitatingly.

Seeing there was to be no respite, no stay of execution, no possible way out, he steeled himself. He twisted his right foot round his left leg, drew himself up on his left foot and stretched out his arm; but just as he touched the dummy, his body, which now had only one foot, tottered on the stool, which had only three; he tried automatically to steady himself on the dummy, lost his balance and fell heavily to the ground, quite deafened by the fatal vibration of the countless bells as the dummy, yielding to the thrust from his hand, rotated once and then swung majestically between the two posts.

'Curse it!' he cried as he fell, and he remained face downwards on the ground, like a corpse.

Meanwhile he could hear the fearful carillon above his head and the satanic laughter of the truants, and the voice of Trouillefou, saying: 'Pick the rogue up and hang him forthwith.'

He got up. They had already unhooked the dummy to make room for him.

The argotiers made him climb on the stool. Clopin came up to him, passed the rope around his neck and tapped him on the shoulder: 'Farewell, friend! You can't escape now, not even if you digested with the bowels of the pope.'

The word 'mercy' died on Gringoire's lips. He took a look around him. But it was hopeless, they were all laughing.

'Bellevigne de l'Étoile,' said the King of Thunes to an enormous truant, who left the ranks, 'climb up on the crosspiece.'

Bellevigne de l'Étoile climbed nimbly up on the crossbeam and a moment later Gringoire raised his eyes in terror to see him crouching above his head.

'Now,' Clopin Trouillefou went on, 'as soon as I clap my hands, Andry le Rouge, you knock the stool away with your knee; François Chante-Prune, you hang on to the scoundrel's feet; and you. Bellevigne, you throw yourself on his shoulders; and all three at once, d'you understand?'

Gringoire shivered.

'Ready?' said Clopin Trouillefou to the three argotiers, who were ready to hurl themselves on Gringoire like three spiders on a fly. The poor victim had a moment of horrible anticipation, while Clopin calmly pushed a few vine-shoots which the flames had not yet reached back into the fire with the end of his foot. 'Ready?' he repeated, and drew back his hands to clap. Another second and it would have been all over.

But he stopped, as if alerted by a sudden idea. 'One minute,' he said, 'I was forgetting! It's customary not to hang a man without asking whether there's a woman who wants him. Comrade, this is your last resort. You must marry either a truant or the rope.'

This law of Bohemia, however bizarre the reader may find it, is still written out in full today in the old English statutes. See *Burington's Observations.*[1]

Gringoire breathed again. This was the second time he had come back to life in the past half hour. So he did not dare place too much trust in it.

'Ho there!' cried Clopin, once more up on his cask. 'Ho there women, females, is there a ribald among you, from the witch down to her she-cat, who will have this ribald? Ho there, Colette la Charonne! Elisabeth Trouvain! Simone Jodouyne! Marie Piédebou! Thonne la Longue! Bérarde Fanouel! Michelle Genaille! Claude Ronge-Oreille! Mathurine Girorou! Ho there, Isabeau le Thierrye! Come and see! A man for nothing! Who'll have him?'

Because of the wretched state he was in, Gringoire was doubtless not very inviting. The truant women showed scant interest in the proposal. The luckless man heard them answer: 'No, no! Hang him, then we shall all enjoy him.'

However, three of them stepped out from the crowd and came to sniff round him. The first was a fat girl with a square face. She carefully inspected the philosopher's lamentable doublet. His tunic was threadbare and had more holes in it than a chestnut roaster. The girl pulled a face: 'Poor stuff!' she grumbled, then, addressing Gringoire: 'Let's see your cape.' 'I've lost it,' said Gringoire. 'Your hat?' 'It was taken away.' 'Your shoes?' 'They're beginning to lose their soles.' 'Your purse?' 'Alas,' Gringoire stammered, 'I haven't a single *denier parisis* left.' 'Let them hang you and be grateful!' answered the truant, turning her back on him.

The second one, old, black, wrinkled and hideous, ugly enough

1. Daines Barrington's *Observations on Statutes* (1766).

to be a blemish even on the Court of Miracles, circled round Gringoire. He was almost trembling in case she took him. But she said between her teeth: 'He's too thin,' and moved off.

The third one was a young girl, quite fresh and not too ugly. 'Save me!' the poor devil said to her in a low voice. She looked at him sympathetically for a moment, then lowered her eyes, made a pleat in her skirt and stood undecided. He followed her every movement with his eyes; she was his last glimmer of hope. 'No,' said the girl finally. 'No! Guillaume Longuejoue would beat me.' She went back amongst the crowd.

'Friend,' said Clopin, 'you're unlucky.'

Then, standing upright on his barrel and imitating the tones of an auctioneer's clerk, much to everyone's amusement: 'No one wants him? No one wants him? Going, going...' And he turned towards the gallows and nodded: 'Gone!'

Bellevigne de l'Étoile, Andry le Rouge and François Chante-Prune approached Gringoire once again.

At that moment a cry went up among the argotiers: 'La Esmeralda! La Esmeralda!'

Gringoire shuddered and turned to where the shouting was coming from. The crowd parted to allow through a pure and dazzling figure.

It was the gypsy girl.

'La Esmeralda!' said Gringoire, amazed, for all his emotion, at the sudden way in which that magic word had tied together all his memories of that day.

The charm and beauty of this rare creature seemed to hold sway even in the Court of Miracles. The men and women of the argot moved quietly back as she passed and their brutal faces broadened into smiles when she looked at them.

She stepped lightly up to the victim. Her pretty Djali was following her. Gringoire was more dead than alive. She considered him for a moment in silence.

'Are you going to hang this man?' she said solemnly to Clopin.

'Yes, sister,' answered the King of Thunes, 'unless you take him for your husband.'

She gave her pretty little pout with her bottom lip.

'I'll take him,' she said.

Whereupon Gringoire firmly believed that he had been living

a dream ever since that morning, and that this was its continuation.

Indeed the sudden change of fortune, though charming, was violent.

The slip knot was removed and the poet made to get off the stool. So overcome was he, he was obliged to sit down.

The Duke of Egypt, without uttering a word, brought a clay pitcher. The gypsy held it out to Gringoire. 'Throw it on the ground,' she told him.

The pitcher broke into four pieces.

'Brother,' the King of Egypt then said, laying his hands on their foreheads, 'she is your wife; sister, he is your husband. For four years. Be gone.'

SEVEN
A Wedding Night

A FEW moments later, our poet found himself in a snug, warm little room with a pointed vault, sitting before a table whose one wish seemed to be to borrow from a meat-safe hanging close beside it, with a good bed in the offing and all alone with a pretty girl. There was an element of magic about the adventure. He was beginning seriously to see himself as a character in a fairy-tale; from time to time he looked around him as if to discover whether the chariot of fire pulled by two winged chimeras, which alone could have borne him so swiftly from Tartarus to paradise, was still there. At other times he fixed his eyes stubbornly on the holes in his doublet, so as to keep tight hold of reality and not lose touch with the earth altogether. This was the one thread by which his reason still held, as it was tossed about in the spaces of his imagination.

The girl seemed to be paying him no attention; she came and went, she moved a stool, she talked to her goat, now and again she pouted. Finally she came and sat by the table and Gringoire could study her in comfort.

You, reader, were once a child or perhaps you are fortunate enough to be one still. In which case, more than once, on a sunny day, beside a quick-flowing stream (and for my own part I spent whole days at it, the most profitable of my life), you will have followed a beautiful green or blue dragonfly as it flew in rapid zigzags from bush to bush, kissing all the tips of the branches. You will remember with what loving curiosity your eyes and thoughts attached themselves to that tiny, hissing, buzzing whirlwind of purple and azure wings, and to the elusive form floating in its midst, veiled by the very rapidity of its motion. The aerial creature dimly outlined behind the flutter of its wings seemed unreal, a fancy, impossible either to touch or to see. But when at last the dragonfly settled on the tip of a reed and, holding your breath, you were able to examine the long gauze wings, the long enamel body, the two crystal eyeballs, how astonished you were and how afraid this form would once more dissolve into a shadow and the creature into a figment! If you recall such impressions, you will be able easily to understand what Gringoire felt as he contemplated the visible, palpable form of Esmeralda, which hitherto he had glimpsed only through a whirlwind of dancing, singing and tumult.

He sank deeper and deeper into his reverie. 'So that's what *La Esmeralda* is,' he said to himself, following her vaguely with his eyes. 'A celestial creature! A dancer off the streets! So much and so little! She dealt my mystery its death-blow this morning, she saved my life this evening. My evil genius! My guardian angel! A pretty woman, I do swear, and who must be madly in love with me to have taken me the way she did. That reminds me,' he said, suddenly standing up, with that feeling for truth which was the basis of his character and his philosophy, 'I don't really know how it came about, but I am her husband!'

With this idea in his head and his eyes, he approached the girl in so amorous and soldierly a fashion that she recoiled.

'What do you want with me?' she said.

'Can you ask me that, adorable Esmeralda?' replied Gringoire, in tones so passionate that even he was surprised as he heard himself speak.

The gypsy's eyes opened wide. 'I don't know what you mean.'

'Well,' Gringoire went on, becoming more and more ardent, and reflecting that the virtue confronting him was only a Court of Miracles virtue, 'am I not yours, my sweet? Are you not mine?'

And, all innocence, he took her by the waist.

The gypsy's bodice slipped through his hands like the skin of an eel. With one bound, she was at the far end of the cell, where she bent down, then straightened up again with a small dagger in her hand, before Gringoire had even had time to see where the dagger came from; angry and proud, her lips puffed out, her nostrils flared, cheeks red as lady-apples, her pupils darting fire. At the same time, the little white goat set itself in front of her and showed Gringoire its battle front, bristling with two pretty, gilded and very pointed horns. And all this in the twinkling of an eye.

The dragonfly had turned into a wasp and was looking only to sting him.

Our philosopher was nonplussed, and his bewildered gaze went from the goat to the girl and back again.

'Holy Virgin!' he said finally, once his surprise allowed him to speak, 'here's a couple of tomboys!'

The gypsy it was who broke the silence.

'You must be asking for trouble!'

'Forgive me, mademoiselle,' said Gringoire smiling. 'But why then did you take me for a husband?'

'Should I have let them hang you?'

'So,' the poet went on, somewhat disappointed in his amorous expectations, 'your only thought when you married me was to save me from the gibbet?'

'What other thought do you expect me to have had?'

Gringoire chewed his lip. 'Come,' he said, 'I'm not yet as victorious in Cupido as I thought. But what was the point of breaking that wretched pitcher then?'

All this time, Esmeralda's dagger and the goat's horns were still on the defensive.

'Mademoiselle Esmeralda,' said the poet, 'let's make a pact. I'm not the Clerk of the Court at the Châtelet and I shan't take issue with you for flying in the face of Monsieur the Provost's orders and prohibitions by carrying a dagger in Paris. You must know, though, that a week ago Noël Lescripvain was fined ten *sols parisis* for carrying a cutlass. But that's none of my business and I'm coming to the point. I swear to you on my share of Paradise that I won't come near you without your leave and permission; but give me some supper.'

At bottom, Gringoire, like M. Despréaux,[1] was none too sensual. He was not one of those swashbuckling cavaliers who take young girls by assault. In love, as in all other matters, he was all for

1. A character in one of Boileau's *Epistles*.

temporization and the middle term; and a good supper, in pleasant intimacy, seemed to him, especially when he was hungry, an excellent interlude between the prologue and dénouement of an amorous adventure.

The gypsy did not answer. She gave her contemptuous little pout, lifted her head like a bird, then burst out laughing, and the dainty dagger disappeared the way it had come, without Gringoire being able to tell where the bee had hidden its sting.

A moment later, a loaf of rye bread, a slice of bacon, a few wrinkled apples and a jug of barley-beer were on the table. Gringoire set to with a will. To judge by the furious clicking of his iron fork on the earthenware plate, it seemed that his love had all turned to appetite.

The girl sat in front of him in silence, watching him eat, obviously preoccupied by some other thought, at which she smiled now and again, while her gentle hand stroked the intelligent head of the goat, which she kept pressed gently between her knees.

This scene of reverie and voracity was illuminated by a candle of yellow wax.

Meanwhile, having appeased the first bleatings of his stomach, Gringoire felt a certain false shame when he saw that all that remained was a single apple. 'Aren't you eating, Mademoiselle Esmeralda?'

She shook her head in reply, and her pensive stare became riveted on the ceiling of the cell.

'What the devil's she got on her mind?' thought Gringoire, looking at what she was looking at. 'It can't possibly be that grinning stone dwarf carved on the keystone that's absorbing her attention like that. Damn it all, I can stand the comparison!'

He raised his voice: 'Mademoiselle!'

She seemed not to hear him.

He resumed, louder still: 'Mademoiselle Esmeralda!'

A waste of effort. The girl's thoughts were elsewhere, and Gringoire's voice did not have the power to recall them. Fortunately, the goat took a hand. It began to tug its mistress gently by the sleeve. 'What do you want, Djali?' the gypsy said quickly, as if starting awake.

'She's hungry,' said Gringoire, delighted to be opening the conversation.

La Esmeralda began to crumble some bread, which Djali ate prettily from her cupped hand.

However, Gringoire did not give her time to resume her day-dreaming. He risked a delicate question.

'So you don't want me for a husband?'

The girl eyed him hard, and said: 'No.'

'For your lover?' Gringoire went on.

She pouted and answered: 'No.'

'For your friend?' Gringoire persevered.

Again she eyed him hard, and after a moment's thought, she said: 'Perhaps.'

This 'perhaps', so dear to philosophers, emboldened Gringoire.

'Do you know what friendship is?' he asked.

'Yes,' answered the gypsy. 'It's being brother and sister, two souls which touch without merging, two fingers on one hand.'

'And love?' Gringoire continued.

'Oh, love!' she said, and her voice trembled and her eye shone. 'That's being two and only one. A man and a woman who merge into an angel. That is heaven.'

As the street-dancer said this, Gringoire was struck by her singular beauty, which he found perfectly in keeping with the almost Oriental exaltation of her words. Her pure, pink lips were half smiling; her serene, child-like brow was clouded over now and again by her thoughts, like a mirror by a breath; a sort of ineffable light came from her long, black, downcast eyelashes, and lent her profile that ideal sweetness which Raphael later discovered at the point of mystical intersection between virginity, motherhood and divinity.

Gringoire persevered just the same.

'What should I be like to please you?'

'You must be a man.'

'Well, what am I now then?' he said.

'A man has a helmet on his head, a sword in his hand and golden spurs at his heels.'

'Good,' said Gringoire, 'without a horse no man. Are you in love with someone?'

'In love?'

'In love.'

She thought for a moment, then said with a peculiar expression: 'I shall know that soon.'

'Why not tonight?' the poet went on, fondly. 'Why not me?'

She looked at him gravely.

'I could only love a man who was able to protect me.'

Gringoire blushed and took the hint. The girl was obviously referring to the poor support he had given her in the critical situation she had found herself in two hours earlier. The memory of it, which had been erased by the evening's other adventures, came back to him. He clapped his hand to his brow.

'That reminds me, mademoiselle, I should have started with that. Forgive me for being so silly and absent-minded. How did you manage to escape the clutches of Quasimodo?'

This question made the gypsy shudder.

'Oh, the horrible hunchback!' she said, hiding her face in her hands; and she shivered as if with severe cold.

'Horrible, indeed!' said Gringoire, not letting go of his idea, 'but how did you get away from him?'

La Esmeralda smiled, sighed and remained silent.

'Do you know why he had followed you?' Gringoire went on, trying to get back to his question by a detour.

'I don't know,' said the girl. And she added quickly: 'But you were following me too, why did you?'

'To be perfectly honest,' answered Gringoire, 'I don't know either.'

There was a silence. Gringoire hacked at the table with his knife. The girl smiled and seemed to be staring at something through the wall. Suddenly she began to sing in a barely articulate voice:

Quando las pintadas aves
Mudas están, y la tierra . . .[1]

She suddenly broke off and started stroking Djali.

'That's a pretty animal you've got there,' said Gringoire.

'She's my sister,' she replied.

'Why do they call you La Esmeralda?' asked the poet.

'I've no idea.'

'You must have.'

1. 'When the coloured birds
Are silent, and the earth . . .'

From her bosom she drew a sort of small oblong sachet hanging round her neck on a chain of margosa seeds. The sachet smelt strongly of camphor. It was covered in green silk and had a big green glass bead at the centre, in imitation of an emerald.

'Perhaps it's because of this,' she said.

Gringoire tried to take the sachet. She moved back. 'Don't touch it. It's an amulet; you would hurt the charm or the charm would hurt you.'

The poet's curiosity was becoming more and more aroused.

'Who gave it to you?'

She put a finger to her lips and hid the amulet in her bosom. He tried other questions, but she scarcely answered.

'What does the word *La Esmeralda* mean?'

'I don't know,' she said.

'What language does it come from?'

'Egyptian, I think.'

'I thought as much,' said Gringoire, 'you don't come from France?'

'I've no idea.'

'Are your parents alive?'

She started to sing, to an old melody:

> My father and mother
> Are birds of the air
> When I cross the water
> No boat need I there
> My father and mother
> Are birds of the air.

'That's nice,' said Gringoire. 'At what age did you come to France?'

'Very young.'

'To Paris?'

'Last year. Just as we were coming in by the Porte Papale I saw a reed-warbler shoot into the air; it was the end of August; I said: It will be a hard winter.'

'It was,' said Gringoire, delighted at the way the conversation had started, 'I spent it blowing on my hands. You have the gift of prophecy then?'

She became uncommunicative again.

'No.'

'That man you called the Duke of Egypt, is he the chief of your tribe?'

'Yes.'

'Yet it's he who married us,' the poet remarked shyly.

She gave her usual pretty grimace. 'I don't even know your name.'

'My name? If you want it, here it is: Pierre Gringoire.'

'I know a better one,' she said.

'Naughty girl!' rejoined the poet. 'Never mind, you shan't annoy me. Here, perhaps you'll like me when you get to know me better; you've told me your story so trustingly that I owe you a bit of mine. You must know then that my name is Pierre Gringoire and I'm the son of the farmer in the tabellionage[1] of Gonesse. My father was hanged by the Burgundians and my mother disembowelled by the Picards, at the time of the siege of Paris, twenty years ago. So at the age of six I was an orphan, and the only sole I had under my feet was the paving-stones of Paris. I don't know how I crossed the gap between six and sixteen. A fruit-seller would give me a plum and a baker throw me a crust. In the evenings I used to be picked up by the constables, who put me in prison, and there I found a bundle of straw. As you can see, none of that prevented me growing older and thinner. In the winter, I used to warm myself in the sun, under the porch of the Hôtel de Sens, and I thought it was quite ridiculous that the Midsummer's Day bonfire should be kept for the dog-days. At sixteen, I tried to find a trade. I tried everything in turn. I became a soldier, but I wasn't brave enough. I became a monk, but I wasn't pious enough. Nor can I hold my drink. In despair, I went as an apprentice in the timberyard; but I wasn't strong enough. I had more of a leaning to be a schoolmaster; it's true I couldn't read, but that was no reason. After a time I realized I lacked something for everything, and finding I was good for nothing, I became of my own free will a poet and composer of rhymes. That's a trade you can always take up when you're a vagabond and it's better than stealing, which is what some young brigands I was friendly with advised me to do. By good fortune, one fine day I met Dom Claude Frollo, the reverend archdeacon of Notre-Dame. He took an interest in me, and it is thanks to him that today I am a true scholar; I

1. A medieval tax district.

know Latin from the *Offices* of Cicero to the *Mortuology* of the Celestine Fathers, and I am no barbarian in either scholastics, poetics, rhythmics, or even hermetics, that wisdom of wisdoms. I am the author of the mystery play they performed today with such signal success and before such great numbers of people in the great hall of the palace itself. I have also written a book which will have six hundred pages, on the prodigious comet of 1465 which sent one man mad. I have had yet other successes. Being something of a gun-smith, I worked on Jean Maugue's great bombard, which as you know burst the day they were trying it out at the Pont de Charenton and killed twenty-four bystanders. As you can see, I'm no bad match. I know lots of very fetching sorts of tricks I can teach your goat; to imitate the Bishop of Paris, for example, that accursed pharisee whose mills splash the passers-by all along the Pont-aux-Meuniers. And then my mystery play will bring me in a lot of silver money, if I get paid. Anyway, I am at your command, I and my wit, and my letters, ready to live with you, demoiselle, any way you wish, chastely or joyously, as husband and wife if you think that right, or brother and sister if you prefer that.'

Gringoire fell silent, watching for the effects of his harangue on the girl. Her eyes were fixed on the ground.

'*Phoebus*,' she said in an undertone. Then, turning to the poet: 'What does *Phoebus* mean?'

Gringoire was not sure he saw any connection between this question and his own allocution, but he was nothing loth to show off his erudition. He answered, preening himself: 'It's a Latin word meaning "sun".'

'Sun!' she went on.

'It was the name of a very handsome archer, who was a god,' added Gringoire.

'God!' the gypsy echoed. And there was something both thoughtful and passionate in her tone.

At that moment, one of her bracelets came undone and fell off. Gringoire quickly bent down to pick it up. When he stood up again the girl and the goat had vanished. He heard the sound of a bolt. A small door, which no doubt led to a neighbouring cell, had been fastened on the outside.

'Has she left me a bed at least?' said our philosopher.

He walked round the cell. The only piece of furniture suitable for sleeping on was a reasonably long wooden chest, but even that had a carved lid, so that when Gringoire stretched himself out on it it made him feel more or less what Micromegas[1] would have felt had he lain down full length on the Alps.

'Come on,' he said, making himself as comfortable as he could. 'We must make do. But what a strange wedding night. Pity. There was something pleasantly naïve and antediluvian about that marriage by broken pitcher!'

1. A giant in one of Voltaire's stories, who was eight leagues tall.

BOOK THREE

ONE
Notre-Dame

THE church of Notre-Dame of Paris is without doubt, even today, a sublime and majestic building. But however much it may have conserved its beauty as it has grown older, it is hard not to regret, not to feel indignation at the numberless degradations and mutilations which time and men have wrought simultaneously on this venerable monument, respecting neither Charlemagne, who laid its first stone, nor Philip-Augustus, who laid the last.

Beside each wrinkle on the face of this old queen of our cathedrals, you will find a scar. *Tempus edax, homo edacior.*[1] Which I would gladly translate as 'Time is blind, man is stupid'.

Had we the leisure to examine, one by one, with the reader, the various traces of destruction imprinted on this ancient church, time's share would be the lesser, that of men the greater, and especially men of 'the art'. I have to say 'men of the art' because in the past two centuries certain individuals have adopted the title of 'architect'.

And first of all, to cite only one or two prime examples, there are certainly few more beautiful pages of architecture than the façade where, successively yet simultaneously, the three recessed and pointed doorways, the jagged and embroidered band of the twenty-eight niches of the kings, the huge central rose-window, flanked by its two side-windows, like the priest by his deacon and subdeacon, the tall, flimsy gallery of trefoiled arches bearing a heavy platform on its slender colonnettes, and finally the two massive black towers with their slate louvres, all harmonious parts of one magnificent whole, superimposed in five gigantic storeys, unfold before the eye in one untroubled mass, the innumerable details of whose statuary, sculptures and carvings are powerfully conjoined to the tranquil grandeur of the whole; a vast symphony in stone, as it were; the colossal handiwork of a man and a people, a whole both one and complex, like its sisters, the *Iliad* and the *Romanceros*;[2] the pro-

1. 'Time erodes, man erodes more.'

2. The corpus of Spanish romances or ballads, which appealed to Romantics like Hugo as at once an exotic and a popular art-form. They were translated into French by his brother Abel.

digious sum contributed by all the resources of an age where, on every stone, you can see, standing out in a hundred ways, the imagination of the workman, disciplined by the genius of the artist; a sort of human creation, in short, as powerful and as fecund as that divine creation whose twin characteristics of variety and eternity it seems to have purloined.

And what we have said here of the façade has to be said of the church as a whole; and what we have said of the cathedral church of Paris has to be said of all the churches of medieval Christendom. Everything is of a piece in this logical, well-proportioned art, which originated in itself. To measure the toe is to measure the giant.

But let us return to the façade of Notre-Dame such as it presents itself to us today, when we go devoutly to admire the solemn, mighty and, according to its chroniclers, terrifying cathedral, *quae mole sua terrorem incutit spectantibus*.[1]

Three important things are missing from that façade today. First, the flight of eleven steps which formerly raised it above the ground; then, the bottom row of statues which occupied the niches in the three portals; and the upper row of the twenty-eight earliest kings of France, which filled the first-floor gallery, from Childebert up until Philip-Augustus, holding the 'apple of empire' in their hands.

It is time that has caused the steps to disappear, by slowly and irresistibly raising the level of the ground in the Cité. But while it may have caused the eleven steps which enhanced the building's majestic height to be swallowed up one by one by the rising tide of Paris's pavements, time has perhaps restored to the church more than it took away, for it is time which has overspread the façade with the sombre colouring of antiquity, which makes the old age of monuments the age of their beauty.

But who overthrew the two rows of statues? Who left the niches empty? Who cut that new and bastard ogive right in the middle of the central doorway? Who had the audacity to hang there, next to Biscornette's arabesques, that heavy, insipid wooden door with its Louis Quinze carvings? Men: the architects, the artists of our own day.

And if we enter the interior of the building, who overthrew that

1. 'Which by its mass fills spectators with terror.'

colossal Saint Christopher, as proverbial among statues as the great hall of the palace was among halls, or the spire of Strasbourg among steeples? And the myriad statues that thronged the bays of the nave and the choir, kneeling, standing, mounted on horseback, men, women, children, bishops, men-at-arms, in stone, marble, gold, silver, bronze, even wax; who swept them brutally away? It was not time.

And who replaced the old Gothic altar, and its splendid clutter of shrines and reliquaries, with that heavy marble sarcophagus, with its angels' heads and clouds, which looks like some oddment from the Val-de-Grâce or the Invalides?[1] Who was foolish enough to set that heavy stone anachronism into Hercandus's Carolingian pavement? Louis XIV, was it not, fulfilling the vow of Louis XIII?[2]

And who put in those cold white windows in place of the stained-glass, 'high in colour', which made our forefathers' gaze hesitate wonderingly between the rose-window above the doorway and the pointed arches of the apse? And what would a sub-cantor of the sixteenth century say if he could see the beautiful yellow distemper with which our archiepiscopal vandals have daubed their cathedral? He would be reminded that that was the colour with which the hangman used to smear 'incriminated' buildings; he would recall the Hôtel du Petit-Bourbon too being coated with yellow after the constable's treason, 'a yellow of such good stamp, after all,' says Sauval, 'and so well recommended, that more than a century has not been able to make it lose its colour.' He would think that the house of God had become infamous and would flee from it.

And if we climb to the top of the cathedral, ignoring on the way countless barbarities of every kind, what have they done with that delightful little spire that stood above the crossing and which, no less frail and no less bold than its neighbour (likewise destroyed) on the Sainte-Chapelle, penetrated deeper into the sky than the towers, slender, pointed, sonorous and transparent? An architect of taste amputated it (1787) and thought it sufficient to disguise the wound with a large lead cataplasm looking like the lid of a saucepan.

Such is the treatment the marvellous art of the Middle Ages has

1. Examples of a later, neo-Classical architecture.

2. Hercandus was supposedly the forty-second Bishop of Paris under Charlemagne; Louis XIII vowed to repair the high altar in 1638, Louis XIV laid the first stone in 1699.

had in almost every country, but especially in France. On its ruins three kinds of lesion can be seen, all of them affecting it to different depths: time, first of all, which has imperceptibly chipped the surface in places and rusted it everywhere; then, political and religious revolutions, blind and wrathful by their very nature, which have dashed against it in a frenzy, rending its rich garment of sculptures and reliefs, bursting in its rose-windows, snapping its necklaces of arabesques and figurines, uprooting its statues, some because of their mitres, others because of their crowns; and lastly, the ever more foolish and grotesque fashions which, since the anarchic but magnificent aberrations of the Renaissance, have succeeded one another in the necessary decadence of architecture. Fashions have done more harm than revolutions. They have cut into the quick, they have attacked the wooden bone-structures of the art, they have hewn and hacked and disorganized, and have killed the building, in its form as well as its symbolism, its logic as well as its beauty. They have also remade it: which neither time nor revolutions had presumed to do. Shamelessly, and in the name of 'good taste', they have stuck their wretched, ephemeral baubles over the wounds in the Gothic architecture, their ribbons of marble, their metal pompoms; and a veritable leprosy of ovolos, scrolls, surrounds, drapery, garlands, fringes, stone flames, bronze clouds, sated Cupids, fat-cheeked cherubims, which was already beginning to engulf the face of the art in Catherine de' Medici's oratory and which caused it to expire, two centuries later, in an agonized grimace, in the Dubarry's boudoir.[1]

To summarize, then, the points we have been making: Gothic architecture is today disfigured by three sorts of devastation. The wrinkles and warts on its skin are the work of time; the acts of violence, the brutalities, bruises and fractures, the work of revolutions, from Luther to Mirabeau. The mutilations, amputations and dislocations of its limbs, the *restorations*, are the Greek, Roman and barbarian work of the professors, following Vitruvius and Vignolo.[2] The magnificent art produced by the Vandals has been

1. Catherine de' Medici was the wife of King Henri II and regent after 1560; she died in 1589. The Comtesse du Barry, the mistress of Louis XV, was guillotined in 1793.

2. Architectural authorities of the High Renaissance. Vitruvius was the great architectural legislator of Rome, and died in 26 BC; Vignolo was an Italian

killed by the academies. To the centuries and the revolutions, which at least laid waste with impartiality and grandeur, has been added the swarm of architects from the schools, licensed, sworn and attested, defacing with the choice and discernment of bad taste, and replacing Gothic tracery with Louis Quinze chicory to the greater glory of the Parthenon. This is the ass kicking the dying lion. This is the old oak tree, in its decline, being stung, bitten and shredded by caterpillars for good measure.

How far we have come from the days when Robert Cenalis compared Notre-Dame of Paris to the famous Temple of Diana at Ephesus, 'so vaunted by the ancient pagans', which immortalized Erostratus, and found the Gallic cathedral 'more excellent in length, breadth, height and construction'.[1]

Notre-Dame of Paris is not, for the rest, what could be called a complete, determinate or classified monument. No longer a Romanesque church, it is not yet a Gothic church. It is not a typical edifice. Notre-Dame of Paris does not have, like the Abbey of Tournus, the solemn, massive build, the broad circular vaulting, the glacial bareness, the majestic simplicity of those buildings engendered by the rounded arch. It is not, like Bourges cathedral, the magnificent, light, multiform, intricate, spiky, efflorescent product of the pointed arch. It is not to be aligned with that ancient family of churches that are sombre, squat, mysterious and as if crushed by the rounded arch; Egyptian almost, but for their ceilings; all hieroglyphic, priestly and symbolic; with more lozenges and zigzags in their ornamentation than flowers, more flowers than animals and more animals than men; the creation not so much of the architect as of the bishop; a first transformation of the art, stamped throughout with a military, theocratic discipline, which took root in the Byzantine Empire and ended with William the Conqueror. Nor is it possible to place our cathedral in that other family of tall, airy churches, rich in stained-glass and sculptures; pointed in their forms and bold in their attitudes; communal and bourgeois as political symbols, free, whimsical and unrestrained as works of art; a second transformation of architecture, no longer hieroglyphic, immutable and priestly, but

---

architect of the sixteenth century and wrote an influential *Treatise on the Five Orders of Architecture.*

1. Erostratus was an Ephesian who burnt the temple down, so as to ensure that his name should survive.

artistic, progressive and popular, which begins with the return from the Crusades and ends with Louis XI. Notre-Dame of Paris is not of pure Roman stock like the first, nor of pure Arab stock like the second.

It is a building of the transition. The Saxon architect was just finishing erecting the first pillars of the nave, when the pointed arch arrived from the Crusades and settled in triumph on those broad, Romanesque capitals, which were to have carried only rounded arches. Thereafter, the pointed arch was master, and built the rest of the church. To start with, however, it was inexperienced and shy, it grew wider and more flared, it held itself back, not daring as yet to soar up in spires and lancets as it was to do later in so many wonderful cathedrals. It was as if it felt the proximity of those heavy Romanesque pillars.

Yet these buildings of the transition from Romanesque to Gothic repay study just as much as the pure types. They express a nuance of the art that would have been lost without them: the grafting of the pointed arch on to the rounded arch.

Notre-Dame of Paris is a particularly curious specimen of this variety. Each face, each stone of this venerable monument is a page not only of our country's history, but also of the history of science and architecture. Thus, to indicate only the main details: whereas the little Porte-Rouge achieves almost the ultimate in fifteenth-century Gothic delicacy, the pillars of the nave, their volume and weightiness, go back to the Carolingian abbey of Saint-Germain-des-Prés. You would think that door and pillars were six centuries apart. In the symbols of the great portal, even the hermeticists can find a satisfying digest of their science, of which the church of Saint-Jacques-de-la-Boucherie was so complete a hieroglyph. Thus, the Romanesque abbey, the philosophical church, Gothic art, Saxon art, the heavy round pillar recalling Gregory VII, the hermetic symbolism by which Nicolas Flamel preceded Luther, papal unity, the schism, Saint-Germain-des-Prés, Saint-Jacques-de-la-Boucherie: all are fused, combined and amalgamated in Notre-Dame. This central, generative church is a sort of chimera among the old churches of Paris: it has the head of one, the limbs of another, the cruppers of a third; something of all of them.

We repeat, these hybrid constructions are not the least interesting for the artist, the antiquary and the historian. They make us aware to what extent architecture is a primitive thing, demonstrating as they do, like the cyclopean remains, the pyramids of Egypt, or the gigantic Hindu pagodas, that architecture's greatest products are less individual than social creations; the offspring of nations in labour rather than the outpouring of men of genius; the deposit left behind by a nation; the accumulation of the centuries; the residue from the successive evaporations of human society; in short, a kind of formation. Each wave of time lays down its alluvium, each race deposits its own stratum on the monument, each individual contributes his stone. Thus do the beavers, and the bees; and thus does man. The great symbol of architecture, Babel, is a beehive.

Great buildings, like great mountains, are the work of centuries. Often architecture is transformed while they are still under construction: *pendent opera interrupta*,[1] they proceed quickly in keeping with the transformation. The new architecture takes the monument as it finds it, is incrusted on it, assimilates it to itself, develops it as it wants and, if possible, finishes it. This is achieved without fuss, or strain, or reaction, in accordance with a tranquil law of nature. A graft occurs, the sap circulates, the vegetation recovers. Indeed, many a massive tome and often the universal history of mankind might be written from these successive weldings of different styles at different levels of a single monument. The man, the individual and the artist are erased from these great piles, which bear no author's name; they are the summary and summation of human intelligence. Time is the architect, the nation the builder.

If we here consider only the architecture of Christian Europe, that younger sister of the great stone structures of the East, it appears to the eye as an immense formation divided into three clearly differentiated zones laid one on top of the other: the Romanesque zone, the Gothic zone and the zone of the Renaissance, which we would gladly call the Greco-Roman. The Romanesque layer, which is the oldest and deepest, is occupied by the rounded arch, which reappears, supported by the Greek column, in the top, modern layer of the Renaissance. The pointed arch comes between the two. Those buildings which belong exclusively to one of these three layers are perfectly distinct, unified and complete. Such are the Abbey of Jumièges, the Cathedral of Rheims, Sainte-Croix at Orléans. But these three zones intermingle and merge at the edges,

1. 'Interrupted works are suspended.'

like the colours in the solar spectrum. Hence those complex monuments, the buildings of nuance and transition. One has Romanesque feet, a Gothic middle, and a Greco-Roman head. This is because it took six hundred years to build. The species is not common. The keep at Etampes is one specimen. But monuments of two formations are more common. Such is Notre-Dame of Paris, a pointed building, whose earliest pillars plunge down into that Romanesque zone in which the portal of Saint-Denis and the nave of Saint-Germain-des-Prés are also plunged. Such is the delightful semi-Gothic chapterhouse at Bocherville, where the Romanesque layer extends halfway up the body. Such is Rouen cathedral, which would be wholly Gothic did not the very tip of its central spire dip into the zone of the Renaissance.

But all these distinctions and differences affect only the surfaces of buildings. Architecture has changed its skin. The actual constitution of the Christian church is unaffected. There is still the same inner framework, the same logical disposition of the parts. The envelope of a cathedral may be sculptured and embroidered but beneath it you always find, at least in an embryonic or rudimentary form, the Roman basilica. It extends over the ground in accordance with the one everlasting law. There are, imperturbably, two naves intersecting in a cross, whose top end is rounded into an apse and forms the choir; there are always side-aisles, for internal processions and for chapels, a kind of lateral promenade into which the nave empties through the bays. Once this has been established, the number of chapels, portals, towers and spires can be varied *ad infinitum*, as the century or the nation, or the style dictates. Once the act of worship has been provided for and ensured, the architecture can do as it pleases. Statues, stained-glass, rose-windows, arabesques, denticulations, capitals, bas-reliefs, it can combine all such flights of fancy according to whatever logarithm suits it. Hence the prodigious external variety of buildings within which there dwells so great an order and unity. The trunk of the tree is immutable, the foliage capricious.

TWO

A Bird's Eye View of Paris

WE have just tried to repair for the reader the admirable church of Notre-Dame of Paris. We have pointed, hurriedly, to most of the beauties which it possessed in the fifteenth century and which it lacks today; but we omitted the chief of these: the view of Paris one then enjoyed from the top of its towers.

When, after groping your way lengthily up the gloomy spiral staircase, which rises vertically up through the thick wall of the bell-towers, you abruptly emerged at last on to one of the two lofty platforms, flooded with air and daylight, a beautiful panorama unfolded itself simultaneously before you on every side: a spectacle *sui generis*, easily imagined by those of our readers lucky enough to have seen a complete, unimpaired, homogeneous Gothic town, a few of which still survive, such as Nuremberg in Bavaria, or Vittoria in Spain; or even smaller specimens, provided they are well preserved, like Vitré in Normandy or Nordhausen in Prussia.

The Paris of three hundred and fifty years ago, the Paris of the fifteenth century, was already a town of vast size. We Parisians generally deceive ourselves over the headway we have made since then. Since Louis XI, Paris has not grown by much more than a third. It has, for a fact, lost much more in beauty than it has gained in size.

Paris was born, as we know, on the old island of the Cité, which is shaped like a cradle. The shoreline of the island was its first city wall, the Seine its first moat. Paris remained an island for several centuries, with two bridges, one to the north, the other to the south, and two bridgeheads, which were at once its gateways and its fortresses, the Grand-Châtelet on the right bank and the Petit-Châtelet on the left. Then, at the time of its first race of kings, too constricted on its island, where it no longer had room to turn round, Paris crossed the water. A first perimeter of walls and towers began to eat into the countryside on either side of the Seine, beyond the Grand and the Petit-Châtelet. A few vestiges of this ancient enclosure still remained in the last century; today, only the memory of it is left, and an occasional tradition; the Porte Baudets or Baudoyer, *Porta Bagauda*. Gradually, the tide of houses, forever thrusting outwards from the heart of the town, swamped, eroded, wore away and obliterated this wall. Philip-Augustus built a fresh dyke for it. He imprisoned Paris in a circular chain of great tall, solid towers. For more than a century, the houses were compressed and accumulated in this basin, and their level rose like water in a reservoir. They began to grow deeper, storey was added to storey, they climbed on top of one another, they spurted upwards like any compressed sap, vying to outreach their neighbours in the quest for air. The streets became more and more narrow and cavernous; the squares were all filled in, and vanished. Finally, the houses leapt over Philip-Augustus's wall and spread across the plain, in glorious disarray, like refugees. Here, they snuggled down, they hacked gardens out of the fields and took their ease. By 1367, the town was spreading so much into the suburb that a new enclosure was needed, especially on the right bank. Charles V built one. But a town like Paris is in perpetual spate. Towns of this kind alone become capital cities. They are craters into which run all of a country's geographical, political, moral and intellectual slopes, all of a people's natural inclinations; wells of civilization, as it were, but also sewers, into which, drop by drop and century by century, trade, industry, intelligence and population, all the sap, all the life, all the soul of a nation, ceaselessly filter and accumulate. Charles V's wall suffered the same fate as Philip Augustus's. By the end of the fifteenth century, it had been overstepped and superseded, and the suburb was expanding. In the sixteenth century, the wall seemed to retreat visibly and to be more and more submerged in the old town, so dense had the new town outside now grown. Thus, as early as the fifteenth century, if we stop there, Paris had already worn out the three concentric circles of wall which, in the days of Julian the Apostate, had existed in embryo, as it were, in the Grand-Châtelet and the Petit-Châtelet. One by one, the mighty town had burst its four belts of wall, like a growing child splitting last year's clothes. Under Louis XI, a few groups of ruined towers from the old containing walls could be seen sticking up here and there through this sea of houses, like the peaks of hills through floodwater, or like an archipelago of the old Paris submerged beneath the new.

Since then, Paris has changed even more, unfortunately for our eyes; but it has only crossed one more wall, that of Louis XV, that miserable wall of mud and spittle, worthy of the king who built it and of the poet who celebrated it:

Le mur murant Paris rend Paris murmurant [1]

In the fifteenth century, Paris was still divided into three quite distinct and separate towns, each with its own physiognomy, speciality, way of life, customs, privileges and history: the City, the University and the Town. The City, which occupied the island, was the oldest and the smallest, and the mother of the other two, between which it was sandwiched, if we be allowed the comparison, like a little old woman between two beautiful, strapping daughters. The University covered the left bank of the Seine, from the Tournelle to the Tour de Nesle, points corresponding in the Paris of today one to the Halle aux Vins, the other to the Mint. Its boundary wall took quite a large bite out of the countryside where Julian had built his baths. Mount Sainte-Geneviève was included in it. The curved walls culminated at the Porte Papale, that is to say roughly the present site of the Panthéon. The Town, which was the largest of the three portions of Paris, had the right bank. Its quay, though it was broken or interrupted at several points, ran along the Seine from the Tour de Billy to the Tour de Bois, that is to say from the place where the Grenier de Réserve now is to where the Tuileries now are. These four points where the Seine cut the ring-wall of the capital, the Tournelle and the Tour de Nesle on the left, the Tour de Billy and the Tour de Bois on the right, were known pre-eminently as 'the four towers of Paris'. The Town had encroached even further on the landscape than the University. The enclosure of the Town (Charles V's enclosure) culminated at the Porte Saint-Denis and the Porte Saint-Martin, whose location has not changed.

As we have just said, each of these three great divisions of Paris was a town, but a town too specialized to be complete, a town which could not do without the other two. Thus three quite separate aspects. The City abounded in churches, the Town in palaces, the University in colleges. Leaving aside here the minor oddities of old Paris and the caprices of local jurisdictions, we can say, in general terms and considering only the overall pattern in that chaos of communal jurisdictions, that the island belonged to the bishop, the

1. 'The wall enclosing Paris makes Paris murmur.'

right bank to the merchants' provost and the left bank to the rector. And over them all, the Provost of Paris, a royal, not a municipal officer. The City had Notre-Dame, the Town the Louvre and the University the Sorbonne. The Town had Les Halles, the City the Hôtel-Dieu, the University the Pré-aux-Clercs. The offence which a student committed on the left bank, in the Pré-aux-Clercs, was tried on the island, in the Palais de Justice, and punished on the right bank, at Montfaucon. Unless the rector, sensing the University to be strong and the king weak, should intervene: for it was a privilege of the students to be hanged in their own part of the town.

Most of these privileges, be it remarked in passing – and there were better ones than this – had been extorted from the king by revolts and mutinies. Such is the immemorial pattern. The king only lets go when the people snatches. There is an old charter which puts the matter of fidelity simple-mindedly: *Civibus fidelitas in reges, quae tamen aliquoties seditionibus interrupta, multa peperit privilegia.*[1]

In the fifteenth century, the Seine washed five islands within the walls of Paris: the Île Louviers, where there were then trees and where there is now only wood; the Île aux Vaches and the Île Notre-Dame, both deserted, one tumbledown house apart, both fiefs of the bishop (in the seventeenth century these two islands were made into one, which was then built on and is now known as the Île Saint-Louis); and finally the Cité, with, at its tip, the cow-ferryman's little island, which has since sunk beneath the esplanade of the Pont-Neuf. In those days the City had five bridges; three on the right, the Pont Notre-Dame and the Pont-au-Change, of stone, and the Pont-aux-Meuniers, of wood; two on the left, the Petit-Pont, of stone, and the Pont Saint-Michel, of wood: all with houses on them. The University had six gates built by Philip-Augustus: starting from the Tournelle, these were the Porte Saint-Victor, the Porte Bordelle, the Porte Papale, the Porte Saint-Jacques, the Porte Saint-Michel, the Porte Saint-Germain. The Town had six gates built by Charles V: starting from the Tour de Billy, the Porte Saint-Antoine, the Porte du Temple, the Porte Saint-Martin, the Porte Saint-Denis, the Porte Montmartre, the Porte Saint-Honoré. All these gates were strong, and beautiful too, for strength is not impaired by beauty. A wide, deep moat, quick-flowing in the

1. 'Loyalty to kings, though interrupted by several uprisings, has procured for the citizens many privileges.'

winter spates, washed the foot of the walls right the way round Paris; the Seine supplied the water. At night, the gates were closed, the river barricaded at either end of the town with huge iron chains, and Paris slept in peace.

Seen from above, these three burghs, the City, the University and the Town, each appeared as an inextricable mesh of weirdly ravelled streets. Yet you could tell at first glance that these three fragments of city formed a single whole. You at once noticed two long, unbroken, undisturbed, parallel streets, which ran almost in a straight line through all three towns at once, from end to end, from south to north, at right angles to the Seine, binding them together and mingling them, infusing, pouring and decanting the inhabitants of one within the walls of another and making the three of them one. The first of these two streets went from the Porte Saint-Jacques to the Porte Saint-Martin; in the University it was known as the Rue Saint-Jacques, in the City as the Rue de la Juiverie, in the Town as the Rue Saint-Martin; it crossed the water twice under the names of the Petit-Pont and the Pont Notre-Dame. The second, which was called the Rue de la Harpe on the left bank, the Rue de la Barillerie on the Island, the Rue Saint-Denis on the right bank, the Pont Saint-Michel on one arm of the Seine and the Pont-au-Change on the other, ran from the Porte Saint-Michel in the University to the Porte Saint-Denis in the Town.

Beneath all these different names, they were still the same two streets, but the two original streets, the generators, the twin arteries of Paris. The other veins of this threefold town all either fed from them or emptied into them.

Independently of these two principal, diametrical thoroughfares, which cut right through Paris from one side to the other and were common to the whole capital, the Town and University each had its own main street, running longitudinally parallel to the Seine and cutting the two arterial streets at right angles as it went. Thus in the Town you descended in a straight line from the Porte Saint-Antoine to the Porte Saint-Honoré; in the University, from the Porte Saint-Victor to the Porte Saint-Germain. These two great thoroughfares intersected with the first two to form the canvas on which rested the densely knotted, labyrinthine network of Paris's streets. By studying the incomprehensible pattern of this network closely, you could make out in addition, like two splayed sheaves of corn, one in the University and the other in the Town, two clumps of large streets fanning outwards from the bridges to the gates.

Something of this geometrical design still survives today. And now, what view of the whole presented itself from on top of the towers of Notre-Dame in 1482? That is what we shall try to say.

As he reached the summit, the out-of-breath spectator was at once bedazzled by roofs, chimneys, streets, bridges, squares, spires, bell-towers. Everything struck him at once, the carved gable, the pointed roof, the turret suspended from the corner of the walls, the stone pyramid from the eleventh century, the slate obelisk from the fifteenth, the bare round tower of the castle-keep, the decorated square tower of the church, the big, the small, the massive and the ethereal. The eye was held long at every level of this labyrinth, where there was nothing which did not have its own originality, its own reason, its own genius, its own beauty, nothing that did not belong to the art of architecture, from the smallest house, with its carved and painted front, its exposed timbers, its rounded doorway, its overhanging upper storeys, to the royal Louvre, which then had a colonnade of towers. But the principal masses visible to the eye once it had begun to adjust to this chaos of buildings, were these.

First, the City. The Île de la Cité, says Sauval, whose farrago sometimes contains these happy accidents of style: 'the Île de la Cité is made like a great ship embedded in the mud and stranded in the current towards the middle of the Seine.' We have just explained that in the fifteenth century this ship was moored to the two banks of the river by five bridges. This nautical shape had also struck the heraldic scribes for, according to Favyn and Pasquier, it was from it and not from the Norman siege that the ship on Paris's old coat of arms derived. For those who can decipher it, blazonry is an algebra, a language. The whole history of the second half of the Middle Ages is written in blazonry, just as the history of the first half is written in the symbolism of Romanesque churches. They are the hieroglyphs of feudalism, succeeding those of theocracy.

The Cité was the first thing you saw then, with its stern to the east and its prow to the west. If you faced the prow, you had before you an innumerable flock of old roofs, above which swelled the broad, leaded chevet of the Sainte-Chapelle, like an elephant carrying a castle on its hindquarters. Only in this case the castle was the most daring, the most highly wrought, the finest carpentered, the most jagged spire ever to show the sky through its cone of tracery. Close at hand, in front of Notre-Dame, three streets flowed into the parvis, a handsome square of old houses. Over its south side leant the sullen, wrinkled façade of the Hôtel-Dieu and its roof, which seemed to be covered in pustules and warts. Then to right, left, east and west, yet all within the narrow confines of the City, rose the belfries of its twenty-one churches, of every date, shape and size, from the low, decrepit Romanesque campanile of Saint-Denys-du-Pas, *carcer Glaucini*, to the slender spires of Saint-Pierre-aux-Bœufs and Saint-Landry.

Behind Notre-Dame, to the north, stretched the cloister, with its Gothic galleries; to the south, the semi-Romanesque palace of the bishop; to the east, the deserted tip of the Terrain. Amidst this jumble of houses the eye could still pick out, by the tall, open-work stone mitres which then crowned the topmost windows of the palace on the roof itself, the hôtel given by the town to Juvénal des Ursins under Charles VI; a little further off, the tarred sheds of the Marché-Palus; elsewhere again the new apse of Saint-Germain-le-Vieux, lengthened in 1458 by a bit of the Rue aux Febvres; and then, at random, a crossroads choked with people; a pillory standing at a street corner; a section of Philip-Augustus's beautiful paving, of magnificent flagstones, laid in the middle of the roadway and scored by the horses' hooves, and so inadequately replaced in the sixteenth century by the wretched cobbles known as the 'pavement of the League'; a deserted backyard with one of those diaphanous staircase turrets such as they built in the fifteenth century and of which you can still see an example in the Rue de Bourdonnais. Finally, to westward, to the right of the Sainte-Chapelle, the towers of the Palais de Justice sat grouped beside the water. The tall trees of the king's gardens, which covered the western tip of the Cité, masked the ferryman's little island. As for the river, from on top of the towers of Notre-Dame, it was scarcely visible on either side of the Cité. The Seine had vanished beneath the bridges, and the bridges beneath the houses.

And once your gaze had crossed these bridges, whose roofs, you could see, had turned green, mildewed before their time by the effluvia from the water, the first building to strike it, if it was directed to the left, towards the University, was a huge, low clump of towers, the Petit-Châtelet, whose yawning porch had swallowed the end of the Petit-Pont; then, as your eye scanned the town from east to west, from the Tournelle to the Tour de Nesle was one long ribbon of houses with sculpted timbers and coloured windows, whose upper storeys overhung the roadway in an interminable zigzag of burgesses' gables, interrupted frequently by the opening of a street, and occasionally by the face or elbow of some great stone hôtel, lolling at its ease, with its courtyards and gardens, wings and *corps de logis*, amidst this populace of shabby, close-packed houses, like a great lord amidst a crowd of villeins. There were five or six such hôtels along the quay, from the Logis de Lorraine, which shared with the Bernardins the great adjoining wall of the Tournelle, to the Hôtel de Nesle, whose principal tower formed the boundary of Paris and whose pointed roofs were empowered, during three months of the year, to obtrude their black triangles on the scarlet disc of the setting sun.

This bank of the Seine, for the rest, was the less commercial of the two, the students were both noisier and more numerous than the artisans, and the only quay, properly speaking, ran from the Pont Saint-Michel to the Tour de Nesle. The remainder of the river-bank was either a bare strand, as beyond the Bernardins, or else a jumble of houses standing with their feet in the water, as between the two bridges. The air was full of the sound of washerwomen, shouting, talking and singing from morning till night along the bank, and pounding away at their washing as they do today. They are not the least of Paris's amusements.

To look at, the University formed a single block. It was one compact and homogeneous whole from one end to the other. Seen from above, those hundreds of close-set, angular, adhesive roofs, almost all of them formed from the one geometrical element, suggested the crystallization of a single substance. The slices into which this slab of houses had been cut by the capricious ravines of the streets were not too disproportionate. The forty-two colleges had been quite evenly distributed, and they were everywhere; the varied and amusing roof-lines of these beautiful buildings were the product of the same style as the simple roofs they dominated, and were merely, in the last resort, a multiplication to the second or third power of the one geometrical figure. Thus they added complexity to the whole without disturbing it, they completed it without weighing it down. Geometry is a harmony. A few handsome hôtels also jutted magnificently out here and there above the picturesque attics of the left bank: the Logis de Nevers, the Logis de Rome and the Logis de Rheims, which have gone; the Hôtel de Cluny, which still survives, for the consolation of the artist, but was so stupidly lopped of its tower a few years ago. Next to Cluny, that Roman palace, with its beautiful rounded arches, were the baths of Julian. There were many abbeys too, no less beautiful or grand than the hôtels, though their beauty was more devout and their grandeur more solemn. The first to strike the eye were: the Bernardins with its three belfries; Sainte-Geneviève, whose square tower, which still exists, makes us regret the rest; the Sorbonne, half-college and half-monastery, of which one quite admirable nave survives, the beautiful quadrilateral cloister of the Mathurins; its neighbour, the cloister of Saint-Benoît, within whose walls they had time to knock up a theatre between the seventh and eighth editions of this book; the Cordeliers, with its three enormous, juxtaposed gables; the Augustins, whose graceful spire was, after the Tour de Nesle, the second piece of denticulation on this side of Paris, starting from the west. The colleges, which were in effect the middle link between the cloister and the world, came midway in the series of monuments between the hôtels and the abbeys; they were severe yet full of elegance, their sculptures were less flighty than those of the palaces, their architecture less earnest than that of the monasteries. Sadly, hardly anything remains of these monuments, in which Gothic architecture so precisely laced opulence with austerity. The churches (which were both numerous and splendid in the University, and which, here too, represented every period of architecture, from the rounded arches of Saint-Julien to the pointed arches of Saint-Séverin), the churches dominated the whole and, as a further harmony in this mass of harmony, they were constantly breaking through the multiple fretwork of the gables with their slashed steeples, their openwork belfries, and their slender spires, whose lines were merely a magnificent exaggeration of the acute angles of the roofs.

The University stood on hilly ground. To the south-east, Mount Sainte-Geneviève formed an enormous blister, and what a sight it made, from on top of Notre-Dame, that crowd of narrow, winding streets (nowadays 'the Latin quarter'), those clusters of houses spilling in every direction from the summit of the hill and hurtling in an almost perpendicular disarray down its sides as far as the water's edge, some looking as if they were falling, others as if they were climbing back up again, all as if they were holding one another back. A continual flow of hundreds of black dots, intersecting on the roadways, made everything seem to be in motion This, seen from on high and from far away, was the people.

Finally, in the gaps between the roofs, the spires and the countless accidents of the architecture, which creased, twisted and indented the outer line of the University in so strange a way, you caught a glimpse, from time to time, of a great slab of moss-grown wall, a stumpy round tower or a crenelated town gate, playing at being a fortress: this was Philip-Augustus's ring-wall. Beyond it, the roads receded into the green of the meadows, with a few suburban houses still spread along them but becoming rarer the further you went. Some of these suburbs had their importance. Starting from the Tournelle, there was first of all the Bourg Saint-Victor, with its single-arched bridge over the Bièvre, its abbey, where you could read Louis the Fat's epitaph, *epitaphium Ludovici Grossi*, and its church, whose octagonal steeple was flanked by four eleventh-century bell-turrets (one like it can be seen at Etampes; it has not yet been knocked down); then the Bourg Saint-Marceau, which already had three churches and a convent. Then, leaving the Gobelins windmill and its four white walls on the left, there was the Faubourg Saint-Jacques with the fine carved cross at its crossroads, and the church of Faubourg Saint-Jacques du Haut-Pas, at that time Gothic, pointed and charming, Saint-Magloire, a beautiful fourteenth-century nave which Napoleon turned into a granary, and Notre-Dame-des-Champs, where there were Byzantine mosaics. Finally, once you had left behind in the open country the Carthusian monastery, an ornate building contemporary with the Palais de Justice, with its little subdivided gardens and the evilly haunted ruins of Vauvert, the eye fell, in the west, on the three Romanesque spires of Saint-Germain-des-Prés. The Bourg Saint-Germain, already a large commune, comprised fifteen or twenty streets behind them. The pointed belfry of Saint-Sulpice marked one corner of the Bourg. Close by could be seen the quadrilateral enclosure of the Foire Saint-Germain, where the market now is; then the abbot's pillory, a pretty little round tower capped by a lead cone. Further on were the tile works, the Rue du Four, which led to the communal oven, the windmill on its hillock, and the leper-house, an isolated small house of evil repute. But what chiefly attracted the eye and kept it fixed on this spot was the abbey itself. And what a truly magnificent sight it made on the horizon, this monastery, which looked the part both as a church and as a manor-house, this abbey palace, where the bishops of Paris considered themselves fortunate to sleep a single night, with its refectory, to which the architect had given the appearance, the beauty and the splendid rose-window of a cathedral, its elegant chapel to the Virgin, its monumental dormitory, its vast gardens, its portcullis, its drawbridge, its envelope of battlements cutting notches into the green of the fields round about, its courtyards, where gleaming men-at arms mingled with gold copes, and all grouped and gathered around the three tall, round-arched spires, set solidly on a Gothic apse.

When at last, after prolonged contemplation of the University, you turned towards the right bank, towards the Town, the prospect abruptly changed its nature. The Town, in fact, was at once much larger and less of a unity than the University. At first glance, it seemed to divide itself into several oddly distinct masses. To the east, first of all, in that part of the Town which still derives its name today from the marsh where Camulogenus embogged Caesar,[1] was a jumble of palaces. They formed a block reaching to the water's edge: Jouy, Sens, Barbeau and the Logis de la Reine, four hôtels almost touching, whose slate roofs, with their slim intervening turrets, were mirrored in the Seine. These four buildings occupied the space between the Rue des Nonaindières and the Celestine abbey, whose spire contrasted prettily with the line of their gables and battlements. A few greenish hovels, leaning over the water in front of these sumptuous hôtels, did not prevent one seeing the beautiful angles of their façades, their broad, square windows with stone mullions, their pointed arches overladen with statues, the sharp edges of their still clean-cut walls, and all those delightful architectural accidents which make it seem that Gothic art can find fresh combinations for each new monument. Behind these palaces, in every direction, at one point loopholed, stockaded

1. i.e. the Marais, just possibly the site of the Gallic defence of Lutetia against a Roman army.

and crenellated like a fortress, at another masked by tall trees like a charterhouse, ran the immense, multiform enclosure of the miraculous Hôtel de Saint-Pol, where the King of France had the wherewithal to lodge in great splendour twenty-two princes of the rank of the dauphin or the Duke of Burgundy, together with their domestics and retinues, not to mention great lords, and the emperor when he came to see Paris, and the lions, who had their own separate hôtel inside the royal hôtel. And we should here say that in those days a princely apartment would not have contained less than eleven rooms, from a reception-room to a private chapel, and not counting the galleries, baths, hot-rooms and other 'superfluous places' with which each apartment was provided; or the private gardens for each of the king's guests; or the kitchens, larders, pantries and general household refectories; the yards where there were twenty-two general workshops, from the bakery to the wine dispensary; games of every kind, mall, fives and tilting at rings; aviaries, fish-tanks, menageries, stables and cattle-sheds; libraries, arsenals and foundries. Such in those days was a king's palace; a Louvre or an Hôtel Saint-Pol. A city within the city.

From the tower where we are standing, the Hôtel Saint-Pol, half hidden almost by the four great houses of which we have just spoken, was still a very considerable and splendid sight. Although they had been cleverly joined on to the main building by long galleries of colonettes and stained-glass, you could still make out quite clearly the three hôtels which Charles V had amalgamated with his palace; the Hôtel du Petit-Muce, its roof prettily ringed by a tracery balustrade; the Hôtel of the Abbot of Saint-Maur, whose lines were those of a fortress, with its great tower, its machicolations, its loopholes, its iron moineaux and, above the wide Saxon gate, between the two grooves of the drawbridge, the abbot's coat of arms; the Hôtel of the Count of Etampes, the top of whose circular keep was in ruins and as jagged as a coxscomb; here, a clump of three or four old oak trees looking like enormous cauliflowers, there, swans disporting themselves in the clear waters of the fishponds, creased all over with light and shade; a great many courtyards, of which picturesque corners could be seen; the lion house, with its low pointed arches on short Saxon piers, its iron portcullises and a perpetual roaring; traversing the whole, the scaly spire of the Ave Maria; to the left, the Provost of Paris's mansion, flanked by four delicately scooped-out turrets; in the centre, in the background, the Hôtel Saint-Pol proper, with its multiple façades, the successive embellishments added since Charles V's time, the hybrid excrescences with which the whims of architects had been burdening it for the past two centuries, all the apses on its chapels, the gables on its galleries, the myriad weathercocks, the two tall, touching towers, whose conical roofs had crenellations round the base and looked like pointed hats with turned-up brims.

Continuing to ascend the storeys of this amphitheatre of palaces, which stretched away into the distance, the eye crossed a deep ravine yawning between the roofs of the Town, and marking the passage of the Rue Saint-Antoine, and came – we are still restricting ourselves to the principal monuments – to the Logis d'Angoulême, a vast structure from different periods, some parts of which were brand new and very white and blended no better with the whole than a red patch on a blue doublet. The peculiarly tall and pointed roof of the modern palace, bristling with carved waterspouts and covered with sheets of lead, on which glittering incrustations of gilded copper were coiled into a thousand fantastic arabesques, this strangely damascened roof, as I say, soared gracefully up from amidst the brown ruins of the earlier building, whose huge old towers were bloated with age, like casks falling in with decay and splitting from top to bottom, and looked like fat, unbuttoned paunches. Behind rose the forest of spires of the Palace of the Tournelles. No prospect in the world, not even at Chambord or the Alhambra, was more magical, more ethereal or more marvellous than this full-grown forest of spires, bell-turrets, chimneys, weathercocks, winding stairs, lanterns that let through the daylight and seemed to have been made with a punch, pavilions and spindle-shaped turrets or, as they were then called, *tournelles*: of every different shape, height and attitude. It was like a gigantic stone chess set.

To the right of the Tournelles, that bundle of enormous ink-black towers, all overlapping each other and roped together, as it were, by a circular moat, that keep with far more loopholes in it than windows, that drawbridge which was always raised, that portcullis which was always lowered; that was the Bastille. The sort of black beaks sticking out between the battlements, which from a distance you took to be waterspouts, were cannon.

At the foot of this formidable edifice, well within their range, was the Porte Sainte-Antoine, huddled between its two towers.

Beyond the Tournelles and right up to Charles V's wall stretched a velvety carpet of cultivated fields and royal gardens, forming a lush pattern of verdure and flowers, in the midst of which could be made out the labyrinth of trees and walks of the Daedalus Garden given by Louis XI to Coictier. Above the maze rose the doctor's observatory, like a huge isolated column with a small house instead of a capital. In this dispensary, many terrible predictions had been made up. Today, it is the site of the Place Royale.

As we have said, the palace quarter, of which we have been attempting to give the reader some idea, though indicating only the crowning glories, filled the angle which Charles V's city wall formed with the Seine to the east. The centre of the Town was occupied by a mound of commoners' dwellings. Here it was, in fact, that the three bridges from the Cité discharged on to the right bank, and bridges create houses before they create palaces. This jumble of bourgeois dwellings, packed tight like the cells of a beehive, had its own beauty. There is a grandeur about the roofs of a capital city, as there is about the waves of the sea. First of all, the skein of intersecting streets divided their mass into a hundred delightful shapes. Around Les Halles, they were like a star with innumerable points. The Rue Saint-Denis and the Rue Saint-Martin, together with their countless ramifications, climbed one behind the other like two huge trees mingling their branches. Then, snaking across the whole area, the tortuous lines of the Rue de la Plâtrerie, the Rue de la Verrerie, the Rue de la Tixanderie, and others. There were some fine buildings, too, breaking through the petrified waves of this sea of gables. At the head of the Pont-aux-Changeurs, behind which could be seen the Seine, frothing beneath the wheels of the Pont-aux-Meuniers, stood the Châtelet, no longer a Roman tower as in Julian the Apostate's time, but a feudal tower of the thirteenth century, of a stone so hard that in three hours the pick-axe could not reduce it by the thickness of a fist. There was the ornate square tower of Saint-Jacques-de-la-Boucherie, its sharp corners blunted by sculptures, admirable even in the fifteenth century though it was not yet finished. It lacked in particular the four monsters who still perch today on the four corners of the roof, looking like four sphinxes setting to the new Paris the riddle of the old; their sculptor, Rault, did not set them up there until 1526, and got twenty francs for his pains. There was the Maison-aux-Piliers, opening on to the Place de Grève, of which we have already given the reader an impression. There was Saint-Gervais, since spoiled by a 'tasteful' portal; Saint-Méry, whose old pointed arches were still almost rounded ones; Saint-Jean, whose magnificent spire was proverbial; and twenty monuments besides which did not disdain to bury their marvels in this chaos of dark, narrow, cavernous streets. To which we can add the carved stone crosses, which even outnumbered the gibbets at the crossroads; the cemetery of the Innocents, whose architectural enclosure could be seen in the distance above the roofs; the pillory of Les Halles, the top of which was visible between two chimneys in the Rue de la Cossonnerie; the gallows of La Croix-du-Trahoir in its crossroads, always black with people; the circular, broken-down buildings of the corn-market; the stumps of Philip-Augustus's ancient enclosure, which you could still see in places, swamped by the houses, towers eaten away by ivy, ruined gateways, slabs of buckled, crumbling wall; the quay with all its shops and its bloody flayers' yards; the Seine, laden with boats from the Port-au-Foin to the For l'Evêque; and now you will have a confused idea of what this central trapezium of the Town looked like in 1482.

The third element in the picture presented by the Town, together with these two districts, one of hôtels and the other of houses, was a long zone of abbeys which lined it almost all the way round, from the east to the west, and formed a second, inner ring of monasteries and chapels behind the ring of fortifications enclosing Paris. Thus, immediately next to the garden of the Tournelles, between the Rue Saint-Antoine and the Rue du Temple, lay Sainte-Catherine, with its vast area of cultivation, bounded only by the wall of Paris. Between the old Rue du Temple and the new stood the Temple, a sinister-looking cluster of towers, tall, upright and isolated in the middle of a vast crenellated ringwall. Between the Rue Neuve-du-Temple and the Rue Saint-Martin, the Abbey of Saint-Martin, in the midst of its gardens, a superb fortified church, whose girdle of towers and tiara of belfries were exceeded, for strength and splendour, only by Saint-Germain-des-Prés. Between the Rue Saint-Martin and the Rue Saint-Denis extended the enclosure of the Trinité. Finally, between the Rue Saint-Denis and the Rue Montorgueil, the Filles-Dieu. Next to it could be made out the mouldering roofs and unpaved precinct of the Cour des Miracles. This was the one profane link to intrude on the sacred chain of monasteries.

Lastly, the fourth self-evident division in the agglomeration of roofs on the right bank, which occupied the western angle formed downstream by the containing-wall and the river, was a second knot of palaces and hôtels crowding round the feet of the Louvre. From a distance, Philip-Augustus's old Louvre, that disproportionate building whose huge tower had gathered twenty-three other towers to it like mistresses, not to mention turrets, seemed to have been embedded in the Gothic roofs of the Hôtel d'Alençon and the Petit-Bourbon. This hydra of towers, the giant watchdog of Paris, with its twenty-four heads constantly erect and its monstrous cruppers, of lead or slate scales, shimmering with a metallic reflection, brought the configuration of the Town to a startling conclusion in the west.

Thus a vast block, what the Romans called an *insula*, of bourgeois houses, flanked to right and left by two groups of palaces, one crowned by the Louvre, the other by the Tournelles, bordered to the north by a long belt of abbeys and enclosed fields, and the whole amalgamated and fused by the eye; above these innumerable buildings, the slates and tiles of whose roofs stood out in weird mountain-ranges one against the other, the tattooed, goffered and guilloched belfries of the forty-four churches of the right bank; traversed by a myriad streets; bounded on one side by an enclosure of high walls with square towers (that of the University had round towers) and on the other by the Seine, divided by bridges and plied by many boats; such was the Town in the fifteenth century.

Outside the walls, a few suburbs pressed around the gates, but they were fewer and more scattered than those of the University. Behind the Bastille, a score of tumbledown houses bunched around the curious sculptures of the Croix-Faubin and the flying buttresses of the Abbey of Saint-Antoine-des-Champs; then Popincourt, lost amidst the corn; then La Courtille, a village gay with taverns; the Bourg Saint-Laurent, whose church tower seemed from the distance to have joined the pointed towers of the Porte Saint-Martin; the Faubourg Saint-Denis, with the huge enclosure of Saint-Ladre; outside the Porte Montmartre, the Grange-Batelière girded with white walls; behind it, the chalk slopes of Montmartre, which in those days had almost as many churches as windmills, but has kept only the windmills, since nowadays society demands only the body's bread. Finally, on the far side of the Louvre, you could see the already very considerable Faubourg Saint-Honoré extending into the meadows, and the green of the Petite-Bretagne, and the Marché-aux-Porceaux, stretching away with, at its centre, the ghastly round oven where forgers were boiled alive. Between the Cortille and Saint-Laurent, your eye had already remarked, on the crown of an eminence squatting above empty plains, a sort of building which looked from a distance like a ruined colonnade standing on an exposed stylobate. This was not a Parthenon, nor a temple to the Olympian Jupiter. It was Montfaucon.

And now, provided the enumeration of so many buildings, brief though we have tried to keep it, has not fragmented the general picture of old Paris in the reader's mind as it was taking shape, we shall sum it up in a few words. In the centre, the Île de la Cité, looking in shape like an enormous tortoise, with its bridges, scaly with tiles, protruding like paws from underneath the grey carapace of roofs. To the left, the compact, dense, tight-packed, bristling, monolithic trapezium of the University. To the right, the vast semicircle of the Town, including many more gardens and monuments. The three blocks, City, University and Town, veined with countless streets. Through it all, the Seine, our 'foster-mother Seine', as Father du Breul puts it, obstructed by islands, bridges and boats. Right the way round, an immense plain, a patchwork of every kind of cultivation dotted with lovely villages: to the left, Issy, Vanvres, Vaugirard, Montrouge and Gentilly with its round tower and its square tower, etc.; to the right, a score of others, from Conflans to La Ville L'Evêque. On the horizon, a fringe of hills set in a circle, like the rim of the bowl. Finally, in the distance, to the east, Vincennes and its seven quadrangular towers; to the south, Bicêtre and its pointed turrets; to the north, Saint-Denis and its spire; to the west, Saint-Cloud and its keep. This was the Paris which rooks living in 1482 could see from on top of the towers of Notre-Dame.

Yet this was the town of which Voltaire has said that 'before Louis XIV it possessed only four fine monuments': the dome of the Sorbonne, the Val-de-Grâce, the modern Louvre and a fourth one which I forget, perhaps the Luxembourg. Happily, Voltaire still wrote *Candide* and was still, of all the men who have succeeded one another in the long sequence of mankind, the one with the most diabolical laugh. Which proves, what is more, that you can be a great genius yet understand nothing of an art which is not your own. Did Molière not fancy he was paying Raphael and Michaelangelo a great compliment by calling them 'those Mignards of their age'?[1]

But we must return to Paris and to the fifteenth century.

At that time it was not only a beautiful town, it was a homogeneous town, the architectural and historical product of the Middle Ages, a chronicle in stone. It was a city formed of only two strata, the Romanesque stratum and the Gothic stratum, for the Roman stratum had long since vanished, apart from Julian's baths, where it still showed through the thick crust of the Middle Ages. As for the Celtic stratum, samples of that no longer turned up even when wells were being dug.

Fifty years later, when the Renaissance came, and added to this very severe yet very varied unity with the dazzling luxury of its fantasies and systems, its riot of rounded Roman arches, Greek columns and Gothic stylobates, its sculpture, so tender and idealized, its characteristic penchant for arabesques and acanthuses, its architectural paganism, and this in the age of Luther, Paris was perhaps more beautiful still, if less harmonious to the eye and the mind. But this splendid moment was short-lived. The Renaissance was not impartial; it was not content merely to put up, it also wanted to knock down. It is true it needed the room. And so Gothic Paris was complete only for a minute. Hardly had they finished Saint-Jacques-de-la-Boucherie before they began to demolish the old Louvre.

Since then, this great town has gone on being disfigured day by day. The Gothic Paris beneath which Romanesque Paris had been obliterated has been obliterated in its turn. But can we say what Paris has replaced them?

There is the Paris of Catherine de' Medici, at the Tuileries,[2] the

1. The brothers Mignard were fashionable but not over-gifted painters of the seventeenth century.

2. We have seen with a mixture of sorrow and indignation that they are thinking of enlarging, recasting, redoing, i.e. destroying this admirable palace. The architects of our own day are too heavy-handed to interfere with these

Paris of Henri II at the Hôtel de Ville – two buildings still in the grand style; the Paris of Henri IV, at the Place Royale: brick façades with stone quoins and slate roofs, tricolour houses; the Paris of Louis XIII, at the Val-de-Grâce: a squat, crumpled architecture, vaulting like the handles of a basket and with a touch of paunchiness about the columns and of a hump about the dome; the Paris of Louis XIV, at the Invalides: grand, ornate, gilded and cold; the Paris of Louis XV, at Saint-Sulpice: scrolls, knotted ribbons, clouds, vermicelli and chicory, all in stone; the Paris of Louis XVI, at the Panthéon: a bad imitation of St Peter's in Rome (the building has settled awkwardly, which has not improved its lines); the Paris of the Republic, at the École de Médecine: a poor Greco-Roman style about as much like the Coliseum or the Parthenon as the Constitution of the Year Three is like the laws of Minos, what is known in architecture as 'the Messidor style';[1] the Paris of Napoleon, at the Place Vendôme: this is sublime, a bronze column made from cannon; the Paris of the Restoration, at the Bourse: a very white colonnade supporting a very smooth frieze, the whole thing square and costing twenty millions.

To each of these characteristic monuments is linked, by a similarity of style, manner and attitude, a certain number of houses scattered in different parts of the town, which the eye of the connoisseur can easily recognize and date. When you know how to look, you can discover the spirit of an age and the physiognomy of a king even in a door-knocker.

Present-day Paris, therefore, has no overall physiognomy. It is a collection of specimens from several centuries, and the most beautiful have vanished. The capital is growing only in houses, and what houses! At the rate Paris is going, it will be renewed every

---

delicate works of the Renaissance. We still hope they will not dare to do so. Moreover, the demolition of the Tuileries now would be not only an act of violence to make a drunken Vandal blush but also an act of treachery. The Tuileries is no longer simply a masterpiece of sixteenth-century art, it is also a page of nineteenth-century history. The palace no longer belongs to the king but to the people. Let us leave it as it is. Our revolution has twice marked its brow. On one of its façades it has the cannon-balls of 10 August, on the other the cannon-balls of 29 July. It is sacred. Paris, 7 April 1831. (V.H.)

1. The Revolutionary calendar began in September 1793; the Year Three was 1796–7, and Messidor the tenth month (June/July).

fifty years. Thus the historical significance of its architecture is being erased every day. Monuments are becoming increasingly rare, and we seem to watch them being gradually engulfed, submerged by the houses. Our fathers had a Paris of stone: our sons will have a Paris of plaster.

As for the modern monuments of the new Paris, we will gladly forgo mentioning them. Not that we do not admire them as is proper. M. Soufflot's Sainte-Geneviève is certainly the finest sponge-cake ever made out of stone. The Palace of the Légion d'Honneur is also a most distinguished slice of patisserie. The dome of the cornmarket is an English jockey's cap on the grand scale. The towers of Saint-Sulpice are two huge clarinets, which is as good a shape as any, while the crooked, grimacing telegraph forms a pleasant accident on their roof. Saint-Roch has a portal comparable in splendour only to Saint-Thomas d'Aquin. It also has a Calvary modelled in the round in a cellar, and a sun of gilded wood. Quite wonderful objects, these. The lantern of the maze in the Jardin des Plantes is likewise most ingenious. As for the Palace of the Bourse, Greek in its colonnade, Roman in the depressed arches of its doors and windows, Renaissance in its great segmental vault, that is indubitably a very correct, very pure monument. And to prove it, it has been crowned with an attic storey such as Athens never knew, a beautiful straight line attractively broken here and there by flue-pipes. Let us add that, if it be the rule that the architecture of a building should be adapted to its function in such a way that this function declares itself merely by looking at the building, then we can hardly wonder enough at a monument which might equally well be a king's palace, a house of commons, a town hall, a college, a riding-school, an academy, a warehouse, a law court, a museum, a barracks, a sepulchre, a temple or a theatre. For the present, it is a stock exchange. A monument should, besides, be suited to the climate. This one was obviously built expressly for our cold and rainy skies. It has an almost flat roof as in the Orient, which means that in winter, when it snows, they sweep the roof, and roofs as we know are made to be swept. As for the function we were talking about a moment ago, it fills that to perfection: it is a stock exchange in France just as it would have been a temple in Greece. It is true that the architect had some difficulty hiding the face of the clock which would have wrecked the pure and beautiful lines of his façade; but to make up for that, we have the colonnade encircling the monument, beneath which, on days of high religious solemnity, the theory of stockbrokers and jobbers can be majestically expounded.

These for sure are very stately monuments. If we add to them many fine streets, as amusing and diverse as the Rue de Rivoli, then I do not despair but that one day a balloon's eye view of Paris will offer us that wealth of lines, that opulence of detail, that diversity of aspect, that somehow grandiose simplicity and unexpected beauty which characterize a draught-board.

Yet, however admirable you may find present-day Paris, rebuild the Paris of the fifteenth century, reconstruct it in your imagination, look, by day, through that astonishing hedge of spires, towers and belfries, spill the Seine through the middle of the immense town, rending it on the tips of the islands, crinkling it against the arches of the bridges, the Seine, with its great yellow and green puddles, more changeable than a serpent's skin, make the Gothic profile of old Paris stand out sharply against an azure horizon, or wreathe its contours in a winter mist, clinging to the innumerable chimneys; submerge it in the depths of night and watch the strange interplay of light and darkness in that sombre labyrinth of buildings; cast over it a ray of moonlight, vaguely to delineate it and to bring the great heads of the towers out from the fog; or take that black silhouette once more, accentuate the innumerable acute angles of its spires and gables with shadow, and make it stand out, more jagged than a shark's jaws, against the copper sky of the sunset. Then, compare.

And if you want to receive, from the old town, an impression which the new can no longer give, climb, on a morning of high festivity, in the rising sun of Easter or Whitsun, to some lofty point from where you can dominate the entire capital, and watch the awakening of the bells. When the signal comes from heaven, for it is the sun which gives it, you will see all those hundreds of churches tremble as one. To start with, there is a scattered ringing, passing from church to church, as when musicians warn each other they are about to begin; then all of a sudden you will see, for there are times when the ear too seems to have eyes, something like a column of sound, a plume of harmony, rising at the same instant from every belfry. At first, the vibration of each bell climbs straight up, pure and, as it were, independently, into the brilliant morning sky. Then, as they swell, they gradually fuse and merge and amalgamate into one magnificent concert. And now there is but a single mass of vibrant sound, issuing ceaselessly from the innumerable belfries, drifting, undulating, leaping, swirling above the town, and extending the deafening orbit of its oscillations far beyond the horizon. Yet this sea of harmony is far from chaotic. Vast and deep it may be, but it has not lost its transparency. Each group of notes as it escapes from the chimes can be seen winding separately upwards; you can follow the dialogue, alternately solemn and shrill, of the tenor bell and the hand-rattle; you can see the octaves leaping from one belfry to the next; you can watch them spring, light, winged and sibilant, from the silver bell and fall, halt and broken, from the wooden one; amongst them, you can admire the rich gamut, rising and falling constantly from the seven bells of Saint-Eustache; you can see quick, clear notes speed across, making three or four zigzags of light and then vanish like flashes of lightning. Here, it is the sour, cracked tones of the Abbey of Saint-Martin; there the sinister and sullen voice of the Bastille; at the far end, the great tower of the Louvre, with its baritone. The royal carillon from the palace launches its resplendent trills unrelentingly on the four winds, and on to them, at regular intervals, fall the heavy notes from the belfry of Notre-Dame, drawing sparks from them like a hammer from an anvil. At times, sounds of every shape can be seen to go past from the triple peal of Saint-Germain-des-Prés. And then this mass of sublime sounds half opens from time to time, to allow through the stretto of the Ave Maria, which bursts and sparkles like a tuft of stars. Down below, in the very depths of the concert, you can dimly perceive the singing from inside the churches, as it transpires through the vibrant pores of the vaulting. Here, indeed, is an opera worth hearing. Generally, the hum which Paris gives off by day is the town talking; by night, it is the town breathing; here, it is the town singing. Harken, then, to this tutti of the bells, add to the ensemble the murmur of half a million men, the eternal lament of the river, the infinite breath of the wind, the solemn and distant quartet of the four forests, standing on the hills of the horizon like vast organ-cases, suppress, as in a half-tone, whatever is too raucous or piercing in the central carillon, and then tell me whether you know of anything in the world more rich, more joyous, more golden or more dazzling than this tumult of bells and chimes; than this furnace of music; than these ten thousand bronze voices singing as one from stone flutes three hundred feet high; than this city which has turned into an orchestra; than this symphony with the sound of a storm.

BOOK FOUR

ONE
The Kind Souls

SIXTEEN years prior to the events of this story, one fine Quasimodo Sunday morning,[1] a living creature was deposited after mass in the church of Notre-Dame on the wooden bed set into the parvis on the left-hand side, facing the 'great image' of St Christopher, at which the carved stone figure of Messire Antoine des Essarts, Knight, had been kneeling staring since 1413, when they took it into their heads to overthrow both saint and worshipper. This was the wooden bed where it was customary to expose foundlings to public charity. Whoever wanted them could take them. In front of the wooden bed was a copper bowl for alms.

The sort of living creature lying recumbent on this plank on the morning of Quasimodo in the Year of Our Lord 1467 seemed to be exciting the liveliest curiosity amongst the quite large group that had collected round the wooden bed. This group largely comprised members of the fair sex. They were nearly all old women.

There were four to be observed in the front row leaning furthest over the bed, whose grey hooded cloaks, rather like cassocks, suggested that they belonged to some religious sisterhood. I see no reason why this history should not hand down to posterity the names of these four discreet and venerable ladies. They were Agnès la Herme, Jehanne de la Tarme, Henriette la Gaultière and Gauchère la Violette, all four of them widows, all four good-wives from the chapel of Etienne-Haudry, who had left their house, by permission of their mistress and in accordance with the statutes of Pierre d'Ailly, to come and hear the sermon.

However, although these worthy *haudriettes*[2] may have been temporarily observing the statutes of Pierre d'Ailly, they were certainly and quite happily transgressing those of Michel de Brache and the Cardinal of Pisa, who had so inhumanely prescribed them to silence.

'What is it, sister?' Agnès was saying to Gauchère, as she ex-

1. Quasimodo is the first Sunday after Easter, or Low Sunday.
2. i.e. inmates of the Haudry chapel.

amined the small creature who was exhibited there, writhing and squealing on its wooden bed, much alarmed by so many pairs of eyes.

'What's going to become of us,' said Jehanne, 'if that's the kind of children they're making nowadays?'

'I don't know much about children,' Agnès went on, 'but it must be a sin to look at that one.'

'It's not a child, Agnès.'

'It's a monkey gone wrong,' remarked Gauchère.

'It's a miracle,' put in Henriette la Gaultière.

'In that case,' observed Agnès, 'it's the third one since Laetare.[1] For not a week since we had the miracle of the mocker of pilgrims, who was divinely punished by Our Lady of Aubervilliers, and that was the second miracle this month.'

'This so-called foundling is a real monster of abomination,' Jehanne resumed.

'His squalling would deafen a cantor,' Gauchère continued. 'Be quiet, will you, you little bawler!'

'And to think that it was the Bishop of Rheims who sent this enormity to the Bishop of Paris!' added la Gaultière, clasping her hands.

'I imagine it's a wild beast,' said Agnès la Herme, 'an animal, fathered by a Jew on a sow; something not Christian in fact, which ought to be thrown into the water or on the fire.'

'I certainly hope no one will postulate it,' resumed la Gaultière.

'Good heavens!' exclaimed Agnès. 'Suppose they took this little monster to be suckled by those poor wet-nurses down in the foundlings' home at the bottom of the alley as you go down river, right next-door to my Lord Bishop's! I'd rather give suck to a vampire.'

'Poor La Herme, you *are* innocent!' Jehanne went on. 'Can't you see, sister, that this little monster is at least four years old and that it'd rather get at a roasting-spit than at your teats.'

'The little monster' (we would be hard put to it ourselves to find another term for him) was indeed no new-born baby. It was a very angular, very restless small lump, imprisoned in a canvas sack stamped with the cipher of Messire Guillaume Chartier, the then Bishop of Paris, and with its head protruding. This head was more

1. The fourth Sunday in Lent.

than a little deformed. All you could see was a forest of red hair, one eye, a mouth and some teeth. The eye was weeping, the mouth yelling, while the teeth seemed anxious only to bite. And all of it threshing about in the sack, to the great amazement of the encircling crowd, which was growing all the time and being replenished.

Dame Aloïse de Gondelaurier, a rich noblewoman, who held the hand of a pretty little girl of about six and wore a long veil trailing from the golden comb in her head-dress, stopped as she passed the bed to examine the unfortunate creature for a moment, while her charming little daughter, Fleur-de-Lys de Gondelaurier, dressed all in silk and velvet, ran her pretty finger along the notice attached permanently to the wooden bed: FOUNDLINGS.

'Really, I thought they only exposed children here,' said the dame, turning away in disgust.

As she turned her back, she tossed a silver florin into the alms-dish, which clinked amidst the *liards* and made the poor goodwives from the Etienne-Haudry chapel open their eyes in wonder.

A moment later, the grave and learned Robert Mistricolle, prothonotary to the king, came past with a huge missal under one arm and his wife (Mistress Guillemette la Mairesse) under the other, being thus flanked by both his governors, the spiritual and the temporal.

'Foundling!' he said, after examining the object. 'Found by the look of it on the parapet of the river Phlegethon!'[1]

'You can only see one eye,' Mistress Guillemette pointed out 'He's got a wen over the other.'

'It's not a wen,' went on Maître Robert Mistricolle. 'It's an egg containing another devil, just the same, and that contains another little egg with another devil inside, and so on.'

'How do you know that?' asked Guillemette la Mairesse.

'I know it for a fact,' answered the prothonotary.

'Monsieur the Prothonotary,' asked Gauchère, 'what do you predict for this supposed foundling?'

'The greatest misfortunes,' replied Mistricolle.

'Oh, goodness gracious!' said an old woman among the onlookers, 'when you think there was all that pestilence last year and they say the English are going to land in force at Harefleu.'[2]

1. A river in the Greek Hades.
2. The old name for Harfleur, in the Seine estuary.

'That will stop the queen coming to Paris in September perhaps,' put in another. 'Trade's bad enough already!'

'It's my opinion,' exclaimed Jehanne de la Tarme, 'that it would be better for the villeins of Paris if this little magician were lying on a faggot rather than on a plank of wood.'

'A beautiful flaming faggot!' added the old woman.

'That would be more sensible,' said Mistricolle.

For the past few moments a young priest had been listening to the *haudriettes*' arguments and the pronouncements of the prothonotary. He had a severe face, with a wide forehead and a penetrating stare. He brushed through the crowd in silence, examined 'the little magician', then stretched out his hand over him. Just in time. For the devout ladies were already licking their lips over 'the beautiful burning faggot'.

'I adopt this child,' said the priest.

He took him into his cassock and carried him off. The onlookers watched him go in amazement. A moment later, he had vanished through the Porte-Rouge, which then led from the church into the cloister.

Once the initial shock had passed, Jehanne de la Tarme lent into La Gaultière's ear:

'Didn't I tell you, sister, that that young clerk Monsieur Claude Frollo was a sorcerer.'

TWO
Claude Frollo

CLAUDE Frollo was, in fact, a man of some distinction. He came from one of those families of middle rank which the impertinent language of the last century referred to alternately as upper bourgeoisie or minor nobility. From the brothers Paclet, his family had inherited the fief of Tirechappe, which came under the Bishop of Paris and whose twenty-one houses had, in the thirteenth century, been the object of a great many lawsuits before the Official.[1] As the owner of this fief, Claude Frollo was one of the 'seven score and one' lords claiming quit-rent in Paris and its suburbs; and as such, his name could long have been seen inscribed, between the Hôtel de Tancarville, which belonged to Maître François le Rez, and the

1. An ecclesiastical judge.

Collège de Tours, in the cartulary held at Saint-Martin-des-Champs.

Claude Frollo had been destined for an ecclesiastical career from early childhood by his parents. He had been taught to read in Latin. He had been brought up to keep his eyes and his voice lowered. He was still a child when his father confined him in the Collège de Torchi at the University. It was there that he had grown up, on the missal and the Lexicon.

He was, besides, a sad, serious and solemn child, who studied zealously and learnt quickly. He was not very vocal at recreation time, took little part in the orgies of the Rue de Fouarre, did not know what it was to *dare alapas et capillos laniare*,[1] and figured not at all in the mutiny of 1463, which the annalists record solemnly under the title of 'sixth disturbance in the University'. He seldom made fun of the poor scholars of Montagu for the *cappettes*[2] from which they derived their name, or the scholarship boys of the Collège de Dormans for their close-cut tonsures and tripartite surcoats of blue, purple and mauve, *azurini coloris et bruni*, as the Cardinal des Quatre-Couronnes's charter puts it.

On the other hand, he attended both upper and lower schools in the Rue Jean-de-Beauvais assiduously. The first student whom the Abbot of Saint-Pierre de Val always saw, pressed against a pillar opposite his rostrum in the Ecole Saint-Vendregesile, as he began his reading from the canon law, was Claude Frollo, armed with his horn inkstand, chewing his quill, scribbling on his threadbare knee and, in the wintertime, blowing on his fingers. The first listener whom Messire Miles d'Isliers, Doctor of Decretals, saw arrive breathing hard each Monday morning, when the doors of the Ecole du Chef-Saint-Denis were opened, was Claude Frollo.

And so, by the age of sixteen, the young clerk could have held his own in mystical theology with a father of the church, in canonical theology with a father of the councils, and in scholastic theology with a doctor from the Sorbonne.

Once past theology, he hurried on to decretals. From the 'Master of the Sentences'[3] he descended to the *Capitularies* of Charlemagne. Then, in his lust for knowledge, he devoured a whole

1. 'To give blows and tear out hair.'
2. A form of cape.
3. Peter Lombard, from his anthology of maxims.

succession of decretals, one after the other: those of Theodore, Bishop of Hispale, those of Bouchard, Bishop of Worms, those of Yves, Bishop of Chartres; then Gratian's *Decree*, which succeeded Charlemagne's *Capitularies*; then the anthology of Gregory IX; then Honorius III's epistle *Super specula*. He elucidated for himself and grew familiar with that vast and turbulent period when civil law and canon law were in travail and at war during the chaos of the Middle Ages, a period that began in 618 with Bishop Theodore and ended in 1227 with Pope Gregory.

Having digested decretals, he threw himself into medicine and the liberal arts. He studied the science of herbs and the science of unguents. He became expert in fevers and contusions, in wounds and impostumes. Jacques d'Espars would have passed him as a physician, Richard Hellain as a surgeon.[1]

He also passed through all the degrees of bachelorhood, mastery and doctorship of arts. He studied languages, Latin, Greek and Hebrew, a triple sanctuary then very little frequented. He had a veritable fever for the acquiring and storing of knowledge. By the age of eighteen, all four faculties had succumbed. The young man could see only one aim in life: to know.

It was around this time that the excessively hot summer of 1466 led to the outbreak of the great plague which carried off more than forty thousand souls in the viscounty of Paris, and among them, according to Jean de Troyes, 'Maître Arnoul, the king's astrologer, who was a most upright man, wise and pleasant'. The word went round the University that the Rue Tirechappe especially had been ravaged by the disease. It was there that Claude's parents resided, in the midst of their fief. The young student ran to his father's house, greatly alarmed. When he went in, his father and mother had been dead since the previous day. His baby brother, not yet out of swaddling clothes, was still alive and was crying abandoned in his cradle. He was the only family Claude had left. The young man picked the child up under his arm and went thoughtfully out. Hitherto he had lived only in science; he was beginning to live in life.

This disaster was a turning-point in Claude's life. An orphan, an elder brother and the head of a family, at the age of nineteen, he felt himself brutally summoned back from the daydreams of school to the realities of the world. Stirred by pity, he became passionately

1. Both doctors in the Sorbonne medical faculty in the fifteenth century.

devoted to this baby brother; and to him, who had so far loved nothing except books, a human attachment was something both strange and sweet.

This attachment developed to a remarkable degree. In a soul so new it was like a first love affair. Separated since childhood from his parents, whom he had hardly known, cloistered and as if immured in his books, eager above all to study and to learn, exclusively concerned up until now with his intellect, which had expanded through science, and his imagination, which had grown through literature, the poor student had not as yet had time to feel the place of his heart. This young brother, without either father or mother, this little child, who had suddenly dropped from the sky into his arms, made a new man of him. He realized there were other things in the world besides the speculations of the Sorbonne and the verses of Homerus, that man has need of affection, that without tenderness and love life was just a harsh and mechanical clockwork, in need of lubrication; only he imagined, being at that age when illusions are as yet replaced only by other illusions, that attachments of blood and family were alone necessary, and that a little brother to love was enough to fill a whole lifetime.

So he threw himself into loving his little Jehan with the passion of a nature already intense, ardent and reserved. This poor, frail creature, pretty, pink and with fair, curly hair, this orphan whose only support was another orphan, moved him to the very depths: and, serious-minded as he was, he began to meditate on Jehan with an infinite compassion. He fussed and fretted over him as over something very fragile which had been entrusted to him. He was more than a brother to the child, he became its mother.

Little Jehan had lost his mother when he was still at the breast. Claude put him out to a wet-nurse. Apart from the fief of Tirechappe, he had inherited from his father the fief of the Moulin, which depended on the square tower of Gentilly. This was a windmill on a hill, near the castle of Winchestre (Bicêtre). The miller's wife there was suckling a beautiful baby; it was not far from the University. Claude carried his little Jehan to her in person.

From then on, he took life very seriously, feeling he had a burden to drag along. The thought of his little brother became not only his recreation but even the aim of his studies. He resolved to dedicate himself entirely to a future for which he would answer before God, and never to have any wife or child other than the happiness and success of his brother. He became more deeply wedded than ever, therefore, to his clerical vocation. His ability, his learning, his rank as the immediate vassal of the Bishop of Paris, opened wide the doors of the church to him. By the age of twenty, through a special dispensation from the Holy See, he was a priest, serving, as the youngest of Notre-Dame's chaplains, the altar known, because of the late mass which is said there, as the *altare pigrorum.*[1]

There, more immersed than ever in his beloved books, which he only left for an hour to hurry to the fief of the Moulin, his mixture of learning and austerity, so uncommon at his age, had promptly won for him the respect and admiration of the cloister. From the cloister, his reputation for learning had spread to the people, where, as then frequently happened, it was distorted somewhat into a reputation for sorcery.

It was as he was returning that Quasimodo Sunday from saying mass for the lazy at their altar, which was next to the door in the choir leading to the nave, on the right, near the image of the Virgin, that his attention was drawn by the group of old women yapping round the foundlings' bed.

It was then that he had gone up to that hapless small creature, so much hated and threatened. Its distress, its deformity, its dereliction, the thought of his young brother, the monstrous fancy that suddenly struck him that, were he to die, his dear little Jehan too might be miserably cast away on the foundlings' wooden plank, all this came into his heart simultaneously, a deep compassion stirred within him and he carried the child off.

When he drew the child from the sack, he found he was deformed indeed. The poor little devil had a wen over his left eye, his head between his shoulders, curvature of the spine, a protruding sternum, and crooked legs; but he seemed lively; and though it was impossible to tell what language he was lisping, his bawling argued a certain health and vigour. Claude's compassion was increased by such ugliness: and in his heart he vowed to bring the child up for love of his brother so that, through it, whatever little Jehan's sins might be in the future, this act of charity would have been performed for his sake. It was a sort of investment of good deeds on his young brother's behalf; a small-holding of shares which he

1. 'The altar of the lazy.'

wanted to amass for him in advance, lest there come a day when the young rogue found himself short of such currency, the only one acceptable at the toll-gate of Paradise.

He baptized his adopted child and named him Quasimodo, either because he wanted to indicate thereby the day on which he had found him, or because he wanted the name to typify just how incomplete and half-finished the poor little creature was. And in fact, Quasimodo, one-eyed, hunchbacked and crook-kneed, was hardly more than an 'approximation'.[1]

THREE

Immanis pecoris custos immanior ipse[2]

NOW, by 1482, Quasimodo was grown up. For several years past he had been bell-ringer at Notre-Dame, thanks to his adoptive father Claude Frollo, who had himself become Archdeacon of Josas, thanks to his suzerain, Messire Louis de Beaumont, who had become Bishop of Paris in 1472, at the death of Guillaume Chartier, thanks to his patron Olivier le Daim, barber, thanks be to God, to King Louis XI.

So Quasimodo was the carillonist of Notre-Dame.

With time, some kind of private bond had been formed, uniting the bell-ringer and the church. Forever cut off from the world by the double fatality of his unknown birth and his bodily deformity, and imprisoned since infancy within this double and impassable ring, the poor devil had grown used to seeing nothing of the world outside the religious walls that had gathered him into their shadow. As he grew bigger and developed, Notre-Dame had been for him in turn egg, nest, house, homeland and universe.

And there was for a fact a sort of mysterious, pre-existing harmony between the creature and the building. When he was still quite small, hauling himself crookedly and jerkily along beneath the gloom of the vaults, he looked, with his human face and his animals' limbs, like the native reptile of these damp and sombre flagstones, where the shadows of the Romanesque capitals cast so many strange shapes.

Later on, the first time he clung unthinkingly to the rope in the

1. i.e. a loose translation of the Latin *quasimodo*.

2. 'Of a monstrous flock a custodian more monstrous still.'

towers, and hung there, and set the bell in motion, the effect on Claude, his adoptive father, was of a child whose tongue has been set free and who has begun to talk.

So it was that, little by little, developing always in harmony with the cathedral, living in it, sleeping in it, hardly ever leaving it, subject day in and day out to its mysterious pressure, he came to resemble it, to be incrusted on it, as it were, to form an integral part of it. His salients fitted into the building's re-entrants, if you will allow the metaphor, and he seemed to be not only its inhabitant but also its natural content. One might almost say that he had taken on its shape, just as the snail takes on the shape of its shell. It was his abode, his hole, his envelope. So deep was the instinctive sympathy between the old church and himself, so numerous the magnetic and material affinities, that he somehow adhered to it like the tortoise to its shell. The gnarled cathedral was his carapace.

There is no need to warn the reader not to take literally the tropes we are obliged to employ here in order to express this peculiar, symmetrical, immediate, almost consubstantial coupling of a man and a building. No need to say either just how familiar he had become with the cathedral during so long and intimate a cohabitation. This abode was his. It had no depths to which he had not penetrated, no heights he had not scaled. Many was the time he had climbed the several elevations of the façade aided only by the asperities of the sculptures. The towers, on the outside surface of which he was often to be seen, crawling like a lizard gliding over a perpendicular wall, those twin giants, so tall, so menacing, so fearsome, held for him no terror or vertigo or attacks of giddiness; seeing them so meek beneath his hand, and so easily scaled, you would have said that he had tamed them. By dint of leaping, climbing and disporting himself amidst the chasms of the gigantic cathedral, he had turned more or less into a monkey and a mountain goat, like the Calabrian child which swims before it can walk and plays as a small child with the sea.

Moreover, not only his body seemed to have been fashioned to fit the cathedral, but his mind too. It would be hard to determine the state of that soul, the habits it had acquired, the form it had taken under that stunted envelope and leading so unsocial a life. Quasimodo had been born one-eyed, hunchbacked and lame. It was with great difficulty and great patience that Claude Frollo had managed to teach him to talk. But a fatality dogged the poor foundling. Having become bell-ringer of Notre-Dame at the age of fourteen, a fresh infirmity had come, to make him complete: the bells had ruptured his eardrums; he had gone deaf. The one door left open on the world for him by nature had been abruptly closed for ever.

As it closed, it cut off the one ray of joy and light which still penetrated to Quasimodo's soul. That soul fell into a profound night. The poor devil's melancholy became as complete and incurable as his deformity. We should add that his deafness made him to some extent dumb. For, so as not to give others cause to laugh at him, the moment he found he was deaf he made up his mind resolutely to a silence which he hardly ever broke except when he was alone. He deliberately tied the tongue that Claude Frollo had had so much trouble loosening. Hence it followed that when necessity constrained him to speak, his tongue was stiff and clumsy, like a door with rusty hinges.

If now we were to try and penetrate to Quasimodo's soul through that hard, thick bark; if we could sound out the depths of that malformed constitution; if it were given to us to shine a torch behind those untransparent organs, to explore the murky interior of that opaque creature, to elucidate its dark corners and absurd cul-de-sacs, and to shine a bright light suddenly on the unhappy psyche chained in the depths of that lair, we should surely find it in the wretchedly stunted and rachitic posture of those prisoners in the leads of Venice, who grew old bent double in a stone box that was too low and too short for them.

The spirit must atrophy in a misbegotten body. Quasimodo could just sense, stirring blindly within him, a soul made in his image. The impressions of objects underwent a considerable refraction before they reached his intelligence. His brain was a peculiar medium: the ideas that passed through it emerged all twisted. The reflections which resulted from this refraction were necessarily warped and divergent.

Hence the countless optical illusions, the countless aberrations of judgement, the countless byways down which his now uncontrolled, now idiot mind strayed.

The first effect this fatal constitution had was to cloud his vision of things. He received almost no immediate perception from them.

To him, the external world seemed much further off than it does to us.

The second effect of his misfortune was to make him vicious. He was vicious in fact because he was anti-social; he was anti-social because he was ugly. There was a logic in his nature as there is in ours.

His abnormally developed physical strength was a further cause of viciousness. *Malus puer robustus*,[1] says Hobbes.

But we must be fair to him, his viciousness was not perhaps inborn. From the time of his earliest steps among mankind, he had first heard himself, then seen himself being jeered at, stigmatized and rejected. For him human speech had always consisted either of mockery or a malediction. As he grew up, he found only loathing all around him. He had acquired it. He had caught the general viciousness. He had picked up the weapon with which he had been wounded.

And now he turned his face towards men only reluctantly. His cathedral sufficed him. It was peopled by marble figures, kings, saints and bishops, who at least did not burst out laughing in his face, but only stared down at him quietly and kindly. The other statues, the ones of monsters and demons, felt no hatred for Quasimodo. He resembled them too closely for that. Rather they mocked other men. The saints were his friends and blessed him; the monsters were his friends, and protected him. Thus he would pour out his heart at length to them. Sometimes he would spend whole hours at a time crouching in front of one of the statues, in solitary conversation with it. Should somebody come, he fled like a lover surprised during his serenade.

The cathedral was not only society for him, but the universe too, the whole of nature. The only espaliers he could conceive were the stained-glass windows, which were always in flower, the only shade that of the stone foliage blossoming in clumps, laden with birds, on the Saxon capitals, the only mountains the colossal towers of the church, the only ocean the Paris that surged at their feet.

What he loved above all else in this maternal edifice, what aroused his soul and made it spread the poor wings it had kept so miserably folded in its cave, what at times made him happy, were the bells. He loved them, he caressed them, he spoke to them, he

1. 'The strong boy is vicious.'

understood them. He cherished them all, from the carillon in the spire over the crossing to the great bell of the portal. For him, the spire above the crossing and the two towers were like three great cages where the birds, which he had raised himself, sang only for him. It was these same bells that had made him deaf, but mothers often love best the child that has made them suffer the most.

True, their voice was the only one he could still hear. And the big bell was thereby his sweetheart. She was his favourite among this rowdy family of girls which fluttered around him on feast-days. The big bell's name was Marie. She hung alone in the south tower, with her sister Jacqueline enclosed in a smaller cage next to hers. This Jacqueline had been so named after the wife of Jean de Montagu, who had given her to the church; not that this had prevented him from appearing minus his head at Montfaucon. In the second tower were six more bells, while the six smallest lived in the spire over the crossing, together with the wooden bell, which was only rung between after dinner on Absolution Thursday[1] and the morning of the Easter vigil. Quasimodo thus had fifteen bells in his harem, but big Marie was the favourite.

You cannot conceive his delight on days when there was a full peal. The moment the archdeacon released him and said 'Go on!' he climbed the spiral stairs of the bell-tower faster than others would have come down them. He went panting into the big bell's aerial chamber; he contemplated her piously and lovingly for a moment; then he softly addressed her and stroked her with his hand, like a good horse about to run a long race. He commiserated with her for what she was about to suffer. After these initial caresses, he shouted to his assistants, on the lower floor of the tower, to begin. They hung from the cables, the windlass gave a groan and the huge metal capsule began slowly to move. Quasimodo trembled as he followed it with his eyes. The first impact of the clapper against the bronze wall brought a shudder from the wooden frame on which it was mounted. Quasimodo vibrated with the bell. 'Yaah!' he cried with a shout of senseless laughter. Meanwhile, the great bell was picking up speed and as its angle began to widen out, so Quasimodo's eyes widened too and glowed like phosphorus. At last the full peal began, the whole tower shook, woodwork, leads, masonry, all rumbled at once, from the piles in the foundations up to the trefoils

1. Or Holy Thursday.

of the coping. Quasimodo now began to bubble over; he came and he went; he trembled from head to foot with the tower. The bell swung furiously and freely, exhibiting to both walls of the tower in turn its bronze jaws, whence came the tempestuous breath audible four leagues away. Quasimodo took up position in front of these gaping jaws. He crouched down, then straightened up as the bell swung back, inhaling its overpowering breath, looking alternately at the teeming square a full two hundred feet beneath him and at the enormous brass tongue which came every second to yell into his ear. This was the one form of speech he could hear, the one sound to disturb his universal silence. He dilated in it like a bird in the sunshine. All of a sudden he caught the bell's frenzy; his eyes became quite extraordinary; he waited for the great bell to come by, like a spider waiting for a fly, and abruptly hurled himself at it full tilt. Then, suspended above the abyss and launched on to the fearsome oscillation of the bell, he seized the bronze monster by its little ears, gripped it between his knees, spurred it on with his heels and renewed the fury of its peal with the full weight and impact of his own body. The tower meanwhile was quaking; he shouted and gnashed his teeth, his red hair bristled, his chest sounded like a blacksmith's bellows, his eyes flashed fire, the monstrous bell whinnied, panting, beneath him; and now it was no longer the great bell of Notre-Dame and Quasimodo but a dream, a whirlwind, a tempest; vertigo bestriding noise; a spirit grappled to a flying croup; a strange centaur, half man, half bell; a sort of horrible Astolphe,[1] borne along on a prodigious hippogryph of living bronze.

The presence of this extraordinary being seemed somehow to infuse the whole cathedral with the breath of life. He seemed to give off, or so at least the increasing superstitions of the crowd had it, a mysterious emanation, which animated all the stones of Notre-Dame and made the innermost bowels of the old church to pulse. People only had to know he was there and they fancied they could see the hundreds of statues in the galleries and portals stirring into life. And, under his hand indeed, the cathedral seemed a docile and obedient creature; it waited on his wishes before raising its great voice; it was possessed and filled by Quasimodo as by a familiar spirit. It was as if he made the vast edifice breathe. He was every-

1. A character in Ariosto's *Orlando Furioso.*

where in it, in fact, in every part of the monument at once. One minute they would be alarmed to see a strange dwarf on the very top of one of the towers, climbing, wriggling, crawling on all fours, descending the outside above the void, leaping from projection to projection, rummaging about in the belly of some sculpted gorgon; this was Quasimodo dislodging some rooks. The next minute, in some dim corner of the church, they would come across a sort of living chimera, squatting sullenly down; this was Quasimodo thinking. Another time, they would espy an enormous head and an unruly bundle of limbs swinging furiously on the end of a rope underneath a belfry; this was Quasimodo ringing for vespers or the angelus. At night a hideous shape was frequently to be seen wandering along the flimsy, open-work parapet which crowns the towers and circles the periphery of the apse; once more it was the hunchback of Notre-Dame. At such times, said the local women, the whole church somehow acquired a fantastic, supernatural and terrifying quality; here and there, an eye or a mouth would come open; the dogs and the serpents and the other stone grotesques which kept watch night and day around the monstrous cathedral were heard to bay, with necks outstretched and jaws agape; and if it was a Christmas night, as the great bell summoned the faithful to mass-ardent at midnight, with what sounded like a death rattle, such was the atmosphere spread across the sombre façade that the great doorway seemed to be swallowing the crowd and the rose-window to be watching it. And all this was Quasimodo's doing. Egypt would have taken him for the god of the temple; the Middle Ages believed he was its demon; in fact he was its soul.

So much so, that for those who know that Quasimodo actually existed, Notre-Dame is today deserted, inanimate, dead. Something, you feel, has gone from it. That vast body is empty; it is a skeleton; the spirit has left it and all you can see is where it was. It is like a skull which still has holes for the eyes but no eyes to look through them.

FOUR
The Dog and his Master

THERE was one human creature, however, whom Quasimodo excluded from the malice and loathing he felt towards others, and whom he loved as much as, and perhaps more than his cathedral; this was Claude Frollo.

There was no mystery about it. Claude Frollo had taken him in, had fed him, had raised him. When he was still tiny, it was against Claude Frollo's legs that he was wont to take refuge when dogs and children barked at him. Claude Frollo had taught him to talk, to read and to write. Claude Frollo had finally made him the bell-ringer. And to give the big bell in marriage to Quasimodo was to give Juliet to Romeo.

Quasimodo was thus profoundly, passionately, boundlessly grateful; and although his adoptive father's face was often stern and overcast, and although his words were generally brusque, harsh and imperious, this gratitude had never for one moment been belied. In Quasimodo the archdeacon had the most submissive of slaves, the most docile of servants, the most vigilant of watchdogs. When the poor bell-ringer went deaf, a mysterious sign language had been established between him and Claude Frollo, which they alone understood. In this way, the archdeacon was the one human being with whom Quasimodo remained in contact. He had only two relationships in the world, with the cathedral and with Claude Frollo.

There are no comparisons for the sway which the archdeacon had over the bell-ringer, or the bell-ringer's attachment to the archdeacon. A sign from Claude, and the thought that it would please him, and Quasimodo would have thrown himself off the top of the towers of Notre-Dame. Remarkably, Quasimodo had placed all that abnormally developed physical strength blindly at the disposal of another. This no doubt was filial devotion and domestic affection; it was also the fascination of one mind by another mind. It was an organism, poor, awkward and maladroit, standing, with bowed head and pleading eyes, before a high intelligence, at once profound, powerful and superior. Finally, and above all, it was gratitude. Gratitude carried to such extremes that there can be no comparison for it. This is not a virtue whose finest examples are to be found amongst men. So we shall say that Quasimodo loved the archdeacon as never dog, horse or elephant loved its master.

FIVE
Claude Frollo (continued)

IN 1482, Quasimodo was some twenty years old, Claude Frollo about thirty-six; the one had grown up, the other had aged.

Claude Frollo was no longer the innocent student of the Collège Torchi, the affectionate protector of a little child, the young and dreamy philosopher who knew many things but was ignorant of a great many more. He was an austere, solemn and forbidding priest; caring for souls; Monsieur the Archdeacon of Josas, second acolyte to the bishop, with the two deaneries of Montlhéry and Chateaufort in his charge and one hundred and seventy-four rural priests. The choirboys in their albs and long coats, the paid choristers, the brothers of Saint-Augustin, the matinal clergy of Notre-Dame, all trembled before this sombre and imposing figure as he passed slowly beneath the tall ogees of the choir, majestic, pensive, arms folded and head sunk so far forward on to his chest that all that could be seen of his face was his great bald forehead.

Dom Claude Frollo, however, had abandoned neither science nor the education of his young brother, the twin preoccupations of his life. But, as time passed, these sweet pleasures had become a little soured. In the end, says Paul Warnefrid,[1] the best bacon goes rancid. As he grew up, young Jehan Frollo, nicknamed 'of the windmill' because of where he had been put out to nurse, had not followed the path Claude had tried to lay down for him. His elder brother had counted on a pupil who was devout, docile, learned and honourable. But, like those young trees which defeat the gardener's efforts and turn stubbornly in the direction from which they receive the air and the sunlight, his young brother grew and multiplied and put out beautifully thick and luxuriant branches only in the direction of idleness, ignorance and debauchery. He was a real devil, and quite unruly, which caused Dom Claude to frown; but also very droll and very artful, which made his big brother smile. Claude had entrusted him to the same Collège de Torchi where he had spent his

1. A poet and historian of the eighth century.

own early years in study and meditation; and it grieved him that this sanctuary, which had once been edified by the name of Frollo, should today be scandalized by it. Sometimes he would give Jehan very long, very stern lectures about it, which the latter endured undaunted. When all was said and done, the young scamp had a kind nature, as is always the case in plays. But once the lecture was over, he went calmly back to his life of sedition and outrage. Once it was a *béjaune* (which was the name given to newcomers to the university) who had got a very warm welcome from him – a valuable tradition which has been carefully perpetuated until our own day. Another time he incited a band of students to storm an inn, in the time-honoured way, *quasi classico excitati*,[1] then drubbed the innkeeper 'with offensive sticks' and joyfully sacked his inn, even staving in the hogsheads of wine in the cellar. Then there had been a fine report in Latin, which the under-monitor from Torchi brought woefully to Dom Claude, bearing the rueful note in the margin: *Rixa: prima causa vinum optimum potatum*.[2] And lastly – which was dreadful for a child of sixteen – it was said that his excesses had many a time led him as far as the Rue de Glatigny.

As a result of all this, Claude, saddened and disheartened in his human affections, had thrown himself the more eagerly into the arms of science, that sister who at least does not laugh in your face and who always pays you for your pains, albeit at times in somewhat hollow coin. Thus he became more and more learned, and at the same time, by a natural consequence, more and more rigid as a priest and more and more unhappy as a man. For each of us, there are certain parallelisms between our intellect, our habits and our character, which develop without interruption and are broken only by life's great upheavals.

Because Claude Frollo had, since his youth, travelled almost the full circle of positive, external and legitimate human knowledge, he was obliged, if he were not to stop *ubi defuit orbis*,[3] to go further, and to seek other nourishment for the insatiable activity of his intellect. The ancient symbol of the serpent biting its own tail is especially appropriate for science. Claude Frollo seemed to have experienced it. Several solemn persons declared that, having ex-

1. 'As if excited by the trumpet.'
2. 'Scuffle: chief cause the very good wine that had been drunk.'
3. 'Where the circle ended.'

hausted the *fas* of human knowledge, he had dared to penetrate into the *nefas*.[1] He had, so it was said, tasted all the apples on the tree of knowledge one after the other and, either from hunger or from disgust, had ended by biting into the forbidden fruit. As our readers have seen, he had attended, by turns, the lectures of the theologians at the Sorbonne, the assemblies of the arts men at the statue of Saint-Hilaire, the disputes of the decretists at the statue of Saint-Martin, and the congregations of the doctors of medicine at the stoup of Notre-Dame, *ad cupam Nostrae Dominae*; he had consumed all the approved and permitted dishes which the four great kitchens, known as the four faculties, could prepare and serve to the intellect, and had been sated by them before his hunger was appeased; he had therefore burrowed further and deeper beneath all this finite, material and limited science; he had risked his soul perhaps, and had sat down in the cave at the mysterious table of the alchemists, the astrologers and the hermeticists, at whose head, in the Middle Ages, sat Averroes, William of Paris and Nicolas Flamel, and which extends eastwards, lit by the seven-branched candelabrum, as far as Solomon, Pythagoras and Zoroaster.

So at least it was assumed, rightly or wrongly.

It is a fact that the archdeacon was a frequent visitor to the graveyard of the Saints-Innocents where, admittedly, his mother and father had been buried along with the other victims of the plague of 1466; but he seemed to show much less reverence towards the cross above their grave than to the strange figures that covered the tomb of Nicolas Flamel and Claude Pernelle,[2] which stood next to it.

It is a fact that he had often been seen to pass along the Rue des Lombards and go furtively into a small house which formed the corner of the Rue des Ecrivains and the Rue Marivaulx. This was the house which Nicolas Flamel had built, in which he had died around 1417, and which had been empty ever since and was now beginning to fall into ruin, all the hermeticists and alchemists from every country having worn away the walls simply by carving their names on them. A few neighbours even declared they had once seen Archdeacon Frollo through a ventilator digging, excavating and shifting the earth in the two cellars whose supports had been scribbled over with countless lines of poetry and hieroglyphics by

1. The *fas* was the divine law, the *nefas* what violated it.
2. Flamel's wife.

Nicolas Flamel himself. It was assumed that Flamel had buried the philosopher's stone in these cellars, and for two centuries, from Magistri to Père Pacifique,[1] the alchemists did not desist from worrying away at the earth until all this relentless digging and searching finally reduced the house to dust beneath their feet.

It is a fact too that the archdeacon had developed a strange passion for the symbolic portal of Notre-Dame, that page from a grimoire written in stone by Bishop William of Paris, who has no doubt been damned for having affixed so infernal a frontispiece to the sacred poem chanted everlastingly by the remainder of the building. Archdeacon Claude was also supposed to have made a profound study of the colossal Saint Christopher and the long, enigmatic statue which then stood at the entrance from the parvis and to which the people had given the derisive name of Monsieur Legris.[2]

But what everyone had been able to observe was the interminable hours he often passed, sitting on the parapet of the parvis, studying the sculptures of the portal, examining first the foolish virgins with their overturned lamps, then the wise virgins with their upright lamps; or calculating at other times the line of sight of the rook standing on the left-hand portal, and staring at some mysterious point inside the church where the philosopher's stone was surely hidden, if it was not in Nicolas Flamel's cellar. It was, be it said in passing, a strange fate for the church of Notre-Dame at that time to be loved with such devotion and to two different degrees by two beings as unalike as Claude and Quasimodo; loved by one, a sort of savage and instinctive half-man, for its beauty, for its stature and for the harmonies that sounded from its magnificent ensemble; loved by the other, with his passionate and erudite imagination, for its meaning, for its myth, for the sense contained in it, for the symbolism dispersed beneath the sculptures of the façade like the first text of a palimpsest beneath the second; in short for the never-ending riddle it posed to the mind.

It is a fact, finally, that in the tower which overlooks the Grève, right next door to the bell-cage, the archdeacon had equipped for

1. The reference to Magistri is problematical; Father Pacifique was a French alchemist of the early seventeenth century.

2. Legris = 'the grey'

himself a small cell, so private that no one, not even, it was said, the bishop, could enter it without his leave. This cell had been built in the old days almost at the top of the tower, among the rooks' nests, by Bishop Hugo of Besançon, who had himself dabbled in the black arts there in his time. No one knew what the cell contained, but often at night, from the shores of the Terrain, they would see a weird, intermittent red light, at a window in the back of the tower, which vanished and then reappeared at short, regular intervals, as if in time to the steady exhalation of a bellows, and which seemed to come from a flame rather than a lamp. In the shadows, and at that height, it produced an odd effect, and the good-wives used to say: 'There's the archdeacon at his alchemy, that's hellfire sparkling.'

None of which constituted any very clear proof of sorcery, but it was as much smoke as they needed, nonetheless, to assume a fire; and the archdeacon had quite a formidable reputation. It must however be said that the sciences of Egypt, necromancy and magic, even of the whitest and most innocent kind, had no more zealous adversary, no one who denounced them more implacably to the officiality of Notre-Dame. Whether this was genuine horror or the play-acting of the thief who shouts 'stop thief', it did not prevent the archdeacon being looked on by the learned heads of the chapter as a soul who had ventured into the vestibule of hell, who was lost in the caverns of the cabbala and was fumbling in the darkness of the occult sciences. The people were in no doubts either: anyone with even a modicum of sound sense saw Quasimodo as the demon and Claude Frollo as the sorcerer. It was obvious that the bell-ringer would serve the archdeacon for a given length of time, at the end of which he would carry off his soul as payment. And so, for all the austerity of his life, the archdeacon was in very bad odour among the devout ladies of the parish, even the least experienced of whom suspected him of being a magician.

And if abysses had opened in his science as he got older, they had opened in his heart too. That at least is what there were grounds for believing when you studied his face, where the soul could be seen shining only through a sombre cloud. Where had he come by that bald forehead, that head forever bowed, that breast forever lifted in a sigh? What secret thought was it which brought such a bitter smile to his lips just as his frowning brows contracted, like two bulls about to do battle? Why was what remained of his hair already grey? What was the inner fire which now and again flared up in his eyes, until they seemed like two holes pierced in the wall of a furnace?

These symptoms of some violent moral preoccupation had become particularly acute at the time we are writing of. So strange and brilliant was his stare that more than once a choirboy had fled in terror when he found him on his own in the church. More than once, in the choir, during a service, his neighbour in the adjoining stall had heard him adding unintelligible parentheses to the plain-chant *ad omnem tonum.*[1] More than once the washer-woman of the Terrain, whose task it was to 'wash the chapter', had been more than a little alarmed to come across the marks of fingernails and clenched fingers in the Archdeacon of Josas's surplice.

He had become, what was more, doubly strict and more exemplary morally. Both his calling and his character had always kept him away from women; now he seemed to dislike them more than ever. The mere rustle of a silk cote-hardie brought his cowl down over his eyes. So jealous was he for his austerity and reticence in this respect that when, in December 1481, the Dame de Beaujeu, the king's daughter, visited the cloister of Notre-Dame, he solemnly opposed her admission, reminding the bishop of the statute in the Black Book, dating from Saint-Bartholomew's Eve, 1334, which forbade access to the cloister by any woman 'whatsoever, old or young, mistress or chambermaid'. Whereupon the bishop had been constrained to quote him the ordonnance of Legate Odo who accepts certain great ladies, *aliquae magnates mulieres, quae sine scandale evitari non possunt.*[2] But he refused to appear before the princess.

It had been noticed besides that for some time past his horror of gypsies and zingari seemed to have intensified. He had solicited an edict from the bishop expressly forbidding gypsies to come and dance or play tambourines on the parvis square, while at this time too he had also gone through the mildewed archives of the Official, so as to collect the cases of sorcerers and sorceresses condemned to the stake or the rope for complicity in the evil arts with he-goats, sows or nanny-goats.

1. 'In every tone.'
2. 'Some great ladies who cannot be turned away without scandal.'

SIX
Unpopularity

THE archdeacon and the bell-ringer were not, as we have said, greatly liked either by the prosperous or by the poor in the neighbourhood of the cathedral. When Claude and Quasimodo went out together, as they often did, and were seen, the pair of them, the servant behind the master, threading the cool, narrow, gloomy streets around Notre-Dame, more than one rude remark, more than one ironic yodel, more than one insulting jibe was aimed at them as they passed, unless, as was seldom the case, Claude Frollo was walking with his head held straight and high and stilled the tongues of the mockers by showing them his severe, almost august forehead.

In their own quarter of the town, the two of them were like Régnier's 'poets':

> All sorts of people walk behind poets
> As behind the owls the warbling fauvettes.

It might be a sly street-urchin, risking skin and bones for the ineffable pleasure of sinking a pin into Quasimodo's hump. Or a buxom, good-looking girl, more forward than she should have been, who brushed against the priest's black robe and sang the sardonic refrain in his face: 'Spite, spite, the devil's been caught.' Sometimes a group of sordid old women squatting in echelon in the shade of some porch steps would grumble loudly as the archdeacon and the bell-ringer passed, and blaspheme and hurl a cheery welcome at them: 'Hm! One of them's soul's like the other one's body!' Or else it was a band of schoolboys playing hopscotch who rose in a body and taunted them with a classical Latin greeting: *Eia! Eia! Claudius cum claudo!*[1] But most often the insults went unheeded either by the priest or the bell-ringer. Quasimodo was too deaf and Claude too sunk in thought to hear all these pleasantries.

1. 'Go on! Go on! Claude and the limper!'

BOOK FIVE

ONE
Abbas Beati Martini[1]

DOM Claude's fame had spread far and wide. At around the time when he refused to meet Madame de Beaujeu, it earned him a visit he long remembered.

It was one evening. He had just retired after service into his canon's cell in the cloister of Notre-Dame. There was nothing strange or mysterious to be seen here, apart perhaps from a few glass phials lying discarded in a corner and full of a rather suspicious-looking powder closely resembling the powder of projection.[2] There were, it was true, one or two inscriptions on the walls, but these were merely scientific or religious maxims culled from the best authors. The archdeacon had just sat down, in the light from a triple brass candlestick, in front of a huge chest full of manuscripts. He had leant his elbow on the open pages of Honorius d'Autun's book *De praedestinatione et libero arbitrio*,[3] and was deep in thought as he leafed through a printed folio he had just fetched, the sole product of the printing-press elsewhere in the cell. In the midst of his meditation, there came a knock at the door. 'Who is it?' shouted the savant, in the graceful tones of a starving mastiff disturbed at its bone. A voice answered from outside: 'Your friend, Jacques Coictier.' He went to open the door.

It was indeed the king's physician, a personage of about fifty, whose hard face was relieved only by the astuteness of his gaze. Another man was with him. Both were wearing long, slate-coloured robes trimmed with Russian squirrel's fur, belted and fastened, with bonnets of the same material and colour. Their hands were concealed by their sleeves, their feet by their robes and their eyes by their bonnets.

'As God is my help, messires!' said the archdeacon as he ushered them in, 'I had not expected so honourable a visit at this late hour.'

1. 'The Abbot of Saint-Martin.'
2. Used by alchemists to assist in the transmutation of metals.
3. 'Of predestination and free will.'

As he spoke which courteous words, his anxious, searching gaze went from the doctor to his companion.

'It's never too late to call on so eminent a scholar as Dom Claude Frollo of Tirechappe,' replied Doctor Coictier, whose Franche-Comté accent dragged all his sentences majestically out like a robe with a train.

There then began between the doctor and the archdeacon one of those congratulatory prologues which, in the custom of the time, preceded any conversation between scholars, but which did not prevent them from heartily detesting one another. For that matter, the same still holds good today, the scholar's mouth that compliments another scholar is a jar of poisoned honey.

Claude Frollo's felicitations to Jacques Coictier related above all to the many temporal advantages that the worthy doctor had managed to derive, in the course of his greatly envied career, from each of the king's illnesses, by exploiting a better and more certain alchemy than the pursuit of the philosopher's stone.

'Indeed, Doctor Coictier, I was delighted to learn of your nephew, my reverend lord Pierre Verse's, bishopric. Is he not Bishop of Amiens?'

'Yes, Archdeacon; by God's blessing and mercy.'

'You looked very well, you know, on Christmas Day, at the head of your company from the Audit office, Monsieur le Président!'

'Vice-president, Dom Claude. Nothing more, alas.'

'And how is your magnificent house in the Rue Saint-André-des-Arcs? It's a veritable Louvre. I love the apricot tree carved over the door with that amusing pun: "the apri-cottage".'

'Alas, Maître Claude, all that building-work is costing me the earth. As the building goes up, I am being ruined.'

'Ha, don't you have your income from the gaol and the palace bailiwick, and the rent from all the houses, stalls, huts and booths in the Clôture? You've a milch-cow there.'

'My lordship of Poissy didn't bring me in a thing last year.'

'But your tolls from Triel, Saint-James, Saint-Germain-en-Laye, they're still good.'

'Six score pounds, and not even *parisis*.'

'You've got your office as king's counsellor. That's a fixed sum.'

'Yes, dear colleague, but that confounded lordship of Poligny you hear so much about, isn't worth sixty gold crowns to me, year in year out.'

Dom Claude's tone as he paid Jacques Coictier these compliments was sour, sardonic and secretly mocking and he wore the sad, cruel smile of a superior but unlucky man absent-mindly playing for a moment with the stolid prosperity of a vulgar one. The other did not notice.

'Upon my soul,' said Claude finally, squeezing his hand, 'it's good to see you in such robust health.'

'Thank you, Maître Claude.'

'By the way,' exclaimed Dom Claude, 'how is your royal patient?'

'He doesn't pay his physician enough,' answered the doctor, glancing sideways at his companion.

'You think not, compère Coictier?' said the companion.

These words, spoken in a tone of surprise and reproach, caused the archdeacon's attention to revert to this unknown personage, from whom, truth to tell, it had not been altogether withdrawn for a single moment since the stranger crossed the threshold of the cell. Indeed, had he not had so many reasons for humouring Doctor Jacques Coictier, the all-powerful physician of King Louis XI, he would not have received him thus accompanied. And so there was nothing particularly cordial about his expression when Jacques Coictier said to him:

'By the way, Dom Claude, I've brought you a colleague who wished to meet you in view of your great reputation.'

'Monsieur is of the science?' asked the archdeacon, fixing Coictier's companion with a piercing stare. Beneath the stranger's eyebrows he found a stare no less wary and penetrating than his own.

As far as he could judge, by the feeble light from the lamp, he was an old man of about sixty and of medium height, who looked rather ill and infirm. There was a certain power and severity about his profile, though its lines were bourgeois enough, and his pupils sparkled in very deep-set eye-sockets like lights in the depths of a cave; and beneath the bonnet, which was pulled down over his face, you had the feeling that a brow of genius was mulling over its expansive schemes.

He undertook to answer the archdeacon's question himself.

'Reverend master,' he said solemnly, 'your fame has reached even me and I wished to consult you. I am only a poor gentleman from the provinces who removes his shoes before entering the house of a scholar. You must be told my name. I am called the Compère Tourangeau.'

'An odd name for a gentleman!' thought the archdeacon. But he felt he was face to face with something strong and serious. The instinct of his own high intelligence made him suspect another no less high beneath the fur-lined bonnet of Compère Tourangeau; and as he studied that solemn face, the ironic grin which the presence of Jacques Coictier had brought to his sullen features gradually faded, like the twilight on the night horizon. He sat down once more, gloomy and silent, in his big armchair, his elbow resumed its customary place on the table, his forehead its place on his hand. After a moment or two's reflection, he gestured to the visitors to be seated and addressed himself to Compère Tourangeau.

'You have come to consult me, maître, about which science?'

'Reverend sir,' answered Compère Tourangeau, 'I am sick, very sick. You are said to be a great Aesculapius, and I have come to ask you for medical advice.'

'Medicine!' said the archdeacon, shaking his head. He seemed to compose himself for a moment, then went on: 'Compère Tourangeau, since that is your name, turn your head. You will find my answer written up on the wall.'

Compère Tourangeau obeyed, and above his head could read this inscription, carved on the wall: 'Medicine is the daughter of dreams – Iamblichus.'

Meanwhile, Doctor Jacques Coictier had heard his companion's question with a resentment which was increased by Dom Claude's reply. He lent towards Compère Tourangeau's ear and said to him, softly enough not to be overheard by the archdeacon: 'I warned you he was a madman. But you would come to see him!'

'The fact is it is very possible the madman may be right, Doctor Jacques!' answered the compère, in the same tone and with a wry smile.

'As you wish!' replied Coictier drily. Then he addressed the archdeacon: 'You are quick with an answer, Dom Claude, and Hippocrates is no more of an obstacle to you than a nut to a monkey. Medicine a dream! I doubt whether the pharmacopolists and master-apothecaries could resist stoning you if they were here. You deny, then, the influence of philtres on the blood and of unguents on the flesh! You deny the eternal pharmacy of flowers and metals we call the world, expressly created for the eternal patient we call man!'

'I deny neither the pharmacy nor the patient,' said Dom Claude coldly, 'I deny the doctor.'

'So it is not true', Coictier went on heatedly, 'that gout is an internal scurf, that a gunshot wound can be cured by applying a roast mouse to it, that young blood properly infused can restore youth to old veins; it's not true that two and two make four, or that the emprosthotonos follows the episthotonos!'[1]

The archdeacon replied, unmoved: 'There are certain things I have my own ideas about.'

Coictier went red with anger.

'There, there, my good Coictier, let's not get angry,' said Compère Tourangeau, 'the archdeacon is our friend.'

Coictier calmed down, grumbling under his breath: 'He's mad, after all!'

'*Pasque-Dieu*, Maître Claude,' Compère Tourangeau went on after an interval, 'you make things very awkward for me. I wanted to consult you on two matters, one concerning my health, the other concerning my stars.'

'If such is your intention, monsieur,' rejoined the archdeacon, 'you would have done well not to waste your breath on my stairs. I do not believe in medicine. I do not believe in astrology.'

'Really!' said the compère in surprise.

Coictier gave a forced laugh.

'You can see he's mad,' he whispered to Compère Tourangeau. 'He doesn't believe in astrology!'

'How can one believe', Dom Claude persevered, 'that each ray from a star is a thread fixed to the head of a man!'

'What do you believe in then?' exclaimed Compère Tourangeau.

The archdeacon remained undecided for a moment, then gave a wintry smile that seemed to contradict his reply: '*Credo in Deum.*'

'*Dominum nostrum*,'[2] added Compère Tourangeau, crossing himself.

1. Emprosthotonos is a sort of muscular contraction; episthotonos, a tetanus.

2. 'I believe in God/Our Lord.'

'Amen,' said Coictier.

'Reverend master,' the compère went on, 'I rejoice in my soul to find you so devout. But you are a great scientist; are you so learned you no longer believe in science?'

'No,' said the archdeacon, seizing Compère Tourangeau by the arm, and a spark of enthusiasm rekindling in his lifeless pupils, 'no, I don't deny science. I have not crawled all this time on my belly with my nails in the earth, along the countless passages of the cavern without glimpsing, far ahead of me, at the end of the unlit gallery, a light, a flame, something, doubtless the reflection from the dazzling central laboratory where the wise and the patient have taken God by surprise.'

'What, then,' interrupted the Tourangeau, 'do you hold to be true and certain?'

'Alchemy.'

Coictier protested. 'Good God, Dom Claude, no doubt alchemy is reasonable enough, but why blaspheme against medicine and astrology?'

'Your science of man is nothing! Your science of the heavens is nothing!' said the archdeacon imperiously.

'So much for Epidaurus[1] and Chaldaea,'[2] answered the doctor with a sneer.

'Listen, Messire Jacques. I speak in good faith. I'm not the king's physician and His Majesty hasn't given me the Daedalus garden to observe the constellations from. Don't be angry, but hear me out. What truth have you derived, I shan't say from medicine, which is far too foolish a thing, but from astrology? Quote me the virtues of the vertical boustrophedon, the discoveries of the number seraph and the number sefiroth.'

'Do you deny', said Coictier, 'the sympathetic force of the Clavicula,[3] and that cabbalism derives from it?'

'Wrong, Messire Jacques! Not one of your formulas leads to reality. Whereas alchemy has made discoveries. Would you dispute results like these? Ice enclosed under the earth for a thousand years turns into rock crystal. Lead is the ancestor of all metals (for gold is not a metal, gold is light). Lead needs only four periods of two

1. The site of a much-frequented temple to Aesculapius, the god of medicine.
2. A country famous for its astrologers.
3. A book of magic falsely attributed to Solomon.

hundred years to pass successively from the state of lead to the state of red arsenic, from red arsenic to pewter, from pewter to silver. Are these facts? But to believe in the Clavicula, the full line and the stars, is as absurd as believing, like the inhabitants of Cathay, that the oriole changes into a worm, or seeds of corn into fish of the carp family!'

'I have studied hermetics,' cried Coictier, 'and I can state...'

The impetuous archdeacon would not let him finish. 'And I have studied medicine, astrology and hermetics. Here only is the truth' (and so saying he picked up from the chest a phial full of the powder to which we referred earlier), 'here only is the light! Hippocrates is a dream, Urania is a dream, Hermes is an idea. Gold is the sun, to make gold is to be God. That is the only science. I have explored medicine and astrology, I tell you. Nothing, nothing at all. The human body, darkness; the stars, darkness!'

And he fell back on to his chair in an attitude both forceful and inspired. Compère Tourangeau observed him in silence. Coictier was trying to snigger. He shrugged his shoulders imperceptibly and repeated in an undertone: 'A madman!'

'And have you attained this miraculous objective?' said the Tourangeau suddenly, 'have you made gold?'

'If I had,' answered the archdeacon, bringing the words out slowly like a man reflecting, 'the King of France would be called Claude and not Louis.'

The compère frowned.

'What am I saying?' Dom Claude went on with a scornful smile. 'What would the throne of France matter to me if I could rebuild the empire of the Orient?'

'I wish you luck!' said the compère.

'Oh, the poor madman!' murmured Coictier.

The archdeacon continued, seemingly in answer only to his own thoughts:

'No indeed, I crawl on; I graze my face and knees on the stones along the subterranean way. I catch glimpses, I do not contemplate! I do not read, I spell out!'

'And when you can read,' asked the compère, 'will you make gold?'

'Who can doubt it?' said the archdeacon.

'In that case, Notre-Dame knows I have great need of money,

and I would like very much to learn to read from your books. Tell me, reverend master, your science is not hostile or displeasing to Notre-Dame?'

To which question from the compère, Dom Claude merely replied with quiet disdain: 'Whose archdeacon I am?'

'That's true, maître. Well, would you like to initiate me? Make me spell out with you.'

Claude adopted the majestic and pontifical attitude of a Samuel.

'Old man, it requires more years than remain to you to venture on this journey through the things of mystery. Your head is very grey! One only emerges from the cave with white hair, but one enters it with black hair. Science knows well how to make a human face look gaunt and withered and wizened, it has no need of old age to bring it faces that are already lined. Yet should you desire to submit yourself to its discipline at your age and to decipher the fearful alphabet of the sages, very well, come to me, I shall try. You are a poor old man, I shall not tell you to go and visit the burial chambers of the Pyramids of which the ancient Herodotus speaks, nor the tower of bricks at Babylon, nor the immense sanctuary of white marble at the Indian temple of Eklinga. I have not seen, any more than you, the Chaldaean stonework built in the sacred form of the Sikra,[1] nor the temple of Solomon which has been destroyed, nor the stone doors of the sepulchre of the kings of Israel that have been broken. We shall content ourselves with the fragments of the book of Hermes which we have here. I will explain the statue of Saint Christopher to you, the symbol of the Sower, and that of the two angels in the portal of the Sainte-Chapelle, one of whom has one hand in a vase and the other in a cloud ...'

At this point, Jacques Coictier, who had been unseated by the archdeacon's fiery rejoinders, got back in the saddle and interrupted him in the triumphant tones of one scholar correcting another: '*Erras, amice Claudi.*[2] Symbols are not numbers. You are mistaking Orpheus for Hermes.'

'It is you who err,' answered the archdeacon solemnly. 'Daedalus is the foundations, Orpheus the wall, Hermes the edifice. The whole. You will come when you wish,' he went on, turning to the Tourangeau, 'I will show you the particles of gold left in the bottom of

1. An Indian round tower, with pinnacle.
2. 'You err, friend Claude!'

Nicolas Flamel's crucible, and you shall compare them with the gold of William of Paris. I will teach you the secret powers of the Greek word *peristera.*[1] But especially shall I make you read one by one the marble letters of the alphabet, the granite pages of the book. We shall go from the portal of Bishop William and Saint-Jean-le-Rond to the Sainte-Chapelle, then to the house of Nicolas Flamel in the Rue Marivaulx, to his tomb, which is in the Saints-Innocents, and to his two hospitals in the Rue de Montmorency. I shall make you read the hieroglyphs covering the four great andirons in the portal of the Hôpital Saint-Gervais and in the Rue de la Ferronnerie. And together we shall spell out the façades of Saint-Côme, Sainte-Geneviève-des-Ardents, Saint-Martin and Saint-Jacques-de-la-Boucherie . . .'

For all the intelligence in his eyes, the Tourangeau did not seem to have understood Dom Claude for quite some while. He broke in.

'*Pasque-Dieu*, what *are* your books?'

'Here is one of them,' said the archdeacon.

And opening the window of the cell, he pointed to the immense church of Notre-Dame, whose black silhouette, with its twin towers, its ribs of stone and its monstrous cruppers, stood out against the starlit sky like an enormous two-headed sphinx sitting in the midst of the town.

The archdeacon contemplated the gigantic cathedral for a time in silence, then he sighed and stretched out his right hand towards the printed book lying open on his table and his left hand towards Notre-Dame, and looked sadly from the book to the church:

'Alas,' he said, 'this will kill that.'

Coictier, who had moved eagerly towards the book, could not help exclaiming: 'But good Lord, what's so dreadful about that: *Glossa in epistolas D. Pauli.*, Norimbergae, Antonius Koburger, 1474?[2] This is not new. It's a book by Peter Lombard, the Master of the Sentences. Is it because it's printed?'

'Exactly,' answered Claude, who seemed engrossed in some profound meditation and stood resting his bent forefinger on the folio that had issued from the famous presses of Nuremberg. Then he added these mysterious words: 'Alas and alack, small things

1. Meaning either a *dove* or *verbena*.

2. 'Commentary on the Epistles of St Paul', Nuremberg, Antony Koburger, 1474.

overcome great ones! A tooth triumphs over a body. The Nile rat kills the crocodile, the swordfish kills the whale, the book will kill the building!'

The curfew sounded in the cloister just as Doctor Jacques was repeating his everlasting refrain to his companion in a low voice: 'He's mad.' To which his companion this time answered: 'I believe he is.'

It was the time of day when no outsiders could remain in the cloister. The two visitors withdrew. 'Maître,' said the Compère Tourangeau, as he took leave of the archdeacon, 'I like scholars and great minds, and I hold you in particular esteem. Come to-morrow to the Palace of the Tournelles and ask for the Abbot of Saint-Martin-de-Tours.'

The archdeacon went back to his room dumbfounded, having at last realized who the Compère Tourangeau was, and recalling this passage from the cartulary of Saint-Martin-de-Tours: *Abbas beati Martini, SCILICET REX FRANCIAE, est canonicus de consuetudine et habet parvam praebendam quam habet sanctus Venantius et debet sedere in sede thesaurarii.*[1]

From then on, so it was declared, the archdeacon frequently conferred with Louis XI when His Majesty came to Paris, and Dom Claude's influence eclipsed that of Olivier le Daim and Jacques Coictier who, as was his way, gave the king the rough edge of his tongue.

TWO
This Will Kill That

OUR female readers will forgive us if we pause for a moment in order to see what the thought might be that lay concealed beneath the archdeacon's enigmatic words: 'This will kill that. The book will kill the building.'

As we see it, this thought had two facets. Firstly, it was the thought of a priest. It was the alarm felt by the priesthood before a new agent: the printing-press. It was the terror and bewilderment felt by a man of the sanctuary before the luminous press of Guten-

1. 'The Abbot of Saint-Martin, to wit the King of France, is by custom a canon; he has the small prebend which Saint Venant has and should sit in the seat of the Treasurer.'

berg. It was the pulpit and the manuscript, the spoken and the written word, taking fright at the printed word; something like the stupor felt by a sparrow were it to see the angel legion unfold its six million wings. It was the cry of the prophet who already hears the restless surge of an emancipated mankind, who can see that future time when intelligence will undermine faith, opinion dethrone belief and the world shake off Rome. The prognosis of a philosopher who sees the human mind, volatilized by the press, evaporate from the theocratic receptacle. The terror of a soldier examining the bronze battering-ram and saying: 'The tower will give way.' It meant that one power was going to succeed another power. It meant: the press will kill the church.

But beneath this first and no doubt simpler thought, there was, in our opinion, a second, newer one, a corollary of the first less easily perceived but more easily challenged, an equally philosophical notion, no longer that of the priest alone but of the scientist and the artist too. This was the presentiment that as human ideas changed their form they would change their mode of expression, that the crucial idea of each generation would no longer be written in the same material or in the same way, that the book of stone, so solid and durable, would give way to the book of paper, which was more solid and durable still. Seen thus, the archdeacon's vague formula had a second meaning: it meant that one art was going to dethrone another art. It meant: printing will kill architecture.

In fact, from the origin of things up to and including the fifteenth century of the Christian era, architecture was the great book of mankind, man's chief form of expression in the various stages of his development, either as force or as intelligence.

When the memory of the first peoples felt itself to be overladen, when the human race's baggage-train of memories became so heavy and confused that language, volatile and unadorned, was in danger of losing it along the road, they were transcribed on to the ground in what was at once the most visible, durable and natural fashion. Each tradition was sealed beneath a monument.

The earliest monuments were simply quarters of rock which 'the iron had not touched', says Moses. Architecture began like any other form of writing. It was first of all an alphabet. A stone was set upright and it was a letter, and each letter was a hieroglyph, and on each hieroglyph a group of ideas rested, like the capital on a column. Such was the way of the first peoples, everywhere at the same moment, across the whole surface of the globe. The 'raised stone' of the Celts is to be found in Asian Siberia and in the pampas of America.

Later on, they formed words. Stone was superimposed on stone, and these granite syllables were coupled together, the word tried out a few combinations. The Celtic dolmen and cromlech, the Etruscan tumulus, the Hebrew *galgal*, are words. Some of them, the tumulus especially, are proper nouns. Sometimes even, when they had plenty of stone and an extensive site, they wrote a sentence. The massive accumulation of Carnac is a complete formula in itself.[1]

Finally, they wrote books. Traditions had given birth to symbols, under which they vanished, like the trunk of a tree under its foliage; mankind had faith in all these symbols and they continued to grow, to multiply, to intersect, to become more and more complex; the early monuments were no longer adequate to contain them; they were swamped on every side; these monuments could barely express the primitive tradition which, like them, was bare, simple and earthbound. The symbol needed to expand into a building. Architecture thus evolved along with the human mind; it became a giant with a thousand heads and a thousand arms, and fixed all this vacillating symbolism in a form at once palpable, visible and eternal. While Daedalus, who is force, measured, and Orpheus, who is intelligence, sang, the pillar which is a letter, the arcade which is a syllable, the pyramid which is a word, simultaneously set in motion both by a law of geometry and a law of poetry, formed groups, they combined and amalgamated, they rose and fell, they were juxtaposed on the ground, and superimposed in the sky, until, at the dictate of the general idea of an epoch, they had written those marvellous books which were also marvellous buildings: the pagoda of Eklinga, the Ramesseum of Egypt, the Temple of Solomon.

The idea that engendered them, the word, was not only the foundation of all these buildings, it was also in their form. The Temple of Solomon, for instance, was not merely the binding of the sacred book, it was the sacred book itself. From each of its concentric ring-walls, the priests could read the word translated and made

1. Carnac is in south Brittany.

manifest to the eye, and could thus follow its transformations from sanctuary to sanctuary until, in its ultimate tabernacle, they could grasp it in its most concrete yet still architectural form: the ark. Thus the word was enclosed in the building, but its image was on the envelope like the human figure on the coffin of a mummy.

And not only the form of buildings but also the site chosen for them revealed the idea which they represented. According to whether the symbol to be expressed was a cheerful or a gloomy one, Greece would crown her mountains with a temple harmonious to the eye, while India disembowelled hers and carved them into those shapeless subterranean pagodas borne by gigantic rows of granite elephants.

Thus, during the world's first six thousand years, from the most immemorial Hindustan pagoda to the cathedral of Cologne, architecture was the great script of the human race. And so true is this, that not only every religious symbol but also every human thought has its own page and its own monument in this immense book.

Every civilization begins in theocracy and ends in democracy. This law, of liberty succeeding to unity, is inscribed in architecture. For, and on this we insist, you must not believe that masonry is capable only of erecting temples, of expressing myth and priestly symbolism, of transcribing the mysterious tablets of the law into hieroglyphs on its stone pages. Were that the case, since there comes a time in every human society when the sacred symbol is outworn and is obliterated by freedom of thought, when man eludes the priest, when the outcrop of systems and philosophies erodes the face of religion, then architecture would be incapable of reproducing this new state of the human mind; its sheets would be covered on the recto and blank on the verso, its work would be abridged, its book incomplete. But such is not the case.

As an example, let us take the Middle Ages, where we can see more clearly because they are closer to us. During their first phase, as theocracy organized Europe, as the Vatican rallied and reordered around itself the elements of a Rome formed from the Rome lying crumbled around the Capitol, as Christianity sifted through the debris of the earlier civilization for all the strata of society and built from its ruins a new, hierarchical universe, with the priesthood as its keystone, then it was that this mysterious Romanesque architecture, sister to the theocratic masonry of Egypt and India, the unvarying emblem of pure Catholicism, the immutable hieroglyph of papal unity, was first heard, welling up amidst the chaos and later, under the impetus of Christianity and the hand of the barbarians, issuing forth from the wreckage of the dead architectures of Greece and Rome. The whole philosophy of the age, in fact, is inscribed in that sombre Romanesque style. In it you everywhere sense authority, unity, the impenetrable and the absolute, Gregory VII; everywhere the priest, never the man; everywhere the caste, never the people. But then came the Crusades. They were a great popular movement; and any great popular movement, whatever its cause or its object, always releases the spirit of liberty from its final precipitate. Innovations were on their way. The stormy age of the Jacqueries, the Pragueries and the Leagues dawned.[1] Authority was shaken, unity split in two. Feudalism demanded to share with theocracy, as it awaited the inevitable advent of the people, who would, as always, take the lion's share. *Quia nominor leo.*[2] Thus, the nobility broke through below the priesthood, the commons below the nobility. The face of Europe was changed. Well, the face of architecture was changed too! Like civilization, it turned the page, and the new spirit of the times found it ready to write at its dictation. It returned from the Crusades with the pointed arch, like the nations with liberty. Then, as Rome was gradually dismembered, Romanesque architecture died. The hieroglyph deserted the cathedral and went to emblazon the castle-keep, so as to lend prestige to feudalism. From now on, the cathedral itself, formerly so dogmatic an edifice, was invaded by the bourgeoisie, by the commons, by liberty; it escaped from the priest and came under the sway of the artist. The artist built to his own fancy. Farewell mystery, myth and law. Now it was fantasy and caprice. Provided the priest had his basilica and his altar, he had no further say. The four walls belonged to the artist. The book of architecture no longer belonged to the priesthood, to religion and to Rome; it belonged to the imagination, to poetry and to the people. Hence the rapid and innumerable transformations of an architecture only three centuries old, so striking after the stagnant immobility of Romanesque architecture, which was six or seven

1. The Jacqueries were peasant revolts in France, the most famous in 1358; the Praguerie was a revolt against Charles VII of France in 1440.

2. 'For my name is lion.'

centuries old. But architecture took giant strides. The genius and originality of the people performed the task the bishops had performed. Each race wrote, in passing, its line in the book; it struck out the old Romanesque hieroglyphs on the frontispieces of the cathedrals, and now the dogma was all but lost to view, except where it showed through the new symbolism laid on top of it. The people's drapery had very nearly obscured the religious bone-structure. And now architects took unimaginable liberties, even towards the Church. Monks and nuns coupled shamefully on capitals, as in the Hall of Chimneys in the Palais de Justice in Paris. The story of Noah was carved *in full*, as beneath the great portal of Bourges. A bacchic monk with asses' ears and glass in hand laughed a whole community to scorn, as above the lavabo in the Abbey of Bocherville. At that time, the thought that was inscribed in stone enjoyed a privilege entirely comparable to our present freedom of the press. This was the freedom of architecture.

That freedom went a long way. Sometimes a portal, a façade or an entire church would display a symbolic meaning utterly alien to the cult, or even hostile to the Church. William of Paris, as early as the thirteenth century, and Nicolas Flamel in the fifteenth, wrote such seditious pages. Saint-Jacques-de-la-Boucherie was an entire anti-church.

At that time, thought was free only in this one mode, and so it was written out in full only in the books known as buildings. But for its architectural form, it would have found itself being burnt in the public squares by the hangman in its manuscript form, had it been rash enough to risk one. Church portal ideas would have witnessed the punishment of book ideas. Masonry being its one way of manifesting itself, thought hastened to it from every side. Hence the immense numbers of cathedrals which covered Europe, their total so prodigious that one can scarcely credit it even after verifying it. The material and intellectual forces of society all converged on the one point: architecture. In this way, on the pretext of building churches to God, that art grew to a magnificent stature.

Whoever was then born a poet became an architect. The genius distributed amongst the masses was everywhere compressed under feudalism, as if under a testudo of bronze shields; architecture was its one outlet, it was released through that art and its Iliads took the form of cathedrals. The other arts all submitted to the allegiance and discipline of architecture. They were the workmen in the great work. In his own person, the architect, the poet and overseer, summated the sculpture that carved his façades, the painting that illuminated his stained-glass and the music which set his bells swinging and breathed air into his organs. And even poor poetry, properly so called, still stubbornly vegetating in manuscripts, was obliged, if it wanted to be something, to enter within the framework of the building in the form of a hymn or of *prose*; the self-same role, after all, which the tragedies of Aeschylus had played in the priestly festivals of Greece, or the book of Genesis in the Temple of Solomon.

Thus, up until Gutenberg, architecture was the chief, the universal form of writing. It was the Middle Ages which wrote the final page in the book of granite, which had been begun in the Orient and carried on by Ancient Greece and Rome. Moreover, this phenomenon, of a popular architecture succeeding a caste architecture, which we have just observed in the Middle Ages, has occurred in every analogous movement of the human intelligence in the other great periods of history. Thus, to enunciate only briefly a law it would require whole volumes to develop: in the high Orient, the cradle of early times, after Hindu architecture, Phoenician architecture, the opulent mother of Arab architecture; in antiquity, after Egyptian architecture, of which the Etruscan style and Cyclopean monuments are only an offshoot, Greek architecture, of which the Roman style is merely an extension, with the Carthaginian dome added; in modern times, after Romanesque architecture, Gothic architecture. And if you divide these three series into two, you will find the same symbol on the three elder sisters, Hindu, Egyptian and Romanesque architecture: theocracy, caste, unity, dogma, God; and the same meaning too, whatever the diversity of form inherent in their nature, for the three younger sisters, Phoenician, Greek and Gothic architecture: liberty, the people, man.

In Hindu, Egyptian or Romanesque buildings, you are conscious always of the priest and of nothing but the priest, whether he be called brahmin, magus or pope. The same does not hold for popular architectures. They are more ornate and less sacred. In Phoenician architecture you are conscious of the merchant; in Greek of the republican; in Gothic of the burgess.

The general characteristics of any theocratic architecture are immutability, the horror of progress, the preservation of traditional lines, the consecration of original types, the constant bending of all the forms of man and nature to the incomprehensible whims of the symbol. They are murky books which initiates alone can decipher. For the rest, every form, every deformity even, has a meaning which makes it inviolable. You must not ask of Hindu, Egyptian or Romanesque buildings that they should amend their design or improve their statuary. To them any improvement is an impiety. In these architectures, the rigidity of dogma seems to have spread across the stonework like a second petrification. The general characteristics of popular buildings on the other hand are variety, progress, originality, opulence, perpetual motion. They are sufficiently detached from religion to think of their beauty, to cultivate it, to be constantly adjusting the statues and arabesques that adorn them. They belong to their century. There is something human about them mixing ceaselessly in with the divine symbol beneath which they are still produced. Hence buildings accessible to every soul, every intelligence, every imagination, still symbolic yet as easily understood as nature. The difference between this architecture and a theocratic one, is that between a sacred and a profane tongue, between hieroglyphs and art, between Solomon and Phidias.

If we now sum up what we have so far said all too hurriedly, omitting many proofs as well as many objections of detail, it amounts to this: that up until the fifteenth century architecture was the principal register of mankind, that during that period all ideas of any complexity which arose in the world became a building; every popular idea, just like every religious law, had its monuments; that the human race, in fact, inscribed in stone every one of its important thoughts. And why? Because every idea, be it religious or philosophical, is concerned to perpetuate itself, because the idea that has moved one generation wants to move others, and to leave some trace. But how precarious was the immortality of a manuscript! While a building is an altogether more solid, lasting and resistant book! It takes only a torch and a Turk to destroy the written word. To demolish the word of stone you need a social, terrestrial revolution. The barbarians passed over the Coliseum, the flood perhaps over the Pyramids.

In the fifteenth century, everything changed.

The human mind discovered a means of perpetuating itself which was not only more lasting and resistant than architecture, but also simpler and easier. Architecture was dethroned. The lead characters of Gutenberg succeeded the stone characters of Orpheus.

The book was to kill the building.

The invention of the printing-press is the greatest event in history. It was the mother of revolutions. It was the total renewal of man's mode of expression, the human mind sloughing off one form to put on another, a complete and definitive change of skin by that symbolic serpent which, ever since Adam, has represented the intelligence.

In its printed form, thought is more imperishable than ever; it is volatile, elusive, indestructible. It mingles with the air. In the days of architecture, thought had turned into a mountain and taken powerful hold of a century and of a place. Now it turned into a flock of birds and was scattered on the four winds, occupying every point of air and space simultaneously.

We repeat: who cannot see that in this guise it is far more indelible? Before, it was solid, now it is alive. It has passed from duration to immortality. You can demolish a great building, but how do you root out ubiquity? Come a flood and the mountain will long ago have vanished beneath the waters while the birds are still flying; let a single ark be floating on the surface of the cataclysm and they will alight on it, will survive on it, and, like it, will be present at the receding of the waters; and as it awakes, the new world which emerges from the chaos will see the ideas of the drowned world soaring above it, winged and full of life.

When you appreciate that this mode of expression is not only the most conservative, but also the simplest and most convenient, the most generally practicable, when you reflect that it has no great baggage-train dragging behind it, nor heavy apparatus to be transported, when you compare the idea which, to translate itself into a building, needed to set in motion four or five other arts and tons of gold, a whole mountain of stones, a whole forest of timber, a whole nation of workmen, when you compare that to the idea which, to become a book, needs only a sheet of paper, some ink and a pen, is it surprising that the human intellect should have deserted architecture for the printing-press? If you suddenly dig a canal through the original bed of a river, at a lower level, the river will abandon its bed.

And so you see how, starting with the discovery of printing, architecture gradually dried up, it atrophied, and was denuded. One can sense that the tide was ebbing, that the sap was departing, that the thought of ages and of nations was withdrawing from it! In the fifteenth century this cooling-down was more or less imperceptible, the press was as yet too weak, and did no more than draw off mighty architecture's superabundance of life. But from the sixteenth century on, architecture's malady was apparent; it was no longer the essential expression of society; it turned miserably into a classical art; once it had been Gallic, European, indigenous, now it became Greek and Roman; once it was true and modern, now it became pseudo-antique. This was the decadence we call the Renaissance. Yet it was a splendid decadence, for the old Gothic genius, that sun which was setting behind the giant press of Mainz, still shed its dying rays for a time into that hybrid mass of Latin arcades and corinthian colonnades.

It was this setting sun which we take to be a dawn.

However, the moment architecture became merely one art among others, once it was no longer the total, the sovereign, the tyrannical art, it no longer had the strength to keep hold of the other arts. So they set themselves free, they broke the architect's yoke and each went its own way. Each of them gained by the divorce. Everything grows in isolation. Sculpture became statuary, imagery became painting, canon became music. It was like an empire which is dismembered when its Alexander dies, and whose provinces become kingdoms.

And so we get Raphael, Michelangelo, Jean Goujon,[1] Palestrina, those glories of the brilliant sixteenth century.

Simultaneously with the arts, thought itself was everywhere being set free. The heresiarchs of the Middle Ages had already made great inroads into Catholicism. The sixteenth century shattered religious unity. Prior to the press, the Reformation would have been only a schism, the press turned it into a revolution. Take away the press and heresy is enervated. Whether it was fate or Providence, Gutenberg was the precursor of Luther.

Meanwhile, once the sun of the Middle Ages was fully set, once

1. French sculptor and architect of the sixteenth century.

the Gothic genius had been extinguished forever on the horizon of the art, architecture became increasingly drab, colourless and self-effacing. The printed book ate its way into buildings like worm, and bled and devoured them. Architecture shed its skin and its leaves, and wasted visibly away. It became mean, impoverished, null. It no longer expressed anything, not even the memory of the art of earlier times. Reduced to itself, abandoned by the other arts because the human mind had abandoned it, it turned to common labourers for want of artists. The plain window replaced stained-glass. The stonemason succeeded the sculptor. It meant farewell to all vitality, all originality, all life, all intelligence. It dragged on, like a pitiable mendicant of the studios, from imitation to imitation. Michelangelo, who had no doubt sensed that it was dying as early as the sixteenth century, had had one last, despairing idea. This Titan of the art piled the Pantheon on the Parthenon and created Saint Peter's of Rome. A master-work which deserved to remain unique, the final originality of architecture, an artistic giant signing his name at the foot of the colossal ledger of stone and closing it. But once Michelangelo was dead, what did this wretched architecture do, which was only the ghost or the spectre of its former self? It took Saint Peter's and traced it, it parodied it. It became a craze. It was pitiful. Every century has its Saint Peter's of Rome; in the seventeenth century the Val-de-Grâce, in the eighteenth Sainte-Geneviève. Every country has its Saint Peter's. London has one. St Petersburg has one. Paris has two or three. A trivial testament, the last ravings of a great art in its decline, which relapsed into infancy before it died.

If, instead of the characteristic monuments like those of which we have just been speaking, we examine the general aspect of the art between the sixteenth and eighteenth centuries, we observe the same phenomena of decline and wasting. From François II on, the architectural form of buildings becomes steadily less noticeable, and allows the geometrical form to show through, like the bone-structure of some emaciated invalid. The beautiful lines of art give way to the cold and inexorable lines of the geometer. A building is no longer a building, it is a polyhedron. Yet architecture is desperate to conceal this bareness. You see Greek pediments inscribed within Roman pediments and vice versa. It is always the Pantheon inside the Parthenon: Saint Peter's of Rome. Look at the brick houses of

Henri IV with their stone quoins: the Place Royale, and the Place Dauphine. Look at Louis XIII's churches, heavy, squat, flattened, thick-set, burdened by their domes as if by a hump. Look at the architecture of Mazarin, at the Quatre Nations, that bad Italian pastiche. Look at Louis XIV's palaces, elongated barracks for courtiers, stiff, glacial, uninteresting. Look finally at Louis Quinze, with its chicory and vermicelli, and all the warts and proud-flesh which disfigure that old, decrepit, toothless and coquettish architecture. Between François II and Louis XV the disease grew in geometrical progression. The art was no longer anything but skin and bone. It died a miserable death.

What, meanwhile, had become of the printing-press? All the vitality which went from architecture came to the press. As architecture waned, the press waxed and grew fat. The capital sums of energy that the human mind had expended on buildings, it henceforth expended on books. And so, as early as the sixteenth century, the press, now the equal of a declining architecture, fought with it and killed it. In the seventeenth century, it was already sufficiently dominant, sufficiently triumphant, sufficiently secure in its victory, to treat the world to the banquet of a great literary age. In the eighteenth century, after its lengthy repose at the court of Louis XIV, it took up Luther's old sword once again, armed Voltaire with it, and ran in tumult to attack the old Europe, whose architectural expression it had already killed. When the eighteenth century came to an end, it had destroyed everything. In the nineteenth century, it was to rebuild.

And now we must ask which of these two arts, over the past three centuries, has truly represented the human mind? Which has translated it? Which has expressed, not only its literary and scholastic obsessions, but its vast, profound and universal movement? Which has constantly superimposed itself without let-up or interruption, on the march of that myriapod monster, the human race? Architecture or printing?

Printing. Let there be no mistake, architecture is dead, dead beyond recall, killed by the printed book, killed because it is less enduring, killed because it is more expensive. Every cathedral is a billion francs. And then imagine what sums it would require to rewrite the book of architecture, to once more cover the earth with thousands of buildings, to return to those ages when, so crowded were the monuments, that, according to an eye-witness, 'it was as if the world had shaken off its old garments so as to clothe itself in a white vestment of churches'. *Erat enim ut si mundus, ipse excutiendo semet, rejecta vetustate, candidam ecclesiarum vestem indueret* (Glaber Radulphus).

A book is so soon made, it costs so little, and it can travel so far! Why wonder that the whole of human thought should flow down this slope? This is not to say that architecture will not now and again have a fine monument, an isolated masterpiece. From time to time, in the reign of printing, we may well still get a column made, I suppose, by a whole army, from the fusing of cannons, as, under the reign of architecture, they had Iliads and Romanceros, Mahabharatas and Nibelungen, made by a whole people from an accumulation and fusion of rhapsodies. The great accident of an architect of genius might occur in the twentieth century just like that of Dante in the thirteenth. But architecture will no longer be the social, the collective, the dominant art. The great poem, the great edifice, the great creation of mankind will no longer be built, it will be printed.

And in future, should architecture accidentally revive, it will no longer be master. It will be subject to the law of literature, which once received the law from it. The respective positions of the two arts will be reversed. It is a fact that during the age of architecture the – admittedly rare – poems resembled the monuments. In India, Vyasa is intricate, strange and impenetrable, like a pagoda. In the Egyptian East, poetry, like the buildings, has a grandeur and tranquillity of line; in ancient Greece, beauty, serenity and calm; in Christian Europe, the majesty of Catholicism, the naïvety of the people, the rich and luxuriant vegetation of an age of renewal. The Bible resembles the Pyramids, the Iliad the Parthenon, Homer Phidias. Dante in the thirteenth century was the last Romanesque church, Shakespeare in the sixteenth the last Gothic cathedral.

Thus, to sum up what we have said so far in a necessarily incomplete and truncated form, the human race has two books, two registers, two testaments: masonry and printing, the bible of stone and the bible of paper. When we study these two bibles, so fully opened through the centuries, it is permissible surely to feel nostalgia for the visible majesty of what was written in granite, those gigantic alphabets formulated as colonnades, pylons and obelisks, those man-made mountains, as it were, which covered the world and the past, from the pyramid to the steeple, from Cheops to Strasbourg. We must re-read the past from these marble pages. We must constantly admire and turn the pages of the book written by architecture; but we must not gainsay the grandeur of the edifice which printing has erected in its turn.

This edifice is colossal. Some maker of statistics or other has calculated that if all the volumes which have issued from the presses since Gutenberg were placed one on top of the other they would occupy the distance from the earth to the moon; but that is not the kind of grandeur we mean. Yet, when we try to compose in our minds a total picture of the sum of the products of the printing-press up till our own day, does the whole not appear to us as a vast construction, with the entire world as its base, at which mankind has been working without respite and whose monstrous head is lost in the profound mists of the future? It is the ant-hill of the intellect. It is the hive to which all the golden bees of the imagination come with their honey. It is an edifice of a thousand storeys. Here and there, on its staircases, one can see the mouths of the murky tunnels of science, which intersect in its bowels. On its surface, everywhere, the luxuriance of art, with its arabesques, its rose-windows and its tracery. Here, each individual work, however isolated or capricious it may appear, has its own place and protuberance. Its harmony comes from the whole. From the cathedral of Shakespeare to the mosque of Byron, innumerable bell-turrets jostle indiscriminately on this metropolis of the universal mind. At its base, a number of the ancient titles of mankind have been rewritten, which architecture had not recorded. On the left of the entrance has been affixed the old white marble bas-relief of Homer, on the right the polyglot bible rears its seven heads. Further on stands the bristling hydra of the Romancero, with other hybrid forms, the Vedas and the Nibelungen. For the rest, this prodigious edifice remains perpetually unfinished. The printing-press, that giant machine, tirelessly pumping the whole intellectual sap of society, is constantly spewing out fresh materials for its erection. The entire human race is on the scaffolding. Each mind is a mason. The humblest can stop up a hole or lay a stone. Restif de la Bretonne[1] contributes his hod-load of plaster. Every day a new course is added. And aside from the

1. Nicolas Restif (1734–1806), a prolific observer of contemporary and especially lower-class life, long thought a salacious writer.

original offerings of individual writers, there are collective contingents. The eighteenth century gives the *Encyclopédie*,[1] the Revolution the *Moniteur*.[2] This indeed is a construction which grows and mounts in spirals without end; here is a confusion of tongues, ceaseless activity, indefatigable labour, fierce rivalry between all of mankind, the intellect's promised refuge against a second deluge, against submersion by the barbarians. This is the human race's second Tower of Babel.

1. The famous attempt by Diderot and others to encompass, in thirty-five volumes, the then state of knowledge of the world. It is now seen as a landmark in the advance of rationalism and the popularization of the scientific attitude.

2. *Le Moniteur universel* was launched in 1789 to publish the debates of the Constituent Assembly.

BOOK SIX

ONE

An Impartial Look at the Old Magistrature

IN the year of grace 1482, the noble Robert d'Estouteville, Chevalier, Sieur of Beyne, Baron of Yvri and Saint-Andry-en-la-Marche, Councillor and Chamberlain to the King, and Keeper of the Provostry of Paris, was a very fortunate man. It was now almost seventeen years since, on 7 November 1465, the year of the comet,[1] he had received from the king the high dignity of Provost of Paris, reputed to be more a lordship than an office, '*dignitas*,' says Joannes Loemnoeus, '*quae cum non exigua potestate politiam concernente, atque praerogativis multis et juribus conjuncta est.*'[2] A gentleman holding a commission from the king whose letters of appointment dated back to the time of the marriage between Louis XI's natural daughter and the Bastard of Bourbon, that was a most remarkable thing in 1482. On the same day as Robert d'Estouteville had replaced Jacques de Villiers in the provostry of Paris, Maître Jean Duvet had replaced Messire Hélye de Thorrettes in the first presidency of the Court of Parliament, Jean Jouvenel des Ursins had ousted Pierre de Morvilliers from the office of Chancellor of France, and Regnault des Dormans had dis-appointed Pierre Puy from the post of Master of Requests in Ordinary to the King's Household. But upon how many heads had the presidency, the chancellery and the mastership not fallen since Robert d'Estouteville got the provostship of Paris! It had been 'bailed in keeping' to him according to the Letters Patent, and he had indeed kept it well. He had clung to it, had incorporated himself into it, had identified himself with it. With the result that he avoided that mania for change that overcame Louis XI, a distrustful, querulous and industrious king, intent on preserving the elasticity of his power by frequent appointments and dismissals. What was more, the gallant chevalier had secured the succession in his post for his

1. This comet, against which Pope Calixtus, uncle of Borgia, ordered public prayers, is the one that will reappear in 1835 (V.H.).

2. 'A dignity which is associated with no small powers of police, and with many prerogatives and rights.'

son, and for two years now the name of the noble Jacques d'Estouteville, Squire, had figured next to his own at the top of the ordinary's register for the provostry of Paris! A rare and notable favour indeed! It is true that Robert d'Estouteville was a good soldier, that he had loyally raised his standard against the 'League of the common weal'[1] and that he had offered the queen a most wonderful stag made from preserves on the day of her entry into Paris in 14... He was moreover the good friend of Messire Tristan l'Hermite, Provost of the Marshals of the King's Household. Life, in fact, was very good and agreeable for Messire Robert. To start with, an excellent salary, to which were attached as a pendant, like additional bunches of grapes on his vine, the revenues from the civil and criminal clerkships of the provostry, plus the civil and criminal revenues from the lower courts of the Châtelet, not to mention certain tolls from the Pont de Mante and Pont de Corbeil, and the profits from the taxes on the *esgrin* of Paris, the bundlers of firewood and the measurers of salt. Add to this the pleasure, as he rode through the town, of eclipsing the half-red, half-tan robes of the syndics and *quarteniers*[2] with his own beautiful military uniform, which you can still admire today carved on his tomb in the Abbey of Valmont in Normandy, and on his badly dented morion at Montlhéry. And was it not something, too, to be in supreme command of the serjeants of the *douzaine*, the porter and watchmen of the Châtelet, the two auditors of the Châtelet, *auditores Castelleti*, the sixteen commissioners of the sixteen districts, the gaoler of the Châtelet, the four enfeoffed serjeants, the 120 mounted serjeants, the 120 tipstaff serjeants, the Chevalier of the Watch, with his watch, under-watch, counter-watch and rear-watch? Was it not something to exercise high and low justice, with the right to turn, hang and draw, not to mention minor jurisdiction in the first instance, *in prima instantia*, as the charters put it, over the viscounty of Paris, so splendidly appanaged with seven noble bailiwicks? What could be imagined more sweet than to pronounce sentences and judgements, as Messire Robert d'Estouteville did each day, in the Grand-Châtelet, beneath the broad, flattened ogees of Philip Augustus? Or to go, as was his way of an evening, to that charming house in the Rue Galilée, in the precincts of the Palais Royal, which

1. A revolt by prominent noblemen against Louis XI in 1464.
2. Officers of a 'quarter', or division of a hundred.

he held in his wife's right, Madame Ambroise de Loré, there to relax from the exertions of sending some poor devil to spend *his* night in 'that small cell in the Rue de l'Escorcherie which the provosts and syndics of Paris were wont to make their prison: it comprising eleven feet in length, seven feet four inches in breadth and eleven feet in height'?

Messire Robert d'Estouteville did not only have his personal justice as Provost and Viscount of Paris, he also had his share, his eye and tooth, in the great justice of the king. All heads of even the slightest eminence passed through his hands before they fell to the executioner. He it was who had gone to the Bastille Saint-Antoine to fetch M. de Nemours to Les Halles, and M. de Saint-Pol to the Grève, the latter having kicked up a fuss and protested, much to the delight of the provost, who did not like the constable.

Which is more, surely, than is required to lead a happy and illustrious life, and to one day earn a distinguished page in the interesting annals of the provosts of Paris, where we learn that Oudard de Villeneuve had a house in the Rue des Boucheries, that Guillaume de Hangest bought Greater and Lesser Savoy, that Guillaume Thiboust gave his houses in the Rue Clopin to the nuns, that Hugues Aubriot lived in the Hôtel du Porc-Épic, and other homely facts.

And yet, with all these reasons for taking life patiently and cheerfully, Messire Robert d'Estouteville had woken up on the morning of 7 January 1482 with a sore head and in a murderous temper. He could not himself have said what had caused this ill temper. Was it because the skies were grey? Because the buckle of his old Montlhéry belt had been wrongly done up and was compressing his provost's paunch in too military a fashion? Because he had seen some ribalds go past in the street beneath his window, who had been cheeky to him, four of them in a group, in doublets but no shifts, hats without crowns, with wallets and bottles by their sides? Or was it some vague foreboding of the 370 *livres* sixteen *sols* eight *deniers* which the future king Charles VIII was to deduct the following year from the revenues of the provostship? The reader may take his choice; for ourselves we are inclined to believe quite simply that he was in an ill temper because he was an ill-tempered man.

Moreover, it was the day following a holiday, a tiresome day for everybody, but especially for the magistrate responsible for sweeping up all the filth, both actual and metaphorical, which holidays cause in Paris. On top of which, he was to sit in judgement at the Grand-Châtelet. Now, we have noticed that judges generally arrange things so that the days when they hold hearings are also the days they are in a bad temper, so that they always have someone on whom they can conveniently vent it, on behalf of the king, of the law and of justice.

The hearing, however, had begun without him. His civil, criminal and particular lieutenants were doing his job for him, as was customary; and by eight o'clock in the morning, several dozen townsmen and townswomen were crammed and squashed into a dark corner of the lower courtroom of the Châtelet, between a strong oak barricade and the wall, blissfully watching the varied and delightful spectacle of civil and criminal justice being meted out somewhat confusedly and quite haphazardly by Maître Florian Barbedienne, Auditor of the Châtelet, and Lieutenant to the Provost.

The room was small, with a low vault. At the far end stood a table covered in fleur-de-lys, together with a big armchair of carved oak which was the provost's and was empty, and on the left a stool for the auditor, Maître Florian. Below sat the Clerk of the Court, scribbling. Opposite was the populace; and in front of the door and the table a great many provost serjeants, in actons of violet camlet with white crosses. Two serjeants from the Parloir-aux-Bourgeois, dressed in their All Saints' Day jackets, half-red and half-blue, stood guard before a low, closed door, visible behind the table at the end. A shaft of wan January daylight, from a single lancet window, tightly set into the thick wall, fell on two grotesque figures: the whimsical stone demon carved as a *cul-de-lampe* on the keystone, and the judge, sitting at the end of the room above the fleur-de-lys.

Picture, in fact, to yourselves, Maître Florian Barbedienne, Auditor of the Châtelet, leaning hunched on the provost's table between two bundles of legal documents, his foot on the train of his brown plain-cloth robe, his face in his white lamb's fur, from which his eyebrows too seemed to have been cut, ruddy, cantankerous, his eyes blinking, and majestically supporting the fat of his cheeks, which met beneath his chin.

Now the auditor was deaf. A slight defect in an auditor. Nonetheless, Maître Florian still passed judgement, without appeal and very fittingly. A judge in actual fact only needs to seem to be listening; and the venerable auditor fulfilled this condition, the one essential of good justice, all the better in that his attention could not be distracted by the slightest sound.

For the rest, he had among the audience a merciless critic of his deeds and gestures in the person of our friend Jehan Frollo du Moulin, the young student from the previous day, that 'wayfarer' you could always be sure of meeting anywhere in Paris, except at the feet of his teachers.

'I say,' he whispered to his companion Robin Poussepain, who was sniggering beside him, as he commented on the scenes taking place before them, 'there's Jehanneton du Buisson. The lovely daughter of that lazy cur at the Marché Neuf! Upon my soul, the old man's convicted her! His eyes are no better than his ears, then. Fifteen *sols* four *deniers parisis*, for carrying two rosaries! That's a bit steep. *Lex duri carminis.*[1] Who's this one? Robin Chief-de-Ville, hauberk-maker! For having been accepted and made a master of the aforesaid trade? It's his entrance money. Ha, two gentlemen among the rabble! Aiglet de Soins, Hutin de Mailly. Two esquires, *corpus Christi*! Ah, they've been playing dice. When shall I see our rector here? Fined one hundred *livres parisis*, to the king! Old Barbedienne won't hear of any nonsense – he can't! If that stops me gambling, gambling by day, gambling by night, living gambling, dying gambling and wagering my soul after my shirt, then I'm my brother the archdeacon! Holy Virgin, all these girls! One after the other, my ewe-lambs! Ambroise Lécuyère! Isabeau le Paynette! Bérarde Gironin! I know them all, for heaven's sake. Fine them, fine them! That'll teach you to wear gilt belts! Ten *sols parisis*, for flirting. What an ugly old deaf idiot of a judge he is! Florian the blockhead! Barbedienne the buzzard! Look at him at table! He eats plaintiffs, he eats lawsuits, he eats, he masticates, he stuffs himself, he's full. Fines, treasure trove, taxes, expenses, legitimate costs, salaries, damages and interests, gehenna, prison, gaol, stocks plus costs, to him they're Christmas buns and marzipan-stuffing. Look at him, the pig! Come on, good, another wanton woman! Thibaud la Thibaude, no more, no less! For leaving the Rue Glatigny! Who's this lad? Gieffroy Mabonne, crossbowman. He's been taking the

1. 'The letter of the law is harsh.'

name of the Father in vain. A fine, for La Thibaude! A fine for Gieffroy! Fine the pair of them! He's as deaf as a post, he must have got the two cases muddled up! Ten to one he makes the girl pay for swearing and the soldier for making love. Look out, Robin Poussepain, what are they going to bring in? Look at all those serjeants! By Jupiter, every greyhound in the pack's here. This must be the big game. A wild boar. It *is* a boar, Robin, it is one! And what a beauty too! *Hercle*,[1] it's our prince from yesterday, our fools' pope, our bell-ringer, our one-eye, our hunchback, our face-puller! It's Quasimodo!'

It was indeed he.

It was Quasimodo, pinioned, swathed, trussed and bound, and under strong guard. The squad of serjeants surrounding him had the help of the Chevalier of the Watch in person, with the arms of France embroidered on his chest and those of the town on his back. Yet apart from his deformity there was nothing about Quasimodo to justify this show of halberds and arquebuses. He was sombre, silent and calm. At most, his one eye squinted angrily down now and again at the bonds that enveloped him.

He looked about him with the same expression, but so dully and sleepily that the women merely laughed as they pointed him out to each other.

Meanwhile, Maître Florian, the auditor, was leafing intently through the documents of the charge laid against Quasimodo, which the clerk had held out to him, and, having glanced at them, he seemed to reflect for a moment. Thanks to this precaution, which he was always careful to take when proceeding to an interrogation, he knew in advance the names, titles and crimes of the accused, could make predictable rejoinders to predictable answers, and could survive all the ins and outs of the interrogation without letting his deafness show overmuch. For him the documents of the case were like the blind man's guide-dog. If it happened now and again that his infirmity was revealed by an incoherent apostrophe or an unintelligible question, then some ascribed this to his profundity, others to his imbecility. In either case, the honour of the magistrature was preserved, since it is better for a judge to be thought profound or an imbecile than deaf. So he took great pains to conceal his deafness from the general notice, and normally succeeded so

1. 'By Hercules!'

well that he had even come to deceive himself. Which is, as it happens, easier than one might think. All hunchbacks hold their heads high, all stammerers make speeches, all deaf people talk quietly. He thought merely that his hearing was somewhat rebellious. That was the one concession he made in the matter to public opinion, during those moments of candour when he examined his conscience.

Having thus ruminated on Quasimodo's case, he threw back his head and half closed his eyes, so as to look more impartial and majestic, with the result that at that moment he was both deaf and blind. Twin conditions without which there can be no perfect judge. In this magisterial pose, he began the interrogation.

'Your name?'

But here was a circumstance which had not been 'foreseen by the law', whereby one deaf man would have to question another.

Quasimodo, totally ignorant that a question had been addressed to him, continued to stare fixedly at the judge and did not answer. The judge, who was deaf and totally ignorant of the deafness of the defendant, thought he had replied, as defendants generally did, and continued, with his stupid and mechanical self-assurance:

'Good. Your age?'

Quasimodo did not reply to this question either. The judge thought it had been answered and went on.

'Now, your trade?'

Still the same silence. The audience, meanwhile, had begun to whisper and exchange glances.

'That will do,' went on the imperturbable auditor, assuming that the defendant had completed his third reply. 'You are accused before us: *primo*, of nocturnal disturbance; *secundo*, of an unlawful act of violence against the person of a loose woman, *in praejudicium meretricis;*[1] *tertio*, of insubordination and disloyalty towards the archers of the ordinance of the king our master. Justify yourself on all these points. Clerk, have you written down what the defendant has said so far?'

At this luckless question, a roar of laughter went up from clerks and spectators alike, so violent, so wild, so contagious, and so universal that the two deaf men could not but be aware of it. Quasimodo turned round with a scornful shrug of his hump-back,

1. 'To the detriment of a harlot.'

while Maître Florian, equally amazed and supposing the laughter to have been provoked by some irreverent rejoinder from the prisoner, made visible for him by that shrug of the shoulders, apostrophized him indignantly.

'The answer you have just given, you scoundrel, deserves the noose. Do you know to whom you are speaking?'

Which outburst was not calculated to stay the general explosion of merriment. Everyone found it so incongruous and absurd that the uncontrollable laughter spread even to the serjeants from the Parloir-aux-Bourgeois, those knaves of spades, as it were, whose stupidity was part of their uniform. Quasimodo alone remained unsmiling, for the good reason that he understood nothing of what was going on around him. The judge was getting more and more irate and thought he should continue in the same vein, thereby hoping to strike a terror into the defendant which would react on the audience and restore some respect amongst them.

'So then, master of depravity and depredation that you are, you presume to show disrespect to the auditor of the Châtelet, to the magistrate entrusted with policing the people of Paris, responsible for the investigation of crimes, misdemeanours and improprieties, for regulating all trades and preventing monopoly, for the upkeep of roadways, for preventing the regrating of poultry, game and wildfowl, for the measurement of firewood and other sorts of wood, for cleansing the town of sewage and the air of contagious diseases, in a word, for continually looking to the common weal, in short, without payment or hope of salary! Do you know that my name is Florian Barbedienne, Personal Lieutenant to the Provost, and Commissioner, Investigator, Controller and Examiner besides, with equal powers in provostry, bailliage, conservation and praesidial...'

There is no reason why one deaf man talking to another deaf man should ever stop. God knows where and when Maître Florian might have come ashore, vigorously launched as he was on the high seas of eloquence, if the low door at the back had not suddenly opened to admit the provost himself.

Maître Florian did not break off when the provost entered, but swung half round on his heel and abruptly aimed the harangue with which a moment before he had been blasting Quasimodo at him instead. 'My lord,' he said, 'I request such penalty as shall please you against the accused here present, for a grave and mirific contempt of court.'

He then sat down again, panting and wiping away large drops of sweat, which dripped from his brow and drenched the parchments spread in front of him like waves from the sea. Messire Robert d'Estouteville frowned and gestured Quasimodo so imperiously and meaningfully to pay attention that the deaf man more or less understood.

The provost addressed him sternly: 'What did you do, then, to find yourself here, scum?'

The poor devil, assuming that the provost had asked him his name, broke the silence he habitually kept, and answered in a raucous, guttural voice: 'Quasimodo.'

The reply was so ill-adapted to the question that the loud laughter began to spread again, and Messire Robert shouted, red with anger: 'Are you making fun of me too, you double-dyed scoundrel?'

'Bell-ringer at Notre-Dame,' replied Quasimodo, thinking he had to explain to the judge who he was.

'Bell-ringer!' went on the provost who, as we have said, had woken up that morning in a bad enough temper and had no need of these weird replies to fan the flames of his wrath. 'Bell-ringer! I'll have them play a carillon on your back with horsewhips round the crossroads of Paris. Do you understand, scum?'

'If it's my age you want to know, I think I shall be twenty at Martinmas,' said Quasimodo.

This was too much to bear; the provost could not contain himself.

'Ah, you are being insolent to the provostry, you wretch! Tipstaff serjeants, you will take this scoundrel to the pillory on the Grève, you will beat him and turn him for one hour. He shall pay for it, by God! And the present sentence will be cried, with the assistance of four sworn trumpeters, in the seven castellanies of the viscounty of Paris.'

The clerk began forthwith to draw up the sentence.

'God's belly, that's what I call a sentence!' cried the little student Jehan Frollo du Moulin, from his corner.

The provost turned round and again fixed his blazing eyes on

Quasimodo: 'I believe the scoundrel said "God's belly!" Clerk, add a fine of twelve *deniers parisis* for swearing, and the fabric of Saint-Eustache shall have half of it. I am particularly devoted to Saint-Eustache.'

Within a few minutes, the sentence had been drawn up. Its purport was short and simple. The custom law of the provostry and viscounty of Paris had not yet been refashioned by President Thibaut Baillet and Roger Barmne, the king's advocate. It was not then obstructed by that upstanding forest of legal niceties and procedures which the two jurisconsults planted in it at the beginning of the sixteenth century. All was clear, prompt and explicit. It went straight to the point, there was no undergrowth and no detours, and at the end of each path you could immediately see the wheel, the gallows or the pillory. At least you knew where you were going.

The clerk handed the sentence to the provost, who affixed his seal to it, then left to continue on his rounds of the courtrooms, in a frame of mind which would that day fill all the gaols of Paris. Jehan Frollo and Robin Poussepain were laughing to themselves. Quasimodo watched it all, looking indifferent and surprised.

However, the clerk, just as Maître Florian Barcedienne was reading the sentence in his turn in order to sign it, felt moved by pity for the poor wretch who had been condemned and, in the hope of obtaining some relaxation of his punishment, he came as close as he could to the ear of the auditor and said, pointing to Quasimodo: 'The man is deaf.'

He had hoped that this common infirmity would arouse Maître Florian's interest in favour of the prisoner. But in the first place, we have already observed that Maître Florian did not like it to be known he was deaf. And he was, secondly, so hard of hearing that he did not hear a single word of what the clerk was saying to him: however, he wanted to appear to have heard, and he answered: 'Ha, ha, that's different! I didn't know that. In that case, one hour extra in the pillory.'

And he signed the sentence so modified.

'That was well done,' said Robin Poussepain, who still bore Quasimodo a grudge, 'that'll teach him to be rough with people.'

TWO
The Rat-Hole

THE reader must now allow us to return him to the Place de Grève, which we left yesterday, with Gringoire, in order to follow La Esmeralda.

It was ten o'clock in the morning. Evidence that the day before had been a public holiday was everywhere. The paving was strewn with detritus: ribbons, chiffons, plumes from crests, drops of wax from torches, crumbs from the public bean-feast. A fair number of burgesses were strolling about, turning over the spent brands of the bonfire with their feet, going into ecstasies in front of the Maison-aux-Piliers as they recalled the beautiful hangings of the day before, and staring today, as a final delight, at the nails. Between the knots of people cider and barley-beer vendors were wheeling their barrows. A few passers-by came and went about their business. Tradesmen were chatting and calling out to one another in the doorways of their shops. The celebrations, the ambassadors, Coppenole, the fools' pope, were on everyone's lips. Each one tried to out-comment and out-laugh the other. But meanwhile, four mounted serjeants had just taken up position on the four sides of the pillory and had already concentrated around them a fair proportion of the 'populace' scattered across the square, who condemned themselves to immobility and boredom in hopes of some minor execution of justice.

If the reader will now, after contemplating the shrill, animated scene being played out in every corner of the square, direct his gaze to that ancient half-Gothic, half-Romanesque house of the Tour-Roland, which forms the corner of the quay to the west, he may observe, at the angle of the façade, a big, richly illuminated public breviary, protected from the rain by a small canopy and from thieves by a grille, through which its pages could still be turned. Beside the breviary was a narrow, pointed window, enclosed behind two crossed iron bars, which looked out on to the square and was the one opening to admit a bit of air and daylight into a small, doorless cell, made on the ground floor of the old house in the thickness of the wall, and filled by a peace and a silence all the more profound and cheerless for being surrounded by a teeming, vociferous public square, the noisiest and most frequented in Paris.

This cell had been famous in Paris for almost three hundred years, ever since Madame Rolande of the Tour-Roland, in mourning for her father who had been killed in the Crusades, had had it excavated from the wall of her own house and shut herself up in it for good, preserving from her palace only this one room, whose door had been walled up and whose window remained open, winter and summer, and giving all the rest to God and to the poor. The desolate maiden had in fact waited twenty years for death in this premature tomb, praying night and day for her father's soul, sleeping amidst ashes, without even a stone for a pillow, dressed in a black sack, and living solely off what the compassion of passers-by placed by way of bread and water on the sill of her window, thus receiving charity after having bestowed it. At her death, when the time came to move on to her second burial-place, she bequeathed this one in perpetuity to women in affliction, to mothers, widows or daughters who would have much praying to do for others or for themselves and wanted to be buried alive, in some great sorrow or great penitence. The poor people of the time had given her a fine funeral with their tears and their blessings; but to their deep regret the pious maiden could not be canonized, for lack of patrons. The slightly more impious amongst them had hoped that the matter might be settled more easily in Paradise than in Rome, and had quite simply prayed to God for the deceased, instead of to the pope. Most had been content to keep the Rolande's memory sacred and to make relics of her rags. The town, for its part, had founded a public breviary in the maiden's honour and installed it next to the window of her cell, so that passers-by might pause there from time to time, if only to pray, so that prayer might turn their thoughts to charity, and so that the poor recluses, who had inherited Madame Rolande's cellar, might not die in earnest of hunger and neglect.

These sort of tombs were, as it happens, far from uncommon in medieval towns. Even in the busiest street, or in the noisiest, most motley marketplace, one often came across, right in the very centre, under the horses' hooves, under the wheels almost of the wagons, a cellar, a well, a walled and grated dungeon, in whose depths a human being prayed night and day, having freely dedicated themselves to some everlasting lamentation or great expiation. All the thoughts that so strange a sight might evoke in us today, the ghastly cell, a sort of cross between a house and a tomb, between the cemetery and the city, a living person cut off from the community of men and to be numbered henceforth among the dead, a lamp consuming its last drop of oil amidst the shadows, the remnants of a life flickering in a grave, a breath, a voice, an everlasting prayer in a stone coffin, a face forever turned towards the next world, an eye already lit by another sun, an ear pressed against the walls of the tomb, a soul imprisoned in a body itself imprisoned in a cell, and beneath that double envelope of flesh and granite the murmuring of a grieved soul: the crowd saw none of this. The crude and none too rational piety of the time could not see all these facets in a single act of religion. It accepted the act as a whole, it honoured, venerated and if need be sanctified the sacrifice but it did not analyse the suffering and felt but little sympathy with it. From time to time it would bring some pittance to the wretched penitent, look through the hole to see whether they were still alive, did not know their name, barely knew how many years it was since they had begun to die, and to the stranger who questioned them about the living skeleton rotting away in the cellar, the locals simply answered 'He's a recluse' if it was a man, or 'She's a recluse' if it was a woman.

In those days they saw everything thus, without metaphysics, without exaggeration, without a magnifying glass, with the naked eye. The microscope had not yet been invented, either for material things or for the things of the spirit.

Moreover, as we have just said, although they caused little stir, examples of this kind of confinement in the centres of towns were, in fact, frequent. In Paris there were a fair number of these cells for praying to God and doing penance; almost all were occupied. True, the clergy did not like leaving them empty, since that implied a lack of zeal among believers, and if there were no penitents they put lepers in them. Apart from the cell on the Grève, there was one at Montfaucon, one at the charnel-house of the Innocents, another I forget where, at the Logis Clichon I believe. And yet others at many sites where, for want of any monument, traces of them can be found in traditions. The University too had one. On Mount Sainte-Geneviève, a sort of medieval Job chanted the seven penitential Psalms for thirty years on a dung-heap at the bottom of a cistern, starting again once he got to the end and chanting more loudly at night, *magna voce per umbras*,[1] and the antiquary who goes down the Rue du Puits-qui-parle[2] today fancies he can still hear his voice.

We shall restrict ourselves to the cell of the Tour-Roland and must tell you that it never lacked for recluses. Since Madame Rolande's death, it had remained empty only for the odd year or two. Many women had come there to weep, until they died, for their parents, their lovers or their sins. Parisian malice, ever active, even when it has no business to be, claimed that not many widows had been seen there.

As was the fashion of the time, a Latin legend, inscribed on the wall, informed the literate passer-by of the devout purpose of the cell. This custom of explaining a building by a brief device written above the door was maintained up until the middle of the sixteenth century. Thus, in France, one can still read, above the wicket-gate of the prison of the manor-house of Tourville: *Sileto et spera*;[3] in Ireland, underneath the shield that surmounts the great gateway of Fortescue Castle: *Forte scutum, salus ducum*;[4] in England, over the main entrance of the hospice of the Counts Cowper: *Tuum est.*[5] In those days, in fact, every building was an idea.

As there was no door to the walled-up cell of the Tour-Roland, the two words TU, ORA[6] had been engraved in large Romanesque characters above the window.

As a result of which the populace, whose common sense ignores fine distinctions and happily translates *Ludovico Magno*[7] as Porte Saint-Denis, had given this black, damp and dismal cavity the name of Trou-aux-rats (Rat-hole). A less sublime explanation perhaps than the other, but a more picturesque one.

1. 'In a loud voice in the darkness.'
2. 'The well-which-talks.'
3. 'Be silent and hope.'
4. 'A strong shield, the saviour of chieftains.'
5. 'It is yours.'
6. 'You, pray.'
7. 'To the Great Louis.'

THREE
The Story of a Maize Cake

At the time of which we are writing, the cell of the Tour-Roland was occupied. If the reader wishes to know by whom, he need only listen to the conversation of three worthy gossips who, just as we fixed his attention on the rat-hole, were walking in that self-same direction, coming up-river from the Châtelet towards the Grève.

Two of the women were dressed like good Paris bourgeoises. Their delicate white gorgets, their skirts of red and blue striped tiretaine, their white knitted stockings, embroidered with coloured clocks, pulled tightly over the leg, their square shoes of tawny leather with black soles, and especially their head-dresses, a sort of tinsel horn weighed down with ribbons and lace such as the women of Champagne still wear, together with the grenadiers of the Russian imperial guard, declared them to belong to that class of rich tradespeople which lies midway between what menials call 'a woman' and what they call 'a lady'. They wore neither rings nor gold crucifixes, and it was easy to see that in their case this was not poverty, but quite simply the fear of being fined. Their companion was got up in more or less the same way, but there was that indefinable something about her clothes and her demeanour which bespeaks the wife of a provincial lawyer. You could tell from the way her belt came up above her hips that she had not been long in Paris. To which must be added a pleated gorget, ribbon bows on her shoes, the fact that the stripes on her skirt went horizontally instead of up and down, and a great many other enormities offensive to good taste.

The first two were walking at a speed peculiar to Parisian women showing provincials the city. The woman from the provinces was holding the hand of a large boy, himself holding a large flat cake.

We are sorry to have to add that, in view of the inclemency of the season, he was using his tongue as a handkerchief.

The child was being dragged along, *non passibus aequis*,[1] as Virgil puts it, and was forever tripping up, and being roundly scolded by his mother. True, he was looking at the cake rather than at the pavement. Some solemn reason had no doubt prevented him

1. 'With unequal steps.'

from biting into it, for he merely gazed at it lovingly. But his mother should have taken charge of the cake. It was cruel to turn this fat, chubby boy into a Tantalus.

Meanwhile the three demoiselles (for the title of *dame* was then reserved for noblewomen) were all talking at once.

'We must hurry, Demoiselle Mahiette,' said the youngest of the three, who was also the fattest, to the woman from the provinces. 'I'm very much afraid we shall get there too late. They told us at the Châtelet they were going to take him to the pillory straight away.'

'Pshaw, what are you talking about, Demoiselle Oudarde Musnier?' put in the other Parisienne. 'He'll be two hours at the pillory. We've got time. Have you ever seen anyone pilloried, my dear Mahiette?'

'Yes,' said the provincial, 'in Rheims.'

'Pshaw, what's your pillory at Rheims? A miserable cage where they only turn peasants. That's nothing!'

'Only peasants!' said Mahiette, 'at the Marché-aux-Draps in Rheims! We've seen some very fine criminals there, who'd killed their fathers and mothers! Peasants! Who do you take us for, Gervaise?'

The provincial was certainly on the point of becoming heated in defence of her pillory. Fortunately, the tactful Demoiselle Oudarde Musnier diverted the conversation in time.

'By the way, Demoiselle Mahiette, what do you think of our Flemish ambassadors. Do you have such fine ones in Rheims?'

'I must admit', answered Mahiette, 'that only in Paris would you see Flemings like that.'

'Did you see that tall ambassador among the embassy who's a hosier?' asked Oudarde.

'Yes,' said Mahiette. 'He looked like a Saturn.'

'And that fat one with a face like a bare belly?' Gervaise went on. 'And the short one with little eyes with red rims round them, all plucked and jagged like a thistle-head?'

'Their horses were a fine sight,' said Oudarde, 'dressed like that in the style of their country!'

'Ah, my dear,' the provincial Mahiette broke in, adopting an air of superiority in her turn, 'what would you have said then if you had seen the horses of the princes and the king's company eighteen years ago, in '61, at the coronation in Rheims! Housings and caparisons of every kind; some of damask, of fine gold cloth, trimmed with sable; others of velvet, trimmed with ermine; and others laden with jewellery and huge gold and silver silk bells! The money it must have cost! And the beautiful page boys on top of them!'

'The fact remains', retorted Demoiselle Oudarde, drily, 'that the Flemings have very fine horses and that they had a magnificent dinner last night with the merchants' provost at the Hôtel de Ville, where they were served sugared almonds, hippocras, spices and other remarkable things.'

'What are you talking about, neighbour?' cried Gervaise. 'The Flemings dined with Monsieur the Cardinal, in the Petit-Bourbon.'

'No they didn't. At the Hôtel de Ville!'

'Yes, they did. At the Petit-Bourbon!'

'It was the Hôtel de Ville all right,' Oudarde went on, acrimoniously, 'because Doctor Secourable made them a speech in Latin, which they were very pleased with. My husband, who's a sworn bookseller, told me so.'

'It was the Petit-Bourbon all right,' replied Gervaise, no less sharply, 'because this is what the cardinal's prosecutor offered them: twelve double quarts of white, claret and vermilion hippocras; twenty-four boxes of golden double Lyon marzipan; the same number of torches weighing two pounds each, and six demijohns of Beaune wine, white and claret, the best they could find. I hope there's no question about that. I have it from my husband, who's a *cinquantenier*[1] at the Parloir-aux-Bourgeois, and this morning compared the Flemish ambassadors with those from Prester John and the Emperor of Trebizond, who came to Paris from Mesopotamia in the last king's time and had rings in their ears.'

'So true is it that they dined at the Hôtel de Ville', replied Oudarde, unimpressed by this catalogue, 'that such a feast of viands and sweetmeats has never before been seen.'

'And I tell you that they were waited on by Le Sec, the town serjeant, at the Hôtel du Petit-Bourbon, and that is what misled you.'

'At the Hôtel de Ville, I tell you!'

'At the Petit-Bourbon, my dear! In fact they lit up the word "Hope" that's written above the great doorway with magic glasses.'

1. Lit. a 'fiftyman', controlling half a hundred.

'At the Hôtel de Ville, at the Hôtel de Ville! Husson le Voir even played the flute!'

'I tell you it wasn't!'

'I tell you it was!'

'I tell you it wasn't!'

The good stout Oudarde was getting ready to retort, and the disagreement might perhaps have led to blows, had Mahiette not suddenly let out a cry: 'Look at those people who've collected there at the end of the bridge! There's something in the middle of them they're looking at.'

'I can hear a tambourine in fact,' said Gervaise. 'I think it's little Smeralda doing her performance with her goat. Quick, Mahiette, walk faster and pull your boy along. You came here to see the curiosities of Paris. Yesterday you saw the Flemings; today you must see the gypsy girl.'

'The gypsy!' said Mahiette turning sharply about and forcibly clutching her son's arm. 'God forbid! She'd steal my child! Come on, Eustache!'

And she started to run along the quay towards the Grève, until she had left the bridge far behind her. The child she was pulling, however, fell to his knees; she paused, panting. Oudarde and Gervaise caught her up.

'That gypsy steal your child?' said Gervaise. 'That's a very odd notion.'

Mahiette shook her head thoughtfully.

'What is odd', remarked Oudarde, 'is that the sachette thinks that about gypsies too.'

'Who's the sachette?' said Mahiette.

'What?' said Oudarde, 'Sister Gudule.'

'Who's Sister Gudule?' Mahiette went on.

'You really must come from Rheims if you don't know that!' answered Oudarde. 'She's the recluse in the Rat-hole.'

'What,' asked Mahiette, 'the poor woman we're taking the cake to?'

Oudarde nodded.

'Exactly. You'll see her in a minute at her window on the Grève. She feels the same as you do about those vagabonds of Egypt who play tambourines and tell people's fortunes. We don't know why she's so terrified of romanies and gypsies. But why do you run away, Mahiette, the minute you set eyes on them?'

'Oh,' said Mahiette, grasping her child's round head in both hands, 'I don't want what happened to Paquette la Chantefleurie to happen to me.'

'Ah, that's a story you must tell us, my good Mahiette,' said Gervaise, taking her by the arm.

'Gladly,' replied Mahiette, 'but you really must come from Paris if you don't know it! I must tell you then – but we don't need to stop for the story to be told – that Paquette la Chantefleurie was a pretty girl of eighteen at the same time as myself, that's to say eighteen years ago, and that it's her own fault if today she isn't, like me, a good, plump, hale mother of thirty-six, with a man and a boy. But it was too late for that even by the time she was fourteen! She was the daughter of Guybertaut, then, a minstrel on the boats at Rheims, the same one who had played before King Charles VII at his coronation, when he went down our river Vesle from Sillery as far as Musion, and even the Maid[1] was in the boat. The old father died when Paquette was still little; so she had only her mother left, the sister of M. Mathieu Pradon, a master coppersmith and tinman in Paris in the Rue de Parin-Garlin, who died last year. She came from a good family, as you can see. Her mother was a simple soul, unfortunately, and all she taught Paquette was a bit of braiding and toy-making which didn't stop the little girl from growing very tall and remaining very poor. They both lived in Rheims by the river, Rue de Folle-Peine. Mark that: I think it was what brought misfortune on Paquette. In '61, the year our King Louis XI, whom God preserve, was crowned, Paquette was so gay and so pretty that she was known everywhere as La Chantefleurie.[2] Poor girl! She had pretty teeth and she loved to display them by laughing. But a girl who loves laughing is on the way to weeping; beautiful teeth are the downfall of beautiful eyes. So, she was La Chantefleurie. She and her mother found it hard to make a living. They had come right down in the world since the fiddler's death. Their braiding now brought them in barely six *deniers* a week, which isn't quite two *liards à l'aigle*. Where were the days when father Guybertaut had earned twelve *sols parisis* at a single coronation with one

1. Joan of Arc. 2. 'Flowersong.'

song? One winter – it was in that same year of '61 – when the two women had neither logs to burn nor faggots, and it was very cold, La Chantefleurie got such a good colour that men called her "Paquette" and some of them "Pâquerette"[1] and she was done for. Eustache, if I see you bite that cake! We saw she was done for straightaway one Sunday when she came to church with a gold crucifix round her neck. At fourteen, did you ever! First it was the young Viscount of Cormontreuil, whose church-tower is three-quarters of a league from Rheims; then Messire Henri de Triancourt, the king's Master of Horse; then, going down in the scale, Chiart de Beaulion, a sergeant-at-arms; then, lower still, Guery Aubergeon, the king's carver, then Macé de Frépus, the dauphin's barber; then Thévenin le Moine, the king's cook; then, getting less young and less noble every time, she descended to Guillaume Racine, a hurdy-gurdy player and Thierry de Mer, a lamp-maker. And then poor Chantefleurie became common property. She was down to the last *sol* of her gold crown. I have to tell you, mesdemoiselles, that at the coronation, in that same year of '61, she it was who made the king of the ribalds' bed! The same year!'

Mahiette sighed and wiped away a tear welling in her eye.

'That's not such an unusual story,' said Gervaise, 'and I don't see any gypsies or children in it.'

'Patience!' resumed Mahiette. 'You are about to see a child. In '66, sixteen years ago this month on Saint Paula's Day, Paquette gave birth to a little girl. The poor thing, she was overjoyed. She'd wanted a child for so long. Her mother, a simple soul who had always turned a blind eye, was dead. Paquette had no one left in the world to love, and no one to love her. In the five years since she had fallen, La Chantefleurie had become a poor creature. She was alone, alone in life, she was pointed out and shouted at in the streets, she was beaten by the serjeants and made fun of by young ragamuffins. And then she was now twenty; and twenty is old age for a woman of easy virtue. Her wanton life was beginning to bring her in no more than had her braiding in the old days; each new wrinkle meant one gold piece the less; the winters got hard for her again, and from then on there was seldom any wood in her hearth or bread in her bread-bin. She couldn't work any more, because when she became sensual she became lazy, and then she suffered even more,

1. 'Daisy.'

because in becoming lazy she became sensual. At least that was the Curé of Saint-Rémy's explanation of why that sort of woman feels the cold and hunger more than other poor women when they get old.'

'Yes,' remarked Gervaise, 'but the gypsies?'

'Wait a minute, then, Gervaise!' said Oudarde, who was not so impatient. 'What would be left for the end if everything came at the beginning? Go on, Mahiette, please. Poor Chantefleurie!'

Mahiette continued.

'So she was very sad, very wretched, and her tears made furrows down her cheeks. But it seemed to her, in her shame, her folly and her forlornness, that she would feel less ashamed, less foolish and less forlorn if there was something or someone in the world she could love and which could love her. It had to be a child, for only a child could be innocent enough to do that. She came to realize this after trying to love a robber, the only man who might have wanted her; but after a short time she could see that the robber despised her. These amorous women need a lover or a child to satisfy their hearts. Otherwise they are very unhappy. Since she couldn't have a lover, she changed over completely to wanting a child, and since she was still devout, she was everlastingly praying to God for one. So the good God took pity on her and gave her a little girl. I can't tell you how happy she was. She was all over it, crying and fondling and kissing it. She nursed the child herself, made baby-clothes for it out of her blanket, the only one she had left on her bed, and no longer felt cold or hungry. Her looks returned. An old maid makes a young mother. She went back to her debauchery, Chantefleurie had visitors once again, she found new purchasers for her wares, and out of such horrors she made layettes, bonnets and bibs, lace vests and little satin hoods, and never even thought of buying herself another blanket. Monsieur Eustache, I've told you once, you're not to eat the cake. In fact, little Agnes – that was the child's name, her baptismal name, because it was a long time since Chantefleurie had had a family name – the little girl was more swaddled in ribbons and embroidery than a dauphin's wife from the Dauphiné! Among other things, she had a pair of little shoes the like of which King Louis XI certainly never had! Her mother sewed and embroidered them for her herself, and put all her skill as a braider into them and all the spangles off a Virgin's robe. They really were the daintiest pink shoes you ever set eyes on. They couldn't have been any longer than my thumb and it was only when you saw the baby's little feet come out of them that you believed they could ever have fitted inside. True, her little feet were so small, so pretty, so pink, pinker than the satin of the shoes! When you have children, Oudarde, you'll find their little hands and feet are the prettiest things of all.'

'If only I could,' said Oudarde with a sigh, 'but I'm waiting for Monsieur Andry Musnier to ask me.'

'Moreover,' Mahiette resumed, 'it wasn't only Paquette's baby's feet that were pretty. I saw her when she was only four months. She was an angel! Her eyes were bigger than her mouth. And the prettiest fine black hair, already going curly. She'd have been a dark-haired beauty by sixteen! Her mother became more and more besotted with her every day. She petted her, she kissed her, she tickled her, she washed her, she dressed her up, she ate her! She was crazy about her and thanked God for her. Especially her pretty pink feet, they were a constant source of amazement to her, she was wild with joy! Her lips were pressed to them all the time and she couldn't get over how small they were. She would put them into the little shoes, take them out again, admire them, marvel at them, hold them up to the light, was moved to pity when she tried to make them walk along the bed, and would happily have spent her whole life on her knees, putting those shoes on and taking them off as if they had been the feet of an infant Jesus.'

'It's a very nice story,' said Gervaise in an undertone, 'but what's it got to do with Egypt?'

'This,' replied Mahiette. 'One day some very strange sorts of horsemen arrived in Rheims. They were beggars and truants who were riding through the district, led by their duke and their counts. They had swarthy skins, very curly hair and silver rings in their ears. The women were even uglier than the men. Their faces were blacker and always uncovered, they wore miserable rochets over their bodies, an old cloth woven from cord tied on their shoulders, and their hair in horsetails. The children, squirming about between their legs, would have frightened a monkey. A band of excommunicates. They had all come in a straight line from lower Egypt to Rheims via Poland. The pope had confessed them, so it was said, and set them as a penitence to travel the world for seven years on end, without sleeping in a bed. So they were called penitents and they stank. It seems that in the old days they had been Saracens, which means they believed in Jupiter, and that they demanded ten *livres tournois* from all croziered and mitred archbishops, bishops and abbots. It was a papal bull that got them that. They had come to Rheims to tell fortunes in the name of the King of Algiers and the Emperor of Germany. As you can imagine, that was all it took for them to be forbidden to enter the town. So the whole band happily camped near the Porte de Braine, on the mound where there's a windmill, next to the craters of the old chalkpits. And everyone in Rheims rushed to go and see them. They looked in your hand and told you marvellous prophecies. They wouldn't have been beyond telling Judas he would be pope. But nasty stories went around about them stealing children, cutting purses and eating human flesh. Prudent people said to the rash ones: "Don't go," then went themselves on the sly. Everyone was quite carried away. The fact is they said things to amaze a cardinal. Mothers showed their children off in triumph after the gypsies had read in their hands all sorts of miracles written in pagan and Turkish. One had an emperor, another a pope, and another a captain. Poor Chantefleurie was seized by curiosity. She wanted to find out what she had got, and whether her pretty little Agnes might not one day be Empress of Armenia or somewhere. So she took her to the gypsies; and how the gypsies admired the child, fondling it, kissing it with their black mouths and marvelling at its tiny hand. To the mother's great delight, alas! They made a special fuss of its pretty feet and shoes. The child was still less than a year old. She already lisped and laughed at her mother like a little demon, she was plump and round, and had ever so many sweet little gestures like an angel from paradise. She was very frightened by the gypsies and cried. But her mother kissed her all the harder and went away overjoyed by what the soothsayers foretold for her Agnes. She was to be a beauty, a virtue, a queen. So she returned to her garret in the Rue Folle-Peine, very proud to be bringing back a queen. The next day, when the child was asleep on her bed, for she always put it to sleep with her, she took the opportunity to leave the door quietly ajar, and ran to tell a neighbour in the Rue de la Séchesserie that the day would come when her daughter Agnes would be waited on at table by the King of England and the Archduke of Ethiopia, and a hundred other surprises. When she returned, she didn't hear any crying as she went up the stairs, and she said to herself: "Good, the baby is still asleep!" She found the door wider open than she had left it, but she went in, the poor mother, and ran to the bed. The baby was no longer there, its place was empty. All that remained of the baby was one of its pretty little shoes. She dashed from the room, threw herself down the stairs and started banging her head against the walls, shouting: "My baby, who's got my baby, who's taken my baby?" The street was deserted, the house isolated; no one could tell her anything. She went through the town, searching every street and running this way and that all day long, wild, distraught, terrible, sniffing at doors and windows like a wild animal that has lost its young. She was panting and dishevelled, a frightening sight, and there was a fire in her eyes that dried her tears. She stopped passers-by and shouted: "My daughter, my daughter, my pretty little daughter! Whoever returns my daughter to me, I will be their servant, their dog's servant and he can eat my heart if he wants." She met the Curé of Saint-Rémy and said to him: "Monsieur le Curé, I will work the soil with my fingernails, but give me back my baby!" It was heart-rending, Oudarde; and I saw one hard-hearted man, Maître Ponce Lacabre, the prosecutor, weeping. The poor mother! That evening, she returned home. While she was out, a neighbour had seen two gypsy women go upstairs on the sly with a package in their arms, then come down again after closing the door and hurry off. Since they left, something like a baby's cries had been heard coming from Paquette's. The mother gave a shriek of laughter, flew up the stairs, burst down her door as if with a cannon, and went in. Something ghastly, Oudarde! In place of her sweet little Agnes, so pink and fresh, who was a gift from God, a sort of hideous little monster, lame, one-eyed and misshapen, was dragging itself across the floor squealing. She hid her eyes in horror. "Oh," she said, "have the witches turned my daughter into this horrible animal?" The little club-footed child was hurriedly removed. He would have driven her mad. It was the monstrous child of some gypsy who had given herself to the devil. He looked about four years old and spoke a language which certainly wasn't human; they were words which aren't possible. La Chantefleurie had hurled herself on the little shoe, all that was left to her of all she had loved. She remained there so long, without moving or speaking, or breathing, that they thought she was dead. Suddenly her whole body shook, she covered her relic with furious kisses and overflowed into sobs as if her heart had just broken. We were crying too, I can assure you. She said: "My little girl, my pretty little girl, where are you?" It wrung the heart. I still weep to think of it. Our children, you know, are the marrow of our bones. My poor Eustache, you're so lovely. If you only knew what a darling he is! Yesterday he said to me, "I want to be a man-at-arms." Oh, Eustache, what if I lost you! La Chantefleurie suddenly got up and began to run through Rheims shouting: "To the gypsy encampment, to the gypsy encampment! Serjeants, to burn the witches!" The gypsies had left. It was pitch black. They couldn't go after them. The following day, two leagues from Rheims, on a heath between Gueux and Tilloy, they found the remains of a big fire, a few ribbons belonging to Paquette's baby, some drops of blood and some goat's droppings. And the night that had just elapsed was a Saturday night.[1] They no longer doubted that the gypsies had celebrated a sabbath on the heath and devoured the baby in company with Beelzebub, as Mahommedans do. When La Chantefleurie learnt these terrible things, she did not cry, she moved her lips as if to speak but she couldn't. The next day her hair was grey. The day after that she vanished.'

'A frightful story, indeed,' said Oudarde, 'and enough to wring tears from a Burgundian!'

'I'm no longer surprised you're so beset by fears of gypsies,' added Gervaise.

'And you were quite right to run away just now with your Eustache,' Oudarde went on, 'because these gypsies are from Poland too.'

'No, they're not,' said Gervaise. 'People say they come from Spain and Catalonia.'

'Catalonia? That's possible,' answered Oudarde. 'Poland, Catalonia, Valognes, I always get those three provinces muddled. What's certain is that they're gypsies.'

'Whose teeth are certainly long enough to eat little children,' added Gervaise. 'And I wouldn't put it beyond La Smeralda to eat a bit too, for all her fastidious ways. The tricks that white goat of hers does are too spiteful, there's something immoral going on there.'

1. i.e. a Sabbath.

Mahiette walked in silence. She was sunk in that reverie that is the prolongation, as it were, of a distressing story and which ceases only once the shock of it has gone on vibrating into the innermost fibres of the heart. Gervaise, meanwhile, was addressing her. 'And did they manage to find out what had become of La Chantefleurie?' Mahiette did not answer. Gervaise repeated her question, shaking her by the arm and calling out her name. Mahiette seemed to awaken from her thoughts.

'What had become of La Chantefleurie?' she said, mechanically repeating the words whose impression was fresh in her ear; then struggling to concentrate again on the meaning of the words: 'Ah,' she went on quickly, 'we never found out.'

She added, after a pause:

'Some said they had seen her leaving Rheims at nightfall by the Porte Fléchembault; others at break of day, by the old Porte Basée. A poor man found her gold crucifix hanging on the stone cross in the field where the fair is held. That was the jewel that had been her downfall in '61. It was a gift from the handsome Viscount of Cormontreuil, her first lover. Paquette would never part with it, however destitute she was. She clung to it like life itself. So when we saw the crucifix thrown away we all thought she was dead. Yet there were people at Le Cabaret-les-Vantes who said they'd seen her go past on the road to Paris walking barefoot over the pebbles. But in that case she'd have had to leave by the Porte de Vesle, which doesn't tally. Or, rather, I think she really did leave by the Porte de Vesle – left this world.'

'I don't follow you,' said Gervaise.

'The Vesle', answered Mahiette with a melancholy smile, 'is the river.'

'Poor Chantefleurie!' said Oudarde, with a shiver. 'Drowned!'

'Drowned!' resumed Mahiette. 'And who could have told old father Guybertaut, as he drifted along underneath the Tinqueux bridge, singing in his boat, that one day his darling little Paquette too would pass under the bridge, without a song and without a boat?'

'And the little shoe?' asked Gervaise.

'Vanished, along with the mother,' replied Mahiette.

'Poor little shoe!' said Oudarde.

Oudarde, fat, susceptible Oudarde, would have been very happy to join with Mahiette in her sighs. But Gervaise was more inquisitive and still had some questions left.

'What about the monster?' she suddenly said to Mahiette.

'What monster?' asked the latter.

'The little gypsy monster the witches left behind at La Chantefleurie's in exchange for her daughter! What did you do with it? I certainly hope you drowned it too.'

'No, we didn't,' replied Mahiette.

'What! Burnt it then? Actually, that's fairer. A baby witch!'

'No, neither, Gervaise. The archbishop took an interest in the gypsy child, he exorcized it, blessed it, carefully removed the devil from its body and sent it to Paris to be exposed on the wooden bed at Notre-Dame, as a foundling.'

'Those bishops!' grumbled Gervaise. 'Because they know a lot they have to be different. I just ask you, Oudarde, putting the devil with the foundlings! Because that little monster was quite certainly the devil. Well, Mahiette, what did they do with it in Paris? I bet no one was charitable enough to want it.'

'I don't know,' answered the woman from Rheims. 'It was just at that time that my husband bought the tabellionage of Beru, two leagues from the town, and we didn't concern ourselves any more about the story; also, in front of Beru there are the two small hills of Cernay, which stop you seeing the towers of Rheims cathedral.'

As they talked, the three worthy bourgeoises had reached the Place de Grève. So preoccupied were they that they had walked past the public breviary of the Tour-Roland without stopping, and were making automatically for the pillory, around which the crowd was constantly growing. It is likely that the spectacle then attracting all eyes to it would have made them forget the Rat-hole and the halt they had intended to make there altogether, if fat, six-year-old Eustache, whom Mahiette was pulling along by the hand, had not abruptly reminded them of their objective. 'Mother,' he said, as if warned by some instinct that the Rat-hole was behind him, 'now can I eat the cake?'

If Eustache had been cleverer, that is to say, less greedy, he would have waited longer and not hazarded that timid question: 'Mother, now can I eat the cake?' until they were back at their lodgings in the University, at Maître Andry Musnier's in the Rue Madame-la-Valence, when the two arms of the Seine and the five bridges of the Cité would have lain between the cake and the Rat-hole.

Put at that moment, it was an untimely question and it alerted Mahiette.

'By the way,' she exclaimed, 'we're forgetting the recluse! Show me your Rat-hole, so I can take her the cake.'

'Right away,' said Oudarde. 'It's a charity.'

Which was not what Eustache wanted at all.

'Here, my cake!' he said, banging his two shoulders alternately with his two ears, which in a case of this sort is the supreme sign of disgruntlement.

The three women retraced their steps and when they had nearly reached the house of the Tour-Roland, Oudarde said to the other two: 'We mustn't all three of us look into the hole at once, in case we frighten the sachette. You two pretend to be reading the *dominus* in the breviary, while I put my face to the window. The sachette knows me slightly. I'll tell you when you can come.'

She went to the window on her own. The moment she could see inside, a profound pity was depicted on each of her features, and her frank, cheerful physiognomy changed its colour and expression as abruptly as if it had passed out of a ray of sunlight and into a ray of moonlight. Her eyes glistened and her lips were pursed, as when we are about to weep. A moment later, she put a finger to her lips and beckoned Mahiette to come and look.

Mahiette was moved and came silently and on tiptoe, as when one approaches the bedside of a dying man.

And it was indeed a sad sight which met the two women's gaze, as they peered, unmoving and unbreathing, through the barred window of the Rat-hole.

The cell was a narrow one, wider than it was deep, with a pointed ceiling, and looking inside not unlike the alveole of a large bishop's mitre. In one corner, on the bare flagstones that formed the floor, sat, or rather squatted, a woman. Her chin was resting on her knees which were clasped tightly against her chest. Thus hunched, clad in brown sacking, whose broad folds completely enveloped her, and with her long grey hair falling forward over her face and down her legs to her feet, she appeared at first glance merely as some strange shape outlined against the murky background of the cell, a sort of blackish triangle, which the shaft of daylight from the window divided crudely into two shades of dark and light. It was one of those spectres, half-shadow and half-light, such as one sees in dreams or in the extraordinary works of Goya, pale, motiónless and sinister, squatting on a grave or leaning against the bars of a prison-cell. It was neither man nor woman, neither a living person nor a definite outline; it was a figure; a sort of vision, where reality and fantasy met, like the shadow and the daylight. A gaunt and severe profile could just be discerned beneath the hair, that reached to the ground; the bare toes, clenched on the hard, freezing stone, just protruded from her robe. What little of human form that could be glimpsed beneath that envelope of mourning brought a shudder.

This figure, which seemed to have been set into the flagstones, appeared to have neither movement, nor thought, nor breath. In the month of January, under that thin sackcloth, lying on the bare granite, without a fire, in the gloom of a prison-cell whose slanting vent let in from outside only the icy north wind and never the sunlight, she seemed not to suffer or even to feel. It was as if she had been turned to stone like the cell, to ice like the season. Her hands were clasped, her eyes fixed. At first glance you would have taken her for a spectre, at second for a statue.

And yet, periodically, her blue lips parted in a breath, and trembled, though as lifelessly and mechanically as leaves blown aside by the wind. While from her expressionless eyes there would come a look, an ineffable look, profound, lugubrious, imperturbable, directed all the time at a corner of the cell invisible from outside; a look that seemed to concentrate all the sombre thoughts of that disconsolate soul on who knows what mysterious object.

Such was the creature who had acquired the name of recluse from her habitation and that of sachette from her garment.

The three women, for Gervaise had joined Mahiette and Oudarde, looked through the window. Their heads cut off the cell's feeble daylight, but the wretched woman they had thus deprived seemed unaware of them. 'Let's not disturb her,' said Oudarde softly, 'she's in her ecstasy, she's praying.'

Meanwhile Mahiette was examining that haggard, wizened and dishevelled head with growing anxiety, and her eyes filled with tears. 'That would be very strange,' she murmured.

She passed her head between the bars of the vent and managed to see right into the corner where the unhappy woman's gaze was invariably concentrated.

When she withdrew her head from the window, her face was bathed in tears.

'What is that woman's name?' she asked Oudarde.

Oudarde answered: 'We call her Sister Gudule.'

'And I call her Paquette la Chantefleurie,' Mahiette went on. Then, putting a finger to her lips, she gestured to the astounded Oudarde to pass her head through the window to take a look.

Oudarde looked, and in the corner on which the recluse's eye was fixed in gloomy ecstasy, she saw a tiny pink satin shoe, embroidered with lots of gold and silver spangles.

After Oudarde, Gervaise looked, then the three women, as they contemplated the unhappy mother, began to weep.

Yet neither their stares nor their tears had distracted the recluse. Her hands remained clasped, her lips mute, her eyes fixed, and the little shoe she was staring at wrung the heart of whoever knew its story.

The three women had yet to utter a single word; they did not dare speak, even in a whisper. That profound silence, that profound grief, that profound oblivion into which everything had vanished apart from a single object, affected them like a high altar at Christmas or Easter. They were silent and thoughtful and ready to kneel down. They felt as if they had just entered a church on Tenebrae Day.[1]

In the end Gervaise, who was the most inquisitive and thus the least sensitive of the three, tried to make the recluse speak:

'Sister, Sister Gudule!'

She repeated this summons no less than three times, raising her voice each time. The recluse did not stir. Neither a word, nor a look, nor a sigh, no sign of life.

Then Oudarde in her turn, in a gentler and more caressing tone: 'Sister,' she said, 'Sister Gudule!'

The same silence, the same immobility.

'Strange woman!' exclaimed Gervaise, 'she wouldn't move if a bombard went off!'

'Perhaps she's deaf,' said Oudarde with a sigh.

'Blind perhaps,' added Gervaise.

1. There is no such day; Tenebrae is a special Holy Week service.

'Dead perhaps,' Mahiette put in.

Certain it is that if the soul had not yet departed that inert, slumbering, lethargic body, it had at least withdrawn inside and hidden itself at a depth beyond the reach of the external organs of perception.

'We shall have to leave the cake on the window-sill then,' said Oudarde. 'Some boy'll take it. What can we do to arouse her?'

Eustache, distracted hitherto by a little cart which had just gone past pulled by a large dog, suddenly noticed that his three guides were looking at something in the window and, gripped by curiosity in his turn, he climbed on a boundary stone, reached up on tiptoe and put his fat, scarlet face to the opening, shouting: 'Come on, Mother, let me look!'

At the clear, fresh, ringing tones of the child, the recluse shuddered. She turned her head with the harsh, abrupt movement of a steel spring, her two long, fleshless hands pushed the hair away from her forehead and she fixed the boy with two bitter, astonished and despairing eyes. That look was instantaneous.

'Oh, my God!' she suddenly exclaimed, hiding her head in her knees, and her croaking voice seemed to rend her breast as it emerged, 'you don't have to show me other people's!'

'Good day, madame,' said the boy gravely.

The shock however had, as it were, awoken the recluse. A prolonged shiver went through her entire body from her head to her feet, her teeth chattered, she half raised her head and said, tucking her elbows into her sides and taking her feet in her hands as if to warm them: 'Oh, it's so cold!'

'Poor woman,' said Oudarde, full of compassion, 'would you like some fire?'

She refused with a shake of the head.

'Well,' Oudarde went on, holding out a flask, 'here's some hippocras that will warm you up. Drink.'

She again shook her head, stared hard at Oudarde and said: 'Water.'

Oudarde insisted. 'No, sister, that's no drink for January. You must drink a little hippocras and eat this maize cake which we've cooked for you.'

She pushed away the cake which Mahiette held out to her and said: 'Black bread.'

'Come,' said Gervaise, overcome by charity in her turn, and unfastening her woollen rochet, 'this surcoat is a bit warmer than yours. Put it over your shoulders.'

She refused the coat as she had refused the cake and flask, and answered: 'A sack.'

'But you must have noticed, surely, that it was a holiday yesterday?' the kindly Oudarde went on.

'I noticed,' said the recluse. 'I've had no water in my jug for the past two days.'

She added after a pause: 'It's a holiday, I am forgotten. They do right. Why should the world think of me when I do not think of it? Cold ashes for a dead coal.'

And as if weary from so much talking, she let her head drop back on to her knees. The simple and charitable Oudarde, who took these last words to mean that she was still complaining of the cold, answered innocently: 'So you'd like some fire then?'

'Fire!' said the sachette in a strange tone; 'and will you also make some for the poor little girl who's been under the earth these fifteen years?'

She trembled in every limb, her voice quavered, her eyes shone, she had raised herself up on to her knees. Suddenly she stretched out her lean white hand towards the child who was looking at her in astonishment: 'Take that child away!' she cried. 'The gypsy's going to come!'

Then she fell forward on to her face and her forehead struck the flags with the sound of stone hitting stone. The three women thought she was dead. But a moment later she stirred, and they watched her drag herself on knees and elbows to the corner where the little shoe was. Then they did not dare to look, they could no longer see her, but they heard a great many sighs and kisses, mixed with heartrending cries and dull thuds like those of a head striking a wall. Then, after one such blow, so violent that it made all three of them give at the knees, they heard no more.

'Can she have killed herself?' said Gervaise, venturing her head through the vent. 'Sister, Sister Gudule!'

'Sister Gudule!' repeated Oudarde.

'Dear God, she's no longer moving!' Gervaise continued, 'Is she dead? Gudule, Gudule!'

Mahiette, hitherto speechless with emotion, now made an effort.

'Wait,' she said. Then, leaning towards the window: 'Paquette!' she said, 'Paquette la Chantefleurie!'

The child who blows innocently on the fuse of a petard when it seems to have gone out, so that it explodes in his face, is no more startled than was Mahiette at the effect this name had, suddenly cast into Sister Gudule's cell.

The recluse's whole body shook, she stood erect on her bare feet and leapt to the window, her eyes blazing, and Mahiette, Oudarde, the third woman and the child retreated as far as the parapet on the quay.

Meanwhile the recluse's sinister face appeared, pressing against the bars of the vent. 'Oh, oh!' she cried with a terrifying laugh, 'it's the gypsy calling me!'

At that moment a scene taking place on the pillory arrested her haggard gaze. Her forehead was creased with horror, she reached her two skeleton-like arms out of her cell and cried in a voice that sounded like a death rattle: 'So it's you again, daughter of Egypt, it's you calling me, you stealer of babies! Well, a curse on you, a curse, a curse, a curse!'

FOUR

A Tear for a Drop of Water

THESE words marked, as it were, the coming together of two scenes which had hitherto been unfolding at the same time but in parallel, each on its own stage, the first, of which you have just been reading, in the Rat-hole, the second, of which you are now about to read, on the ladder of the pillory. The only witnesses to the first scene were the three women whose acquaintance the reader has just made; the second had for spectators all the people we earlier saw gathering on the Place de Grève, around the pillory and the gibbet.

The presence of the four serjeants, stationed since nine o'clock that morning at the four corners of the pillory, had led the crowd to anticipate some kind of punishment, doubtless not a hanging, but a flogging, or the cutting off of an ear, or something of the sort, and it had increased so rapidly that the four serjeants became too hemmed in and had had more than once to 'compress' it, as the saying then was, with blows from their *boullayes* and the rumps of their horses.

The populace was well trained when it came to waiting for public punishments and did not exhibit too great an impatience. It amused itself by gazing at the pillory, a very simple sort of monument consisting of a cube of masonry some ten feet high and hollow inside. A very steep flight of steps of unhewn stone, known pre-eminently as the 'ladder', led to the platform on top, on which could be seen a horizontal wheel of plain oak. To this wheel the victim was tied, kneeling down and with his hands behind his back. A wooden shaft, worked from a capstan hidden inside the little building, made the wheel rotate, keeping it always in the horizontal plane and presenting the prisoner's face to all four corners of the square in turn. This was known as 'turning' a criminal.

As can be seen, the pillory on the Grève was far from offering all the delights of the pillory at Les Halles. Nothing architectural. Nothing monumental. No roof of iron crosses, no octagonal lantern, no slender columns widening out at the roofline into acanthus-leaf and floral capitals, no chimeras or monsters to spout rainwater, no carved timbers, no delicate sculptures incised deeply into the stone.

They had to make do with these four slabs of rubble and two sandstone backwalls, and with a miserable stone gibbet, standing thin and bare beside them.

It would have made but a poor banquet for lovers of Gothic architecture. But then no one could have been less interested in monuments than the good bystanders of the Middle Ages, little exercised by the appearance of a pillory.

The victim finally arrived, lashed to the tailgate of a wagon, and once he had been hoisted on to the platform, where he could be seen from all parts of the square, bound with ropes and straps to the wheel of the pillory, a prodigious hooting broke out in the square, mingled with laughter and applause. They had recognized Quasimodo.

It was in fact he. It was a strange reversal. He was being pilloried on the self-same square where the day before he had been saluted, acclaimed and conclaimed pope and prince of fools, in procession with the Duke of Egypt, the King of Thunes and the Emperor of Galilee. But what is certain is that not a soul in that crowd, not even he, who had been by turns victor and victim, formed any clear idea of the contrast. Gringoire and his philosophy were absent from the spectacle.

Soon Michel Noiret, sworn trumpeter of our master the king, summoned the villeins to silence and proclaimed the sentence, in accordance with the orders and regulations of the provost. Then he fell back behind the wagon, together with his men in their livery actons.

Quasimodo was impassive and unblinking. All resistance had been made impossible for him by what was then known, in the language of the criminal chancellery, as 'the vehemence and firmness of the bonds', which means that the thongs and chains were probably biting into his flesh. We have not yet, as it happens, given up this tradition of the gaol and the chain-gang, which we, a gentle, civilized and humane people (forgetting for a moment forced labour and the guillotine), still keep alive with the handcuffs.

He had let himself be led and pushed, carried, perched, tied and retied. There was nothing to be read on his physiognomy but the astonishment of a savage or an imbecile. They knew he was deaf, he might have been blind.

He was made to kneel on the circular plank and he offered no resistance. He was stripped of his shirt and doublet down to the waist, and he offered no resistance. He was enmeshed in a fresh system of straps and hooks, and he let himself be buckled and attached. Every so often he merely gave a loud snort, like a calf with its head dangling and bobbing about over the side of the butcher's cart.

'The dolt,' said Jehan Frollo du Moulin to his friend Robin Poussepain (for the two students had followed the victim as a matter of course), 'he understands about as much as a cockchafer shut up in a box!'

A great laugh went up from the crowd when Quasimodo's hump, his camel's chest, and his horny, hairy shoulders were exposed to view. During which merriment, a short, stocky-looking man, in the town's livery, climbed on to the platform and took up his position beside the victim. His name circulated swiftly among the spectators. This was Maître Pierrat Torterue, sworn torturer at the Châtelet.

He began by setting down a black hour-glass at one corner of the pillory whose upper bulb was full of red sand, which it allowed to flow into the receptacle below, then he removed his particoloured surcoat and a thin, tapering whip could be seen dangling from his right hand, with long, gleaming white thongs, knotted and plaited and studded with metal claws. With his left hand he casually folded his shirt round his right arm, up to the armpit.

Meanwhile Jehan Frollo had raised his fair, curly head above the crowd (he had climbed on to Robin Poussepain's shoulders for the purpose) and was yelling: 'Roll up, roll up, messieurs, mesdames! We are about to see the peremptory flogging of Maître Quasimodo, bell-ringer to my brother the Archdeacon of Josas, a curious piece of oriental architecture, with a dome for a back and twisted columns for legs!'

Loud laughter from the crowd, especially the children and young girls.

Finally, the torturer stamped his foot. The wheel started to turn. Quasimodo quivered under his bonds. The stupefaction suddenly depicted on his misshapen face brought renewed laughter from the crowd round about.

Suddenly, as the wheel revolved and offered him Quasimodo's mountainous back, Maître Pierrat raised his arm, the slender thongs hissed sharply through the air like a handful of serpents and came furiously down on the poor devil's shoulders.

Quasimodo jumped where he knelt, as if starting from sleep. He was beginning to understand. He twisted about in his bonds; a violent contraction of surprise and pain distorted the muscles of his face; but no complaint from him. He merely turned his head behind him, then swung it both right and left, like a bull stung on the flank by a horsefly.

A second stroke followed the first, then a third, then another and another, and so on. The wheel did not cease from turning nor the blows from raining down. Soon the blood spurted, it could be seen running in innumerable rivulets down the hunchback's black shoulders, and the slender thongs spattered drops of it amongst the crowd as they swished through the air.

Quasimodo, in appearance at least, had resumed his earlier impassivity. First, he had tried stealthily, without any great visible exertion, to burst his bonds. They had seen his eye kindle, his muscles go tense, his limbs gather themselves, and the straps and chains grow taut. It was a mighty, a prodigious, a desperate effort; but the ancient trammels of the provostry withstood it. They creaked, but that was all. Quasimodo fell back exhausted. The stupefaction on his features gave way to a sense of bitter and profound discouragement. He closed his solitary eye, let his head fall forward on to his chest and was as if dead.

Thereafter he did not move. Nothing was able to wrest any movement from him. Not the blood that continued to flow, not the lashes in their redoubled fury, not the torturer's anger as he grew excited and intoxicated by the punishment, not the sound of the terrible thongs, shriller and more piercing than the legs of a hornet.

Finally an usher from the Châtelet, dressed in black and riding a black horse, who had been stationed beside the ladder since the punishment began, stretched out his ebony rod towards the hour-glass. The torturer stopped. The wheel stopped. Quasimodo's eyes slowly reopened.

The flogging was over. Two of the sworn torturer's attendants washed the victim's bleeding shoulders and rubbed them with some ointment or other which at once closed up all the wounds, and threw over his back a sort of yellow loincloth cut like a chasuble. Pierrat Torterue meanwhile was shaking out his red, blood-soaked thongs on to the pavement.

Quasimodo was not yet done with. He still had to undergo the hour in the pillory which Maître Florian Barbedienne had so judiciously added to the sentence of Messire Robert d'Estouteville; and all to the greater glory of John Comenius's old physiological and psychological play on words: *surdus absurdus*.[1]

The hour-glass was therefore reversed and the hunchback left tied to the plank so that justice might be fully done.

As the child is in the family, so the common people in society, and never more so than in the Middle Ages. For as long as it remains in this state of primal ignorance, of moral and intellectual minority, we can say of it as we do of the child: 'That age is without pity.'[2]

We have already shown how widespread was the dislike of Quasimodo, for more than one good reason, admittedly. There was hardly a spectator in that crowd who did not either have or think he had cause to complain of the evil hunchback of Notre-Dame. The

1. 'Deaf absurd.'
2. La Fontaine: 'Les deux pigeons.

joy was universal when they saw him appear on the pillory, and the harsh punishment he had just undergone and the pitiful state it had left him in, far from moving the populace to pity, had rendered its hatred more spiteful still, by giving it an edge of gaiety.

And so once the *vindicte publique* had been satisfied, as the academic jargon still has it, it was the turn for many private acts of revenge. Here, as in the great hall, it was the women above all who gave vent. They all bore him some grudge, some for his spitefulness, others for his ugliness. The latter were the fiercest.

'Oh, mask of Antichrist!' said one.

'Rider on broomsticks!' shouted a second.

'That's a lovely tragic face,' yelled a third, 'it'd make you fools' pope if today was yesterday.'

'That's good,' put in an old woman. 'That's his pillory face. When do we get the gallows one?'

'When will you be a hundred feet underground with your big bell on your head, you accursed bell-ringer?'

'Yet it's that devil who rings the angelus!'

'Oh, he's deaf, he's one-eyed, he's hunchbacked, he's a monster!'

'A face like that'd give you an abortion faster than any medicine or pharmicals!'

The two students, Jehan du Moulin and Robin Poussepain were roaring out the popular old refrain:

He's no use
Fetch a noose!
What a sight,
Set him alight!

Other insults rained down on him by the score, with catcalls, and imprecations and laughter, and now and again a stone.

Quasimodo may have been deaf but he could see well enough, and the popular fury was no less energetically depicted on their faces than in their words. The stones, moreover, explained the outbursts of laughter. He did not respond at first, but then his patience, steeled by the torturer's whip, gradually weakened and gave way before all these gnat-bites. The Asturian bull, little troubled by the onrushes of the picador, is irritated by the dogs and the *banderillas*.

He first of all cast a threatening glance around the crowd. But pinioned as he was, his eye was powerless to dispel these flies that were biting his wounds. Then he wrestled with his fetters and his furious convulsions caused the old pillory wheel to groan on its planks. All of which added to the jeers and the derision.

Then the poor devil, unable to snap the collar that tethered him like a wild animal, became still again. Only now and again did a sigh of rage swell all the cavities of his chest. On his face there was neither shame nor blushes. He was too far from the state of society and too close to that of nature to know what shame was. With that degree of deformity, moreover, can one have any sense of infamy? But anger, hatred and despair slowly descended on that hideous face in an ever more sombre cloud, full of an electricity that flashed unendingly from his cyclop's eye.

That cloud lifted for a moment, however, when a mule came through the crowd, carrying a priest. The moment he saw the mule and the priest in the distance, the poor victim's face softened. From being distorted with fury, it now wore a strange smile, full of an ineffable sweetness, docility and tenderness. As the priest drew nearer, this smile became clearer, more distinct, more radiant. It was as if the poor man were greeting the advent of a saviour. Nevertheless, once the mule came close enough to the pillory for its rider to be able to recognize the victim, the priest lowered his gaze, turned abruptly about and dug in both his heels, as if he were in a hurry to be spared humiliating entreaties and not at all anxious to be greeted and recognized by a poor wretch in such a situation.

The priest was the archdeacon, Dom Claude Frollo.

The cloud redescended blacker still on Quasimodo's brow. For a time a smile was still mixed in with it, but a bitter, discouraged, profoundly sad smile.

Time was passing. He had been there at least an hour and a half, had been lacerated, abused, mocked without respite and nearly stoned.

Suddenly he again writhed around in his chains with a renewed desperation, which caused the whole timber frame supporting him to shake, and, breaking the silence he had obstinately kept up until that moment, he shouted in a furious, raucous voice which sounded more like a dog's bark than a human cry and was drowned by the sound of jeering: 'A drink!'

Far from evoking compassion, this exclamation of distress merely added to the amusement of the good people of Paris surrounding the ladder, who, it must be said, taken in the mass and as a multitude, were hardly any less cruel or debased than the horrible tribe of truants to whom we have already directed the reader's steps and who were, quite simply, the bottom-most stratum of the people. Not a voice was raised around the wretched victim, unless it was to rail at him for his thirst. He was, for a fact, even more repulsive and grotesque than pitiable at that moment, with his streaming, purple face, his frenzied eye, his mouth frothing with rage and pain, and his tongue hanging half out. It must also be said that, had that mob contained some pious and charitable Parisian or Parisienne, tempted to carry a glass of water to that poor tormented creature, the prejudice of shame and ignominy prevailing around the infamous steps of the pillory would have been enough to drive the good Samaritan away.

After a few minutes, Quasimodo looked despairingly around the crowd and repeated in an even more heart-rending tone: 'A drink!'

At which they all laughed.

'Drink this!' shouted Robin Poussepain, throwing a sponge that had been dragged in the gutter at his face. 'Take it, you deaf brute, I owe you a debt!'

A woman threw a stone at his head: 'That'll teach you to wake us up at nights with your infernal peals of bells.'

'Well, sonny,' screamed a cripple trying to get at him with his crutch, 'are you going to go on casting spells on us from on top of the towers of Notre-Dame?'

'Here's a bowl to drink from!' added a man, letting fly at his chest with a broken jug. 'You made my wife give birth to a two-headed baby just by walking past her!'

'And my cat to a six-legged kitten!' squealed an old woman, hurling a tile at him.

'A drink!' panted Quasimodo for the third time.

Just then, he saw the populace draw back. A strangely dressed young girl stepped out from the crowd. She was accompanied by a little white goat with gilded horns and was carrying a tambourine in her hand.

Quasimodo's eye glinted. It was the gypsy girl he had tried to abduct the night before, an assault for which he dimly sensed he was being chastised at this very moment; which was, as it happens, very far from being the case, since he was being punished only for the misfortune of being deaf and of having been judged by a deaf man. He did not doubt but that she too had come to get her revenge and to let fly at him like all the others.

And in fact he saw her climb quickly up the ladder. He was choked by rage and resentment. He would have liked to be able to bring the pillory crashing to the ground and if the lightning of his eye could have struck her down, the gypsy would have been pulverized before she reached the platform.

Without uttering a word, she approached the victim, who was writhing about in a vain attempt to escape her, then she unfastened a gourd from her belt and raised it gently to the wretched man's parched lips.

And then, in that hitherto dry, burnt eye, a large tear was seen to form, which rolled slowly down his deformed face, for so long contorted by despair. It was perhaps the first tear the luckless man had ever shed.

But he was forgetting to drink. The gypsy gave her little impatient pout and smilingly leant the neck of the bottle against Quasimodo's protruding teeth. He took long draughts. His thirst was burning.

When he had finished, the poor devil extended his black lips, no doubt to kiss the fair hand that had just come to his aid. But the girl may still have felt suspicion or been remembering the violent attempt on her the night before; she withdrew her hand with the frightened gesture of a child afraid of being bitten by an animal.

The poor deaf man then fixed her with a stare full of reproach and an inexpressible sadness.

This beautiful, pure, fresh, charming and yet at the same time frail girl would have been a touching sight anywhere, coming piously to the aid of so much destitution, deformity and viciousness. On a pillory it was sublime. The crowd was itself affected and began to clap its hands, shouting, 'Nowel, nowel!'

It was at that moment that the recluse noticed the gypsy on the pillory from the window of her cell and hurled her sinister imprecation at her: 'A curse on you, daughter of Egypt! A curse, a curse!'

FIVE

The Story of a Cake (concluded)

LA Esmeralda turned pale and stumbled down from the pillory. The recluse's voice still pursued her: 'Down you go, you robber from Egypt! You'll go back up!'

'It's one of the sachette's whims,' muttered the people, but took it no further. For such women were feared and that made them sacred. In those days, they didn't willingly attack someone who prayed day and night.

The time had come for Quasimodo to be led off. He was untied and the crowd broke up.

Near the Grand-Pont, Mahiette, who was coming away with her two companions, suddenly stopped. 'By the way, Eustache, what have you done with the cake?'

'While you were talking with that lady in the hole, mother,' said the child, 'there was a big dog and it bit my cake. So I ate some too.'

'What, monsieur,' she went on, 'you've eaten it all?'

'It was the dog, mother. I told him but he wouldn't listen to me. So I had a bite as well!'

'Terrible child,' said the mother, smiling and scolding him at one and the same time. 'Do you know, Oudarde, he already eats the whole cherry-tree in our field in Charlerange on his own. That's why his grandfather says he'll be a captain. Don't let me catch you again, Monsieur Eustache. Come on, you great big lion!'

BOOK SEVEN

ONE

Of the Danger of Entrusting Your Secret to a Goat

SEVERAL weeks had elapsed.

It was now early March. The sun, which Du Bartas,[1] that classical forefather of the periphrasis, had yet to name 'the grand-duke of candles', was no less joyful and radiant for that. It was one of those lovely soft spring days, when the whole of Paris flocks to the squares and promenades and celebrates as if it were a Sunday. On such clear, warm, cloudless days, there is one moment in particular for admiring the portal of Notre-Dame. When the sun is already sinking in the west and strikes the cathedral almost full on. As its rays become more and more horizontal, they slowly retreat from the paving-stones of the square and ascend the precipitous façade, causing the innumerable sculptures to stand away from their shadows, while the great central rose-window flames like the eye of a cyclops ablaze with the reflection from the forge.

It was that moment now.

The tall cathedral was ruddy in the setting sun; opposite it, on a stone balcony built on top of the porch of an ornate Gothic house, which formed the corner of the square and the Rue du Parvis, were laughing and chattering, full of charm and high spirits, a number of beautiful young girls. From the length of the veils that hung right to their heels from the tops of pointed head-dresses, wound round with pearls, from the fineness of the embroidered chemisettes which covered their shoulders, displaying, in the attractive fashion of the time, the cleavage of their lovely virgin breasts, from the opulence of their under-skirts, which were of even costlier stuff than their outer garments (a splendid refinement!), from the gauze, the silk and the velvet from which it was all confected, and above all from the whiteness of their hands, which declared them to be young ladies of leisure, it was simple to guess that these were rich and aristocratic heiresses. They were, in fact, Demoiselle Fleur-de-Lys de Gondelaurier and her companions, Diane de Christeuil, Amelotte de Montmichel, Colombe de Gaillefontaine and the little De Champchevrier; all of them girls of good family, gathered at

1. Guillaume de Salluste, Seigneur du Bartas (1544–90), diplomat and poet.

this moment in the house of the widowed Dame de Gondelaurier because of my lord de Beaujeu and his lady wife, who were to come to Paris in April and there choose companions of honour for the Dauphine Marguerite, when they went to receive her in Picardy from the hands of the Flemings. All the country squires for thirty leagues around had schemed for this favour for their daughters, and a good many had already brought or sent them to Paris. They had been entrusted by their parents to the discreet and venerable protection of Madame Aloïse de Gondelaurier, widow of a former Master of the King's Crossbowmen, who had withdrawn with her only daughter into her house on the square of the parvis of Notre-Dame in Paris.

The balcony where the girls were sitting opened on to a chamber richly hung in a tawny Flanders leather printed with gold scrolls. The beams made parallel stripes across the ceiling, amusing the eye with the strangeness of their innumerable painted or gilded carvings. Here and there, on top of worked chests, glinted splendid enamels; a boar's head in faïence crowned a magnificent dresser, whose two steps proclaimed that the mistress of the house was the wife or widow of a knight-banneret. At the far end, beside a tall chimney-piece emblazoned from top to bottom with coats of arms, sat the Dame de Gondelaurier, in an ornate armchair of red velvet, her fifty-five years as much in evidence in her clothing as in her face. Next to her stood a young man of somewhat haughty mien, if a trifle vain and boastful, one of those good-looking boys about whom women are all of the same mind though they bring a shrug of the shoulders from any man who is both serious and a student of physiognomy. This young cavalier wore the brilliant uniform of a captain of archers of the king's bodyguard, far too similar to the costume of Jupiter, which the reader was able to admire in Book One of this history, for us to weary him with a second description of it.

The young ladies were seated, some in the room, the others on the balcony, some on pillows of Utrecht velvet with gold corner-pieces, the others on oak stools carved with flowers and figures. Each of them held on her knees a portion of a huge needlework tapestry, on which they were collaborating and of which a considerable length trailed across the matting that covered the floor.

They were talking among themselves with the lowered voices

and suppressed giggles of any conclave of girls with a young man in their midst. The young man, whose presence had sufficed to bring so much feminine vanity into play, seemed for his part to be little concerned by it; and while the pretty girls vied in attracting his attention, he seemed occupied above all in shining up the buckle of his belt with his kid glove.

From time to time the old lady would say something to him in an undertone and he answered as best he could, with a sort of stiff and awkward good manners. From Madame Aloïse's smiles, from her little gestures of complicity, from the winks she despatched in the direction of her daughter Fleur-de-Lys as she whispered to the captain, it was easy to see that a betrothal was involved, some forthcoming marriage no doubt between the young man and Fleur-de-Lys. And from the officer's embarrassed indifference, it was easy to tell that, at least on his side, love was no longer involved. His whole bearing expressed an idea of embarrassment and tedium which our second lieutenants on garrison duty today would convey admirably by the words: 'What a ghastly bore!'

The good lady, quite besotted by her daughter, like any poor mother, had not noticed the officer's lack of ardour, and was doing her utmost, in a whisper, to make him observe the infinite perfection with which Fleur-de-Lys inserted her needle or unwound her thread.

'There, young cousin,' she said to him, pulling him by the sleeve so she could talk into his ear. 'Look at her! She's bending over.'

'So she is,' answered the young man, and relapsed into his icy, absent-minded silence.

A moment later, he had to lean across again, as Dame Aloïse said to him:

'Have you ever seen a more comely or cheerful figure than your betrothed? Was anyone ever so white and fair? Aren't those clever hands? And her neck, doesn't it move ravishingly, just like a swan's? There are times when I do envy you! You're so lucky to be a man, you wicked libertine you! Isn't it a fact that my Fleur-de-Lys is adorably beautiful and that you're head over heels in love with her?'

'Surely,' he replied, his mind on other matters.

'But talk to her, then,' said Madame Aloïse all of a sudden, pushing him by the shoulder. 'Say something to her, then. You've got very shy.'

We can assure our readers that shyness was neither the captain's virtue nor his weakness. However, he tried to do as he had been asked.

'Fair cousin,' he said, going up to Fleur-de-Lys, 'what is the subject of that piece of tapestry you are doing?'

'Fair cousin,' replied Fleur-de-Lys in a resentful tone, 'I have told you three times already. It's Neptunus's grotto.'

It was obvious that Fleur-de-Lys saw more clearly than her mother into the captain's cold and indifferent ways. He felt the need to make conversation.

'And who is all this neptunery for?' he asked.

'For the Abbey of Saint-Antoine-des-Champs,' said Fleur-de-Lys, without looking up.

The captain picked up a corner of the tapestry: 'Who's this fat soldier, fair cousin of mine, blowing so hard into a trumpet?'

'That's Triton,' she replied.

There was still a slightly piqued tone to Fleur-de-Lys's brief words. The young man realized it was essential for him to whisper something into her ear, some sweet nothing or piece of gallantry, anything would do. He therefore leant towards her, but the tenderest and most intimate invention he could find was: 'Why does your mother still wear a cote-hardie with a coat of arms on like our grandmothers in Charles VII's time? Tell her, fair cousin, that it is no longer fashionable these days, and that the hinge-pin[1] and bay-tree[2] emblazoned on her dress make her look like a walking chimney-piece. I swear people don't sit on their banners like that any more, truly.'

Fleur-de-Lys raised two beautiful and reproachful eyes to him: 'Is that all you swear to me?' she said softly.

Meanwhile the good Dame Aloïse, overjoyed at seeing them leaning together and whispering like this, said as she fiddled with the clasps on her book of hours: 'A touching picture of love!'

The captain grew more and more embarrassed and fell back on the tapestry: 'It really is a delightful piece of work!' he exclaimed.

In which connection, Colombe de Gaillefontaine, another beautiful fair-haired girl with white skin and a blue damask collar,

1. *Gond.* 2. *Laurier.*

shyly ventured a remark which she addressed to Fleur-de-Lys in hopes that the captain might answer: 'Dear Gondelaurier, have you seen the tapestries in the Roche-Guyon's hôtel?'

'Isn't that the hôtel that encloses the wardrobe-mistress of the Louvre's garden?' laughingly asked Diane de Christeuil, who had beautiful teeth and so laughed at the least provocation.

'And where there's that huge old tower of the ancient wall of Paris,' added Amelotte de Montmichel, a fresh and pretty dark girl with curly hair, who made a habit of sighing, just as the other laughed, without knowing why.

'My dear Colombe,' put in Dame Aloïse, 'do you mean the hôtel that belonged to Monsieur de Bacqueville, in King Charles VI's days? There are indeed some magnificent high-warp tapestries there.'

'Charles VI, King Charles VI!' muttered the young captain, twirling his moustache. 'Good God, what old things the good woman remembers!'

Madame de Gondelaurier continued: 'Fine tapestries, indeed. Work so highly regarded, it is thought to be unique!'

Just then, Bérangère de Champchevrier, a slender little girl of seven, who was looking down into the square through the trefoils of the balcony, cried out: 'Oh, look, godmother Fleur-de-Lys, the pretty dancer dancing there on the paving and playing her tambourine in the middle of the common burgesses!'

They could indeed hear the resonant trembling of a tambourine.

'Some gypsy from Bohemia,' said Fleur-de-Lys, turning casually towards the square.

'Let's see, let's see!' cried her companions, animatedly; and they all ran to the edge of the balcony, while Fleur-de-Lys, her thoughts on her fiancé's indifference, slowly followed, and the latter, relieved by this incident, which had cut short a difficult conversation, went back to the far end of the apartment with the contented look of a soldier coming off duty. And yet what a charming and congenial duty the fair Fleur-de-Lys was, as he himself indeed had once thought; but the captain had gradually become blasé; the prospect of an imminent marriage caused his ardour to abate daily. Moreover, he was fickle by nature, and – must we say it? – of somewhat vulgar tastes. Although very well-born, he had contracted in the army more than one old soldier's habit. He liked the tavern, and what it led to. He was at ease only amongst the crude talk and the womanizing of soldiers, amongst easy beauties and easy conquests. His family had given him some education and manners, but at too early an age he had travelled the country and served in garrisons, and day by day the veneer of the gentleman had rubbed away under the vigorous chafing of his man-at-arm's cross-belt. Although he still called on her from time to time, out of some vestige of human respect, he felt doubly awkward with Fleur-de-Lys; first because, having distributed his favours in all sorts of places, he had kept very few for her; and secondly because he was always afraid, in the midst of all those stiff, starched and respectable ladies, in case his habitually foul tongue should suddenly take the bit between its teeth and break out into the language of the tavern. With what effect may be imagined!

For the rest, all this went with great pretensions to elegance, to fine clothes and a distinguished appearance. Which you must explain as best you can; I am merely a historian.

For the past few moments, he had been leaning in silence, in thought or not in thought, against the carved mantelpiece, when Fleur-de-Lys suddenly turned and addressed him. After all, the poor girl had only snubbed him in self-defence.

'Fair cousin, did you not tell us about a little gypsy girl whom you saved one night, two months ago, when you were on the counter-watch, from the hands of a dozen robbers?'

'I think I did, fair cousin,' said the captain.

'Well,' she went on, 'perhaps it was that gypsy dancing there in the parvis. Come and see if you recognize her, fair cousin Phoebus.'

He detected a secret desire for reconciliation in this gentle invitation to move closer to her, and in the care she had taken to call him by name. Captain Phoebus de Châteaupers (for he it is whom the reader has had before him since the beginning of this chapter) walked slowly towards the balcony. 'Look,' Fleur-de-Lys said to him, placing her hand affectionately on Phoebus's arm, 'look at that girl dancing there in the circle. Is that your gypsy?'

Phoebus looked and said:

'Yes, I recognize her by her goat.'

'Oh, isn't it a pretty little goat!' said Amelotte, clasping her hands in admiration.

'Are its horns real gold?' asked Bérangère.

Dame Aloïse spoke, without getting up from her armchair:

'Isn't she one of those gypsies who arrived last year by the Porte Gibard?'

'These days it's known as the Porte d'Enfer, mother,' said Fleur-de-Lys quietly.

Mademoiselle de Gondelaurier knew just how offended the captain was by her mother's dated way of speaking. Indeed, he had begun to snigger and mutter under his breath: 'Porte Gibard, Porte Gibard! That's so King Charles VI can enter!'

'Godmother,' exclaimed Bérangère, whose eyes were never still and had suddenly been raised to the tops of the towers of Notre-Dame, 'who's that man in black up there?'

The girls all looked upwards. A man was in fact leaning over the topmost balustrade of the north tower, overlooking the Grève. It was a priest. They could clearly make out his garb, and his face, cupped in his two hands. For the rest, he was as motionless as a statue. He was staring intently down into the square.

There was about him something of the stillness of a hawk that has just discovered a nest of sparrows and is watching it.

'It's the Archdeacon of Josas,' said Fleur-de-Lys.

'You've got good eyesight if you can recognize him from here!' remarked la Gaillefontaine.

'How he's staring at the little dancer!' put in Diane de Christeuil.

'Gypsy beware!' said Fleur-de-Lys, 'because he doesn't like Egypt!'

'What a pity that man's looking at her like that,' added Amelotte de Montmichel, 'because she dances brilliantly.'

'Fair cousin Phoebus,' said Fleur-de-Lys suddenly, 'since you know the little gypsy, signal her to come up. It would be fun.'

'Oh, yes!' cried all the girls, clapping their hands.

'But that's silly,' answered Phoebus. 'She's no doubt forgotten me, and I don't even know her name. However, since you wish it, mesdemoiselles, I shall try.' And leaning over the balustrade of the balcony, he began shouting: 'Little one!'

The dancer was not playing her tambourine just at that moment. She turned her head towards the point whence the summons had come, her brilliant eyes fell on Phoebus and she stopped dead.

'Little one!' the captain repeated, beckoning to her.

The girl looked at him again, then blushed as if a flame had risen into her cheeks and, taking her tambourine under her arm, she walked with slow, faltering steps, through the flabbergasted spectators, towards the door of the house from which Phoebus had called to her, with the disquieted gaze of a bird succumbing to the fascination of a snake.

A moment later, the door-curtain was raised and the gypsy appeared in the doorway of the room, bewildered, red-faced, panting, her big eyes lowered, not daring to take another step.

Bérangère clapped her hands.

The dancer, however, stood without moving in the doorway. Her appearance had had a singular effect on the group of girls. The fact is that every one of them had been animated by some vague, shadowy desire to please the good-looking officer, whose splendid uniform was the mark at which all their coquetries were aimed, and since his arrival there had been a certain secret, unspoken rivalry between them, which they would scarcely have admitted even to themselves yet which was constantly manifesting itself in their gestures and remarks. Nevertheless, because they were all more or less of the same degree of beauty, they fought on equal terms and any one of them might hope to win. The gypsy's arrival abruptly destroyed the balance. She was so uncommonly beautiful that the instant she appeared in the doorway of the apartment she seemed to diffuse a kind of light peculiar to herself. In that confined room, with its sombre frame of hangings and panelling, she was incomparably more beautiful and radiant than in the public square. She was like a torch that had just been carried from the daylight into the shadows. The noble maidens were dazzled in spite of themselves. Each of them felt somehow injured in her own beauty. And so their battlefront, if you will permit the expression, changed instantly, without a word being spoken. But they understood one another perfectly. Women's instincts understand and answer one another quicker than men's intellects. An enemy had just come upon them; they all sensed it and they closed ranks. One drop of wine is enough to turn a whole glass of water red; to tinge an entire gathering of pretty women with a certain ill-humour, all it takes is the arrival of a prettier woman still – especially when there is only one man.

Thus the gypsy's reception was wonderfully chilly. They looked her up and down, then looked at each other, and all had been said.

They had understood each other. The girl meanwhile waited to be spoken to, so agitated that she did not dare raise her eyelids.

The captain was the first to break the silence. 'Upon my word,' he said in a fearlessly fatuous voice, 'what a delightful creature! What do you think of her, fair cousin?'

This remark, which a more tactful admirer would at least have spoken in an undertone, was not of a kind to dispel the feminine jealousies keeping one another under observation in front of the gypsy.

Fleur-de-Lys answered the captain with a honeyed affectation of disdain: 'Not bad.'

The others were whispering.

At last Madame Aloïse, who was not the least jealous because she was jealous for her daughter, addressed the dancer: 'Come here, little one.'

'Come here, little one!' repeated Bérangère with comic dignity, she who would have come up to her hip.

The gypsy went towards the noble lady.

'Fair child,' said Phoebus emphatically, taking a few steps towards her from his side, 'I don't know if I have the supreme good fortune to be recognized by you...'

She interrupted him by raising on to him a smile and a look full of an infinite sweetness:

'Oh, yes!' she said.

'She has a good memory,' remarked Fleur-de-Lys.

'Well then,' Phoebus went on, 'you ran off very nimbly the other evening. Do I frighten you?'

'Oh no!' said the gypsy.

Fleur-de-Lys felt hurt by something ineffable in the tone in which this 'Oh no!' had been said, following the 'Oh yes!'

'You left me a pretty surly customer in your stead, my beauty,' continued the captain, whose tongue had been loosened now that he was talking to a girl from the streets, 'with a hump and only one eye, the bishop's bell-ringer, I believe. I'm told he was the bastard of an archdeacon and was born a devil. He's got a charming name, he's called Ember-Days, Palm Sunday, Shrove Tuesday, I don't remember which! Some church festival anyway! So he presumed to abduct you, as if you were made for beadles, that's a bit much! What the devil did that owl want with you, then? Tell me that!'

'I don't know,' she answered.

'What insolence, I ask you! A bell-ringer abducting a girl, just like a viscount! A villein poaching gentlemen's game. Did you ever hear the like. Anyway, he paid dearly for it. Maître Pierrat Torterue's the toughest groom who ever curried a horse, and I can tell you, what you might be pleased to know, that your bell-ringer's hide got a thorough drubbing from him.'

'Poor man!' said the gypsy, whose memory of the scene at the pillory had been revived by these words.

The captain burst out laughing. '*Corne-de-bœuf*, sympathy's just about as appropriate in his case as a feather up a pig's arse! Give me a pot-belly and call me pope, if...'

He pulled himself up. 'Forgive me, mesdames, I think I was about to say something foolish.'

'Shame on you, monsieur!' said La Gaillefontaine.

'He talks his own language to that creature!' added Fleur-de-Lys in an undertone, her resentment increasing by the minute. This resentment did not lessen when she saw the captain, delighted by the gypsy but above all by himself, spin on his heel and repeat, with a soldier's crude and naïve gallantry: 'A good-looking girl, upon my soul!'

'Somewhat primitively dressed,' said Diane de Christeuil, showing her fine teeth as she laughed.

This thought was a ray of light for the others. It showed them where the gypsy was vulnerable. Unable to criticize her looks, they hurled themselves on her clothes.

'That's true, little one,' said La Montmichel, 'how come you roam the streets like that without a wimple or a gorget?'

'That skirt is frighteningly short,' added La Gaillefontaine.

'You will be picked up by the serjeants of the *douzaine*, my dear, for your gilt belt,' Fleur-de-Lys continued, rather sourly.

'If you were to put a proper sleeve over your arm, little one,' went on La Christeuil, with an implacable smile, 'it wouldn't get so sunburnt.'

It was in truth a sight worthy of a more intelligent spectator than Phoebus, to watch these beautiful girls, with their waspish, venomous tongues, as they slithered and slipped and wriggled round the dancer from the streets. They were both graceful and cruel. They searched and probed her cheap, silly costume of spangles and tinsel with their malevolent remarks. There was no end to the laughter, the ironies, the humiliations. Sarcasms, a haughty benevolence, and spiteful glances rained down on the gypsy. One might have been watching the young ladies of Rome, who used to amuse themselves by sticking pins into beautiful slave-girls. They were like graceful whippets circling, with flared nostrils and blazing eyes, round some poor woodland hind, which the eye of their master forbids them to devour.

What was a wretched dancer from the public square, after all, compared to these girls of high breeding? They seemed to ignore her presence, they discussed her out loud, in front of her, to her face, as if she were something rather unclean, rather abject, but rather pretty.

The gypsy was not immune to these pinpricks. Now and again, her eye or her cheeks would flare angrily or colour with shame; a disdainful word seemed to tremble on her lips; contemptuously, she made that little grimace the reader knows already; but she did not speak. Unmoving, she fixed Phoebus with a sad, gentle, resigned stare. There was happiness and tenderness too in that stare. It was as if she were restraining herself, for fear of being sent away.

Phoebus himself laughed and took the gypsy's part with a mixture of impertinence and sympathy.

'Don't listen to them, little one!' he repeated, clinking his gold spurs, 'your costume is a shade wild and extravagant no doubt; but what does that matter, charming girl that you are?'

'Goodness!' exclaimed the fair-haired Gaillefontaine, raising her swanlike neck with a bitter smile, 'I see that the archers of the king's bodyguard are easily inflamed by the beautiful eyes of gypsies.'

'Why not?' said Phoebus.

At this answer, casually tossed away by the captain, like some aimless stone whose fall one does not even follow, Colombe began to laugh, so did Diane, so did Amelotte and so did Fleur-de-Lys, into whose eye there came at the same time a tear.

The gypsy, who had dropped her eyes to the floor at Colombe de Gaillefontaine's words, raised them again radiant with joy and pride and fixed them once more on Phoebus. At that moment she was very beautiful.

The old lady, who had been observing the scene, felt offended and did not understand.

'Holy Virgin!' she suddenly exclaimed, 'what's that moving about round my legs? Oh, the horrid creature!'

It was the goat, which had just arrived in search of its mistress and, as it dashed towards her, had begun by catching its horns in the pile of material which the noble lady's clothes formed on her feet when she was sitting down.

This was a distraction. The gypsy freed it without a word.

'Oh, it's the little goat with gold hooves!' exclaimed Bérangère, jumping for joy.

The gypsy squatted down on her knees and leant the goat's affectionate head against her cheek. It was as if she were saying she was sorry for having left it behind.

Meanwhile Diane had leant into Colombe's ear.

'Good heavens, why didn't I think of it sooner! It's the gypsy with the goat. They say she's a witch and that her goat does really miraculous tricks.'

'Well,' said Colombe, 'the goat must amuse us in its turn, and do a miracle for us.'

Diane and Colombe spoke quickly to the gypsy: 'Little one, make your goat do a miracle.'

'I don't know what you mean,' replied the dancer.

'A miracle, some magic, some witchcraft if you like.'

'I don't know.' And she went back to stroking the pretty creature, repeating: 'Djali! Djali!'

Just then, Fleur-de-Lys noticed an embroidered leather sachet hanging from the goat's neck. 'What's that?' she asked the gypsy.

The gypsy raised her big eyes to her and answered solemnly: 'That's my secret.'

'I'd love to know what your secret is,' thought Fleur-de-Lys.

The good dame meanwhile had stood up crossly. 'Now then, gypsy, if neither you nor your goat has a dance for us, what are you doing in here?'

The gypsy made slowly for the door without answering. But her step grew slower and slower as she neared it. An invincible magnet seemed to be holding her back. Suddenly she turned her tearful eyes on Phoebus and stopped.

'God's truth!' exclaimed the captain, 'you can't just leave like that. Come back and dance something for us. By the way, my lovely, what's your name?'

'La Esmeralda,' said the dancer, not taking her eyes off him.

A loud laugh went up from the girls at this strange name.

'That's an awful name for a young lady!' said Diane.

'You can tell she's an enchantress,' put in Amelotte.

'Your parents didn't fish that name up for you from the baptismal font, my dear,' exclaimed Dame Aloïse solemnly.

A few minutes earlier, however, without anyone noticing, Bérangère had lured the goat into a corner of the room with some marzipan. They had instantly become firm friends. The inquisitive child had removed the sachet that hung round the goat's neck, had undone it and had emptied its contents on to the matting. It was an alphabet, each letter of which had been separately inscribed on a small boxwood cube. Hardly had these playthings been spread out on the mat when the child was surprised to see the goat, one of whose 'miracles' this no doubt was, extract certain letters with its gilded hoof and arrange them with little nudges in a particular order. A moment later they made a word, which the goat seemed to have been trained to write, so unhesitating had it been in forming it, and Bérangère suddenly exclaimed and clasped her hands in admiration:

'Godmother Fleur-de-Lys, look what the goat has just done!'

Fleur-de-Lys ran up and gave a shudder. The letters arranged on the floor formed the word PHOEBUS.

'Did the goat write it?' she asked in a changed voice.

'Yes, godmother,' answered Bérangère.

There could be no doubt; the child could not write.

'That's her secret!' thought Fleur-de-Lys.

Meanwhile everyone had come hurrying up at the child's shout, the girls, the gypsy and the officer.

The gypsy saw the folly which the goat had just committed. She went red, then white and began to tremble like a guilty woman in front of the captain, who stared at her with an astonished and self-satisfied smile.

'"Phoebus",' whispered the astounded girls, 'that's the captain's name!'

'You have a wonderful memory!' said Fleur-de-Lys to the petrified gypsy. Then, bursting into sobs: 'Oh, she's a magician!' she stammered, hiding her face in her lovely hands. And she heard an even more bitter voice say deep within her: 'She's a rival!'

She dropped in a faint.

'Daughter, daughter!' cried her terrified mother. 'Get out, you gypsy from hell!'

Quick as a flash, La Esmeralda gathered up the ill-starred letters, signalled to Djali and went out through one door as Fleur-de-Lys was being carried out by the other.

Captain Phoebus was left on his own; he hesitated for a moment between the two doors, then he followed the gypsy.

TWO
The Difference between a Priest and a Philosopher

THE priest whom the girls had observed on top of the north tower, leaning over the square and so intent on the gypsy's dancing, was in fact the archdeacon, Claude Frollo.

Our readers will not have forgotten the mysterious cell he had reserved for himself in this tower. (It might, let me say in passing, be the same one whose interior can still be seen today, through a small, square window facing east at eye-level, on the platform from which the towers spring: a garret, now bare, empty and dilapidated, whose badly plastered walls are, at the time of writing, 'adorned' here and there with a few wretched yellowed engravings showing the fronts of cathedrals. This hole is, I imagine, inhabited concurrently by bats and spiders, so that a double war of extermination on flies is waged in it.)

Each day, one hour before sunset, the archdeacon used to climb the staircase to the tower and shut himself up in his cell, where he sometimes spent the whole night. On this particular day, just as he reached the low door to his den and was inserting into the lock the intricate small key he always carried on him in the wallet hanging at his side, the sound of a tambourine and of castanets reached him. It came from the square in front of the cathedral. The cell, as we have said, had only one window, overlooking the rear of the church. Claude Frollo hurriedly recovered his key and a moment later he was on top of the tower, in that attitude of sombre concentration in which the young ladies had noticed him.

He stood there, grave and unmoving, absorbed in a look and a thought. The whole of Paris lay at his feet, with the countless spires of its buildings and its circular horizon of gently undulating hills, with the river snaking beneath its bridges and the population rippling through the streets, with its clouds of smoke and the mountain-range of its roofs, pressing in on Notre-Dame like chain-mail. But in that whole town, the archdeacon had eyes for only one point: the Place du Parvis; in that whole crowd, for only one figure: the gypsy.

It would have been hard to say what kind of look it was, and whence the flame came that sprang from it. It was a fixed look, yet full of anxiety and turmoil. And so utterly motionless was his whole body, though stirred imperceptibly now and again by an involuntary tremor, like a tree in the wind, so rigid were his elbows, more marmoreal than the balustrade on which they were propped, so petrified was the smile that contracted his features, that it seemed as if the only part of Claude Frollo which was still alive was his eyes.

The gypsy was dancing. She spun her tambourine round the tip of one finger and tossed it into the air as she danced sarabands from Provence; nimble, light of foot, joyous, she felt nothing of the weight of that formidable stare falling perpendicularly down on her head.

The crowd milled about her; from time to time, a man attired in a red and yellow cassock formed them into a circle, then went back and sat on a chair a few feet away from the dancer, and took the goat's head on his knees. This man seemed to be the gypsy's companion. From his lofty vantage-point, Claude Frollo could not make out his features.

The moment the archdeacon noticed the stranger, he seemed to divide his attention between him and the dancer, and his face grew more and more grim. Suddenly he straightened up, his whole body trembled and: 'Who is that man?' he muttered to himself. 'I've always seen her on her own!'

He then plunged back underneath the tortuous vault of the spiral staircase and went down again. As he passed the half-open door of the bell-chamber, he saw something which gave him pause, he saw Quasimodo leaning at one of the vents in the slate louvres, which are like huge venetian blinds, also staring down into the square. So profoundly lost in contemplation was he that he paid no heed to his adoptive father as he went past. There was a strange expression in his wild eye. Its gaze was gentle and entranced. 'How odd!'

murmured Claude. 'Is it the gypsy he's staring at like that?' He continued on down. A few minutes later, the preoccupied archdeacon emerged into the square through the door at the foot of the tower.

'What's happened to the gypsy?' he said, as he mingled with the group of spectators attracted by the tambourine.

'I don't know,' replied one of his neighbours, 'she's just vanished. I think she's gone to dance some fandango in the house opposite, where they called to her.'

In place of the gypsy, on that same carpet whose arabesques had been obliterated a moment earlier beneath the capricious figures of her dance, the archdeacon could see only the man in red and yellow who, to earn a few *testons* in his turn, was walking round the circle, elbows on hips, head thrown back, face flushed and neck straining, with a chair between his teeth. On to the chair he had tied a cat lent him by a local woman, which was hissing out its terror.

'Mother of God!' exclaimed the archdeacon, just as the acrobat, sweating profusely, passed in front of him with his pyramid of chair and cat, 'what's Maître Pierre Gringoire doing here?'

The poor devil was so flustered by the archdeacon's stern tones that he lost his balance, together with his entire edifice, and chair and cat came down anyhow on to the heads of the onlookers, amidst inextinguishable boos.

Maître Pierre Gringoire (for it was indeed he) would most likely have had an awkward account to settle with the neighbour whose cat it was, and with all the scratched and bruised faces around him, had he not hastily taken advantage of the uproar to seek refuge in the church, whither Claude Frollo had signalled him to follow.

The cathedral was already in gloom and deserted. The side-aisles were full of darkness and the lamps in the chapels were beginning to twinkle like stars, so black had the vault become. Only the great rose-window in the façade, its thousand colours drenched in a horizontal ray of sunlight, shone in the shadows like a heap of diamonds, its dazzling spectre reflected at the far end of the nave.

After they had walked a few paces, Dom Claude leant against a pillar and fixed Gringoire with his eye. This was not the look Gringoire had feared, in his shame at having been surprised in his buffoon's costume by someone so grave and erudite. There was nothing mocking or ironic in the priest's glance; it was serious, calm and penetrating. The archdeacon was the first to break the silence.

'Come here, Maître Pierre. You must explain many things to me. And first of all, how comes it that you have not been seen for getting on for two months and that you now turn up at the crossroads, very handsomely fitted out, I must say, half-red and half-yellow like a Caudebec apple?'

'An amazing outfit, as you say, messire,' said Gringoire piteously, 'and I'm no more proud of it than a cat with a saucepan on its head. It's quite wrong, as I am aware, to expose messieurs the serjeants of the watch to taking their sticks to the humerus of a Pythagorean philosopher, underneath this cassock. But what could I do, reverend master? It was the fault of my old jerkin which cravenly deserted at the beginning of the winter, on the pretext that it was falling to bits and needed to go and rest in the rag-and-bone man's basket. What was to be done? Civilization hasn't yet reached the stage where we can go around stark naked, as old Diogenes wanted. Add to which a mighty cold wind was blowing, and January is no month to succeed in making humanity take this new step forward. This cassock turned up. I took it and left behind my old black smock which, for a hermeticist like myself, was far from hermetically sealed. So here I am dressed as a play-actor, like Saint Genet. What could I do? It was an eclipse. Apollo guarded Admetus's flocks after all.'

'A fine profession you follow!' the archdeacon rejoined.

'I agree it would be better to philosophize or poeticize, master, to fan the flames in the furnace or receive them from on high, rather than carry cats aloft in triumph. And so when you apostrophized me I felt as stupid as a donkey in front of a turnspit. But what could I do, messire? One has got to live, and when you're starving, a piece of Brie's worth more than even the finest alexandrines. I wrote that famous epithalamium for Madame Marguerite of Flanders, as you know, and the town hasn't paid me for it, on the grounds that it wasn't very good, as if one could provide a tragedy by Sophocles for four crowns. So I was about to die of hunger. Luckily, I found I was quite strong in the maxillary region and I said to my jaw: "Do balancing tricks and feats of strength, provide your own food. *Ale te ipsam.*" A gang of beggars, who have become my good friends, taught me twenty kinds of Herculean tricks, and now every evening I give my teeth the bread they've earned during the day by the sweat of my brow. *Concedo*, I concede that it's a poor employment of my intellectual powers, and that man wasn't made to spend his life tambourining and biting chairs. But it's not enough to spend your life, reverend master, you've got to earn it.'

Dom Claude had been listening in silence. Suddenly his deep-set eyes took on an expression so shrewd and penetrating that Gringoire felt them probe him to the very depths of his soul, as it were.

'Very good, Maître Pierre, but how comes it that you are now the companion of the dancer from Egypt?'

'Good gracious,' said Gringoire, 'the fact is she's my wife and I am her husband.'

The priest's sinister eye kindled.

'Can you have done that, you wretch?' he cried, angrily seizing Gringoire by the arm; 'can you have been so godforsaken as to lay hands on that girl?'

'I swear to you on my share of Paradise, my lord,' replied Gringoire, trembling in every limb, 'that I have never touched her. if that's what's worrying you.'

'Why do you talk about husband and wife, then?' said the priest.

Gringoire hastily told him, as succinctly as he could, all that the reader knows already, his adventure in the Court of Miracles and his wedding with the broken pitcher. It appeared, for the rest, that this wedding had not yet had any outcome and that each evening the gypsy whisked his wedding night away from him as she had on the first day. 'It's disappointing,' he said in conclusion, 'but that's the unfortunate result of marrying a virgin.'

'What do you mean?' asked the archdeacon, who had gradually calmed down during this narrative.

'It's rather difficult to explain,' answered the poet. 'It's a superstition. According to an old bandit who's known among us as the Duke of Egypt, my wife is a foundling, or lostling, which comes to the same thing. She wears an amulet round her neck which, we're assured, will one day lead her to her parents but which would lose its virtue if the young girl lost hers. From which it follows that we both of us remain very chaste.'

'So,' Dom Claude went on, the clouds lifting more and more

from his brow, 'you don't think, Maître Pierre, that any man has ever approached this creature?'

'What do you expect a man to do against a superstition, Dom Claude? She's taken it into her head. I reckon it a rare thing, to be sure, that she can stay as ferociously chaste as a nun among those easy-to-tame gypsy girls. But she's got three things to defend her: the Duke of Egypt, who's taken her under his wing, perhaps reckoning to sell her to some lord abbot; her whole tribe, which holds her in particular veneration, like a Virgin Mary; and a certain dainty little dagger, which the hoyden always carries somewhere about her, despite the provost's regulations, and which you can get her to bring out by squeezing her waist. She's a regular hornet!'

The archdeacon pressed Gringoire with questions.

La Esmeralda was, in Gringoire's judgement, an inoffensive and charming creature, and pretty, apart from a peculiar way she had of pouting; an innocent and passionate girl, ignorant of everything and enthusiastic about everything; unaware as yet of the difference between a man and a woman, even in her dreams; made that way; mad above all about dancing, noise and the open air; a sort of bee-woman, with invisible wings on her feet and living in a whirlwind. She owed her nature to the wandering life she had always led. Gringoire had managed to find out that as a young child she had travelled all over Spain and Catalonia, as far as Sicily; he even thought that the caravan of zingaris to which she belonged had taken her to the kingdom of Algiers, a country situated in Achaia, Achaia itself being bordered on one side by lesser Albania and Greece and on the other by the Sea of the Sicilies, which is the route to Constantinople. The Bohemians, said Gringoire, were vassals of the King of Algiers, in his capacity as chief of the race of white Moors. What was certain was that La Esmeralda had come to France when still very young, via Hungary. From all these countries, the young girl had brought back shreds of weird dialects, songs and alien notions, which had turned her language into something as motley as her half-Parisian, half-African costume. For the rest, the people in the quarters she frequented loved her for her gaiety, her kindness, her lively manner, her dancing and her singing. She thought there were only two people in the whole town who disliked her and of whom she often spoke fearfully: the sachette of the Tour-Roland, a horrible recluse who had some grievance or other against gypsies and cursed the poor dancer whenever she passed her window; and a priest who always had a frightening word or glance for her when they met. This last particular greatly perturbed the archdeacon, but Gringoire paid little heed to his agitation; two months had more than sufficed for the carefree poet to forget the strange circumstances of the evening of his first encounter with the gypsy and of the archdeacon's part in it. Otherwise, the little dancer had no fears; she did not tell fortunes, which meant she was safe from the accusations of witchcraft so frequently made against gypsy women. And then Gringoire acted as her brother if not as her husband. The philosopher had in fact borne with this sort of Platonic marriage very patiently. It meant a roof over his head and a crust to eat. He used to leave the truantry each morning, most often with the gypsy, and help her gather in her crop of *targes* and *petits-blancs* at the crossroads; each night he returned home with her under the one roof, let her bolt herself into her little retreat and slept the sleep of the just. A very easy existence, all things considered, he said, and most conducive to meditation. And in any case, in his soul and conscience, the philosopher was not at all sure he was madly in love with the gypsy. He was almost equally fond of the goat. It was a charming animal, gentle, intelligent and witty, a performing goat. Such performing animals were common enough in the Middle Ages, they were objects of great wonder and often led their mentors to the stake. The sorcery of the goat with the gilded hooves, however, was a quite innocent mischief. Gringoire explained this to the archdeacon, who showed a keen interest in the details. In most cases, the tambourine merely had to be held out to the goat in one way rather than another for it to perform the desired routine. It had been trained by the gypsy, who had so rare a gift for such delicate tasks that in two months she had taught the goat to write the word 'Phoebus' with moveable letters.

'Phoebus!' said the priest. 'Why Phoebus?'

'I don't know,' answered Gringoire. 'It may be a word she thinks is endowed with some magic and secret virtue. She often repeats it under her breath when she thinks she's alone.'

'Are you sure it's only a word and not a name?' Claude went on, with his penetrating stare.

'Whose name?' said the poet.

'How should I know?' said the priest.

'What I imagine is this, messire. These gypsies are a bit Zoroastrian and worship the sun. Hence Phoebus.'

'It doesn't seem as clear to me as it does to you, Maître Pierre.'

'I don't care, anyway. Let her go on mumbling about her Phoebus. What is sure is that Djali already likes me almost as much as her.'

'What's Djali?'

'That's the goat.'

The archdeacon leant his chin on his hand and seemed to ponder for a moment. All of a sudden he swung abruptly round towards Gringoire.

'And you swear to me you haven't touched her?'

'Who?' said Gringoire. 'The goat?'

'No, that woman.'

'My wife! I swear I haven't.'

'And you are often alone with her?'

'Every evening, for a good hour.'

Dom Claude frowned.

'Ha! *Solus cum sola non cogitabantur orare Pater noster*.'[1]

'By all that's holy, I could say the *Pater*, the *Ave Maria* and the *Credo in Deum patrem omnipotentem*,[2] and she'd pay no more attention to me than a hen to a church.'

'Swear to me on your mother's womb', the archdeacon repeated violently, 'that not even your fingertips have touched that creature.'

'I'd swear it on my father's head too, for the two things have more than a little in common. But, reverend master, allow me to ask one question in return.'

'Go ahead, monsieur.'

'What is all this to you?'

The archdeacon's pallid face went as red as a maiden's cheek. He remained for a moment without answering, then with evident embarrassment:

'Listen, Maître Pierre Gringoire. You are not yet damned, so far as I know. I am interested in you and I wish you well. But the slightest contact with that devil's gypsy will make you into Satan's

1. 'He alone with her, they will not be thought to be saying the Lord's Prayer.'

2. 'I believe in God the Father Almighty.'

vassal. You know that it is always the body which condemns the soul. Woe betide you if you approach that woman! That is all.'

'I tried to once,' said Gringoire scratching his ear. 'It was the first day, but I got stung.'

'You were shameless enough for that, Maître Pierre?' And the priest's brow darkened once more.

'Another time,' the poet continued, smiling, 'I looked through her keyhole before I went to bed, and I certainly saw the most delectable lady in a chemise who ever made the webbing of a bed creak under her bare foot.'

'Go to the devil!' cried the priest with a terrible look and, pushing the amazed Gringoire by the shoulders, he strode off beneath the gloomiest arcades of the cathedral.

THREE
The Bells

SINCE the morning at the pillory, the neighbourhood of Notre-Dame thought it had noticed that Quasimodo's ardour for his chimes had cooled. Previously, they had rung out at the least provocation, long aubades lasting from Primes to Complines, peals from the belfry for a high mass, rich scales produced on the hand-bells for a wedding or a baptism, and intermingling in the air in an embroidery of all sorts of captivating sounds. The old church everywhere shook and resounded, in a perpetual merriment of bells. One could sense the constant presence of a spirit of noise and caprice singing through all these bronze mouths. But now this spirit seemed to have vanished; the cathedral seemed mournful and wilfully silent. On festivals and at funerals there was simply the harsh, bare tolling required by the ritual, and nothing more. Of the twofold sounds made by a church, the organ within and the bells without, only the organ remained. It was as if there were no longer a musician in the bell-towers. Yet Quasimodo was still there. So what had taken place inside him? Was it that the shame and despair of the pillory were still lodged deep within him, that the lashes of the torturer's whip were reverberating endlessly in his soul, and that the sadness of such treatment had extinguished everything in him, even his passion for the bells? Or was it that Marie had a rival for the bell-ringer of Notre-Dame's affections, and that the big bell and her fourteen sisters were being neglected for someone more lovable and more beautiful?

It so happened that in that year of grace 1482, the Annunciation fell on a Tuesday, 25 March.[1] On that day, the air was so pure and so light that Quasimodo felt something of his love for the bells return. He therefore climbed up inside the north tower as down below the verger was throwing open wide the doors of the church, which at that time were vast panels of stout wood covered in leather, edged with gilded iron nails and framed by 'very artificially elaborated' sculptures.

Having arrived in the lofty cage of the bell-chamber, Quasimodo contemplated the six campaniles [*sic*] for a time with a sad shaking of the head, as if lamenting some alien presence in his heart which had come between him and them. But once he had set them in motion, once he felt this bunch of bells stir under his hand, once he saw, for he could not hear, the throbbing octave climb and descend the ladder of sound like a bird hopping from branch to branch, once the devil music, that demon who brandishes a glittering sheaf of stretti, trills and arpeggios, had taken possession of the poor deaf man, then he was happy once again, he forgot everything and his heart as it dilated caused his face to break into a smile.

He came and he went, he clapped his hands, he ran from one rope to the next, he incited his six singers by voice and by gesture, like a conductor spurring on intelligent virtuosi.

'Come on, come on, Gabrielle,' he said. 'Pour all your sound down into the square. It's a festival today. No laziness, Thibauld. You're slowing down. Come on, come on, have you gone rusty, you shirker? That's good! Quick, quick, I don't want to see your clapper. Make them all as deaf as me! That's right, Thibauld, bravo! Guillaume, Guillaume, you're the biggest and Pasquier is the smallest, and Pasquier's doing better! I'll wager that the people listening can hear him better than you. Good, good, Gabrielle, loudly, more loudly! Hey, what are you two Sparrows doing up there? I can't see you making any noise at all. What are those bronze beaks that look as if they're yawning when they should be singing? There, to work! It's the Annunciation. There's a beautiful sun shining. We want a beautiful carillon. Poor fat Guillaume, you're all out of breath!'

1. In fact, it is a fixed festival.

He was wholly absorbed in goading on his bells, all six of whom were leaping about as hard as they could go, shaking their gleaming rumps like a rowdy team of Spanish mules which now and again gets the rough edge of the muleteer's tongue.

All of a sudden, looking down between the broad, fish-scale slates which cover the perpendicular wall of the tower at a certain height, he saw a strangely attired girl stop in the square and unroll a carpet along the ground, on which a little goat came and stood as a knot of spectators gathered round in a circle. This sight abruptly changed his train of thought, congealing his musical fervour the way a puff of air congeals molten resin. He stopped, turned his back on the chimes, and squatted down behind the slate louvre, fixing the dancer with that gentle, tender and dreamy stare which had once before astonished the archdeacon. The forgotten bells, meanwhile, suddenly all died away at once, to the great disappointment of the lovers of church-bells, who had been listening trustingly to their peals from above the Pont-au-Change and now walked away in bewilderment, like a dog that has been shown a bone then given a stone.

FOUR
'ΑΝΆΓΚΗ

IT happened that one fine morning in this same month of March, I think it was Saturday the 29th, Saint Eustache's Day, our young friend the student, Jehan Frollo du Moulin, noticed as he was getting dressed that the breeches containing his purse did not give off any metallic clink. 'Poor purse!' he said, pulling it from its fob pocket. 'What, not even one little *denier parisis*! How cruelly the dice, the jugs of beer and Venus have disembowelled you! How empty, wrinkled and limp you are! You're like a harpy's breasts! I put it to you, Messer Cicero and Messer Seneca, dog-eared copies of whom I see strewn across the floor, what is the good of knowing as I do, better than a comptroller-general or a Jew from the Pont-au-Change, that one gold crown equals thirty-five *unzains* of twenty-five *sous* eight *deniers parisis* each, or that one gold crescent is worth thirty-six *unzains* of twenty-six *sous* and six *deniers tournois* each, if I haven't got a single miserable black *liard* to stake on the double six! That, Consul Cicero, is not a calamity from which one can extract oneself with periphrases, with *quemadmodums*[1] and *verum enim veros*!'[2]

He got dressed sadly. A thought occurred to him just as he was lacing up his ankle-boots, but at first he rejected it; it returned however, and he put on his waistcoat inside out, an obvious sign of some violent inner conflict. In the end he threw his bonnet roughly on the ground and exclaimed: 'Too bad! Let it turn out as it may. I shall go and see my brother. I'll get a sermon, but I'll also get a gold piece.'

He then hurriedly donned his cassock with the padded, fur-lined shoulders, picked up his bonnet and went out like a desperate man.

He went down the Rue de la Harpe towards the Cité. As he passed the Rue de la Huchette, the smell from the admirable spits constantly rotating there tickled his olfactory apparatus, and he bestowed a fond look on the cyclopean roaster which one day drew from the Franciscan friar Calatagirone this pathetic exclamation: *Veramente, queste rotisserie sona cosa stupende!*[3] But Jehan lacked the wherewithal to dine and giving a deep sigh plunged beneath the porch of the Petit-Châtelet, a huge double-cloverleaf of massive towers which guarded the entrance to the Cité.

He did not even take time as he passed to cast the customary stone at the wretched statue of Périnet Leclerc, who had delivered Charles VI's Paris up to the English, a crime which his effigy, its face flattened by stones and smeared with mud, expiated through three centuries at the corner of the Rue de la Harpe and the Rue de Bussy, as if in an everlasting pillory. After crossing the Petit-Pont and straddling the Rue Neuve-Sainte-Geneviève, Jehan de Molendino found himself in front of Notre-Dame. His indecision then seized him again, and he walked round the statue of M. Legris for a minute or two, repeating anxiously to himself: 'The sermon is certain, the gold piece doubtful!'

He stopped a verger who was coming from the cloister. 'Where is the Archdeacon of Josas?'

'I think he's in his cell in the tower,' said the verger, 'and I advise you not to disturb him there, unless you've come on behalf of someone like the pope or the king.'

1. 'In the same way as.'
2. 'But in actual fact.'
3. 'Truly, these roasters are a marvellous thing!'

Jehan struck his palm. 'Dammit, this is a splendid opportunity to see the famous den of sorcery!'

This thought having decided him, he entered resolutely beneath the small black doorway and began to ascend Saint-Gilles's spiral, which leads to the upper storeys of the tower. 'Now I shall see!' he told himself as he did so. 'By the corbels of the Holy Virgin, this cell that my reverend brother hides like his pudendum must be a curious affair! They say he lights his infernal kitchen-fire up there and cooks the philosopher's stone over a hot flame. *Bédieu*, the philosopher's stone's no more to me than a pebble. I'd rather find a bacon omelette made with Easter eggs on his stove than the biggest philosopher's stone in the world!'

When he reached the gallery of colonnettes, he drew breath for a moment, invoked I don't know how many million wagonloads of devils against the interminable stairs, then resumed his ascent by the narrow door in the north tower which is today forbidden to the public. A moment or two after passing the cage of bells, he encountered a small landing recessed into the side-wall and a low, pointed door under the vaulting, whose huge lock and powerful iron bracing he could make out in the light from a loophole opening in the curved wall of the staircase opposite. Those curious enough to visit that door today will recognize it by this inscription, carved in white letters on the black wall: I ADORE CORALIE. 1823. SIGNED UGÈNE. The word 'signed' being part of the text.

'Phew!' said the student; 'this must be it.'

The key was in the lock. The door was right beside him. He pushed it gently, and stuck his head through the opening.

The reader must surely have perused the admirable works of Rembrandt, that Shakespeare of painting. Among so many marvellous engravings, there is one etching in particular, depicting, or so one assumes, Doctor Faustus, which is wonderful to behold. It shows a cell in darkness. In the centre a table laden with hideous objects: skulls, globes, alembics, compasses, hieroglyphic parchments. The doctor is at the table, dressed in his huge greatcoat and with his fur-trimmed bonnet pulled down over his eyebrows. Only the top half of him is visible. He has half risen from his enormous armchair, his clenched fists are resting on the table, and he looks both curious and terrified as he contemplates a great circle of light, formed from magic letters, shining on the far wall like the solar spectrum in a camera obscura. This cabbalistic sun seems to tremble as you look at it and fills the pale cell with its mysterious radiance. It is both horrible and beautiful.

Something rather similar to Faustus's cell presented itself to Jehan's gaze once he had risked his head inside the half-open door. It was, like the other, a gloomy retreat, very dimly lit. Here too there was a big armchair and a big table, compasses, alembics, the skeletons of animals hanging from the ceiling, a globe rolling across the stone floor, horses' heads in disorder and glass jars with gold leaves trembling inside them, skulls standing on parchments scrawled over with figures and characters, fat manuscripts lying open in piles with no thought for the brittle corners of the parchment: all the debris of science in fact, and everywhere, on top of the clutter, dust and spiders' webs; but there was no circle of luminous letters, and no doctor ecstatically contemplating the flaming vision like an eagle gazing at the sun.

Yet the cell was not empty. A man sat in the armchair, bent over the table. He had his back to Jehan, who could see only his shoulders and the back of his skull; but he had no trouble in recognizing that bald head, to which nature had given a perpetual tonsure, as if wanting to mark the archdeacon's irresistible clerical vocation with some external symbol.

Jehan recognized his brother, then. But the door had opened so quietly that Dom Claude had had no warning of his presence. The inquisitive student took advantage of this to examine the cell for a moment or two at his leisure. To the left of the armchair, below the window, was a large furnace, which he had not noticed straight away. The shaft of daylight entered the room through a circular spider's web, whose delicate rose had been tastefully inscribed in the pointed arch of the window, and at its centre, motionless, sat the insect architect, like the hub of a lacework wheel. On the furnace were heaped, anyhow, vessels of every kind, earthenware phials, glass retorts and matrasses of charcoal. Jehan noticed with a sigh that there was no saucepan. 'The kitchen utensils are like new!' he thought.

For the rest, there was no fire in the furnace, and it looked in fact as if it had not been lit for a long time past. A glass mask, which Jehan noticed among the alchemist's utensils, and which no doubt served to protect the archdeacon's face as he manufactured some fearsome substance, lay in a corner, covered in dust, seemingly forgotten. Next to it, no less dust-covered, lay a bellows, whose upper leaf bore this legend, incrusted in brass letters: SPIRA, SPERA.[1]

Other mottoes had been inscribed in great profusion on the walls, as was the fashion with hermeticists: some written in ink, others carved with a metal point. For the rest, Gothic characters, Hebrew characters, Greek characters and Roman characters all higgledy-piggledy, the inscriptions overflowing haphazardly one on top of the other, the most recent obliterating the earlier ones, and all intertwined with each other like the branches of a thicket or the pikes of skirmishing soldiers. It was, in fact, a somewhat confused skirmish between all the philosophies, the daydreams and lore of mankind. Here and there, one shone out above the rest like a flag among lance-heads. Generally, this was some short device in Latin or Greek, such as the Middle Ages were so adept at formulating: *Unde? Inde?*[2] *Homo homini monstrum*;[3] *Astra, castra, nomen, numen*;[4] Μεγα βιβλιον, μεγα κακόν;[5] *Sapere aude*;[6] *Flat ubi vult*;[7] etc.; sometimes a word apparently devoid of meaning: 'Αναγκοφαγία,[8] perhaps concealing some bitter reference to the regime of the cloister; or a simple maxim of clerical discipline formulated in a regulation hexameter: *Coelestum dominum, terrestrem dicito domnum.*[9] There were also, *passim*, Hebrew incantations of which Jehan, who knew little enough Greek, understood nothing, while the whole was traversed, at every opportunity, by stars, figures of men and animals, and intersecting triangles, which helped not a little to make the defaced wall of the cell resemble a sheet of paper over which a monkey had drawn an ink-laden pen.

The whole cell presented an appearance of general neglect and decay, for that matter, while the poor condition of the utensils gave one to suppose that for some time past its master had been distracted from his work by other concerns.

This master, meanwhile, was poring over an enormous manu-

1. 'Blow, hope.'
2. 'From whence? From thence?'
3. 'Man is a monster for men.'
4. 'Stars, camp, name, divinity.'
5. 'A great book, a great evil.'
6. 'Dare to learn.'
7. 'Blows where it listeth.'
8. 'Strict discipline.'
9. 'Call [God] the *dominum* of Heaven, the *domnum* of earth.'

script adorned with weird paintings, seemingly tormented by a thought that intruded constantly on his meditations. Or so at least Jehan concluded as he heard him exclaim, with those intervals for thought of the seer dreaming out loud:

'... Yes, Manou says so, and Zoroaster taught so, the sun is born from fire, the moon from the sun. Fire is the soul of the great whole. Its elementary atoms pour forth and stream incessantly over the world in infinite currents. At the points where these currents intersect in the sky, they produce light; at their points of intersection on earth, they produce gold ... Light, gold, the same thing. Fire in its concrete state ... The difference between the visible and the palpable, the fluid and the solid, for the same substance, between water vapour and ice, that's all ... These aren't dreams ... it's the universal law of nature ... but how to draw off the secret of that universal law into science? What, this light flooding my hand is gold! The same atoms dilated in accordance with a certain law, all you have to do is condense them in accordance with a certain other law! How? ... Some have had the idea of burying a ray of sunlight ... Averroës ... yes, it was Averroës ... Averroës buried one underneath the first pillar on the left of the sanctuary of the Koran in the great Mahounery of Córdoba; but it will be eight thousand years before they can open up the cavity to see whether the operation has been a success.'

'Dammit!' said Jehan aside, 'that's a long time to wait for a gold piece!'

'... others have thought', the archdeacon went on dreamily, 'that it would be better to work with a ray from Sirius. But it is far from easy to get a pure one, because of the simultaneous presence of the other stars which interfere with it. Flamel considers that it is simpler to work with terrestrial fire ... Flamel, the name of a man predestined, *Flamma*! ... Yes, fire. That's all ... The diamond is in the charcoal, gold is in the fire ... But how to extract it? ... Magistri asserts that there are certain women's names whose charm is so sweet and mysterious that you need only utter them during the operation ... Let's read what Manou says about them: "Where women are honoured, the divinities are greatly pleased; where they are scorned, it is useless to pray to God ... A woman's mouth is constantly pure; it is running water, it is a ray of sunlight ... A woman's name must be pleasing, soft, imaginary; end on long vowels and resemble words of benediction." ... Yes, the sage is right; indeed, Maria, Sophia, Esmeral ... Curse it, that same thought all the time!'

And he snapped the book shut.

He passed his hand over his brow, as if to chase away the idea that obsessed him. Then, he picked up from the table a nail and a small hammer whose handle was curiously painted with cabbalistic characters.

'For some time now,' he said with a bitter smile, 'I've failed in all my experiments! I am in the grip of an obsession which has made my brain shrivel like clover in a fire. I haven't even managed to rediscover the secret of Cassiodorus, whose lamp burned without wick or oil. A simple enough matter, too!'

'The plague!' said Jehan under his breath.

'... So all it takes to make a man feeble and crazy is one miserable thought!' the priest went on. 'Oh, how Claude Pernelle would laugh at me, who could not distract Nicolas Flamel from his pursuit of the Great Work for a moment! What, in my hand I am holding the magic hammer of Ezechiel! Every time the redoubtable rabbi brought this hammer down on this nail, in the depths of his cell, that particular enemy whom he had condemned, even if he was two thousand leagues away, sank another cubit deeper into the earth that was devouring him. The King of France himself one evening knocked out of turn on the thaumaturge's door and sank up to his knees into the paving-stones of Paris ... That happened not three centuries since ... Well, I have the hammer and the nail, but in my hands these tools are no more formidable than a mallet in the hands of a smith ... Yet all it needs is to rediscover the magic word that Ezechiel uttered, as he hit his nail.'

'Balderdash!' thought Jehan.

'Come on, let's try,' the archdeacon went on quickly. 'If I succeed, I shall see the blue spark spurt from the head of the nail. *Emen-hétan*, *emen-hétan!* That's not it. *Sigéani*, *Sigéani!* May this nail open up the grave for whoever bears the name of Phoebus! ... Curse it! Still the same everlasting idea!'

And he threw the hammer angrily down. Then he slumped down on to the chair and table until he was lost to view behind the enormous chair-back. For a few minutes, Jehan could see only his fist clenched convulsively on a book. Suddenly Dom Claude stood up, took a compass and silently carved the Greek word 'ΑΝΆΓΚΗ on the wall in capital letters.

'My brother's mad,' said Jehan to himself, 'it would have been simpler to write *Fatum*. Not everyone is obliged to know Greek.'

The archdeacon went and sat down again on his chair, and leant his head on his hands, like a sick man whose forehead feels heavy and burning.

The student observed his brother in surprise. He, who wore his heart on his sleeve, who observed none of the world's laws except the good law of nature, who allowed his passions to escape through his inclinations, and in whom the reservoir of strong emotion was always dry, so many fresh drains did he dig for it each morning, he had no idea of how the sea of human passions rages and ferments and boils once it is refused all outlet, of how it accumulates and increases and flows over, of how it scours the heart and breaks out into inward sobs and dumb convulsions, until it has torn down its dykes and burst its bed. Jehan had always been deceived by Claude Frollo's austere and icy exterior, that chill surface of precipitous and inaccessible virtue. That this seething, raging lava bubbled deep beneath the snowclad brow of Etna had never occurred to the cheerful student.

We do not know whether he suddenly became conscious of such thoughts but, empty-headed though he was, he realized he had witnessed something he should not have witnessed, that he had just surprised his elder brother's soul in one of its most secret attitudes and that Claude must not know. Noticing that the archdeacon had relapsed into his earlier immobility, he withdrew his head very quietly and shuffled his feet outside the door, like someone just arrived and giving notice of his arrival.

'Come in!' cried the archdeacon from inside the cell. 'I was expecting you. I left the key in the door on purpose. Come in, Maître Jacques.'

The student entered boldly. The archdeacon, much put out by such a visit in such a place, trembled on his chair. 'What, it's you, Jehan?'

'It's still a J,' said the student with his cheerful, ruddy, insolent face.

Dom Claude's own face had resumed its stern expression.

'What have you come here for?'

'Brother,' replied the student, struggling to achieve a decent, pitiable and modest expression, and spinning his bycoket round in his hands with a look of innocence, 'I came to ask you for...'

'What?'

'A little moral philosophy, of which I have great need.' Jehan did not dare add out loud: 'And a little money, of which I have even greater need.' This last member of his sentence remained unpublished.

'Monsieur,' said the archdeacon coldly, 'I am not at all pleased with you.'

'Oh dear!' sighed the student.

Dom Claude pivoted his chair through a quarter of a circle and eyed Jehan intently. 'You come at a good moment.'

The exordium was forbidding. Jehan steeled himself for a rude impact.

'Jehan, every day they bring me complaints against you. What's this fight you had when you laid about a young Viscount Albert de Ramonchamp with a stick?...'

'Oh, nothing much!' said Jehan. 'A worthless page-boy who was having fun driving his horse through puddles and spattering the students.'

'And who's this Mahiet Fargel, whose robe you tore?' the archdeacon resumed. '*Tunicam dechiraverunt* says the complaint.'

'That? Oh, some Montagu's miserable cappette, that's all!'

'The complaint says *tunicam* not *cappettam*. Do you know Latin?'

Jehan made no reply.

'Yes, that's what education and letters are coming to,' continued the priest, with a shake of the head. 'Latin is barely understood, Syriac unknown, Greek so detested that it's not adjudged ignorant even for the most learned to skip a Greek word without reading it, and people say: *Graecum est, non legitur*.'[1]

The student looked resolutely up. 'Brother, would you like me to explain in simple French that Greek word written on the wall there?'

'Which word?'

''ANÁΓKH.'

A faint blush spread over the archdeacon's yellow cheekbones,

1. 'It is Greek, it will not be read.'

like the puff of smoke which is the outward sign of the secret commotions of a volcano. The student hardly noticed it.

'Well, Jehan,' stammered the elder brother with an effort, 'what does that word mean?'

'Fatality.'

Dom Claude went pale again, and the student continued heedlessly:

'And that word underneath it, carved by the same hand, 'Aναγνεία, means "uncleanliness". You can see we know our Greek.'

The archdeacon remained silent. This Greek lesson had set him musing. Young Jehan, who had all the finesse of a spoilt child, judged the moment right to risk putting his request. So he adopted a very meek tone and began:

'Kind brother, do you dislike me so much that you are going to get worked up when I deal out a few trivial slaps and punches in fair combat to unknown boys and street urchins, *quibusdam mormosetis*? You can see we know our Latin, good brother Claude.'

But all this wheedling hypocrisy failed of its usual effect on the stern elder brother. Cerberus would not take the honey-cake. The archdeacon's brow was as creased as ever.

'What are you trying to say?' he said drily.

'Well, I'll out with it,' replied Jehan gallantly. 'I need money.'

At this shameless declaration, the archdeacon's countenance assumed an altogether pedagogic and paternal expression.

'You know, monsieur Jehan, that our fief of Tirechappe only brings in, if you add together the quit-rent and the income from the twenty-one houses, thirty-nine *livres* eleven *sous* six *deniers parisis*. That's half as much again as in the days of the Paclet brothers, but it's not much.'

'I need money,' said Jehan stoically.

'You know that the Official has decided that our twenty-one houses were fully infeudated to the fief of the bishopric, and that we can only redeem this homage by paying the reverend bishop two marks of silver gilt worth six *livres parisis*. But I haven't yet managed to get the two marks together. You know that.'

'I know I need money,' repeated Jehan for the third time.

'And what do you mean to do with it?'

This question brought a gleam of hope to Jehan's eyes. He resumed his sly, saccharine expression.

'Look, dear brother Claude, I would not come to you if my intentions were bad. Your *unzains* are not for playing the dandy in the taverns or parading the streets of Paris dolled up in gold brocade with my lackey, *cum meo laquasio*. No, brother, it's for a good cause.'

'What good cause?' asked Claude, somewhat surprised.

'Two of my friends want to buy baby-clothes for the child of a poor *haudriette* widow. It's charity. It will cost three florins, and I'd like to contribute mine.'

'What are your two friends' names?'

'Pierre the slaughterman and Baptiste Croque-Oison.'

'Hm!' said the archdeacon, 'two names about as suitable for good works as a bombard on a high altar.'

Jehan's choice of names for his two friends was certainly a bad one. As he appreciated now that it was too late.

'And then,' Claude went on shrewdly, 'what sort of baby-clothes are they which cost three florins? And for the child of a *haudriette*? Since when have *haudriette* widows had brats still in swaddling-clothes?'

Jehan broke the ice once again. 'Well, all right! I need money to go and meet Isabeau la Thierrye this evening at the Val d'Amour!'

'Unclean wretch!' exclaimed the priest.

''Αναγνεία,' said Jehan.

This quotation, which the student had borrowed, maliciously perhaps, from the wall of the cell, had a strange effect on the priest. He bit his lip, and his anger abated in a blush.

'You must go,' he then said to Jehan. 'I'm expecting someone.'

The student tried once more. 'Brother Claude, at least give me one small *parisis*, for food.'

'Where have you got to in Gratian's decretals?' asked Dom Claude.

'I've lost my school-books.'

'Where have you got to with the Latin humanities?'

'My copy of Horace was stolen from me.'

'Where have you got to in Aristotle?'

'Good Lord, brother! Which church father is it who says that the undergrowth of Aristotle's metaphysics has ever been a covert for the errors of heretics? A fig for Aristotle! I shall not tear my religion on his metaphysics.'

'Young man,' the archdeacon resumed, 'at the king's last entry there was a gentleman called Philippe de Commynes, who wore his motto embroidered on his horse's saddle-cloth, and I recommend you to reflect on it: *Qui non laborat non manducet.*[1]

The student remained in silence for a moment, his finger to his ear, his eye fixed on the ground, his expression angry. He suddenly turned to Claude as quick and agile as a wagtail.

'So, kind brother, you refuse me one *sol parisis* to go and buy a crust from the baker?'

'*Qui non laborat non manducet.*'

At this reply from the immovable archdeacon, Jehan hid his face in his hands, like a woman sobbing, and exclaimed with an expression of despair: Οτοτοτοτοτοτοτ!

'What does that mean, monsieur?' asked Claude, surprised by this outburst.

'What? Well,' said the student, raising two insolent eyes to Claude into which he had just stuck his fists so as to make them look red from weeping, 'it's Greek! It's an anapaest from Aeschylus which perfectly expresses grief.'

At which he let out such a violent and comic shout of laughter that it brought a smile from the archdeacon. It was Claude's fault in fact; why had he spoiled the boy so?

'Oh, kind brother Claude,' Jehan went on, emboldened by this smile, 'look at the holes in my boots. Could there be a more tragic buskin anywhere than a boot whose sole is sticking its tongue out?'

The archdeacon had promptly reverted to his earlier severity. 'I will send you some new boots. But no money.'

'Just one little *parisis*, brother,' persevered the supplicant Jehan. 'I will learn Gratian by heart, I will really believe in God, I shall be a veritable Pythagoras of learning and virtue! But one little *parisis*, for pity's sake! Do you want famine to bite me with its jaws, which gape before me, blacker, deeper and more evil-smelling than a Tartarus or a monk's nose?'

Dom Claude shook his wrinkled head. '*Qui non laborat . . .*'

Jehan would not let him finish.

'All right,' he cried, 'to the devil! Long live pleasure! I shall go

1. 'He who does not work, let him not eat.'

taverning, I shall fight, I shall break pots and I shall visit the girls!'

Whereupon, he threw his bonnet at the wall and clicked his fingers like castanets.

The archdeacon eyed him gloomily.

'Jehan, you have no soul.'

'In that case, according to Epicurius, I lack an I don't know what made from something without a name.'

'Jehan, you must think seriously of mending your ways.'

'Bah!' cried the student, looking alternately at his brother and at the alembics on the stove, 'so everything's got horns on here, the ideas as well as the bottles!'

'Jehan, you are on a very slippery slope. Do you know where you are headed?'

'To the inn,' said Jehan.

'The inn leads to the pillory.'

'It's as good a lantern as any, and one Diogenes might have found his man with.'

'The pillory leads to the gallows.'

'The gallows is a pair of scales with a man on one end and the whole earth on the other. It's good to be that man.'

'The gallows leads to hell.'

'Which is a big fire.'

'Jehan, Jehan, you will end badly.'

'But I shall have begun well.'

Just then, the sound of footsteps came from the stairs.

'Silence!' said the archdeacon, putting a finger to his lips, 'here's Maître Jacques. Listen, Jehan,' he added in a whisper, 'be sure never to speak about what you've seen and heard here. Quickly, hide under the stove and don't breathe.'

The student took cover underneath the stove, where a likely thought occurred to him.

'Incidentally, brother Claude, a florin to keep me from breathing.'

'Silence! I promise.'

'You must give it to me.'

'Take it then!' said the archdeacon, angrily tossing him his purse. Jehan dived back under the stove and the door opened.

FIVE
The Two Men in Black

THE figure that now entered wore a black robe and a gloomy expression. What at once struck our friend Jehan (who, as can easily be imagined, had so arranged himself in his hiding-place as to be able to see and hear at his convenience) was the unrelieved sadness of the newcomer's clothes and features. There was mildness, too, in his face, but the mildness of a cat or a judge, a false mildness. He was approaching sixty, very grey, lined, with narrowed eyes, white eyebrows, a pendulous lip and large hands. Once Jehan had seen that this was all it was, a doctor no doubt, or a magistrate, he backed down into his hole, in despair at having to spend an indeterminate length of time in such an uncomfortable posture and such poor company.

The archdeacon meanwhile had not even stood up for the other man. He gestured to him to sit down on a stool near the door and after a moment or two's silence, seemingly in continuation of an earlier meditation, he said to him somewhat patronizingly: 'Good day, Maître Jacques.'

'Greetings, maître!' replied the man in black.

The difference between that 'Maître Jacques' on the one hand and the heartfelt 'maître' on the other, was the difference between 'my lord' and 'monsieur', between *domine* and *domne*. It was clearly a meeting between teacher and disciple.

'Well, have you succeeded?' went on the archdeacon, after a fresh silence, which Maître Jacques took good care not to disturb.

'Alas, *mon maître*,' said the other, with a sad smile, 'I'm still at my furnace. All the ash I need. But not a spark of gold.'

Dom Claude gestured impatiently. 'That's not what I meant, Maître Jacques Charmolue, but the case of your magician. Marc Cenaine, didn't you say his name was, the steward from the audit-house? Has he confessed his magic? Was the question successful?'

'Alas, no,' answered Maître Jacques, still with his sad smile. 'We have not had that consolation. The man is a stone. We shall boil him at the Marché-aux-Pourceaux before he says anything. But we shall spare nothing to get at the truth. His body's already broken.

We've tried everything under the sun, as that old comedian Plautus says:

> *Advorsum stimulos, laminas, crucesque, compedesque,*
> *Nervos, catenas, carceres, numellas, pedicas, boias.*[1]

To no avail. A terrible fellow. I'm at my wits' end.'

'You haven't found anything new in his house?'

'Yes indeed,' said Maître Jacques, fumbling in his pouch, 'this parchment. There are words on it we can't understand. But the criminal advocate Philippe Lheulier knows a bit of Hebrew which he learnt during the case of the Jews of the Rue Kantersten in Brussels.'

So saying, Maître Jacques unrolled a parchment.

'Give it here,' said the archdeacon. Then, running his eye over the document: 'Pure magic, Maître Jacques! *Emen-hétan* is the cry of the vampires when they arrive at the sabbath. *Per ipsum, et cum ipso, et in ipso*[2] is the command which chains the devil up in hell again. *Hax, pax, max*, that's medicine. A formula against the bite of rabid dogs. Maître Jacques, you're Crown Prosecutor in the Ecclesiastical Court, this parchment is an abomination.'

'We will put the man to the question again. And we found this in Marc Cenaine's house too,' added Maître Jacques, fumbling once again in his satchel.

It was a vessel of the same family as those that littered Dom Claude's furnace. 'Ah!' said the archdeacon, 'an alchemist's crucible.'

'I must confess', resumed Maître Jacques, with his awkward, diffident smile, 'that I tried it out on the furnace, but I was no more successful than with my own.'

The archdeacon began to examine the vessel. 'What's he engraved on his crucible? *Och, och*! the word that drives fleas away! This Marc Cenaine is an ignoramus! I can well believe you won't make gold with this. All it's good for is putting beside your bed in the summer!'

'Talking of errors,' said the crown prosecutor, 'I was examining the portal downstairs before I came up; is your reverence quite sure

1. 'Against goads, red-hot irons, crosses and double rings, Fetters, chains, prisons, gyves, shackles, iron collars.'
2. 'Through him, and with him and in him.'

that the beginning of the book of physics is represented on the Hôtel-Dieu side, and that of the seven naked figures at the feet of Our Lady the one with wings at its heels is Mercurius?'

'Yes,' replied the priest. 'Augustin Nypho wrote that, the Italian doctor who had a bearded demon who taught him everything. Let's go down, anyway, and I will explain it to you from the text.'

'Thank you, maître,' said Charmolue, bowing to the ground. 'By the way, I was forgetting! When would you like me to apprehend the little magician?'

'Which magician?'

'That gypsy girl, as you know very well, who comes and dances every day on the parvis despite the Official's prohibition! She has a goat which is possessed and has horns from the devil, which can read and write and knows as much mathematics as Picatrix, and would be enough to hang the whole of Bohemia. The case is all prepared. It won't take long, come on! A pretty creature, I do declare, that dancer. The most beautiful black eyes! Two carbuncles from Egypt! When do we start?'

The archdeacon was exceedingly pale.

'I shall tell you when,' he stammered in a barely articulate voice. Then he went on with an effort: 'You concern yourself with Marc Cenaine.'

'Don't worry,' said Charmolue with a smile. 'I'll have him strapped to the leather bed again when I get back. But he's a devil of a fellow. He's worn out Pierre Torterue himself, who's got bigger hands than I have. As good old Plautus says:

Nudus vinctus, centum pondo, es quando pendes per pedes.[1]

The question with the hoist, it's the best we've got. He shall endure that.'

Dom Claude seemed plunged in gloomy distraction. He turned to Charmolue.

'Maître Pierrat . . . Maître Jacques I mean, you concern yourself with Marc Cenaine!'

'Yes, yes, Dom Claude. Poor man, he must have suffered like Mummol. What an idea, too, going to the witches' sabbath. A steward from the audit-house, who ought to have known Charle-

1. 'Naked, strangled, one hundredweight you weigh, hanging by the feet.'

magne's text, *Stryga vel masca.*[1] As for the girl... Smelarda as they call her... I shall await your orders... Ah, as we go underneath the portal, you must explain to me too what that painted gardener means whom you see as you enter the church. The Sower, isn't it? Hey there, maître, are you still with me?'

Dom Claude, engrossed in his own thoughts, was no longer listening. Charmolue followed the direction of his gaze and saw that it had settled mechanically on the big spider's web curtaining the window. At that moment, an unthinking fly in quest of the March sunlight threw itself against this net and became enmeshed. As its web quivered, the enormous spider made a sudden dart from its central cell, then leapt on the fly, which it bent in two with its front antennae, as its hideous proboscis excavated the head. 'Poor fly!' said the crown prosecutor and raised his hand to rescue it. The archdeacon, as if starting awake, stayed his arm with convulsive force.

'Maître Jacques,' he cried, 'let fatality take its course!'

The prosecutor turned round in alarm. His arm seemed to have been seized in an iron pincer. The priest's haggard, blazing eye was riveted on the ghastly small tableau of the fly and the spider.

'Ah, yes!' the priest went on, in a voice that seemed to come from his very entrails, 'it symbolizes everything. She flies, she is happy, she has just been born; she seeks the springtime, the open air, liberty; oh, yes! But then she comes up against the fatal rosace, the spider emerges, the hideous spider! Poor dancer, poor predestined fly! Let them be, Maître Jacques, it's fate! Alas, Claude, you are the spider. Claude, you are the fly too! You flew towards knowledge, towards the light, towards the sun, your one concern was to reach the open air, the broad daylight of eternal truth; but as you sped towards the dazzling window that opens on to the other world, the world of clarity, intelligence and knowledge, your learning did not save you, you did not see, blind fly, the ingenious web fate had spun between you and that light, you hurled yourself against it with all your might and now, poor fool, you are writhing between the iron antennae of fatality, your head smashed and your wings dismembered. Maître Jacques, Maître Jacques, let the spider be!'

'I shan't touch it, I assure you,' said Charmolue, staring at him

1. 'A vampire or a mask.'

uncomprehendingly. 'But for pity's sake let go of my arm, maître, you've a grip like a vice.'

The archdeacon did not hear him. 'Madman!' he went on, not taking his eyes from the window. 'You fancy you would have reached that light if only you had been able to break that terrible web with your gnat's wings. But how would you have got past that further pane of glass, that transparent obstacle, that wall of crystal, harder than bronze, which divides all philosophies from the truth? Oh, the vanity of science! So many wise men have come winging from afar and have dashed their heads against it! So many systems have banged and buzzed in vain against that everlasting window!'

He stopped. These last thoughts had led him imperceptibly back from science to himself, and seemed to have calmed him. Jacques Charmolue brought him back to a full awareness of reality by asking him this question: 'Now then, maître, when are you going to come and help me make gold? It's time I succeeded.'

The archdeacon shook his head with a bitter smile. 'Read Michael Psellus, *Dialogus de energia et operatione daemonum*,[1] Maître Jacques. What we are doing is not altogether innocent.'

'Not so loud, maître! I suspect not,' said Charmolue. 'But one is bound to dabble in hermetics when one is only a crown prosecutor in the ecclesiastical court, at thirty *écus tournois* a year. Only let's keep our voices down.'

At that very moment, a sound of masticating jaws caught Charmolue's apprehensive ear, coming from underneath the furnace.

'What's that?' he asked.

It was the student, very bored and very uncomfortable in his hiding-place, who had managed to find an old crust of bread and a triangle of mildewed cheese and had begun unceremoniously to eat them, by way of consolation and of dinner. Because he was ravenously hungry he was making a lot of noise and emphasizing each mouthful loudly, and this had both alerted and alarmed the prosecutor.

'It's a cat I've got,' said the archdeacon hastily, 'feasting off some mouse or other under there.'

This explanation satisfied Charmolue.

'Indeed, maître,' he said, with a respectful smile, 'all the great

1. 'Dialogue of the energy and workings of devils.'

philosophers have had their familiar. You know what Servius says: *Nullus enim locus sine genio est.*[1]

Dom Claude meanwhile, fearing some fresh devilry from Jehan, reminded his worthy disciple that they had some figures on the portal to examine and together they left the cell, to a loud 'phew!' from the student, who had begun seriously to fear that his knee might take on the imprint of his chin.

SIX

The Possible Effect of Seven Oaths in the Open Air

'*Te Deum laudamus!*' exclaimed Maître Jehan as he emerged from his hole, 'the two owls have flown. Och och! Hax, pax, max! Fleas and mad dogs! The devil, I've had enough of their conversation! My head's ringing like a belfry. And mouldy cheese to boot! Come on, let's go downstairs, let's take big brother's wallet, and convert all those coins into bottles!'

He cast a fond and admiring glance inside the precious wallet, straightened his clothes, brushed his boots, dusted his poor padded sleeves, which were grey with ash, whistled a tune, cut a caper, looked to see whether there was anything else he could take from the cell, pocketed one or two glass amulets from off the furnace, which would do as jewelry for Isabeau la Thierrye, and finally opened the door which his brother, as a last indulgence, had left unfastened, and which he left unfastened as a last piece of mischief, then hopped down the circular staircase like a bird.

In the darkness of the stairs, his elbow met something which drew back muttering; he assumed it was Quasimodo and found this so comic that he held his sides with laughing as he descended the remaining stairs. He was still laughing when he came out into the square.

When he found himself back on the ground he stamped his foot. 'Oh, kind and honourable paving of Paris!' he said. 'That confounded staircase would put the angels on Jacob's ladder out of breath! What was I thinking of sticking my nose into that stone gimlet that bores through the sky, just so I could have some cheese that had whiskers on and see the bell-towers of Paris through a skylight!'

1. 'There is no place but has its spirit.'

He took a few steps, then noticed the two owls, Dom Claude and Maître Jacques Charmolue that is, meditating on a sculpture in the portal. He tiptoed up to them and heard the archdeacon say to Charmolue in an undertone: 'It was William of Paris who had a Job carved on that lapis lazuli stone with the gilded edges. Job appears on the philosopher's stone, which has to be tested as well as martyrized in order to become perfect, as Ramon Llull says: *Sub conservatione formae specificae salva anima*.'[1]

'Who cares,' said Jehan, 'I've got the purse.'

At that moment he heard a loud, ringing voice behind him utter a formidable string of oaths: 'God's blood! God's belly! By God! God's body! Beelzebub's navel! Name of a pope! Horn and thunder!'

'Upon my soul,' exclaimed Jehan, 'that can only be my friend Captain Phoebus!'

The name Phoebus came to the archdeacon's ear just as he was explaining to the crown prosecutor the dragon hiding its tail in a bath which has smoke and a king's head coming from it. Dom Claude gave a shudder, stopped short, to Charmolue's astonishment, and turned round, to see his brother Jehan greeting a tall officer by the door of the Gondelaurier house.

It was indeed Captain Phoebus de Châteaupers. He was leaning against the corner of his fiancée's house, swearing like a heathen.

'My word, Captain Phoebus,' said Jehan, taking him by the hand, 'you blaspheme with admirable enthusiasm.'

'Horn and thunder!' answered the captain.

'Horn and thunder yourself!' retorted the student. 'Whence this effusion of handsome words, gentle captain?'

'Forgive me, comrade Jehan,' exclaimed Phoebus, shaking his hand, 'a charging horse does not stop dead and I was swearing at full gallop. I've just come out from those prudes, and whenever I leave my throat's always full of swear-words; I have to spit them out or I'd choke, belly and thunder!'

'Do you want to come for a drink?' asked the student.

This proposal calmed the captain down.

'Love to, but I haven't any money.'

'I have!'

1. 'Under the conservation of the specific form, the soul is intact.' Llull (1233–1315) was a Majorcan mystic and alchemist.

'Bah, let's see!'

Simply and majestically, Jehan exhibited the wallet to the captain. Meanwhile the archdeacon had left Charmolue standing open-mouthed and had moved closer; he stopped a yard or two away to watch them, but so rapt were they in contemplation of the wallet that they never noticed him.

Phoebus exclaimed: 'A purse in your pocket, Jehan, is the moon in a bucket of water. You can see it but it isn't there. There's only its shadow. By God, I bet they're pebbles!'

Jehan answered frostily: 'Here are the pebbles I pave my pocket with.'

And without another word, he emptied the wallet on to a nearby boundary-stone, with the air of a Roman saving the fatherland.

'God's truth!' muttered Phoebus, '*targes*, *grands-blancs*, *petits-blancs*, *mailles* at two to the *tournois*, *deniers parisis*, real eagle *liards*! It hurts the eyes!'

Jehan remained dignified and impassive. A few *liards* had rolled into the mud; the captain, in his enthusiasm, bent down to pick them up. Jehan restrained him: 'Shame on you, Captain Phoebus de Châteaupers!'

Phoebus counted the coins and turned solemnly to Jehan. 'Do you know, Jehan, that there are twenty-three *sols parisis*? So who did you waylay last night in the Rue Coupe-Gueule?'

Jehan threw back his fair head of curls, and said, half closing his eyes in disdain: 'We have a brother who is an archdeacon and an idiot.'

'God's horn, estimable man!' cried Phoebus.

'Let's go and drink,' said Jehan.

'Where shall we go?' said Phoebus. 'To the Pomme d'Eve?'

'No, Captain. Let's go to La Vieille Science. An old woman sawing a jug.[1] It's a rebus. I like it.'

'None of your rebuses, Jehan! The wine's better at the Pomme d'Eve. Next to the door, what's more, there's a sunlit vine which cheers me up when I'm drinking.'

'All right! I'll settle for Eve and her apple,' said the student; then, taking Phoebus's arm: 'By the way, my dear captain, you said Rue

1. *Une vieille qui scie (une) anse;* the last two words have the same sound as *science* in French.

Coupe-Gueule just now. That's no way to talk. We're not so barbaric these days. We say Rue Coupe-Gorge.'

The two friends set off for the Pomme d'Eve. Needless to say, before they did so they picked up the money and the archdeacon followed them.

The archdeacon followed them, sombre and haggard. Was this the Phoebus whose accursed name had entered into all his thoughts since his conversation with Gringoire? He did not know, but at least it was *a* Phoebus, and this magic name was enough to make the archdeacon follow stealthily behind the two carefree companions, listening to what they said and watching their least movement with an anxious attentiveness. He had no difficulty, as it happened, overhearing every word they spoke, for they talked at the tops of their voices, quite unconcerned that the passers-by were sharing half their secrets. The talk was of escapades, of duels, of women, and of wine.

At a bend in the street, the sound of a tambourine reached them from a near-by crossroads. Dom Claude heard the officer say to the student:

'Blast! Let's walk faster.'

'Why, Phoebus?'

'I'm afraid the gypsy may see me.'

'Which gypsy?'

'The young one with a goat.'

'La Smeralda?'

'Exactly, Jehan. I always forget her infernal name. Hurry up, she would recognize me. I don't want that girl accosting me in the street.'

'Do you know her, Phoebus?'

At this point the archdeacon saw Phoebus snigger, lean towards Jehan's ear and say a few words to him in a low voice. Then Phoebus burst out laughing and shook his head in seeming triumph.

'Truly?' said Jehan.

'I swear it!' said Phoebus.

'This evening?'

'This evening.'

'Are you sure she'll come?'

'Are you crazy, Jehan? Does one doubt such things?'

'Captain Phoebus, you're a lucky soldier!'

The archdeacon overheard the whole of this conversation. His teeth chattered. A visible shudder went through his entire body. He paused for a moment, leant on a boundary-stone like a drunken man, then again took up the trail of the two merrymakers.

He caught them up just as they changed the subject. He heard them lustily singing the old refrain:

The children of the Petits-Carreaux[1]
End up on the gallows.

SEVEN
The Spectral Monk

THE celebrated tavern of the Pomme d'Eve was situated in the University, where the Rue de la Rondelle met the Rue du Bâtonnier. It was a vast ground-floor room, with a very low, vaulted ceiling whose central springing rested on a huge wooden pillar painted yellow; tables everywhere, gleaming pewter hanging from the wall, never any shortage of customers, girls by the score, a glass front on to the street, a vine by the door, and above this door a gaudy metal plate, decorated with a woman and an apple, which had gone rusty in the rain and swung in the wind on an iron hinge-pin. This sort of weathercock overhanging the pavement was the inn-sign.

Night was falling. The crossroads was in darkness. From a distance, the tavern full of candles blazed in the shadows like a forge. Through the broken window-panes came the sound of glasses, of carousing, of swearing and quarrelling. Through the mist formed by the heat of the room on the glass front, dozens of blurred figures could be seen milling about, from whom there now and again came a resounding shout of laughter. The passers-by did not look in through those turbulent window-panes as they went about their business. Except, from time to time, when some small ragamuffin stretched up on tiptoe to the window-rail and hurled into the tavern the mocking old cry with which drunkards were then pursued:

'Halloo, halloo, you're boozy.'

Yet one man walked imperturbably to and fro past the rowdy

1. The name of a Paris street.

tavern, who looked in constantly and strayed no further from it than a pikeman from his sentry-box. A cloak was pulled up round his eyes. This cloak he had just purchased from the old-clothes man next door to the Pomme d'Eve, no doubt to ward off the chill of a March evening, or perhaps to conceal his costume. From time to time, he stopped in front of the clouded window with its lead lattice-work, to listen, to watch and to stamp his feet.

The door of the tavern finally opened. This was what he seemed to have been waiting for. Two customers emerged. The ray of light from the doorway shone purple for a moment on their jovial faces. The man in the cloak took up a vantage-point under a porch on the other side of the street.

'Horn and thunder!' said one of the two drinkers. 'It's going to strike seven. That's when we were to meet.'

'I tell you,' put in his companion thickly, 'I don't live in the Rue des Mauvaises Paroles, *indignus qui inter mala verba habitat.*[1] My lodgings are in the Rue Jean-Pain-Mollet, *in vico Johannis-Pain-Mollet.* And you're cornier than a unicorn if you say otherwise. Everyone knows that whoever rides a bear once is never afraid, but you're too fond of sweet things like Saint-Jacques de l'Hôpital.'

'Jehan, my friend, you're drunk,' said the other.

The other staggered as he replied: 'You like to say that, Phoebus, but it's been proved that Plato had the profile of a hunting-dog.'

The reader has no doubt already recognized our two worthy friends, the captain and the student. The man lying in wait for them in the shadows seemed to have recognized them too, for he slowly retraced all the zigzags which the student forced the captain to make, the latter, a more hardened drinker, still having all his wits about him. The man in the cloak listened attentively and was able to catch the following interesting conversation in its entirety:

'*Corbacque!* Try and walk straight, mister bachelor of arts. You know I've got to leave you. There's seven o'clock. I've got a date with a woman.'

'Leave me alone, will you! I can see stars and spears of flame. You're like the Château of Dampmartin which has split its sides laughing.'

'By my grandmother's warts, Jehan, you really are much too

1. 'Unworthy the man who lives amidst rude words.'

keen on talking rubbish. By the way, Jehan, have you no money left?'

'No one's to blame, Monsieur le Recteur, just a small shambles, *parva boucheria.*'

'Jehan, friend Jehan! You know I arranged to meet this girl at the end of the Pont Saint-Michel and I can only take her to La Falourdel's, that harpy on the bridge, and I shall have to pay for the room. The old ribald with white whiskers won't give me credit. Please, Jehan, have we drunk the whole of the priest's wallet? Haven't you got one little *parisis* left?'

'Knowing one has spent the other hours well is a just and savoury condiment for the table.'[1]

'Belly and guts, stop your nonsense! Tell me, you infernal Jehan, have you any money left? Give it to me, for God's sake, or I shall search you, even if you're as leprous as Job and as mangy as Caesar!'

'Monsieur, the Rue Galiache is a street with one end at the Rue de la Verrerie and the other at the Rue de la Tixeranderie.'

'Yes, all right, my good friend Jehan, my poor comrade, the Rue Galiache, that's good, very good. But in heaven's name, pull yourself together. All I need is one little *sou parisis*, and by seven o'clock.'

'Silence round about, attend to the chorus:

'When rats shall eat cats
The king will be lord of Arras;
When the sea which is big and wide
Is frozen at midsummertide
The people of Arras will leave their place
And walk across the ice.'

'All right, student of Antichrist, may you be strangled with your mother's tripes!' cried Phoebus, giving the drunken student a rough shove, who slid down the wall and fell limply on to Philip Augustus's paving-stones. Out of a vestige of that fellow-feeling that never deserts a drinker's heart, Phoebus rolled Jehan with his foot on to one of those poor man's pillows which providence keeps in readiness at the corner of all the boundary-stones of Paris, and which the rich stigmatize disdainfully as 'piles of filth'. The captain

1. The quotation is from Montaigne.

arranged Jehan's head on an incline of cabbage stalks and at the same moment the student began to snore in a magnificent basso-profundo. However, not all resentment had been extinguished in the captain's heart: 'Too bad if the devil's wagon picks you up on its way past!' he said to the poor sleeping scholar, then walked away.

The man in the cloak, who had not ceased to follow him, paused for a moment in front of the prostrate student, as if torn by indecision; then he fetched a deep sigh and moved off after the captain.

Like them, we shall leave Jehan to sleep beneath the benevolent gaze of the stars and shall, if it please the reader, follow them.

As he came out into the Rue Saint-André-des-Arcs, Captain Phoebus realized someone was following him. Chancing to look round, he saw a sort of shadow creeping along the walls behind him. He stopped, it stopped. He set off again, the shadow set off again. This did not worry him greatly. 'Bah!' he said to himself, 'I haven't a *sou.*'

He came to a halt in front of the façade of the Collège d'Autun. It was at this college that he had set out on what he called his studies, and out of an irreverent habit left over from his schooldays, he never passed by without subjecting the statue of Cardinal Pierre Bertrand, carved to the right of the doorway, to the sort of indignity of which Priapus complains so bitterly in Horace's satire *Olim truncus eram ficulnus.*[1] So zealous had he been that the inscription *Eduensis episcopus*[2] had been almost obliterated. He stopped in front of the statue, therefore, as was his wont. The street was completely deserted. Just as he was nonchalantly retying his laces, and gazing up at the stars, he saw the shadow slowly approaching, so slowly that he had ample time to remark that this shadow wore a cloak and a hat. When it came close, it stopped and remained more motionless than the statue of Cardinal Bertrand. Meanwhile it had fixed on Phoebus two eyes full of that uncertain light which the pupils of a cat give off at night.

The captain was a brave man and would have been little worried by a robber brandishing a sword. But his blood ran cold at this walking statue, this man of stone. There were current at that time

1. 'In olden times I was the trunk of a fig-tree.'
2. 'Bishop of Autun.'

rumours of some kind of spectral monk who roamed the streets of Paris at night, and these now came dimly back to him.

For a minute or two he remained in a daze, then he broke the silence, with an attempt at laughter:

'Monsieur, if you are a thief, as I hope, you remind me of a heron attacking a nutshell. I am the son of a ruined family, my dear fellow. Try next door. In the chapel of this college there is some wood from the true cross, set in silver.'

The shadow's hand came out from beneath its cloak and descended on Phoebus's arm with the weight of an eagle's claw. At the same time, the shadow spoke: 'Captain Phoebus de Châteaupers!'

'What the devil, you know my name!' said Phoebus.

'I don't only know your name,' the man in the cloak went on in a sepulchral tone. 'You have a rendezvous this evening.'

'Yes,' replied Phoebus in utter amazement.

'At seven o'clock.'

'In a quarter of an hour.'

'At La Falourdel's.'

'Absolutely right.'

'The bawd on the Pont Saint-Michel.'

'Saint Michael archangel as the paternoster puts it.'

'Blasphemer!' muttered the spectre. 'With a woman?'

'*Confiteor*.'[1]

'Whose name is . . .'

'La Smeralda,' said Phoebus gaily. All his insouciance had gradually returned.

At this name, the shadow's claw shook Phoe bus's arm in rage.

'Captain Phoebus de Châteaupers, you are lying!'

Whoever could have seen at that moment the captain's fiery cheeks, his backward leap, so violent that he broke free from the vice in which he had been held, the proud expression with which his hand flashed to the hilt of his sword, and, confronted by such anger, the gloomy immobility of the man in the cloak – whoever could have seen this would have been terrified. It was rather like the combat between Don Juan and the statue.

'Christ and Satan!' cried the captain. 'That's a word that seldom assails the ear of a Châteaupers! You would not dare repeat it.'

1. 'I confess.'

'You are lying!' said the shadow coldly.

The captain gnashed his teeth. Phantom monk, ghost, superstitions, he had forgotten them all at this moment. He could see only a man and an insult.

'Ha, that's what we need!' he stammered in a voice choking with rage. He drew his sword, then stuttered, since anger, like fear, makes us tremble: 'Here! This instant! Have at you. The swords, the swords! Blood on these stones!'

The other, however, did not move. When he saw his adversary on guard and ready to make a thrust: 'Captain Phoebus,' he said, his voice vibrant with bitterness, 'you are forgetting your rendezvous.'

The rages of men like Phoebus are a pan of boiling milk, which subsides under one drop of cold water. These few words caused the sword that had been glinting in the captain's hand to be lowered.

'Captain,' the man continued, 'tomorrow, the day after, in a month from now, in ten years, you will find me again ready to cut your throat; but go first to your rendezvous.'

'Indeed,' said Phoebus, as if seeking a compromise with himself, 'a sword and a girl are two delightful things to come across at one rendezvous; I don't see why I should give one up for the other when I can have both.'

He put his sword back in its scabbard.

'Go to your rendezvous,' the stranger went on.

'Many thanks for your courtesy, monsieur,' replied Phoebus with some embarrassment. 'Tomorrow will indeed still be time enough to pink one another and slash the doublets we came into the world wearing. I am grateful to you for allowing me to spend one more pleasant quarter of an hour. I very much hoped to put you to sleep in the gutter and still arrive in time for my beauty, especially since it's the done thing in these matters to keep the lady waiting a bit. But you look a robust fellow to me and it's safer to defer the contest until tomorrow. So I shall go to my rendezvous. It's for seven o'clock, as you know.' At this point, Phoebus scratched his ear. 'Ah, *Corne-Dieu*, I was forgetting! I haven't a *sou* to settle the bill for the attic, and the old harridan will want to be paid in advance. She distrusts me.'

'Here's something to pay with.'

Phoebus felt the stranger's cold hand slip a large coin into his own. He could not prevent himself from taking the money and shaking his hand.

'Goddam it, you're a good fellow!' he cried.

'On one condition,' said the man. 'Prove to me that I was wrong and that you were telling the truth. Hide me in some corner where I can see whether the woman really is the one whose name you spoke.'

'Oh,' answered Phoebus, 'that's quite all right with me. We'll take the Saint-Martha room. You can watch comfortably from the dog-kennel next door.'

'Come on then,' the shadow rejoined.

'At your service,' said the captain. 'I don't know whether you may not be Mister Diabolus in person. But this evening let's be friends. Tomorrow I will pay back all my debts, with my purse and my sword.'

They set quickly off again. After a few minutes, the sound of the river told them they were on the Pont Saint-Michel, which had houses on it in those days. 'I'll let you in first,' said Phoebus to his companion; 'then I'll go and look for the beauty who should be waiting for me near the Petit-Châtelet.'

His companion made no reply. He had not uttered a word since they had been walking side by side. Phoebus stopped in front of a low door and knocked roughly on it. A light appeared through the cracks in the door. 'Who is it?' cried a toothless voice. 'God's body! God's head! God's belly!' answered the captain. The door opened at once and the visitors could see an old woman and an old lamp, both of them shaking. The woman was bent double and dressed in rags, and her doddering head was done up in a duster; her eyes were like slits, she had wrinkles everywhere, on hands, face and neck, her lips went in underneath her gums and she had tufts of white hair all round her mouth which made her look like a cat with whiskers. The interior of the hovel was as derelict as she. It had chalk walls, black beams in the ceiling, a broken-down fire-place, spiders' webs in every corner, a rickety flock of tables and lame stools in the centre, a filthy child in the ashes, and at the far end a staircase, or rather a wooden ladder ending in a trapdoor in the ceiling. As he penetrated into this lair, Phoebus's mysterious companion pulled his cloak up to his eyes. The captain meanwhile, still blaspheming like a Saracen, hastened to 'make the sun to shine in a golden crown' as our admirable Régnier has it. 'The Saint Martha room,' he said.

The old woman addressed him as 'my lord' and shut the coin away in a drawer. It was the coin the man in the black cloak had given Phoebus. When she had her back turned, the ragged, long-haired little boy who had been playing in the ashes went nimbly up to the drawer, took the crown out and replaced it with a dry leaf he had pulled off a faggot.

The old woman gestured to the two gentlemen, as she called them, to follow her, and preceded them up the ladder. When they reached the floor above, she set her lamp down on a chest and Phoebus, as an habitué of the establishment, opened a door giving on to a dark recess. 'Go in, my dear fellow,' he said to his companion. The man in the cloak obeyed without answering a word. The door closed behind him. He heard Phoebus bolt it again and a moment later go back down the stairs with the old woman. The light had vanished.

EIGHT

The Usefulness of Windows which Open on to the River

CLAUDE Frollo (for we assume that the reader is cleverer than Phoebus and has recognized the phantom monk in this adventure to be none other than the archdeacon), Claude Frollo groped around for a moment or two in the murky fastness into which the captain had bolted him. It was one of those crannies such as architects sometimes effect at the point where the roof joins a side-wall. A vertical section of this dog-kennel, as Phoebus had quite rightly called it, would have formed a triangle. For the rest, it had neither window nor skylight, and the sloping roof meant you could not stand upright. Claude therefore squatted in the dust and the plaster, which crunched underfoot. His head was on fire. As he rummaged around with his hands he found a piece of broken glass on the ground which he pressed against his forehead and whose coolness afforded him some relief.

What was taking place at that moment in the archdeacon's darkling soul? He and God alone can have known.

In what fatal order had he arranged in his mind La Esmeralda, Phoebus, Jacques Charmolue, his beloved young brother whom he had abandoned in the mud, his archdeacon's cassock, his reputation perhaps, dragged with him to La Falourdel's, all these images and adventures? I cannot say. But these ideas certainly formed a dreadful constellation in his mind.

He had been waiting for a quarter of an hour; he felt he had aged a hundred years. All of a sudden he heard the boards creak on the wooden stairs. Someone was coming up. The trap-door opened again and the light reappeared. There was a widish crack in the worm-eaten door of his garret. He pressed his face to it. In this way he could see all that was going on in the bedroom next door. The cat-faced old woman emerged from the trap-door first, her lamp in her hand, then Phoebus, twirling his moustache, then a third person, the lovely, graceful figure of La Esmeralda. The priest saw her emerge from the ground like a dazzling apparition. Claude shook, a cloud came over his eyes, his arteries throbbed violently, everything spun noisily around him. He saw and heard nothing more.

When he came to, Phoebus and La Esmeralda were alone, sitting on the wooden chest next to the lamp, which threw into relief for the archdeacon their two young bodies, together with a miserable pallet at the far end of the attic.

Beside the pallet was a window whose glass had fallen in, like a spider's web that has been exposed to the rain, and through its broken lattice could be seen a patch of sky, with the moon in the distance, resting on an eiderdown of fleecy clouds.

The girl was quite overcome, red-faced and trembling. Her long eyelashes were lowered, shading her purple cheeks. The officer, on whom she did not dare raise her eyes, was beaming. Mechanically, and with a charming gaucherie, she was tracing incoherent patterns on the seat with her fingertip, and staring at her finger. Her feet were hidden from view, the little goat having squatted on top of them.

The captain was very dashingly got up, with clusters of ribbons at his throat and wrists, at that time the height of elegance.

Dom Claude found it hard to hear what they said through the surging of the blood that bubbled in his temples.

(Love-talk is a somewhat pedestrian business, being nothing but 'I love you's: a very bare and insipid refrain for the disinterested listener, unless it be embellished with a few *fioriture*. But Claude was no disinterested listener.)

'Oh!' said the girl, without lifting her eyes, 'don't despise me, my lord Phoebus. I feel that what I'm doing is wrong.'

'Despise you, you beautiful child!' replied the officer, with an air of superior and distinguished gallantry. 'Despise you, God's head, why should I?'

'For having followed you.'

'There we don't agree, my beauty. I shouldn't despise you, I should hate you.'

The girl looked at him in alarm. 'Hate me! What have I done then?'

'For having taken so much persuading.'

'Oh dear!' she said. 'The fact is I am betraying a vow ... I shan't find my parents again ... the amulet will lose its virtue. But what does it matter? What do I need a mother and father for now?'

As she said which, she fixed the captain with her great black eyes, moist with joy and tenderness.

'Damned if I understand you!' exclaimed Phoebus.

La Esmeralda remained silent for a moment, then a tear came from her eyes and a sigh from her lips, and she said: 'Oh, my lord, I love you!'

There was about the girl such an aura of chastity, such a fascination of virtue, that Phoebus did not feel altogether at ease beside her. But these words gave him courage. 'You love me!' he said, ecstatically, and threw his arm round the gypsy's waist. This was the opportunity he had been waiting for.

The priest saw and ran his fingertip over the point of a dagger concealed against his breast.

'Phoebus,' the gypsy continued, gently removing the captain's tenacious hands from her waist, 'you are kind, you are generous, you are handsome. You rescued me, I who am simply a poor child lost in Bohemia. I have long dreamt of an officer who would save my life. It was you I was dreaming of before I met you, my Phoebus. My dream had a beautiful uniform like you, and a noble bearing, and a sword. You're called Phoebus, that's a beautiful name. I like your name and I like your sword. Draw your sword, Phoebus, so I can see it.'

'Child!' said the captain and smilingly unsheathed his rapier. The gypsy looked at the handle and at the blade, examined the monogram on the hilt with an adorable inquisitiveness, then kissed the sword and said: 'You are the sword of a brave man. I love my captain.'

Phoebus seized the opportunity once more to bestow a kiss on that beautiful, bowed neck, which caused the girl to straighten up as scarlet as a cherry. The priest gnashed his teeth in the darkness.

'Let me talk to you, Phoebus,' the gypsy went on. 'Walk up and down a little, so I can see how tall you are and hear your spurs jangle. You are so handsome!'

To humour her, the captain got up, chiding her with a self-satisfied smile: 'What a child you are! By the way, my charmer, have you seen me in my ceremonial acton?'

'No, alas!' she replied.

'That really is handsome!'

Phoebus came and sat beside her again, but much closer than before.

'Listen, my love...'

Like the gay, graceful, silly child she was, the gypsy gave him a few little taps on the mouth with her pretty hand. 'No, no, I shan't listen to you. Do you love me? I want you to tell me whether you love me.'

'Do I love you, angel of my life!' exclaimed the captain, half kneeling. 'My body, my blood, my soul, all are yours, all are for you. I love you and have never loved anyone but you.'

The captain had rehearsed this phrase so many times, in a great many similar situations, that he now delivered it in one breath and word-perfect. At his passionate declaration, the gypsy raised two eyes full of an angelic happiness to the filthy ceiling, which was where the sky should have been. 'Oh!' she murmured, 'this is the moment to die!' Phoebus considered the 'moment' ripe to steal another kiss, which was agony for the wretched archdeacon in his hiding-place.

'Die!' said the amorous captain. 'What are you saying, my fair angel? This is a time to live, or Jupiter's just a scoundrel! To die at the start of something so sweet! *Corne-de-bœuf*, a poor joke! That's not right. Listen, my dear Similar... Esmenarda... Forgive me, but you've got such a prodigiously Saracen name I can't extricate myself from it. It's so overgrown it stops me dead.'

'Good heavens,' said the poor girl, 'and I thought it was a

pretty name because it was so strange! But since you don't like it, I would like to be called Goton.'

'Ah, let's not weep over such a trifle, my charmer! It's a name we must get used to, that's all. Once I know it by heart, it'll come of its own accord. So listen, my dear Similar, I adore you passionately. I love you truly, miraculously. I know one girl who'll be beside herself with rage . . .'

The jealous girl interrupted him: 'Who's that?'

'What's that to us?' said Phoebus. 'Do you love me?'

'Oh!' she said.

'Right, that's all. You'll see how I love you too. May the great devil Neptunus spear me with his fork if I don't make you the happiest creature in the world. We'll have a pretty little room somewhere. I shall parade my archers beneath your windows. They're all mounted, so they taunt Captain Mignon's archers. There are halberdiers, crossbowmen and culverineers. I'll take you to the Parisians' great displays at the barn of Rully. It's very splendid. Eighty thousand armed men, thirty thousand white harnesses, jacks or brigandines; the sixty-seven guild banners; the standards of the parliament, the audit-house, the paymaster-general and the mint; a devilish array in fact! I'll take you to see the lions at the Hôtel du Roi, they're wild animals. Women all love that.'

For the past few moments, the girl had been absorbed in her own delightful thoughts, and had been dreaming to the sound of his voice without attending to the meaning of his words.

'Oh, you'll be happy!' the captain continued, and at the same time he gently unbuckled the gypsy's belt.

'What are you doing?' she said quickly. This 'act of violence' had snatched her from her rêverie.

'Nothing,' answered Phoebus. 'I was just saying that you will have to give up all these silly street-corner clothes when you're with me.'

'When I'm with you, my Phoebus!' said the girl tenderly.

She became silent and thoughtful once again.

The captain was emboldened by her meekness and she offered no resistance when he took hold of her by the waist, then began very quietly to unlace the poor child's bodice, disarranging her gorget to the point where the priest, breathing hard, saw the gypsy's lovely bare shoulder emerge from the gauze, round and brown, like the moon rising out of the mist on the horizon.

The girl let Phoebus do as he wanted. She seemed not to notice. There was a bold glint in the captain's eye.

Suddenly she turned to him: 'Phoebus,' she said with an expression of infinite love, 'instruct me in your religion.'

'My religion!' cried the captain and burst out laughing. 'I, instruct you in my religion! Horn and thunder! What do you want with my religion?'

'So we can be married,' she replied.

The captain's face took on an expression of mingled surprise, disdain, nonchalance and lechery. 'Pshaw!' he said, 'do people get married?'

The gypsy turned pale and allowed her head to drop disconsolately on to her breast.

'What sort of silliness is that, my loving beauty,' Phoebus went on tenderly. 'Marriage is nothing! Are we any less devoted because we haven't been to spout Latin in the priest's shop?'

As he said which, in his most intimate voice, he moved as close as he could to the gypsy, his hands once more encircled that slender, supple waist in a caress, his eye grew brighter and brighter, and all the signs were that Monsieur Phoebus was evidently about to experience one of those moments when Jupiter himself behaves so foolishly that the good Homer is obliged to summon a cloud to his assistance.

Dom Claude, however, could see everything. The door was made of rotten puncheon staves and his predator's gaze could pass easily through the gaps. This brown-skinned, broad-shouldered priest, condemned hitherto to the austere virginity of the cloister, trembled, his senses on fire, at this scene of love, darkness and voluptuousness. That young and beautiful girl, succumbing, in disarray, to an ardent young man, caused molten lead to flow in his veins. Extraordinary changes were taking place inside him. His jealous and lascivious eye plunged beneath all those undone pins. Whoever could have seen the unhappy man's face at that moment, pressed against the worm-eaten bars, would have thought he was seeing the face of a tiger, watching from inside a cage as some jackal devoured a gazelle. His pupils flared like a candle through the cracks in the door.

Suddenly and quickly, Phoebus removed the gypsy's gorget. The poor child had been pale and dreaming, now she seemed to wake up with a start. She backed abruptly away from the presumptuous officer, became red, confused and speechless with shame at the sight of her bare breasts and shoulders, and folded her lovely arms across her bosom so as to hide it. Seeing her thus silent and unmoving, one might have thought her a statue of modesty, but for the flame that blazed in her cheeks. Her eyes remained lowered.

Meanwhile, the captain's action had uncovered the mysterious amulet she wore round her neck. 'What's this?' he said, using it as an excuse to move closer to the beautiful creature whom he had just scared away.

'Don't touch it!' she answered rapidly, 'it's my guardian. It will make me find my family again if I remain worthy of it. Oh, leave me alone, *monsieur le capitaine*! Mother! My poor mother! Mother! Where are you? Help me! Please, Monsieur Phoebus, give me back my gorget!'

Phoebus recoiled and said coldly: 'Oh, mademoiselle! I can see clearly you don't love me!'

'Not love you!' cried the poor wretched child, hanging on to the captain at the same time, and making him sit down beside her. 'Not love you, my Phoebus! What are you saying, you wicked man, you will break my heart. Oh, come, take me, take everything! Do what you like with me. I am yours. What does the amulet matter! What does my mother matter? You are my mother, because I love you! Phoebus, my beloved Phoebus, do you see me? It's me, look at me. It's the girl you won't reject, she's coming, she's coming herself to find you. My soul, my life, my body, my person, they all belong to you, *mon capitaine*! All right, let us not get married, that annoys you. What am I in any case, a poor girl from the gutter, whereas you, my Phoebus, are a gentleman. Really. What an idea, a dancer marrying an officer! I was crazy! No, Phoebus, no, I shall be your mistress, your amusement, your pleasure, whenever you like, a girl who will be yours, that's all I was meant to be, soiled, despised, dishonoured, but what does that matter, loved! I shall be the proudest and happiest of women. And when I'm old or ugly, Phoebus, when I'm no longer any good for loving you, my lord, you will still let me wait on you. Others will embroider sashes for you. I shall be the servant, I shall look after them. You will let me polish your spurs, brush your acton and clean your riding boots. You'll take pity on me and let me, won't you, Phoebus? Meanwhile, take me! Here, Phoebus, all this belongs to you, love me alone! That's all we gypsies need, air and love.'

So saying, she threw her arms about the officer's neck, looked up at him beseechingly and, giving a lovely, tearful smile, rubbed her delicate breasts against his woollen doublet with its coarse braid. Her lovely half-naked body writhed on his knees. The captain, beside himself, pressed his burning lips to those beautiful African shoulders. The girl lay back, seeing only the ceiling, trembling and palpitating beneath that kiss.

Suddenly, above Phoebus's head, she saw another head, a livid, green, convulsed face, with the eyes of a damned soul. Beside this face was a hand holding a dagger. It was the face and the hand of the priest. He had burst down the door and there he stood. Phoebus could not see him. The girl remained frozen, immobile, struck dumb by this dreadful apparition, like a dove that raises its head to find the round eyes of the osprey staring into its nest.

She was unable even to utter a cry. She watched the dagger descend on Phoebus and rise again, smoking. 'Curses!' said the captain, and fell.

She fainted.

Just as her eyes were closing and she was losing all sensation she thought she felt a touch of fire being imprinted on her lips, a kiss more burning than the red-hot irons of the hangman.

When she came to her senses, she was surrounded by soldiers from the watch, the captain was being carried out drenched in his own blood, the priest had vanished, the window at the far end of the room, which opened on to the river, was wide open, they were picking up a cloak which they assumed was the officer's, and she heard them saying around her: 'It's a witch who's stabbed a captain.'

BOOK EIGHT

ONE

The Gold Crown that Turned into a Dried Leaf

GRINGOIRE and the whole Court of Miracles were worried to death. For a good month now they had heard nothing of La Esmeralda, much to the distress of the Duke of Egypt and his friends the truants, nor anything of her goat, which made Gringoire doubly sad. The gypsy had vanished one evening, since when she had given no sign of life. All their inquiries had been fruitless. A few truants teased Gringoire by telling him they had met her that evening in the vicinity of the Pont Saint-Michel, going off with an officer; but this Bohemian-style husband was an incredulous philosopher and knew, moreover, better than anyone, just how virginal his wife was. He had been able to judge what an unassailable modesty resulted from the combined virtues of the amulet and the gypsy, and had computed the resistance of that chastity mathematically to the second power. So his mind was easy on that score.

Thus he could find no explanation for her disappearance. It made him profoundly sad. Had it been possible, he would have lost weight. He neglected everything, even his literary proclivities, even his magnum opus, *De figuris regularibus et irregularibus*,[1] which he counted on having printed as soon as he got some money. (For he had been going on about printing ever since seeing Hugues de Saint-Victor's *Didascolon*, printed with the celebrated characters of Vindelin of Spire.)

One day, as he was walking sadly past the criminal Tournelle, he noticed a small crowd at one of the doors of the Palais de Justice.

'What is it?' he asked a young man who was coming out.

'I don't know, monsieur,' replied the young man. 'They say a woman's being tried for murdering a man-at-arms. Since it seems there's witchcraft involved, the bishop and the Official have intervened in the case, and my brother, who is the Archdeacon of Josas, spends his whole life there. I wanted to speak to him, but I couldn't get to him because of the crowds, which is extremely vexing, because I need money.'

1. 'Of regular and irregular figures.'

'Alas, monsieur,' said Gringoire, 'I wish I could lend you some; but it's not gold pieces that have made these holes in my breeches.'

He did not dare tell the young man that he knew his brother the archdeacon, whom he had not revisited since the scene in the church; an omission which embarrassed him.

The student went on his way, and Gringoire began to follow the crowd mounting the stairs to the great chamber. He reckoned that there was nothing like the spectacle of criminal proceedings to drive away melancholy, so entertainingly stupid as a rule are the judges. The public whom he had joined were walking and jostling one another in silence. After a slow and uninteresting trudge beneath a long, gloomy corridor, which wound through the palace like the old building's intestinal canal, he arrived outside a low door opening into a hall which he was tall enough to see into above the swaying heads of the mob.

The hall was vast and in gloom, which made it seem vaster still. The daylight was fading; a single pale shaft entered through the long, pointed windows but was spent before it reached the vaulting, an enormous trellis of carved timbers, with hundreds of faces that seemed to stir vaguely in the shadows. In places, several candles had already been lit on tables, and shone on the heads of clerks slumped over their paperwork. The front of the hall was occupied by the crowd; to right and left were lawyers at tables; at the far end, on a platform, a great many judges, the rear ranks of whom were lost in the murk; sinister and unmoving faces. The walls were strewn with innumerable fleur-de-lys. Above the judges a big Christ could be dimly discerned, and there were pikes and halberds everywhere, with points of fire at their tips from the candlelight.

'Monsieur,' Gringoire asked one of his neighbours, 'who are all those people in rows, like prelates at a council?'

'Monsieur,' said the neighbour, 'on the right are the councillors of the great chamber, on the left the investigating councillors; the maîtres in black-robes, the messires in red robes.'

'Who's that fat, red-faced man sweating up there above them?' Gringoire went on.

'That's Monsieur the President.'

'And those sheep behind him?' continued Gringoire, who, as we nave already said, was no friend of the magistracy. Which may have had something to do with the grievance he had nursed against the Palais de Justice ever since the mishap to his play.

'Those are the Maîtres des Requêtes from the king's household.'

'And that wild boar in front of him?'

'That's the Clerk to the Court of Parliament.'

'And that crocodile on the right?'

'Maître Philippe Lheulier, Advocate Extraordinary to the King.'

'And that big black cat on the left?'

'Maître Jacques Charmolue, Crown Prosecutor in the Ecclesiastical Court, with the gentlemen of the Officiality.'

'And what are all these good men doing here, monsieur?' said Gringoire.

'Trying someone.'

'Trying who? I see no prisoner.'

'It's a woman, monsieur. You can't see her. She's got her back to us and she's hidden by the crowd. Look, she's there where you can see a group of partisans.'

'Who is the woman?' asked Gringoire. 'Do you know her name?'

'No, monsieur. I've only just arrived. I can only assume it involves witchcraft, because the Official is present at the trial.'

'So!' said our philosopher, 'we are going to see all these men of law eat human flesh. As good a spectacle as any.'

'Monsieur,' observed his neighbour, 'don't you think Maître Jacques Charmolue looks a very mild man?'

'Hmm!' answered Gringoire. 'I don't trust mildness which has pinched nostrils and thin lips.'

At this point those near by enjoined silence on the two chatterers. An important deposition was being heard.

'My lords,' an old woman was saying, in the middle of the hall, her face so obscured by her clothing that she looked like a walking heap of rags, 'my lords, the thing is as true as it's true that I'm La Falourdel, established these forty years on the Pont Saint-Michel, and paying promptly rents, lods[1] and quit-rent, the door facing the house of Tassin-Caillart, the dyer, who's next door as you go up river. A poor old woman these days, a pretty young girl once upon a time, my lords! For the past few days, they'd been telling me: "La Falourdel, don't spin your spinning-wheel too

1. A tax on inheritance.

much in the evenings, the devil likes to comb old women's distaffs with his horns. It's a fact that the phantom monk, who last year was over Temple way, is roaming round the Cité now. Watch out he doesn't bang on your door, La Falourdel." One evening, I'm spinning and there's a knocking on my door. I ask who. They swear. I open it. Two men come in. A black one with a good-looking officer. You could only see the black one's eyes, two live coals. All the rest was cloak and hat. Then they say to me: "The Saint Martha room." That's my upstairs room, my lords, my cleanest one. They give me a gold crown. I shut the crown away in my drawer and I say: "That'll do to buy some tripe tomorrow from La Gloriette the flayers." We go up. When we get to the upstairs room, while my back's turned, the man in black vanishes. That amazes me somewhat. The officer, who's as handsome as a great lord, comes back down with me. He goes out. Time to spin a quarter of a skein and back he comes with a beautiful young girl, a doll who'd have shone like a sun if she'd had something on her head. She had a billy-goat with her, a big billy-goat, black or white, I can't remember which. That sets me thinking. The girl's none of my business, but the goat! . . . I don't like those creatures, they've got a beard and horns. They look like a man. Moreover, there's a smack of the witches' sabbath about them. However, I say nothing. I had the crown. That's right, isn't it, *monsieur le juge*? I show the girl and the captain up to the upstairs room and leave them on their own, with the goat that is. I go down again and go back to my spinning. I must tell you that my house has got a ground floor and a first floor, it overlooks the river at the back, like the other houses on the bridge, and the window on the ground floor and the window on the first floor open on to the water. I was busy spinning then. I don't know why but I was thinking of the phantom monk, the goat had reminded me of it, and then the girl was dressed pretty outlandishly. All of a sudden, I hear a cry from upstairs, something falling on the floor and the window being opened. I run to mine, which is underneath it, and I see a black shape go past my eyes and fall into the water. It was a phantom dressed as a priest. It was bright moonlight. I saw it as clear as clear. It swam towards the Cité. Then, all of a tremble, I call the watch. In come the gentlemen of the *douzaine*, and straight off, not knowing what it's about, because they're so merry, they lay about me. I explain to them. We go up and what do we find? My poor room all covered in blood, the captain stretched out full length with a dagger in his neck, the girl acting dead, and the billy-goat terrified. "Right," I say, "it'll take me a fortnight or more to scrub the floorboards. I'll have to scrape, it'll be terrible." They carry out the officer, poor young man, and the girl all indecent. Wait. The worst of it was the next day, when I wanted to take the crown and buy tripe, I found a dried leaf in its place.'

The old woman ceased. A murmur of horror went round the audience. 'The phantom and the billy-goat, it all reeks of magic,' said one of Gringoire's neighbours. 'And the dried leaf,' added another. 'No question, she's a witch and she's in league with the phantom monk to rob officers,' rejoined a third. Gringoire himself was close to finding the whole thing both frightening and probable.

'Mistress Falourdel,' said the president majestically, 'have you nothing more to tell the court?'

'No, my lord,' answered the old woman, 'except that in the report they described my house as crooked, ramshackle and stinking, which is an outrageous thing to say. The houses on the bridge don't look much, because there are such swarms of people in them, but the butchers go on living there, and they're rich men and married to very clean and beautiful women.'

The magistrate who had reminded Gringoire of a crocodile stood up. 'Silence!' he said. 'I beg you not to lose sight of the fact, messieurs, that a dagger was found on the accused. Mistress Falourdel, have you brought the dried leaf into which the crown the demon gave you was turned?'

'Yes, my lord,' she replied, 'I found it again. Here it is.'

An usher handed the dead leaf to the crocodile, who gave a lugubrious nod of the head and passed it to the president, who returned it to the Crown Prosecutor in the Ecclesiastical Court, until it had travelled right round the room. 'It's a birch-leaf,' said Maître Jacques Charmolue. 'A further proof of magic.'

A councillor began speaking. 'Witness, two men went up your stairs at the same time. The man in black, whom you saw first of all disappear then swimming in the Seine in priest's clothing, and the officer. Which of them handed you the crown?'

The old woman pondered for a moment, then said: 'It was the officer.' A buzz went round the crowd.

'Ah!' thought Gringoire, 'now my conviction is shaken.'

However, Maître Philippe Lheulier, Advocate Extraordinary to the King, intervened once more. 'I would remind you, messieurs, that in the deposition taken down at his bedside, the murdered officer, stating that he had had a vague idea, at the time when the man in black accosted him, that it might very well be the phantom monk, added that the phantom was very keen that he should be intimate with the accused, and he, the captain remarking that he had no money, gave him the crown with which the said officer paid La Falourdel. The coin therefore came from hell.'

This conclusive remark seemed to dispel all the doubts felt by Gringoire and the other sceptics in the audience.

'You have the dossier of evidence, messieurs,' added the king's advocate as he sat down, 'you can consult the statement of Phoebus de Châteaupers.'

At this name, the accused stood up. Her head showed above the crowd. The terrified Gringoire recognized La Esmeralda.

She was pale; her hair, previously so elegantly plaited and spangled with sequins, hung unkempt; her lips were blue, her eyes alarmingly sunken. Alas!

'Phoebus!' she said distraught, 'where is he? O, my lords, please, before you kill me, tell me whether he is still alive!'

'Silence, woman,' replied the president. 'That's none of our concern.'

'Oh, for pity's sake, tell me if he is alive!' she resumed, clasping her beautiful wasted hands; and her chains could be heard brushing against her robe.

'Very well,' said the king's advocate drily, 'he's dying. Does that satisfy you?'

The wretched girl slumped back onto her stool, without speaking and without crying, as white as a wax dummy.

The president bent towards a man standing below him, with a gold bonnet, a black robe, a chain round his neck and a staff in his hand.

'Usher, bring in the second accused.'

All eyes turned towards a small door, which opened to allow through – and Gringoire's heart beat violently – a pretty she-goat with gilded horns and hooves. The graceful animal paused for a moment in the doorway, craning her neck as if she were perched on top of a rock, with an immense horizon before her. Suddenly, she caught sight of the gypsy and, in two bounds, had cleared the table and the head of a clerk to be at her knee. She then curled gracefully up on her mistress's feet, soliciting a word or a caress; but the prisoner remained motionless, and poor Djali did not get so much as a glance.

'But . . . that's my horrid animal,' said the old Falourdel, 'I recognize the pair of them all right!'

Jacques Charmolue intervened. 'If it please you, messieurs, we shall proceed to the interrogation of the goat.'

Which was indeed the second accused. Nothing was simpler in those days than to bring an animal to trial for witchcraft. Among others, you will find in the accounts of the provostry for 1466 a curious detail in the expenses of the trial of Gillet-Soulart and his sow, 'executed for their demerits, at Corbeil'. It is all there, the cost of digging holes to put the sow in, the five hundred bundles of faggots brought from Morsant, the three pints of wine and the bread, the victim's last meal, shared fraternally with the executioner, and even the eleven days' guarding and feeding of the sow, at eight *deniers parisis* per day. Sometimes they went one better even than animals. The capitularies of Charlemagne and Louis the Debonair inflict grave punishments on fiery phantoms rash enough to materialize in the air.

Meanwhile, the Crown Prosecutor in the Ecclesiastical Court had exclaimed: 'If the demon which possesses this goat and which has resisted all exorcisms persists in its malefices, and if it alarms the court by them, we warn it that we shall be obliged to demand the gallows or the stake for it.'

Gringoire was in a cold sweat. Charmolue took the gypsy's tambourine off the table and, holding it out in a particular way to the goat, he asked it: 'What time is it?'

The goat looked at him knowingly, raised its gilded hoof and gave seven kicks. It was indeed seven o'clock. A movement of terror went through the crowd.

Gringoire could not restrain himself.

'She's condemning herself!' he shouted loudly. 'You can see she doesn't know what she's doing.'

'Silence, the villeins at the end of the hall!' said the usher shrilly.

With the help of these same manoeuvres with the tambourine, Jacques Charmolue made the goat perform several more tricks, involving the date and the month of the year, etc., which the reader has witnessed already. And, by an optical illusion peculiar to judicial proceedings, these same spectators, who may more than once have applauded Djali's innocent wiles at the crossroads, were terrified by them beneath the vault of the Palais de Justice. Decidedly, the goat was the devil.

Worse still was to come when, the Crown Prosecutor having emptied on to the floor a certain leather bag full of movable letters which Djali wore round her neck, the goat was seen to pick out the fatal name of Phoebus with its hoof from the scattered alphabet. The spells of which the captain had been the victim seemed to have been irresistibly proven, and everyone now saw the gypsy, the ravishing dancer who had so often dazzled the passers-by with her grace, as nothing less than a terrible vampire.

She, for the rest, gave no sign of life. Nothing, not the graceful motions of Djali, nor the threats of the lawyers, nor the muffled imprecations of the spectators, impinged any longer on her mind.

To arouse her, a serjeant had to shake her mercilessly and the president solemnly to raise his voice:

'Girl, you are of the Bohemian race, given to malefice. On the night of 29 March last, you did, in complicity with the bewitched goat implicated in this trial, stab and kill, in concert with the powers of darkness, and with the help of charms and practices, a captain of archers of the king's bodyguard, Phoebus de Châteaupers. Do you continue to deny it?'

'Horrors!' cried the girl, hiding her face in her hands. 'My Phoebus! Oh, this is hell!'

'Do you continue to deny it?' asked the president coldly.

'Yes, I deny it!' she said in a terrible voice; she had stood up and her eyes were glittering.

The president went bluntly on: 'How then do you explain the facts you are charged with?'

She answered in a halting voice: 'I've already said. I don't know. It was a priest. A priest I don't know. An infernal priest who pursues me!'

'That's right,' the judge went on. 'The phantom monk.'

'Oh my lords, be merciful! I'm only a poor girl...'

'Of Egypt,' said the judge.

Maître Jacques Charmolue spoke softly: 'In view of the accused's distressing obstinacy, I request the application of the question.'

'Granted,' said the president.

The wretched girl trembled all over. However, she stood up at an order from the halberdiers, and walked steadily enough, preceded by Charmolue and the priests of the Officialty, between two lines of halberds, towards a single door which abruptly opened then closed again behind her, and to the unhappy Gringoire it was as if she had been swallowed by some terrible pair of jaws.

As she vanished, a plaintive bleating was heard. It was the little goat crying.

The hearing was suspended. One councillor having remarked that they were tired and would have a long wait before the torture was finished, the president replied that a magistrate should be prepared to sacrifice himself to his duty.

'What a beastly nuisance the slut is,' said an old judge, 'getting given the question before we've had dinner!'

TWO

The Gold Crown that Turned into a Dried Leaf (continued)

AFTER she had been up and down several sets of steps, in corridors so gloomy that they were lit by lamps even in the middle of the day, La Esmeralda, still surrounded by her grim cortège, was thrust by the palace serjeants into a sinister chamber. This chamber was circular and it occupied the ground floor of one of those huge towers which still, in our own century, break through the layer of modern buildings with which the new Paris has covered the old. There was no window in this cellar, and no other opening apart from the entrance, which was low and guarded by an enormous iron door. Yet there was no lack of light. A furnace had been let into the thickness of the wall. In it, a fierce fire was burning, whose red glow filled the entire cellar and deprived a miserable candle standing in a corner of all its radiance. The iron portcullis that served to close the furnace had been raised and all that could be seen, in that fiery orifice opening in a dark wall, were the very bottoms of its bars, like a row of pointed and gappy black teeth, so that the furnace looked like one of those dragon's mouths which breathe fire in legends. By its light, the prisoner could see, all around the chamber, dreadful instruments whose uses she did not understand. In the centre, almost touching the floor, lay a leather mattress; above it hung a strap with a buckle, which was attached to a brass ring held in the mouth of a flat-nosed monster carved in the keystone of the vault. The inside of the furnace was littered haphazardly with tongs, pincers and huge plough-irons, reddening on the coals. Wherever it fell in the chamber, the blood-red glow from the furnace showed only a clutter of terrible objects.

This Tartarus was known simply as 'the question chamber'.

Pierrat Torterue, the sworn torturer, was sitting nonchalantly on the bed. His attendants, two gnomes with square faces, leather aprons and canvas drawers, were moving the irons about on the coals.

In vain did the poor girl summon up all her courage. As she entered the chamber, she felt panic.

The palace bailiff's serjeants lined up on one side, the priests of the Officialry on the other. In a corner were a clerk, an inkstand and a table. Maître Jacques Charmolue approached the gypsy with the sweetest of smiles. 'So, my dear child,' he said, 'you persist in your denials?'

'I do,' she answered in an already inert voice.

'In that case,' Charmolue went on, 'it will grieve us greatly to question you more insistently than we would have wished. Kindly take the trouble to sit down on that bed. Maître Pierrat, make way for mademoiselle, and close the door.'

Pierrat grumbled and got up. 'If I shut the door,' he muttered, 'my fire will go out.'

'Very well, my dear fellow,' rejoined Charmolue, 'leave it open.'

La Esmeralda meanwhile had remained standing. The leather bed, where so many poor devils had writhed, appalled her. Terror froze the marrow of her bones. She stood there, frightened and stupefied. At a signal from Charmolue, the two attendants took hold of her and sat her down on the bed. They did not hurt her at all, yet as first the men and then the leather touched her, she felt all her blood flow back towards her heart. She gave a frantic look around the chamber. She thought she could see all those shapeless instruments of torture moving and walking towards her from every side, in order to climb along her body and bite and pinch her; amongst all the various implements she had met with up till now, these were what bats, millipedes and spiders are amongst the birds and the insects.

'Where is the doctor?' asked Charmolue.

'Here,' answered a black robe she had not so far noticed.

She shuddered.

'For the third time, mademoiselle,' went on the silky voice of the Prosecutor in the Ecclesiastical Court, 'do you persist in denying the deeds of which you are accused?'

This time she could only nod. Her voice failed her.

'You persist?' said Jacques Charmolue. 'Then, I am very sorry, but I must carry out the duties of my office.'

'What shall we start with, *monsieur le procureur*?' said Pierrat brusquely.

Charmolue hesitated for a moment with the equivocal grimace of a poet hunting for a rhyme.

'With the boot,' he said finally.

The hapless girl felt herself so profoundly forsaken by both God and man that her head fell forward on to her breast like an inert object without any strength of its own.

The torturer and the doctor approached her simultaneously. At the same time, the two attendants began to rummage through their hideous arsenal.

At the clank of the terrible irons, the poor child shuddered, like a dead frog being galvanized. 'Oh,' she murmured, so quietly that no one heard her, 'oh, my Phoebus!' Then she relapsed into silence and a marble-like stillness. Any heart but that of a judge would have been rent by such a spectacle. It was like some poor, sinful soul being questioned by Satan beneath the scarlet grille of hell. The wretched body to which that terrible ant-swarm of saws, wheels and racks was about to attach itself, the living being on whom the harsh hands of the pincers and the executioners were about to be laid, was this soft, white, fragile creature. A poor grain of millet fed by human justice to the frightful millstones of torture to be ground!

Meanwhile the calloused hands of Pierrat Torterue's attendants had brutally laid bare that adorable leg, and that tiny foot, so graceful and so lovely that they had often filled the passers-by at Paris's crossroads with wonder.

'It's a shame!' mumbled the torturer, as he contemplated those neat and delicate contours. Had the archdeacon been present he would surely have recalled, at that moment, his symbolism of the spider and the fly. Soon, through a cloud that had formed before her eyes, the poor girl saw the 'boot' approaching, saw her foot, encased between the iron plates, vanish into the dreadful apparatus. And now terror gave her back her strength. 'Take it off!' she shouted desperately. Then, sitting up, all dishevelled: 'Mercy!'

She started up from the bed so as to throw herself at the crown prosecutor's feet, but her leg was held in the heavy block of iron and oak, and she collapsed on to the boot, more broken than a bee with a lead weight on its wing.

At a signal from Charmolue, she was replaced on the bed, and two huge hands attached the strap hanging from the ceiling to her slender waist.

'For the last time, do you confess the facts in the case?' asked Charmolue with his unshakeable benignity.

'I am innocent.'

'How then, mademoiselle, do you explain the circumstances you are charged with?'

'Alas, my lord; I don't know!'

'You deny them then?'

'All of them!'

'Go on,' said Charmolue to Pierrat.

Pierrat turned the handle of the winch, the boot tightened and the poor girl let out one of those terrible cries that cannot be written down in any human language.

'Stop,' said Charmolue to Pierrat. 'Do you confess?' he said to the gypsy.

'Everything!' cried the wretched girl. 'I confess, I confess! Mercy!'

She had not estimated her capacity to withstand the question. Up till now, the poor child's life had run so happily, so smoothly and so sweetly, that this first pain was too much for her.

'Humanity obliges me to inform you', remarked the crown prosecutor, 'that by confessing you must expect to die.'

'I hope I do,' she said. And she fell back on to the leather bed, inert, bent double, dangling from the strap buckled against her chest.

'Come on, my beauty, up with you,' said Maître Pierrat, raising her upright. 'You look like the golden fleece round the Duke of Burgundy's neck.'

Jacques Charmolue raised his voice.

'Clerk, write. Young Bohemian girl, you confess to having taken part in agapes, sabbaths and infernal malefices, together with larvae, masks and vampires? Answer.'

'Yes,' she said, so softly that the word was drowned by her breathing.

'You confess to having seen the ram which Beelzebub causes to appear in the clouds to convene the sabbath, and which is only seen by sorcerers?'

'Yes.'

'You admit to having worshipped the heads of Bophomet, those abominable idols of the templars?'

'Yes.'

'To having had habitual commerce with the devil in the shape of a familiar she-goat, your fellow-accused?'

'Yes.'

'Finally, you admit and confess to having, on the night of the twenty-ninth of March last, with the help of the demon and of the spectre commonly known as the phantom monk, killed and murdered a captain, Phoebus de Châteaupers by name?'

She raised her big, staring eyes to the magistrate and answered, as if automatically, without any great stress or agitation: 'Yes.' Everything had clearly snapped inside her.

'Write, clerk,' said Charmolue. Then, addressing himself to the torturers: 'Let the prisoner be untied and taken back to the hearing.'

Once the prisoner had been 'unshod', the crown prosecutor examined her foot, still numb from the pain. 'Come on!' he said, 'there's no great harm done. You cried out in time. You could still dance, my beauty!'

Then he turned to the acolytes from the Officialty: 'Justice, finally, has been enlightened! That is a consolation, messieurs! Mademoiselle will witness to the fact that we acted with the greatest possible gentleness.'

THREE
The Gold Crown that Turned into a Dried Leaf (concluded)

SHE came back into the courtroom, pale-faced and limping, to be greeted by a general murmur of pleasure. In the audience's case, this was that feeling of impatience satisfied which one gets in the theatre at the conclusion of the final interval, when the curtain goes up again and the end is about to begin. In the case of the judges it was the hope of an early supper. The little goat too bleated for joy. She tried to run towards her mistress, but she had been tethered to the bench.

Night had fallen in earnest. The candles, whose number had not been increased, gave so little light that you could not even see the walls of the hall. The gloom enveloped everything in a sort of haze. From it, there emerged dimly a few apathetic judges' faces. Facing them, at the very end of the long hall, a vague white blob was visible against the dark background. This was the prisoner.

She had dragged herself to her place. Once Charmolue had installed himself magisterially in his, he sat down, then he stood up again and said, not allowing his vanity at his success to be too apparent: 'The accused has admitted everything.'

'Bohemian girl,' the president put in, 'you have confessed all your acts of magic, prostitution and murder against Phoebus de Châteaupers?'

Her heart shrank. She could be heard sobbing in the shadows.

'Whatever you like,' she replied feebly, 'only kill me quickly!'

'*Monsieur le procureur*,' said the president, 'the court is ready to hear your requisition.'

Maître Charmolue brandished an alarming-looking dossier and began to read, with a great many gestures and the exaggerated emphases of the advocate, a Latin oration in which all the proofs of the charges were erected on Ciceronian periphrases, flanked by quotations from Plautus, his favourite humorist. We are sorry not to be able to offer our readers this remarkable morsel. The orator delivered it with wonderful actions. He had not finished the exordium before the sweat was already starting from his brow and his eyes from his head. Suddenly, right in the middle of a period, he broke off, and his normally rather mild and even rather stupid gaze became one of thunder. 'Messieurs,' he cried (in French this time, for this was not in his notes), 'so involved is Satan in this affair that he is present at our deliberations and apes their solemnity. See there!'

And so saying, he pointed to the little goat, which had seen Charmolue gesticulating and thought in fact it would be a good moment to do the same, so she sat down on her backside to imitate, as best she could, with her front hooves and her bearded face, the pathetic pantomime of the Crown Prosecutor in the Ecclesiastical Court. This, you may remember, was one of her most charming accomplishments. This incident, this final *proof*, made a great stir. The goat's feet were tied together and the crown prosecutor picked up the threads of his eloquence.

It was a very long, but admirable peroration. Here is the final sentence; to it must be added the hoarse voice and breathless gestures of Maître Charmolue: 'Ideo, Domni, coram stryga demonstrata, crimine patente, intentione criminis existente, in nomine sanctae ecclesiae Nostrae-Dominae Parisiensis, quae est in saisina habendi omnimodam altam et bassam justitiam in illa hac intemerata Civitatis insula, tenore praesentium declaramus nos requirere, primo, aliquandam pecuniariam indemnitatem; secundo, amendationem honorabilem ante portalium maximum Nostrae-Dominae, ecclesiae cathedralis; tertio, sententiam in virtute cujus ista stryga cum sua capella, seu in trivið vulgariter dicto *la Grève*, seu in insula exeunte in fluvio Sequanae, juxta pointam jardini regalis, executatae sint!'[1]

He put his bonnet on again and sat down.

'*Eheu!*' sighed the heartbroken Gringoire, '*bassa latinitas!*'[2]

1. 'That is why, gentlemen, in the presence of a confessed vampire, the crime being patent, the criminal intention existent, in the name of the holy church of Notre-Dame of Paris, which is in seisin of having justice of all kinds, high and low, in this stainless island of the Cité, by the tenor of those present we declare that we demand, firstly, some pecuniary indemnity; secondly, honourable amends before the great portal of the cathedral church of Notre-Dame: thirdly, a sentence by virtue of which this vampire and her goat be executed, either on the place commonly known as the Grève, or at the point where you leave the island on the Seine river, near the end of the royal garden!'

2. 'Alas, low Latinity!'

Another man in a black robe stood up beside the prisoner. It was her advocate. The judges were starving and were beginning to mutter.

'Counsel, be brief,' said the president.

'The defendant having confessed to the crime, *monsieur le président*,' answered the lawyer, 'I have only one word to say to the court. There is a text in the salic law: "If a vampire has eaten a man and been convicted of it, she shall pay a fine of eight thousand *deniers*, which make two hundred gold *sous*." May it please the court to sentence my client to the fine.'

'An abrogated text,' said the Advocate Extraordinary to the King.

'*Nego*,'[1] replied counsel.

'A vote!' said a councillor. 'The crime is blatant, and it's late.'

They proceeded to a vote without leaving the hall. The judges 'made a show of bonnets', they were in a hurry. They could be seen baring their hooded heads one after another in the shadows as the president put the grim question to them in an undertone. The poor prisoner seemed to be watching them, but her troubled gaze no longer saw.

The clerk began to write; then he handed a long parchment to the president.

The poor girl now heard movements in the crowd, the clash of pikes, and a wintry voice, saying:

'Girl of Bohemia, on whatever day it please our master the king, at the hour of noon, you will be taken in a tumbril, in a shift, barefoot, with a rope around your neck, before the great portal of Notre-Dame, and there make honourable amends with a torch of wax to the weight of two pounds in your hand, and from thence be taken to the Place de Grève, where you will be hanged and strangled on the town gibbet; likewise your goat; and will pay the Official three lions of gold, in reparation for the crimes committed and confessed by you of witchcraft, magic, lewdness and murder on the person of Sir Phoebus de Châteaupers. May God have your soul!'

'Oh, I'm dreaming!' she murmured, and felt rough hands carry her away.

1. 'I deny it.'

FOUR
Lasciate ogni speranza[1]

IN the Middle Ages, once a building was complete, there was almost as much of it in the ground as outside it. Unless it was built on piles, as Notre-Dame was, a palace, fortress or church always had a false bottom. In the cathedrals, this was rather like a second, subterranean cathedral, low, dark, mysterious, blind and dumb, underneath the upper nave, which overflowed with light and echoed night and day to bells and organs; sometimes it was a burial-place. In palaces and fortresses, it was a prison, or sometimes a burial-place again; and sometimes both. These mighty fabrics, whose mode of formation and of 'vegetation' we have explained elsewhere, did not simply have foundations, they had roots, so to speak, ramifying off into the earth as chambers, galleries and staircases, like the structure above them. Thus churches, palaces and fortresses had earth up to their waists. The cellars of a building were a second building into which you went down instead of up, and whose subterranean storeys adhered to the pile of visible storeys, like the forests and mountains reflected upside-down in the waters of a lake beneath the forests and mountains on the shore.

At the Bastille Saint-Antoine, at the Palais de Justice in Paris, and at the Louvre, these subterranean buildings were prisons. As they tunnelled deeper into the earth, each floor of these prisons became darker and more confined. They were so many zones, and each one a further gradation of horror. Dante found no better model for his Inferno. These funnels of prison-cells usually ended in a bottle-shaped dungeon, into which Dante put his Satan and society its condemned prisoners. Once some wretched existence had been interred there, farewell daylight, air, life, *ogni speranza*. It re-emerged only for the gallows or the stake. Sometimes it rotted away there. Human justice called that 'to forget'.[2] Between himself and humankind, the prisoner felt a mass of stones and gaolers pressing down on his head, and the whole prison, the massive

1. 'Abandon all hope.' The legend inscribed above the entrance to Dante's Inferno.

2. i.e. *oublier*, hence the word *oubliette* for dungeon.

fortress, was simply one enormous, complicated lock, barring him from the world of the living.

It was in just such a dungeon, in the oubliettes dug by Saint Louis, in the *in-pace* of the Tournelle, that they had, fearful no doubt she might escape, lodged La Esmeralda, condemned to the gallows and with the colossal Palais de Justice above her head. A poor fly who could not have dislodged the least of its rubble-stones!

Both Providence and society had been equally unjust, such a superfluity of torture and misfortune was not needed to crush so frail a creature.

She lay there, lost in darkness, buried, entombed, immured. Whoever could have seen her in that state, after seeing her laugh and dance in the sunlight, must have shuddered. Cold as night, cold as death, no breath of air in her hair any more, no human sound in her ear, no gleam of daylight in her eyes, broken in half, crushed by chains, squatting beside a jug and a loaf of bread on a bit of straw, in the puddle formed beneath her by the oozing of the cell, unmoving, almost unbreathing, she was no longer even capable of suffering. Phoebus, the sunshine, the noonday, the fresh air, the streets of Paris, the applause for her dancing, the sweet nothings exchanged with the officer, and then the priest, the old hag, the dagger, the blood, the torture, the gallows, they all came back to her still, sometimes as a golden, harmonious vision, at others as a formless nightmare; but it was simply a confused and terrible struggle fading into the darkness, or else a distant music playing up there on the surface, and no longer audible at the depths into which the poor girl had descended.

All this time, she had been neither asleep nor awake. In her misfortune and in that dungeon, she could no more distinguish sleeping from waking, or a dream from reality, than night from day. Everything had merged and lay broken, shifting and scattered in confusion about her mind. She no longer felt, or knew, or thought. At most she dreamt. Never had a living creature progressed so far towards oblivion.

Benumbed, frozen, petrified as she was, she had hardly noticed on the two or three occasions when a trap-door was heard to open somewhere above her, though without letting any light through, and a hand tossed down a crust of black bread. Yet this, the periodic visit of her gaoler, was her one remaining contact with mankind.

Only one thing still automatically filled her ears: above her head, the moisture had filtered through the mildewed stones of the ceiling, and at regular intervals a drop of water would break away. She listened in a stupor to the sound this drop of water made as it fell into the pool beside her.

The drop of water falling into the pool was the one source of movement around her, the one clock measuring out the hours, the one sound to reach her out of all the sounds that are made on the surface of the earth.

Though truth to tell, she also felt, now and again, in that cloaca of darkness and slime, something cold pass across an arm or a foot; and then she shuddered.

She had no idea how long she had been there. She could recall a sentence of death being pronounced on someone somewhere, then that it was she who had been taken away and who had woken up, frozen, in the darkness and the silence. She had dragged herself along on her hands, then iron rings had cut into her ankles and there had been the clank of chains. She had discovered that all around her was wall, that beneath her was a flagstone covered in water and a bundle of straw. But no lamp and no air-vent. So she sat on the straw, or sometimes, in order to change her position, on the lowest step of some stone stairs which there were in the dungeon. She had tried, briefly, to count the minutes of blackness measured out by the dripping water, but this unhappy labour of a sick brain soon broke off of its own accord and left her in a stupor.

Finally, one day or one night (for midday and midnight wore the same colour in this sepulchre), she heard above her a sound louder than that the turnkey generally made when bringing her her water-jug and her bread. She raised her head and saw a reddish beam of light coming through the cracks in the sort of door or trap in the ceiling of the *in-pace*. At the same moment, the heavy iron-work groaned, the trap-door squeaked on its rusty hinges and opened, and she saw a lantern, a hand and the bottom halves of the bodies of two men, the door being too low for her to be able to see their heads. So painful was the light to her eyes that she closed them.

When she opened them again, the door had been closed, the lantern set down on one of the stairs and in front of her stood a man, alone. A hooded black gown fell right to his feet, a *caphardum*[1] of the same colour masked his face. No part of his body was visible, neither his face nor his hands. He was a long, black shroud standing upright beneath which something could be heard moving. She stared fixedly at this kind of spectre for a minute or two. But neither she nor it spoke. It was as if two statues had been facing one another. Only two things in the cellar seemed to be alive: the wick of the lantern, as it guttered in the damp atmosphere, and the water which dripped from the ceiling, interrupting the irregular crepitation with its own monotonous splash and making the light from the lantern to tremble in moiré rings on the oily surface of the pool.

At last, the prisoner broke the silence. 'Who are you?'

'A priest.'

The word, the intonation, the sound of his voice, made her shudder.

The priest continued, in muffled tones: 'Are you prepared?'

'For what?'

'To die.'

'Oh,' she said, 'will it be soon?'

'Tomorrow.'

Her head, having been raised in joy, fell back against her chest. 'That's still a long time!' she murmured. 'Couldn't they have done it today?'

'Are you very unhappy then?' asked the priest, after a silence.

'I'm very cold,' she replied.

She took her feet in her hands, a gesture habitual to any poor wretch who is cold and which we have already seen made by the recluse in the Tour-Roland, and her teeth chattered.

The priest seemed to be casting an eye round the cell from underneath his cowl.

'Without light! Without fire! In the water! It's horrible!'

'Yes,' she answered with that look of surprise which misfortune had given her. 'The daylight belongs to everybody. Why do they only give me the dark?'

'Do you know why you are here?' the priest resumed after another silence.

'I think I did know,' she said, passing her emaciated fingers over her eyebrows as if to aid her memory, 'but I don't know now.'

1. A low-Latin term for an academic garment of the fourteenth century.

She suddenly began to cry like a child. 'I want to get out of here, monsieur. I'm cold, I'm frightened, and there are creatures that climb up my body.'

'Very well, follow me.'

So saying, the priest took her by the arm. The wretched girl was chilled to the very marrow yet still that hand felt cold.

'Oh,' she murmured, 'that is the icy hand of death. Who are you then?'

The priest lifted his cowl. She looked. It was the same sinister face that had been pursuing her for so long, the same demon's head that had appeared to her at La Falourdel's above the head of her adored Phoebus, the same eye she had last seen glinting beside a dagger.

This apparition, which had always proved so fatal to her and had driven her on from one misfortune to another until her torture, aroused her from her numbed state. The kind of veil that had obscured her memory seemed to tear. All the details of her dismal adventure, from the nocturnal scene at La Falourdel's to her condemnation at the Tournelle, came back to her at once, not vague and muddled as hitherto, but distinct, vivid, unequivocal, pulsating, terrible. These half-erased memories, almost obliterated by the excess of her sufferings, were revived by this sombre figure standing in front of her, just as the invisible characters traced with sympathetic ink on a blank sheet of paper re-emerge afresh when held up to the fire. She felt as if all the wounds in her heart had reopened as one and were bleeding.

'Ha!' she cried, her hands over her eyes and trembling convulsively, 'it's the priest!'

Then she dropped her arms dispiritedly, and remained sitting, her head bowed, her eyes on the ground, unspeaking, still shaking.

The priest eyed her like a kite which has long been circling high in the sky round a poor lark huddled amidst the corn, which has long and silently been contracting the fearsome circles of its flight, and then suddenly pounces on its prey like a lightning flash and holds it palpitating in its claws.

She began to murmur softly: 'Finish me, finish me! The final blow!' And she hunched her head in terror between her shoulders, like the ewe-lamb waiting for the butcher's club to fall.

'Do I horrify you then?' he said finally.

She made no answer.

'Do I horrify you?' he repeated.

Her lips drew back as if in a smile. 'Yes,' she said, 'the executioner mocks the condemned man. For months now he has been pursuing me, threatening me, terrifying me! Oh God, how happy I would have been but for him! It is he who has cast me into this abyss! Oh, great Heaven, it was he who killed ... he who killed him! My Phoebus!'

At this point, she burst into sobs and looked up at the priest: 'Oh, wretched man, who are you? What have I done to you? Do you hate me so much then? Alas, what have you got against me?'

'I love you!' cried the priest.

Her tears suddenly ceased. She stared at him like an idiot. He had fallen to his knees and was gazing at her intently with eyes of fire.

'Do you understand? I love you!' he cried again.

'What a love!' said the poor girl with a shudder.

He went on: 'The love of a damned soul!'

Both of them remained silent for a minute or two, crushed beneath the weight of their emotions, he demented, she stupefied.

'Listen,' said the priest finally, and a strange calm had returned to him. 'You shall know everything. I am going to tell you what up till now I have hardly dared tell myself, as I questioned my conscience furtively in the very dead of night, when it is so dark that God seems no longer able to see us. Listen. Before I met you, a young girl, I was happy...'

'So was I!' she sighed weakly.

'Don't interrupt me. Yes, I was happy, or so at least I thought. I was pure, my soul was full of a limpid clarity. No head was raised more proudly or radiantly than mine. The priests consulted me on chastity, the doctors on doctrine. Yes, science was everything to me. It was a sister, and a sister was all I needed. Only with age did other ideas come to me. More than once my flesh was excited by the passing form of a woman. More than once, the virility of my sex and my blood which, as a foolish adolescent, I thought I had suffocated once and for all, brandished convulsively the chain of the iron vows fixing me, poor wretch, to the cold stones of the altar. But prayer, fasting, study and the mortifications of the cloister made the soul mistress of the body once again. I shunned women in any case. Moreover, I needed only to open a book for the impure fumes of my brain to be dispelled by the splendours of science. Within a few minutes I could feel the turbid things of earth receding into the distance, and I was calm, dazzled and serene once more, in the presence of the tranquil radiance of everlasting truth. For as long as the demon sent to assail me only vague women's shadows, who straggled past me in church, in the streets or in the fields, and seldom reappeared in my dreams, I overcame him easily. Alas, if the victory did not remain with me, the fault is God's, who did not give man a strength equal to that of the demon. Listen. One day . . .'

Here the priest paused, and the prisoner could hear sighs, which sounded as if they were being torn from his chest, like a death-rattle.

He resumed: 'One day, I was leaning at the window of my cell... What book was I reading? Oh, my head's all in a whirl . . . I was reading. The window looked out on to a square. I heard the sound of music and of a tabor. Annoyed at having my meditations disturbed like this, I looked out into the square. Others beside myself could see what I saw, yet it was a sight not meant for human eyes. There, in the middle of the paving – it was midday – bright sunlight – a creature was dancing. A creature so lovely that God would have preferred her to the Virgin, would have chosen her for his mother, would have wished to be born of her, if she had existed when he was made man! She had splendid black eyes, and where the sunlight had penetrated her black hair, a few strands were as fair as gold thread. Her feet moved invisibly like the spokes of a fast-turning wheel. Around her head, in her black tresses, she wore metal plaques, which sparkled in the sun and made a wreath of stars on her forehead. Her dress was blue and sequined, and glistened, studded with a thousand sparks, like a summer's night. Her brown and supple arms she wrapped and unwrapped round her waist like two scarves. The lines of her body were of a startling beauty. Oh, a resplendent figure which stood out like something luminous in the light of the very sun itself! . . . Alas, that girl was you. I was surprised, intoxicated, spellbound and I allowed myself to look at you. I looked at you so hard that I suddenly shivered with fright, I felt that fate had seized hold of me.'

The priest's breathing was laboured and he paused for a moment. Then he continued.

'I was already half fascinated, I tried to clutch on to something and to stay myself from falling. I remembered the ambushes Satan had already laid for me. The creature I was looking at had that superhuman beauty which can come only from heaven or from hell. This was no mere girl created from a clod of earth, and meanly lit within by the flickering beam of a feminine soul. It was an angel! But of darkness, of flame, not of light! And just as I was thinking this, I saw beside you a goat, a beast of the sabbath, which was looking at me and laughing. The noonday sun made its horns flash fire. Then I glimpsed the demon's snare, and I no longer doubted but that you had come from hell and had come for my perdition. I believed that.'

At this point, the priest looked the prisoner in the face and added coldly:

'I believe it still. Yet the spell was slowly working, your dancing spun around in my brain, I could feel the mysterious malefice being accomplished within me, everything that should have been keeping vigil in my soul slept, and like someone dying in the snow I found pleasure in being overcome by sleep. Suddenly, you began to sing. What could I do, poor wretch? Your singing was even more enchanting than your dancing. I tried to escape. Impossible. I was nailed, I was rooted to the ground. The marble slabs seemed to reach to my knees. I had to stay till it was finished. My feet were like ice, my head was on fire. Finally, perhaps you took pity on me, you stopped singing, you vanished. The reflection of that dazzling vision, the echoes of that bewitching music, faded by degrees from my eyes and ears. Then I fell in the window corner, stiffer and more feeble than an overturned statue. The bell for vespers aroused me. I got up, I fled, but something had fallen within me, alas, which could not get up, something had come to pass from which I could not flee.'

He paused once more, then went on:

'Yes, from that day on, there was a man within me whom I did not know. I sought to employ all my remedies, the cloister, the altar, work, books. Madness! Oh, how hollow science rings when a head full of passions runs despairingly against it! Do you know what I always saw, girl, from then on, between the book and myself? You, your shadow, the image of the luminous apparition that had one day crossed my field of vision. But this image no longer had the same colour; it was sombre, funereal, dark, like the black disc that long haunts the vision of the man unwise enough to fix his eye on the sun.

'Unable to rid myself of it, hearing your song still ringing in my head, seeing your feet still dancing over my breviary, feeling your form still sliding across my flesh at night in my dreams, I sought to see you again, to touch you, to find out who you were, to see whether I should find you like the ideal image that still remained to me of you, to shatter my dream perhaps on the reality. At all events, I hoped that a new impression would erase the old one, and the old one had become unbearable. I searched you out. I saw you again. Woe! Now I had seen you twice, I wanted to see you a thousand times, I wanted to see you always. Then, how to check myself on the infernal slope? I was no longer my own master. The other end of the thread which the demon had fixed to my wings had been tied to your foot. I became, like you, a wandering vagabond. I waited for you under porches, I spied on you from street corners, I watched for you from on top of my tower. Each evening, I re-entered myself more fascinated, more desperate, more bewitched, more damned!

'I had found out who you were, a gypsy, a Bohemian, a zingara, a romany, so how could I doubt it was magic? Listen. I hoped that a trial would release me from the spell. A witch enchanted Bruno of Asti, he had her burnt and was cured. I knew that. I would try his remedy. First I tried to have you banned from the Parvis of Notre-Dame, hoping I would forget you if you did not return. You paid no heed. You returned. Then I had the idea of abducting you. One night I attempted it. There were two of us. We already had you when that wretched officer appeared. He freed you. In doing so he began your misfortunes, and mine and his. Finally, no longer knowing what to do or what would become of me, I denounced you to the Official. I thought I would be cured, like Bruno of Asti. I also had a vague notion that a trial would deliver you over to me, that in a prison I would have you, you would be mine, that you could not escape me there, that you had possessed me for so long that I should possess you in my turn. When one does evil one must do the whole evil. To be only half a monster is insanity! There is ecstasy in an extreme of crime. A priest and a sorceress can melt in delight together on the straw of a dungeon floor!

'So I denounced you. It was then that I terrified you when we came face to face. The plot I was hatching against you, the storm I was heaping up above your head, escaped from me as threats and flashing glances. But still I hesitated. My scheme had its frightening aspects and I recoiled from it.

'Perhaps I would have abandoned it, perhaps my ghastly idea would have withered in my brain without coming to fruition. I believed it would always depend on me whether to go on with the case or to stop it. But every evil thought is inexorable and seeks to become a deed; where I thought myself all-powerful, fatality proved more powerful than I. Alas and alas, it was fatality which took you and delivered you up to the gear-wheels of the grim and terrible machine I had constructed! Listen. I am nearly at an end.

'One day, of bright sunshine once again, I saw a man pass by me who pronounced your name and laughed and had lechery in his eyes. Damnation! I followed him! You know the rest.'

He fell silent. The girl could find only one word:

'Oh my Phoebus!'

'Not that name!' said the priest, grabbing her violently by the arm. 'Don't utter that name! Oh, wretches that we are, that was the name that destroyed us! Or rather we have all destroyed each other through the inexplicable play of fatality! You're suffering, aren't you? You are cold, the darkness makes you blind, the dungeon envelops you, but perhaps deep inside you still have some light, be it only your childish love for that empty man who trifled with your affections! Whereas I carry the dungeon inside me, inside me is winter, ice, despair, I have the darkness in my soul. Do you know all I have suffered? I was present at your trial. I was sitting on the Official's bench. Yes, beneath one of those priest's cowls were the contortions of a damned soul. When they brought you in, I was there; when they interrogated you, I was there. A den of wolves! It was my crime, my gallows that I saw being slowly erected on your brow. At each witness, each proof, each speech by counsel, I was there; I was able to count each one of your steps along the *via dolorosa*; I was even there when that ravening beast . . . Oh, I had not foreseen torture! Listen. I followed you into the chamber of pain. I saw you undressed, saw the torturer lay his vile hands on you, half-naked. I saw your foot, that foot on which I would have given an empire to plant a single kiss and then die, that foot it would have been such sweet delight to feel crushing my head, I saw it squeezed in the terrible iron boot which turns the limbs of a living creature into a bloody pulp. Oh, misery! As I watched, I had a dagger under my shroud with which I was furrowing my breast. At the cry you let out, I dug it into my flesh; another cry and it would have entered my heart! Look, I think it is still bleeding.'

He undid his cassock. His chest indeed had been lacerated as if by a tiger's claw, and in his side he had a considerable wound that was not yet closed.

The prisoner recoiled in horror.

'Oh, have pity on me, girl!' said the priest. 'You think you are unhappy. Alas and alas, you do not know what unhappiness is. Oh, to love a woman! To be a priest! To be hated! To love her with all the fury of your soul, to feel that you would give your blood, your entrails, your reputation, your salvation, immortality and eternity, this life and the next, for the least of her smiles; to regret that you are not a king, a genie, an emperor, an archangel, a god, so as to be a greater slave at her feet; to clasp her night and day in your dreams and thoughts; and to see her fall in love with a soldier's uniform! And to have nothing to offer her but a filthy priest's cassock which will frighten and disgust her! To be present, with your jealousy and your rage, while she squanders treasures of love and beauty on a wretched, brainless braggart! To see that body whose contours scorch you, that breast with all its softness, that flesh throb and redden beneath the kisses of another! Oh God! To love her foot, her arm, her shoulder, to dream of her blue veins and her brown skin, until you writhe for whole nights at a time on the stone floor of your cell, only to see all the caresses you have dreamt of for her end in torture! To have succeeded only in laying her down on the leather bed! Oh, those are the real pincers heated red-hot in hellfire! Oh, happy the man sawn between two planks, or quartered by four horses. Do you know the torture you can be made to endure, through long nights, by bubbling arteries, by a bursting heart, by a breaking head, by teeth that bite into your hands? Zealous tormentors turning you without respite, as if on a red-hot grill, on a thought of love, jealousy and despair! Have mercy, girl! A moment's truce! A few ashes on this glowing coal! I beg you to wipe away the sweat streaming in great drops down my brow! Torture me with one hand, child, but caress me with the other! Have pity, girl, oh have pity on me!'

The priest was rolling about on the flagstones in the water and hammering his skull against the corners of the stone steps. The girl listened and watched. When, exhausted and breathless, he became silent, she repeated softly: 'Oh my Phoebus!'

The priest dragged himself towards her on both knees.

'I implore you, if you have any compassion,' he cried, 'do not reject me! I love you! I am a wretch! When you say that name, unhappy girl, it is as if you were grinding all the fibres of my heart between your teeth! Mercy! If you come from hell, I will go there with you. All I have done was for that. The hell where you are is my paradise, the sight of you more delightful to me than that of God! Say, then, will you not have me? The day when a woman rejects such a love, I would have thought the mountains would move. Oh, if only you wanted! . . . How happy we could be! We should flee – I would make you flee – we should go somewhere, we should seek the place on earth where there is the most sunshine, the most trees, the most blue sky. We should love one another, we should pour out our two souls one into the other, we should feel an unquenchable thirst which together we should slake unceasingly from the inexhaustible cup of our love!'

She interrupted him with a terrible, shrill laugh. 'Look, father, you've got blood on your fingernails!'

For a moment or two the priest remained as if petrified, staring at his hand.

'Very well, yes!' he went on finally, with a strange gentleness, 'outrage me, mock me, crush me! But come, come! We must hurry. It's for tomorrow, I tell you. The gallows on the Grève, you realize? It's always ready. How horrible, to see you step into the tumbril! Oh, I beg you! Never have I felt how much I love you up till this moment. Oh, follow me! You will take your time loving me after I have saved you. You can hate me for as long as you like. But come. Tomorrow, tomorrow! The gallows, your execution! Oh, save yourself! Spare me!'

He took her arm, he was beside himself, he tried to drag her along.

She fixed her staring eyes on him.

'What has happened to my Phoebus?'

'Ah,' said the priest, letting go of her arm, 'you are without pity.'

'What's happened to my Phoebus?' she repeated coldly.

'He's dead!' cried the priest.

'Dead!' she said, still icy and unmoving. 'Then why do you talk to me of living?'

But he was not listening. 'Oh, yes,' he said, as if talking to himself, 'he must certainly be dead. The blade went in deep. I think I touched the heart with the tip. Oh, I was alive down to the very end of the dagger!'

The girl hurled herself at him like a raging tigress and pushed him on to the steps of the stairs with supernatural strength. 'Go, monster! Go, murderer! Leave me to die! May both our bloods mark your brow everlastingly! Be yours, priest? Never! Never! Nothing shall reunite us, not even hell! Go, you are accursed! Never!'

The priest had stumbled on the stairs. Silently, he disengaged his feet from the folds of his robe, picked up his lantern again and began slowly to mount the steps leading to the door; he reopened the door and went out.

Suddenly, the girl saw his face reappear, it wore a terrifying expression and he cried to her, in a voice croaking with rage and despair: 'He's dead, I tell you!'

She fell face downward on the ground; and now the only sound in the dungeon was the sigh of the dripping water as it ruffled the pool in the darkness.

FIVE
The Mother

THERE can be nothing in the world more pleasing, I imagine, than the thoughts awakened in a mother's breast by the sight of her baby's tiny shoe. Especially if it is its best shoe, for Sundays or baptism, embroidered even on the sole, a shoe in which the baby has yet to take a single step. So tiny and graceful is it, so impossible for it to walk, that for the mother it is as if she could see her baby. She smiles at it, she kisses it, she talks to it. She asks herself whether in fact it is possible for a foot to be so small; and should her baby not be there, the pretty shoe is enough to restore the soft and fragile creature to her sight. She imagines she can see him, she does see him, all of him, alive, joyful, with his delicate hands, his round face, his pure lips, the bluey white of his unclouded eyes. If it is wintertime, he is with her, he crawls on the carpet, he clambers laboriously up on a stool, and the mother trembles lest he go too near the fire. If it is summer, then he is crawling about the yard, or the garden, pulling up the grass between the paving-stones, staring innocently at the huge dogs and horses, unafraid, playing with the ornamental shells and the flowers, and causing the gardener to grumble when he finds sand in the flower-beds or earth on the paths. Around him everything is laughing, shining, playing like him, even the faint breeze and the ray of sunlight which frolic enviously in his stray curls. All this the mother sees in the shoe and it melts her heart, just as fire melts a taper.

But once the baby has been lost, all these images of joy, of fascination and tenderness, which cluster round the tiny shoe, become so many sources of horror. Now, the pretty, embroidered shoe is nothing more than an instrument of torture, eternally grinding the mother's heart. It is still the same fibre of it which vibrates, the deepest and most sensitive of all; but instead of being caressed by an angel, now it is plucked by a demon.

One morning, just as the May sun was rising into one of those dark blue skies against which Garofolo likes to set his Descents from the Cross, the recluse of the Tour-Roland heard the sound of wheels, horses and rattling chains from the Place de Grève. She paid it little heed but plaited her hair over her ears to shut it out and went back to contemplating, on her knees, the inanimate object she had been worshipping in this way for the past fifteen years. For her, as we have said, the tiny shoe was the entire universe. Her mind was locked inside it and would come out again only with death. The grim cavity of the Tour-Roland alone knew how many embittered imprecations, how many poignant laments, how many sobs and entreaties she had cast up at the heavens over this pretty, pink satin bauble. Never has more despair been expended on an object so dainty and so graceful.

That morning, she seemed to be venting her grief even more violently than usual, and could be heard from outside lamenting in a high, monotonous voice that wrung the heart:

'Oh, my daughter!' she was saying, 'my daughter! My poor dear little baby! So I shan't see you again. It's over, then! It still seems only yesterday it happened! Better not to have given her to me, God, just to take her back so soon. Do you not know that our babies come from our wombs and that a mother who has lost her baby no longer believes in God? Oh wretch that I am, for going out that day! Lord, Lord, never would you have taken her away like that, if you had seen me with her, as I warmed her, all smiles, by my fire, or as she laughed at me and took the breast, or as I made her little feet climb up my chest to my lips! Oh, if you had seen that, God, you would have had pity on my joy, you would not have taken away from me the one love that remained in my heart! Was I such a miserable creature then, Lord, that you could not have watched me before you condemned me? Alas and alas, here is the shoe; but where is the foot? Where is the rest? Where is my baby? My daughter, my daughter, what have they done with you? Lord, give her back to me. Fifteen years have I been scraping my knees praying to you, God, is that not enough? Give her back to me for a day, an hour, a minute, one minute, Lord! Then cast me to the demon for all eternity! Oh, if I knew where the hem of your robe was trailing I would cling to it with both hands, and you would have to give me back my baby! Do you feel no pity, Lord, for her pretty little shoe? Can you condemn a poor mother to fifteen years of such torment? Good Virgin, good Virgin in heaven, my child-Jesus was taken from me, they stole him, they ate him on a heath, they drank his blood, they chewed his bones! Good Virgin, have pity on me! My daughter, I need my daughter! What is it to me that she's in paradise? I don't want your angel, I want my baby. I am a lioness, I want my cub. Oh, I shall writhe on the ground, I shall smash the stone with my forehead, I shall damn myself, I shall curse you, Lord, if you keep my baby! You can see, Lord, that my arms are all bites! Will the good God not take pity? Oh, give me only salt and black bread, provided I have my daughter and she warms me like a sun! Alas, Lord God, I am only a vile sinner; but my daughter made me pious. I was full of religion through love of her: and I could see you through her smile as if heaven had opened. Oh, if only I could once, once more, just one more time, put this shoe on her pretty little pink foot, then I should die blessing you, good Virgin! Ah, fifteen years, she would be grown-up now! Unhappy child! It's quite true, then, I shan't see her again, not even in heaven! For I won't go there. Oh what misery, to think that all I have is her shoe!'

The unhappy woman had thrown herself on the shoe, her consolation and despair during all these years, and her inmost heart was wracked with sobbing as on the first day. For it is always the first day for a mother who has lost her baby. That is a sorrow that does not grow old. Her mourning-clothes may become threadbare and white: her heart remains black.

Just then, the fresh and joyful voices of children passed by her cell. Every time her eye or her ear fell on a child, the poor mother would rush into the darkest corner of her tomb and seemed to try and drive her head into the stone so as not to hear them. This time, on the contrary, she sat up as if with a start, and listened eagerly. One of the little boys had just said: 'It's because they're going to hang a gypsy today.'

With a sudden bound, like the spider we saw hurling itself on a fly at the trembling of its web, she ran to the window, which, as we know, looked out on the Place de Grève. A ladder had indeed been erected next to the permanent gallows, and the executioner was busy readjusting the chains, made rusty by the rain. A few of the people stood round.

The merry band of children was already in the distance. The sachette looked around for a passer-by to question. Right beside her cell, she noticed a priest pretending to read from the public breviary, but who was much less concerned with the 'trellised iron lectern' than with the gallows, at which from time to time he cast a gloomy and ferocious glance. She recognized the Archdeacon of Josas, a holy man.

'Who are they going to hang there, father?' she asked.

The priest looked at her without answering; she repeated her question. Then he said: 'I don't know.'

'There were some children here who said it was a gypsy,' the recluse went on.

'I believe it is,' said the priest.

Paquette la Chantefleurie then broke out into a hyena-like laugh.

'Do you really hate the gypsies then, sister?' said the archdeacon.

'Do I hate them?' cried the recluse. 'They are vampires, child stealers! They devoured my little daughter, my baby, my only child! I have no heart left. They ate her!'

She was a terrifying sight. The priest looked at her coldly.

'There's one in particular I hate, and who I've cursed,' she went on. 'She's a young one, the age my daughter would have been, if her mother hadn't eaten my daughter. Every time that young viper passes my cell, she curdles my blood!'

'Well, rejoice, sister,' said the priest, glacial as a statue on a tomb, 'she it is you will see die.'

His head fell forward on to his chest and he walked slowly off.

The recluse hugged herself in delight. 'I told her she'd go up there! Thank you, priest!' she cried.

And she began to pace up and down past the bars of her window, dishevelled, her eyes blazing, banging against the wall with her shoulders, with the air of some tawny she-wolf in a cage, which has long felt hungry but senses that feeding-time is near.

SIX
Three Men's Hearts Differently Formed

PHOEBUS, meanwhile, had not died. Men of his kind are not easily killed. When Maître Philippe Lheulier, Advocate Extraordinary to the King, told poor Esmeralda 'He's dying', he was either mistaken or in jest. When the archdeacon repeated to the condemned girl 'He's dead', the fact is he did not know, but believed he was dead, was banking on it, did not doubt it and certainly hoped he was. It would have been too much to bear to give the woman he loved good news of his rival. In his position, any man would have done the same.

Not that Phoebus's wound was not serious, but it was less serious than the archdeacon liked to think. The master-apothecary, to whose house the soldiers of the watch had carried him in the first instance, had feared for his life for a week and even told him so in Latin. Nevertheless, youth had regained the upper hand; and, as often happens, prognoses and diagnoses notwithstanding, nature had amused itself by saving the patient and spiting the doctor. It was while he still lay prostrate on the master-apothecary's pallet that he had undergone his first interrogations by Philippe Lheulier and the Official's investigators, which he found very irksome. And so, one fine morning, feeling better, he left the pharmacopolist his gold spurs by way of payment, and sneaked off. This, as it happens, in no way disturbed the preparation of the case. In those days, justice was little concerned with the accuracy or propriety of a criminal trial. Provided the accused was hanged, that was all it needed. Now the judges had sufficient proof against La Esmeralda. They thought Phoebus was dead, and everything had been said.

Phoebus, for his part, had not fled very far. He had simply gone to rejoin his company, in garrison at Queue-en-Brie, in the Ile-de-France, a few stages from Paris.

He had absolutely no wish after all to appear at the trial in person. He felt vaguely he would cut a ridiculous figure there. At bottom, he was none too sure what to make of the whole business. Like all soldiers who are nothing but soldiers, he was both irreligious and superstitious, and when he questioned himself about his adventure, he did not feel sure about the goat, about the weird way in which he had made La Esmeralda's acquaintance, about the no less strange way in which she had given him to understand her love, about her being a gypsy, and finally about the phantom monk. He saw much more magic than love in the affair, probably a witch, perhaps the devil; a drama in fact, or, to use the language of the time, a most unpleasant mystery play, in which he had taken the very clumsy role of the recipient of the blows and the ridicule. The captain felt decidedly sheepish. He experienced that sort of shame which La Fontaine has defined so admirably: 'Ashamed as a fox captured by a hen.'

He hoped, in any case, that the affair would not become public, and that if he were not present then his name would hardly arise or at least would not reverberate outside the judgement-chamber of the Tournelle. In this he was not mistaken; there was in those days no *Gazette des Tribunaux*, and since hardly a week went by without some forger being boiled alive, or a witch hanged, or a heretic burnt at one of Paris's innumerable 'justices', people were so accustomed to seeing the old feudal Themis, arms bared and sleeves rolled up, going about his business at the gibbets, ladders and pillories on every street-corner, that they took scant notice of him. The fashionable society of the time scarcely knew the name even of the victim passing by at the end of the street, and the populace alone regaled itself on this brutal fare. An execution was an habitual incident of the thoroughfares, like the baker's brazier or the butcher's slaughter-yard. The hangman was nothing more than a butcher of a rather darker hue than the others.

So Phoebus's mind was soon at rest on the enchantress Esmeralda, or Similar as he had it, on being stabbed by the gypsy or by the phantom monk (it mattered little which), and on the outcome of the trial. But as soon as his heart was vacant in that direction, the image of Fleur-de-Lys returned to it. Captain Phoebus's heart, like the physics of the time, abhorred a vacuum.

Queue-en-Brie, in any case, was a very dull posting, a village of blacksmiths and cow-girls with chapped hands, a long ribbon of tumbledown houses and thatched cottages lining the high-road on either side for half a league: a *queue*[1] in fact.

Fleur-de-Lys had been his last passion but one, a pretty girl and an attractive dowry; so one fine morning, completely cured, and assuming that after two months the affair of the gypsy must be well and truly dead and buried, the amorous cavalier swaggered up to the door of the Gondelaurier house.

He paid no attention to quite a large crowd that had assembled in the parvis square, in front of the portal of Notre-Dame; he remembered it was May, assumed a procession, some Whitsun or feast-day, tethered his horse to the ring in the porch and went gaily up to see his lovely fiancée.

She was alone with her mother.

Fleur-de-Lys was still troubled by the scene of the witch, her goat, and her accursed alphabet and by the long absences of Phoebus. However, when she saw her captain enter, she found him so imposing, with his brand-new acton, gleaming cross-belt and passionate expression, that she blushed with pleasure. The noble damsel was herself more charming than ever. She wore her magnificent blonde hair in ravishing plaits, she was dressed from head to foot in sky-blue, a colour so becoming to fair-haired girls, and a coquetry learnt from Colombe, while her eyes were suffused with that amorous languor which is more becoming still.

Phoebus, who had seen nothing by way of beauty since the drabs of Queue-en-Brie, was bowled over by Fleur-de-Lys, and this lent our officer a manner so zealous and gallant that his peace was made there and then. Madame de Gondelaurier herself, still sitting matron-like in her great armchair, did not have the strength to upbraid him. As for the reproaches of Fleur-de-Lys, they died away into affectionate murmurings.

The girl was sitting by the window, still embroidering her

1. 'Tail.'

Neptunus's grotto. The captain stood leaning on the back of her chair, and she addressed her fond scoldings to him in an undertone.

'What have you been doing these two whole months, you naughty man?'

'I swear you are so beautiful you would give an archbishop dreams,' answered Phoebus, somewhat embarrassed by the question.

She could not forbear smiling.

'All right, all right, monsieur. Forget about my beauty and answer me. A fine beauty indeed!'

'Well, dear cousin, I was recalled for garrison duty.'

'And where, please? And why did you not come to say goodbye to me first?'

Phoebus was delighted that the first question should have helped him to evade the second.

'In Queue-en-Brie.'

'But that's no distance, monsieur. Why have you not been to see me one single time?'

Phoebus was now in serious difficulties. 'The fact is ... on duty ... and then, charming cousin, I have been ill.'

'Ill?' she repeated, in alarm.

'Yes ... wounded.'

'Wounded!'

The poor child was quite overcome.

'Oh, don't be alarmed,' said Phoebus casually, 'it was nothing. A quarrel, a sword-wound; why should you worry?'

'Why should I worry?' cried Fleur-de-Lys and raised two beautiful eyes brimming with tears. 'Oh, you are not saying what you are thinking when you say that. What sword-wound? I want to hear all about it.'

'Well, my lovely, I fell out with Mahé Fédy, you know? The lieutenant from Saint-Germain-en-Laye, and we unstitched a few inches of one another's skin. That's all.'

The mendacious captain knew very well that an affair of honour always increases a woman's respect for a man. And in fact Fleur-de-Lys was staring straight at him, quivering with fear, pleasure and admiration. However, she was not altogether reassured.

'So long as you are completely cured, my Phoebus!' she said. 'I don't know your Mahé Fédy, but he's a horrid man. And what started the quarrel?'

At this Phoebus, whose imagination was not notably creative, began not to know how to extricate himself from his exploit.

'Oh, how should I know? . . . A trifle, a horse, a remark! . . . Fair cousin,' he cried in order to change the subject, 'what's all that noise in the parvis?'

He went to the window. 'Good heavens, fair cousin, look at all the people on the square!'

'I don't know,' said Fleur-de-Lys: 'it seems there's a witch who's going to make honourable amends this morning in front of the church and be hanged afterwards.'

The captain was so sure that the affair of La Esmeralda was finished that he was troubled hardly at all by Fleur-de-Lys's words. He did ask her one or two questions, however.

'What's the witch's name?'

'I don't know,' she replied.

'And what is she said to have done?'

Again she shrugged her white shoulders.

'I don't know.'

'Oh, dear God Jesus!' said her mother, 'there are so many sorcerers these days, I believe they burn them without finding out their names. As well try to find out the name of every cloud in the sky. After all, we need not worry. The good God keeps his own accounts.' At this point the venerable dame got up and came to the window. 'Lord, you're right, Phoebus!' she said. 'Such a mob of the people. God be blessed, they're on the roofs, even! Do you know, Phoebus, it reminds me of my heyday. The entry of King Charles VII, there were so many people then too. I no longer remember the year. When I talk to you about it, it strikes you as something old, doesn't it, and me as something young. Oh, it was a much finer crowd than nowadays. They were on the machicolations of the Porte Saint-Antoine even. The king had the queen in pillion, and behind their Highnesses all the ladies rode pillion behind all the lords. I remember how we laughed, because next to Amanyon de Garlande, who was very short in stature, there was Sir Matefalon, a knight of gigantic size who had killed heaps of Englishmen. It was very fine. All the gentlemen of France in procession with their fiery red oriflammes. There were those with pennons and those with banners. I don't know. Lord de Calan with a pennon; Jean de Châteaumorant with a banner; Lord de Coucy, with a banner, larger than any of the others, except for the Duke of Bourbon... Alas, how sad to think that it all existed once and now it's no more!'

The two lovers had not been listening to the worthy dowager. Phoebus had come and leant again on the back of his betrothed's chair, a delightful position from which his lascivious gaze could plunge down all the gaps in Fleur-de-Lys's collarette. Her gorget hung open so conveniently, allowing him to see a great many exquisite things and to guess at a great many more, that Phoebus was dazzled by the satin sheen of her skin and said to himself: 'How could one love anyone except a fair girl?' Both maintained their silence. Now and again, the girl raised her soft, ecstatic eyes to him, and their hair intermingled in a ray of spring sunshine.

'Phoebus,' said Fleur-de-Lys suddenly in a low voice, 'we are to be married in three months' time, swear to me you have never loved any other woman but me.'

'I swear it, my angel!' replied Phoebus, and the passionate look he gave her joined with his sincere tone to convince Fleur-de-Lys. He may even have believed it himself at that moment.

The good mother, meanwhile, delighted to see the betrothed couple on such excellent terms, had just left the apartment in order to attend to some domestic detail. Phoebus saw they were alone and this so emboldened the adventurous captain that some very peculiar notions rose into his brain. Fleur-de-Lys loved him, he was her betrothed, she was alone with him, his former liking for her had reawakened, in all its ardour if not all its freshness; after all, it is no great crime to eat a bit of your corn while it is still on the stalk; I do not know whether these thoughts really were passing through his mind, but what is certain is that Fleur-de-Lys suddenly took fright at the expression in his eyes. She looked about her and could no longer see her mother.

'Good heavens!' she said, red-faced and anxious, 'I'm very hot!'

'It's not far off the middle of the day, I think, in fact,' answered Phoebus. 'The sun is troublesome. We need only draw the curtains.'

'No, no,' cried the poor girl, 'on the contrary, I need air.'

And, like a hind that has heard the panting of the hounds, she got up, ran to the window, opened it and hastened on to the balcony.

Phoebus followed her, somewhat put out.

The balcony, as we know, overlooked the square of the Parvis Notre-Dame, which offered at that moment a strange and sinister spectacle that abruptly altered the nature of the timid Fleur-de-Lys's fear.

The square proper was choked by an immense crowd, which had flowed back up the adjoining streets. The little wall which surrounded the parvis at waist-height would not have been enough to keep it clear, had it not been duplicated by a dense hedge of serjeants of the *onze-vingts* and of hackbuteers, culverins in hand. Thanks to this thicket of pikes and arquebuses, the parvis was empty. The entrance to it was guarded by a mass of halberdiers, wearing the arms of the bishop. The great doors of the church were closed, unlike the innumerable windows in the square, which were open even up in the gables, to reveal thousands of heaped-up heads, not unlike the piles of cannon-balls in an artillery park.

The surface of the crowd was grubby, grey, ashen. The spectacle it was awaiting was clearly one of those which have the privilege of selecting and attracting the lowest elements of the population. Nothing could have been more hideous than the sound that came from those teeming yellow headdresses and filthy heads of hair. In this crowd, there was more laughter than shouting, and more women than men.

From time to time, a shrill, resonant voice would pierce the general uproar.

'Hey, there, Mahiet Baliffre! Are they going to hang her here?'

'Idiot! It's the honourable amends here, in a shift! The good God's going to cough Latin in her face! They always do it here, at noon. If it's the gallows you want, go to the Grève.'

'I shall go afterwards.'

'I say, La Boucandry, is it true she's refused a confessor?'

'It seems so, La Bechaigne.'

'Well I never, the heathen!'

'It's the custom, monsieur. The Bailiff of the Palais is responsible for handing over the malefactor once he's been sentenced, for the execution; if he's a layman, to the Provost of Paris; if he's a cleric, to the Official of the Bishopric.'

'Monsieur, I thank you.'

'Oh, good heavens, the poor creature!' said Fleur-de-Lys.

This thought filled the eyes she had been casting over the populace with sorrow. The captain, who was far more taken up with her than with the rabble below, was amorously rumpling her waistband from behind. She turned round, pleading and smiling: 'Please, leave me alone, Phoebus! If my mother came back she would see your hand!'

Just then, the clock of Notre-Dame slowly struck twelve. A murmur of satisfaction burst from the crowd. The last vibration of the twelfth stroke had hardly died away before white crests appeared on that sea of heads, as if whipped up by a gust of wind, and a great shout arose from pavement, windows and roofs: 'There she is!'

Fleur-de-Lys put her hands over her eyes so as not to see.

'Do you want to go back inside, my sweet?' said Phoebus.

'No,' she replied; and the eyes she had just closed out of fear she reopened out of curiosity.

A tumbril, drawn by a sturdy Norman shaft-horse and completely surrounded by horsemen in mauve uniforms with white crosses, had just emerged into the square from the Rue Saint-Pierre-aux-Bœufs. The serjeants of the watch struck out with their whips to make a passage for it through the crowd. Beside the tumbril rode legal and police officers, recognizable by their black costumes and their awkward seat. At their head paraded Maître Jacques Charmolue.

In the fatal wagon sat a young girl, her arms tied behind her back, without any priest at her side. She wore a shift, and her long black hair (the fashion in those days was to cut it only at the foot of the gallows) fell loose about her bosom and her half-uncovered shoulders.

Through its undulations, glossier than a raven's plumage, could be seen, twisting and clinging, a thick, gnarled, grey rope, which chafed the poor girl's fragile collar-bones and lay coiled around her charming neck like an earthworm round a flower. Beneath the rope there gleamed a small amulet, set with green glass beads, which she had been allowed to keep no doubt because those about to die are refused nothing. In the bottom of the tumbril, the onlookers at the windows could see her bare legs, which she was trying to conceal beneath her as if by some last feminine instinct. At her feet was a small, pinioned goat. Her shift was not done up and the condemned girl was trying to hold it up with her teeth. It was as if, despite her dereliction, it still pained her to be offered to the public gaze half-naked. But modesty, alas, was not meant for trembling such as hers.

'Jesus!' said Fleur-de-Lys quickly to the captain. 'Look, fair cousin, it's that horrid gypsy with the goat!'

So saying, she turned to Phoebus. His eyes were fixed on the tumbril. He was ashen-faced.

'What gypsy with the goat?' he stammered.

'What!' Fleur-de-Lys went on; 'don't you remember?'

Phoebus broke in: 'I don't know what you mean.'

He made as if to go back inside. But Fleur-de-Lys, her jealousy, so keenly aroused once before by this very gypsy, now reawakened, gave him a look full of penetration and mistrust. She vaguely remembered now having heard that a captain was mixed up in the affair of the gypsy.

'What's the matter?' she said to Phoebus. 'Anyone would think that woman has upset you.'

Phoebus gave a forced sneer.

'Me, not in the least! Well, yes!'

'Stay then,' she went on imperiously, 'and let's watch to the end.'

The hapless captain had no choice but to stay. He was somewhat reassured by the fact that the prisoner had not taken her eyes off the floor of the tumbril. It was only too obviously La Esmeralda. Even on this final rung of opprobrium and misfortune, she was still beautiful, her big black eyes were made to seem bigger still by the sunkenness of her cheeks, her livid profile was both pure and sublime. Before she had been like a Madonna by Raphael, now she was like a Madonna by Masaccio: frailer, thinner, more wasted.

So utterly broken had she been, moreover, by stupor and despair, there was nothing that was not, as it were, being tossed about, nothing, apart from her modesty, which she had not abandoned to chance. At each jolt of the tumbril her body bounced like some dead or broken object. Her stare was crazed and melancholy. A tear could still be seen in her eye, but motionless and as if frozen.

Meanwhile, the dismal cavalcade had passed through the crowd, amidst cries of delight and craning necks. Though, as a faithful historian, we have to say that some, even among the hardest, seeing her so beautiful and so downcast, were moved to pity. The tumbril had entered the parvis.

It halted before the central doorway. The escort lined up on either side. The crowd fell silent, and in the midst of a solemn and expectant hush, the two panels of the great door swung back, as if of their own accord, and their hinges squeaked with a sound like a fife. Now they could look down the full length of the church, sombre, draped with mourning, dimly lit by a few candles sparkling in the distance on the high altar, and opening like the mouth of a cave in the blinding light of the square. At the far end, in the shadows of the apse, they caught a glimpse of a gigantic silver cross, splayed against a black drape which stretched from the vaulting to the pavement. The nave was completely deserted. But the heads of one or two priests could just be discerned moving about in the distant choir-stalls, and as the great door opened a solemn and monotonous chanting sounded from the church, and cast lugubrious fragments of psalms at the condemned girl's head, as if in gusts.

'*Non timebo millia populi circumdantis me; exsurge, Domine; salvum me fac, Deus!*'[1]

'*Salvum me fac, Deus, quoniam intraverunt aquae usque ad animam meam.*

'*Infixus sum in limo profundi; et non est substantia.*'[2]

At the same time another voice, not a part of the chorus, was intoning this melancholy offertory from the steps of the high altar:

'*Qui verbum meum audit, et credit ei qui misit me, habet vitam aeternam et in judicium non venit; sed transit a morte in vitam.*'[3]

The chant, which a few old men, remote and unseen in their darkness, were singing over that lovely creature, full of youth and

1. 'I will not be afraid of ten thousands of people, that have set themselves against me round about. Arise O Lord; save me, O my God ...' (Psalms, III, 6–7).

2. 'Save me, O God; for the waters are come in unto my soul. I sink in deep mire, where there is no standing ...' (Psalms, LXIX, 1–2).

3. 'He that heareth my word, and believeth on him that sent me, hath everlasting life, and shall not come into condemnation; but is passed from death into life' (John, V, 24).

life, caressed by the warm spring air and inundated with sunlight, was the mass for the dead.

The people listened devoutly.

The poor girl was afraid, and her eyes and thoughts seemed lost in the darkened bowels of the church. Her bloodless lips moved as if in prayer, and when the executioner's attendant approached to help her down from the tumbril, he heard her softly repeating the word 'Phoebus'.

Her hands were untied and she was made to get down, accompanied by her goat, which had also been untied and bleated with joy at finding itself free, and then to walk barefoot across the hard pavement to the foot of the steps of the portal. The rope round her neck trailed behind her. It was like a serpent following her.

Then the chanting in the church broke off. A great gold cross and a file of tapers got under way in the shadows. The halberds of the gaudily dressed beadles rang out, and a few moments later a long procession of priests in chasubles and deacons in dalmatics came in view of the prisoner and of the crowd, and advanced towards her, solemnly intoning. But her gaze settled on the man walking at its head, immediately after the cross-bearer. 'Oh!' she whispered, with a shudder, 'it's him again. The priest!'

It was indeed the archdeacon. To his left he had the sub-cantor and to his right the cantor, armed with his rod of office. He advanced, head thrown back, eyes open and staring, chanting in a loud voice:

'*De ventre inferi clamavi, et exaudisti vocem meam,*

Et projecisti me in profundum in corde maris, et flumen circumdedit me.'[1]

When he emerged into the broad daylight under the tall, pointed archway, swathed in a huge silver cope with a black cross barring it, he looked so pale that more than one member of the crowd thought that one of the marble bishops had risen from his knees on a tombstone in the choir and come to receive the girl who was about to die on the threshold of the grave.

She was equally pale and statuesque and had hardly noticed when

1. 'Out of the belly of hell cried I, and thou heardest my voice. For thou hadst cast me into the deep, in the midst of the seas; and the floods compassed me about' (Jonah, II, 2–3).

they put a heavy lighted taper of yellow wax into her hand; nor had she listened to the clerk's braying voice as he read out the fateful tenor of the honourable amends; when told to answer '*Amen*', she had answered '*Amen*'. She only recovered some life and strength when she saw the priest signal to her guards to withdraw and come towards her on his own.

Then she felt her blood boil in her head, and a remnant of indignation rekindled in her already cold and numbed soul.

The archdeacon approached her slowly. Even in this extremity, she saw him cast an eye glittering with lust, jealousy and desire over her nakedness. Then he said to her loudly: 'Young girl, have you asked God's pardon for your faults and failings?' He leaned towards her ear and added (the onlookers thought he was receiving her last confession): 'Will you have me? I can still save you!'

She eyed him fixedly. 'Begone, demon, or I shall denounce you.'

He began to smile a horrible smile. 'You won't be believed. You will only be adding a scandal to a crime. Answer me quickly! Will you have me?'

'What have you done with my Phoebus?'

'He's dead,' said the priest.

At that moment, the wretched archdeacon raised his head automatically and saw, at the far end of the square, on the balcony of the Gondelaurier house, the captain, standing next to Fleur-de-Lys. He reeled back, passed a hand over his eyes, looked again, muttered a curse, and all his features contracted violently.

'Right, you shall die,' he said between his teeth. 'No one shall have you.'

Then he raised his hand over the gypsy and cried in a funereal voice: '*I nunc, anima anceps, et sit tibi Deus misericors!*'[1]

Such was the awful formula with which it was customary to conclude these grim ceremonies. It was the agreed signal from priest to executioner.

The people knelt.

'*Kyrie Eleison*,' said the priests who had remained underneath the archway of the portal.

'*Kyrie Eleison*,' the crowd repeated, and the sound passed over its surface like the poppling of a choppy sea.

1. 'Go now, uncertain soul, and may God have mercy on you.'

'*Amen*,' said the archdeacon.

He turned his back on the condemned girl, his head fell forward on to his chest, his arms were crossed and he rejoined his cortège of priests; a moment later, together with the cross, the tapers and the copes, they saw him vanish beneath the misty arches of the cathedral, and his echoing voice slowly died away into the choir, as he chanted the despairing verset: '*Omnes gurgites tui et fluctus tui super me transierunt!*'[1]

At the same time, the intermittent clanging of the iron-tipped shafts of the beadles' halberds gradually expired beneath the bays of the nave, as if they had been the hammer of a clock striking the condemned girl's last hour.

Meanwhile the doors of Notre-Dame remained open, revealing the empty, desolate church, in mourning, without either tapers or voices.

The girl remained where she was, without moving, waiting for them to dispose of her. One of the tipstaff serjeants had to arouse Maître Charmolue, who, throughout this scene, had been studying the bas-relief in the main portal which, according to some, shows the sacrifice of Abraham, or, according to others, the alchemists at work, the angel representing the sun, the faggots the fire and Abraham the artisan.

They had some difficulty tearing him away from this examination, but finally he turned around and at a signal from him two men dressed in yellow, the executioner's attendants, went up to the gypsy to retie her hands.

As she was climbing back into the fatal tumbril, to make her way to her last stopping-place, the poor girl was seized perhaps by some agonized longing for life. She raised her unweeping, bloodshot eyes to the heavens, to the sun, to the silver clouds, broken here and there by trapeziums and triangles of blue, then she lowered them round about her, on to the earth, the crowd, the houses ... Suddenly, as the man in yellow was tying her elbows, she let out a terrible cry, a cry of joy. On that balcony there, at the corner of the square, she had just caught sight of him, her friend, her lord, Phoebus, the other apparition of her life! The judge had lied! The priest had lied! It was him beyond any doubt, there he stood, handsome,

1. 'All thy billows and thy waves passed over me' (Jonah, II, 4).

alive, clad in his dazzling uniform, his plume on his head, his sword at his side.

'Phoebus!' she shouted, 'my Phoebus!'

And she tried to hold out to him two arms trembling with love and rapture, but they had been tied.

Then she saw the captain's brow darken and the beautiful girl on his arm look at him with curled lip and flashing eyes; Phoebus now spoke a few words which did not carry to her and the pair of them vanished hurriedly behind the latticed window of the balcony, which then closed again.

'Phoebus!' she cried, distraught, 'do you believe it?'

A monstrous thought had just occurred to her. She remembered that she had been condemned for murder on the person of Phoebus de Châteaupers.

She had endured everything up till now. But this final blow was too much for her. She fell senseless on to the pavement.

'Come on,' said Charmolue, 'put her in the cart, and let's get it over with!'

So far no one had noticed, in the gallery of royal statues, carved immediately above the ogees of the portal, a strange onlooker who had, up till now, been studying everything so impassively, his neck so outstretched and his face so deformed that, but for his half-red, half-mauve tunic, he might have been mistaken for one of the stone monsters through whose jaws the long gutters of the cathedral have been disgorging these past six hundred years. This onlooker had missed nothing of what had taken place since midday in front of the entrance to Notre-Dame. And no one had thought to watch him when, right at the outset, he attached a thick, knotted rope firmly to one of the colonnettes in the gallery, whose other end dangled down on to the entrance steps. After which, he settled calmly down to watch and to whistle now and again when a blackbird flew past. Suddenly, just as the executioner's assistants were getting ready to carry out Charmolue's phlegmatic order, he stepped over the balustrade of the gallery, and gripped the rope with feet, knees and hands; and then they saw him slip down the façade like a raindrop sliding down a window-pane, run towards the two executioners with the speed of a cat that has fallen off a roof, flatten them with two enormous fists, pick up the gypsy in one hand, like a child picking up a doll, and take a single leap back inside the church, raising the girl above his head and shouting in a formidable voice: 'Asylum!'

It happened so fast that, had it been nighttime, one might have seen everything in a single lightning-flash.

'Asylum! Asylum!' the crowd took up, and ten thousand clapping hands brought a gleam of joy and pride to Quasimodo's one eye.

The jolt brought the condemned girl to. She raised an eyelid, looked at Quasimodo, then abruptly lowered it again, as if appalled by her saviour.

Charmolue remained stunned, as did the executioners and the entire escort. Within the precincts of Notre-Dame, the condemned girl was indeed inviolable. The cathedral was a place of refuge. All human justice expired on its threshold.

Quasimodo had paused beneath the main doorway. His broad feet looked as solid on the pavement of the church as the heavy Romanesque piers. His huge shaggy head was sunk between his shoulders like a lion's, for lions too have a mane and no neck. He held the trembling girl in his horny hands like a white drapery; but so circumspectly did he carry her that he seemed afraid of breaking or sullying her. It was as if he sensed that this was something delicate, exquisite and precious, intended for other hands than his. There were moments when he seemed not to dare to touch her, even with his breath. Then, without warning, he would clutch her tightly in his arms, against his angular chest, as his property, his treasure, the way the child's mother might have done; his gnome's eye looked down at her, smothering her in tenderness, grief and compassion, then was suddenly raised again, flashing fire. And now the women laughed and wept, and the crowd stamped its enthusiasm, for at that moment Quasimodo was genuinely beautiful. He, the orphan, the foundling, the outcast, was beautiful, he felt august and strong, as he stood facing the society from which he had been banished and in which he had intervened so powerfully, facing that human justice which he had just robbed of its prey, all those tigers now forced to bite on air, the policemen, the judges, the executioners, the full might of the king which he, a nobody, had just smashed with the might of God.

That protection for a creature so unfortunate should have come from another creature so deformed, that a condemned girl should have been saved by Quasimodo, this too had its poignancy. The extremes of natural and social deprivation had met and were aiding one another.

Meanwhile, after a minute or two of triumph, Quasimodo had abruptly entered the church with his burden. The people, who loved an act of valour, looked for him in the gloom of the nave, sorry that he should have slipped away so soon from their applause. Suddenly they saw him reappear at one end of the gallery of the kings of France; he ran along it like a madman, his conquest upraised, shouting 'Asylum!' Again the crowd burst into applause. Having traversed the gallery, he plunged back inside the church. A moment later, he reappeared on the upper platform, the gypsy still in his arms, still running crazily, still shouting 'Asylum!' And the crowd applauded. Finally, he appeared for a third time on top of the great bell's tower; from there he seemed to show the girl whom he had rescued proudly to the whole town, and his thunderous voice, that voice that was so seldom heard and which he himself never heard, repeated three times, frenziedly, to the very clouds themselves: 'Asylum, asylum, asylum!'

'Nowel, nowel!' shouted the people for their part, and on the other bank of the river this deafening acclamation startled the crowd in the Grève; and the recluse, who was still waiting, her eye fixed on the gallows.

BOOK NINE

ONE
Fever

CLAUDE Frollo was no longer in Notre-Dame when his adoptive son so abruptly severed the fatal noose in which the archdeacon had ensnared the gypsy and been ensnared himself. Once back in the sacristy, he had snatched off his alb, his cope and his stole, thrown the lot of them into the hands of the amazed beadle, made his escape through the secret door in the cloister, ordered a boatman from the Terrain to row him across to the left bank of the Seine, and dived into the steep streets of the University, not knowing where he was going but encountering at every step bands of men and women hurrying happily towards the Pont Saint-Michel in the hope of 'still being in time' to see the witch hang, pale, distraught, and blinder, more nervous and more unsociable than a night-bird that has been released and then pursued by a gang of children in broad daylight. He no longer knew where he was, what his thoughts were, or whether he was dreaming. But he went on, at a walk or a run, taking streets at random without choosing them, urged onwards only by the Grève, the terrible Grève, which he felt confusedly to lie behind him.

In this way he skirted the hill of Sainte-Geneviève and finally left the town by the Porte Saint-Victor. He continued his flight for as long as he could see, when he looked back, the ring of towers of the University and the scattered houses of the suburb; but when, at last, a fold in the ground hid the loathsome Paris from him altogether, when he could feel it was a hundred leagues away, in the fields, in a desert, he stopped and seemed to breathe again.

And now dreadful thoughts crowded into his mind. He saw clearly into his soul once more, and shuddered. He thought of the unhappy girl who had destroyed him and whom he had destroyed. His haggard eye retraced the tortuous, double path their twin destinies had been made to follow by fatality, to that point of intersection where it had smashed them mercilessly one against the other. He reflected on the folly of eternal vows, on the futility of chastity, science, religion and virtue, on the uselessness of God. He revelled in these evil thoughts and as he plunged deeper and deeper heard a shout of satanic laughter burst from within him.

And as he thus probed his own soul and saw what a large place nature had prepared in it for passion, his laughter grew more bitter still. He turned over all the hatred and malice in the bottom of his heart and realized, with the detached eye of a doctor examining a patient, that this hatred and malice were nothing but a vitiated love; that love, the source of all virtue in man, could turn into something terrible in the heart of a priest, that when a man constituted as he was became a priest then he became a demon. He gave a ghastly laugh and went suddenly white again as he contemplated the most sinister aspect of his fatal passion, of that corrosive, venomous, hateful, implacable love which had merely led one of them to the gallows and the other to hell: she had been condemned, he damned.

Then his laughter returned as he reflected that Phoebus was alive, that in spite of everything the captain lived, was merry and contented, wore more handsome actons than ever and had a new mistress whom he had taken to see the old one hanged. He laughed more hollowly still at the thought that, of all the human beings whose death he had desired, the gypsy, the one creature whom he did not hate, was the only one whose death he had accomplished.

His thoughts then turned from the captain to the crowd and jealousy of an unheard-of kind came over him. He reflected that the crowd too, the whole of it, had set eyes on the woman he loved, almost naked, in her shift. He wrung his arms at the thought that this woman, a mere glimpse of whose form in the shadows would have been for him the supreme happiness, had been delivered up in broad daylight, at the very noonday, to an entire crowd, dressed as if for a night of love. He wept with rage at all the mysteries of love that had been forever profaned, sullied, denuded, blighted. He wept with rage as he imagined to himself how many unclean pairs of eyes had found satisfaction in that unfastened shift; and that this beautiful girl, this virgin lily, this chalice of modesty and delight which he would have trembled to raise to his lips, had just been transformed into a sort of public trough, where the lowest elements of Paris, thieves, beggars, lackeys, had come as one to taste a shameless, impure and depraved pleasure.

When he tried to form an idea of the happiness he might have found on earth if she had not been a gypsy and he a priest, if Phoebus had not existed and she had loved him; when he figured to himself that a life of love and serenity might have been possible for him too, that at that very moment there were, scattered over the earth, happy couples lost in long conversations under the orange-trees, beside streams, in the presence of a setting sun, or a starlit night; and that, if God had so willed, he and she might have been one such blessed couple, then his heart melted in tenderness and despair.

'It's her, oh, it's her!' was the idea that haunted him unceasingly, the idea which tormented him, which gnawed at his brain and tore at his entrails. He had no regrets, he did not repent; all he had done he would do again; he would rather she were in the hands of the executioner than on the arm of the captain, but he was in torment; such torment that now and again he snatched out handfuls of hair to see whether they might not have turned white.

There was one moment in particular when it crossed his mind that at that very minute perhaps the hideous chain he had seen that morning was drawing its iron noose tight around a neck so slender and graceful. This thought brought the sweat spurting from every pore.

There was another moment when, even as he laughed at himself satanically, he could see La Esmeralda simultaneously as he had seen her on that first day, quick, devil-may-care, joyous, in her finery, dancing, winged, harmonious, and La Esmeralda on her last day, in a shift, the rope around her neck, slowly climbing, in bare feet, the angular ladder of the gallows; so clear was this double image that he let out a terrible cry.

While this hurricane of despair was overturning, breaking, uprooting, bending, tearing everything in his soul, he looked around him at nature. At his feet, a few hens were pecking away in the bushes, enamelled beetles scurried about in the sun, overhead a few groups of dappled grey clouds scudded across a blue sky, on the horizon the spire of the Abbaye Saint-Victor cut the arc of the hillside with its slate obelisk, while the miller on the Butte Copeaux was whistling as he watched the sails of his mill industriously turning. All this active, organized, tranquil life, whose countless forms were reproduced around him, caused him pain. He resumed his flight.

Thus he sped across country until evening. His flight from nature, from life, from himself, from God, from everything, lasted all day. At times he would throw himself face downwards on the earth and uproot the young corn with his fingernails. At other times he paused in a deserted village street, and so unbearable were his thoughts that he took his head in both hands and tried to wrench it from his shoulders, so as to smash it on the paving-stones.

About the time when the sun was going down, he examined himself again and considered he was almost mad. The storm that had been raging in him since the moment when he had lost the hope and the will to save the gypsy had left not a single sound idea, not a single upright thought, in his consciousness. His reason lay prostrate, more or less wholly destroyed. He had only two distinct images in his mind: La Esmeralda and the gallows. The rest was blackness. These two juxtaposed images formed a terrible group, and the more he concentrated what was left of his mind and attention on them, the more he saw them grow, in a fantastic progression, the one in grace, charm, beauty and light, the other in horror; so that La Esmeralda finally appeared to him as a star, and the gallows as a huge, fleshless arm.

Remarkably enough, at no time during all this torment did the thought of death seriously cross his mind. Such was his miserable way. He clung to life. Perhaps he could really see hellfire behind him.

Meanwhile the daylight continued to fade. The living being who still existed within him thought confusedly of returning. He believed he was a long way from Paris; but as he took his bearings, he realized that all he had done was to follow the ring-wall of the University. The steeple of Saint-Sulpice and the three tall spires of Saint-Germain-des-Prés stuck up above the horizon to his right. He made towards them. When he heard the challenge of the abbot's men-at-arms round the crenellated circumvallation of Saint-Germain, he turned aside, and took a path that opened between the abbey mill and the leper-house of the burg, and after a few minutes he found himself on the edge of the Pré-aux-Clercs. This was a meadow famous for the disturbances that took place there by both day and night; it was the 'hydra' of the poor monks of Saint-Germain, '*quod monachis Sancti-Germani pratensis hydra fuit*, *clericis nova semper dissidiorum capita suscitantibus'*.[1] The archdeacon feared he might meet someone there; he was afraid of any human face; he had just avoided the University and the Bourg Saint-Germain, and he did not want to return to the streets until as late as possible. He skirted the Pré-aux-Clercs, took the deserted path that divided it from the Dieu-Neuf, and finally came to the edge of the water. There, Dom Claude found a boatman who, for a few *deniers parisis*, took him up the Seine as far as the tip of the Cité, and set him ashore on that abandoned tongue of land where the reader has already seen Gringoire dreaming, and which extended beyond the royal gardens, parallel with the island of the Passeur-aux-Vaches.

The monotonous rocking of the boat and the lapping of the water had to some extent numbed the unhappy Claude. Once the boatman had rowed off, he remained standing in a daze on the shore, looking ahead of him and seeing things only through oscillations which magnified everything and turned it into a sort of phantasmagoria. The fatigue of some great pain quite often produces these effects on the mind.

The sun had set behind the tall Tour de Nesle. It was the moment of twilight. The sky was white, the water of the river was white. The left bank of the Seine, on which his gaze was fixed, projected its dark mass between these two whitenesses and tapered away into the distance like a black arrow, until it was lost in the mists of the horizon. It was covered in houses, of which only the dark silhouettes could be seen, standing sharply out in black against the light background of the sky and the water. Here and there windows were beginning to twinkle like glowing embers. This huge black obelisk, isolated between the two white sheets of the sky and the river, which was very wide at this point, had a peculiar effect on Dom Claude, comparable to what a man might feel who lay flat on his back at the foot of the bell-tower of Strasbourg and looked at the enormous spire sticking up into the crepuscular gloom above his head. Only in this case it was Claude who was upright and the obelisk that was on its side; but because the river mirrored the sky, so extending the abyss underneath it, the huge promontory seemed to soar as boldly up into the void as any cathedral spire; the effect

1. 'Which meadow for the monks of Saint-Germain was a hydra, the clerks always introducing new topics for debate.'

was the same. What was strange and even more profound about this effect was that it was indeed the spire of Strasbourg, but the spire of Strasbourg two leagues high, something extraordinary, gigantic, disproportionate, an edifice such as no human eye has ever seen, a tower of Babel. The chimneys of the houses, the crenellations of the walls, the carved gables of the roofs, the spire of the Augustins, the Tour de Nesle, all the projections on the irregular profile of the colossal obelisk added to the illusion with the weird play of their jagged, dense and fantastic sculpture. Hallucinated as he was, Claude thought he was seeing, with his living eye, the bell-tower of hell; the innumerable lights scattered all the way up the awful tower looked to him like so many porches to the immense furnace within; the hum and the voices coming from it were so many shrieks and death-rattles. He took fright, he blocked his ears with his hands, turned his back so as not to see, and strode away from the terrible vision.

But the vision was inside him.

When he re-entered the streets, the passers-by, jostling in the dim light from the shop-fronts, appeared to him as spectres, eternally coming and going around him. There was a strange dinning in his ears. Extraordinary fantasies disturbed his mind. He did not see houses, or the pavement, or barrows, or men and women, but a chaos of indeterminate objects that fused together at the edges. At the corner of the Rue de la Barillerie stood a grocer's shop, the rim of whose canopy was, in accordance with the age-old custom, set with tin hoops from which hung a ring of wooden candles that knocked together in the wind with a sound like castanets. He thought he could hear a sheaf of skeletons banging together in the shadows of Montfaucon.

'Oh!' he muttered, 'the night-wind is driving them against each other, and merging the sound of their chains with the sound of their bones! Perhaps she's there amongst them!'

He was distraught and did not know where he was going. A few yards more and he found himself on the Pont Saint-Michel. There was a light in a ground-floor window. He went up to it. Through a cracked pane of glass, he could see a sordid room, which awoke some vague memory in his mind. Inside the room, poorly lit by a feeble lamp, a fresh, cheerful-looking, fair-haired young man had his arms round a very brazenly bedecked girl, and was laughing uproariously. Beside the lamp, an old woman sat spinning, and singing in a quavering voice. Since the young man did not laugh continuously, the priest caught snatches of the old woman's song. It was something unintelligible and awful.

Grève roar, Grève grin
Spin, my distaff, spin
Spin the hangman his cord
While he strolls the prison yard
Grève roar, Grève grin.

The fine cord of tow!
It's hemp they should sow
Not corn in the fields.
The thief never steals
The fine cord of tow.

Grève grin, Grève roar!
If you'd see the whore
Hang from the rheumy gallows,
For eyes you've your windows.
Grève grin, Grève roar!

Whereat the young man laughed and fondled the girl. The old woman was La Falourdel; the girl was a common prostitute; the man was his young brother Jehan.

He continued to watch. As well this spectacle as any other.

He saw Jehan go to a window at the end of the room, open it, look out on to the quay, where hundreds of lighted casements shone in the distance, and heard him say as he closed the window again: 'Upon my soul, it's getting dark. The townsfolk are lighting their candles and the good God his stars.'

Then Jehan came back towards the ribald and smashed a bottle standing on the table, exclaiming:

'Empty already, *corbœuf*! And I've no money left! Isabeau, my sweet, I shan't be pleased with Jupiter till he's turned your two white titties into two black bottles, where I can suck Beaune wine all day and night.'

The girl laughed at this good joke and Jehan went out.

Dom Claude only just had time to throw himself to the ground, so as not to come face to face with his brother and be recognized.

Luckily, the street was unlit and the student drunk. But he noticed the archdeacon lying on the roadway in the filth.

'Ha, ha!' he said, 'here's someone who's been enjoying himself today.'

He prodded him with his foot and Dom Claude held his breath.

'Dead drunk,' Jehan went on. 'Come on, he's full. A genuine leech pulled off a barrel. He's bald,' he added as he bent down; 'it's an old man! *Fortunate senex!*'[1]

Then Dom Claude heard him walking away, saying, 'Why worry, reason is a fine thing and my brother the archdeacon is very lucky to be wise and to have money.'

The archdeacon then got up and ran in a single breath to Notre-Dame, whose huge towers he could see looming up in the darkness above the houses.

When he arrived, gasping for breath, on the parvis square, he recoiled and did not dare look up at the fateful building. 'Oh!' he said in a low voice, 'is it really true then that such a thing took place here, today, this very morning!'

He ventured a look at the church, however. The façade was in shadow. The sky behind was bright with stars. The crescent of the moon, which had just taken flight from the horizon, was poised at that moment on the summit of the right-hand tower, seemingly perched there, like a luminous bird, on the edge of the balustrade with its jagged black trefoils.

The door into the cloister was locked. But the archdeacon was still carrying the key to the tower where his laboratory was. He used it to let himself into the church.

Inside, it was as dark and silent as a cave. From the tall shadows which hung on every side in broad folds, he could tell that the hangings from that morning's ceremony had not yet been removed. In the depths of the darkness there twinkled the great cross of silver, scattered with a few points of light, like the Milky Way of this sepulchral night. Above the black drapes the tips of the tall lancet windows of the choir showed and a ray of moonlight, passing through the stained glass, lent it the doubtful colours of the night, a sort of violet, whitish blue, of a shade to be found only on the face of a corpse. Seeing the pallid tips of the arches all around the choir, the archdeacon thought he was looking at the mitres of damned

1. 'O fortunate old man.'

bishops. He closed his eyes and when he reopened them he thought it was a ring of pale faces, staring at him.

He began to run through the church. Then it seemed to him that the church too was rocking, was moving, was animate and alive, that each great pier had become an enormous hoof, pawing the ground with its great stone spatula, that the gigantic cathedral was nothing but a kind of prodigious elephant, breathing and walking, with pillars for its feet, the two towers for trunks and the immense black hangings for a housing.

To such a pitch had the unfortunate man's fever or madness now arrived, that the external world was nothing but a sort of visible, palpable, terrifying apocalypse.

For a moment, he found relief. As he penetrated beneath the side-aisles he noticed, behind a clump of pillars, a reddish glow. He ran to it as if to a star. It was the feeble lamp which burned day and night by the public breviary of Notre-Dame under its wire grating. He threw himself eagerly on the holy book, in the hopes of finding some consolation or encouragement in it. The book was open at this passage from Job, which he perused with staring eyes: 'Then a spirit passed before my face, and I heard a little breath, and the hair of my flesh stood up.'[1]

At which dismal words, he felt what the blind man feels when he pricks himself on the stick he has picked up. His knees gave way beneath him and he collapsed on to the pavement, his mind on the girl who had died during that day. He felt so many monstrous fumes pass and overflow into his brain that his head seemed to have become one of the chimneys of hell.

He seemingly remained in this posture for a long time, no longer thinking, crushed and passive under the hand of the demon. Finally, a little strength returned to him and it occurred to him to go and take refuge beside his faithful Quasimodo in the tower. He stood up, and being afraid, took the lamp from the breviary to light his way. This was sacrilege; but he could no longer concern himself with such trifles.

He slowly mounted the staircase in the towers, full of a secret terror which must have been communicated to the rare passers-by

1. The first and third clauses of this quotation are Job, IV, 15; the second clause is, so far as the Authorized Version is concerned, an interpolation.

on the parvis by the mysterious light of his lamp, rising loophole by loophole up the bell-tower so late at night.

Suddenly he felt some freshness on his face and found he was below the door on to the topmost gallery. The air was cold; great white billows of cloud were sweeping across the sky and crumpling at the corners as they overflowed one into the other; they looked like winter drift-ice breaking up in a river. The moon's crescent was stranded in the midst of the clouds, as if it were some celestial ship trapped between these ice-floes of the air.

He dropped his eyes to contemplate for a moment, in the distance, between the railing of colonnettes which links the two towers, and through a gauze of mist and smoke, the silent crowd of the rooftops of Paris, as pointed, innumerable, small and close-packed as the ripples of a calm sea on a summer's night.

Both earth and sky wore an ashen hue from the feeble light of the moon.

Just then the clock raised its thin, cracked voice. Midnight struck. The priest remembered midday. It was twelve o'clock again. 'Ah, she must be cold by now!' he told himself under his breath.

A gust of wind suddenly extinguished his lamp and at almost the same moment he saw a shadow appear, a whiteness, a shape, a woman, at the opposite corner of the tower. He shivered. At the woman's side was a little goat, adding its own bleating to the final bleat of the clock.

He found the strength to look. It was her.

She was pale and sombre. Her hair lay round her shoulders as in the morning. But there was no longer any rope around her neck, no longer were her hands tied. She was free, she was dead.

She was dressed in white and had a white veil on her head.

She came slowly towards him, looking at the sky. The supernatural goat followed her. He felt of stone, too heavy to escape. At each step she took forwards, he took a step back, that was all. In this way, he returned beneath the unlit vault of the staircase. His blood ran cold at the thought that she too perhaps would enter there; had she done so, he would have died of terror.

In fact, she arrived in front of the door into the staircase, paused there for a moment or two, peered into the shadows, apparently without seeing the priest, and passed on. She seemed taller than she had been in life; he could see the moon through her white robe; he could hear her breathing.

Once she had gone past, he started to descend the stairs once again, as slowly as he had seen the spectre go, believing himself to be a spectre, haggard, his hair on end, still holding his extinguished lamp; and as he went down the spiral stairs, he distinctly heard a voice in his ear, laughing and repeating: '. . . A spirit passed before my face, and I heard a little breath, and the hair of my flesh stood up.'

TWO
Hunchbacked, One-eyed, Lame

EVERY town in the Middle Ages and, up until Louis XII, every town in France, had its places of asylum. Amidst the deluge of penal laws and barbaric jurisdictions which inundated the city, these places of asylum were a sort of island standing up above the surface of human justice. Any criminal who landed on one was safe. In a suburb, there were almost as many places of asylum as of execution. The abuse of impunity went hand in hand with the abuse of punishment, two evils attempting to rectify one another. Above all, royal palaces, the hôtels of princes and churches had the right of asylum. Sometimes an entire town was made into a temporary place of asylum when it needed repopulating. Louis XI made Paris an asylum in 1467.

Once he had set foot in an asylum, the criminal was sacred; but he had to be careful not to leave it. Take one step outside his sanctuary and he fell back again into the waters. The wheel, the gibbet and the strappado kept careful watch around the place of refuge, constantly on the look-out for their prey, like sharks around a ship. Thus, it had been known for condemned prisoners to grow white-haired in a cloister, on the staircase of a palace, in the tilled fields of an abbey, under the porch of a church; in its way, the asylum was just as much a prison as the other. It sometimes happened that a solemn decree of parliament violated the refuge and handed the prisoner back to the hangman; but this was rare. The parliaments were chary of the bishops, and when these two robes came into conflict, the simarre stood little chance against the cassock. Occasionally however, as in the case of the murderers of Petit-Jean, the Paris hangman, or that of Émery Rousseau, the murderer of Jean Valleret, justice overruled the Church and proceeded to carry out its sentence; but, short of a parliamentary decree, woe to the man who went armed into a place of asylum! We know the manner of death of Robert de Clermont, Marshal of France, and Jean de Châlons, Marshal of Champagne;[1] yet the man they had hanged was one Perrin Marc, a money-changer's errand-boy and a despicable murderer; but the two marshals had forced the doors of the church of Saint-Méry; that was the enormity.

Such was the respect surrounding these asylums that, according to tradition, it sometimes even affected animals. Aymoin tells of a stag, pursued by Dagobert, which took refuge beside the tomb of Saint Denys; the hounds stood and bayed.

Churches generally kept a small cell ready to receive supplicants. In 1407, Nicolas Flamel made them build, above the vaulting of Saint-Jacques-de-la-Boucherie, a room which cost him four *livres*, six *sols*, sixteen *deniers parisis*.

At Notre-Dame, a cell had been created over the lofts of the side-aisle underneath the flying buttresses and facing the cloister, at the precise spot where the wife of the present concierge of the towers has made herself a garden which, compared to the hanging gardens of Babylon, is like a lettuce compared to a palm-tree, or a porter's wife compared to Semiramis.

Here it was, after his frenzied and triumphal dash over the towers and galleries, that Quasimodo had put Esmeralda down. While he had been running with her, the girl had not been able to collect her wits; half dozing, half waking, she had felt nothing except that she was rising into the air, was floating there, was flying, that something had raised her above the earth. Now and again she heard Quasimodo's echoing laugh and loud voice in her ear; she half-opened her eyes; then, beneath her, she could vaguely see Paris, inlaid with its countless roofs of slates and tiles, like a blue and red mosaic, and above her head the joyous and terrifying face of Quasimodo. Then her eyelids closed again; she thought that it was all over, that she had been executed while she was in a faint, and that the misshapen spirit that had presided over her destiny had recaptured her and was

1. They were put to death in 1358, but not, strictly speaking, for violation of an asylum.

bearing her off. She did not dare look at him, she let herself go limp.

But once the panting and dishevelled bell-ringer had put her down in the cell of asylum, once she felt his huge hands gently untying the rope that had been bruising her arms, she felt the sort of jolt that brings the passengers on a ship starting awake when it grounds in the middle of a moonless night. Her thoughts awoke too, and came back to her one by one. She saw that she was in Notre-Dame, she remembered having been snatched out of the hangman's hands, that Phoebus was alive, that Phoebus no longer loved her; these two thoughts, one of which cast so much bitterness over the other, occurring together to the poor condemned girl, she turned to Quasimodo, who was standing in front of her and who frightened her. She said to him: 'Why did you rescue me?'

He looked at her anxiously as if trying to guess what she had said to him. She repeated her question. He then threw her a profoundly unhappy glance and fled.

She remained astonished.

A moment or two later he reappeared, carrying a package which he threw at her feet. It was clothing left for her by some charitable ladies in the doorway of the church. She then looked down at herself, saw she was nearly naked and blushed. Life was returning.

Quasimodo seemed to share some of this modesty. He veiled his eyes behind a large hand and once more walked away, though slowly.

She lost no time getting dressed. It was a white robe with a white veil. A novice's habit from the Hôtel-Dieu.

Hardly had she finished before she saw Quasimodo returning. He was carrying a basket under one arm and a mattress under the other. In the basket were a bottle, a loaf and a few provisions. He put the basket down on the ground and said: 'Eat.' He spread the mattress out on the flagstones and said: 'Sleep.' It was his own meal, and his own bed that the bell-ringer had been to fetch.

The gypsy raised her eyes to him in order to thank him; but no words would come. The poor devil was a truly horrible sight. She lowered her head with a frightened shudder.

Then he said to her: 'I frighten you. I'm very ugly, aren't I? Don't look at me. Only listen to me. During the day you must stay here; at night, you can go all over the church. But don't leave the church by night or by day. You would be doomed. They would kill you and I should die.'

Touched, she raised her head to answer him. He had vanished. She found herself alone again, pondering the strange words of this almost monstrous being, and struck by the sound of his voice, so harsh and yet so gentle.

Next, she examined her cell. It was a room some six feet square, with a little window and a door on to the gently sloping roof of flat stones. Several gargoyles with animal faces seemed to lean out around her, craning their necks to see her through the window. At the edge of her roof, she could see the tops of innumerable chimneys from which, as she watched, rose the smoke from all the fires of Paris. A sad spectacle for the poor gypsy, a foundling, under sentence of death, an unhappy creature, without homeland, family or hearth.

As she was thus being made aware, more poignantly than ever, of her isolation, she felt a shaggy, bearded head slip into her hands, on her knees. She gave a shudder (everything frightened her now) and looked. It was her poor goat, the agile Djali, who had escaped after her, at the moment when Quasimodo was routing Charmolue's brigade, and had been rubbing itself against her feet for nearly an hour now without managing to obtain a single glance. The gypsy smothered her in kisses. 'Oh, Djali,' she said, 'and I had forgotten you! You still think of me then! Oh, you at least aren't ungrateful!' At the same time, as if an invisible hand had removed the weight that had for so long been compressing the tears in her heart, she began to cry; and as her tears flowed, she felt all that was harshest and most bitter in her sorrow go with them.

When evening came, she found the night so beautiful and the moonlight so sweet, that she walked round the raised gallery that encircles the church. So calm did the earth seem, seen from this height, that she felt a certain solace.

THREE
Deaf

WHEN she awoke the next morning, she realized she had been asleep. She was astonished by this remarkable event. She had long grown unaccustomed to sleeping. A joyful ray from the rising sun came through her window and struck her face. At the same time as the sun, she saw something at the window which terrified her, the unhappy face of Quasimodo. Involuntarily, she closed her eyes again, but in vain; she still fancied she could see that gnome's mask, with its one eye and its broken teeth, through her pink eyelids. Then, still keeping her eyes shut, she heard a rough voice say to her very gently: 'Don't be afraid. I'm your friend. I came to watch you sleeping. It doesn't harm you, does it, if I come and watch you sleeping? What does it matter to you that I should be there when you've got your eyes shut? Now I shall go away. Look, I've put myself behind the wall. You can open your eyes again.'

Even more plaintive than the words themselves was the tone they were uttered in. The gypsy was moved and opened her eyes. He was in fact no longer at the window. She went to the window and saw the poor hunchback huddled in a corner by the wall, in an attitude of sorrow and resignation. She tried hard to overcome the feeling of repugnance he inspired in her. 'Come,' she said to him gently. When he saw the gypsy's lips move, Quasimodo thought she was driving him away; so he got up and limped slowly off, head bowed, not daring even to raise his despairing eyes to the girl. 'Come, then,' she cried. But he continued to withdraw. Then she dashed from her cell, ran to him and took him by the arm. Feeling himself touched by her, Quasimodo trembled in every limb. He raised his pleading eye, and finding that she was leading him back beside her, his whole face radiated joy and tenderness. She tried to make him come into her cell, but he insisted on remaining in the doorway. 'No, no,' he said, 'the owl doesn't go into the lark's nest.'

Then she squatted prettily down on her bed with her sleeping goat at her feet. The two of them remained for a few moments without moving, in silent consideration, he of so much grace, she of so much ugliness. She discovered some fresh deformity in Quasimodo every second. Her eyes travelled from his knock knees to his humped back, from his humped back to his one eye. She could not understand how so clumsily moulded a creature could exist. Yet he was imbued with such sadness and gentleness that she was beginning to accept him.

He was the first to break the silence. 'You were telling me to come back, then?'

She nodded her head and said: 'Yes.'

He understood her nod. 'Alas!' he said, as if doubtful whether to finish, 'it's because . . . I'm deaf.'

'Poor man!' exclaimed the gypsy, with an expression of kindly compassion.

He began to smile ruefully. 'You think that's the last straw, don't you? Yes, I'm deaf. That's the way I'm made. It's truly horrible, isn't it? While you are so beautiful!'

So profound a sense of his own wretchedness was there in the poor man's voice that she lacked the strength to say a single word. In any case, he would not have heard it. He continued.

'Never have I seen my ugliness as I do now. When I compare myself to you, I feel very sorry for myself, poor unhappy monster that I am! To you I must seem like an animal . . . But you, you are a ray of sunshine, a drop of dew, the song of a bird! While I am something frightful, neither man nor animal, but something else, harder, more downtrodden, more misshapen than a stone!'

And now he began to laugh, and his laugh was the most heart-rending sound you ever heard. He went on:

'Yes, I'm deaf. But you can talk to me in gestures, in signs. I have a master who talks with me like that. Anyway, I shall soon know what you want from the movement of your lips, from your eyes.'

'All right!' she went on, with a smile, 'tell me why you rescued me.'

He watched her closely as she was speaking.

'I've understood,' he answered. 'You're asking me why I rescued you. You have forgotten a poor devil who attempted to abduct you one night, a poor devil to whom the very next day you brought succour on their infamous pillory. A drop of water and a little compassion, I would pay for less than that with my life. You forgot that poor devil, but he remembered.'

She listened to him, deeply moved. A tear had formed in the bell-ringer's eye but it did not fall. He seemed to make it a sort of point of honour to choke it back.

'Listen,' he went on, once he was no longer afraid the tear might escape, 'we have got very high towers here, a man who fell from them would be dead before he struck the pavement; when you want me to fall, you won't have to say a single word, a look will do.'

Then he stood up. However unhappy the gypsy may have felt,

this strange creature still aroused her compassion. She gestured him to stay.

'No, no,' he said. 'I mustn't stay too long. I feel uncomfortable when you look at me. It's out of pity that you don't look away. I shall go somewhere from where I can see you without you seeing me. That will be better.'

He pulled a small metal whistle from his pocket. 'Take it,' he said. 'When you need me, when you want me to come, when you won't feel too horrified by the sight of me, you must blow into this. That is a sound I can hear.'

He put the whistle down on the ground and fled.

FOUR
Earthenware and Crystal

DAY followed day.

Calm had gradually returned to La Esmeralda's soul. An excess of sorrow, like an excess of joy, is a violent and a shortlived thing. The human heart cannot remain for long in an extremity. So much had the gypsy suffered that all that was left was astonishment.

Hope had returned now that she was safe. She was outside society and outside life, but she sensed vaguely that it would not perhaps be impossible to re-enter them. She was like a dead person holding in reserve a key to her tomb.

Little by little, she felt the terrible images that had haunted her for so long leaving her. All those hideous phantoms, Pierrat Torterue, Jacques Charmolue, faded from her mind, all of them, even the priest.

And then, Phoebus was alive, of that she was sure, she had seen him. Phoebus's life was everything. After the series of fatal tremors that had brought everything in her crashing down, she had found only one thing still standing in her soul, only one feeling, her love for the captain. For love is like a tree, it grows of its own accord, it puts down deep roots into our whole being, and often continues to put out leaves over a heart in ruins.

And what is inexplicable is that the blinder the passion, the more tenacious it is. It is never more solid than when it is unreasonable.

No doubt La Esmeralda felt some bitterness towards the captain. No doubt it was terrible that he too should have been deceived, that he should have believed that impossible thing, and thought the dagger-thrust to have come from her, who would have given a thousand lives for him. But she must not hold it against him: had she not confessed *her crime?* Was she not a weak woman who had succumbed to torture? The blame was hers alone. She ought to have let them wrench out her fingernails rather than the words she had spoken. And if she were to see Phoebus again, just once, for only a minute, a single word, a single glance would suffice to undeceive him, to win him back. Of that she was in no doubt. She thought dazedly of many other odd circumstances too, Phoebus's chancing to be present on the day of her honourable amends, and the girl he had been with. No doubt it was his sister. An unreasonable explanation, but one that satisfied her, for she needed to believe that Phoebus still loved her and loved no one but her. Had he not sworn as much? What more did she need, naïve and credulous as she was? Moreover, were appearances, in this affair, not much more against her than against him? So she waited. She hoped.

We should add that the church, that vast church which enfolded her on every side, which guarded her and had saved her, was itself a sovereign calmative. The solemn lines of its architecture, the attitude of devotion of all the objects that surrounded her, the godly and untroubled thoughts exuded, as it were, by every pore of its stonework, worked on her unconsciously. The edifice had sounds too of such blessedness and majesty that they pacified that ailing soul. The monotonous chanting of the officiants, the responses of the congregation to the priests, now inarticulate, now thunderous, the harmonious trembling of the stained-glass, the organ blaring out like a hundred trumpets, the three bell-towers humming like the hives of huge bees, this whole orchestra, above which there leapt, constantly rising and falling between the congregation and the bell-towers, a gigantic musical scale, deadened her memory, her imagination, her pain. The bells above soothed her. It was as if those enormous instruments poured wave after wave of a powerful magnetism over her.

And so each sunrise found her more at peace, breathing more freely, less pale. As her inner wounds healed, her grace and her beauty flowered once again on her face, only more composed now and more sedate. Her former character returned too, and even something of her gaiety, her pretty pout, her love for her goat, her taste for singing, her modesty. She took care in the mornings to get dressed in the corner of her little room, lest some inhabitant of the neighbouring attics should see her through the window.

Whenever the thought of Phoebus left her the time, the gypsy's mind sometimes turned to Quasimodo. He was the one link, the one connection, the one communication left to her with mankind, with the living. Unhappy girl, she was more of an outcast than Quasimodo! She understood nothing of the strange friend chance had given her. Often she reproached herself for not feeling a gratitude that would close her eyes to him, but she simply could not accustom herself to the poor bell-ringer. He was too ugly.

She had left the whistle he had given her on the ground. This did not stop Quasimodo reappearing from time to time in the early days. She did her utmost not to avert her eyes with too much repugnance whenever he brought her the basket of provisions or the pitcher of water, but he always noticed any least movement of the kind and then he would walk sadly away.

Once he appeared as she was stroking Djali. He remained pensive for a moment or two before the graceful tableau of the gypsy and the goat. Finally he said, shaking his heavy, ill-formed head: 'My misfortune is that I still look too much like a man. I wish I were all animal, like that goat.'

She looked up at him in astonishment.

He answered her look: 'Oh, I know very well why!' And went away.

On another occasion, he appeared at the door of the cell (where he never entered) just as La Esmeralda was singing an old Spanish ballad, whose words she did not understand, but which had remained in her ear because the gypsy women had lulled her to sleep with it as a little child. At the sight of that villainous face suddenly appearing in the midst of her song, the girl broke off with an involuntary movement of fright. The poor bell-ringer fell to his knees in the doorway and clasped his huge shapeless hands beseechingly. 'Oh!' he said sadly, 'I beg you, go on and don't drive me away.' She did not want to hurt him, and, trembling all over, she resumed her romance. But by degrees her fear was dispelled and she gave herself up completely to the impression of the languid and melancholy melody she was singing. He remained kneeling, his hands clasped, as if in prayer, intent, scarcely breathing, his gaze fixed on the gypsy's shining pupils. He seemed to hear her song in her eyes.

On yet another occasion, he came to her looking shy and awkward. 'Listen to me,' he said with an effort, 'I have something to say to you.' She indicated to him that she was listening. He then began to sigh, parted his lips, seemed about to speak for a moment, then looked at her, shook his head and, to the gypsy's amazement, slowly backed away, his forehead in his hand.

Among the grotesque figures carved in the wall, there was one to which he seemed especially attached and with which he often seemed to exchange a fraternal look. Once the gypsy heard him saying to it: 'Oh, why am I not of stone like you!'

At length, one day, one morning, La Esmeralda had advanced to the edge of the roof and was gazing down into the square over the pointed roof of Saint-Jean-le-Rond. Quasimodo was there, behind her. He would stand thus of his own accord, so as to spare the girl as far as possible from the unpleasantness of looking at him. All of a sudden, the gypsy trembled, a tear and a flash of joy shone simultaneously in her eye, she knelt at the edge of the roof and held out her arms in anguish towards the square, crying: 'Phoebus! Come, come! A word, one single word, in heaven's name! Phoebus! Phoebus!' Her voice, her face, her gesture, her whole person bore the heartrending expression of a shipwrecked sailor making a distress signal to the ship sailing gaily past in a ray of sunlight on the distant horizon.

Quasimodo leant out over the square and saw that the object of this tender, frenzied entreaty was a young man, a captain, a handsome cavalier, agleam with armour and with braid, prancing about on his horse at the far end of the square and saluting with his plumes a beautiful lady smiling on her balcony. However, the officer had not heard the poor girl's appeal. He was too far away.

But poor deaf Quasimodo had heard. His breast heaved a deep sigh. He turned round. His heart was swollen with all the tears he had choked back; his two fists struck convulsively against his head and when he removed them he had a handful of red hair in either hand.

The gypsy had no eyes for him. He said, quietly, grinding his teeth: 'Damnation! That's the way you need to be! You need only be handsome on the outside!'

She meanwhile was still kneeling and cried in extreme agitation: 'Oh, there, he's getting off his horse! He's going to go into that house! Phoebus! He can't hear me! Phoebus! That woman is wicked talking to him at the same time as me! Phoebus! Phoebus!'

Quasimodo looked at her. He had followed her pantomime. The poor bell-ringer's eye had filled with tears but not one did he allow to flow. Suddenly he tugged her gently by the hem of her sleeve. She turned round. He had taken on a look of calm. He said to her: 'Do you want me to go and fetch him for you?'

She let out a cry of joy. 'Oh, go on, go on, run, quickly! The captain, the captain! Bring him to me! I shall love you!' She embraced his knees. He could not prevent himself shaking his head in sorrow. 'I shall bring him to you,' he said in a faint voice. Then he turned his head and strode hurriedly off under the staircase, choked by sobs.

When he reached the square, all he could see was the handsome horse tethered at the door of the Gondelaurier house. The captain had just gone in.

He looked up towards the roof of the church. La Esmeralda still stood in the same spot and in the same position. He shook his head sadly at her. Then he leant against one of the stone posts of the Gondelauriers' porch, resolved to wait until the captain came out.

Inside the Gondelaurier house, it was one of those gala days which precede weddings. Quasimodo watched many people enter and saw none come out. From time to time he looked up at the roof. The gypsy had not budged any more than he had. A groom came and untied the horse and led it away to the stables.

The whole day went by like this, with Quasimodo against the post, La Esmeralda on the roof and Phoebus no doubt at Fleur-de-Lys's feet.

Finally, night came; a moonless night, a dark night. In vain did Quasimodo stare intently at La Esmeralda. Soon she was only a blob of white in the dusk; then nothing. All was obliterated, all was black.

Quasimodo saw the windows in the front of the Gondelaurier house light up from top to bottom. He saw the other windows in the square light up one after the other; he also saw every last one of them go dark again. For he remained at his post all evening. The officer had not emerged. Once the last passers-by had gone home, and all the windows of the other houses were in darkness, Quasimodo was left all alone, in complete darkness. In those days there was no lighting in the Parvis of Notre-Dame.

However, the windows of the Gondelaurier house remained lit, even after midnight. Quasimodo watched, motionless and intent, as a host of shadows flitted quickly past the multi-coloured glass. If he had not been deaf, he would have heard, more and more distinctly, from inside the house, as the hum of a sleeping Paris died away, a sound of revelry, of laughter and music.

Around one o'clock in the morning, the guests began to withdraw. Ensconced in the darkness, Quasimodo watched them all pass beneath the torch-lit porch. None of them was the captain.

He was full of sad thoughts. At times he would stare into the air, as people do when they are bored. Great heavy, black clouds hung, split and tattered, from the starlit vault of the night, like crêpe hammocks. They might have been spiders' webs on the ceiling of the heavens.

At one such moment, he suddenly saw the French window open mysteriously on the balcony, whose stone balustrade was outlined above his head. The thin glass door opened for two figures, then closed noiselessly behind them. It was a man and a woman. Only with difficulty was Quasimodo able to recognize the man as the handsome captain and the woman as the young lady whom he had seen that morning welcoming the officer from on top of this selfsame balcony. The square was pitch-dark, and a double crimson curtain, which had fallen back behind the door as it closed again, allowed scarcely any light to reach the balcony from the apartment.

As far as the deaf man could tell, without being able to hear a single word, the young man and the girl appeared to be indulging in a very affectionate tête-à-tête. The girl seemed to have allowed the officer to make a belt for her with his arm, but was gently resisting being kissed.

Quasimodo watched the scene from below, all the more charming to see in that it was not meant to be seen. He felt bitterness as he contemplated such happiness and beauty. Nature, after all, was not dumb in the poor devil, and his spinal column, wretchedly warped though it may have been, was as well able to shiver as anyone else's. He reflected on the miserable portion Providence had given him, that women, love, sensuality, would forever pass before his eyes, but that the only felicity he would see would be that of others. But what afflicted him most about the spectacle, what added indignation to his resentment, was the thought of what the gypsy must have suffered had she been able to see. But the fact is that it was a very dark night, La Esmeralda, if she had remained where she was (and he did not doubt she had), was a long way off, and it was as much as he could do himself to make out the lovers on the balcony. This consoled him.

Meanwhile, their conversation was becoming more and more animated. The young lady seemed to be begging the officer not to ask anything more of her. All Quasimodo could make out being the lovely clasped hands, the smiles mingled with tears, the girl's gaze upturned to the stars, the captain's eyes lowered ardently on her.

Fortunately, for the girl's resistance was beginning to weaken, the door of the balcony reopened abruptly, an old lady appeared, the girl seemed abashed, the officer looked resentful and all three went back inside.

A moment later, a horse pawed the ground underneath the porch and the dashing officer passed rapidly in front of Quasimodo, wrapped in his night-cloak.

The bell-ringer let him turn the corner of the street, then began to run after him with his monkey-like agility, shouting, 'Hey, Captain!'

The captain reined up.

'What's this scum want with me?' he said, discerning a sort of disjointed figure jerking quickly towards him in the shadows.

Quasimodo meanwhile had come up with him and had boldly laid hold of the bridle of his horse: 'Follow me, Captain, there's someone here who wants to speak to you.'

'*Cornemahom!*' muttered Phoebus, 'here's a villainous scarecrow I seem to have seen somewhere. Hey, there, maître, would you kindly let go of the bridle of my horse?'

'Aren't you going to ask me who, Captain?' the deaf man replied.

'Let go of my horse, I tell you,' rejoined Phoebus impatiently. 'What's the rascal want hanging on to my charger's chamfrain? Do you take my horse to be a gallows?'

Far from leaving go of the horse's bridle, Quasimodo was preparing to make it turn about. Unable to explain the captain's resistance, he was quick to say to him: 'Come, Captain, it's a woman who's waiting for you.' He added with an effort: 'A woman who loves you.'

'A rare cur,' said the captain, 'who thinks I'm obliged to go and call on all the women who love me! Or say they do! And just supposing she looked like you, owl-face? Tell her who sent you I'm going to be married, and she can go to the devil!'

'Listen,' cried Quasimodo, thinking a single word would overcome his hesitation. 'Come, my lord, it's the gypsy you know of!'

The word did indeed have a great impact on Phoebus but not that which the deaf man had been expecting. It will be recalled that our gallant officer had withdrawn with Fleur-de-Lys a moment or two before Quasimodo rescued the condemned girl from the hands of Charmolue. He had been careful, during his subsequent visits to the Gondelaurier house, not to mention the woman again, the memory of whom, after all, was painful to him; and for her part Fleur-de-Lys had not thought it politic to tell him that the gypsy was alive. Phoebus therefore believed poor 'Similar' to be dead, and dead this past month or more. We should add that for the past few moments the captain had been reflecting on the profound darkness of the night, on the supernatural ugliness and sepulchral tones of this strange messenger, that it was past midnight, that the street was as deserted as on the evening when the phantom monk had accosted him, and that his horse was snorting as it looked at Quasimodo.

'The gypsy!' he cried, almost frightened. 'Have you come from the next world, then?'

And his hand went to the hilt of his dagger.

'Quick, quick,' said the deaf man, seeking to drag the horse along. 'This way!'

Phoebus landed him a hearty kick in the chest with his boot.

Quasimodo's eye glinted. He moved as if to hurl himself on the captain. Then he stiffened and said: 'Oh, how fortunate you are that there is someone who loves you!'

He emphasized the word *someone* and let go of the horse's bridle: 'Go!'

Phoebus swore and dug in both heels. Quasimodo watched him disappear into the mist down the street. 'Oh,' said the poor hunchback to himself, 'to refuse that!'

He went back into Notre-Dame, lit his lamp and climbed back up the tower. As he expected, the gypsy was still in the same spot.

The moment she caught sight of him, she ran to him. 'Alone!' she exclaimed, clasping her lovely hands in sorrow.

'I couldn't find him,' said Quasimodo coldly.

'You should have waited all night!' she went on, angrily.

He saw her angry gesture and understood her reproach. 'Another time I will keep a better look-out for him,' he said, lowering his head.

'Go!' she said to him.

He left her. She was displeased with him. He had preferred being abused by her to hurting her. He had kept all the pain for himself.

From that day forth, the gypsy saw him no more. He stopped coming to her cell. At most she would sometimes glimpse the bell-ringer's melancholy face staring at her from on top of a tower. But as soon as she caught sight of him, he vanished.

Truth to tell, she was not greatly distressed by the poor hunchback's voluntary absence. Deep down, she was grateful to him for it. Quasimodo, in any case, was under no illusions on that score.

She no longer saw him but she felt the presence of a good genie around her. Her stores were replenished by an invisible hand while she slept. One morning, she found a bird-cage on her window. Above her cell there was a sculpture which frightened her. She had given evidence of this more than once in front of Quasimodo. One morning (for all these things were done at night) it was no longer to be seen. It had been smashed. Whoever had climbed up to that sculpture must have risked his neck.

Sometimes, of an evening, she would hear a voice hidden under the penthouse on the tower, singing a strange, sad song, as if lulling her to sleep. The lines were unrhymed as if whoever had made them up were deaf:

> Don't look at the face,
> Young girl, look at the heart.
> The heart of a handsome young man is often deformed.
> There are hearts where love does not keep.
>
> Young girl, the fir-tree is not beautiful,
> Not beautiful like the poplar,
> But it keeps its leaves in winter.

Alas, what's the good of saying that?
What isn't beauty does wrong to exist;
Beauty loves only beauty,
April turns its back on January.

Beauty is perfect,
Beauty can achieve anything,
Beauty is the one thing that cannot exist by halves.

The crow flies only by day,
The owl flies only by night,
The swan flies by night and day.

One morning, when she awoke, she saw, on her window, two vases full of flowers. One was of very fine, very brilliant crystal, but cracked. It had allowed the water with which it had been filled to run out and the flowers it contained had wilted. The other was an earthenware pot, rough and ordinary, but it had kept all its water and its flowers were still of a fresh, bright vermilion.

I do not know whether she intended it, but La Esmeralda took the wilted bunch and wore it all day against her breast.

That day, she did not hear the voice singing from the tower.

This did not worry her greatly. She spent her days stroking Djali, keeping watch on the door of the Gondelaurier house, conversing quietly with herself about Phoebus, and crumbling her bread for the swallows.

She had ceased altogether to see or to hear Quasimodo. The poor bell-ringer seemed to have vanished from the church. One night, however, because she was not asleep but was dreaming of her handsome captain, she heard sighing close beside her cell. Frightened, she got up, and, by the light of the moon, saw a shapeless mass lying across her doorway. It was Quasimodo, sleeping there on the stone.

FIVE

The Key of the Porte-Rouge

THE archdeacon meanwhile had heard rumours of the miraculous rescue of the gypsy. He did not know what to feel. He had come to terms with La Esmeralda's death. With her dead, his mind was at rest, he had plumbed the depths of possible sorrow. The human heart (Dom Claude had pondered these questions) can contain only a limited amount of despair. Once the sponge is saturated, the sea can pass over it without another drop entering.

And with the death of La Esmeralda, his sponge was saturated, all was over for Dom Claude on this earth. Now, knowing her to be alive, and Phoebus too, the torments would begin again, the shocks and the alternatives: life itself. And Claude was weary of all that.

When he learnt the news, he shut himself up in his cell in the cloister. He appeared neither at the congregations of the chapter nor at services. His door was closed to everybody, even the bishop. He remained walled up in this way for several weeks. They imagined he was sick; and so he was.

What was he doing behind that locked door? With what thoughts was the luckless man wrestling? Was he locked in some final struggle against his redoubtable passion? Was he working out some final scheme of death for her and perdition for himself?

Once his Jehan, his darling brother, his spoilt child, came to his door, knocked, swore, pleaded and stated his name ten times. Claude did not open it.

He spent days on end with his face pressed against the window-panes. From his window, which was in the cloister, he could see the little cell, and frequently saw La Esmeralda herself with her goat, or sometimes with Quasimodo. He remarked the vile hunchback's little attentions, his obediences, his tactful and submissive manner with the gypsy. He remembered, for he had a good memory and memory is the jealous man's torturer, the peculiar way in which the bell-ringer had been staring down at the dancer on a certain evening. He asked himself what motive could have impelled Quasimodo to rescue her. He witnessed countless small scenes between the gypsy and the deaf man whose pantomime, seen from a distance and interpreted by his passion, he found very affectionate. He distrusted the vagaries of women. Then, confusedly, he felt a jealousy come alive in him that he could never have anticipated, a jealousy that made him redden with shame and indignation. 'The captain's all very well, but him . . .!' This thought overwhelmed him.

His nights were dreadful. Now that he knew the gypsy was alive, those chilling notions of spectres and tombs that had haunted him for the whole of one day had faded, and the flesh renewed its prompting. He writhed about on his bed knowing the brown-skinned girl to be so close at hand.

Each night, his delirious imagination showed him La Esmeralda in all the attitudes that had most inflamed his senses. He saw her stretched out on the captain after he had been stabbed, eyes closed and her lovely bare breasts covered with Phoebus's blood, at that moment of ecstasy when the archdeacon had bestowed on those bloodless lips the kiss whose burning touch the poor girl had felt even though she was half-dead. He saw her being undressed once again by the bestial hands of the torturers, as she let them bare her tiny foot, her slender, rounded leg, her white, supple knee and encase them in the boot with its iron screws. He saw again the ivory knee that alone remained outside Torterue's terrible apparatus. And finally he pictured the girl in her shift, with the rope about her neck, her shoulders bare, her feet bare, almost naked, as he had seen her on that last day. These voluptuous images made him clench his fists and sent a shiver down his vertebrae.

One night in particular, they inflamed the blood in his arteries so cruelly that this virgin priest bit into his pillow, leapt from his bed, threw a surplice over his nightshirt, and left his cell, lamp in hand, half-naked, distraught, his eyes afire.

He knew where to find the key to the Porte-Rouge, which led from the cloister into the church, and he always carried on him, as we know, a key to the staircase in the towers.

SIX

The Key of the Porte-Rouge (continued)

THAT night, La Esmeralda had gone to sleep in her little cell, full of forgetfulness, of hope and of sweet thoughts. She had been asleep for some time, dreaming, as ever, of Phoebus, when she thought she heard a noise around her. Her sleep was light and nervous, like a bird's. The slightest thing woke her up. She opened her eyes. The night was pitch-black. However, she could see a face at her window, staring at her. This apparition was lit by a lamp. The minute it realized it had been observed by La Esmeralda, the face blew out the lamp. Nevertheless, the girl had had time to catch a glimpse of it. Her eyelids closed again in terror. 'Oh,' she said in a spent voice, 'the priest!'

All her past misfortunes came back to her in a flash. She fell back on her bed, as cold as ice.

A moment later, she felt a contact down her whole body and gave such a shudder that she came bolt upright, wide awake now and furious.

The priest had just slipped in beside her. His two arms were about her.

She tried to cry out but couldn't.

'Go away, monster! Go away, murderer!' she said, in a voice made low and tremulous by anger and terror.

'Mercy! Mercy!' murmured the priest, pressing his lips to her shoulders.

She seized his bald head in both hands by what was left of its hair and strove to fend off his kisses as if they had been bites.

'Mercy!' the unfortunate man repeated. 'If only you knew what my love for you is like! It's fire, molten lead, a thousand knives in my heart!'

And he held back her two arms with superhuman force. Distraught, 'Let go of me,' she said, 'or I shall spit in your face!'

He let go of her. 'Humiliate me, strike me, be vicious! Do what you like! But please, love me!'

Then she struck him, in a childlike fury. She clenched her beautiful hands so as to bruise his face. 'Go away, demon!'

'Love me! Love me! Have pity!' cried the poor priest, writhing on top of her and answering her blows with caresses.

Suddenly, she felt him overpower her. 'We must put an end to this!' he said, gnashing his teeth.

She was in his arms, broken, subjugated, quivering, at his mercy. She felt a lascivious hand stray over her. She made one last effort and began to shout: 'Help! Help me! A vampire, a vampire!'

No one came. Only Djali had been aroused and was bleating anxiously.

'Be quiet!' panted the priest.

Suddenly, in her struggles, as she crawled across the floor, the gypsy's hand encountered a cold, metallic object. It was Quasimodo's whistle. She grabbed it in a convulsion of hope, carried it to her lips and blew into it with all her remaining strength. The whistle made a clear, high-pitched, piercing sound.

'What's that?' said the priest.

At almost the same instant, he felt himself being lifted off by a powerful arm; the cell was in shadow and he could not make out clearly who it was holding him in this way; but he could hear teeth chattering with rage, and there was just enough light scattered in the shadows for him to see the broad blade of a cutlass gleaming above his head.

The priest thought he could make out the form of Quasimodo. He supposed it could only be him. He remembered that as he entered he had stumbled over a bundle lying stretched across the doorway outside. However, since the newcomer had not uttered a single sound, he did not know what to believe. He threw himself at the arm holding the cutlass, shouting: 'Quasimodo!' In this moment of distress, he had forgotten that Quasimodo was deaf.

In a trice the priest was flat on the ground and could feel a knee of lead pressing against his chest. From the angular imprint of that knee, he recognized Quasimodo. But what was he to do? How to be recognized *by* him? The darkness made the deaf man blind.

He was doomed. The girl, like an angry tigress, felt no mercy and had not intervened to save him. The cutlass was approaching his head. The moment was critical. Suddenly, his adversary seemed gripped by a hesitation. 'No blood on her!' he said in a muffled voice.

It was indeed the voice of Quasimodo.

The priest then felt a huge hand drag him out of the cell by his foot. It was there he was to die. Fortunately for him, in the last few minutes the moon had risen.

Once they had crossed the threshold of the cell, its pale rays fell on the priest's face. Quasimodo looked at him, was seized by trembling, let go of the priest and stepped back.

The gypsy, who had advanced into her doorway, was surprised to see the roles abruptly reversed. Now it was the priest who was threatening, Quasimodo who was the supplicant.

The priest, who had been heaping gestures of anger and reproach on the deaf man, signalled him violently to withdraw.

The deaf man bowed his head, then came and knelt before the gypsy's door. 'My lord,' he said in a solemn and resigned tone, 'afterwards you can do what you will; but kill me first.'

So saying, he offered the priest his cutlass. The priest was beside himself and threw himself on it, but the girl was quicker. She snatched the knife from Quasimodo's hands and burst out into a furious laugh. 'Come closer!' she said to the priest.

She held the blade aloft. The priest was undecided. She would certainly have struck. 'You wouldn't dare come closer, you coward!' she shouted at him. Then she added, with a pitiless expression, knowing full well she was about to pierce the priest's heart with a thousand red-hot irons: 'Ah, I know that Phoebus isn't dead!'

The priest sent Quasimodo sprawling with a kick, then plunged back, trembling with rage, under the vault of the staircase.

When he had gone, Quasimodo picked up the whistle which had just saved the gypsy. 'It was getting rusty,' he said, handing it back. Then he left her on her own.

The girl, overcome by this violent scene, fell exhausted on to her bed, and began to sob. Her horizon had darkened once again.

For his part, the priest had groped his way back into his cell.

It had happened. Dom Claude was jealous of Quasimodo!

Thoughtfully, he repeated the fateful words: 'No one shall have her!'

BOOK TEN

ONE

Gringoire has Several Good Ideas in a Row in the Rue des Bernardins

ONCE he had seen how the whole business was turning out, and that there would certainly be ropes, hangings and other unpleasantnesses for the principal characters in the play, Pierre Gringoire was no longer anxious to be mixed up in it. The truants, among whom he had remained, reckoning that in the last resort they were the best company in Paris, had continued to worry about the gypsy. He found that simple enough for people, like her, whose one perspective was Charmolue and Torterue and who did not, like him, take horse in the realms of the imagination between the two wings of Pegasus. He had learnt from what they said that his broken-pitcher wife had taken refuge in Notre-Dame, and he was glad to hear it. But he did not even feel tempted to go and visit her there. Now and again, his thoughts turned to the little goat, but that was all. By day, for the rest, he performed feats of strength in order to live, and by night he toiled away at a memorandum against the Bishop of Paris, for he remembered being inundated by the wheels of his mills and still bore him a grudge. He was also busy on a commentary to the *De Cupa Petrarum*,[1] that fine work by Baudry the Red, Bishop of Noyon and of Tournay, which had filled him with a violent love of architecture; an enthusiasm that had taken the place in his heart of his passion for hermeticism, of which it was, as it happens, simply the natural corollary, since there are intimate links between hermetics and masonry. Gringoire had passed from love of an idea to love of the form of that idea.

One day, he had paused beside Saint-Germain-l'Auxerrois, at the corner of a house known as the 'For l'Evêque', which stood opposite another known as the 'For-le-Roi'. The For l'Evêque possessed a delightful fourteenth-century chapel, whose chevet overlooked the street. Gringoire was piously examining its external sculptures. He was experiencing one of those moments of egotistical, exclusive and supreme delight, when the artist sees only

1. 'Of the shaping of stones.'

art in the world and sees the world in art. Suddenly, he felt a hand laid solemnly on his shoulder. He turned round. It was his former friend, his former master, the archdeacon.

He stood there amazed. He had not seen the archdeacon in a long while, and Dom Claude was one of those solemn and passionate men an encounter with whom always upsets the equilibrium of a sceptical philosopher.

The archdeacon kept silent for a moment or two, and Gringoire had time to study him closely. He found Dom Claude much altered, as pale as a winter morning, his eyes sunken, his hair almost white. It was the priest who finally ended the silence by saying in a calm but glacial voice: 'How are you, Maître Pierre?'

'My health?' replied Gringoire. 'Ha, so so. Good overall though. Moderation in all things. You know, maître, the secret of good health according to Hippocrates, *id est: cibi, potus, somni, Venus, omnia moderata sint.*'[1]

'You have no worries then, Maître Pierre?' the archdeacon went on, eyeing Gringoire intently.

'Indeed, no.'

'And what are you doing now?'

'As you can see, *mon maître.* I am examining the carving of the stone here, and the way this bas-relief has been undercut.'

The priest began to smile that bitter smile which raises only one corner of the mouth. 'And that amuses you?'

'It's paradise!' exclaimed Gringoire. Then, bending over the sculptures with the awed look of a scientist demonstrating living phenomena: 'For instance, don't you consider that this bas-relief of a metamorphosis has been executed with great skill, fastidiousness and patience? Look at this colonnette. Round what capital have you seen tenderer or more lovingly chiselled leaves than those? See these three figures in the round by Jean Maillevin. Not that great genius's finest work. Nevertheless, the innocence and sweetness of the faces, the gaiety of the attitudes and the drapery, and the inexplicable charm which is inseparable from all their faults make them very cheerful and delicate figurines, too much so perhaps. Amusing, don't you find?'

'Yes indeed!' said the priest.

'And if you saw the interior of the chapel!' the poet went on,

1. 'That is food, drink, sleep, Venus, all things in moderation.'

with his garrulous enthusiasm. 'Sculptures everywhere. It's as dense as a cabbage-heart! The apse is in a very devout style and quite unique; I've never seen its like anywhere else!'

'You're happy then?' Dom Claude interjected.

Gringoire replied excitedly: 'On my honour, I am! First I loved women, then animals. Now I love stones. They're just as amusing as animals or women, and less treacherous.'

The priest put a hand to his brow, in a habitual gesture: 'Indeed?'

'Look!' said Gringoire, 'I can't tell you the enjoyment!' He took the priest's arm, who let himself be led, and made him enter the stair-turret of the For l'Évêque. 'Look at that staircase! I feel happy every time I see it. Those stairs are the simplest and most uncommon in Paris. Each step is chamfered underneath. Their beauty and simplicity come from the treads, which are a foot or so apart, and are interlaced, interlinked, embedded, enchased, enclosed and enchained one inside the other, and dovetailed together really firmly and attractively!'

'And you desire for nothing?'

'No.'

'And you regret nothing?'

'Neither regret nor desire. I have ordered my life.'

'What men order', said Claude, 'things disorder.'

'I am a pyrrhonian philosopher,' replied Gringoire, 'and I hold everything in equilibrium.'

'And how do you earn your living?'

'I still write epics and tragedies now and again; but what brings me in the most is the industry you know of, maître. Carrying pyramids of chairs in my teeth.'

'A crude calling for a philosopher.'

'It's still equilibrium,' said Gringoire. 'Once you have an idea you find it everywhere.'

'That I know,' said the archdeacon.

After a pause, the priest went on: 'You are quite poor, even so?'

'Poor, yes; unhappy, no.'

At that moment there was a sound of horses, and our two interlocutors saw a company of archers of the king's bodyguard ride past at the end of the street, lances raised and with an officer at their head. The paving echoed to their brilliant cavalcade.

'You're staring very hard at that officer!' said Gringoire to the archdeacon.

'That's because I think I recognize him.'

'What do you call him?'

'I think his name's Phoebus de Châteaupers,' said Claude.

'Phoebus! A curious name! There's Phoebus, Count de Foix, too. I remember meeting a girl who swore only by Phoebus.'

'Come away,' said the priest. 'I've something to say to you.'

Since the troop had ridden by, a certain agitation was visible beneath the archdeacon's frigid exterior. He started walking. Gringoire followed, used to obeying him, like everyone else who had once come into contact with this superior man. They came in silence to the Rue des Bernardins, which was more or less deserted. There Dom Claude halted.

'What have you got to say to me, maître?' Gringoire asked him.

'Do you not find', replied the archdeacon, looking deeply thoughtful, 'that the costume of those horsemen we have just seen is more handsome than yours or mine?'

Gringoire shook his head. 'Bless me! I prefer my yellow and red surcoat to those iron and steel fish-scales. Where's the pleasure in walking about sounding like an ironmonger's shop in an earthquake!'

'So, Gringoire, you've never felt envious of those fine-looking boys in their soldier's actons?'

'Envious of what, Monsieur the Archdeacon? Their strength, their armour, their discipline? Better philosophy and independence, in rags. I'd rather be the head of a fly than the tail of a lion.'

'That's strange,' mused the priest. 'Yet a beautiful uniform's beautiful!'

Gringoire saw he was preoccupied, and left him to go and admire the porch of a near-by house. He came back clapping his hands. 'If you were less taken up with the fine clothes of the military, Monsieur the Archdeacon, I would beg you to go and look at that door. I have always said that the entrance to the Lord Aubry's house is the most splendid in the world.'

'Pierre Gringoire,' said the archdeacon, 'what have you done with that little gypsy dancer?'

'La Esmeralda? You're changing the subject very abruptly.'

'Was she not your wife?'

'Yes, by means of a broken pitcher. Four years of it we were to have. So, then,' added Gringoire, looking at the archdeacon half-mockingly, 'you still think about her?'

'And you, don't you think about her?'

'Seldom, I've so many things . . .! Lord, the little goat was so pretty!'

'Didn't the gypsy save your life?'

'That's true, by God.'

'Well, what's become of her? What have you done with her?'

'I couldn't say. I think they hanged her.'

'You think so?'

'I'm not sure. When I saw they wanted to hang people, I retired from the game.'

'Is that all you know about her?'

'Wait, though. I was told she'd taken refuge in Notre-Dame, and that she was safe there, and I was delighted, and I haven't been able to discover whether the goat was rescued with her, and that's all I know about her.'

'I am going to tell you something more,' cried Dom Claude, and his voice, hitherto slow, soft and almost secretive, had become thunderous. 'She did indeed take refuge in Notre-Dame. But in three days' time justice will take her back again and she will be hanged on the Grève. There is a judgement of parliament.'

'That's a nuisance,' said Gringoire.

In a trice, the priest had become cold and calm again.

'And who the devil saw fit to ask for a judgement of reintegration?' the poet went on. 'Couldn't they have let the parliament be? What does it matter if one poor girl takes shelter under the flying buttresses of Notre-Dame next to the swallows' nests?'

'There are satans in the world,' answered the archdeacon.

'It's a devilish bad beginning,' remarked Gringoire.

The archdeacon went on after a pause: 'So, she saved your life?'

'Among my good friends the truants. It was touch and go whether they hanged me. They would have been annoyed now if they had.'

'Wouldn't you like to do something for her?'

'There's nothing I'd like better, Dom Claude. But what if I was to get something nasty wound round my neck?'

'What matter!'

'What matter! I like that! I've two major works under way, *mon maître*!'

The priest clapped his brow. For all the calm he was affecting, a violent gesture now and again revealed the convulsions within. 'How can we save her?'

Gringoire said to him: 'My answer, maître, is: *Il padelt*, which is Turkish for "In God is our hope".'

'How can we save her?' repeated Claude, thoughtfully.

Gringoire clapped his brow in turn.

'Listen, *mon maître*. I have imagination. I'll think of expedients for you. Supposing we asked the king for a pardon?'

'Louis XI? A pardon?'

'Why not?'

'Go and take its bone away from a tiger!'

Gringoire began to search for other solutions.

'Very well! Wait! Would you like me to address a request to the matrons, declaring the girl to be pregnant?'

This brought a spark from the priest's sunken pupils.

'Pregnant, you scoundrel! Do you know something?'

Gringoire was alarmed by his expression. He hurriedly said: 'Oh, not I! Our marriage was a true *forismaritagium*.[1] I was left outside. But at least we would get a reprieve.'

'Foolishness! Infamy! Hold your tongue!'

'You're wrong to be angry,' grumbled Gringoire. 'It doesn't hurt anybody to get a stay of execution and it would earn the matrons forty *deniers parisis*, and they're poor women.'

The priest was not listening. 'She's got to get out of there, though!' he muttered. 'The judgement takes effect in three days. What's more, even if there was no judgement, that Quasimodo! What depraved tastes women have!' He raised his voice: 'Maître Pierre, I've been thinking it over. There's only one way to save her.'

'What is it? I see none.'

'Listen, maître Pierre, remember you owe her your life. I'm going to tell you frankly what my plan is. The church is watched night and day. They only allow out those they've seen go in. So you'll be able to get in. You will come. I will take you in to her. You will change clothes with her. She will take your doublet, you will take her skirt.'

1. 'Marriage with an outsider.'

'So far, so good,' remarked the philosopher. 'What then?'

'What then? She will leave in your clothes; you will stay in hers. They may hang you, but she will be safe.'

Gringoire scratched his ear, and looked very serious.

'I say, that's a plan that would never have occurred to me,' he said.

The poet's genial, trusting face had suddenly darkened at Dom Claude's unexpected suggestion, like some cheerful Italian landscape when an untimely gust of wind arrives and flattens a cloud across the sun.

'Well, Gringoire, how does my method strike you?'

'What I say, maître, is that they will not hang me perhaps, they will hang me indubitably.'

'That's no concern of ours.'

'The devil!'

'She saved your life. It's a debt you're paying.'

'There are plenty of others I haven't paid!'

'Maître Pierre, you have no choice.'

The archdeacon had spoken imperiously.

'Listen, Dom Claude,' answered the poet in dismay. 'You hold by your plan and you are wrong. I don't see why I should get myself hanged in place of someone else.'

'Why are you so attached to life, then?'

'Ah, a thousand reasons!'

'What, may I ask?'

'What? The air, the sky, the morning, the evening, the moonlight, my good friends the truants, our slanging-matches with the old bawds, the beautiful architecture of Paris to study, three fat books to be written, one of them against the bishop and his mills, and I don't know what else. Anaxagoras said he was in the world to admire the sun. Moreover, I am fortunate enough to spend all my days from morn till night with a man of genius, to wit myself, and that is very agreeable.'

'Oh man of little brain!' grumbled the archdeacon. 'Tell me, this so delightful life you lead, who preserved it for you? To whom do you owe it that you are breathing this air, seeing that sky, and can still amuse your lark's brain with fads and frivolities? Where would you be, but for her? Do you want her to die, when it's through her you are alive? To die, that lovely, sweet, adorable creature, necessary to the light of the world, more divine than God? While you, semi-sage and semi-madman, you vain apology for a man, a sort of vegetable which thinks it walks and thinks, you will continue to live with the life you have stolen from her, as useless as a candle in broad daylight? Come, Gringoire, a little compassion! It's your turn to be generous! She was the first.'

The priest spoke vehemently. Listening to him, Gringoire looked first uncertain, then moved, and ended up wearing a tragic grimace which made his pallid face look like that of a new-born baby with the colic.

'You move me,' he said, wiping away a tear. 'Very well, I'll think it over. It's a queer plan of yours. After all,' he went on, after a pause, 'who knows? Perhaps they won't hang me. Not everyone who is betrothed gets married. When they find me in the cell, so grotesquely got up in a skirt and a coif, they may burst out laughing. And then, if they do hang me, well, the rope's a death just like any other, or, rather, not just like any other. It's a death worthy of a sage who has oscillated all his life, a death that is neither flesh nor fowl, like the mind of the true sceptic, a death firmly stamped with pyrrhonism and hesitancy, which comes halfway between heaven and earth, which leaves one in suspense. It's a philosopher's death and maybe I was predestined to it. It's splendid to die as you have lived.'

The priest broke in: 'It's agreed?'

'What is death, when all's said and done?' continued Gringoire exaltedly. 'A nasty moment, a toll-gate, the passage from very little to nothing at all. Someone having asked Cercidas, the Megalopolitan, if he would die happily: "Why not," he replied; "for after my death I shall see those great men, Pythagoras among the philosophers, Hecateus among the historians, Homer among the poets, Olympus among the musicians."'

The archdeacon offered him his hand. 'It's settled then, you'll come tomorrow?'

This gesture brought Gringoire back to earth.

'No, damn it, it isn't!' he said, in the tone of a man waking from sleep. 'Be hanged! That's too ridiculous. I won't.'

'Farewell, then!' And the archdeacon added between his teeth: 'We shall be seeing each other!'

'I don't want to see that devilish man again,' thought Gringoire;

and ran after Dom Claude. 'Look, Monsieur the Archdeacon, no unpleasantness between old friends! You are interested in the girl, in my wife, I mean, all right. You have thought of a stratagem for getting her safely out of Notre-Dame, but your method is extremely disagreeable for me, Gringoire. Supposing I had a different one! I must warn you that a quite blinding inspiration has just this minute come to me. Supposing I had an expedient for extricating her from her plight without risking my own neck in even the smallest noose? What would you say? Would that not satisfy you? Is it absolutely necessary that I should be hanged for you to feel happy?'

In his impatience, the archdeacon was wrenching the buttons from his cassock. 'A river of words! What is your way?'

'Yes,' Gringoire went on, talking to himself and touching his nose with his index-finger to show he was deep in thought. 'That's it! The truants are good lads. The tribe of Egypt are very fond of her. They'll rise up at a word. Nothing simpler. By surprise. Under cover of the disorder, we can easily abduct her. Tomorrow evening. They'll be only too ready.'

'The means, tell me!' said the priest, shaking him.

Gringoire turned to him majestically. 'Let go of me, then! You can see very well I'm composing.' He pondered for a moment or two longer. Then he began to applaud his own scheme, crying: 'Admirable, it can't fail!'

'The means!' Claude went on angrily.

Gringoire was beaming.

'Come, I'll whisper it to you. It's a really bold countermine and it'll solve all our problems. You must agree, by God, that I'm not an idiot!'

He broke off: 'Ah, yes, is the little goat with the girl?'

'Yes. Devil take you!'

'Because they'd have hanged her too, wouldn't they?'

'Why should I care?'

'Yes, they would have hanged her. They hanged a sow last month. The hangman loves that. He eats the beast afterwards. Hang my pretty Djali! Poor little lamb!'

'Damnation!' exclaimed Dom Claude. 'It's you who are the hangman. What means have you found of saving her, you scoundrel? Must I pull your plan out of you with the forceps?'

'A splendid one, maître! It's this.'

Gringoire leant towards the archdeacon's ear and spoke to him in a low voice, casting an anxious look up and down the street, though no one was passing. When he had finished, Dom Claude took him by the hand and said coldly: 'Good. Till tomorrow.'

'Till tomorrow,' echoed Gringoire. And as the archdeacon walked off in one direction, he went off in the other, saying quietly to himself: 'This is a fine business, Monsieur Pierre Gringoire. Never mind. It's not said, because one's small, that one will shrink from great enterprises. Bito[1] carried a great bull on his shoulders; wagtails, warblers and chats cross the ocean.'

TWO
Become a Truant

WHEN he got back to the cloister, the archdeacon found his brother Jehan du Moulin waiting for him at the door of his cell, having been whiling away his boredom by drawing his elder brother's profile on the wall in charcoal, embellished with an outsize nose.

Dom Claude barely glanced at his brother. He had other things in mind. The happy, rascally face whose beaming smile had so many times gladdened the priest's own sombre countenance was powerless now to dissolve the mists that grew thicker each day above that corrupt, mephitic and stagnant soul.

'Brother,' said Jehan diffidently, 'I've come to see you.'

The archdeacon did not even look up at him. 'Well?'

'Brother,' went on the hypocrite, 'you're so kind to me and you give me such good advice that I always come back to you.'

'So?'

'Alas, brother, the fact is you were quite right when you said to me: "Jehan, Jehan, *cessat doctorum doctrina, discipulorum disciplina.*[2] Jehan be good, Jehan be studious, Jehan don't stay out of college all night without legitimate excuse and your master's permission. Don't beat the Picards, *noli, Joannes, verberare Picardos.* Don't rot on the straw of the classroom like an illiterate donkey, *quasi asinus illitteratus.* Jehan, let yourself be punished at your master's discretion. Jehan, go to chapel every evening and sing an

1. A Greek mathematician of the third century BC.

2. 'The doctrine of the doctors, the discipline of the disciples have grown slack.'

anthem with a verse and a prayer to Our Glorious Lady the Virgin Mary." Alas, that was excellent advice!'

'And so?'

'Brother, you see before you a guilty man, a criminal, a wretch, a libertine, an outrageous man! My dear brother, Jehan turned your gracious counsels into straw and dung, to be trampled underfoot. I have been well punished for it, and the good Lord is extraordinarily just. For as long as I had money, I revelled, I led a wild, carefree life. Oh, debauchery looks so attractive from in front, and so sour and ugly from behind! Now I haven't a farthing, I've sold my tablecloth, my shirt and my towel, and the gay life is over! The fine candle is spent and all I've got left is the horrid tallow wick, smoking in my face. The girls laugh at me. I drink water. I'm tormented by remorse and by creditors.'

'The rest?' said the archdeacon.

'Alas, my very dear brother, I would like very much to lead a better life. I come to you full of contrition. I am penitent. I confess myself. I pound my breast with my fists. You are quite right to want me one day to become a licentiate and sub-monitor of the Collège de Torchi. I now feel a splendid vocation for that way of life. But I've no ink left, I shall have to buy some more; I've no quills left, I shall have to buy some more; I've no paper left, no books, I shall have to buy some more. To do that, I badly need funds. And I come to you, brother, with a heart full of contrition.'

'Is that all?'

'Yes,' said the student. 'A little money.'

'I haven't got any.'

The student then said with an air both grave and resolute: 'Well, brother, I'm sorry to have to tell you that I've been made very good offers and proposals from another quarter. You refuse to give me any money? No? In that case, I shall become a truant.'

As he uttered these monstrous words, he took up a pose like Ajax, expecting to see the thunderbolt descend on his head.

The archdeacon said to him coldly: 'Become a truant.'

Jehan gave him a deep bow and whistled as he redescended the stairs to the cloister.

Just as he was passing into the courtyard of the cloister below the window of his brother's cell, he heard the window open, looked up and saw the archdeacon's stern face appear at the aperture. 'Go to the devil!' said Dom Claude. 'This is the last money you'll get from me.'

At the same moment, the priest threw Jehan a purse which raised a large lump on the student's forehead, and Jehan bore it away, at once annoyed and pleased, like a dog that has been pelted with marrow-bones.

THREE
Long Live Pleasure!

THE reader will not perhaps have forgotten that the Cour des Miracles was partly enclosed by the ancient ring-wall of the town, a good many of whose towers were, by this time, falling into ruin. One of these towers the truants had converted into a place of entertainment. There was a tavern in the lower room, amusement of another kind on the upper floors. This tower was the most vital and consequently most repulsive spot in the entire truantry. It was a sort of monstrous beehive, which buzzed both night and day. At night, when all the rest of beggardom was asleep, when there were no more lighted windows to be seen in the grimy house-fronts of the square, no more yelling to be heard coming from the innumerable households, those ant-hills of robbers, whores and stolen or illegitimate children, the tower of delight could always be recognized by the noise it made, and by the scarlet light radiating simultaneously from air-vents, windows and fissures in the gaping walls, escaping, as it were, from its every pore.

The cellar, then, was the tavern. One descended to it through a low doorway and then down a staircase as unbending as a classical alexandrine.[1] Above the door, by way of an inn-sign, was an amazing daub depicting newly minted *sols* and slaughtered chickens, with underneath it a pun: *Aux sonneurs pour les trépassés*.[2]

One evening, as the curfew sounded from all the belfries of Paris, the serjeants of the watch, had it been given them to enter

1. The conventional dodecasyllabic line of classical French poetry and poetic drama. As a legislator of Romanticism, Hugo helped to subvert the authority of this very strict form over French poetic practice.

2. Not a very impressive pun. The legend (meaning: 'To the bell-ringers for the departed') is intended to sound like 'les sols neufs et les poulets tués' or 'newly minted sols and slaughtered chickens'. The word *poulet* in French has the additional slang meaning of 'policeman'.

the fearful Court of Miracles, might have observed that the uproar coming from the truants' tavern was louder than usual, that they were drinking more and swearing more roundly. Outside, the square was full of groups of men conferring in low voices, as when some great design is afoot, with the odd rogue squatting on his haunches, sharpening a wicked-looking iron blade on the paving-stones.

In the tavern itself, however, wining and gambling offered such a powerful distraction from the ideas preoccupying the truantry that evening that the remarks of the drinkers offered little clue to what was in the air. They merely seemed merrier than usual, and between every pair of legs there gleamed some kind of weapon: a bill-hook, an axe-handle, a broad-sword or the hook of an old hackbut.

The room was circular and absolutely vast, but so close-packed were the tables and so numerous the drinkers that the entire contents of the tavern, men, women, benches, beer-jugs, whoever was drinking, sleeping or gambling, the fit and the crippled, seemed piled up anyhow, with all the orderliness and harmony of a heap of oyster-shells. On the tables burnt a few tallow candles; but the true luminary of the tavern, which fulfilled here the role of the lustre in an opera-house, was the fire. The cellar was so damp that not even at the height of summer was the hearth allowed to go out; an immense fireplace with a carved mantel, bristling all over with heavy iron firedogs and cooking utensils, with one of those mixed peat and log fires which, at night, in a village street, casts the ruddy spectre of the windows of the forge on to the wall opposite. Sitting solemnly in the ashes in front of the embers was a large dog, turning a spit laden with viands.

After a first glance, you could pick out in this multitude, for all its confusion, three main groups, pressing around three figures whom the reader has already met. One of these figures, weirdly got up in much Oriental-looking tinsel, was Mathias Hungadi Spicali, Duke of Egypt and of Bohemia. The villain was sitting cross-legged on the table, finger upraised, loudly sharing out his knowledge of black and white magic among the many gawping faces round about. Another crowd was growing round our old friend the valiant King of Thunes, who was armed to the teeth. Clopin Trouillefou, looking very serious and speaking in an undertone, was directing the plunder of an enormous cask full of weapons which stood, split wide open, in front of him, and from which spilled axes, swords, bassinets, coats of mail, platers, lance-heads, spear-heads, arrows and crossbow bolts in profusion, like apples and grapes from a cornucopia. Each man chose from the pile, one a morion, another a short-sword, a third a dagger with a cross hilt. The children too were being armed and there were even legless men in bards and breastplates moving between the legs of the drinkers like huge beetles.

A third audience, finally, the rowdiest, most jovial and most numerous of all, was choking the benches and tables, in whose midst there perorated and blasphemed a fluting voice, coming from beneath a weighty suit of armour, complete from casque to spurs. This individual, who had screwed an entire panoply on to his body, had vanished so far beneath his martial costume that all that was to be seen of him was an insolent, red, turned-up nose, a lock of fair hair, a pink mouth and two audacious eyes. His belt was full of daggers and poniards, a large sword hung at his side, to his left was a rusty crossbow, in front of him an enormous jug of wine, not to mention, to his right, a plump and dishevelled girl. Around him every mouth was laughing, swearing or drinking.

Add to these a score of subsidiary groups, the serving boys and girls dashing about with jugs on their heads, the gamblers squatting over their marbles, their merils, and their dice, or over the excitements of trinquet, arguments in one corner, embraces in another, and you will have some general idea of the scene, over which there played the light from a great blazing fire, which set a thousand grotesque and disproportionate shadows dancing on the tavern walls.

As for the din, it was the inside of a bell in full peal.

A shower of fat frizzled in the dripping-pan and its continuous shrilling filled in the gaps in the innumerable dialogues which were being conducted right across the room.

Amidst the uproar, at the far end of the tavern, on the seat inside the fireplace, was meditating a philosopher, his feet in the ashes and his eye on the brands. This was Pierre Gringoire.

'Come on, quick! Hurry up and arm yourselves! We march in one hour!' Clopin Trouillefou was telling his argotiers.

A girl was humming:

Good night, mother and father
The last out cover the fire.

Two cardplayers were arguing. 'Knave!' cried the more purple-faced of the two, showing the other his fist. 'I'll club you. Then you could take the place of the knave of clubs in my lord the king's pack of cards.'

'Phew!' yelled a Norman, recognizable by his nasal twang, 'we're packed in as tight as the saints of Caillouville!'[1]

'Boys,' the Duke of Egypt was saying to his audience in a falsetto, 'the witches of France go to the sabbath without broomsticks, grease or animals to ride, but only a few magic words. The witches of Italy always have a billy-goat waiting for them at the door. All of them have to leave up the chimney.'

The voice of the young rogue armed cap-à-pie dominated the uproar. 'Nowel, Nowel!' he shouted. 'My first arms today! Truant, I'm a truant, Christ's belly! Pour me a drink! Friends, my name is Jehan Frollo du Moulin and I'm a gentleman. It's my opinion that if God was a man at arms he'd become a looter. Brothers, we're going to go on a fine expedition. We're brave fellows. Lay siege to the church, force the doors, extract the beautiful girl, save her from the judges, save her from the priests, demolish the cloister, burn the bishop in his palace, we shall do all that in less time than it takes a burgomaster to eat a spoonful of soup. Our cause is a just one, we shall loot Notre-Dame and that will be that. We shall hang Quasimodo. Do you know Quasimodo, mesdemoiselles? Have you seen him panting away on the great bell on some Whitsun day? *Corne du père*, a fine sight! Like a devil astride a pair of jaws. Listen to me, my friends. I'm a truant through and through, a true argotier, a born palliard. I've been very rich, but I've run through my patrimony. My mother wanted to make me an officer, my father a subdeacon, my aunt an investigating councillor, my grandmother Protonotary to the King, my great aunt a short-robed paymaster. But I became a truant. I told my father and he spat his curse in my face, I told my mother and she began, the old woman, to weep and drool like that log on the fire-dog. Long live pleasure! I'm a great destroyer! Some different wine, mine lovely hostess! I

1. Where, up until the Revolution, there was a chapel with four or five hundred statues of saints.

can still pay. No more of that Suresnes. It offends my gullet. *Corbœuf*, I'd as soon gargle with a basket!'

The company, meanwhile, roared with laughter and clapped, and finding the tumult renewed around him, the student shouted: 'Ah, a lovely sound! *Populi debacchantis populosa debacchatio*!'[1] He then began to sing, his eyes brimming as if with ecstasy, in the accents of a canon intoning vespers: '*Quae cantica! quae organa! quae cantilenae! quae melodiae hic sine fine decantantur! sonant mellifIua hymnorum organa, suavissima angelorum melodia, cantica canticorum mira!*'[2] He broke off. 'Where's that infernal barmaid, bring me some supper.'

There was a moment of semi-silence, during which the shrill voice of the Duke of Egypt rose in its turn, instructing his gypsies: 'The weasel's known as Aduine, the fox as Blue-Foot or Forest-Ranger, the wolf as Grey-Foot or Gold Foot, the bear as the Old Man or Grandfather. A gnome's bonnet makes you invisible and shows you invisible things. Every tcad that's baptized has to be dressed in red or black velvet, with a small bell round its neck and another on its feet. The godfather holds its head and the godmother its backside. The demon Sidragasum has the power to make girls dance stark naked.'

'By the mass, I'd like to be the demon Sidragasum,' Jehan broke in.

Meanwhile the truants went on whispering and arming themselves at the other end of the tavern.

'Poor Esmeralda!' said one Bohemian. 'She's our sister. We must get her out of there.'

'Is she still in Notre-Dame, then?' put in a Jewish-looking merchant.

'Yes, by God!'

'Well then, comrades,' cried the merchant, 'to Notre-Dame! Especially because in the chapel of Saints Féréol and Ferrution there are two statues, one of St John the Baptist and the other of St Anthony, solid gold, together weighing seventeen gold marcs

1. 'Of a people making merry, a popular merry-making.'

2. 'What canticles! What instruments! What chants! What melodies are here sung without end! There sounds the mellifluous instrument of the hymns, the most sweet melody of the angels, admirable songs of songs' (St Augustine).

fifteen estellins, with plinths of silver gilt, seventeen marks, five ounces. I know, I'm a goldsmith.'

At this point Jehan's supper was brought. He sprawled against the breasts of the girl beside him and exclaimed:

'By St Voult of Lucca, whom the people call St Goguelu, I am perfectly happy. Before me I see an idiot, staring at me with the clean-shaven face of an archduke. To my left another whose teeth are so long they hide his chin. And then I'm like the Marshal of Gié at the siege of Pontoise, my right is resting on a small protuberance. Mahomet's belly, comrade! You look like a man who sells tennis-balls, yet you come and sit next to me! I'm an aristocrat, my friend. Trade is not compatible with nobility. Out of it. Hey, you there, don't fight! What, Baptiste Croque-Oison, are you going to risk that beautiful nose of yours against the huge fists of that buzzard? Idiot! *Non cuiquam datum est habere nasum.*[1] You're truly divine, Jacqueline Ronge-Oreille, it's a shame you haven't got any hair! Hallo, my name is Jehan Frollo and my brother's an archdeacon. He can go to the devil. Everything I am telling you is the truth. When I became a truant, I happily gave up half a house situated in paradise which my brother had promised me. *Dimidiam domum in paradiso.* I quote from the text. I've got a fief in the Rue Tirechappe, and women are all in love with me, which is as true as it's true that St Eloy was an excellent goldsmith, and that the five trades of the good town of Paris are tanners, tawers, baldric makers, purse-makers and cord-wainers and that St Laurence was grilled on egg-shells. I swear to you, comrades,

> I'll drink no piment for one full year
> If this is a lie I tell you here.

It's bright moonlight, my charmer, look through that air-vent there, how the wind is ruffling the clouds! As I'm ruffling your gorget. Girls, snuff the children and the candles! Christ and Mahomet, what am I eating, Jupiter? Hey, you old hag, the hairs you can't find on the heads of your whores turn up in the omelettes. I like my omelettes bald, old woman! May the devil give you a snub-nose! A hostelry fit for Beelzebub where the whores comb their hair with the forks!'

1. 'It has not been given to everyone to have a nose.'

Having said which, he smashed his plate on the stone floor and began to sing at the top of his voice:

God's blood, I've got
No faith, no law,
No fire, no place,
Or king,
Or God!

Clopin Trouillefou had meanwhile finished distributing the weapons. He approached Gringoire, who seemed plunged in some profound meditation, his feet on a fire-dog. 'What the devil's on your mind, friend Pierre?' said the King of Thunes.

Gringoire turned to him with a mournful smile. 'I like fire, my dear lord. Not for the base reason that fire warms our feet or cooks our soup, but because it has sparks. I sometimes spend hours staring at the sparks. I find hundreds of things in the stars dotted over the black of the fire-back. Those stars are worlds too.'

'Damned if I understand you,' said the truant. 'Do you know what time it is?'

'I don't know,' answered Gringoire.

Clopin then went up to the Duke of Egypt.

'Comrade Mathias, quarter past isn't good. They say King Louis XI's in Paris.'

'One more reason to extricate our sister from his clutches,' answered the old Bohemian.

'You talk like a man, Mathias,' said the King of Thunes. 'Anyway we shall act swiftly. We need fear no resistance in the church. The canons are rabbits and we are in force. The parliament will be well and truly caught tomorrow when they come to fetch her! Pope's guts! I don't want them to hang that pretty girl!'

Clopin left the tavern.

During this time, Jehan had been shouting hoarsely: 'I drink, I eat, I'm drunk, I'm Jupiter! Hey, Pierre the Slaughterman, if you look at me like that again, I'll flick the dust from your nose with my fingers.'

Gringoire, for his part, had been torn from his meditations and had begun to contemplate the gaudy, animated scene around him, murmuring under his breath: '*Luxuriosa res vinum et tumultuosa ebrietas.*[1] How right I am, alas, not to drink and what an ad-

1. 'Wine and turbulent drunkenness are things of luxury.'

mirable saying of St Benedict's: *Vinum apostatare facit etiam sapientes.*'[1]

Just then Clopin returned and shouted in a voice of thunder: 'Midnight!'

The effect of this word was like that of the 'mount' being sounded in a resting regiment; all the truants, men, women and children, rushed as one from the tavern with a great clatter of arms and of iron.

The moon had gone in.

The Court of Miracles was in total darkness. Not a light to be seen. Yet it was far from deserted. One could make out a crowd of men and women, conversing in low voices. One caught the hum of voices and the gleam of every kind of weapon in the darkness. Clopin climbed up on a huge stone. 'Form up, the argotiers!' he yelled. 'Form up, Egypt! Form up, Galilee!' There was a movement in the shadows. The vast multitude seemed to be forming into a column. A minute or two later, the King of Thunes's voice was again raised: 'And now silence as we cross Paris! The password is "Blazing bayonets." The torches won't be lit till Notre-Dame! Quick march!'

Ten minutes later, the horsemen of the watch were fleeing in terror before a long procession of silent, black-clad men descending towards the Pont-au-Change, along the tortuous streets that lead in every direction through the heavily built-up quarter of Les Halles.

FOUR
A Friend Blunders

THAT same night, Quasimodo was not asleep. He had just made his final round of the church. As he closed the doors, he had not noticed the archdeacon go past and evidence some displeasure as he saw him bolting and padlocking the vast iron armature which lent their broad panels the solidity of a wall. Dom Claude seemed even more preoccupied than usual. For the rest, since the nocturnal episode in the cell, he was always abusing Quasimodo; but though he berated and even on occasions struck him, nothing could shake the submissiveness, patience and devoted resignation of the

1. 'Wine makes even wise men abjure their faith.'

faithful bell-ringer. He withstood everything from the archdeacon, insults, threats or blows, without a murmur and without complaint. At most, when Dom Claude climbed the staircase to the tower, his eye would follow him uneasily, but the archdeacon had abstained of his own accord from reappearing before the gypsy.

That night, then, after glancing in at his poor, forsaken bells, at Jacqueline, Marie and Thibauld, Quasimodo climbed to the top of the north tower, closed his dark lantern tightly and laid it on the leads, and began to gaze at Paris. The night, as we have said, was very dark, and Paris, at that time, was not, properly speaking, lit, but appeared to the eye as a confused jumble of black shapes, broken here and there by the whitish curve of the Seine. Quasimodo could see no lights except in one window of a far-off building, whose dim and sombre profile stood out high above the roofs, over by the Porte Saint-Antoine. There, too, someone was keeping vigil.

As he let his single eye drift across that horizon of mist and blackness, the bell-ringer felt within him an inexpressible anxiety. For several days now, he had been on his guard. He had seen sinister-looking men prowling constantly round the church, who never took their eyes off the girl's asylum. He thought that some plot was perhaps being hatched against the poor fugitive. He imagined that she, like himself, was an object of popular hatred, and that soon something might very well happen. So he stood on his bell-tower, on the look-out, 'thinking in his thinkery' as Rabelais puts it, his eye alternately on the cell and on Paris, standing guard like a faithful hound, his mind full of mistrust.

Suddenly, as he peered at the town out of that one eye which Nature, by a kind of compensation, had made so keen that it was almost a substitute for the other organs that Quasimodo lacked, he thought there was something odd about the outline of the Quai de la Vieille Pelleterie, that there was movement at that point, that the line of the parapet, etched in black against the whiteness of the water, was not still and straight like that of the other quays, but undulating as he watched, like the waves of a river or the heads of a marching crowd.

This seemed to him strange. He grew doubly attentive. The movement seemed to be coming towards the Cité. But no light of any kind. It remained on the quay for a time, then slowly tailed off, as if whatever was going past had entered the interior of the island;

then it ceased altogether and the line of the quay went back to being straight and immobile.

Just as Quasimodo was wearing himself out in conjectures, the movement seemed to reappear in the Rue du Parvis, which extends into the Cité at right angles to the façade of Notre-Dame. Finally, pitch-dark though it was, he saw the head of a column emerge from the street and in no time at all a crowd flood into the square, of which all that he could make out in the blackness was that it was a crowd.

The sight had its terror. It is probable that this strange procession, seemingly so concerned to move under cover of total darkness, was observing a silence no less total. Some kind of sound must however have escaped it, if only the tramp of feet. But this did not reach the deaf Quasimodo, on whom this vast multitude, of which he could see very little and hear nothing, yet which was moving and marching so near by, had the effect of a gathering of corpses, dumb, impalpable and wreathed in vapour. He seemed to see a mist full of men advancing towards him, to see shadows moving about in the shadows.

Then his fears returned, and the idea of an attempt against the gypsy recurred to him. He sensed dimly that he was approaching some violent situation. At this moment of crisis, he conferred with himself, and more promptly and rationally than might have been expected from a brain so ill-organized. Should he arouse the gypsy? Make her escape? Which way? The streets were besieged, the church backed on to the river. No boat! No way out! Only one course was open, to defend access to Notre-Dame to the death, to resist at least until help came, if help was to come, and not to disturb La Esmeralda's sleep. The poor girl would be aroused soon enough, to die. This resolution once made, he began to examine the 'enemy' more calmly.

The crowd on the parvis seemed to be swelling all the time. But he presumed it must be making very little noise, since the windows in the streets and the square remained closed. All of a sudden a light shone out, and instantly seven or eight torches were being waved overhead, brandishing their bouquets of flame in the shadows. Now Quasimodo could distinctly see a terrifying herd of men and women in rags milling about in the parvis, and the glinting points of innumerable scythes, pikes, bill-hooks and partisans. Here and there a black pitchfork put horns on a hideous face. He vaguely remembered this populace and thought he recognized all the faces which, a few months earlier, had acclaimed him pope of fools. A man who held a torch in one hand and a bull-whip in the other climbed on to a boundary-stone and seemed to harangue them. At the same time this strange army performed a number of manoeuvres, as if taking up position round the church. Quasimodo picked up his lantern and went down on to the platform between the towers to get a closer look and to see to his means of defence.

Clopin Trouillefou, when he arrived before the tall portal of Notre-Dame, had indeed deployed his troops for battle. Although he was not anticipating any resistance, he wanted, as a prudent general, to maintain a disposition which would enable him, if need be, to withstand a sudden attack by the watch or the constables. He had therefore disposed his brigade in depth, in such a way that, seen from above and from a distance, it looked like the Roman triangle at the battle of Ecnoma, like Alexander's pig's head, or like Gustavus Adolphus's famous wedge. The base of the triangle rested on the far end of the square, so as to block the Rue du Parvis; one of the sides faced the Hôtel-Dieu, the other the Rue Saint-Pierre-aux-Bœufs. Clopin Trouillefou had placed himself at the apex, together with the Duke of Egypt, our friend Jehan and the boldest of his beggars.

An enterprise such as the truants were attempting at that moment against Notre-Dame was by no means a rarity in medieval towns. What today we call 'police' did not then exist. In populous, and especially capital cities, there was no single, central, regulating authority. Feudalism had constructed these great communes in a strange way. A city was an assemblage of countless lordships which divided it up into compartments of every shape and size. Hence there were countless contradictory polices, or in other words no police. In Paris, for example, independently of the 141 lords claiming quit-rent, there were twenty-five who claimed both justice and quit-rent, from the Bishop of Paris, who had 105 streets, down to the Abbot of Notre-Dame des Champs, who had four. All these feudal justiciaries recognized the suzerain authority of the king only in name. All of them had rights of hundred. All of them were their own masters. Louis XI, that indefatigable worker who began the wholesale demolition of the feudal edifice, which was carried on by Richelieu and Louis XIV in the interests of the monarchy, and completed by Mirabeau in those of the people, Louis XI, as I say, tried hard to break up this network of lordships that covered Paris, by violently controverting it with two or three ordinances of general police. Thus, in 1465, an order to the inhabitants to put lighted candles in their windows at nightfall and to lock up their dogs, on pain of the noose; in the same year, an order to close the streets each evening with iron chains, and a prohibition on the carrying of daggers or offensive weapons in the streets at night. But all these attempts at communal legislation quickly fell into disuse. The burgesses let the wind extinguish the candles in their casements, and let their dogs run wild; the iron chains were stretched across only during a siege; the only change brought about by the ban on daggers was one of nomenclature: the Rue Coupe-Gueule becoming the Rue Coupe-Gorge,[1] which was obviously an improvement. The old scaffolding of feudal jurisdictions was still in place; a vast accumulation of bailiwicks and lordships meeting above the town, hampering one another, encroaching on one another and becoming entangled and enmeshed; a futile thicket of watches, under-watches and counter-watches, through which brigandage, rapine and sedition passed by force of arms. Given this chaos, it was by no means unheard-of for part of the populace to rise up against a palace, an hôtel or a private house in the more populous quarters. In most cases, the neighbours did not intervene unless their own houses were threatened by pillage. They turned a deaf ear to the shooting, closed their shutters and barricaded their doors, and allowed the quarrel to be resolved with or without the watch; and the following day in Paris, it would be: 'They broke in to Etienne Barbette's last night', 'they seized the Marshal of Clermont bodily', etc. And so not only the royal residences, the Louvre, the Palais, the Bastille, the Tournelles, but also merely seignorial dwellings, the Petit-Bourbon, the Hôtel de Sens, the Hôtel d'Angoulême, and so on, had their battlemented walls and machicolations over the gates. Churches were protected by their sanctity. Yet a few of them, of which Notre-Dame was not one, were fortified. The Abbot of Saint-Germain-des-Prés was crenellated like a baron, and expended even more of his bronze on bom-

1. An equivalent change might be from Cut-throat Street to Den-of-Thieves Street.

bards than on bells. His fortress was still to be seen in 1610. Today even his church barely survives.

But back to Notre-Dame.

Once the first deployments were completed, and we owe it to the honour of truant discipline to say that Clopin's orders were carried out in silence and with admirable precision, the worthy leader of the band climbed on to the parapet of the parvis and raised his hoarse, sullen voice, standing with his face to Notre-Dame, whose ruddy façade came and went in the light of the torch he was waving, as it was buffeted by the wind and masked continually by its own smoke.

'Louis de Beaumont, Bishop of Paris, Councillor in the Court of Parliament, I, Clopin Trouillefou, King of Thunes, Grand Coëzra, Prince of the Argots, Bishop of Fools, I say to you: Our sister, wrongly convicted of magic, has taken refuge in your church; you owe her asylum and safekeeping; but the court of parliament seeks to remove her from there and you have agreed; so that if God and the truants were not here, tomorrow she would be hanged on the Grève. And so we come to you, bishop. If your church is sacred, so is our sister; if our sister is not sacred, then neither is your church. That is why we call on you to return the girl to us if you want to save your church, or we shall take the girl back and will sack the church. Which will be right. As a pledge of which, I hereby plant my banner, and may God protect you, Bishop of Paris!'

Quasimodo, unfortunately, could not hear these words, uttered with a sort of wild and sombre majesty. A truant offered Clopin his banner and he solemnly set it up between two paving-stones. It was a pitchfork from whose prongs there dangled a quarter of bleeding carrion.

Having done which, the King of Thunes turned round and ran an eye over his army, a hostile-looking multitude whose eyes gleamed almost as brightly as their pikes. After a moment's pause: 'Forward, lads!' he shouted. 'To work, my rowdies.'

Thirty sturdy men, with square limbs and the look of locksmiths, stepped from the ranks, carrying hammers, pincers and iron bars over their shoulders. They went towards the main entrance to the church, climbed the steps, and soon could be seen crouching under the archway, working on the door with pincers and crowbars. A crowd of truants followed them either to help or to watch. They blocked the eleven steps of the portal.

But the door stood firm. 'Damn it, it's tough and stubborn!' said one. 'It's old,' said another, 'its cartilages are like leather.' 'Courage, comrades!' Clopin went. 'I'll wager my head against a slipper that you'll have opened the door, taken the girl and stripped the high altar before a single beadle's woken up! There, I think the lock's giving.'

Clopin was interrupted by a terrible crash that rang out at that moment behind him. He turned round. A huge beam had just fallen from the sky, crushing a dozen truants on the steps of the church, and then rebounded on to the paving with a sound like a cannon-ball, breaking one or two more legs among the crowd of beggars, who drew back with cries of alarm. In a trice, the enclosed area of the parvis was deserted. Although they were protected by the deeply recessed doorway, the 'rowdies' abandoned the door and Clopin himself fell back to a respectful distance from the church.

'That was a near thing!' shouted Jehan. 'I felt the wind of it, *tête-bœuf*! But Pierre the Slaughterman's been slaughtered!'

Words cannot describe the amazement, mixed with terror, that fell on the bandits along with the beam. For several minutes they remained staring into the air, more dismayed by this lump of wood than by twenty thousand royal archers. 'Satan!' mumbled the Duke of Egypt, 'this smacks of magic!' 'It was the moon that threw the log at us,' said Andry the Red. 'Yes, because they say the moon's a friend of the Virgin!' put in François Chante-Prune. 'A thousand popes!' cried Clopin, 'you're idiots, the lot of you!' But he could not explain the falling beam.

Meanwhile, there was nothing to be discerned on the façade, because the light from the torches would not reach to its top. The heavy beam lay in the middle of the parvis, and one could hear the groans of the poor devils who had received the first impact and had had their bellies cut in two against the edges of the stone steps.

The King of Thunes, his first astonishment past, finally hit on an explanation that his companions found plausible: 'God's teeth, are the canons defending themselves? Sack the church, then, sack it!'

'Sack it!' the mob took up with a furious hurrah. And a volley of crossbows and hackbuts was loosed off against the façade of the church.

At the detonation, the peaceable inhabitants of the houses round about woke up, several windows were seen to open and nightcaps and hands holding candles appeared at the casements. 'Aim at the windows!' shouted Clopin. The windows closed again instantly, and the poor burgesses, who had barely had time to cast a bewildered look on this scene of lights and uproar, returned to sweat with fear next to their wives and to wonder whether the sabbath was now held in the Parvis of Notre-Dame or whether it was a raid by the Burgundians like in '64. Husbands thought of rapine, wives of rape, and both trembled.

'Sack it,' the argotiers took up. But they did not dare come any closer. They looked at the church, they looked at the beam. The beam did not move. The building preserved its calm and deserted air, yet something froze the truants' blood.

'To work, then, rowdies!' shouted Trouillefou. 'Break in the door.'

No one moved.

'Beard and belly!' said Clopin, 'there are men here afraid of a rafter.'

An old 'rowdy' addressed him.

'It's not the rafter that's worrying us, captain, it's the door, it's all stitched up with iron bars. The pincers are useless.'

'So what do you need to break it down?' asked Clopin.

'Ah, we'd need a battering-ram!'

The King of Thunes ran boldly to the formidable beam and put his foot on it. 'Here's one,' he cried; 'the canons have sent it to you.' And with a derisive bow in the direction of the church: 'Thank you, canons!'

His bravado had the right effect, the spell of the beam was broken. The truants plucked up courage again and soon the heavy beam, raised like a feather in two hundred sturdy arms, was thudding furiously against the great door that they had already tried to loosen. Seen thus, in the half-light shed over the square by the scattered torches of the truants, the long beam looked like some monstrous millipede, charging, head down, against the stone giant, as the crowd of men ran and dashed it against the church.

The half-metal door resounded like a vast drum under the impact of the beam; it did not break open but the entire cathedral shuddered, and rumblings could be heard from the edifice's deep cavities. At the same moment, a shower of huge stones began to fall on the assailants from on top of the façade. 'Damn it!' shouted

Jehan, 'are the towers shaking their balustrades down on our heads?' But the momentum had been given, the King of Thunes was in the forefront, it was certainly the bishop defending himself, and they beat against the door all the more furiously, despite the stones, which were splitting skulls to right and to left.

Remarkably enough, these stones were falling one at a time, yet in rapid succession. The argotiers were always aware of two at any given moment, one amongst their legs, the other above their heads. There were few who were unmarked, and a thick layer of dead and wounded already lay bleeding and heaving under the feet of the attackers, raging now and constantly taking one another's place. The long beam continued to beat against the door as regularly as the hammer of a bell, the stones to rain down, the door to bellow.

The reader will doubtless have guessed before now that this unexpected resistance, which had exasperated the truants, came from Quasimodo.

Luck had unfortunately come to the deaf man's aid.

When he went down on to the platform between the two towers, his mind was in a turmoil. For a minute or two he had run up and down the gallery like a madman, looking down at the serried mass of truants preparing to rush the church, and asking God or the devil to save the gypsy. It had crossed his mind to climb into the south belfry and sound the tocsin; but before he could have set the bell in motion, before Marie's great voice could have uttered a single cry, would there not have been time for the door of the church to be broken in ten times over? At that very moment the 'rowdies' were advancing on it with their tools. What should he do?

He suddenly remembered that builders had been at work all that day, repairing the wall, the framework and the roof of the south tower. This was a ray of light. The wall was of stone, the roof of lead and the framework timber. That prodigious framework, so intricate that it was known as 'the forest'.

Quasimodo ran to the tower. The lower rooms were indeed full of materials. There were piles of rubble-stones, coiled sheets of lead, bundles of lathes, stout rafters already notched by the saw, heaps of plaster. An entire arsenal.

Time was of the essence. The pincers and hammers were at work below. With a strength redoubled by his sense of danger, he lifted the heaviest and longest of the beams, pushed it out through a window, took hold of it again outside the tower, slid it over the edge of the balustrade that surrounds the platform and launched it into the void. As it fell the one hundred and sixty feet, the vast piece of timber scraped against the wall, snapping off the sculptures, and turned end over end several times like the sail of a windmill spinning off through the air on its own. Finally it struck the ground, a terrible cry went up and the black beam looked like a leaping serpent as it rebounded on to the paving.

Quasimodo saw the truants scatter as the beam fell, like ashes blown by a child. He took advantage of their terror, and as they stared superstitiously at this bludgeon that had fallen from the sky and shot out the eyes of the stone saints in the portal with a volley of arrows and buck-shot, Quasimodo was silently accumulating plaster, stones, rubble and even bags of building tools on the edge of the balustrade from which the beam had already been launched.

And so, as soon as they began to batter at the great door, the hail-storm of stones began to fall, and it seemed to them that the church was demolishing itself of its own accord above their heads.

Whoever could have seen Quasimodo at that moment would have been terrified. Quite apart from the projectiles he had heaped up on the balustrade, he had also amassed a pile of stones on the platform itself. As soon as the rubble accumulated on the outer ledge was exhausted, he resorted to the pile. Thus he stooped and straightened, stooped and straightened, with incredible activity. His huge gnome's head leant over the balustrade, then an enormous stone would fall, and another, and another.

Now and again his eye would follow a stone down, and when it killed he let out an 'Aah!'

The beggars had not lost heart, however. The stout door against which they were exerting themselves had already trembled a score of times under the weight of their oaken battering-ram, multiplied by the strength of a hundred men. The panels were cracking, the carvings flew in splinters, the hinges leapt on their eye-bolts at each impact, the planks were giving way, the wood was being pounded to sawdust between the iron ribs. Luckily for Quasimodo, there was more iron than wood.

He sensed, though, that the great door was giving. Although he couldn't hear it, each blow of the battering-ram echoed through both the cavernous church and his own entrails. From up above he could see the truants, full of triumph and fury, shaking their fists at the murky façade, and both for the gypsy and for himself he envied the owls their wings as they flew off above his head.

His shower of rubble-stones was not sufficient to drive the attackers off.

At this moment of anguish, he noticed, just below the balustrade from which he had crushed the argotiers, two long stone rain-spouts which disgorged immediately above the great door. The opening to them was in the floor of the platform. He had an idea. He ran to his bell-ringer's den to fetch a faggot, laid a great many bundles of lathes and coils of lead on it, ammunition he had not so far used, then, having arranged this pyre neatly in front of the hole of the two rain-spouts, he set light to it with his lantern.

In the meanwhile, since the stones were no longer falling, the truants had stopped staring upwards. The bandits, panting like a pack of hounds that has bearded a wild-boar in its lair, were pressing noisily round the great door, forced out of shape by the battering-ram but still standing. They quivered in anticipation of the decisive blow, the blow that was going to eviscerate it. They fought to get closer so that when it opened they would be among the first to rush inside the opulent cathedral, a vast depository where the wealth of three centuries had accumulated. They roared with cupidity and delight as they reminded each other of the lovely silver crucifixes, the lovely brocade copes, the lovely silver-gilt tombstones, the great splendour of the choir, the dazzling feast-days, the sparkling torches of Christmastime, the brilliant sunlight of Easter, all those splendid solemnities when the altars were embossed and encrusted with the gold and diamonds of reliquaries, candelabra, ciboria, tabernacles and shrines. At this beautiful moment, palliards and malingerers, rufflers and clapper-dogens were certainly much less preoccupied with freeing the gypsy than with sacking the church. We are perfectly ready to believe that for a good many of them La Esmeralda was merely an excuse, that is if robbers need excuses.

Suddenly, as they were forming up round the battering-ram for one last effort, each one holding his breath and tensing his muscles so as to lend his full strength to the decisive blow, a screaming even more frightful than the one that had arisen and then expired underneath the beam rose from their midst. Those who were not yelling, those who were still alive, looked. Two jets of molten lead were falling from on top of the building into the very thick of the crowd. That sea of men had just subsided beneath the boiling metal which, at the two points where it was falling, had made two black, smoking holes in the crowd, such as hot water might make in snow. Dying men could be seen twitching, half incinerated and bellowing with pain. Around the two principal jets, drops of this terrible rain were splashing over the attackers and entered their skulls like gimlets of flame. The poor devils were being riddled by the innumerable pellets of that ponderable fire.

The screams were harrowing. They fled in disorder, throwing the beam down on the corpses, the boldest and most fearful alike, and the parvis was emptied for a second time.

All eyes were raised to the top of the church. There an extraordinary sight met them. On the summit of the topmost gallery, higher than the central rose-window, a great flame was rising from between the two towers amidst eddying sparks, a great ragged, furious flame, a shred of which would be borne off by the wind now and again into the smoke. Below this flame, below the sombre balustrade and its fiery trefoils, two gargoyles were unremittingly spewing out the burning rain, which showed as a stream of silver against the blackness of the façade. As they neared the ground, the twin jets of liquid lead spread out into a spray, like the water that gushes from the rose of a watering-can. Above the flame, each of the enormous towers displayed two harsh, sharp-edged faces, one quite black, the other quite red, and seemed taller still by the full immensity of the shadows they cast up into the very sky itself. Their countless sculptures of devils and dragons wore a dismal aspect. As one watched, the uncertain brilliance of the flame set them in motion. There were serpents that appeared to be laughing, gargoyles one seemed to hear yapping, salamanders blowing into the flames, dragons sneezing in the smoke. And amongst the monsters thus awoken from their stone sleep by the flame and the din, there was one who was walking about and was seen now and again to pass across the fiery brow of the pyre like a bat before a candle.

Far away on the hills of Bicêtre, this untoward beacon would no doubt awaken the woodcutter, who would be terrified to see the gigantic shadow of the towers of Notre-Dame flickering across his heath.

A terrified silence fell on the truants, broken only by the cries of alarm of the canons, shut up in their cloister and more apprehensive than horses in a burning stable, by the furtive sound of windows quickly opening then closing again more quickly still, by the shifting of furniture inside the houses and the Hôtel-Dieu, by the wind in the flames, by the death-rattles of the truants, and by the constant sizzle of the lead showering on to the pavement.

The truant leaders had meanwhile withdrawn underneath the porch of the Gondelaurier house and were conferring. The Duke of Egypt sat on a boundary-stone. staring at the fantastic bonfire, blazing two hundred feet up in the air, with a religious awe. Clopin Trouillefou was chewing his great fists in fury. 'Impossible to get inside!' he muttered between his teeth.

'Old hag of a church!' growled the old Bohemian Mathias Hungadi Spicali.

'By the pope's moustaches!' put in an irreverent and grizzled veteran, 'those church drainpipes are better at spitting molten lead at you than the machicolations of Lectoure.'

'Do you see that demon going to and fro in front of the fire?' exclaimed the Duke of Egypt.

'It's that damned bell-ringer, by God, said Clopin. 'It's Quasimodo.'

The Bohemian shook his head. 'And I tell you it's the spirit Sabnac, the great marquis, the demon of fortifications. He has the shape of an armed soldier and the head of a lion. Sometimes he rides a hideous horse. He turns men into stones and builds towers with them. He commands fifty legions. It's him all right. I recognize him. Sometimes he's dressed in a fine robe of figured gold like the Turks wear.'

'Where's Bellevigne de l'Etoile?' asked Clopin.

'Dead,' answered a truant.

Andry the Red gave an idiot laugh. 'Notre-Dame is making work for the Hôtel-Dieu,' he said.

'Is there no way of forcing that door, then?' cried the King of Thunes, stamping his foot.

The Duke of Egypt pointed sadly to the twin streams of boiling lead that continued to streak the black façade like two long distaffs of phosphorus. 'It's been known for churches to defend themselves like this on their own,' he remarked with a sigh. 'Santa Sophia in Constantinople, forty years ago, overthrew Mahom's crescent three times in succession by shaking its domes, which are its heads. William of Paris, who built this one, was a magician.'

'Must we slink ignominiously off like so many running footmen?' said Clopin. 'And leave our sister here to be hanged tomorrow by those wolves in monks' cowls?'

'And the sacristy, where there are wagonloads of gold!' added a truant, whose name, we are sorry to say, we do not know.

'By the beard of the Prophet!' cried Trouillefou.

'Let's try one more time,' the truant went on.

Mathias Hungadi shook his head. 'We shan't get in through the door. We must find the chink in the old hag's armour. A hole, a false postern, some join or other.'

'Who's with me?' said Clopin. 'I'm going back. By the way, where's the young student Jehan and all that scrap-iron?'

'Dead no doubt,' someone replied. 'We can't hear his laugh any more.'

The King of Thunes frowned.

'Pity. There was a stout heart under the scrap-iron. And Maître Pierre Gringoire?'

'He sneaked off, Captain Clopin,' said Andry le Rouge, 'when we were still only at the Pont-aux-Changeurs.'

Clopin stamped his foot. '*Gueule-Dieu!* He urges us into it, then he deserts us in mid-stream! Cowardly bag of wind, with a slipper for a helmet!'

'Captain Clopin,' cried Andry the Red, who was looking down the Rue du Parvis, 'here's the little student.'

'Pluto be praised!' said Clopin. 'But what the devil's he dragging behind him?'

It was indeed Jehan, hastening along as fast as his heavy paladin's outfit and the long ladder he was pulling gallantly along the pavement would allow; he was more out of breath than an ant harnessed to a blade of grass twenty times its own length.

'Victory! *Te Deum!*' cried the student. 'This is the dockers' ladder from the Port Saint-Landry.'

Clopin went up to him.

'*Corne-Dieu*, boy, what do you intend doing with that ladder?'

'I've got it,' answered Jehan breathlessly. 'I knew where it was. Under the lean-to at the lieutenant's house. There's a girl there I know, who thinks I'm as handsome as a Cupid. I used that to get the ladder, and I've got the ladder, *Pasque-Mahom*! The poor gir came and opened the door to me in her nightshirt.'

'Yes,' said Clopin, 'but what do you intend doing with the ladder?'

Jehan gave him a cunning, capable look and clicked his fingers like castanets. At that moment he was sublime. On his head he wore one of those overladen helmets of the fifteenth century, which struck fear into the enemy with the monsters on their crests. His own bristled with ten iron beaks, so that Jehan could have claimed the fearsome epithet of δεκέμβολος[1] from Nestor's ship in Homer.

'What do I intend doing with it, august King of Thunes? You see that row of idiotic-looking statues there above the three doorways?'

'Yes. What of them?'

'That's the gallery of the kings of France.'

'What's that to me?' said Clopin.

'Wait, will you! At the end of that gallery there's a door that's never more than latched, I climb up there with this ladder and I'm inside the church.'

'Let me go up first, boy.'

'No, comrade, the ladder's mine. Come on, you'll be second.'

'May Beelzebub strangle you!' said the surly Clopin. 'I don't want to be behind anyone.'

'Find a ladder then, Clopin!'

Jehan began to run about the square, dragging his ladder and shouting: 'To me, lads!'

In no time at all, the ladder was raised and propped against the balustrade of the lower gallery, above one of the side doors. The crowd of truants cheered loudly and ran to the foot of it, to climb up. But Jehan maintained his privilege and was the first to set foot on the rungs. It was quite a long climb. Today the gallery of the kings of France stands some sixty feet above the pavement. The eleven steps of the perron raised it higher still. Jehan climbed slowly, somewhat hampered by his heavy armour, gripping the rungs with one hand and his crossbow in the other. When he reached the middle of the ladder he cast a mournful glance down at the corpses of the poor argotiers littering the steps. 'Alas!' he said, 'a mound of bodies worthy of the fifth canto of the *Iliad*!' Then he

1. 'Ten-spurred.'

resumed his ascent. The truants came behind him. There was one on every rung. As that line of armour-plated backs rippled upwards in the shadows, it looked just like a steel-scaled serpent rearing up against the church. Jehan, who formed its head and was whistling, made the illusion complete.

The student finally reached the balcony of the gallery and vaulted it nimbly enough, to the applause of the entire truantry. As master of the citadel he let out a whoop of joy, then suddenly broke off, petrified. He had just seen Quasimodo, lurking in the darkness behind the statue of a king, his eye glittering.

Before a second assailant could set foot on the gallery, the formidable hunchback leapt to the head of the ladder, seized the two ends of the uprights wordlessly in his powerful hands, raised them, pushed them away from the wall, balanced the long, flexible ladder, encumbered from top to bottom with truants, for a moment, amidst yells of anguish, then suddenly, with superhuman strength, hurled that cluster of men down into the square. For a second, the more resolute ones still hoped. The ladder, once thrown backwards, remained upright for a moment and seemed to hesitate, then it swayed, suddenly described a terrifying quarter of a circle eighty feet in radius, and smashed its load of bandits down on the paving more swiftly than a drawbridge whose chains have snapped. A vast imprecation went up, then everything was extinguished, and a few maimed wretches crawled out from beneath the pile of dead.

Amongst the attackers, a murmur of grief and anger succeeded the earlier yells of triumph. Quasimodo stared impassively, both elbows resting on the balustrade. He looked like some shaggy old king at his window.

Jehan Frollo, for his part, was in a critical situation. He found himself alone on the gallery with the redoubtable bell-ringer, cut off from his companions by a vertical eighty-foot wall. While Quasimodo was toying with the ladder, the student had run to the postern thinking it was open. It was not. The hunchback had locked it behind him when he entered the gallery. So Jehan had hidden behind a stone king, not daring to breathe, his scared face fixed on the monstrous hunchback, like the man who, when paying court to a menagerie-keeper's wife, scaled the wrong wall one night to keep a rendezvous with her and abruptly came face to face with a white bear.

To start with, the deaf man paid him no heed; but at last he turned his head and suddenly drew himself up. He had just noticed the student.

Jehan steeled himself for a rude impact, but the deaf man did not move; he merely turned to stare at the student.

'Ha!' said Jehan, 'why are you staring at me with that one melancholy eye of yours?'

And so saying, the young rogue surreptitiously strung his cross-bow.

'Quasimodo!' he shouted, 'I'm going to change your nickname. They'll call you the blind man.'

He let fly. The feathered bolt went whirring off to lodge in the hunchback's left arm. Quasimodo was no more troubled by it than if it had scratched King Pharamond. He put his hand to the arrow, wrenched it from his arm and calmly snapped it over his huge knee. Then he dropped rather than threw the two halves on the ground. But Jehan got no chance to fire a second time. After snapping the arrow, Quasimodo snorted loudly, sprang like a grasshopper and fell on the student, whose armour was flattened against the wall by the blow.

And then, in the penumbra round the wavering light of the torches, they half-glimpsed something terrible.

With his left hand, Quasimodo was holding both Jehan's arms, who had given himself up for lost and was not struggling. With his right hand, the hunchback removed his entire armour piece by piece, in silence and with a sinister deliberation, sword, daggers, helmet, breastplate, brassards. It was like a monkey peeling a nut. Quasimodo threw the student's iron shell down at his feet, bit by bit.

When the student found himself disarmed, unclothed, feeble and naked in those redoubtable hands, he did not try to talk to the deaf man, but began to laugh insolently in his face and to sing a then popular refrain, blithe and fearless as a boy of sixteen:

> The town of Cambrai
> Was in fine array
> Till Marafin one day . . .[1]

He never finished. They saw Quasimodo erect on the parapet of

1. Marafin was Governor of Cambrai and despoiled it.

the gallery, holding the student's feet in only one hand and whirling him round above the drop like a sling. Then they heard a noise like a bone box bursting against a wall and something was seen to fall which was arrested a third of the way down by a projection of the architecture. It was a dead body, which remained caught there, bent double, its back broken, its skull empty.

A cry of horror arose from the truants. 'Vengeance!' yelled Clopin. 'Sack the church!' answered the multitude. 'To the attack, to the attack!' And a prodigious howling went up, in a mixture of every known language, dialect and accent. The poor student's death filled the crowd with a burning fury. It was seized by shame, and anger at having been held in check for so long in front of a church by a hunchback. Their fury found ladders and multiplied the torches, and a few minutes later the distraught Quasimodo saw this terrifying army of ants climbing to assault Notre-Dame from every quarter. The ones without ladders had knotted ropes, and the ones without ropes climbed by the reliefs of the sculptures. They dangled from one another's rags. There was no resisting this rising tide of terrifying faces. Their savage features glowed red with fury; their grimy foreheads streamed with sweat; their eyes flashed fire. All these grimaces, all this ugliness was besieging Quasimodo. It was as if some other church had despatched its gorgons, its mastiffs, its drees, its demons, its most fantastic sculptures, to the assault of Notre-Dame. They were like a layer of living monsters on top of the stone monsters of the façade.

The square, meanwhile, had been starred by a thousand torches. This scene of disorder, hitherto shrouded in darkness, had suddenly became a blaze of light. The parvis was resplendent and cast its radiance into the sky. The pyre still burnt on the upper platform and lit up the town in the distance. The enormous silhouette of the twin towers stretched away into the distance over the rooftops of Paris, its shadow biting deeply into the light. The town seemed to be stirring. Tocsins were complaining in the distance. The truants were yelling, panting, swearing, climbing, and Quasimodo, powerless against so many enemies and trembling for the gypsy, as he saw the furious faces drawing closer and closer to his gallery, asked heaven for a miracle and wrung his hands in despair.

FIVE

The Retreat where Monsieur Louis of France Says his Hours

THE reader has not perhaps forgotten that, just before he sighted the nocturnal band of truants, Quasimodo, inspecting Paris from on top of his tower, could see only one light burning, starring a pane of glass on the topmost storey of a tall, sombre building next to the Porte Saint-Antoine. The building was the Bastille. The star was Louis XI's candle.

King Louis XI had been in Paris in fact for the past two days. He was to leave again for his citadel of Montilz-lès-Tours in two days' time. He only ever made rare and brief appearances in his fair town of Paris, feeling there were too few trap-doors, gallows and Scottish archers about him there.

Today he had come to the Bastille to sleep. He did not much care for the great bedchamber, five *toises* square, which he had at the Louvre, with its tall chimney-piece, laden with twelve huge animals and the thirteen major prophets, and its great bed, eleven foot by twelve. He felt lost amidst such grandeur. This very bourgeois king preferred the Bastille, with a small bedchamber and a small bed. The Bastille, moreover, was stronger than the Louvre.

The 'small' bedchamber which the king kept for himself in the famous state prison was still spacious enough and occupied the top storey of a turret set into the keep. This redoubt was circular in shape, the walls were hung with shiny straw matting, the ceiling beams were enhanced with fleur-de-lys of gilded tin and painted spaces between, the panelling was ornately carved, strewn with rosettes of white tin and painted a beautiful bright green, made from orpiment and finest indigo.

There was only one window, a tall lancet latticed with brass wire and iron bars, and obscured still further by the beautiful coats of arms of the king and queen painted on the glass, each pane of which had cost twenty-two *sols*.

There was only one entrance, a modern doorway, with a semicircular arch, decorated on the inside with a tapestry and on the outside with one of those porches of Irish wood, frail and curiously carpentered edifices, still to be seen in a good many old houses 150 years ago. 'Although they encumber and disfigure places,' says Sauval despairingly, 'yet our old men will not do away with them and preserve them in spite of everyone.'

There were none of the usual furnishings of an apartment in the room, no benches, no trestle-tables, no forms, no common drum-shaped stools, no fine stools supported on columns and counter-columns at four *sols* apiece. All that could be seen was a very magnificent folding armchair; the woodwork was painted with roses on a red background, the seat was of scarlet Cordoban leather, decorated with long silk fringes and studded with hundreds of gold nails. The chair's isolation showed that one person alone had the right to be seated in this room. Next to the chair and right beside the window stood a table, covered by a cloth with birds on it. On the table an ink-stained inkhorn, a few parchments, a few pens and a goblet of chased silver. Just beyond, a chafing-dish and a prie-Dieu of crimson velvet, set off with small gold studs. Finally, at the far end, a simple bed of yellow and rose-pink damask, with neither tinsel nor braid, and plain fringes. This bed, famous for having supported the sleep or the insomnia of Louis XI, was still on view, two hundred years ago, in the house of a councillor of state, where it was seen by old Madame Pilou, celebrated in the *Cyrus* under the names of 'Arricidie' and 'the living morality'.

Such was the room they called 'the retreat where Monsieur Louis of France says his hours'.

At the moment we introduced the reader into this retreat, it was in semi-darkness. The curfew had sounded an hour previously, it was nighttime, and there was only a single wax candle flickering on the table to give light to the five figures grouped variously around the room.

It fell first of all on a nobleman splendidly dressed in a scarlet doublet and hose with silver stripes, and a cassock with padded shoulders made from gold-cloth with black designs on. Where the light played on it, this opulent costume seemed glazed with fire in every crease. The man who wore it had his coat of arms embroidered on his chest in bright colours: a chevron accompanied in point by a deer passant. The escutcheon was *accosted* on the right by an olive branch and on the left by a deer's horn. In his belt, this man wore an ornate dagger, whose silver-gilt handle was carved in the shape of a cimier, surmounted by a ducal coronet. He looked evil but bore himself proudly, with head erect. At first glance you read arrogance on his face, at the second cunning.

He stood bare-headed, holding a long scroll, behind the arm-chair, on which there sat, his body bent inelegantly double, his knees crossed, his elbow on the table, a very shabbily dressed figure. Picture to yourselves, in fact, against the plush Cordoba leather, two knock knees, two scrawny thighs cheaply clad in knitted black hose, a torso wrapped in a fustian surcoat whose fur trimmings displayed more leather than hair; and finally, as a crowning glory, a greasy old hat of the most miserable black cloth with a band of lead figurines round it. Which, together with a dirty skull-cap, that allowed scarcely a single hair to protrude, was all one could make out of the person sitting down. He kept his head so bent over his chest that his face was lost in shadow and one could see nothing of it but for the tip of his nose, on which a ray of light fell and which must have been a long one. The gauntness of his wrinkled hand gave one to suppose an old man. It was Louis XI.

Some little way behind them, two men in clothes of a Flemish cut were conversing in an undertone, and were not so shrouded in gloom that anyone who was present at the performance of Gringoire's mystery play could not have recognized them as two of the leading Flemish envoys, Guillaume Rym, the shrewd Pensioner of Ghent, and Jacques Coppenole, the popular hosier. It will be recalled that both men were party to Louis XI's secret diplomacy.

Finally, at the far end, next to the door, standing in the shadows, as still as a statue, was a robust-looking man with square limbs, soldier's equipment and an emblazoned cassock, whose square face was a cross between a dog's and a tiger's, with its bulging eyeballs, its immense slit of a mouth, ears concealed beneath two broad windshields of straight hair, and absence of forehead.

All were uncovered, apart from the king.

The nobleman standing beside the king was reading some kind of lengthy memorandum, to which His Majesty seemed to be listening attentively. The two Flemings were whispering.

'By the Holy Cross!' grumbled Coppenole. 'I'm tired of standing up. Are there no chairs here?'

Rym's answer was a shake of the head, accompanied by a discreet smile.

'By the Holy Cross!' Coppenole went on, very unhappy at

having to keep his voice down in this way. 'I feel an urge to sit cross-legged on the ground, hosier-fashion, like I do in my shop.'

'For heaven's sake don't, Maître Jacques!'

'So one can only be on one's feet here, Maître Guillaume?'

'Or your knees,' said Rym.

At that moment the king's voice was upraised. They became silent.

'Fifty *sols* for our valets' robes, and twelve *livres* for the cloaks of the clerks of our crown! That's right, lash out gold by the ton! Are you mad, Olivier?'

As he spoke, the old man had raised his head. The gold cockle-shells of the collar of St Michael could be seen gleaming at his throat. The candlelight fell full on his morose and fleshless profile. He snatched the paper from the other's hand.

'You are ruining us!' he cried, running his sunken eyes over the accounts. 'What is all this? Where's the need for such a prodigious establishment? Two chaplains at the rate of ten *livres* a month each, and a clerk of chapel at a hundred *sols*! A *valet de chambre* at ninety *livres* a year! Four squires of the kitchen at a hundred and twenty *livres* a year each! A roaster, a pottinger, a saucer, a master chef, an armoury-keeper, two sumptermen at the rate of ten *livres* a month each! Two kitchen boys at eight *livres*! A groom and his two helpers at twenty-four *livres* a month! A porter, a pastry-cook, a baker, two wagoners, each sixty *livres* a month! And the forge-marshal one hundred and twenty *livres*! And the master of our exchequer, twelve hundred *livres*, and the comptroller five hundred! I don't know, it has got out of hand! The wages of our servants are putting France to the sack! All the secret reserves in the Louvre will melt away at this rate of expenditure! We shall be selling our plate: and next year, if God and Our Lady (here he raised his hat) spare us, we shall be drinking our tisane from a pewter mug!'

As he said which, he glanced at the silver goblet sparkling on the table. He coughed and went on:

'Maître Olivier, princes who govern great lordships, like kings and emperors, must not allow luxury to breed in their courts: for the flames spread from there to the provinces. So take this as said, Maître Olivier. Our expenditure is increasing every year. That displeases us. *Pasque-Dieu*, until '79 it never exceeded thirty-six thousand *livres*. In '80 it reached forty-three thousand six hundred and nineteen *livres* – I have the figures in my head – in '81, sixty-six thousand six hundred and eighty *livres*; and this year, as I live and breathe, it will reach eighty thousand *livres*! Double in four years! Monstrous!'

He stopped to regain his breath, then went on, heatedly: 'All around me I see only men waxing fat on my leanness! You suck gold crowns out of my every pore!'

They all kept silent. This was one of those fits of temper one allows to take their course. He continued:

'It's like that Latin request from the seigniory of France, that we should restore what they call the great charges of the crown! Charges is right! Crippling charges! Ah, messieurs, you say we are not a king, because we reign *dapifero nullo, buticulario nullo*![1] We shall show you whether we're a king or not, *pasque-Dieu*!'

At this point he smiled, conscious of his own authority, his bad temper was assuaged and he turned to the Flemings:

'You see, Compère Guillaume? The grand pantler, the grand butler, the grand chamberlain and the grand seneschal are not worth the meanest valet. Mark this, Compère Coppenole, they serve no purpose. So useless are they as they stand around the king they remind me of the four evangelists who surround the dial of the great clock in the Palais, which Philippe Brille has just renovated. They are gilded but they don't tell the time, and the hands can do without them.'

He paused for a moment in thought, then added, shaking his old head: 'Ha, ha, by Our Lady, I'm not Philippe Brille and I shan't regild the great vassals. I am of King Edward's[2] opinion: save the people and kill the lords. Continue, Olivier.'

The person so designated took the document back and began once more to read it out:

'... to Adam Tenon, Clerk to the Keeper of the Seals of the Provostry of Paris, for the silver, working and engraving of the said seals, these having been renewed on account the previous ones through great age and decrepitude, were no longer serviceable. Twelve *livres parisis*.'

'To Guillaume Frère, the sum of four *livres* four *sols parisis*, for his pains and wages, he having nourished and fed the doves in the

1. 'Without either squire-carver or butler.'
2. King Edward IV of England, who died that same year.

two dovecotes of the Hôtel des Tournelles, during the months of January, February and March of this year; having given for this purpose seven sextiers of barley.'

'To a cordelier, for confessing a criminal, four *sols parisis.*'

The king was listening in silence. Now and again he gave a cough. Then he raised the goblet to his lips and grimaced as he swallowed a mouthful.

'In this year, fifty-six cries made at the crossroads to the sound of trumpets by order of justice. Account to be settled.'

'To having sought and searched in certain places, in Paris and elsewhere, for moneys said to have been concealed there, but nothing discovered; forty-five *livres parisis.*'

'Bury a gold crown to dig up a *sou*!' said the king.

'To having prepared six panes of white glass at the Hôtel des Tournelles, at the place where the iron cage is, thirteen *sols.* To having made and delivered, by the king's command, on the day of monsters, four escutcheons with the arms of the said lord, enchased with chaplets of roses all about, six *livres.* To two new sleeves for the king's old doublet, twenty *sols.* To a box of grease for greasing the king's boots, fifteen *deniers.* A new stable to house the king's black hogs, thirty *livres parisis.* To sundry partitions, planks and traps made for the custody of the lions close by Saint-Paul, twenty-two *livres.*'

'Expensive animals, those,' said Louis XI. 'No mind, it's a very kingly extravagance. There's one big tawny lion I like because he's mischievous. Have you seen him, Maître Guillaume? Princes need to keep these marvellous animals. We kings need lions as dogs and tigers as cats. Size goes with the crown. In the days of Jupiter's pagans, when the people offered the churches a hundred oxen and a hundred ewe-lambs, the emperors used to give a hundred lions and a hundred eagles. That was very grand and barbaric. The kings of France have always kept beasts to roar around their throne. It will be allowed to me, nonetheless, that I spend even less money on them than they did, and that I possess fewer lions, bears, elephants and leopards. Go on, Maître Olivier. We wanted to say that to our friends the Flemings.'

Guillaume Rym gave a deep bow, whereas Coppenole, with his sullen expression, looked like one of those bears of which His Majesty had just been speaking. The king took no notice. He had just wet his lips from the goblet and now spat the beverage out, saying: 'Ugh! Filthy tisane!' The man who was reading went on:

'To feeding a rogue and vagabond locked up these six months in the cell in the flayers' yard, until it be known what to do with him. Six *livres* four *sols*.'

'What's that?' the king broke in. 'Feeding what should be hanged! *Pasque-Dieu*, I shan't give another *sol* for his food. Olivier, arrange the matter with Monsieur d'Estouteville, and make preparations this evening for this swain to be married off to a gallows. Continue.'

Olivier made a mark with his thumb at the item of the 'rogue and vagabond' and proceeded.

'To Henriet Cousin, Chief Executioner of the Justice of Paris, the sum of sixty *sols parisis*, taxed and ordered to him by my lord Provost of Paris, for having bought, at the command of the said Sir Provost, a large broadsword for the purpose of executing and beheading those persons condemned by justice for their demerits, it having been fitted with a scabbard and all pertaining to it; and likewise to having repaired and restored the old sword, it being broken and notched when carrying out sentence on Messire Louis de Luxembourg, as may more fully appear . . .'

The king broke in: 'That's enough. I gladly authorize the sum. These are expenses I shan't quibble over. I've never begrudged that money. Continue.'

'To making a large new cage . . .'

'Ah!' said the king, gripping the two arms of his chair, 'I knew I'd come here to the Bastille for a purpose. Wait, Maître Olivier, I want to see the cage myself. You can read the cost to me while I am inspecting it. Come and see it, Messieurs the Flemings. It's interesting.'

He then stood up, leant on his interlocutor's arm, signalled to the sort of mute standing in front of the door to go ahead of him and to the two Flemings to follow, and left the room.

At the door of the retreat, the royal party recruited men-at-arms weighed down with iron and slim pageboys carrying torches. It wended its way for a time through the grim interior of the keep, honeycombed by staircases and corridors even in the thickness of the walls. The Captain of the Bastille walked ahead, having the wickets opened in front of the stooping, sickly old king, who coughed as he walked.

At each wicket, every head was obliged to be lowered, except the old man's, already bowed by age. 'Hmm!' he said between his gums, for he had no teeth left, 'we're quite ready now for the door into the tomb. For a low door, a stooping visitor.'

At last, after negotiating a final wicket so encumbered with locks it took them a quarter of an hour to get it open, they entered a vast hall with a tall, pointed vault, in the centre of which the torchlight revealed a huge solid-looking cube of stonework, iron and wood. It was hollow inside. This was one of the famous cages for state prisoners known as 'the little daughters of the King'. In the side-walls were two or three tiny windows, so closely latticed with thick iron bars that no glass was visible. The door was a tall, flat slab of stone, as in a burial vault. One of those doors only ever used as an entrance. In this case, though, the corpse was a living person.

The king began walking slowly round this little edifice, examining it carefully, while Maître Olivier followed behind reading from the memorandum:

'To having made a great new wooden cage of large joists, ribs and stringers, comprising nine feet in length by eight in width, and a height of seven feet between two wooden floors, smoothed and bolted with large iron bolts, the which was installed in a chamber being in one of the towers of the blockhouse of Saint-Antoine, in which cage has been put and detained, at the command of our lord the king, a prisoner who had previously dwelt in an old, decayed and decrepit cage. Employed in the said new cage ninety-six horizontal beams and fifty-two upright beams, ten stringers three *toises* in length; and occupied twenty days in squaring, working and shaping all the aforesaid wood in the courtyard of the Bastille nineteen carpenters . . .'

'Good heart of oak,' said the king, banging the timbers with his fist.

'There went into this cage', the other continued, 'two hundred and twenty great iron bolts, of nine and eight feet, the remainder of middle length, together with the rowels, pommels and counter-bands serving the said bolts, the aforesaid iron weighing in all three thousand seven hundred and thirty-five *livres*; besides eight great iron brackets serving to attach the said cage, together with the crampons and nails, together weighing two hundred and eighteen *livres* of iron, not counting the iron of the lattice for the windows of the chamber wherein the cage was placed, the iron bars for the door of the chamber, and sundry other things . . .'

'A lot of iron,' said the king, 'to contain the lightness of a spirit!'

'. . . The whole amounting to three hundred and seventeen *livres* five *sols* seven *deniers*.'

'*Pasque-Dieu!*' exclaimed the king.

At this, Louis XI's favourite oath, someone seemed to come awake inside the cage, chains could be heard scraping loudly across the wooden floor and a feeble voice arose that seemed to come from the grave: 'Mercy, sire, mercy!' It was impossible to see who it was who spoke.

'Three hundred and seventeen *livres*, five *sols*, seven *deniers*!' Louis XI resumed.

The pitiful voice that had come from the cage froze the blood of everyone present, Maître Olivier included. Only the king seemed not to have heard it. At his order, Maître Olivier resumed his reading, while His Majesty went coldly on with his inspection of the cage.

'Besides which, there was paid to a mason who made the holes for inserting the bars of the windows, and the floor of the room wherein stands the cage, for the floor would have been unable to support this cage because of its weight, twenty-seven *livres* fourteen *sols parisis* . . .'

The voice began to moan again: 'Mercy, sire! I swear it was Monsieur the Cardinal of Angers who committed this treason, and not I.'

'The mason's overdoing things!' said the king. 'Go on, Olivier.'

Olivier went on: '. . . To a joiner, for windows, close-stool, bed and sundry other matters, twenty *livres* two *sols parisis* . . .'

The voice continued too: 'Alas, sire, will you not hear me? I protest to you that it was not I who wrote these things to my lord of Guyenne, but Monsieur the Cardinal La Balue!'

'The joiner is expensive,' remarked the king. 'Is that the lot?'

'No, sire. "To a glazier, for the windows of the said chamber, forty-six *sols* eight *deniers parisis*."'

'Have mercy, sire. Is it not enough that they have given all my belongings to my judges, my plate to Monsieur de Torcy, my library to Maître Pierre Doriolle, my tapestry to the Governor of Roussillon? I am innocent. For fourteen years I have been shivering in an iron cage. Have mercy, sire! You will be repaid in heaven.'

'The total, Maître Olivier?' said the king.

'Three hundred and sixty-seven *livres*, eight *sols*, three *deniers parisis*.'

'*Notre-Dame*,' cried the king. 'An outrageous cage!'

He snatched the accounts from Maître Olivier's hands and began to calculate for himself on his fingers, looking first at the paper and then at the cage. The prisoner meanwhile could be heard sobbing. It was a dismal sound in that gloom, and their faces went pale as they eyed one another.

'Fourteen years, sire! It's fourteen years! Since April 1469. In the name of the Holy Mother of God, sire, hear me! All this time you have enjoyed the warmth of the sun. And I, a poor caitiff, shall I ever see the daylight again? Mercy, sire! Be merciful. Clemency is a fine virtue in kings, which stems the flow of anger. Does Your Majesty believe that it is a great satisfaction for a king, at the hour of his death, not to have left a single offence unpunished? What is more, sire, I did not betray Your Majesty; it was Monsieur of Angers. And on my foot I have a very heavy chain, with a great ball of iron at the end, weighing much more than is right. Have mercy on me, sire!'

'Olivier,' said the king, shaking his head, 'I notice they are charging me twenty *sols* a barrel for plaster, which is only worth twelve. You will make this account out again.'

He turned his back on the cage and prepared to leave the room. As the torches and the noise withdrew, the wretched prisoner concluded that the king was leaving. 'Sire, sire!' he cried despairingly. The door closed once more. He could no longer see a thing and all he could hear was the hoarse voice of the jailer, singing this refrain into his ear:

Maître Jean Balue
Has lost from view
Every bishop's see;
Monsieur of Verdun
No longer has one;
All are now set free.

The king reascended to his retreat in silence and his cortège followed, appalled by the prisoner's final lamentation. All of a sudden, His Majesty turned to the Governor of the Bastille: 'By the way,' he said, 'wasn't there someone in that cage?'

'Good God, sire!' answered the governor, astounded by the question.

'Who was it then?'

'Monsieur the Bishop of Verdun.'

The king knew this better than anyone. But it was a compulsion. 'Ah!' he said innocently, as if it had not occurred to him before. 'Guillaume de Harancourt, the friend of Monsieur the Cardinal La Balue. A right devil of a bishop!'

A few moments later, the door of the retreat reopened then closed again behind the five persons whom the reader has seen there at the beginning of this chapter, and who now resumed their places, their hushed conversations and their attitudes.

During the king's absence, some despatches had been laid on the table, whose seals he broke himself. He then set promptly to reading them one after the other, gestured to 'Maître Olivier', who seemed to be acting as his minister, to take a quill and, without disclosing the contents of the despatches, began to dictate the answers to him in an undertone, which the other took down kneeling somewhat uncomfortably in front of the table.

Guillaume Rym watched.

So quietly did the king speak that the Flemings could hear nothing of what he dictated, except for an occasional isolated and more or less unintelligible fragment, such as: '. . . Maintain the fertile districts by trade and infertile ones by manufacture . . . Show the English lords our four bombards, the London, the Brabant, the Bourg-en-Bresse, the Saint-Omer . . . Artillery is the reason why war is waged more circumspectly these days . . . To M. des Bressuire, our friend . . . Armies cannot be kept up without tributes . . . etc.'

Once he raised his voice: '*Pasque-Dieu!* Monsieur the King of Sicily seals his letters on yellow wax, like a king of France. Perhaps we are wrong to allow him to. My good cousin of Burgundy did not grant coats of arms on a field gules. A house's greatness is ensured by the integrity of its prerogatives. Make a note of that, Compère Olivier.'

Another time: 'Ha, ha, a bulky missive! What does our brother the emperor ask from us?' And as he perused the letter, he broke off to interject: 'True, the Germanies are so large and powerful it's scarcely credible. But we don't forget the old saying: "The fairest county is Flanders, the fairest duchy Milan, the fairest kingdom France." Is that not so, Messieurs the Flemings?'

This time, Coppenole bowed as well as Guillaume Rym. The hosier's patriotism had been flattered.

A final despatch brought a frown from Louis XI. 'What's this?' he exclaimed. 'Complaints and grievances against our garrisons in Picardy? Olivier, write forthwith to Monsieur the Marshal of Rouault. That discipline has grown slack. That the men-at-arms of the ordonnances, the nobles of the ban, the free archers and the Swiss are doing untold damage to the villeins. That the soldiery, not satisfied with the belongings they find in the ploughmen's houses, take their sticks and halberds to them and force them to go to the town in search of wine, fish and groceries, as well as other excesses. That Monsieur the King knows this. That we mean to protect our people from harassment, larceny and pillage. That such is our will, by Our Lady! That he will not allow, furthermore, any musician, barber or *valet de guerre* to dress like a prince, in velvet, silk and gold rings. That such vanities are hateful to God. That we who are gentlemen are content with a doublet of cloth from Paris at sixteen *sols* the ell. That messieurs the camp-followers can also descend to that level. Order and command. To Monsieur de Rouault, our friend. Good.'

He dictated this letter in a loud firm voice, in short bursts. Just as he was finishing the door opened to admit a new personage, who rushed into the room in great alarm, shouting: 'Sire, sire! There is an uprising of the people in Paris!'

Louis XI's grave face contracted, but his emotion was visible only for a brief second. He controlled himself and said, with quiet severity: 'You enter very abruptly, Compère Jacques!'

'Sire, sire, there's a revolt!' Compère Jacques went on, breathlessly.

The king, who had stood up, took him roughly by the arm and said into his ear, so that only he should hear him, with a concentrated anger and a sidelong glance at the Flemings: 'Shut up, or talk quietly!'

The new arrival understood and began in a whisper to give him a terrified account, which the king listened to calmly, while Guillaume Rym pointed out to Coppenole the newcomer's face and clothes, his furlined hood, *caputia fourrata*, his short epitoga, *epitogia curta*, and his black velvet robe, which bespoke a president of the audit-house.

Scarcely had this personage given the king a few explanations before Louis XI burst out laughing and exclaimed: 'Really! Speak up, Compère Coictier! What's the matter with you, whispering like that? Our Lady knows we have nothing to hide from our good friends the Flemings.'

'But sire ...'

'Speak up!'

'Compère Coictier' remained speechless with surprise.

'You say then, monsieur,' the king went on, 'that there is unrest among the villeins in our fair town of Paris?'

'Yes, sire.'

'And which is directed, you say, against Monsieur the Bailiff of the Palais de Justice?'

'So it would seem,' stammered the compère in reply, still quite stunned by the king's sudden and inexplicable change of mind.

Louis XI went on: 'Where did the watch encounter the mob?'

'Making its way from the Grande-Truanderie towards the Pont-aux-Changeurs. I encountered it myself as I was coming here in obedience to Your Majesty's orders. I heard some of them shouting "Down with the Bailiff of the Palace".'

'And what grievances do they have against the bailiff?'

'Ah,' said Compère Jacques, 'that he is their lord.'

'Really!'

'Yes, sire. They're scum from the Court of Miracles. They've been complaining about the bailiff for a long time now, they're his vassals. They refuse to recognize him either as justiciary or as hundredman.'

'Is that so!' the king rejoined, with a contented smile that he strove in vain to disguise.

'In all their requests to parliament,' Compère Jacques went on, 'they claim to have only two masters, Your Majesty and their God, who is, I believe, the devil.'

'Ha, ha!' said the king.

He rubbed his hands and laughed inwardly with that laugh which brings a broad smile to the face. He could not conceal his delight, although he tried off and on to compose himself. None of them understood, not even 'Maître Olivier'. He remained for a moment in silence, looking thoughtful but pleased.

'Are they in strength?' he asked, all of a sudden.

'Yes, indeed, sire,' answered Compère Jacques.

'How many?'

'At least six thousand.'

The king could not help saying 'Good!' He went on: 'Are they armed?'

'With scythes, pikes, hackbuts and pickaxes. All sorts of very violent weapons.'

The king seemed not at all put out by such a display. Compère Jacques felt he should add: 'If Your Majesty doesn't send help promptly the bailiff is doomed.'

'We shall send,' said the king with a false air of seriousness. 'Good. Certainly we shall send. The bailiff is our friend. Six thousand! They're determined rascals. Their audacity is astounding and we are much angered by it. But we have few men about us tonight. Tomorrow morning will be time enough.'

Compère Jacques protested. 'Straight away, sire! There'll be time for the bailiff's house to be plundered, the seigniory broken into and the bailiff hung twenty times over. For God's sake, sire! Send before tomorrow morning.'

The king stared straight at him. 'Tomorrow morning, I said.'

It was one of those looks to which one does not retort.

After a pause, Louis XI again raised his voice. 'Compère Jacques, you must know this. What was . . .' He corrected himself: 'What is the bailiff's feudal jurisdiction?'

'Sire, the Bailiff of the Palace has the Rue de la Calandre as far as the Rue de l'Herberie, the Place Saint-Michel and the places vulgarly known as the Mureaux, near the church of Notre-Dame-des-Champs (here Louis XI raised the brim of his hat), the which hôtels number thirteen, also the Court of Miracles, also the leper-house known as the Banlieue, also the whole thoroughfare which starts at the leper-house and finishes at the Porte Saint-Jacques. Of which divers places he is hundredman, high, middle and low justiciary, and lord in full.'

'Indeed!' said the king, scratching his left ear with his right hand, 'that's quite a large piece of my town! Ah, Monsieur the Bailiff *was* king of all that!'

This time he did not correct himself. He continued, thoughtfully, as if talking to himself: 'Very fine, Monsieur the Bailiff, you had a nice slice of our Paris between your teeth there.'

Suddenly, he exploded: '*Pasque-Dieu!* What are these people who claim to be hundredmen, justiciaries, lords and masters in our house? Who have their toll-gate at the end of every field, their justice and their hangman at every crossroads amongst our people? The Greeks thought they had as many gods as fountains, and the Persians as many as they could see stars, so the French reckon up as many kings as they see gallows. That's not right, by God! I don't like such confusion. I should very much like to know whether it's God's grace that there should be a hundredman in Paris other than the king, a justice other than our parliament, an emperor other than ourself in this empire. The day must come in France, upon the faith of my soul, when there's only one king, one lord, one judge and one executioner, just as there's only one God in paradise!'

He raised his bonnet again and went on, still ruminating, with the look and the tones of a huntsman urging on and launching his hounds: 'Good! My people! Bravo! Smash these false lords! Go about your work. At them, at them! Pillage them, hang them, plunder them! So you want to be kings, my lords? Go on, people, go on!'

At which point he suddenly broke off, bit his lip, as if to take back a thought already half escaped, rested his penetrating gaze on each of the five persons around him in turn, then, suddenly seizing his hat in both hands, he stared straight at it and said: 'Oh, I should burn you if you knew what's in my head!'

Then, again casting about him the anxious and attentive look of a fox stealthily returning to its earth: 'Never mind! We shall succour Monsieur the Bailiff! Unhappily, we have only a few troops here at this moment against all that populace. We must wait until tomorrow. Order will be restored in the City and whoever is captured will quite simply be hanged.'

'By the way, sire!' said Compère Coictier, 'in my anxiety earlier I forgot, the watch seized two stragglers from the band. If Your Majesty would like to see these men, they are here.'

'Like to see them!' cried the king. 'What? *Pasque-Dieu!* You can forget something like that! Olivier, run, go and fetch them!'

Maître Olivier left and returned a moment later with the two prisoners, surrounded by archers of the bodyguard. The first one's face was fat, stupid, drunken and surprised. He was dressed in rags and walked with one knee bent and dragging his foot. The second had a sallow, smiling face that the reader knows already.

The king studied them for a moment without speaking, then abruptly addressed the first man:

'What's your name?'

'Gieffroy Pincebourde.'

'Your trade?'

'Truant.'

'What were you going to do in this damnable sedition?'

The truant looked at the king, arms dangling and with a vacant expression. His was one of those maladjusted heads in which intelligence is about as much at ease as a flame under a snuffer.

'I don't know,' he said. 'They were going, I was going.'

'Were you not going, outrageously, to attack and pillage our lord the Bailiff of the Palace?'

'I know they were going to take something from someone's house. That's all.'

A soldier showed the king a bill-hook that had been found on the truant.

'Do you recognize this weapon?' asked the king.

'Yes, it's my bill-hook. I grow grapes.'

'And do you acknowledge this man as your companion?' added Louis XI, indicating the other prisoner.

'No, I don't know him.'

'That'll do,' said the king. And beckoning to the silent figure standing motionless by the door, to whom we have already drawn the reader's attention: 'Compère Tristan, here's a man for you.'

Tristan l'Hermite bowed. He whispered an order to two archers, who led the poor truant away.

The king meanwhile had gone up to the second prisoner, who was sweating profusely. 'Your name?'

'Sire, Pierre Gringoire.'

'Your trade?'

'Philosopher, sire.'

'What do you mean, you scoundrel, by going and besieging our friend Monsieur the Bailiff of the Palace, and what do you have to say about this popular disturbance?'

'Sire, I was not part of it.'

'What, *paillard*, were you not apprehended by the watch in such evil company?'

'No, sire, there's been a mistake. It's a fatality. I write tragedies. Sire, I entreat Your Majesty to hear me. I'm a poet. It's the melancholy of men of my profession to walk the streets at night. This evening I was passing that way. It was pure chance. I was wrongly arrested. I'm innocent of this civil storm. Your Majesty saw that the truant didn't recognize me. I beseech Your Majesty ...'

'Silence!' said the king between two sips of tisane. 'You talk too much.'

Tristan l'Hermite stepped forward and pointed to Gringoire: 'Sire, can this one be hanged too?'

It was the first word he had uttered.

'Bah!' answered the king casually. 'I see no objections.'

'I see plenty!' said Gringoire.

At that moment our philosopher was greener than an olive. He could see from the king's cold and indifferent expression that his only recourse now was something of high pathos, and he hurled himself at Louis XI's feet, crying out with despairing gesticulations:

'Sire, Your Majesty must deign to hear me! Sire, do not call down your thunder on something as unimportant as myself. God's great thunderbolts do not bombard lettuces. Sire, you are an august and very mighty monarch, have mercy on a poor, law-abiding man, who could no more foment a revolt than a lump of ice could give off sparks! Very gracious sire, good humour is a virtue in lions and kings. Severity, alas, strikes only fear into the mind, the impetuous blasts of the north wind could never make the passer-by remove his coat, but the sun provides its rays and slowly warms him up until it has him in a shirt. You, sire, are the sun. I protest to you, my sovereign lord and master, that I am not a thieving and disorderly associate of truants. Rebellion and brigandry are not part of the baggage of Apollo. *I* would never hurl myself into those clouds which burst in noises of sedition. I am Your Majesty's loyal vassal.

The husband's jealousy for the honour of his wife, the reciprocal love of a son for his father, that is what a good vassal must feel for the glory of his king, he must be consumed with zeal for his house and for the increase of his service. Any other passion that transports him is mere fury. Those, sire, are my maxims of state. Do not adjudge me to be seditious or a looter because I am out at elbows. If you grant me mercy, sire, I shall be out at knees too, praying God for you morning and evening! It's true, alas, I'm not excessively rich. In fact I'm rather poor. But not vicious for all that. It's not my fault. Everyone knows that great wealth does not accrue from literature, and that those who write great masterpieces do not always have a warm fire in winter. The legal fraternity alone takes all the wheat and leaves the other learned professions only the chaff. There are forty most excellent proverbs about the tattered mantle of the philosophers. Oh, sire, clemency is the one light that can illuminate the inside of a great soul. Clemency bears the torch ahead of all the other virtues. Without it, they are blind men groping for God. Mercifulness, which is the same thing as clemency, makes loving subjects, who are the strongest of bodyguards for the person of a prince. What is it to you, a majesty by whom all eyes are dazzled, that there should be one more poor man on earth? A poor innocent philosopher, floundering in the darkness of calamity, with his empty fob re-echoing against his hollow belly? Moreover, sire, I am a man of letters. Great kings add a pearl to their crown by patronizing letters. Hercules did not spurn the title of Musagetes. Mathias Corvinus encouraged Jean de Monroyal, the glory of mathematics. But to hang men of letters is no way to patronize literature. What a stigma on Alexander had he hanged Aristoteles! Such an act would not have been a small patch on the face of his reputation, embellishing it, but a malignant ulcer disfiguring it. Sire, I wrote a most timely epithalamium for Mademoiselle of Flanders and My Lord the most august dauphin. No troublemaker would do that. Your Majesty can see that I am not a hack, that I was excellently educated and have great natural eloquence. Have mercy on me, sire. By so doing, you will be acting gallantly towards Our Lady, and I swear to you that the thought of being hanged frightens me greatly!'

So saying, the woebegone Gringoire kissed the king's slippers, and Guillaume Rym whispered to Coppenole: 'He does well to crawl on the ground. Kings are like the Cretan Jupiter, they only have ears in their feet.' But, unconcerned by the Cretan Jupiter, the hosier replied with a heavy smile, his eye fixed on Gringoire: 'This is rich! I fancy I hear the chancellor Hugonet begging me for mercy.'

Once Gringoire finally ceased, for lack of breath, he looked tremulously up at the king, who was scratching a stain on the knee of his hose with a fingernail. Then His Majesty began to drink from the goblet of tisane. For the rest, he spoke not a word and his silence was agonizing for Gringoire. At last the king looked at him. 'He's got a voice like a corncrake!' he said. Then, turning to Tristan l'Hermite: 'Bah, let him go!'

Gringoire fell on his backside, terrified with joy.

'Free!' grumbled Tristan. 'Wouldn't Your Majesty like us to keep him in a cage for a bit?'

'Compère,' Louis XI rejoined, 'do you think it is for birds of his feather that we have cages made costing three hundred and sixty-seven *livres*, eight *sols*, three *deniers*? Let the *paillard* go forthwith (Louis XI was fond of this word, which, together with *Pasque-Dieu*, constituted the entire stock of his joviality), put him out with your fists!'

'Phew!' exclaimed Gringoire, 'there speaks a great king!'

And fearing a countermand, he hastened towards the door, which Tristan opened for him with a somewhat ill grace. The soldiers went out with him, punching him hard as they drove him ahead of them, the which Gringoire bore like a true Stoic philosopher.

The king's good humour, since being informed of the revolt against the bailiff, showed in everything. This unwonted clemency was no small sign of it. In his corner, Tristan l'Hermite wore the grumpy look of a mastiff that has seen but has not had.

The king meanwhile was merrily tapping out the 'March of Pont-Audemer' with his fingers on the arm of his chair. He was a secretive prince, but he was far better at concealing his sorrows than his joys. These outward manifestations of joy at all good news sometimes led him to extremes; thus, at the death of Charles the Bold,[1] to the dedication of silver balustrades in Saint-Martin's at Tours; at his accession to the throne, to forgetting to give orders for his father's funeral.

1. The Duke of Burgundy, long an enemy of Louis XI.

'Sire!' Jacques Coictier suddenly exclaimed, 'what about those sharp pains for which Your Majesty had me summoned?'

'Oh!' said the king, 'I'm far from well in fact, Compère. I've got a hissing in my ears and rakes of fire scraping my chest.'

Coictier took the king's hand and began to feel his pulse, wearing an air of efficiency.

'Look, Coppenole,' said Rym quietly. 'Look at him between Coictier and Tristan. That's his entire court. A doctor for him and a hangman for everyone else.'

As he felt the king's pulse, Coictier began to look more and more alarmed. Louis XI stared at him in some anxiety. Coictier's brow darkened visibly. The worthy man had no other source of profit but the king's health. He made the most of it.

'Oh!' he murmured finally. 'This is serious, in fact.'

'It is?' said the king, anxiously.

'*Pulsus creber, anhelans, crepitans, irregularis*,'[1] the doctor went on.

'*Pasque-Dieu!*'

'It can carry a man off in less than three days.'

'By Our Lady!' cried the king. 'And the remedy, Compère?'

'I'm considering, sire.'

He made Louis XI stick out his tongue, shook his head, pulled a face, then, in the midst of all this play-acting: 'By God, sire,' he said suddenly, 'I must tell you that there's a receivership of regalia[2] vacant and that I have a nephew.'

'I give my receivership to your nephew, Compère Jacques,' answered the king, 'but get this fire out of my chest.'

'Since Your Majesty is so clement,' the doctor went on, 'he will not refuse me a little assistance in the building of my house in the Rue Saint-André-des-Arcs.'

'Hmmm!' said the king.

'My funds are at an end,' the doctor continued, 'and it would be a great pity if the house had no roof. Not because of the house, which is just a simple burgess's house, but because of Jehan Fourbault's paintings, which adorn the wainscotting. There's a Diana flying in the air, so perfect, so tender, so delicate, moving so artlessly, her hair so beautifully dressed and crowned with a crescent, and her flesh so white, that those who examine her too closely

1. 'The pulse is racing, gasping, noisy, irregular.'
2. 'Royal dues.'

feel tempted. There's a Ceres too. Another very beautiful divinity. She is seated on sheafs of corn and has a graceful wreath on her head of ears of grain interwoven with salsify and other flowers. Nothing could look more amorous than her eyes, or more rounded than her legs, or more noble than her expression, or better draped than her skirts. She is one of the most perfect and innocent beauties that ever paint-brush produced.'

'Hang it all,' grumbled Louis XI, 'when will you get to the point?'

'I need a roof over those paintings, sire, and though it's only a trifling sum, I've no money left.'

'How much is your roof?'

'Well ... an ornamental roof of gilded copper, two thousand *livres* at the most.'

'Ah, the assassin!' cried the king. 'Every tooth he pulls from me is a diamond.'

'Do I get my roof?' said Coictier.

'Yes, and go to the devil, but cure me!'

Jacques Coictier bowed deeply and said: 'Sire, a repercussive will save you. We shall apply the great defensive to the small of the back, composed of cerate, kaolin from Armenia, white of egg, oil and vinegar. Keep on with your tisane and we shall answer for Your Majesty.'

A lighted candle attracts more than one moth. Maître Olivier, seeing the king so generous and judging the moment to be ripe, approached in his turn: 'Sire ...'

'What is it now?' said Louis XI.

'Sire, Your Majesty knows that Maître Simon Radin has died?'

'Well?'

'The fact is he was King's Councillor for the Execution of Justice in the Treasury.'

'Well?'

'Sire, his place is vacant.'

As he spoke, Maître Olivier's haughty face had exchanged its arrogant expression for a fawning one: the one change of which a courtier's face is capable. The king stared him straight in the eyes and said drily: 'I understand.'

He went on: 'Maître Olivier, the Marshal of Boucicaut used to say: "There are no gifts except from the king, there are no fishermen except on the seas." I can see that you are of the same mind as Monsieur de Boucicaut. And now hear this. We have a good memory. In '68 we had you made Groom of the Bedchamber; in '69 Warden of the Castle of the Pont de Saint-Cloud at a salary of one hundred *livres tournois* (you wanted *livres parisis*). In November '73, by letters given at Gergeole, we had you installed as Keeper of the Forest of Vincennes, in place of Gilbert Acle, esquire; in '75, Forester of the Forest of Rouvray-lez-Saint-Cloud, in place of Jacques le Maire. In '78 we graciously settled on you, by letters patent double sealed with green wax, an annuity of ten *livres parisis*, for yourself and your wife, on the Place aux Marchands, situated at the Ecole Saint-Germain; in '79 we had you made Forester of the Forest of Senart, in place of poor Jehan Daiz; then Captain of the Castle of Loches; then Governor of Saint-Quentin; then Captain of the Pont de Meulan, of which you call yourself Count. Out of the five *sols'* fine paid by any barber giving shaves on a feast-day, three *sols* come to you and we get what you leave. We were kind enough to change your name from The Bad, which was too close to what you looked like. In '74, to the great displeasure of our nobles, we granted you a coat of arms of many colours, which gives you a chest like a peacock's. *Pasque-Dieu*, have you not drunk your fill? Has the draught of fishes not been miraculous enough? Are you not afraid that one more salmon might capsize your boat? Pride will be your downfall, Compère. Shame and ruin always follow close behind pride. Think on that, and be silent.'

These words, spoken with severity, brought the insolence back into Maître Olivier's resentful features. 'Good,' he muttered, quite audibly, 'it's easy to see the king is sick today. He is giving everything to the doctor.'

Far from taking offence at this outburst, Louis XI went on quite mildly: 'And I was forgetting, I made you my ambassador to Madame Marie in Ghent. Yes, messieurs,' the king added, turning to the Flemings, 'this man has been an ambassador. There, Compère,' he continued, addressing Maître Olivier, 'let's not be angry, we are old friends. It's getting very late. We've finished our work. Shave me.'

Our readers will surely not have waited until now to recognize in 'Maître Olivier' the terrible Figaro whom Providence, that great playwright, introduced so artistically into the long and bloody drama of Louis XI. This is not the place to expatiate further on this strange figure. The king's barber had three names. At court, he was known politely as Olivier le Daim; amongst the people as Olivier the Devil. His real name was Olivier the Bad.

Olivier the Bad remained then without moving, snubbing the king and looking askance at Jacques Coictier. 'Yes, yes, the doctor!' he said between his teeth.

'Yes, the doctor,' Louis XI went on, with strange good humour, 'the doctor has even more credit than you. It's quite simple. He has a hold over our whole body, while you have a hold only on our chin. Come, my poor barber, it's not so unusual. What would you say and what would become of your office, if I were a king like King Chilpéric, whose gesture it was to hold his beard in his hand? Come, *mon compère*, see to your office, shave me. Go and fetch what you need.'

Olivier, seeing that the king was set on being humorous and that there was no way even of making him angry, went out, grumbling, to execute his orders.

The king got up and went to the window, which he suddenly threw open in extraordinary agitation. 'Oh, yes!' he cried, clapping his hands, 'there's a red glow in the sky above the City. That's the bailiff burning. It couldn't be anything else. Ah, my good people, at last you are helping me to demolish the lordships!'

Then, turning to the Flemings: 'Messieurs, come and look at this. Is that not the glow from a fire?'

The two men of Ghent came up.

'A big fire,' said Guillaume Rym.

'Aha!' added Coppenole, his eyes suddenly sparkling, 'it reminds me of the burning-down of the house of the Lord d'Hymbercourt. It must be a big revolt.'

'You think so, Maître Coppenole?' And Louis XI looked almost as cheerful as the hosier.

'It will be hard to resist, will it not?'

'By the Holy Cross, sire, Your Majesty will dent a good many companies of men-of-war on it!'

'I? Ah, that's another matter,' rejoined the king. 'If I so wished ...'

The hosier answered boldly: 'If this revolt is as I imagine, you would wish in vain, sire!'

'Compère,' said Louis XI, 'a populace of villeins is no match for two companies of my bodyguard and a volley from the serpentines.'

Despite Guillaume Rym's signals to him, the hosier seemed determined to oppose the king.

'The Swiss were villeins too, sire. Monsieur the Duke of Burgundy was a great gentleman, and despised them for a rabble. At the battle of Grandson, sire, he shouted: "Canoneers, fire on the villeins!" And he swore by Saint George. But the *avoyer*[1] Scharnachtal rushed on the fine duke with his club and his people, and when it encountered those peasants in their buffalo skins, the glittering Burgundian army shattered like a pane of glass struck by a stone. A great many knights were slain by churls; and Monsieur de Château-Guyon, the greatest lord in Burgundy, was found dead with his great grey horse in a small marshy field.'

'My friend,' the king returned, 'you are talking of a battle. Here we have a mutiny. Which I shall put down whenever it pleases me to wear a frown.'

The other replied, unmoved: 'Maybe, sire. In that case, it will mean that the people's hour has not yet come.'

Guillaume Rym felt he should intervene. 'Maître Coppenole, you are talking to a powerful king.'

'That I know,' replied the hosier solemnly.

'Let him speak, Monsieur Rym, my friend,' said the king, 'I like such candid talk. My father Charles VII used to say that the truth was sick. I myself thought it was dead and had not found a confessor. Maître Coppenole is proving me wrong.'

Then, laying his hand familiarly on Coppenole's shoulder: 'You were saying, then, Maître Jacques?'

'I say, sire, that perhaps you were right, that the people's hour has not come in your country.'

Louis XI looked at him keenly.

'And when will that hour come, maître?'

'You will hear it strike.'

'From which clock, pray?'

Coppenole, with his calm, countryman's features, drew the king to the window. 'Listen, sire! Here there is a keep, a belfry, cannon, burgesses, soldiers. When the belfry booms, when the cannon

1. A Swiss term for a chief magistrate.

rumble, when the keep crashes noisily to the ground, when burgesses and soldiers are yelling and killing one another, then the hour will have struck.'[1]

Louis's face became sombre and thoughtful. He remained for a moment in silence, then patted the thick wall of the keep gently with his hand, as one might stroke the cruppers of a war-horse. 'Never!' he said. 'You won't fall so easily, will you, my good Bastille?'

And turning abruptly to the outspoken Fleming: 'Have you ever seen a revolt, Maître Jacques?'

'I have made them,' said the hosier.

'How do you go about making a revolt?' said the king.

'Ah,' said Coppenole, 'it's not very difficult. There are a hundred ways. First, there must be discontent in the town. Which is not so very rare. Next, there's the character of the inhabitants. Those of Ghent lend themselves to revolts. They always like the prince's son, the prince never. Well, one morning, let's assume, they come into my shop, they say to me: Père Coppenole, there's this, there's that, the Demoiselle of Flanders is trying to save her ministers, the high bailiff is doubling the vegetable tax, or something. Anything you like. I drop what I'm working at, I leave my shop, I go into the street and shout: "Pillage!" There's always some broken barrel handy. I climb on to it and shout out the first words that come, whatever's on my heart; and when you are of the people, sire, you always have something on your heart. Then they gather, they shout, they sound the tocsin, they arm the villeins from the disarming of the soldiers, the men from the market join us and off we go! And that is how it will always be, as long as there are lords in the lordships, burgesses in the burgs and landsmen on the land.'

'And who do you rebel against like this?' asked the king. 'Against your bailiffs? Against your lords?'

'Sometimes. It all depends. Against the duke too, sometimes.'

Louis XI went and sat down again, then said with a smile: 'Ah, here, they've only got as far as the bailiffs!'

Just then Olivier le Daim returned. He was followed by two pages carrying the king's toilets; but what struck Louis XI was that he was accompanied in addition by the Provost of Paris and the

1. The reference, of course, is to the fall of the Bastille at the start of the French Revolution in 1789.

Chevalier of the Watch, both looking dismayed. The rancorous barber too looked dismayed, if secretly pleased. He it was who spoke: 'Sire, I ask Your Majesty's pardon for the calamitous news I bring you.'

As he turned quickly round, the king scraped the matting with the legs of his chair: 'What is it?'

'Sire,' Olivier le Daim resumed, with the spiteful look of a man delighted to be delivering a violent blow, 'this popular uprising is not directed against the Bailiff of the Palace.'

'Against whom then?'

'Against you, sire.'

The old king stood up, as straight as a young man. 'Explain yourself, Olivier, explain yourself! And keep your head, Compère, because I swear to you on the cross of Saint-Lô that if you lie to us at this time, the sword which cut off the head of Monsieur de Luxembourg is not so dented that it can't still saw through yours!'

The oath was a formidable one. Only twice in his life had Louis XI sworn on the cross of Saint-Lô.

Olivier opened his mouth to reply: 'Sire...'

'On your knees!' the king broke in violently. 'Tristan, keep an eye on this man!'

Olivier fell to his knees and said coldly: 'Sire, a witch was sentenced to death by your court of parliament. She has taken refuge in Notre-Dame. The people want to get her out by force. Monsieur the Provost and Monsieur the Chevalier of the Watch, who have come from the rioting, are here to contradict me if that is not the truth. The people are besieging Notre-Dame.'

'Indeed!' said the king quietly, white-faced and shaking with anger. 'Notre-Dame! They are besieging Notre-Dame, my good mistress, in her cathedral! Get up, Olivier. You're right. I give you Simon Radin's place. You're right. It's me they are attacking. The witch is under the protection of the church, the church is under my protection. And I thought it was over the bailiff! It's against me!'

Then, rejuvenated by his fury, he began to stride up and down. He was no longer laughing, but made a terrifying sight as he walked back and forth, the fox had turned into a hyena, he seemed incapable of speech, his lips were moving and his bony fists were clenched. All of a sudden he looked up, his cavernous eyes appeared full of light and his voice rang out like a bugle: 'Set about them,

Tristan! Set about the scoundrels! Go, Tristan my friend! Kill, kill!'

Once this eruption was over, he went and sat down again, and said with a cold and concentrated rage:

'Here, Tristan! With us in the Bastille are the fifty lances of the Viscount of Gif, which makes three hundred horse;[1] take them. There is also Monsieur de Châteaupers's company of archers of our bodyguard; take them. You are Provost of the Marshals, you have the men from your provostry; take them. At the Hôtel Saint-Pol, you will find forty archers of Monsieur the Dauphin's new guard; take them; take all of them and make haste to Notre-Dame. So, messieurs the villeins of Paris, you would thwart the crown of France, the sanctity of Notre-Dame and the peace of the republic! Exterminate, Tristan, exterminate! No one must escape unless for Montfaucon.'

Tristan bowed: 'As you say, sire!'

He added after a silence: 'And what shall I do with the witch?'

The question gave the king pause.

'Ah!' he said, 'the witch! Monsieur d'Estouteville, what did the people want to do with her?'

'Sire,' replied the Provost of Paris, 'since the people have gone to snatch her from her asylum in Notre-Dame I presume her impunity offended them and they want to hang her.'

The king seemed to ponder deeply, then addressed himself to Tristan l'Hermite. 'Well, Compère, exterminate the people and hang the witch.'

'That's right,' said Rym to Coppenole in a whisper, 'punish the people for wanting, then do what they want.'

'Enough, sire,' answered Tristan. 'If the witch is still in Notre-Dame, should I take her there in spite of the asylum?'

'*Pasque-Dieu*, the asylum!' said the king scratching an ear. 'Yet the woman has got to be hanged.'

At which point, as if seized by a sudden idea, he knelt rapidly down in front of his chair, took off his hat, laid it on the seat, then, staring devoutly at one of the lead amulets which weighed it down: 'Oh, Notre-Dame of Paris, my gracious patroness, forgive me!' he said with hands clasped. 'I shall do it only this once. This criminal

1. A *lance* was a team of six soldiers.

must be punished. I assure you, Madame Virgin, my good mistress, that she is a witch who is not worthy of your kind protection. You must know, madame, that many devout princes have transgressed the privilege of the churches for the glory of God and necessities of state. Saint Hugh, Bishop of England, allowed King Edward to seize a magician in his church. Saint Louis of France, my master, violated the church of Monsieur Saint Paul for the same purpose; and Monsieur Alphonse, son of the King of Jerusalem, the church of the Holy Sepulchre itself. So forgive me this one time, Notre-Dame of Paris. I shall not do it again, and shall give you a fine silver statue, like the one I gave last year to Notre-Dame of Ecouys. So be it.'

He crossed himself, stood up, put his hat back on and said to Tristan: 'Act swiftly, Compère. Take Monsieur de Châteaupers with you. Have the tocsin sounded. Crush the populace. Hang the witch. I have spoken. And I intend that the execution be performed by you. You will account to me for it. Come, Olivier, I shall not go to bed tonight. Shave me.'

Tristan l'Hermite bowed and went out. The king then dismissed Rym and Coppenole with a gesture: 'God go with you, my good friends the Flemings. Go and get some rest. The night is drawing on, we are nearer morning than evening.'

The pair withdrew, and as they were conducted back to their apartments by the Captain of the Bastille, Coppenole said to Guillaume Rym: 'I've had enough of this king who coughs. I saw Charles of Burgundy drunk, he wasn't as vicious as Louis XI sick.'

'The fact is with kings, Maître Jacques,' replied Rym, 'their wine is less cruel than their tisane.'

SIX
Blazing Bayonets

AFTER leaving the Bastille, Gringoire descended the Rue Saint-Antoine at the speed of a runaway horse. When he reached the Porte Baudoyer, he walked straight up to the stone cross that stood in the middle of the square, as if able to discern in the darkness the figure of the man dressed and hooded in black who was sitting on the steps of the cross. 'Is that you, maître?' said Gringoire.

The figure in black got up. 'Death and passion, you make my

blood boil, Gringoire! The man on the tower of Saint-Gervais has just cried half-past-one in the morning.'

'Oh, it wasn't my fault!' rejoined Gringoire, 'but the watch's and the king's. I've just had a narrow escape! I'm always just missing being hanged. I'm predestined.'

'You miss everything,' said the other. 'But we must be quick. Have you got the password?'

'Just fancy, maître, I've seen the king. I've come from him. He's got fustian breeches. Quite an adventure.'

'Oh, stop spinning words. What do I care about your adventure? Have you got the truants' password?'

'I've got it. Don't worry. "Blazing bayonets".'

'Good. Otherwise we should never get through to the church. The truants have blocked the streets. Luckily they seem to have met with resistance. We may still arrive in time.'

'Yes, maître. But how shall we get into Notre-Dame?'

'I've got the key to the towers.'

'And how shall we get out?'

'Behind the cloister there's a little door that opens on to the Terrain and from there on to the water. I've taken the key to it and I moored a boat there this morning.'

'I was jolly nearly hanged!' Gringoire went on.

'Quickly, come on!' said the other.

Together they strode down towards the Cité.

SEVEN

Châteaupers to the Rescue!

THE reader will perhaps recall the critical situation in which we left Quasimodo. The brave hunchback, assailed on every side, had lost, if not all heart, then at least all hope of saving, not himself, he had no thought for himself, but the gypsy. He ran about the gallery in bewilderment. Notre-Dame was about to be stormed by the truants. Suddenly, a great galloping of horses filled the adjoining streets, then, together with a long line of torches and a dense cavalcade of horsemen with lances and bridles lowered, the furious sound issued into the square like a hurricane: 'France, France! Cut down the villeins! Châteaupers to the rescue! The provostry! The provostry!'

The startled truants turned about.

Quasimodo could not hear but he saw the unsheathed swords, the torches, the pikeheads, all the horsemen, at whose head he recognized Captain Phoebus, he saw the truants' confusion, the terror of some, the apprehension of the braver ones, and such was the strength he derived from this unhoped-for succour that he hurled down from the church the first assailants, who were already stepping over the gallery.

The king's troops, in fact, had arrived.

The truants fought stoutly. They defended themselves like desperate men. Taken in the flank from the Rue Saint-Pierre-aux-Bœufs, and in the rear from the Rue du Parvis, and with their backs against Notre-Dame, which they were still assaulting and which Quasimodo was defending, they were in that strange situation of being both the besiegers and the besieged in which Count Henri d'Harcourt was later to find himself, in 1640, at the siege of Turin, between Prince Thomas of Savoy, whom he was besieging, and the Marquis of Leganez, who was blockading him: *Taurinum obsessor idem et obsessus*, as his epitaph puts it.

The encounter was terrible. For the flesh of the wolf, the fang of the dog, as P. Mathieu says. The royal cavalry, amongst whom Phoebus de Châteaupers acquitted himself valiantly, gave no quarter, and whoever escaped a thrust fell to a cut. The ill-armed truants stormed and bit. Men, women and children hurled themselves on the breasts and cruppers of the horses and hung there like cats by teeth, fingernails and toenails. Others jabbed their torches into the archers' faces. Others sank iron hooks into the necks of the horsemen and dragged them down. Those who fell were hacked to pieces.

One man in particular had a great gleaming scythe, and mowed away at the legs of the horses. A terrifying sight. He sang through his nose as he relentlessly launched and pulled in his scythe. With each sweep, he described around him a great swathe of severed limbs. In this way, he advanced into the very thick of the cavalry, with the calm deliberation, the swing of the head and the regular breathing of a reaper attacking a field of corn. It was Clopin Trouillefou. He was felled by an arquebus.

Meanwhile, the windows had reopened. Having heard the battle-cries of the king's men, the locals were now taking a hand, and balls rained down on the truants from every storey. The parvis was full of a dense smoke, streaked with flame by the musket-fire. One could dimly make out the façade of Notre-Dame and the dilapidated Hôtel-Dieu, with a few haggard patients looking down from on top of its scaly, dormered roof.

The truants finally yielded, overcome by weariness, their lack of proper weapons, the shock of this surprise attack, the musket-fire from the windows and the bold impact of the king's men. They broke through the line of attackers and began to flee in all directions, leaving the parvis littered with their dead.

Quasimodo had not stopped fighting for a moment, and when he saw they were routed, he fell to his knees and raised his hands heavenwards; then, drunk with delight, he ran, he climbed swiftly as a bird to the cell whose approaches he had defended so intrepidly. His one thought now was to kneel before the girl whom he had just saved for a second time.

When he entered the cell he found it empty.

BOOK ELEVEN

ONE
The Little Shoe

WHEN the truants launched their attack on the church, La Esmeralda was asleep.

She was soon aroused by the steadily increasing uproar round the church and the anxious bleating of her goat, which had woken up first. She sat bolt upright, listened, looked, and then, frightened by the glow and the din, she ran from her cell and went to see. The appearance of the square, the vision that was astir on it, the confusion of the nocturnal assault, that hideous crowd, jumping about like an army of frogs, half glimpsed in the darkness, the croaking of that raucous multitude, the few red torches hurrying about and passing each other against the shadows, like the night fires that streak the surface of a bog, the whole scene affected her like some mysterious battle being waged between the phantoms of the witches' sabbath and the stone monsters of the church. Imbued since childhood with the superstitions of the tribe of Bohemia, her immediate thought was that she had surprised the strange creatures peculiar to the night at their evil practices, and she ran back in terror to cower in her cell, begging her pallet for some less horrible nightmare.

But the first vapours of fear were gradually dispelled; with the constantly growing noise and several other indications of reality, she came to feel she was beset not by spectres but by human beings. At this her fright did not increase but it changed its nature. It seemed possible this might be a mutiny of the people to snatch her from her asylum. The thought of once again losing her life, her hopes, Phoebus, whom she could still glimpse in her future, the utter nothingness of her frailty, all escape barred, without support, abandoned, isolated, these and a thousand other thoughts overwhelmed her. She fell to her knees, her head on her bed, hands clasped over her head, full of anxiety and trembling, and although she was a gypsy, an idolatress and a heathen, she began, sobbing, to beg the Christian God for mercy and to pray to Notre-Dame her hostess. For, even if we believe in nothing, there are moments in life when we are always of the religion of the temple nearest to hand.

For a long time, she remained prostrate, trembling, if the truth be told, rather than praying, turned to ice by the steadily approaching breath of that raging multitude, understanding nothing of this explosion, ignorant of what they were plotting, what they were doing, what they wanted, but with a foreboding of some terrible outcome.

And then, in the midst of her anguish, she heard footsteps close by. She looked round. Two men, one of them carrying a lantern, had just entered her cell. She let out a feeble cry.

'Don't be afraid,' said a voice that was not unknown to her, 'it's I.'

'Who? You?' she asked.

'Pierre Gringoire.'

This name reassured her. She looked up and saw that it was indeed the poet. But next to him stood a figure veiled from head to foot in black, who reduced her to silence.

'Ah!' Gringoire went on reproachfully, 'Djali recognized me before you did!'

Indeed, the little goat had not waited for Gringoire to name himself. Scarcely had he entered before she was rubbing affectionately up against his knees, covering the poet with caresses and white hairs, for she was moulting. Gringoire returned her caresses.

'Who's that with you?' said the gypsy in a low voice.

'Don't worry,' answered Gringoire. 'A friend of mine.'

Then the philosopher set his lantern down on the ground, squatted on the flagstones and exclaimed enthusiastically as he hugged Djali in his arms: 'Oh, she's a pretty creature, more notable for her cleanliness than her size no doubt, but as ingenious, subtle and literate as a grammarian! Come on, Djali, you haven't forgotten any of your pretty tricks? How does Maître Jacques Charmolue go? . . .'

The man in black did not let him finish. He went up to Gringoire and pushed him roughly by the shoulder. Gringoire stood up. 'True,' he said, 'I was forgetting we're in a hurry. But that's no reason to be so rough with a man, *mon maître*. My dear lovely child, your life is in danger, and Djali's. They want to take you back. We're your friends and we've come to rescue you. Follow us.'

'Is that true?' she cried, overcome.

'Yes, very true. Come quickly!'

'I will, I will,' she stammered. 'But why doesn't your friend speak?'

'Ah,' said Gringoire, 'that's because his father and mother were fanciful people who gave him a taciturn nature.'

She had to be satisfied with this explanation. Gringoire took her by the hand, his companion picked up the lantern and walked in front. The girl was dazed with fear. She let herself be led. The goat bounded after them, so happy to see Gringoire once more that she made him stumble again and again by poking her horns between his legs. 'That's life!' said the philosopher each time he nearly fell, 'it's often our best friends who bring us down!'

They went quickly down the staircase of the towers, passed through the church, where all was darkness and solitude but full of the sound of tumult, which formed so dreadful a contrast, and emerged into the courtyard of the cloister through the Porte-Rouge. The cloister was deserted, the canons having fled into the bishop's palace, to say a communal prayer; the courtyard was empty, with a few terrified servants huddled in dark corners. They made for the little door that led from the courtyard into the Terrain. The man in black opened it with a key he was carrying. As our readers know, the Terrain was a tongue of land, enclosed by walls on the Cité side and belonging to the chapter of Notre-Dame, which formed the eastern end of the island behind the church. They found the enclosure completely deserted. Here, the air was already less full of the uproar. The sounds that reached them from the truants' assault were more confused and less strident. They could distinctly hear the cool wind that blows down river rustling in the leaves of the solitary tree planted on the tip of the Terrain. Yet the danger was still close at hand. The two nearest buildings were the bishop's palace and the church. It was obvious there was a great turmoil inside the palace. Its dark mass was everywhere furrowed by lights, hurrying from window to window; just as, after one has just burnt some paper, a sombre edifice of ash is left, across which hundreds of live sparks travel haphazardly.

Beside it, the black outline of the enormous towers of Notre-Dame, seen thus from behind, towering above the long nave, looked, against the huge red glow that filled the parvis, like two gigantic andirons in some cyclopean hearth.

What could be seen of Paris wavered on every side in a mixture of light and shadow. It was a background from a Rembrandt.

The man with the lantern walked straight to the point of the Terrain. There, on the very edge of the water, stood the rotting remains of a hedge of stakes trellised with slats, to which clung a low vine, its few meagre branches extended like the fingers of an open hand. Behind it, in the shadow cast by the trellis, a small boat had been concealed. The man gestured to Gringoire and his companion to step into it. The goat followed them. The man was the last to step down. Then he cut the boat's moorings, pushed it off from the shore with a long crook, seized two oars and sat down in the bows, rowing for all he was worth towards the open river. At that point, the Seine is very fast-flowing and he had some difficulty getting away from the point of the island.

Gringoire's first concern on getting into the boat was to place the goat on his knees. He took up position in the stern and the girl, whom the stranger filled with an indefinable anxiety, came and sat pressed against the poet.

When our philosopher felt the boat get under way, he clapped his hands and kissed Djali between the horns. 'Now all four of us are safe!' he said. He added, with the look of a profound thinker: 'We are indebted, sometimes to fortune, sometimes to subterfuge, for bringing great enterprises to a successful conclusion.'

The boat edged slowly towards the right bank. The girl studied the stranger in secret terror. He had carefully stopped up the light of his dark lantern. In the darkness, he could just be discerned in the bows, like a spectre. His cowl was still lowered and formed a sort of mask, and each time, in rowing, he half-extended his arms, from which hung ample black sleeves, they looked like two huge bats' wings. For the rest, he had not yet spoken a word or let out a breath. The only sound in the boat was the motion of the oars, mingled with the rustle of innumerable ripples along the side.

'Upon my soul!' Gringoire suddenly exclaimed, 'we're as bright and as cheerful as so many Ascalaphuses![1] We are observing a

1. Son of Acheron, changed into an owl by Persephone.

Pythagorical or fish-like silence! *Pasque-Dieu*, my friends, I'd love someone to talk to me. The human voice is music to the human ear. Nor is it I who say that, but Didymus of Alexandria, and they are celebrated words. Didymus of Alexandria, indeed, was no mean philosopher. A word, my lovely child, speak one word to me, I beseech you! Incidentally, you used to have a funny peculiar little pout; do you still make it? Do you know, my love, that the parliament has full jurisdiction over places of asylum, and that you were in grave danger in your cell in Notre-Dame? Alas, the little trochilus bird makes its nest in the crocodile's jaws. Maître, the moon's coming out again. Let's hope they don't spot us! We are doing a laudable thing by rescuing mademoiselle, yet we would be hanged by order of the king if they caught us. Human actions, alas, have two handles to them! They stigmatize in me what they reward in you. Who admires Caesar blames Cataline. Is that not so, *mon maître*? What do you say to that philosophy? I myself possess the philosophy of instinct, of nature, *ut apes geometriam.*[1] Come on, no one's answering. What an annoying mood you two are in! I shall have to talk to myself. In tragedy that's what we call a monologue. *Pasque-Dieu!* I must warn you I've just met King Louis the Eleventh and I've kept that swear-word. So *pasque-Dieu*! They're still yelling their heads off in the Cité. He's a nasty, vicious old king. He's all hunched up in furs. He still owes me the money for my epithalamium, and he all but had me hanged this evening, which would have been most inconvenient. He's stingy towards men of merit. He should certainly read the four books of Salvian of Cologne *Adversus avaritiam.*[2] In fact, he's a king who's very mean in his treatment of men of letters and commits very barbaric cruelties. He's a sponge for soaking up money laid on the people. His savings are the spleen, which waxes fat on the thinness of all the other organs. And so complaints against the severity of the times turn into mutterings against the prince. Under this gentle, godfearing master, the gallows are groaning with bodies, the executioner's blocks are rotten with blood, and the prisons split open like bloated bellies. This king takes with one hand and hangs with the other. He's the procurator of Dame Gabelle[3] and my lord

1. 'As bees do geometry.'
2. 'Against avarice.'
3. The hated tax on salt.

Gibbet. The great are despoiled of their dignities and the small ceaselessly crushed beneath new burdens. He is an exorbitant prince. A monarch whom I do not like. What about you, *mon maître?*'

The man in black allowed the garrulous poet to pursue his strictures. He continued to struggle against the fierce, compressed current that divides the poop of the Cité from the prow of the Ile Notre-Dame, known today as the Ile Saint-Louis.

'By the way, maître,' resumed Gringoire suddenly. 'As we came on to the parvis through those berserk truants, did your reverence notice the poor young devil whose brains your hunchback was busy dashing out against the balustrade of the gallery of kings? I'm short-sighted, I didn't recognize him. Any idea who it might have been?'

The stranger answered not a word. But he abruptly left off rowing, his arms slumped as if broken, his head fell on to his chest, and La Esmeralda heard him give a convulsive sigh. For her part, she shuddered. She had heard those sighs before.

Left to itself, the boat drifted with the current for a few moments. But the man in black finally drew himself up, took hold of the oars again and began to work back upstream. He rounded the point of the Ile Notre-Dame, and made for the landing-stage of the Port-au-Foin.

'Ah!' said Gringoire, 'there's the Logis Barbeau. Look, maître, see, that group of black roofs making funny angles there, underneath that heap of low, wispy, soiled, filthy clouds, in which the moon's squashed and spread out like an egg-yolk whose shell has burst. It's a handsome house. There's a chapel crowned by a small vault full of beautifully carved decoration. On top you can see the very delicately pierced spire. There's also a pleasing garden, consisting of a pond, an aviary, an echo, a mall, a maze, a house for the wild animals, and a number of overgrown walks very agreeable to Venus. There is also a rascally tree known as 'the tree of lust', having served for the pleasures of a famous princess and a gallant, witty constable of France. Alas, we poor philosophers are to a constable what a bed of cabbages and radishes is to the garden of the Louvre. What does it matter, after all? For the great as for us, human life is a mixture of good and bad. Sorrow is always next to joy, like the spondee to the dactyl. I must tell you a story about the

Logis Barbeau, *mon maître*. It ends tragically. It was in 1319, in the reign of Philip V, the longest of any king of France. The moral of the story is that the temptations of the flesh are pernicious and malignant. We must not allow our eyes to dwell for too long on our neighbour's wife, however susceptible our senses may be to her beauty. Fornication is a very lewd thought. Adultery is a curiosity into other men's delights . . . Listen, the noise is intensifying over there!'

The tumult was indeed increasing around Notre-Dame. They listened. Shouts of victory were quite clearly audible. Suddenly, a hundred torches, reflecting on the helmets of men-at-arms, spilled across the church at every height, on the towers and galleries, and below the buttresses. These torches seemed in search of something; and soon the distant yelling came distinctly to the fugitives' ears: 'The gypsy! The witch! Death to the gypsy!'

The poor girl let her head fall on to her hands and the stranger began to row furiously for the bank. Our philosopher meanwhile was thinking. He hugged the goat to him and edged gently away from the gypsy, who had been pressing closer and closer against him, as if to her one remaining refuge.

Gringoire was truly in a cruel quandary. It had occurred to him that the goat too, 'in accordance with the existing legislation', would be hanged if she were recaptured, that that would be a great shame, poor Djali, that to have two condemned women clinging to him like this was too much and that there was nothing his companion would like better in any case than to take care of the gypsy. A violent combat was being fought out between his thoughts, in which, like Jupiter in the *Iliad*, he alternately weighed up the gypsy and the goat: he looked at them, one after the other, his eyes moist with tears, and said under his breath: 'Yet I can't save both of you.'

A bump finally told them that the boat had reached the bank. The Cité was still full of a sinister hubbub. The stranger stood up, went over to the gypsy and tried to take her arm to help her ashore. She pushed him away and clung on to the sleeve of Gringoire, who, for his part, was busy with the goat and almost pushed her away. She then jumped down from the boat unaided. So agitated was she, she did not know what she was doing or where she was going. She remained for a moment in a daze, watching the water flow past. When she recovered her senses somewhat, she was alone on the quayside with the stranger. Gringoire must have taken advantage of the disembarkation to slip away with the goat into the block of houses on the Rue Grenier-sur-l'Eau.

The poor gypsy shivered at finding herself alone with this man. She tried to speak, to cry out, to call Gringoire, but her tongue lay inert in her mouth and no sound came from her lips. Suddenly she felt the stranger's hand on hers. It was a cold, strong hand. Her teeth chattered and she became paler than the ray of moonlight shining down on her. The man said not a word. He began to stride up towards the Place de Grève, holding her by the hand. At that moment, she felt dimly that destiny was an irresistible force. She had no resistance left, she let herself be dragged along, running while he walked. The quay led uphill at this point, yet it seemed to her she was descending a slope.

She looked all round her. No one about. The quay was utterly deserted. The only sounds she could hear, the only human activity, were in the lurid and turbulent Cité, from which she was divided only by an arm of the Seine and from which her name carried to her, mingled with shouts of death. The rest of Paris lay spread round about her in great blocks of shadow.

Meanwhile the stranger was still hauling her along in the same silence and with the same rapidity. She could not discover any of the places where she was walking in her memory. As she passed a lighted window, she aroused herself, stiffened suddenly and shouted 'Help!'

The burgess whose window it was opened it, appeared in his nightshirt with his lamp, stared vacantly along the quay, uttered a few words she could not catch, then closed his shutter again. Her last glimmer of hope had been extinguished.

The man in black proffered not a single syllable, but held her tight and set off walking again even faster. She no longer resisted but followed him, brokenly.

Every so often she summoned enough strength to say, in a voice broken by the jolting of the pavement and breathless from running: 'Who are you? Who are you?' He made no answer.

In this way, still on the quayside, they came to quite a large square. There was a pale moonlight. It was the Grève. Standing in the centre could be discerned a sort of black cross. It was the gallows. She recognized it, and realized where she was.

The man stopped, turned to her and raised his cowl. 'Oh,' she stammered, petrified, 'I knew it was him again!'

It was the priest. He looked like his own ghost. This is an effect of moonlight, in which one seems to see only the spectres of things.

'Listen,' he said to her, and she shuddered at the sound of that fateful voice, which she had not heard for so long. He continued. The words came in short, breathless gasps, and their irregularity betrayed the tremors deep within. 'Listen. We are here. I am going to speak to you. This is the Grève. It is an extreme point. Destiny has delivered us up to one another. I shall determine your life, you my soul. Beyond this square and this night, nothing can be seen. Listen to me therefore. I'm going to tell you . . . First of all, don't talk to me of your Phoebus.' (He was walking up and down as he spoke, like a man unable to remain in one place, and pulling her behind him.) 'Don't talk to me of him. You see, if you pronounce that name, I don't know what I shall do but it will be terrible.'

Having said this, he became still again, like a body recovering its centre of gravity. But his words displayed just as much agitation. His voice grew softer and softer.

'Don't turn your head away like that. Listen to me. This is a serious matter. First, here is what happened. I swear none of this will be laughed at. What was I saying, then? Remind me. Ah! There's a judgement of parliament giving you back to the scaffold. I've just got you out of their hands. But they are there, pursuing you. Look.'

He extended his arm towards the Cité. The search in fact seemed to be continuing. The sound was drawing closer. The tower of the lieutenant's house, opposite the Grève, was full of noise and of lights, and soldiers could be seen running along the quay opposite with torches, shouting: 'The gypsy! Where's the gypsy? Death! Death!'

'You can see well enough they're pursuing you and that I'm not lying. I love you. Don't open your mouth, say nothing rather than tell me you hate me. I am determined not to hear that again. I've just saved you. Let me finish first. I can save you altogether. I've prepared everything. It's up to you to will it. As you will, so I can.'

He broke off violently. 'No, that's not what I must say.'

Then he ran, and made her run, for he had not let go of her, straight to the gallows, and pointed to it with his finger: 'Choose between the two of us,' he said coldly.

She wrenched herself free from his hands and fell at the foot of the gallows, clasping this dismal support. Then she half-turned her lovely head and looked at the priest over her shoulder. She was like a Holy Virgin at the foot of the cross. The priest had remained motionless, his finger still raised towards the gallows, maintaining his gesture, like a statue.

Finally, the gypsy said to him: 'It doesn't horrify me as much as you do.'

Then he allowed his arm to drop slowly and he stared at the pavement utterly crushed. 'If these stones could speak,' he murmured, 'yes, they would say that here stands a very unhappy man.'

He resumed. The girl knelt before the gallows, submerged in her long hair, and allowed him to speak without interrupting. He now had a gentle, plaintive tone which contrasted painfully with the harsh disdain of his features.

'I love you. Oh, how true that is! So nothing of the fire consuming my heart shows on the outside! Alas, young girl, night and day, yes night and day, is that not deserving of some sympathy? It is a love of night and day, I tell you, a torment. Oh, the pain is too great, my poor child! It is something worthy of compassion, I assure you. You see, I speak softly to you. I don't want you to feel that horror for me. After all, a man who loves a woman, it's not his fault. Oh my God! Will you never forgive me? Will you always hate me? It's over then! That's what makes me wicked, you see, and abhorrent to myself! You don't even look at me! Your thoughts are elsewhere perhaps as I speak to you, as I stand trembling on the brink of our two eternities! Above all, don't speak to me of the officer! I would throw myself at your knees and kiss, not your feet, you would not like that, but the ground beneath your feet! I would sob like a baby, I would pluck from my breast, not words but my heart and entrails, to tell you that I love you, but all to no avail, to no avail! Yet your soul is all tenderness and clemency, you are radiant with the most lovely sweetness, you are nothing but softness, goodness, mercifulness and charm. You are unkind only to me, alas! Oh, what a fatality!'

He buried his face in his hands. The girl could hear him weeping. It was the first time. Standing thus, wracked by sobs, he seemed even more wretched and supplicant than on his knees. He wept for some considerable time.

'Come!' he continued, these first tears over, 'I can find no words. Yet I had thought carefully of what I would say to you. Now I tremble and shake, I grow weak at the decisive moment, I feel something supreme envelop us and I stammer. Oh, I shall fall to the pavement if you don't take pity on me, take pity on yourself. Don't condemn us both. If only you knew how much I love you! What a heart is mine! Oh, I have abandoned all virtue, have abandoned my self in despair! I am a doctor but I sneer at learning, a gentleman but I dishonour my name, a priest, but I have made my missal into a pillow of debauchery, I spit in the face of my God! All this for you, you enchantress! To be worthier of your hell! And you refuse a damned man! Oh, I must tell you everything! There is more yet, something more horrible, oh, more horrible! . . .'

As he uttered these last words, his expression became completely distraught. He was silent for a moment, then he went on, as if talking to himself, but in a loud voice: 'Cain, what hast thou done with thy brother?'

There was another pause, then he continued: 'Done, Lord? I took him in. I raised him, I fed him, I loved him, I idolized him and I slew him! Yes, Lord, his head has just been crushed before me against the stones of your house, and all because of me, because of this woman, because of her . . .'

His eye was haggard. His voice grew fainter, as he again repeated several times, mechanically, at quite long intervals, like a clock prolonging its last vibration: 'Because of her . . . because of her . . .' Then his tongue no longer articulated any perceptible sound, though his lips were still moving. Suddenly he crumpled up like a falling building and lay on the ground without moving, his head between his knees.

The girl touched him lightly with her foot as she drew it back from underneath him, and brought him to. He ran his hand slowly over his sunken cheeks and gazed in amazement for a moment or two at the moisture on his fingers: 'What!' he murmured, 'I've been crying!'

And turning suddenly to the gypsy with an inexpressible

anguish: 'Alas, you watched unmoved as I wept! Child, do you know that these tears are lava? Is it really true, then? That we feel no pity for the man we hate? You could watch me die, and laugh. But I don't want to watch you die! A word, a single word of forgiveness! Don't tell me that you love me, simply tell me you are willing, that will do, I shall save you. If not . . . Oh, time is passing, I beseech you by all that's sacred, don't wait until I have become stone again, like that gibbet that is also claiming you! Remember that I hold our two destinies in my hand, that I am insane, how terrible, that I may let everything drop, and that beneath us there is a bottomless abyss, my poor girl, into which my fall will follow yours through all eternity! One word of kindness! Say one word! Just one word!'

She opened her mouth to reply. He fell hurriedly to his knees to gather up adoringly the word – the word of compassion perhaps – that would come from her lips. She said to him: 'You're a murderer!'

The priest took her furiously in his arms and began to laugh an abominable laugh. 'Right, yes! A murderer!' he said, 'and I shall have you. You refuse me as a slave, you shall have me as a master. I shall have you. I've got a lair I shall drag you to. You will follow me, you must follow me, or I shall give you up! You must die, my beauty, or be mine! Be the priest's! Be the apostate's! Be the murderer's! This very night, do you understand? Come! Joy! Come, kiss me, foolish girl! The grave or my bed!'

His eye glinted with anger and with lust. His lascivious mouth reddened the girl's neck. She struggled in his grasp. He covered her with slavering kisses.

'Don't bite me, you monster!' she cried. 'Oh, the vile, loathsome monk! Let me go! I shall tear out your horrible grey hairs and throw them in your face by handfuls!'

He went red, then white, then he released her and looked at her gloomily. She thought she had won and continued: 'I belong to my Phoebus, I tell you, it's Phoebus I love, it's Phoebus who is handsome! You, priest, you are old! You are ugly! Go away!'

He let out a violent cry, like the poor wretch who feels the touch of the red-hot iron. 'Die, then!' he said through gritted teeth. She saw his terrible eyes and tried to flee. He caught hold of her, shook her, threw her to the ground and walked rapidly towards the corner of the Tour-Roland, dragging her behind him along the pavement by her lovely hands.

When he got there, he turned to her: 'One last time, will you be mine?'

She replied vigorously: 'No.'

Then he cried out loudly: 'Gudule! Gudule! Here's the gypsy! Take your revenge!'

The girl felt herself suddenly seized by the elbow. She looked. A gaunt arm had come from a window in the wall and was holding her in a grip of iron.

'Hold her tight!' said the priest. 'It's the gypsy who escaped. Don't let go of her. I'm going to fetch the serjeants. You'll see her hanged.'

A guttural laugh answered these bloodthirsty words from inside the wall. 'He, he, he!' The gypsy saw the priest run off in the direction of the Pont Notre-Dame. Hoofbeats could be heard from that quarter.

The girl had recognized the spiteful recluse. Panting with terror, she tried to free herself. She twisted about, she gave several agonized and despairing jerks, but the other woman held her with incredible strength. The lean, bony fingers that were bruising her clenched on her flesh and encircled it. It was as if the hand had been riveted to her arm. It was more than a chain, more than a carcan, more than an iron ring, it was an intelligent, living pincer emerging from a wall.

She fell back exhausted against the wall and then the fear of death possessed her. She thought of the loveliness of life, of youth, of the sight of the sky, of the aspects of nature, of love, of Phoebus, of all that was receding and all that was approaching, of the priest who was denouncing her, of the executioner who would come, of the gallows standing there. Then she felt her terror rise into the very roots of her hair, and heard the dismal laugh of the recluse muttering to her: 'He, he, he! You're going to be hanged!'

Half-dead, she turned towards the window, and saw the savage face of the sachette through the bars. 'What have I done to you?' she said, almost unconscious.

The recluse did not answer, but began to mumble in an angry and derisive sing-song: 'Daughter of Egypt! Daughter of Egypt! Daughter of Egypt!'

The wretched Esmeralda let her head fall back beneath her hair, realizing she was not dealing with a human being.

Suddenly the recluse exclaimed, as if the gypsy's question had taken all this time to penetrate to her mind: 'What have you done to me, you say! Ah, what you've done to me, gypsy! Well, listen. I had a baby, do you see? Yes I did, a baby, a baby I tell you! A pretty little daughter! My Agnes,' she went on distraught, kissing something in the darkness. 'Well, do you see, daughter of Egypt? My baby was taken, my baby was stolen, my baby was eaten. That's what you've done to me.'

The girl answered like the little lamb: 'Alas, I may not even have been born then!'

'Oh, yes, you must have been born!' rejoined the recluse. 'You were one of them. She would have been your age. So! Fifteen years I have been here, fifteen years have I suffered, fifteen years have I prayed, fifteen years have I been knocking my head against these four walls. I tell you it was the gypsies who stole her from me, do you understand that? And who ate her with their teeth. Have you a heart? Picture to yourself what it's like, a baby playing, a baby taking the breast, a baby asleep. It's so innocent! Well, that's what they took from me, that's what they killed! The good God knows that! Today, it's my turn, I'm going to eat gypsy. Oh, how I'd sink my teeth into you if the bars didn't prevent me. My head's too big! Poor little one, while she was asleep! And if they woke her up when they took her, it would have been no good her crying, I wasn't there! Ah, gypsy mothers, you've eaten my baby! Come and see yours.'

Then she began either to laugh or to gnash her teeth, on that furious face it was impossible to tell which. Day was beginning to break. An ashen glimmer cast a dim light over the scene, and the gibbet stood out more and more distinctly in the square. Over the other side, towards the Pont Notre-Dame, the poor condemned girl thought she could hear the sound of horsemen approaching.

'Madame!' she cried, clasping her hands and dropping to her knees, dishevelled, distraught, crazed with fear. 'Madame! Have pity on me. They are coming. I've done nothing to you. Do you want to see me die in that horrible fashion before your eyes? You can feel pity, I am sure you can. It's too horrible. Let me run away. Let me go! I beg you! I don't want to die like that!'

'Give me back my baby!' said the recluse.

'Please, please!'

'Give me back my baby!'

'Let me go, in the name of heaven!'

'Give me back my baby!'

Again the girl fell back, broken and exhausted, with the glassy stare of someone already in the grave. 'Alas,' she stammered, 'you are looking for your baby, whereas I am looking for my parents.'

'Give me back my little Agnes!' continued Gudule. 'You don't know where she is? Die, then. I'll tell you. I was a harlot, I had a baby, they took my baby away. They were gypsies. You can see you've got to die. When your mother the gypsy comes to claim you, I shall say to her: "Mother, look at that gallows!" Or else, "Give me back my baby." Do you know where she is, my little girl? Wait, I'll show you. There is her shoe, all I have left of her. Do you know where its pair is? If you do, tell me, and if it's only at the other end of the earth, I shall walk there on my knees to fetch it.'

As she was speaking, she stretched her other arm through the window and showed the gypsy the little embroidered shoe. There was already enough daylight for its shape and colours to be visible.

'Show me that shoe,' said the gypsy, trembling. 'Oh God!' And at the same time, with her one free hand, she rapidly opened the little sachet decorated with green beads which she wore round her neck.

'Go on, go on!' grunted Gudule, 'search in your demon's amulet!' Suddenly she broke off, her whole body shook and she cried out in a voice that came from the uttermost depths of her being: 'My daughter!'

The gypsy had just drawn from the sachet a little shoe similar in every respect to the other one. To the shoe was pinned a parchment on which this 'charm' had been written:

When for me you find the pair
Then your mother's arms you'll share.

Quicker than a flash of lightning, the recluse compared the two shoes, read the writing on the parchment and pressed her face, radiant with a celestial joy, against the bars of the window, crying: 'My daughter! My daughter!'

'Mother!' replied the gypsy.

And here we forbear to describe further.

The wall and the iron bars were between them. 'Oh, the wall!' cried the recluse. 'Oh, to see her yet not to embrace her! Your hand, your hand!'

The girl passed her arm through the window, the recluse threw herself on her hand, pressed her lips to it and remained there, absorbed in the kiss, giving no other sign of life but an occasional sob which lifted her haunches. But she wept torrents, in silence, in the shadows, like a nocturnal rainstorm. On to that adored hand, the poor mother poured out the deep, black well of tears that was inside her, and into which all her grief had been filtering, drop by drop, these past fifteen years.

Suddenly, she straightened up, parted her long grey hair from over her forehead and, without saying a word, began to shake the bars of her den with both hands, more furiously than a lioness. The bars held firm. Then she went to a corner of the cell to fetch a huge paving-stone that served her for a pillow, and dashed it against them so violently that one of the bars snapped, amidst a great shower of sparks. A second blow and the old iron cross barring the window collapsed completely. Then she finished off breaking and separating the rusty stumps of the bars with her bare hands. There are moments when a woman's hands have a superhuman strength.

The hole once made, and it took her less than a minute, she seized her daughter round the waist and pulled her into the cell. 'Come, let me fish you up from the abyss!' she murmured.

Once her daughter was in the cell, she set her gently on the ground, then picked her up again and carried her in her arms as if she were still her little Agnes, pacing up and down in the confined cell, ecstatic, frenzied, joyful and excitedly shouting, singi g, kissing her daughter, talking to her, bursting out laughing, dissolving into tears, at one and the same time.

'My daughter! My daughter!' she said. 'I've got my daughter! There she is. The good God has given her back to me. Come, all of you! Is there anyone there to see that I've got my daughter! Lord Jesus, she's so beautiful! You made me wait fifteen years for her, my good God, but it was so she'd be beautiful when you gave her back. So the gypsies didn't eat her! Who said they had? My little daughter, my little daughter! Kiss me! Those kind gypsies! I love the gypsies. It really is you. That's why my heart leapt every time you went past. And I thought it was hatred! Forgive me, my Agnes, forgive me. You thought I was very spiteful, didn't you? I love you. Have you still got that little mark on your neck? Let's see. She's still got it. Oh, how beautiful you are! It was I who gave you those great big eyes, mademoiselle. Kiss me. I love you. I don't mind other mothers having babies, they don't worry me now. They need only come here. Here's mine. There's her neck, her eyes, her hair, her hand. Find me something else as beautiful as that! Oh, I promise you she'll have lovers, this one! For fifteen years I wept. All my beauty has gone, and hers has come. Kiss me!'

She made her a thousand other extravagant speeches, whose whole beauty lay in their tone, she disarranged the poor girl's clothing until she made her blush, she smoothed down her silken hair with her hand, she kissed her on the foot, the knee, the brow, the eyes, she went into ecstasies over everything. The girl let her do as she liked, merely repeating now and again, very quietly and with an infinite gentleness, 'Mother!'

'You see, my little girl,' the recluse went on, interjecting a kiss after every word, 'you see, I shall love you. We shall go away from here. We are going to be so happy. I have inherited something in Rheims, our own homeland. You know Rheims? Ah, no, you don't know it, you were too small! If only you knew how pretty you were, at four months! Little feet they came to look at out of curiosity from Epernay, seven leagues away! We shall have a field and a house. I will put you to sleep in my bed. Dear God, who would have believed it? I've got my daughter!'

'Oh mother!' said the girl, at last finding the strength to speak in her emotion, 'the gypsy told me so. There was a kind gypsy with us who died last year and who had always looked after me like a foster-mother. It was she who put this sachet round my neck. She always used to say to me: "Little one, take good care of this jewel. It's a treasure. It will make you find your mother again. You are wearing your mother round your neck." She foretold it, the gypsy!'

The sachette again hugged her daughter to her. 'Come, let me kiss you! You say that so prettily. When we get back to our own country, we shall put the little shoes on an infant Jesus in church.

We certainly owe it to the kind Holy Virgin. Dear God, what a pretty voice you've got! When you were talking to me just now, it was pure music! Ah, dear Lord God! I've found my baby again! But could anyone believe such a story? We can't die of anything, because I haven't died of joy.'

Then she again began clapping her hands, laughing and shouting: 'We're going to be happy!'

At that moment, the cell resounded to the clatter of arms and the galloping of horses, which seemed to be issuing from the Pont Notre-Dame and to be advancing further and further along the quay.

The gypsy threw herself into her mother's arms in anguish.

'Save me! Save me, mother! They're coming!'

The recluse turned pale.

'Great heavens, what are you saying? I'd forgotten, they are pursuing you! What have you done, then?'

'I don't know,' answered the unhappy child, 'but I've been condemned to death.'

'To death!' said Gudule, staggering as if under a thunderbolt. 'To death!' she went on slowly, staring fixedly at her daughter.

'Yes, mother,' went on the distraught girl, 'they want to kill me. They're coming to take me. That gallows is for me! Save me! Save me! They're coming! Save me!'

For a few moments, the recluse remained immobile, as if turned to stone, then she shook her head unbelievingly and suddenly let out a loud laugh, but it was her terrifying laugh of old. 'He, he, no! It's a dream you're telling me. Oh, yes, I'd have lost her, that would have lasted fifteen years, then I'd have found her again and that would last one minute! And they'd take her back from me! And it's now, now that she's beautiful, now that she's grown up, now that she talks to me, now that she loves me, it's now they would come to eat her, under my very eyes, and I her mother! Oh, no, such things aren't possible. The good God does not allow them.'

At this point, the cavalcade seemed to come to a halt, and a voice could be heard in the distance, saying: 'This way, Messire Tristan! The priest says we shall find her in the Rat-hole.' The sound of horses began again.

The recluse drew herself up with a cry of despair. 'You must fly, my child, you must fly! It's all coming back to me. You're right. It's your death! Oh, horrors! Curses! Fly!'

She put her head through the window and quickly withdrew it.

'Stay,' she said rapidly in a low, grim voice, convulsively squeezing the hand of the gypsy, who was more dead than alive. 'Stay! Not a sound! There are soldiers everywhere. You can't leave. It's too light.'

Her eyes were dry and burning. She remained a moment without speaking. She merely strode up and down her cell, stopping now and again to snatch out handfuls of grey hair which she then tore with her teeth.

Suddenly she said: 'They're getting closer. I shall talk to them. Hide in this corner. They won't see you. I shall tell them you escaped, that I let you go!'

She laid her daughter down, for she was still carrying her, in a corner of the cell invisible from outside. She made her crouch down, carefully settled her so that neither her feet nor her hands protruded from the shadows, unfastened her black hair and spread it over her white robe so as to hide it, then placed her jug and her paving-stone, the only furniture she possessed, in front of her, imagining that a jug and a paving-stone might conceal her. This done, she was calmer, and knelt down to pray. The day was only just coming up and plenty of dark corners remained in the Rat-hole.

At that instant, the voice of the priest, that hellish voice, passed close by the cell, shouting: 'This way, Captain Phoebus de Châteaupers!'

At that name, and that voice, La Esmeralda, huddled in her corner, made a movement. 'Be still!' said Gudule.

Scarcely had she finished before a tumult of men, swords and horses halted around the cell. The mother got rapidly to her feet and went and stationed herself in front of the window so as to block it. She could see a large troop of armed men, on foot and on horseback, lined up on the Grève. The man in command of them dismounted and came towards her. 'Old woman,' said the man, whose face was repulsive, 'we're looking for a witch to hang her; we've been told you had her.'

The poor mother looked as unconcerned as she could and replied: 'I really don't know what you mean.'

The other went on: 'God's head! What was that archdeacon so excited about then? Where is he?'

'He's vanished, my lord,' said a soldier.

'Now then, no lies, you crazy old woman,' the commander went on. 'You were given a witch to guard. What have you done with her?'

The recluse did not want to deny everything, for fear of arousing suspicion, and answered in a sincere but surly tone: 'If you're talking about a tall girl they hung on my hands just now, I can tell you that she bit me and I let go of her. There. Leave me in peace.'

The commander gave a disappointed grimace.

'Don't you lie to me, you old spectre,' he resumed. 'My name is Tristan l'Hermite, and I am the king's friend. Tristan l'Hermite, do you hear?' He added, as he looked about him at the Place de Grève: 'It's a name with a certain resonance here.'

'Even if you were Satan l'Hermite,' answered Gudule, who was beginning to hope again, 'I should have nothing else to tell you and I would not be afraid of you.'

'God's head!' said Tristan, 'what a crone! So, the young witch has escaped! Which way did she go?'

Gudule replied carelessly:

'By the Rue du Mouton, I think.'

Tristan turned and signalled to his troop to be ready to move off. The recluse breathed again.

'My lord,' said an archer suddenly, 'ask the old hag why the bars of her window have been smashed in like that.'

This question filled the poor mother's heart with anguish once again. But she did not lose all her presence of mind. 'They've always been like that,' she stammered.

'Rubbish!' rejoined the archer, 'only yesterday they formed a fine black cross that filled us with devotion.'

Tristan threw the recluse a sidelong glance.

'I think the old crone's worried!'

The hapless woman felt that everything depended on showing a bold front, and, sick at heart, she began to snigger. Mothers have such resources. 'Bah!' she said, 'the man's drunk. It's a year or more since the tail-end of a cart of stones hit my window and stove in the grating. What didn't I say to the driver!'

'That's right,' said another archer. 'I was there.'

Always, wherever one goes, there is someone who has seen everything. The archer's unexpected corroboration gave fresh heart to the recluse, who had been crossing an abyss on a knife-edge during this interrogation.

But she was doomed to alternate continually between hope and alarm.

'If a cart did it,' retorted the first soldier, 'the stumps of the bars ought to be pushed inwards, whereas they point outwards.'

'Ha!' said Tristan to the soldier, 'you've got the nose of an investigator from the Châtelet. Answer what he says, old woman!'

'Great heaven!' she exclaimed, desperately, in a voice which, in spite of herself, was full of tears, 'I swear to you, my lord, that it was a cart that broke the bars. You've heard that that man saw it. In any case, what's it got to do with your gypsy?'

'Hmm!' grunted Tristan.

'Damn it!' the soldier went on, flattered by the provost's praises, 'the breaks in the iron are quite fresh!'

Tristan shook his head. She went pale. 'How long do you say it is since that cart?'

'A month, a fortnight perhaps, my lord. I don't remember.'

'She said more than a year to start with,' observed the soldier.

'That's highly suspicious!' said the provost.

'My lord,' she cried, still pressed against the window and fearful lest suspicion might induce them to pass their heads through and look into the cell, 'my lord, I swear to you it was a cart that broke the grating. I swear it by all the holy angels of paradise. If it was not a cart, may I be eternally damned and I deny God!'

'You swear very vigorously,' said Tristan, with his inquisitorial look.

The poor woman could feel her self-assurance ebbing fast. She was getting clumsy now and realized to her terror that she was not saying what she ought to have said.

At this point, another soldier came up, crying: 'The old hag's lying, my lord. The witch didn't escape down the Rue du Mouton. The chain's been stretched across the street all night, and the chain-keeper hasn't seen anyone go past.'

Tristan, whose expression was becoming more sinister by the instant, challenged the recluse: 'What have you got to say to that?'

She tried once again to withstand this fresh incident: 'That I don't know, my lord, that I may have been mistaken. I think she crossed the water in fact.'

'That's in the opposite direction,' said the provost. 'It hardly seems likely she would have wanted to go back into the Cité where she was being hunted. You're lying, old woman!'

'Anyway,' added the first soldier, 'there's no boat either on this side of the water or on the other.'

'She could have swum across,' answered the recluse, contesting every inch of ground.

'Do women swim?' said the soldier.

'God's head, old woman, you're lying, you're lying!' Tristan went on angrily. 'I've a good mind to forget the witch and hang you instead. A quarter of an hour of the question may drag the truth from your gizzard perhaps. Come on, you will follow us.'

She seized on these words eagerly. 'As you wish, my lord. Go on, go on. The question, I'm ready. Take me away. Quick, quick, let's go straight away!' During which time, she was telling herself: 'My daughter will escape.'

'God's death!' said the provost, 'she's greedy for the rack! This crazy old woman's beyond me.'

An old, grey-haired serjeant of the watch stepped from the ranks and addressed the provost: 'Crazy indeed, my lord! If she did let the gypsy go it wasn't her fault, because she doesn't like gypsies. Fifteen years I've been in the watch, and every night I hear her endlessly blaspheming and execrating Bohemian women. If the one we're after is, as I believe, the little dancer with the goat, she hates her above all.'

Gudule made an effort and said: 'Her above all.'

The unanimous testimony of the men of the watch confirmed the old serjeant's words for the provost. Tristan l'Hermite, despairing of ever getting anything out of the recluse, turned his back on her and, with an inexpressible anxiety, she saw him go slowly towards his horse. 'Come on,' he said between his teeth, 'on our way! We shall resume the search. I shan't sleep till the gypsy's been hanged.'

However, he hesitated some little while longer before mounting. Gudule palpitated between life and death as she saw him cast around the square the restless look of a hunting-dog who senses that the beast's hide is close by and is reluctant to move away. At last, he shook his head and jumped into the saddle. Gudule's heart, from being so terribly compressed, dilated and she said quietly, glancing at her daughter, whom she had not dared look at during the time they were there: 'Safe!'

All this time the poor child had remained in her corner, neither breathing nor moving, with the thought of death standing before her. She had missed nothing of the scene between Gudule and Tristan, and each of her mother's anguishes found its echo in her. She heard each successive twanging of the thread that held her suspended above the gulf and thought a score of times she could see it breaking; now at last she began to breathe freely and to feel her feet were on *terra firma* again. Just then, she heard a voice saying to the provost:

'*Corbœuf*, Monsieur the Provost, I'm a soldier, hanging witches is none of my concern. The rabble has been put down. I leave you to perform your task on your own. You will not object if I rejoin my company, since it is without a captain.' The voice was that of Phoebus de Châteaupers. Something ineffable took place within her. So he was there, her friend, her protector, her support, her refuge, her Phoebus! She stood up, and before her mother could prevent her, had hurled herself at the window shouting: 'Phoebus! Help me, my Phoebus!'

Phoebus was there no longer. He had just turned the corner into the Rue de la Coutellerie at a gallop. But Tristan had not yet left.

The recluse dashed at her daughter with a roar. She pulled her violently backwards, her nails digging into her neck. A tigress is none too gentle with her cubs. But it was too late. Tristan had seen.

'Ha, ha!' he cried, with a laugh that bared all his teeth and made his face look like the muzzle of a wolf, 'two mice in the mouse-trap!'

'I thought as much,' said the soldier.

Tristan patted him on the shoulder. 'You're a good cat! Come on,' he added, 'where's Henriet Cousin?'

A man without either the clothes or the bearing of a soldier stepped from their ranks. He wore a half-grey, half-brown tunic, and had straight hair, leather sleeves and a bundle of cords in his huge fist. This man was always at Tristan's side, just as Tristan was always at Louis XI's side.

'My friend,' said Tristan l'Hermite, 'I assume that's the witch we were looking for. You'll hang it for me. Have you got your ladder?'

'There's one under the lean-to at the Maison-aux-Piliers,' answered the man. 'Shall we do the job at this gallows?' he continued, pointing to the stone gibbet.

'Yes.'

'Good!' the man went on, with a coarse, even more bestial laugh than that of the provost, 'we shan't have far to go.'

'Hurry!' said Tristan. 'You can laugh afterwards.'

Meanwhile, since Tristan caught sight of her daughter and all hope was lost, the recluse had not said a word. She had thrown the poor half-dead gypsy into the corner of the cellar, and taken up her position by the window again, her hands resting on the edge of the sill like two talons. In this attitude, they saw her eyes, now wild and crazed once more, move fearlessly round all the soldiers. When Henriet Cousin approached the cell, she showed him a face so savage he recoiled.

'Which one must I take, my lord?' he said, returning to the provost.

'The young one.'

'That's good. The old one looks awkward.'

'Poor little dancer with the goat!' said the old serjeant of the watch.

Henriet Cousin went back up to the window. The mother's eyes made him lower his own. He said rather diffidently: 'Madame . . .'

She interrupted him in a very low, furious voice: 'What do you want?'

'Not you,' he said, 'the other one.'

'What other one?'

'The young one.'

She began to shake her head and shout: 'There's no one here! No one! No one!'

'Yes, there is!' the hangman went on, 'you know there is. Let me take the young one. I don't want to hurt you.'

She said with a strange, sneering laugh: 'Ah, you don't want to hurt me!'

'Let me have the other one, madame; it's the provost's will.'

She repeated crazily: 'There's no one here.'

'I tell you there is!' replied the hangman. 'We've all seen there were two of you.'

'Well look, then!' said the recluse with a sneer. 'Poke your head through the window.'

The hangman contemplated the mother's fingernails and did not dare to.

'Hurry up!' cried Tristan, who had just formed his troop into a circle around the Rat-hole and was sitting on his horse beside the gibbet.

Henriet returned once again to the provost, deeply embarrassed. He had put his rope down on the ground and was rolling his hat awkwardly in his hands. 'How do we get in, my lord?' he asked.

'Through the door.'

'There isn't one.'

'Through the window.'

'It's too narrow.'

'Widen it,' said Tristan angrily. 'Haven't you got pick-axes?'

From the depths of her cavern, the mother watched, still motionless. She no longer felt any hope, she no longer knew what she wanted, but she did not want them to take her daughter away.

Henriet Cousin went to fetch his executioner's box of tools from beneath the lean-to of the Maison-aux-Piliers. He also pulled out the double ladder, which he at once set against the gallows. Five or six of the provost's men armed themselves with picks and crow-bars and Tristan made his way with them towards the window.

'Old woman,' said the provost sternly, 'will you kindly hand the girl over to us.'

She gave him an uncomprehending look.

'God's head!' Tristan went on, 'what's the matter with you, preventing the witch being hanged at the king's pleasure?'

The poor woman began to laugh her inhuman laugh.

'What's the matter? It's my daughter.'

The tone in which she uttered these words brought a shiver from Henriet Cousin himself.

'I'm sorry about that,' rejoined the provost. 'But it's the king's good pleasure.'

Her terrible laugh was renewed as she cried: 'What do I care about your king? I tell you it's my daughter!'

'Break through the wall,' said Tristan.

All that was needed, to make a wide enough opening, was to dislodge one course of stone underneath the window. When the mother heard the picks and crowbars undermining her fortress, she let out a frightful cry, then began to circle her cell at a terrifying rate, a wild animal's habit instilled in her by her cage. She no longer spoke but her eyes were blazing. The soldiers' blood ran cold.

Suddenly, she picked up her stone, laughed and hurled it with both hands at the workmen. Her hands were trembling and the ill-aimed stone hit no one, but came to rest under the feet of Tristan's horse. She ground her teeth.

Meanwhile, although the sun had not yet risen, it was broad daylight, and the battered old chimneys of the Maison-aux-Piliers were tinged a lovely bright pink. It was that hour of the day when the great town's earliest risers throw their windows cheerfully open over the rooftops. A few villeins, a few fruiterers going to market on their donkeys, were beginning to cross the Grève; they halted for a moment before the knot of soldiers amassed round the Rat-hole, considered it in astonishment, then proceeded on their way.

The recluse had gone to sit beside her daughter, in front of her, shielding her with her own body, her eyes staring as she listened to the poor child, who did not move and could only give a low murmur of 'Phoebus! Phoebus!' As the work of demolition seemed to progress, the mother automatically retreated, pressing her daughter tighter and tighter against the wall. Suddenly she saw the stone shift (for she was standing sentry and had not taken her eyes off it) and heard the voice of Tristan urging the workmen on. Then she emerged from the stupor into which she had sunk for the past few moments and cried out, and her voice, as she spoke, first rent the ear like a saw, then stammered, as if every malediction had crowded to her lips at once so as to burst forth simultaneously. 'He, he, he! It's horrible. You're brigands! Are you really going to hang my daughter? She's my daughter, I tell you! You cowards! Heartless lackeys! Base and miserable murderers! Help! Help! Fire! But are they going to take my child like this? Who is it they call the good God, then?'

Then, foaming at the mouth, hollow-eyed, on all fours like a panther, and bristling all over, she addressed Tristan: 'Come a bit closer and take my daughter! Don't you understand, this woman is telling you it's her daughter? Do you know what it's like to have a child? Have you never lain with your mate, you lynx? Have you never had a cub? And if you've got little ones, doesn't it do something to your insides when they scream?'

'Lower the stone,' said Tristan, 'it's no longer fixed.'

The crowbars raised the heavy course. It was, as we have said, the mother's last rampart. She threw herself on top of it, and tried to hold it back, her fingernails scrabbling at the stone, but the massive block, set in motion by six men, escaped from her and slid gently to the ground down the crowbars.

When she saw the entry was made, the mother fell across the opening and filled the breach with her own body, wringing her arms, beating her head on the floor and shouting in a barely audible voice, hoarse with fatigue: 'Help! Fire, fire!'

'Now, take the girl,' said the still impassive Tristan.

The mother gave the soldiers a look so formidable that they felt more like retreating than advancing.

'Come on, then,' the provost went on. 'Henriet Cousin, you!'

No one came forward.

The provost swore: 'Christ's head! My soldiers! Afraid of a woman!'

'You call that a woman, my lord?' said Henriet.

'She's got a lion's mane!' said another.

'Come on,' rejoined the provost, 'the bay's wide enough! Go in three abreast, like at the breach of Pontoise. Let's get it over with, *mort-Mahom*! The first man who backs away, I'll cut him in two!'

Caught between the provost and the mother, both of them threatening, the soldiers hesitated for a moment then, their decision made, advanced towards the Rat-hole.

Seeing this, the recluse abruptly drew herself to her knees, parted the hair from her face and then allowed her scratched and wasted arms to drop on to her thighs. And now huge tears came from her eyes one by one, and ran down a furrow in her cheeks, like a torrent down the bed it has scooped out. At the same time she began to speak, but in a voice so beseeching, so soft, so submissive and so poignant, that around Tristan more than one old turnkey who would have eaten human flesh was wiping his eyes.

'My lords! Messieurs the serjeants, one word! There is something I must tell you. It's my daughter, you see, my dear little daughter who I'd lost! Listen. It's a story. Just fancy, I know messieurs the serjeants very well. They were always kind to me in the days when little boys threw stones at me because of the wanton life I led. Do you see? You'll let me keep my child, when you hear! I'm a poor harlot. It was the gypsies who stole her from me. I even kept her shoe for fifteen years. Look, there it is. That was her foot. In Rheims! La Chantefleurie! Rue Folle-Peine! Perhaps you knew that. It was me. When you were young, those were good times. We passed some good quarters of an hour. You'll have pity on me, won't you, my lords? The gypsies stole her from me, they hid her from me for fifteen years. I thought she was dead. Just imagine, my kind friends, I thought she was dead. I've spent fifteen years here in this cellar, without a fire in the winter. That's hard, that is. The poor dear little shoe! I cried so much the good Lord heard me. Last night he gave me my daughter back. It was a miracle from the good Lord. She wasn't dead. I'm sure you won't take her away from me. I wouldn't say that if it was me, but her, a child of sixteen! Give her time to see the sunlight! What's she done to you? Nothing at all. Nor have I. If only you knew, she's all I've got, I'm an old woman, she's a blessing the Holy Virgin has sent me. And you're all so kind! You didn't know it was my daughter, and now you do know. Oh, I love her! Monsieur the High Provost, I'd rather a hole in my own entrails than a scratch on her finger! You look such a kind lord! What I've been saying explains everything, isn't that so? Oh, if only you had had a mother, my lord! You are the captain, leave me my child! Just think, I am praying to you on my knees, like we pray to Jesus Christ! I ask nothing from anyone, I'm from Rheims, my lords, I've got a little field from my uncle Mahiet Pradon. I'm not a beggar. I don't want anything, but I want my child! Oh, I want to keep my child! The good God, who is the master, did not give her back to me for nothing! The king, you say the king! It won't give him very much pleasure if my little daughter is killed! Anyway, the king is kind! She's my daughter! She's my daughter! Mine! She's not the king's! She's not yours! I want to leave! We want to leave! After all, two women walking along, one the mother and the other her daughter, you let them pass! Let us pass, we're from Rheims! Oh, you're so kind, messieurs the serjeants, I love you all. You won't take away my darling little one, you can't! It's quite impossible, isn't it? My child, my child!'

We shall not attempt to convey her gestures, or her accents, or the tears she swallowed as she spoke, or the hands which she clasped and then wrung, or the heart-rending smiles, the tearful glances, the groans, the sighs, the harrowing cries of distress, with which she interspersed her crazed, chaotic and disjointed words. When she ceased, Tristan l'Hermite was frowning, but only so as to hide the tear welling in his tiger's eye. He overcame this weakness, however, and said shortly: 'It's the will of the king.'

Then he leant into Henriet Cousin's ear and said to him quietly: 'Get it over with quickly!' Perhaps even the formidable provost felt his heart failing him.

The executioner and the serjeants entered the cell. The mother offered no resistance, she merely dragged herself towards her daughter and threw herself bodily on top of her. The gypsy saw the soldiers approaching. The horror of death revived her. 'Mother!' she cried, with a note of inexpressible distress, 'Mother! They're coming! Defend me!' 'Yes, my darling, I'll defend you!' answered the mother in a spent voice and, clutching her tightly in her arms, she smothered her with kisses. The pair of them made a pitiable sight, thus prostrate, the mother on top of the daughter.

Henriet Cousin picked the girl up round the middle, below her beautiful shoulders. At the touch of his hand, she went 'huh!' and fainted. The executioner, who was letting great tears fall on her, drop by drop, sought to pick her up in his arms. He tried to release the mother, who had, as it were, tied both her hands around her daughter's waist, but so powerfully did she cling to her child that to separate them was impossible. So Henriet Cousin dragged the girl from the cell and the mother behind her. The mother too had her eyes closed.

The sun was just coming up and already on the square there was quite a gathering of the people, watching from a distance to see who it was being dragged across the paving to the gallows. For such was Provost Tristan's custom at executions. He was obsessed with preventing onlookers from coming too close.

There was no one at the windows. But way off, on top of the

tower of Notre-Dame which overlooks the Grève, two men could be seen, outlined in black against the clear morning sky, who seemed to be watching.

Henriet Cousin stopped with what he was dragging at the foot of the fatal ladder and, scarcely breathing, such was the pity he felt, he passed the rope about the young girl's adorable neck. The poor child felt the terrible contact of the hemp. She raised her eyelids and saw the gaunt arm of the stone gibbet extended above her head. Then she shook herself and cried out in a loud, heart-rending voice: 'No, no, I won't!' The mother, whose head was buried and lost to view under her daughter's clothes, said nothing; but they saw her whole body quiver and heard her redouble her kisses on her child. The hangman took advantage of that moment quickly to untie the arms which she had clasped around the condemned girl. Either from exhaustion or despair, she let him do it. Then he picked the girl up over his shoulder, whence the fair creature hung gracefully down, bent double over his broad head. Then he set foot on the ladder to climb it.

At that moment, the mother, crouching on the paving, opened her eyes wide. She uttered no cry, but straightened up with a terrible expression and then, like a wild animal pouncing on its prey, she sprang on the hangman's hand and bit him. It happened in a flash. The hangman shrieked with pain. Men ran up. With difficulty they withdrew his bloody hand from between the mother's teeth. She maintained a profound silence. They thrust her back brutally enough, then noticed that her head had fallen heavily on the paving. They picked her up. She fell back again. She was dead.

The hangman, who had not let go of the girl, began to reascend the ladder.

TWO

La creatura bella bianco vestita (Dante)[1]

WHEN Quasimodo found that the cell was empty, that the gypsy was no longer there, that while he had been defending her she had been abducted, he seized his hair in both hands and stamped the ground in surprise and grief. Then he began to run all over the

1. 'The fair creature dressed in white.

church, in search of his Bohemian, uttering strange cries to every corner of the walls, and strewing the pavement with his red hair. It was at this precise moment that the king's archers entered Notre-Dame in triumph, also searching for the gypsy. Quasimodo helped them, little suspecting, deaf as he was, their fatal intentions: he thought that the gypsy's enemies were the truants. He led Tristan l'Hermite to all the possible hiding-places personally, opening secret doors, the false bottoms of altars and the back-sacristies. If the poor girl had still been there, it was he who would have betrayed her. Once Tristan, who was not easily discouraged, had grown weary and discouraged at not finding anything, Quasimodo continued the search on his own. Twenty times, a hundred times, wild with desperation, he combed the church from top to bottom and from side to side, mounting, descending, running, calling, shouting, sniffing, rummaging, ferreting, sticking his head into every aperture, thrusting a torch up to every ceiling. An animal that has lost its mate could not have roared more loudly nor looked more haggard. Finally, once he was sure, quite sure, that she was no longer there, that it was all over, that she had been smuggled out, he slowly reascended the staircase to the towers, that staircase which he had scaled so excitedly and triumphantly on the day he rescued her. He passed the same places, head lowered, without speaking, without weeping, almost without breathing. The church was deserted once again and had relapsed into silence. The archers had left, to hunt the witch in the Cité. Quasimodo was left alone in the vastness of Notre-Dame, so tumultuously besieged only a moment before, and he made his way once more to the cell where for so many weeks the gypsy had slept under his protection. As he neared it, he imagined that perhaps he would find her there. When, at a bend in the gallery that overlooks the roof of the side-aisle, he saw the narrow cell with its little window and its little door, huddled under a flying buttress like a bird's nest beneath a branch, the poor man's heart failed him and he leant against a pillar to stop himself from falling. He fancied that perhaps she had returned there, that a good genie had no doubt brought her back, that the cell was too tranquil, too safe and too charming for her not to be in it, and he did not dare take another step, for fear of shattering the illusion. 'Yes,' he told himself, 'perhaps she's asleep, or praying. Let's not disturb her.'

Finally, he plucked up courage, went forward on tiptoe, looked and entered. Empty! The cell was still empty. The poor hunchback walked slowly round it, lifted up the bed to look underneath, as if she might have been hiding between the mattress and the flagstones, then shook his head and remained in a stupor. Suddenly, he ground his torch furiously underfoot then, without saying a word or uttering any sigh, he ran full tilt against the wall with his head and fell unconscious to the floor.

When he came to, he threw himself on the bed, rolling about on it and frantically kissing the place, still warm, where the girl had been sleeping. For a minute or two he remained motionless, as if about to expire there, then he got up, pouring sweat, panting, demented, and began to butt the walls with his head with the terrifying regularity of the clapper of one of his bells, and the determination of a man who wants to break his skull. Finally he fell for a second time, exhausted; he dragged himself out of the cell on his knees and crouched down facing the door, in an attitude of astonishment. He remained like this for more than an hour, without a single movement, his eye fixed on the abandoned cell, grimmer and more pensive than a mother sitting between an empty cradle and a full coffin. No word passed his lips; only very occasionally, his body convulsed in a violent sob, but a sob without tears, like the summer lightning that makes no sound.

It was now, seemingly, as he searched the depths of his disconsolate reverie for who the gypsy's unexpected ravisher might be, that he thought of the archdeacon. He remembered that Dom Claude alone had a key to the staircase leading to the cell, he recalled his nocturnal attempts on the girl, the first of which he, Quasimodo, had abetted, and the second of which he had foiled. He remembered countless details, and soon he no longer doubted but that the archdeacon had taken the gypsy from him. Yet such was his respect for the priest, so deeply engrained in his heart were his gratitude, devotion and love for the man, that even at this juncture they withstood the talons of jealousy and despair.

He reflected that the archdeacon had done this thing, yet the moment Claude Frollo was involved, the mortal, bloody anger that he would have felt against anyone else turned in the poor hunchback into an increase of grief.

And as his thoughts thus became fixed on the priest, and the dawn light blanched the flying buttresses, he saw, on the upper storey of Notre-Dame, at a bend in the outer balustrade that encircles the apse, a figure, walking. The figure was coming towards him. He recognized it. It was the archdeacon. Claude was moving slowly and solemnly. He did not look ahead of him as he walked, making for the north tower, but his face was turned to one side, towards the right bank of the Seine, while his head was held high, as if he were trying to see something above the roofs. Owls often have this sideways attitude. They look at one point and fly towards another. The priest thus passed above Quasimodo without seeing him.

The hunchback, petrified by this sudden apparition, saw him go in under the doorway of the stairs in the north tower. The reader knows that it is from this tower that one can see the Hôtel de Ville. Quasimodo got up and followed the archdeacon.

Quasimodo climbed the stairs of the tower merely in order to climb them, to find out why the priest had climbed them. For the rest, the poor bell-ringer did not know what he would do, what he would say, what he wanted. He was filled with rage and with fear. The archdeacon and the gypsy had collided in his heart.

When he reached the top of the tower, before he emerged from the shadows of the staircase on to the platform, he looked carefully to see where the priest was. The priest had his back to him. The platform of the tower is surrounded by an open-work balustrade. The priest was staring down into the town, his chest resting on the balustrade on the side overlooking the Pont Notre-Dame.

Quasimodo came up stealthily behind him, to see what he was looking at. The priest's attention was so engaged elsewhere that he never heard the muffled tread of the hunchback close beside him.

Paris, and especially the Paris of those days, made a fascinating and magnificent spectacle, seen from on top of the towers of Notre-Dame in the fresh radiance of a summer dawn. That day, it might have been July. The sky was quite cloudless. Above various points, a few belated stars were fading, with one very brilliant one to the east, in the brightest part of the sky. The sun was on the point of coming up. Paris was beginning to stir. To the east, each plane of its innumerable roofs was set in sharp relief by a very pure, very white light. The giant shadows of its church-towers advanced from roof to roof, from one end of the great town to the other. Already some districts were giving voice. Here a bell sounded, there a hammer, somewhere else again the complicated clatter of a moving cart. Already too, from everywhere on that surface of roofs, smoke was issuing, as if from the fissures in some immense sulphur spring. The river, whose waters are corrugated by the arches of so many bridges and the points of so many islands, wore a sheen of silvery pleats. Beyond the ramparts, around the town, the eye lost itself in a great ring of flaky vapour through which one could dimly perceive the indefinite line of the plains and the graceful swelling of the hills. All sorts of sounds drifted up to disperse above the half-awake city. To the east, a few puffs of white cotton-wool, torn from the misty fleece on the hills, were being driven across the sky by the morning breeze.

In the parvis some goodwives, milk-jugs in hand, were pointing in astonishment to the strange devastation in the main portal of Notre-Dame and to the two rivulets of congealed lead between the cracks in the sandstone. This was all that remained of the night's disturbance. The pyre lit by Quasimodo between the towers had died out. Tristan had already cleared the square and had the bodies thrown into the Seine. Kings of Louis XI's kind are careful to wash the pavements down quickly after a massacre.

Beyond the balustrade of the tower, exactly underneath the point where the priest had stopped, was one of those fantastically carved stone waterspouts which bristle on Gothic buildings; in one of its crevices two pretty gillyflowers had blossomed, and as they shook and seemed to come alive in the passing breeze, they bowed to one another playfully. From high above the towers, in the furthest reaches of the sky, there came faint bird-calls.

But the priest's eyes and ears were closed to all this. He was one of those men for whom there are neither mornings nor birds nor flowers. In all that vast horizon, and all its manifold aspects, his gaze was concentrated on a single point.

Quasimodo longed to ask him what he had done with the gypsy. But at that moment the archdeacon seemed not of this world. He had obviously reached one of those violent moments in life when the earth could crumble without one's being aware of it. His eyes fixed unwaveringly on a certain spot, he stood silent and motionless; and there was about this silence and immobility something so forbidding that the solitary bell-ringer shuddered and did not dare confront them. He merely, which was still a way of interrogating the archdeacon, followed the direction of his line of sight, and in this way the wretched hunchback's gaze fell on the Place de Grève.

Thus he saw what the priest was staring at. The ladder had been erected alongside the permanent gallows. There were a few of the people in the square and lots of soldiers. A man was dragging something white across the paving with something black clinging to it. This man stopped at the foot of the gallows.

Here, something took place which Quasimodo could not properly see. It was not that the range of his one eye was any less, simply that the crowd of soldiers prevented him getting a full view. At that moment, moreover, the sun appeared, and such was the flood of light that overflowed the horizon that it was as if everything pointed in Paris, spires, chimneys and gables, had caught fire simultaneously.

The man meanwhile had begun to climb the ladder. Now Quasimodo could see him clearly once more. He was carrying a woman over his shoulder, a young girl dressed in white, and this girl had a noose round her neck. Quasimodo recognized her. It was her.

In this way the man reached the top of the ladder. There he fixed the noose. And now the priest knelt on the balustrade so as to have a better view.

Suddenly the man kicked the ladder roughly away with his heel, and Quasimodo, who had been holding his breath for the past few moments, saw the poor child dangling at the end of the rope, two fathoms above the paving, with the man squatting with his feet on her shoulders. The rope spun round several times and Quasimodo saw terrible convulsions travel down the gypsy's body. The priest, for his part, neck craning and eyes starting from his head, was studying the ghastly tableau of the man and the girl, the spider and the fly.

At this moment of extreme horror, a fiendish laugh, a laugh only possible for someone no longer a man, broke out on the priest's livid face. Quasimodo could not hear that laugh but he could see it. The bell-ringer retreated one or two steps behind the archdeacon then suddenly charged at him in a fury and pushed him in the back with his two huge hands, into the abyss over which Dom Claude had been leaning.

'Damnation!' cried the priest, and fell.

The waterspout, above which he had been kneeling, broke his fall. He hung to it with despairing hands, but just as he opened his mouth to give a second cry, he saw Quasimodo's formidable and vindictive face come to the edge of the balustrade, above his head. He was silent.

Below him was the abyss. A drop of more than two hundred feet, and then the paving. In this terrible situation, the archdeacon said not a word and let out no groans. He merely twisted about on the spout in a prodigious effort to climb back up. But his hands could find no holds on the granite and his feet scored the blackened wall without gripping it. Anyone who has climbed the towers of Notre-Dame will know that the stonework bulges immediately below the balustrade. It was against this re-entrant that the wretched archdeacon was exhausting himself. He had to deal not with a perpendicular wall but with one that receded beneath him.

Quasimodo could have hauled him up from the gulf merely by extending a hand, but he was not even looking at him. He was looking at the Grève. He was looking at the gibbet. He was looking at the gypsy. The hunchback's elbows rested on the balustrade in the place where the archdeacon had been a moment before and there he remained, mute and immobile, like one thunderstruck, his gaze never straying from the one object there was in the world for him at that moment, as a long river of tears flowed silently from that eye which had hitherto shed but a single tear.

The archdeacon meanwhile was breathing heavily. His bald brow ran with sweat, his fingernails bled against the stonework, his knees scraped on the wall. His soutane was caught on the waterspout and each time he jerked it he could hear it splitting and coming unstitched. And as if that were not enough, the spout ended in a lead pipe which was sagging under the weight of his body. The archdeacon could feel the pipe slowly bending. The poor devil told himself that once his hands were overcome by fatigue, once his soutane was torn, once the lead had sagged, he must fall, and terror seized his vitals. More than once he cast a frantic eye at a sort of narrow platform which the sculptures happened to form about ten feet below him, and he asked heaven, from the very bottom of his tormented soul, to be able to end his days on that space two feet square, were he to live a hundred years.

Once, he looked beneath him into the square, into the abyss; the head he raised again had its eyes shut and its hair on end.

The silence of the two men was a terrifying thing. While, a few feet away, the archdeacon was in the throes of a horrible death, Quasimodo wept and gazed at the Grève.

Realizing that all his convulsions were serving only to disturb the one fragile point of support left to him, the archdeacon had made up his mind not to move any more. And so he clasped the waterspout, scarcely breathing, no longer moving, his only movement that automatic twitching of the belly which we experience in dreams when we imagine we can feel ourselves falling. His staring eyes were open in a way both morbid and astonished. Slowly, however, he was giving ground, his fingers were sliding across the spout, more and more he could feel the weakness of his arms and the weight of his body, while the curved lead supporting him was constantly inclining another degree towards the abyss. Below him he could see a terrible sight, the roof of Saint-Jean-le-Rond, no bigger than a playing-card folded in two. One by one he looked at the impassive sculptures on the tower, suspended like him above the precipice, but without either terror for themselves or compassion for him. Around him everything was of stone: before his eyes, the gaping monsters; far beneath him, in the square, the paving; above his head, the weeping Quasimodo.

In the parvis, a few groups of onlookers were calmly trying to guess who the madman might be amusing himself in this singular fashion. The priest heard them say, for their voices carried up to him, faint but clear: 'But he'll break his neck!'

Quasimodo wept.

At last, beside himself with rage and terror, the archdeacon realized it was hopeless. Yet he summoned up all the strength he had left for one final effort. He tensed himself on the waterspout, pushed the wall away with his knees, clung by his hands from a crack in the stones, and succeeded in climbing back by perhaps a foot; but the commotion caused the lead spout that was supporting him to bend suddenly. At the same time his soutane split right open. Then, feeling everything give way beneath him and with only his cramped and enfeebled hands to hold on with, the luckless man closed his eyes and let go of the waterspout. He fell.

Quasimodo watched him fall.

A fall from that height is seldom perpendicular. Once launched into the void, the archdeacon first of all fell headlong with hands outstretched, then turned over and over several times. The wind carried him on to the roof of a house, where the poor devil began to break up. Yet he was not dead when he struck it. The bell-ringer could see him still trying to stop himself on the roof-tree with his fingernails. But the incline was too steep and his strength was gone. He slid rapidly down the roof like a tile coming loose, then rebounded on to the pavement. There he moved no more.

Quasimodo then raised his eye to the gypsy, whose body he could see in the distance, hanging from the gibbet, and shuddering beneath its white robe in the final throes of death; then he lowered it again on to the archdeacon, stretched out at the foot of the tower and no longer with the form of a man; and he said, with a sob that caused his deep chest to heave: 'Oh, all that I have loved!'

THREE
Phoebus's Marriage

TOWARDS evening that same day, when the bishop's judicial officers came to take up the archdeacon's dislocated corpse from the pavement of the parvis, Quasimodo had vanished from Notre-Dame.

The episode gave rise to many rumours. No one doubted but that the day had come when, in fulfilment of their pact, Quasimodo, that is the devil, had to carry off Claude Frollo, that is the sorcerer. It was assumed that he had broken the body as he took the soul, just as monkeys break open the shell to eat the nut.

And that was why the archdeacon was not interred in consecrated ground.

Louis XI died the following year, in August 1483.

As for Pierre Gringoire, he managed to save the goat and achieved success as a tragedian. It seems that after dabbling in astrology, philosophy, architecture, hermetics, and every kind of folly, he went back to tragedy, which is the greatest folly of them all. This is what he called 'coming to a tragic end'. Here, on the subject of his dramatic triumphs, is what can be read in the accounts of the Ordinary for 1483: 'To Jehan Marchand and Pierre Gringoire, carpenter and composer, who made and composed the mystery play created at the Châtelet of Paris at the entry of Monsieur the Legate, ordered the characters, these being clothed and costumed as required by the said mystery, and similarly, for having made the scaffolding necessary to it; for doing this, one hundred *livres*.'

Phoebus de Châteaupers too came to a tragic end; he got married.

FOUR
Quasimodo's Marriage

WE have just said that Quasimodo vanished from Notre-Dame on the day of the gypsy's and the archdeacon's deaths. In fact he was never seen again, and it was not known what had become of him.

On the night following La Esmeralda's execution, the executioner's men took her body down from the gibbet and carried it, as was customary, to the cellar of Montfaucon.

Montfaucon was, in Sauval's words, 'the most ancient and superb gibbet in the kingdom'. Between the suburbs of the Temple and of Saint-Martin, some one hundred and sixty *toises* from the walls of Paris, and a few crossbow shots from the Courtille, there could be seen, on top of a gentle, imperceptible rise, high enough to be visible for several leagues around, an edifice of a strange shape, looking not unlike a Celtic cromlech; here, too, sacrifices were performed.

Picture to yourselves, crowning a mound of plaster, a huge parallelepiped of masonry, fifteen feet high, thirty feet wide and forty feet long, with a door, an outside ramp and a platform; on this platform, sixteen huge pillars of rough stone, standing thirty feet tall, arranged in a colonnade around three of the four sides of the block that supported them, and joined at the top by strong beams from which, at intervals, there hung chains; on every chain, a skeleton; near by, on the plain, a stone cross and two second-class gibbets, seeming to sprout like buds around the central fork; above, in the sky, a perpetual wheeling of crows. Such was Montfaucon.

By the end of the fifteenth century, the fearsome gibbet, which dated from 1328, was already very dilapidated. The beams were worm-eaten, the chains rusty, the pillars green with mould. The courses of shaped stones were all cracked at the joins and grass grew on the platform that no foot ever trod. The monument stood out in gruesome profile against the sky; at night, especially, when the moon shone palely on the white skulls, or when the cold evening wind rustled the chains and the skeletons and set them all stirring in the shadows. The presence of this gibbet was enough to make the whole area roundabout a place of foreboding.

The block of stone that formed the base of this loathsome edifice was hollow. A huge cellar had been made in it, enclosed by an old broken-down iron grille, into which they threw not only the human remains taken down from the chains of Montfaucon, but also the bodies of all the poor wretches executed on the other permanent gallows of Paris. To this subterranean charnel-house, where so much human dust and so many crimes rotted together, many of the great of this world as well as many innocents came, one by one, to lay their bones, from Enguerrand de Marigni, who christened Montfaucon and was a just man, to Admiral de Coligny, who brought it to a close and was also a just man.[1]

As for the mysterious disappearance of Quasimodo, here is all that we have been able to discover.

About eighteen months or two years after the concluding events of this history, when they came to the cellar of Montfaucon to fetch the corpse of Olivier le Daim, who had been hanged two days earlier and to whom Charles VIII had granted the favour of burial at Saint-Laurent, in better company, they found amongst all those hideous carcasses two skeletons, one of which was clasping the other in a strange embrace. One of the two skeletons was that of a woman and still wore a few shreds of a robe of what must have been white material, while round its neck could be seen a necklace of margosa seeds, together with a little silk sachet, decorated with green glass beads, which lay open and empty. These objects were of such small value that the executioner had doubtless not wanted them. The second skeleton, which had enfolded the first in a tight embrace, was that of a man. They noticed that its spinal column was curved, that its head was between the shoulder-blades and that one leg was shorter than the other. But the vertebrae of the neck

1. Marigni, a financier and politician, was unjustly executed in 1315; Admiral de Coligny was the eminent victim of the Massacre of Saint-Bartholomew, in 1572.

showed no fracture, and it had obviously not been hanged. The man to whom it had belonged must therefore have come there and have died there. When they tried to release him from the skeleton he was embracing, he crumbled into dust.

CHRONOLOGY

1802 Born in Besançon, the third son of an army officer, Leópold-Sigisbert Hugo, who was himself the son of a carpenter.

1811 Following postings in Elba, Paris, Italy and then Paris again, the family moves to Madrid, where the father, now a General, is serving with the Napoleonic army in the war against the British. The young Victor is captivated by the exoticism of Spanish life.

1812 Return to Paris.

1814–18 As a pupil at a Parisian boarding-school and then at the lyceé Louis-le Grand, writes his first literary essays, poems (on Napoleon) and historical dramas.

1819 Proposes to a childhood friend, Adèle Foucher. Continues to write poetry, and, with his brothers, launches a bi-monthly review, Royalist in inspiration, entitled *Le Conservateur littéraire*, which runs for fifteen months.

1822 Publishes his first poetry collection, *Odes et poésies diverses*; and marries Adèle Foucher. His brother Eugène becomes insane.

1823 Publishes his gory and melodramatic first novel, *Hans d'Islande* (*Hans of Iceland*), and collaborates on a new monthly review, *La Muse française*. Birth of his first son, who lives for only three months.

1824 Publishes *Nouvelles Odes*. Birth of a daughter, Léopoldine.

1825 Appointed to the Légion d'Honneur and attends the coronation of the last Bourbon King, Charles X. Travels in eastern France.

1826 Publishes a second, equally violent and exotic novel, *Bug-Jargal*, set during the 1791 slave revolt in Santo Domingo. Publishes *Odes et ballades*, which attracts the attention of the leading critic, Sainte-Beuve. Birth of a second son, Charles.

1827 Publishes his drama *Cromwell*, with a long preface that proves the most powerful and influential manifesto of the new Romanticism and the aesthetic revolution it aimed to bring about, in literature as in the theatre.

1828 Death of General Hugo. His historical drama *Amy Robsart* fails in the theatre. Birth of another son, François-Victor.

1829 Publishes *Le Dernier jour d'un condamné*, a novel in the form of an interior monologue, whose hero is awaiting execution. Hugo was later to claim it had been intended as an argument against capital punishment.

1830 February: the first night of his new drama *Hernani* becomes known as the 'battle of *Hernani*', as young Romantics in the audience provoke its more staid and reactionary members by their support for the liberties Hugo has taken, politically, morally and artistically. In July, the 'three glorious days' of rioting in Paris force the hated Charles X into exile, to be replaced by Louis-Philippe, the more liberal 'Citizen King'. Hugo, fast becoming a Republican sympathizer, withdraws to write *Notre-Dame de Paris*. Birth of a second daughter, Adèle.

1831 16 March: *Notre-Dame de Paris* published.

Publishes one of his best-known poetry collections, *Les Feuilles d'automne*.

1832 Sets up house in what is now the Place des Vosges, near the Marais. His play *Le Roi s'amuse* is put on and banned after one performance, reinforcing his new-found liberalism.

1833 Starts a love affair with an actress, Juliette Drouet, who was to remain his mistress for fifty years.

1835 Publishes another poetry collection, *Les Chants du crépuscule*.

1836 Fails to get elected to the Académie Française. The first of numerous musical versions of *Notre-Dame* flops.

1837–40 Years of extensive travels, in France, Belgium, Germany and Switzerland.

1841 Finally elected to the Académie Française.

1843 His daughter Léopoldine and her husband are drowned in a boating accident on the Seine.

1843 Becomes a Pair de France, i.e. a member of the French Upper House.

1843 Following the February Revolution in Paris, becomes Mayor of the eighth arrondissement and is elected in June to the Constituent Assembly. Launches a newspaper, *L'Evénement*, with his sons.

December: Louis-Napoléon becomes the first President of the new Republic.

1849 Elected to the new legislative Assembly as a *député* for Paris.

1850 Moves further to the political left.

1851 December: Louis-Napoléon seizes power in a coup d'état. Hugo tries to organize the popular resistance to him but is forced to leave France secretly and take refuge in Brussels.

1852 His 'expulsion' from France is promulgated. Leaves Belgium and takes up residence in Jersey. Publishes *Napoléon-le-Petit*, a robust broadside against the illiberal new Emperor, Napoleon III, seen as unfit to be compared with his uncle, Napoleon I.

1853 Publishes *Les Châtiments*, a vituperative collection of poems likewise attacking the new regime. Goes in for 'table-turning' with a medium.

1855 Declares his support for a group of French exiles expelled from Jersey for publishing a letter attacking Queen Victoria. Leaves Jersey for Guernsey.

1856 Publishes another collection of poetry, *Les Contemplations*. Settles into Hauteville House, now a Hugo museum.

1859 Rejects the offer of an amnesty from the Emperor. Publishes the first part of *La Légende des siècles*, a vast sequence of poems tracing the historical and spiritual progress of humanity.

1862 Publishes *Les Misérables*, his longest and finest novel.

1863 Publication of *Victor Hugo raconté par un témoin de sa vie*, a memoir purportedly written by Mme Hugo but usually thought to be the work of its subject. Publishes a set of engravings made after his own drawings.

1866 Publishes *Les Travailleurs de la mer* (*The Toilers of the Sea*) another huge novel, set in and around the Channel Islands.

1869 Publishes *L'Homme qui rit* (*The Laughing Man*), a novel set this time in seventeenth-century England.

1870 Plants an oak tree dedicated to 'The United States of Europe'.

July: war breaks out between France and Prussia.

After learning of serious French setbacks, Hugo travels to Brussels and, following the disastrous defeat at Sedan and the surrender of the Emperor, to Paris, where he remains during the Prussian siege. Addresses public appeals in turn to the Prussians, the French and Parisians.

1871 Elected to the National Assembly following the armistice but resigns a month later, after strong disagreements with the conservative majority. Sudden death of his son, Charles.

March: the left-wing insurrection of the Paris Commune breaks out.

Hugo moves back to Brussels, where he offers asylum to refugee Communards. Expelled from Belgium by the authorities. Returns to Paris.

1873 Death of his last son, François-Victor. His mentally unstable daughter, Adèle, (the subject of François Truffaut's film *Adèle H.*) is by now in an asylum.

1874 Publishes his last novel, *Quatre-Vingt Treize* ('93), a story set in Brittany during the Revolutionary Terror.

1875 Becomes a member of the Senate.

1877 Publishes the second part of *La Légende des siècles*, and a collection of 68 poems celebrating his grandchildren, *L'Art d'être grand'père*. Finally publishes his *Histoire d'un crime*, his account of Louis-Napoléon's coup d'état.

1883 Death of Juliette Drouet. Publishes third and final part of *La Légende*.

1885 22 May: Dies of congestion of the lungs.

His coffin is displayed beneath the Arc de Triomphe before a state funeral at the Panthéon.

FURTHER READING

For a life of Victor Hugo in English, there is nothing to compare with Graham Robb's *Victor Hugo* (Picador, 1997), which is thorough without being massive, excellent on the historical background and written with humour. Of Hugo's other novels, there is a good modern translation by Norman Denny of *Les Misérables* in Penguin Classics (1982). *Les Travailleurs de la mer* was retranslated into English to mark Hugo's bicentenary in 2002: *The Toilers of the Sea*, tr. James Hogarth, Modern Library. *Le Dernier jour d'un condamné* has recently appeared in English as *The Last Day of a Condemned Man* (Hesperus, 2003). Three bilingual selections from Hugo's enormous output of poetry are: *Selected Poems*, tr. Steven Monte (Routledge, 2002), *Selected Poems*, tr. Brooks Haxton (Penguin US, 2002) and, best of all perhaps, *Selected Poems*, tr. E. H. and A. M. Blackmore (University of Chicago Press, 2001).

WILKIE COLLINS

The Woman in White

'In one moment, every drop of blood in my body was brought to a stop ... There, as if it had that moment sprung out of the earth ... stood the figure of a solitary Woman, dressed from head to foot in white'

The Woman in White famously opens with Walter Hartright's eerie encounter on a moonlit London road. Engaged as a drawing master to the beautiful Laura Fairlie, Walter is drawn into the sinister intrigues of Sir Percival Glyde and his 'charming' friend Count Fosco, who has a taste for white mice, vanilla bonbons and poison. Pursuing questions of identity and insanity along the paths and corridors of English country houses and the madhouse, *The Woman in White* is the first and most influential of the Victorian genre that combined Gothic horror with psychological realism.

Matthew Sweet's introduction explores the phenomenon of Victorian 'sensation' fiction, and discusses Wilkie Collins's biographical and societal influences. Included in this edition are appendices on theatrical adaptations of the novel and its serialization history.

Edited with an introduction and notes by MATTHEW SWEET

HUGO

Les Misérables

'He was no longer Jean Valjean, but No. 24601'

Victor Hugo's tale of injustice, heroism and love follows the fortunes of Jean Valjean, an escaped convict determined to put his criminal past behind him. But his attempts to become a respected member of the community are constantly put under threat: by his own conscience, when, owing to a case of mistaken identity, another man is arrested in his place; and by the relentless investigations of the dogged policeman Javert. It is not simply for himself that Valjean must stay free, however, for he has sworn to protect the baby daughter of Fantine, driven to prostitution by poverty. A compelling and compassionate view of the victims of early nineteenth-century French society, *Les Misérables* is a novel on an epic scale, moving inexorably from the eve of the battle of Waterloo to the July Revolution of 1830.

Norman Denny's introduction to his lively English translation discusses Hugo's political and artistic aims in writing *Les Misérables*.

'A great writer – inventive, witty, sly, innovatory' A. S. BYATT

Translated and with an introduction by NORMAN DENNY

DUMAS

The Three Musketeers

'Now, gentlemen, it's one for all and all for one. That's our motto, and I think we should stick to it'

Dumas's tale of swashbuckling and heroism follows the fortunes of d'Artagnan, a headstrong country boy who travels to Paris to join the Musketeers – the bodyguard of King Louis XIII. Here he falls in with Athos, Porthos and Aramis, and the four friends soon find themselves caught up in court politics and intrigue. Together they must outwit Cardinal Richelieu and his plot to gain influence over the King, and thwart the beautiful spy Milady's scheme to disgrace the Queen. In *The Three Musketeers*, Dumas breathed fresh life into the genre of historical romance, creating a vividly realized cast of characters and a stirring dramatic narrative.

The introduction examines Dumas's historical sources, the balance between fact and fiction, and the figures from history that formed the basis for the central characters of *The Three Musketeers*.

Translated and with an introduction by LORD SUDLEY

DUMAS

The Count of Monte Cristo

'On what slender threads do life and fortune hang'

Thrown in prison for a crime he has not committed, Edmond Dantes is confined to the grim fortress of If. There he learns of a great hoard of treasure hidden on the Isle of Monte Cristo and he becomes determined not only to escape, but also to unearth the treasure and use it to plot the destruction of the three men responsible for his incarceration. Dumas's epic tale of suffering and retribution, inspired by a real-life case of wrongful imprisonment, was a huge popular success when it was first serialized in the 1840s.

Robin Buss's lively English translation remains faithful to the style of Dumas's original. This edition includes an introduction, explanatory notes and suggestions for further reading.

'Robin Buss broke new ground with a fresh version of *Monte Cristo* for Penguin' *Oxford Guide to Literature in English Translation*

Translated with an introduction by ROBIN BUSS

CHARLES DICKENS

A Tale of Two Cities

'Liberty, equality, fraternity, or death; – the last, much the easiest to bestow, O Guillotine!'

After eighteen years as a political prisoner in the Bastille, the ageing Doctor Manette is finally released and reunited with his daughter in England. There the lives of two very different men, Charles Darnay, an exiled French aristocrat, and Sydney Carton, a disreputable but brilliant English lawyer, become enmeshed through their love for Lucie Manette. From the tranquil roads of London, they are drawn against their will to the vengeful, bloodstained streets of Paris at the height of the Reign of Terror, and they soon fall under the lethal shadow of La Guillotine.

This edition uses the text as it appeared in its first serial publication in 1859 to convey the full scope of Dickens's vision, and includes the original illustrations by H. K. Browne ('Phiz'). Richard Maxwell's introduction discusses the intricate interweaving of epic drama with personal tragedy.

Edited with an introduction and notes by
RICHARD MAXWELL

CHARLES DICKENS

Oliver Twist

'Let him feel that he is one of us; once fill his mind with the idea that he has been a thief, and he's ours, – ours for his life!'

The story of the orphan Oliver, who runs away from the workhouse only to be taken in by a den of thieves, shocked readers when it was first published. Dickens's tale of childhood innocence beset by evil depicts the dark criminal underworld of a London peopled by vivid and memorable characters – the arch-villain Fagin, the artful Dodger, the menacing Bill Sikes and the prostitute Nancy. Combining elements of Gothic romance, the Newgate novel and popular melodrama, in *Oliver Twist* Dickens created an entirely new kind of fiction, scathing in its indictment of a cruel society, and pervaded by an unforgettable sense of threat and mystery.

This is the first critical edition to use the *Bentley's Miscellany* serial text of 1837–9, showing *Oliver Twist* as it appeared to its earliest readers. It includes Dickens's 1841 introduction and 1850 preface, the original illustrations and a glossary of contemporary slang.

'The power of [Dickens] is so amazing, that the reader at once becomes his captive' WILLIAM MAKEPEACE THACKERAY

Edited with an introduction and notes by PHILIP HORNE

CHARLES DICKENS

Bleak House

'Jarndyce and Jarndyce has passed into a joke. That is the only good that has ever come of it'

As the interminable case of Jarndyce and Jarndyce grinds its way through the Court of Chancery, it draws together a disparate group of people: Ada and Richard Clare, whose inheritance is gradually being devoured by legal costs; Esther Summerson, a ward of court, whose parentage is a source of deepening mystery; the menacing lawyer Tulkinghorn; the determined sleuth Inspector Bucket; and even Jo, a destitute little crossing-sweeper. A savage but often comic indictment of a society that is rotten to the core, *Bleak House* is one of Dickens's most ambitious novels, with a range that extends from the drawing-rooms of the aristocracy to the poorest of London slums.

This edition follows the first book edition of 1853. Terry Eagleton's preface examines characterization and considers *Bleak House* as an early work of detective fiction.

'Perhaps his best novel . . . when Dickens wrote *Bleak House* he had grown up' G. K. CHESTERTON

'One of the finest of all English satires' TERRY EAGLETON

Edited with an introduction and notes by NICOLA BRADBURY
With a new preface by TERRY EAGLETON